N

W9-BNF-188

14.37

Ins
2.99

N

RIDE

THE MOON

DOWN

BANTAM BOOKS

New York
Toronto
London
Sydney
Auckland

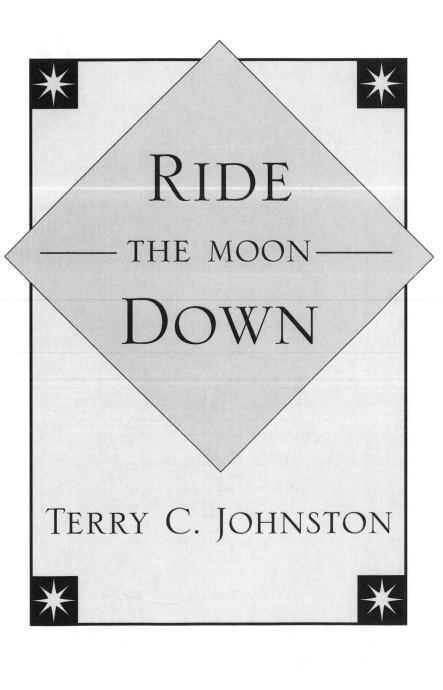

RIDE

THE MOON

DOWN

TERRY C. JOHNSTON

RIDE THE MOON DOWN
A Bantam Book / November 1998

Map by Jeffrey L. Ward

Library of Congress Cataloging-in-Publication Data
Johnston, Terry C.
Ride the moon down / Terry Johnston.
p.   cm.
ISBN 0-553-09082-8
I. Title.
PS3560.O392R53   1998
813'.54—dc21   98-8721
                                                    CIP

Published simultaneously in the United States and Canada

Bantam Books are published by Bantam Books, a division of Bantam
Doubleday Dell Publishing Group, Inc. Its trademark, consisting of the
words "Bantam Books" and the portrayal of a rooster, is Registered in
U.S. Patent and Trademark Office and in other countries. Marca
Registrada. Bantam Books, 1540 Broadway, New York, New York 10036.

PRINTED IN THE UNITED STATES OF AMERICA

BVG   10 9 8 7 6 5 4 3 2 1

For more than a decade now
he has opened doors
and joined me across the miles,
not just selling my books but
showing me how much he believed in me.
With admiration and respect,
I dedicate this book to

HAL SCHLEGEL,

my friend in Washington.

Here is the hardy mountain veteran who has ranged these wilds for more than thirty years. Pecuniary emolument was perhaps his first inducement, but now he is as poor as at first. Reckless of all provision for the future, his great solicitude is to fill up his mental insanity by animal gratification. Here is the man, now past the meridian of his life, who has been in the country from his youth, whose connections and associations with the natives have identified his interests and habits with theirs.

—Philip Edwards,
missionary to Oregon in 1834

RIDE

THE

MOON

DOWN

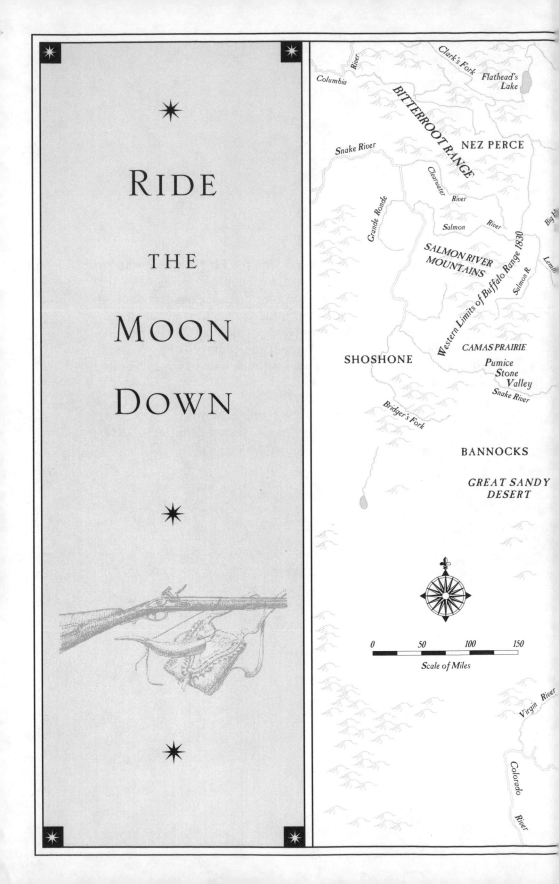

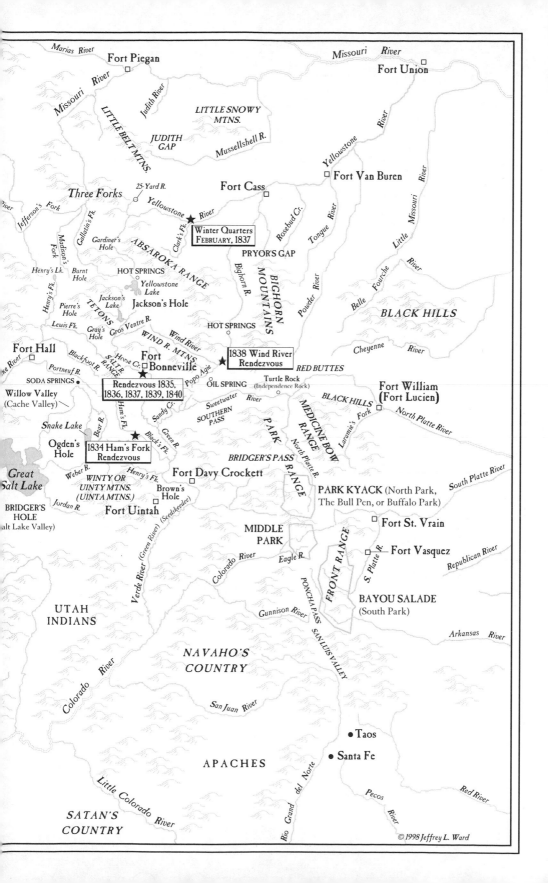

RIDE

THE MOON

DOWN

ONE

The baby stirred between them.

She eventually fussed enough to bring Bass fully awake, suddenly, sweating beneath the blankets.

Without opening her eyes, the child's mother groggily drew the infant against her breast and suckled the babe back to sleep.

Titus kicked the heavy wool horse blanket off his legs, hearing one of the horses nicker. Not sure which one of the four it was, the trapper sat up quiet as coal cotton, letting the blanket slip from his bare arms as he dragged the rifle from between his knees.

Somewhere close, out there in the dark, he heard the low, warning rumble past the old dog's throat. Bass hissed—immediately silencing Zeke.

Several moments slipped by before he heard another sound from the animals. But for the quiet breathing of mother and the *ngg-ngg* suckling of their daughter, the summer night lay all but silent around their camp at the base of a low ridge.

Straining to see the unseeable, Bass glanced overhead to search for the moon in that wide canopy stretching across the treetops. Moonset already come and gone. Nothing left but some puny starshine. As he blinked a third time, his groggy brain finally remembered that his vision wasn't what it had been. For weeks now that milky cloud covering his left eye was forcing his right to work all the harder.

Then his nose suddenly captured something new on the night wind. A smell musky and feral—an odor not all that familiar, just foreign enough that he strained his recollections to put a finger on it.

Then off to the side of camp his ears heard the padding of the dog's big feet as Zeke moved stealthily through the stands of aspen that nearly surrounded this tiny pocket in the foothills he had found for them late yesterday afternoon.

And from farther in the darkness came another low, menacing growl—

Titus practically jumped out of his skin when she touched him, laying her fingers against his bare arm. He turned to peer back, swallowing hard, that lone eye finding Waits-by-the-Water in what dim light seeped over them there beneath the big square of oiled Russian sheeting he had lashed between the trees should the summer sky decide to rain on them through the night.

He could hear Zeke moving again, not near so quietly this time, angling farther out from camp.

Bass laid a lone finger against her lips, hoping it would tell her enough. Waits nodded slightly and kissed the finger just before he pulled it away and rocked forward onto his knees, slowly standing. Smelling. Listening.

Sure enough, the old dog was in motion, growling off to his right— not where he had heard Zeke a moment before. Yonder, toward the horses at the edge of the gently sloping meadow.

Had someone, red or white, stumbled upon them camped here? he wondered as he took a first barefooted step, then listened some more. Snake country, this was—them Shoshone—though Crow were known to plunge this far south, Arapaho push in too. Had some hunting party found their tracks and followed them here against the bluff?

Every night of their journey north from Taos, Bass had damn well exercised caution. They would stop late of the lengthening afternoons and water their horses, then let them graze a bit while he gathered wood for a small fire he always built directly beneath the wide overhang of some branches to disperse the smoke. Waits nursed the baby, and when her tummy was full, Bass's Crow wife passed the child to him. If his daughter was awake after her supper, the trapper cuddled the babe across his arm or bounced her gently in his lap while Waits cooked their supper. But most evenings the tiny one fell asleep as the warm milk filled her tummy.

So the man sat quietly with the child sleeping against him, watching his wife kneel at the fire, listening to the twilight advancing upon them, his nostrils taking in the feral innocence of this land carried on every breeze. With all the scars, the slashes of knife, those pucker holes from bullets and iron-tipped arrows too, with the frequent visits of pain on his old joints and the dim sight left him in that one eye . . . even with all those infirmities, this trapper, fondly named Scratch, nonetheless believed Dame Fortune had embraced him more times than she had shunned him.

Every morning for the past twenty-five days they loaded up their two packhorses and the new mule he had come to call Samantha, dividing up what furs Josiah Paddock had refused to take for himself, what necessaries of coffee, sugar, powder, lead, and foofaraw he figured the three of them would need, what with leaving Taos behind for the high country once more. By the reckoning of most, he hadn't taken much. A few beaver plews to trade with Sublette at the coming rendezvous on Ham's Fork where he would buy a few girlews and geegaws to pack off to Rotten Belly up in Absaroka, Crow country—when Bass returned Waits-by-the-Water to the land of her people for the coming winter.

Josiah. Each time he thought on the one who had been his young partner, thought too on that ex-slave, Esau, they had stumbled across out in Pawnee country,* on the others he had left behind in the Mexican settlements . . . it brought a hard lump to Scratch's throat.

For those first few days after bidding them that difficult farewell, Titus would look down their backtrail, fully expecting to find one or more of them hurrying to catch up, to again try convincing him to remain where it was safe, maybe even to announce that they were throwing in with him once more. After some two weeks he had eventually put aside such notions, realizing he and Josiah had truly had their time together as the best of friends, realizing too that their time lay in the past.

Time now for a man to ride into the rest of his tomorrows with his family.

One of the ponies snorted in that language he recognized as nervousness edging into fear. Whoever it was no longer was staying downwind of the critters.

Kneeling, Bass swept up one of the pistols from where he'd laid them when he'd settled down to sleep. After stuffing it into the belt that held up his leggings and breechclout, Scratch scooped up a second pistol and poked it beneath the belt with the first.

Gazing down at the look of apprehension on the woman's face, he whispered in Crow, "Our daughter needs a name."

He stood before Waits could utter a reply and pushed into the dark.

The babe needed a name. For weeks now his wife said it was for the

---

* One-Eyed Dream

girl's father to decide. Never before could he remember being given so grave a task—this naming of another. A responsibility so important not only to the Crow people, but to him as well. The proper name would set a tone for her life, put the child's feet on a certain path as no other name could. Now that his daughter was almost a month old, he suddenly realized he could no longer put this matter aside, dealing each day with other affairs, his mind grown all the more wary and watchful now that there were these two women to think of, to care for, to protect.

More than his own hide to look after, there were others counting on him.

No one was going to slink on in and drive off their horses—

Suddenly Zeke emitted more than a low rumble. Now it became an ominous growl.

One of the ponies began to snort, another whinnying of a sudden. And he could hear their hooves slam the earth.

Where was that goddamned dog? Zeke was bound to get himself hurt or killed mixing with them what had come to steal their horses. In his gut it felt good, real good, to know that he wasn't going into this alone. The dog was there with him. Bass quickened his pace.

As that strong, feral odor struck him full in the face, Scratch stepped close enough to the far side of the meadow to see their shadows rearing. The struggling ponies were frightened, crying out, straining at the end of their picket pins right where he had tied them to graze their fill until morning.

He stopped, half crouching, searching the dark for the intruders, those horse thieves come to run off with his stock—

A dim yellow-gray blur burst from the tree line. His teeth bared, Zeke pounced, colliding noisily with one of the thieves just beyond the ponies.

There had to be more, Scratch knew—his finger itchy along the trigger. With Zeke's roar the thieves had to expect the owner of the horses to be coming.

But as Bass looked left and right, he couldn't spot any others. Perhaps only one had stolen in alone.

Then in the midst of that growling and snapping Scratch suddenly realized the dog hadn't pounced on a horse thief at all. It was another four-legged. A predator. A goddamned *wolf.*

"Zeke!" he roared as he bolted forward toward the contest. Remembering that dog fight Zeke was slowly losing in front of the waterfront tippling house back in St. Louis when Scratch stepped in and saved the animal's life.

The damned boneheaded dog didn't know when he was getting the worst of a whipping.

Three of the ponies whipped this way and that, kicking and snorting at the ends of their picket ropes where he had secured them. Dodging side to side, Bass rushed into their midst, ready to club the wolf off Zeke when the battle-scarred dog tumbled toward him under the legs of a packhorse, fighting off two of them.

Two goddamned wolves!

At that moment Samantha set up a plaintive bawl, jerking him around as if he were tied to her by a strip of latigo.

Again and again she thrashed her hind legs, flailing at a third wolf that slinked this way and that, attempting to get in close enough to hamstring her.

He'd fought these damned critters before, big ones too, high in the mountains and on the prairies.

Taking a step back as Samantha connected against her attacker with a small hoof, Scratch jammed the rifle against his shoulder, staring down the long, octagonal barrel to find the target. Then set the back trigger.

As the predator clambered back to all fours and began to slink toward the mule once more, Scratch shut both eyes and pulled the front trigger. With a roar the powder in the pan ignited and a blinding muzzle flash jetted into the black of night.

On opening his eyes, Titus heard the .54-caliber lead ball strike the wolf, saw it bowl the creature over.

Whipping to his left, the trapper upended the rifle, gripping the muzzle in both hands as he started for the mass of jaws and legs and yelps where Zeke was embroiled with two lanky-limbed wolves, getting the worst of it. Slinging the rifle over his shoulder and preparing to swing the buttstock at one of the dog's attackers, a fragment of the starlit night tore itself loose and flickered into the side of his vision.

Landing against Scratch with the force of its leap, a fourth wolf sank its teeth deep into the muscle at the top of his bare left arm. Struggling on the ground beneath the animal as it attempted to whip its head back and forth to tear meat from its prey, Bass yanked a pistol from his belt as the pain became more than he could bear—fearing he was about to lose consciousness at any moment.

He fought for breath as he rammed the pistol's muzzle against the attacker's body and pulled the hammer back with his thumb, dragging back the trigger an instant later. The roar was muffled beneath the furry attacker's body, nonetheless searing the man's bare flesh with powder burns as the big round ball slammed through the wolf and blew a huge, fist-sized hole out the attacker's back in a spray of blood.

Pitching the empty pistol aside, Scratch pried at the jaws death-locked on his torn shoulder, savagely tearing the wolf's teeth from his flesh. He rolled onto his knees shakily, blood streaming down the left arm, finding Zeke struggling valiantly beneath his two attackers, clearly growing weary. Bass pulled the second pistol from his belt and clambered to his feet. Lunging closer, praying he would not miss, he aimed at the two darker forms as they swarmed over their prey.

The moment the bullet struck, the wolf yelped and rolled off the dog, all four of its legs galloping sidelong for a moment before they stilled in death. The last wolf remained resolutely twisted atop Zeke. The dog had one of the attacker's legs imprisoned in his jaws, but the wolf clamped down on Zeke's throat, thrashing its head side to side in its brutal attempt to tear open its prey, assuring the kill.

Rocking down onto his hands, Bass frantically searched the grass for the rifle knocked from his grip, tears of frustration stinging his eyes. By Jehoshaphat! That dog was a fighter to the end. He had known it from the start back there in St. Louis when Zeke hadn't run out of fight, even when he was getting whipped—

Scratch's fingers found the rifle, dragged it into both hands as he leaped to his feet, swinging his arms overhead as he rushed forward, yelling a guttural, unintelligible sound that welled up from the pit of him as he lunged toward the wolf and dog.

The cool air of that summer night fairly hissed as it was sliced with such force—driving the butt of his long full-stock Derringer flintlock rifle against the wolf's backbone. The creature grunted and yelped but did not relinquish its hold on Zeke. Yellow eyes glared primally at the man.

"You goddamned sonuvabitch!" he roared as he flung the rifle overhead again.

Driving it down into the attacker a second time, Bass forced the wolf to release its hold on Zeke. Now it staggered around to face the man on three legs, that fourth still imprisoned in the dog's jaws. Then with a powerful snap the wolf seized Zeke's nose in his teeth, clamping down for that moment it took to compel the dog to release the bloody leg.

Whimpering, Zeke pulled free of this last attacker, freeing the wolf to whirl back around. It crouched, its head slung between its front shoulders, snarling at the man.

Once more Scratch brought his rifle back behind his head, stretching that torn flesh in the left shoulder.

He was already swinging the moment the wolf left the ground. The rifle collided with the predator less than an arm's span away. With a high-pitched yelp the wolf tumbled to the ground. Scratch was on him, slamming the rifle's iron butt-plate down into the predator's head again, then again.

Remembering other thieves of the forest, he flushed with his hatred of their kind.

Over and over he brought the rifle up and hurtled it down savagely, finally stopping as he realized he had no idea how long he had been beating the beast's head to pulp.

"Zeke," he whispered even before he turned.

Staggering toward the dog, Bass knelt beside the big gray animal. Weakly the dog raised its head, whimpered a bit, then laid its bloody muzzle in Scratch's hand. He quickly ran a hand over the animal's throat, fingers finding warm, sticky blood clotting in the thick hair. Then he dragged his hand over much of the rib cage, the soft underbelly, finding no other wounds to speak of.

"Can you get up, boy?" he asked in a hopeful whisper. "Can you?"

Patting the dog on the head, Titus stood shakily himself. "C'mon now, you can get up, cain't you?"

God, how his heart ached—not wanting to lose this dog the way he had lost Hannah, the way he lost so many other good friends—the way he almost lost Josiah.

"C'mon, boy," he urged as if it were a desperate prayer.

With a struggle Zeke dragged his legs under him, thrashed a bit, then lurched upward onto all four. The dog staggered forward a few steps as Bass crouched, welcoming the animal into his arms. Zeke collapsed again, panting, his breath shallow and ragged.

"Good ol' boy!" he cried louder now, his face wet with tears. "We got 'em, didn't we? Got 'em all!"

He needed light to look over the dog's wounds.

Gazing east, he figured it was nowhere near getting time for dawn. They could light a fire and he could see to Zeke before packing up and setting out early. Be gone by the time anyone who had spotted their fire could get close.

For several minutes he knelt there stroking the animal as it laid against him, its breath growing more regular. Then he remembered Waits. She would have heard the shots and could well be near out of her mind with fright by now.

"We ought'n go back," he whispered as he bent over, stabbing his arms under the big animal, pulling the dog against him as he staggered to his feet.

Its fur was warm and damp against the one arm as he started back toward their shelter in the dark, his bare feet feeling their way through the grass.

She was standing there against the trees in front of their blankets, holding a rifle ready as he emerged from the gloom. With a tiny shriek she dropped the heavy weapon and dashed toward him, throwing her arms around his neck, clinging against Bass and the dog.

"He is wounded?" she asked in Crow as she drew back, swiping tears away with both hands.

8 TERRY C. JOHNSTON

"Yes, but I won't know how bad until I get a fire going."

"Your daughter is sleeping," she said as she began to turn. "I will start the fire. You stay with the dog."

"That sure as hell is one ugly critter of a dog!"

From the way the speaker was smiling, Bass could easily see the man meant no harm by his critical judgment.

"I take it you're a man what knows his dogs?" Titus asked as he neared the bare-chested white trapper who had stepped out from the trees and willows that lined the south side of Ham's Fork of the Green River where every shady, cloistered spot was littered with canvas tents, lean-tos, and bowers made of blankets and oiled sheeting.

Awful quiet here for a rendezvous, Titus had been thinking ever since their tiny procession marched off the bluff and made their way into the gently meandering valley. But, after all, it was the middle of a summer afternoon and a smart man laid out that hottest time of the day.

The stranger whistled to the dog and knelt. "He your'n?"

Bass reined to a halt as Waits came up beside him. "Zeke's his name."

Patting and scratching the big dog's head, the man observed, "He been in a scrap of recent, ain't he?"

"Pertecting our camp from a pack of wolves."

The man cupped Zeke's jaw in a hand and peered into the dog's eyes. "Had me a dog not too different'n this'un back in the States when I was a growing lad." Then he sighed. "Likely he's gone under by now. Be real old if he ain't."

"My name's Bass. Titus Bass," and Scratch held down his hand to the stranger.

"You're a free man, I take it?" the stranger asked as they shook.

"Trap on my own hook," he replied.

"Then you're likely the Bass a feller was lookin' for, asking if you'd come in when they arrived a week or so back."

His eyes warily squinted as he searched the nearby groves of trees and canvas. "Someone asking after me?"

"Big feller, English-tongued he was—"

"By damn, them Britishers here again this summer?"

"They are for sure."

"Where's their camp?"

"Off yonder," and he pointed. "My name's Nels Dixon. Ride with Drips."

"He that booshway with American Fur?"

Dixon threw a thumb, gesturing over his shoulder. "Him and Font'nelle. That's us over there."

"Good to know you," Bass replied. "Where the free men camped?"

"Some here and some there. Rocky Mountain Fur settled in on upstream 'bout eight miles or so. Sublette come in with his goods to trade, with 'nother feller too." Then, after he glanced quickly at the woman and the child she had lashed inside that Flathead cradleboard swinging from the tall pommel at the front of her saddle, Dixon asked, "How long you been out here to the mountains?"

Scratch smiled. "Come out spring of twenty-five."

"Damn—you mean to tell me you was a Ashley man for that first ronnyvoo?"

Wagging his head, Bass replied, "Didn't see my first ronnyvoo till twenty-six. But I made ever' one since."

"That makes nine of 'em, Bass."

Drawing himself up, Scratch sighed. "Time was, I didn't figure I'd ever see near this many ronnyvooz, Dixon. S'pose it's nigh onto time for us to make camp."

"That sure is a handsome woman," the man declared, backing one step to grab himself a last admiring look at Waits-by-the-Water. "I take it she yours."

"My wife. Crow. They are a handsome people. We been together for more'n a year now," then he nudged his heels into the buffalo runner's ribs.

"Handsome woman, Titus Bass," Dixon repeated. "But, like I said, that sure is one ugly dog!"

"Thankee kindly," Scratch replied with a wide, brown-toothed grin. "Thankee on both counts!"

As the infant suckled at her breast, Waits-by-the-Water watched her husband call the dog over to have it lay beside him as he squatted at their small fire. She studied how the man scratched its torn ears, the scarred snout, that thick neck the wolf tried vainly to crush—seeing how gently her husband's hands treated the big dog, recalling how his hands ignited a fire in her.

Her husband loved his animals, the buffalo pony and mule, and now this dog too. Almost as much as she knew he loved her and their daughter.

"Have you decided upon a name?" she asked.

He stared at the flames awhile. The only sound besides the crackling of their fire were the shouts and laughter from down the valley where the many white men camped and celebrated. How the white man could celebrate!

"No," he finally admitted, not taking his eyes off the fire. "This is so important, I do not want to make a mistake."

"Who do you want to name her if you don't?" she asked.

Her husband turned to look at her. "Isn't it the father who gives a name among your people?"

"It is one of the father's family."

Wagging his head, Bass peered back at the flames. "Besides the two of you, I don't have any family out here. I might as well not have any family left back there anyway. So there is no one to name our daughter but me."

"Arapooesh calls you his brother."

Nodding, Bass replied, "Yes, Rotten Belly is like a brother."

"Perhaps he can help us when we return to my people for the winter, *chil'ee,* my husband." She sighed and gently pulled her wet nipple from the babe's slack mouth. Waits laid the sleeping infant beside her and pulled the corner of a blanket over the child.

"I am anxious to see Rotten Belly," Scratch admitted. "It will be two winters since we have talked and smoked together."

"A good man, my uncle is," she said, scooting over to sit alongside him. "You have decided where we will go when we leave this place of many white men?"

"We will ride north when we go. There are beaver still to trap in Absaroka. We can take our time and work slowly north through the mountains while the flat-tails put on their winter fur, then find Rotten Belly's camp for the winter."

She grinned. "I will be going back to my people a married woman."

"And a mother," he added, looping an arm over her shoulder and pulling her against him. "Mother of a beautiful daughter."

"You still think of me as beautiful too?"

Staring her full in the face, his brow knit with concern. "I don't ever want you to feel anything less than beautiful—for you are all my sunrises and all my sunsets. The way the light strikes a high-country pool."

"You still think of me as your lover?" she asked, slipping her fingers beneath the flap of his breechclout to barely brush his manhood lying there under the layer of wool.

Waits wanted him now. All too fleeting were their moments alone. How desperately she wanted to know that he still thought of her as a woman, that the fire between them had not diminished now that she had given birth to their daughter.

"Feel what you are doing to that-which-rises," he said with a groan of pleasure. "Then you tell me if I could ever forget you were the lover I've searched for all my life."

Strange how it made it hard to breathe each time she felt him stiffen beneath her touch, sensing how her heart started to gallop. Then too, she always felt a tensing, a teasing flutter, that heated warmth begin down below where she craved him so. Now she snaked her fingers beneath the breechclout and touched his flesh. Just stroking him like this made her grow ready for him.

She nestled her head into the crook of his shoulder as his hand probed through the large open sleeve of her dress and found her breast. He found her nipple hardened in anticipation.

"How long are you going to do that?" he asked. "Do you want to feel me explode in your hand?"

"No," she answered, and pulled her hand away from his quivering flesh, leaning back so that she freed her breast from his hand.

Onto her knees she rocked, bending over to yank aside his breech-clout, there beside the firepit where she could gaze at the hardness of him. It made her wetter in anticipation as Waits-by-the-Water seized both sides of her buckskin dress and yanked it up to her hips as she swiveled herself atop him on her knees. Taking that rigid flesh in one hand, she planted the head of him against her dampness as she guided his other hand back into the wide, loose sleeve of her dress where he could fondle her breast.

He responded savagely, imprisoning that firm, milky mound so roughly that she would have cried out in pain had she not already grown accustomed to his all-consuming hunger, his passion when they coupled.

Both of them groaned together as she eased down upon his shaft, descending far too slowly for him.

Her husband suddenly thrust his hips upward against her, seating himself inside her warmth with a feral grunt of pleasure before he began to sway beneath her.

Interlacing her fingers behind his neck, she leaned back to the full length of her arms as he bent forward to bite at one of her breasts through the thin hide of her dress. How she loved to feel the rhythmic bouncing of her breasts as the two of them rocked together, locked as one.

But of a sudden he pulled his head away from the breast and yanked at the dress, shoving it up from her hips and over her shoulders as she stretched her arms to the starlit sky where the fireflies of sparks rose beyond the tops of the cottonwood trees. First to one side, then to the other they leaned, struggling to get her dress off her arms and over her head . . . until he held the rumpled mass in one hand, and tossed it toward their bedding.

Again she locked her fingers behind his arms as he bent forward to lick at her nipples, first one, then the other. She knew he was lapping at the warm milk that she could sense oozing from them as she neared the peak of her passion. Inside her he was growing even bigger, ready to explode and fill her with his release. He told her how he loved to suckle at her breasts, just enough to taste the milk her body fed their daughter. In little more than a moon since the birth, she had come to know how passionate her husband grew as he nursed on her. How mad it made him as he drove in and out of her with a rising fury.

Then she heard his rapid breathing become ragged, as if the sound caught on something low in his throat—knowing that he was close. And with that realization she suddenly reached her peak, sensing a flood sweep through her just as surely as there would be if he had torn down a high-country dam and what had been a flooded meadow rushed downslope between two narrow banks.

Her quivering thighs.

She felt as if her legs were the banks of that mountain stream suddenly released. Starting somewhere inside her belly where she had carried their daughter, Waits sensed the gushing wave wash downward, down, down over his manhood imprisoned inside her, on down as it swept over them both while their rhythm slowed like the passing of a stampede.

Not the hurtling passage of massive, lumbering, ground-shaking buffalo . . . but the breathless, fleeting passage of wild horses—their nostrils flaring, their eyes wide with wind-borne lust, their manes and tails blowing free in the wind.

She could tell he had enjoyed it as he pulled back from her and gazed into her eyes. He didn't have to speak for her to know.

Her husband licked his lips and said, "There is no finer woman than you in all this world. With all I have done wrong, with all the folks I didn't mean to hurt but ended up hurting anyway over the years . . . I don't know how I ever became worthy of your love."

"The Grandfather Above has smiled on us both," she whispered against his cheek, closing her eyes and wishing this moment would never end. Then of a sudden she rocked back and smiled at him, saying, "One Above smiled on me a little earlier in my life than he did in yours!"

"That doesn't mean I'm going to die anytime soon, woman."

Holding his face between her hands as she felt him continue to soften within her, Waits said, "You have lived through so many deaths already, I grow so afraid you won't live through any more."

Bass pulled her against him fiercely, kissing her wet, warm mouth. When he could no longer hold his breath, he pulled away, gasping, and said, "I have so much to live for now, I wouldn't dare go and poke a stick in death's hornet's nest, woman."

Resting her cheek against his shoulder, Waits felt guilty that his words gave her so little relief.

Finally she said, "I will consider those words as your vow to me, husband."

"You have my promise—till the day we part in death."

TWO

"Maybe I should catch this strange-looking fish!"

At her giggle Bass turned his head to find his wife standing among the willows on the creekbank. "You already caught your fish, woman. Come in with me—the water feels almost as good as you this morning."

Before ever worrying about breakfast this morning, he had tagged along with her to a secluded part of the stream where she would have a little privacy to bathe the baby. There he tied off their two horses while Waits-by-the-Water pushed through a gap in the willows to reach the edge of the creek where she found a small strip of open ground covered with grass, shaded by some young cottonwood saplings.

As she began to unwind all the swaddling wrapped around the child, he pulled off his grimy calico shirt, moccasins, and leggings, then dropped his breechclout on the bank before tiptoeing into the cool water. Finding it cold enough that morning to make him shiver with those first few steps, Titus finally eased himself beneath the surface until he sat submerged, water lapping up to his shoulders.

But he was standing now, scrubbing his skinny legs with creek-bottom sand, when she called him an odd-looking fish.

Scratch stopped, peered down, studying himself a moment there in the new day's light. "You afraid to come in here and swim with this fish you caught?"

"Never did I realize how truly white you are for a white man!" she snorted, putting her fingers over her lips to stifle a giggle.

Looking down at himself again, Titus had to agree. His legs might see the sun only once a year, come his annual rendezvous scrubbing. From his neck up and his wrists down, the man was tanned brown as a twice-smoked Kentucky ham. But the rest of his skinny, scarred, bony body was about as pale as a translucent winter moon.

"Downright stupefying, ain't I?" he said in English as he worked at scrubbing that second leg before settling back into the stream.

Waits had finished pulling off all the fouled grass and moss she had packed around the baby's genitals at sundown the night before, and now held the girl just above the surface of the water to gently wash the child's skin. Finally she laid the infant back on the blankets, patted the child dry, then leaned over to yank up long blades of summer-cured grass from the bank. These clumps of dry stalks she placed under the girl's bottom, packed them between the child's legs, then methodically rewrapped the long sections of cloth and, finally, an antelope hide around her daughter's body.

Once done with that, Waits-by-the-Water returned the bundled child to the open flaps of the small cradleboard as the girl began to fuss. Watching her care for their child there on the bank, Titus smiled, enjoying the round fullness of her rump as it strained against her leather dress, the way her full breasts swayed against the buckskin yoke as she knotted the cradleboard strings.

"You coming, woman?"

Picking up the cradleboard, then settling cross-legged on the bank, Waits pulled aside the loose dress sleeve and partially exposed a breast, guiding it into the girl's mouth. "As soon as she has eaten some more breakfast."

"By the stars, woman—that child eats more than . . . more than—"

"More than you?" she interrupted with a big grin.

He slapped at the water with one hand. "Seems she's eating most all the time."

"That's what babies do, husband. They eat and sleep, and mess their cradleboards too." She looked at him a long moment, then gazed up- and downstream before she added, "As soon as she is asleep, I'll join you. If no one will see me, I will come in to swim with you."

That delicious anticipation was enough to slowly arouse him.

Once she had set the cradleboard aside to let the child sleep with her full tummy, Waits quickly yanked off her moccasins. Taking a moment to glance both ways along the creek, she hurriedly pulled her dress over her head and stepped off the bank, sucking in a gush of air as the sudden cold shocked her.

"You'll get used to it. Come on over here," he begged.

She settled beside him, then turned so that he could pull her back against his chest. There they sat in the middle of the creek as the valley gradually came alive on all sides of them. In the quiet of this early morning, it took little effort to hear sounds drifting from far-off trapper camps and Indian villages too: grumbling, hungover men, mothers scolding children in foreign tongues, the whinnying of horses and braying of mules, the crack of axes and the occasional boom of a rifle against the far bluffs where someone had gone in search of game.

Time was he had never seen a rendezvous sunrise unless he was stumbling back to his robes after a long, long night of liquoring and devilment. Many were the summers he drank himself into oblivion, hardly rousing from his stupor to vomit right where he lay, then passing right out again—repeatedly convincing himself he was having a fine time of it. After all, weren't the rest of his friends doing the very same thing, day after day until the rendezvous was over and the traders headed east, or at least until he and his friends ran out of money and pelts and it was time to face down their hangovers, time to haul their aching heads back to the high country where they would work up enough plews to pay for another summer spree?

The last real drunk he'd given himself was no more than two summers before, back to Pierre's Hole in thirty-two. By then the hangovers had begun to hurt him something terrible. And last year both he and Josiah took it easy on the whiskey, choosing not to punish the barleycorn that much, what with their both having new wives with them.

Wives. Most white folks just wouldn't ever understand, he figured. There'd been no ceremony between him and Waits-by-the-Water. Hell, when he'd ridden off for the western sea more than a year and a half ago, Titus had gone to sulking and licking his wounds, figuring her vows of love weren't worth much at all. But come the next spring—there she had been, tagging along with Josiah his own self, clearly intending to find Titus, to show him just how devoted she truly was.

No, there had been no civil-folks preacher to say the proper words over the two of them as they stood before their families and friends as they did back among the settlements. Such folks in the States would likely mule up their eyes and scrunch their lips in a sneer at the very thought that a man like him and a creature such as Waits could be so much in love that they would privately vow to one another every bit as strong as any white folks' ceremony, promising they would be there until death ultimately parted them.

One more reason why he figured he'd made his last trip back east. St. Louis was in the past, and all those white folks too. Titus figured he wouldn't live long enough to ever want to see settlements again, their sprawl stretching farther and farther west the way they always had.

Maybe he wouldn't live long enough to see settlers and wagons, white women and preachers, reach the high plains, much less make it to the Shining Mountains. Why—a mountain man sure as hell ought'n die a'fore he had to witness such a goddamned confabulation as that! Damn if it wouldn't likely pull the heart right out of a feller to see all this get ruin't with settlers and civilizing.

By bloody damn, he prayed there'd still be plenty of wild in the wilderness, enough to last him all the rest of his days.

"You are going to see your tall friend this morning?" Waits asked him in a whisper as she gently scrubbed his grimy fingers one by one, scratching at the layers of grease and blood, grit and camp-black that had encrusted itself down deep into every knuckle, hardened into dark crescents at the base of every fingernail.

"Yes. Jarrell," he said in English.

"Jer-rel," she repeated.

"Jarrell Thornbrugh," he completed the friend's name with just the proper burr to the last name. "A John Bull Englishman."

"That is more of his name?"

He chuckled and explained in Crow, "Just Jarrel Thornbrugh. Englishman is where he's from, what he is. Like I'm American from the States, and you're a Crow from Absaroka."

"It was good to have a friend near when death loomed close last summer,"* she reflected.

"He saved our lives," Bass agreed. "Saved Josiah's life. Mine too."

"This man, he comes to trade his furs like you?"

"No. Last summer Jarrell told me that his boss, a man I met out to the western sea, sent him to rendezvous all alone only to look things over. That boss, a white-headed eagle named McLoughlin, had plans to send a brigade of men here this summer."

"More of the English white men?"

"Yes, woman—all sent by a man who wants to carve off a piece of this rendezvous trade for himself."

Worry tinged her voice. "Will the English push the Americans out of these mountains?"

Bass snorted, shaking his long, damp hair. "Not a chance of that. If the English know what's good for them, they'll stay to their own country and leave this to the rest of us."

"You will go this morning to throw the tall white man out of this country?"

---

* *BorderLords*

After some hesitation Bass said, "I don't figure I got the right to throw any man out of what country isn't mine."

"But many times you've told me this land is your home."

"True, woman. But it still isn't mine, the way folks put down claims on the ground back east. No, I'm content to live out here where none of this is really mine, to pass on through a lot of country where I'm only visiting."

"There is Crow country farther north," she tried to explain as she wrapped his arms over the tops of her heavy breasts. "And this country is the land of the Shoshone and Bannock. All fight to keep the powerful Blackfoot from taking away their lands. So why aren't you going to fight the English now that they have come to take this country from you?"

"I don't think they have come here to take any land from me," he declared.

"But they came for the beaver," she maintained. "And some of that beaver is yours."

He leaned to the side so he could gaze closely at her face. "You trying to stir up some trouble between me and that big Englishman?"

With a smile she replied in Crow, "No. I am only trying to make sense of why you do what you do sometimes. Make sense of what you don't do at times. You Americans and the Englishmen are confusing to me: you say you don't want this country out here, but you both want to be free to take what you want from the land."

Beginning to fuss, the child began a muted squawl from the bank.

"You're right, woman," Bass admitted. "This land ain't mine, but the beaver I take with my own sweat, with my hands—they're mine. I don't allow I have any right to fight for this country because it's not mine. But I will fight for what is mine: my beaver, my animals and traps, my family. No man will ever take them from me."

She turned slightly and kissed him, then pulled away, wading to the bank. He stood too, allowing the water to sluice off his cold white flesh, marveling at just how pale he was now that the sun had climbed fully above the ridge to the east.

As she pulled her dress over her head and tugged it down over her hips, Waits-by-the-Water laughed again. "I am happy a strange fish like you is the father of my child."

"Even if you don't understand me at times?"

The woman nodded, dragging the cradleboard into her lap and stroking the infant's cheek with a fingertip. "I may not always understand the way things rumble around inside your head, husband. But I always know just how your heart works."

"Is that the back of Jarrell Thornbrugh's head I've got my pistol pointed at?"

At first the tall Englishman froze, daring not to turn his head, his eyes instead glancing at the other company employees nearby, hoping to find them ready to defend him.

"And you're the booshway of this here bloody Hudson's Bay bunch, ain'cha?"

With his pounding heart rising to his throat and his hands held out from his body, Thornbrugh turned just enough to level his eyes at his antagonizer.

Plain to see that the man had no pistol trained on the back of his head.

Jarrell's eyes climbed to the stranger's face.

"By the stars! It can't be!" Thornbrugh roared as he whirled around, his booming voice like the clangor on a huge cast-iron bell.

Bass slapped both his open hands on his chest, then spread his arms wide. "In the flesh, you god-blame-ed Englishman!"

They crashed together, hugging fiercely, slapping backs and shoulders, dancing side to side and around and around.

"I've asked after you," Thornbrugh admitted breathlessly as they ground to a halt, their forearms locked fraternally. "No one heard evidence of you since last summer on the Green. No one's come across you in their travels."

"I stayed south ever since ronnyvoo," Bass explained. "And I went east for a time too."

"The States?" and Jarrell rocked back a bit, closely studying his friend's face. "You didn't think of giving up the mountains?"

"Hell, I couldn't give up the mountains," he declared with a reassuring smile. "Wouldn't be happy anyplace else."

Then he spotted the left eye and leaned close to have himself a look at it. "So tell me about this eye of yours."

"Don't rightly know what to think of it, Jarrell. Just come on me few months back. Been seeing stars shootin' out of it for some time, howsoever. But this last spring it got so ever'thing's real fuzzy."

He peered closely at the milky film over the iris and pupil. "Looks cloudy. You see anything with it?"

"A little," Bass answered. "I can tell light from dark. Not much else. For most part, I ain't in a bad way, what with this other eye doing more'n its share."

"Tie your horse off and come on in here, you old one-eyed reprobate," he said with relief, gesturing for Titus to follow him beneath the canvas sheeting Thornbrugh's men had strung up for shade in the middle of their encampment.

He watched the American ground-hobble his animal where it could graze nearby, then patted the blanket beside him. "Sit."

"You John Bulls got any tobaccy wuth smoking?" Bass inquired.

"Get me some tobacco for this guest with such terrible manners," Thornbrugh roared, laughing.

As the American filled his pipe, Jarrell said, "As soon as I arrived here, I asked after you. But as the days slipped past, I feared more and more you'd lost your hair."

"Wagh! If'n that half-breed giant named Sharpe couldn't raise this nigger's hair last summer, ain't a Injun gonna take what's left of this poor scalp!"

He slapped Bass on the leg, sensing such an exquisite joy in seeing this friend after a long, long year of separation. "You've brought many pelts to trade?"

"Nope, I ain't got but a few left to barter off."

"Not a good year for you and young Paddock?"

The American smiled. "It was a damn fine year for the two of us, Jarrell. But I left most all of them plews behind in Taos with Josiah."

"Taos," he repeated, confused. "Josiah's not here with you?"

Having puffed on his pipe to get it started with a twig from the nearby fire, Titus Bass began to tell the story of all that had taken place since last summer's raucous trading fair. From that chase after an old Shoshone friend turned horse thief, through their deadly hunt for an Arapaho war party in the Bayou Salade, on to those Christmas and New Year's celebrations in the little village of San Fernando de Taos, where Scratch had run onto an old friend believed dead. A chance meeting that spurred Scratch all the way back to St. Louis through the maw of winter, then off to the west again for the massive mud fort the Bent brothers had erected beside the Arkansas River—completing that deadly journey in hopes of putting some old ghosts to rest.

"This Silas Cooper shot you?"

The American tugged up the hem of his cloth shirt to show the vividly pink bullet wounds.

A dark-skinned stranger stepped beneath the shady bower, leaning in to inspect one of the puckers as he commented, "You got nothing better to do, Jarrell—but go and look at this man's bullet holes?"

Thornbrugh snorted, "By the stars, the bullet made that wound came a hairsbreadth from killing my friend here. Introduce yourself proper, Thomas."

"Thomas McKay," the man declared, holding his hand out as he backed a step.

Watching the American grab McKay's hand, Jarrell explained, "This be Titus Bass—"

"Yes, I've heard of you," McKay replied, his dark Indian eyes narrowing. "You come to Vancouver to visit the Doctor."

"Two winters back it was," Bass stated. "A good man, the Doctor. He is what you see of him."

"Thomas here is leading the Doctor's brigade this year," Thornbrugh explained.

"We ain't been doing much in the way of trading," McKay confessed as he took a dipper of water from one of the company's laborers and drank. Wiping the dribble from his chin, he said, "But we didn't figure to scare up much trading from you Americans anyway."

Bass looked at Thornbrugh. "Company men bound to deal with their own traders. Them what trap for American Fur gonna trade for company supplies. And Rocky Mountain Fur gotta trade with Sublette."

"Last year them Rocky Mountain Fur partners had contracted with that Yank named Wyeth to buy supplies off him this summer," McKay said. "But Sublette come in a couple days ahead of Wyeth, so Fitzpatrick started trading off pelts even before Wyeth got to the valley."

Thornbrugh wagged his head. "So now Wyeth has all those goods Rocky Mountain Fur said they'd take off his hands, with no one to trade with."

"How 'bout the free men?" Bass inquired. "Where they been trading their furs?"

Jarrell could tell by the set of Scratch's jaw that the unfairness of Sublette's actions didn't sit well with his American friend. "Sadly, from what I have been witness to myself, it appears most of your American free men are conducting their business with Sublette."

"Damn 'em," Bass growled, his brow furrowing. "But it don't s'prise me none. Most of 'em knowed Sublette for years now. Some trapped with him back when, or they been trading with him for the last few ronnyvooz. Natural, I s'pose, for 'em to stick with what they know. But it damn well sours my milk to see a man break his vow with another, like Fitz and the rest done to Wyeth."

"Is there no honor among you Americans?" McKay inquired with a wry grin.

"Not when you're speaking of prime pelts and beaver country," Bass confessed. "For years now there's been a war on between Rocky Mountain Fur and Astor's company."

"From what I've learned over the past few days," Thornbrugh injected, "no longer is there any war between them. Instead, they've divided up the fur country on the east side of the mountains."

Bass bellowed, "Divided it between 'em!"

Finally settling on the ground beside Thornbrugh, McKay declared, "Astor's retired and turned his business on the upper Missouri over to Pierre Chouteau in St. Louis—so that Upper Missouri Outfit's gonna run things up there from here on out."

"They'll have that country all to themselves now that Sublette and Campbell are pulling out," Thornbrugh continued. "In turn, American

Fur won't give Sublette's company any competition for a year down here in these central and southern mountains."

Bass wagged his head as if it was incomprehensible to him. "They made 'em a truce? Dividing up the beaver country a'tween 'em . . . and here it was not so long ago the free men were hoping McKenzie would come on down here from his American Fur post to give Sublette some competition—his prices were so goddamned high!"

"Still are," Jarrell replied. "And what he offers for fur is terribly low."

"So Sublette's got this cat skinned two ways of Sunday, don't he?" Bass observed.

McKay explained, "McLoughlin sent us here to sell our goods at prices lower than what any American trader sells for, and to buy beaver at a price higher than Americans would pay."

Bass looked around him a moment. "Don't see no crowd lining up to sell you their beaver, fellas."

Scratching at his cheek, the bearded Thornbrugh said, "Appears your Americans will trade with Sublette, no matter how black-hearted his business ethics."

"You gotta dance the way Sublette dances: ain't you offered them trappers any of your whiskey?" Bass inquired.

McKay exploded in laughter. "We didn't bring any liquor! The Doctor's an honorable man, so he wouldn't hear of any whiskey trade."

"Which puts us at a decided disadvantage," Thornbrugh stated. "Sublette opened his packs and his whiskey kegs three days before Wyeth ever came in. Which meant that Rocky Mountain Fur was dead and buried by the time that Yank showed up to sell them his goods—"

"Rocky Mountain Fur's . . . d-dead?" Bass sputtered.

"Sublette bought them out, one at a time I hear," Jarrell said. "There were five partners, but by the time Sublette got through offering them this or offering them that for their shares, only two of them decided to stay on with Sublette."

"Which ones?" Bass inquired.

"Thomas Fitzpatrick is one," McKay answered. "Don't know who the other one is."

"Rocky Mountain Fur, dead," Bass repeated, staring at the trampled grass. "Hard for that to make sense to me."

"So where's your future lie, Titus Bass?" Jarrell asked. "You want to bring your pelts over here and trade with Hudson's Bay?"

The American regarded Thornbrugh a long and thoughtful moment, then admitted, "I figure I owe first crack to the Americans."

McKay roared, "You're gonna give in to Sublette's temptations too?"

"No." Bass wagged his head. "Feel I ought'n see what Wyeth's got to offer a man like me what's come in late too, after Sublette's bamboozled all the rest into backing out on their word. What the Yankee can't trade for, I'll be over to see if you can help me out, fellas."

Thornbrugh slapped his hand down on Bass's thigh. "Good man, Titus Bass. Perhaps there is a bit of honor left in a few of you Americans after all."

"We still got lots of honor, Jarrell," Titus snapped. "A man ain't nothing without his honor. Pulling something so underhanded like that goddamned Sublette done makes all us Americans look bad."

By the time Scratch had pushed more than three miles downstream that afternoon, what had been a faint, far-off hodgepodge of sounds became the familiar revelry of rendezvous as he drew closer.

Down from the bluffs lining both sides of the valley wound small groups of hunters leading pack animals, carcasses of deer, antelope, and elk lashed securely athwart their sturdy backs. In the bottoms men competed with warriors from the visiting Nez Perce and Flathead camps in horse races, handsome fleet geldings as the champion's prize. Even greater numbers of the trappers stripped down to no more than breech-clout and moccasins as they pitted themselves against one another in drunken footraces. Cheered on by foggy-headed companions, the finish line judged by the unsteadiest among them, most of the contests erupted into a drunken brawl as knots of men rolled about in the tall grass.

Behind it all arose the periodic boom of rifle fire echoing from the meandering hemline of bluffs where others shot at the mark for a trea-sured prize or another cup of Sublette's whiskey. Thin, ghostly wisps of gun smoke intertwined to trail lazily on the breezeless air that hot after-noon, its whitish gray captured among the branches of leafy cottonwood and willow. From creekside and meadow alike came the constant din of whoops and hurrahs, loud voices raised in cheer, mingling with a few strident calls made in heat and anger as men fell to gouging eyes and kneeing groins, urged on by their backers.

More than six hundred white men—company and free—languished and played, celebrating their survival, toasting their having met the chal-lenge for another year even though the greater number of them hadn't trapped near enough to pay off the entirety of last year's debt, much less be free to purchase everything needed for the coming season without hanging oneself on the company's hook. Six hundred, not as many as last year for sure, but still more than had gathered for that high-water mark in Pierre's Hole two summers ago.

Horses grazed, while some took a dusty roll, freed now for long days when they would not suffer the heavy burdens of the fur trade. A time for saddle sores, cinch ulcers, and herd bites to heal before making that climb to the autumn high country.

Off in the distance through the afternoon's haze he could make out the tops of the lodgepole swirls, faint fingers of wood smoke still rising from fires tended by the squaws in that camp. Of a sudden he wondered if that were the Flathead village, and if chance dictated it might be the people Looks Far Woman left when she chose to find Josiah, the father of her child. Perhaps he would see before rendezvous played itself out, if only to tell her kin she was safer in that Mexican town on the border of Comanche country than she was living at the edge of the Blackfoot domain.

Then again, that band might well be Nez Perce. A man couldn't really tell from this distance. Not with all the dust raised by the teeming crowds in the Rocky Mountain Fur camp he was about to enter, a veritable town with its streets laid out among the shady trees, the grass trampled by hundreds of feet as groups came and went of some serious purpose.

"Got furs to trade with Sublette, do ye?"

Bass reined up, staring down at the face of an old companion.

"Elbridge?"

"Get down here and shake my paw, Titus Bass."

Behind Gray the others streamed, a handful in all as Scratch leaped to the ground, dropping Samantha's lead rope. Breathless when he finished hugging these dear old friends, done pounding backs and withstanding the blows of doubled fists hurled his way, he stood back and stared at the semicircle of their faces.

Dragging a hand beneath the dribble at the end of his nose, he sighed, "You ugly boys sure make a sight for these ol' eyes."

"So where's that pretty wife of your'n?" Rufus Graham asked, his auburn hair just hinting at turning gray. He was missing those four front teeth, both top and bottom. "The gal you had roped to you last ronnyvoo finally get smart and run off with a good-looking man?"

"Naw," Titus said with a big grin. "She's back yonder to our camp, upstream. We had us a girl-child."

"Merciful heavens! A girl?" Caleb Wood echoed.

"Purty as her mother," Bass declared.

"God bless!" exclaimed Solomon Fish, rubbing the long ringlets of his blond beard. "Pray God saw to it the little child didn't take after her homely pap!"

Bass suddenly looped an arm around Solomon's neck and playfully rubbed the top of his mangy blond hair with a handful of knuckles before allowing the struggling man to go free.

"Where's Wyeth?" Bass asked. "I heard tell when we come in yestiddy that the Yank was already in from the East."

None of them answered at first, until the stocky Isaac Simms said,

"He's yonder. More'n a couple miles on down the creek. On past them Nepercy what's camped close to Sublette's tents."

"That's Sublette off yonder, eh?"

Caleb nodded. "He's doing a handsome business."

Of a sudden it struck Titus. "Why you boys camped in here with Rocky Mountain Fur? You ain't throwed in with the company men, have you?"

Wood toed the grass a moment before answering. "It ain't been so good for us since losing . . . J-jack," he said quietly.

Bass looked around at the others, most of whom did not meet his gaze. "Been two summers now, ain't it, boys?"

Graham swallowed and answered, "Y-yeah. Two year, Scratch— since them god-blamed Blackfoot got him in the Pierre's Hole fight."

"But when I saw you fellers last summer on the Green, seemed you'd done fair for that first year 'thout Jack Hatcher in the lead," Titus declared.

"The more we talked about it last ronnyvoo," Elbridge explained, "the more we figured we ought'n try some new country up north when we pulled away from ronnyvoo."

Solemnly, Isaac said, "But a man'd be stupid to ride north 'thout a brigade round him."

"So you boys throwed in with one of the outfits, eh?" Bass inquired.

"Bridger's, it were," Caleb volunteered. "Fitzpatrick was going to the Powder, so we signed on with Bridger."

Titus could see it written on their faces—how the toll of losing their leader had marked every man jack of them. No matter how they had spouted and spumed in protest at Mad Jack Hatcher, not a one of them was leader enough to take the reins and make an outfit of them once again. They were good men, hard-cased and veterans all. But they were followers still. No man could fault them for realizing that before every last one of them lost his hair.

"It's a good thing," Scratch told them, "for the easy beavers been took already. To go where the beaver still plays, a man needs to go in goodly numbers. Wise you boys chose to throw in with Bridger's brigade."

And he watched how his words visibly struck each one, bringing relief and smiles to eyes and faces.

"Where's that Josiah, the young'un you brung with you to the Pierre's Hole fight?" Simms asked.

"He was with you last year on the Green," Rufus said.

Bass sucked down some wind. "Left him in Taos with his wife and boy, 'long with some trade goods to set up shop."

Caleb eyed him. "You figger to be a trader now?"

With a wag of his head Titus answered, "Just Josiah. He'd tempted

Lady Fate's fickle hand enough while we rode together. Time was for me to give him his leave."

Scratching the beginnings of his potbelly, Elbridge asked, "Who you riding with come autumn?"

"On my own hook, boys."

"By jam—just you and the woman?" Isaac inquired.

"And our girl."

"You ought'n throw in with us, Scratch," Caleb observed.

"That's right," Gray said. "Bridger knows you. He ain't got nothing 'gainst a man packing a squaw along."

With a shake of his head, Titus quieted their suggestions. "Time's come for me to go it alone. Moseying with a brigade's gonna be the best for most fellas. But there's hard-assed pricknoses like me what're better off on their lonesome. Thanks for the asking. If I was to lay down my traps with any bunch, it'd be you boys . . . and only you boys."

Solomon asked, "Got time for some whiskey?"

Titus looked at the five slowly, his eyes narrowing. "You figger this here nigger got stupid in the last year? Course I got time for some whiskey and some stories. Then I ought'n be on my way to find Wyeth."

"But Billy Sublette's got his trade tents just past the bend in the creek," Caleb said. "Hell, he's so close I could throw a rock and likely hit one of his whiskey kegs!"

"No thanks," Bass said as he turned around and took up both the reins to the horse and Samantha's lead rope. "From what I heard 'bout the underhanded jigger-pokey Sublette pulled on Wyeth—I don't care to have nothing more to do with Billy Sublette."

"So I s'pose you've heard there ain't no more Rocky Mountain Fur?" Isaac asked.

"But we're still working for Bridger's company," Rufus explained.

"From the sounds of things," Bass said, "Fitzpatrick and Bridger can call their company what they want . . . but Billy Sublette still owns 'em and calls their tune."

Elbridge suddenly placed the flat of his hand against Bass's chest to bring Scratch to a halt. "Then I take it you're a nigger what won't drink none of Billy Sublette's whiskey."

Titus thought on it a moment, careful that his face remained gravely pensive. "Is Sublette's whiskey as good an' powerful as it ever was?"

"Damn right it is!" Caleb roared.

"Then I ain't above accepting a free drink of that low-down thieving Sublette's whiskey," Bass declared boldly, "not when I get me the chance to drink that whiskey with the likes of you boys!"

THREE

As the sun had eased down on rendezvous that day of revel and reunion, Bass had crawled atop the bare back of the buffalo-runner, looped Samantha's lead rope around his hand, and groggily pointed them north. It was twilight before he reached their tiny camp where Waits-by-the-Water had a fire going and thick slabs of antelope tenderloin sizzling in his old iron skillet.

"You find the trader you went in search of?"

"No," he said to her voice at his back as he loosened knots securing those packs he had tied to the back of the mule. Crow words came hard with his thick, swollen tongue that wasn't near as nimble as it had been when he left camp hours ago, so he settled for English. "Ran onto some old friends."

She stepped up to him, their daughter straddling one of Waits's hips, clinging like a possum kit to her mother. For a moment she only stared at her husband's eyes, then leaned in close, inches from his face, and sniffed.

Bass jerked his head back. "What you doing?"

With a tinkle of laughter Waits replied, "You've been drinking the white man's *bi'li'ka'wii'taa'le,* the real bad water!"

"Just because you don't like whiskey don't mean I cain't enjoy having some ever' now and then!" he protested slowly, struggling to keep his tongue from getting as tangled as were the knots his fingers fought.

"Here," she said, taking his hand and turning him, starting toward their fire. Waits convinced him to settle upon their blanket-and-robe bedding. "Take our daughter," and she passed the infant down to him. "I'll see to the animals."

"Y-you're a good woman," he said to her back as she yanked free the first of the ropes and pulled off one of the beaver packs.

It was a few moments before he grew aware of his daughter's chatter. There on his lap she played with her fingers, popped them into her mouth, licked them, then pulled them out and played with them again as she babbled constantly. Struck dumb, he listened with rapt attention, concentrating on the infant as she played and talked, talked and played, her skin turned the color of copper by the fire there at twilight.

Why had he never really listened to her until now? Was it the whiskey that had numbed most of his other senses, dulling them so that her chatter somehow pricked his attention? He laughed—and the baby stopped her babble, gazing up at him with widening eyes.

In English he said, "For weeks now I been wondering what we was gonna name you, little one."

The moment he finished she gurgled happily again, which made him laugh once more, causing her in turn to stare at him in wonder.

"You and me can have us a talk, cain't we?" he asked, bouncing her on a thigh. "I talk and laugh, just like you, pretty one. So you understand me. And you're gonna grow up talking your pap's tongue, 'long with your mama's tongue too. Gonna talk happy in both!"

As soon as his voice drifted off, the infant set right in with her cheery babble. "So when your mama gets mad at me and don't wanna talk, or when she don't wanna have nothing to do with speaking the white man's tongue I'm trying to teach her—why, you and me can have us all the talk we want!"

"Talk?" Waits repeated the word in English as she stepped up, then knelt beside him on the blankets.

"Yes," he replied in English, and slowly continued in his own language, "we're gonna see which one of you learns my tongue first. Mama, or daughter."

"You will teach her to talk the white man's words the way you are teaching me?"

He nodded, feeling the fuzziness creep across his forehead there by the warmth of the fire. "I'm hoping she'll want to talk to me when you're angry at something I've done or said."

"Do I hurt your feelings when I won't talk to you?"

The girl reached out for her mother, so he settled the baby in Waits-by-the-Water's lap. "I don't like letting things go," he confessed. "I want to get things settled quick. Get shed of those bad feelings soon as we can. Only way to do that is to talk."

She brushed the babe's short hair with a palm as she considered that. "Yes," Waits agreed. "When you make me angry with you, I don't want to hurt your feelings because I am so mad I don't know what to say. Now I know that you want me to talk."

"That's the only way to . . . to . . ." But he lost track of what he had wanted to say.

"The white man's real bad water made you forget, husband," she said, then leaned in to kiss his hairy cheek.

"No, the whiskey just makes me stupid," he admitted in English. "Better I sleep now."

"Sleep," she echoed the English word, and reached down to stuff a blanket under his head as he settled back onto the robes.

"Like I said, you're a good woman," Bass whispered in English as he closed his eyes.

"You . . . good man," she said the words quietly, haltingly, in her husband's tongue.

He smiled and sighed, and listened to the baby softly chatter as he sank into sweet oblivion.

It was late of the next morning when he awoke, his head tender as a raw wound, his temples thumping louder and louder still as he fought to sit up without his brain sloshing around inside his skull.

But at the fire where she was carefully cutting pieces of winter moccasins from a section of smoked buffalo hide, she heard him moving, groaning. In her cradleboard their daughter was asleep, propped against a bale of beaver hides. Without a word Waits laid her work aside and kneed up to the fire, pouring coffee into a dented tin cup.

"Drink this," she said to him in Crow, holding the cup out between them. Then, as he peered up at her with grateful eyes, Waits spoke in English. "Coffee . . . for husband's s-sick head."

He tapped his puckered lips with a fingertip. After she leaned over to kiss him, Bass whispered, "What'd this ol' bonehead ever do to deserve such a good woman like you?"

After swilling down several pint cups of coffee and gnawing on some flank steak from the antelope carcass they had hanging in a nearby tree, Titus started to feel halfway human again. By early afternoon the roll of thunder had eased at his temples, and that greasy pitch and heave to his belly had departed.

"Do you want my help?" she asked when he brought the mule into camp and dragged over the two small bales of beaver he had to trade.

"You're a pure delight," he said in English.

"Dee-light?" she repeated.

Grinning, "Do you know the word *smile?*"

"Smile, yes," and her whole face lit up.

"You make me smile in here," he said using her tongue, tapping his chest. "A big, big smile in here."

"Too, me," she attempted in English as she pulled up the thick, woolly packsaddle pad made from a mountain sheep and lapped it over the mule's back.

Minutes later beneath the painful glare of a summer sun he encountered a pack train on the move that afternoon, migrating toward him, moving up Ham's Fork.

"This here Wyeth's outfit?" he asked as he brought his pony alongside three of the horsemen who were wrangling less than a dozen horned cows at the far side of the march.

"It is," one answered.

"Where's Wyeth?"

"At the head, yonder," and that second man gestured toward the front of the cavalcade stirring dust from every hoof into the still, hot air.

"Thankee," Bass replied as he kicked heels into the pony and they bolted into a lope, crossing the narrow bottomland that meandered between bare bluffs and the twisting stream.

In no time he was standing in the wide cottonwood stirrups, hollering, "Wyeth! Wyeth!"

One of the figures ahead turned in the saddle, bringing a hand to his brow as he peered from beneath the brim of his hat. "I'm Wyeth."

Slowing his pony to match the pack train's pace, Bass found himself suddenly grown anxious that his afternoon of reunion and celebration had put him one day late in trading for what the three of them would need through the coming year. The Yank's brigade was clearly on its way.

"You pulling out?" he asked of the leader. "Leaving ronnyvoo?"

"Not yet," the man answered. His small eyes in that overly narrow face squinted in the shade beneath his hat brim. "That time will come soon," and he sighed with resignation. "But for now, we're only migrating upstream to find more grass for our stock."

"Them cows I see'd over there?"

Wyeth grinned. "That's what's left of the herd we started with."

"You gonna open for trading?"

That question plainly startled Wyeth. His eyes blinked in surprise as he appeared to consider his response. "W-why, there hasn't been anyone wanting to . . . not a soul's come to me, our tents to trade. Suppose I would be willing to trade. Uh, yes—well, we do have near everything we brought west with us from Missouri to supply Rocky Mountain Fur." Wyeth grinned. "Yes, mister—I'll be open for business tomorrow morning after breakfast."

With great relief Bass inquired, "You eat early or late of a morning, Wyeth?"

The trader smiled even bigger, the sharply chiseled edges to his lean face easing somewhat with mirth. "I'm one to eat early."

Bass held out his hand and shook with the Yankee before he loped away. "I'll see you after breakfast."

"I said it last year, and I've said it more than once this summer already," Wyeth declared to Bass that following morning, "but most of these men out here in the mountains are nothing less than a low breed of scoundrel."

"You countin' me in that bunch?"

Wyeth slung his head back and laughed heartily. "Not by a long shot, Mr. Bass."

Titus thumbed through some more of the lighter amber-colored flints. "If'n you had yourself whiskey to trade, I'd be one to give you all my business."

"Looking to give yourself a celebration, are you?" Wyeth asked. "And a good-sized headache when you're done too?"

"Maybe a good carouse, but the days are past when Titus Bass gets so far down in his cups he can't crawl back out till a morning or two later. Gimme a dozen of them wiping sticks," and he shoved a double handful of flints across the top of a wooden box at Wyeth's clerk.

"How many winters you been out here, Bass?"

"Twenty-five were my first summer."

"An Ashley man."

"No," and he wagged his head emphatically. "Come west on my own hook and paid dearly for it, I s'pose. Lost some hair to some red niggers down to Bayou Salade, but I ain't gone under yet."

Wyeth clucked sadly, then said, "Appears the only ones making any real money out of the mountain fur trade was Ashley and now Sublette. Damn him, damn him."

"Heard how he finagled the Rocky Mountain Fur boys to break their agreement with you."

"Sublette overtook my supply train not far out of the western settlements," Wyeth declared, "and he stayed ahead of me the rest of the way."

"Knowed the trail better, I'd s'pose," Bass stated as he rubbed a thumb across the edge of a camp ax.

"I couldn't travel as fast as he with the cattle," Wyeth explained. "Started out with more. But what I have left we'll put to good use eventually."

"How much for an ax?"

"Two-fifty," Wyeth said.

"Gimme two. What you figger to do for fur season?" Titus said as he inched down the rows of crates and blankets Wyeth's men had opened and spread across a shady patch of ground beside Ham's Fork—not all that far south of where Bass had camped with his family so that he might stay as far away as he could from the loud and raucous company camps pitched downstream toward Black's Fork.

"I may send some of the men out. I've been struggling to convince more to sign on with me when I venture into the Snake River country."

"Beaver country there."

"Yes," Wyeth exclaimed, beaming. "I want to get as far as I can from that country where Sublette and Campbell are building their fort on the Platte."

"Jehoshaphat!" he exclaimed, coming to a stop. "W-where on the Platte?"

"Mouth of La Ramee's Fork, right there on the trail to the mountains."

Nodding, Bass said, "I know the place. Damn, a fort just east of the mountains. And you know them two Bent brothers got theirs down south on the Arkansas. So you're gonna trap west of the mountains, eh?"

"I've got these men in my employ, and a supply train filled with trade goods," Wyeth explained. "I'll put them to work in the Snake country before the end of August, then go on to the mouth of the Columbia. Plan to return to the Snake before winter sets in hard."

"All the way down the Columbia," Bass repeated. "Going to see that white-headed Doctor there?"

"No. I'm meeting a ship there. Our enterprise plans to catch enough salmon to fill the belly of that ship before we turn it around for Boston and I turn east to rendezvous with my brigade."

"I got a friend what's come here with Hudson's Bay," Bass explained. "It was him told me about how Sublette dealt you off the bottom of the deck with Rocky Mountain Fur."

"Ah, but Doctor McLoughlin's spies don't realize that I'll be up there on the Columbia real soon to take for myself some of their salmon!" Wyeth spouted with glee.

Titus ran his thumbnail down a bar of lead. "What's your lead going for?"

"Dollar the pound."

"Gimme twenty pounds," Bass advised. "Tell me, how you figure them Hudson's Bay men are spies?"

"Hell," Wyeth gushed, "they couldn't come here expecting to do much business at all. You take a look at their camp?"

"I was there yestiddy."

"See much in the way of trade goods?" Wyeth prodded. "Anything anywhere close to what I got laid out for you here?"

Scratch looked it over, side to side, and had to admit the Yankee was right. "Didn't see nowhere near what you got."

"And you won't—because they didn't bring but enough to make a little show. They aren't here to trade, not really. They come to be Mc-Loughlin's eyes and ears. Ever since Jedediah Smith stumbled into Vancouver, the Doctor wants to stay informed of just what Americans will be trapping this side of the mountains—in what Hudson's Bay claims is their country."

"Maybeso," Bass replied, not really wanting to admit that Jarrell Thornbrugh could be there for the unexpressed purpose of spying in the American fur country for McLoughlin.

And this was American fur country, no matter what Hudson's Bay believed, no matter what treaty some government fellas had signed their names to in jointly occupying this ground. But if the central Rockies ever began to run out of beaver, Bass was damned sure the American trapping brigades would push farther and farther west, bumping right up against the British outfits with greater frequency.

Mayhaps that would leave the northern rivers for him to trap with little crowding to speak of.

Scratch turned to find one of those who had been grading his pelts now coming up behind Wyeth. "What you gonna give me for my beaver?"

Wyeth took the slip of paper, glanced at it, then stuffed it into the pocket of his canvas breeches. "You didn't have much in the way of fur."

"Already took care of most down to Taos."

"Didn't leave you with much in the way to outfit you for another year," Wyeth explained.

"I don't need much. 'Sides, I got some possibles cached up on the Yallerstone," Bass replied. Then he gestured toward all that he had chosen so far. "My plews gonna cover what's here? And still leave me a little for at least one good whiskey headache?"

"Believe me, Mr. Bass," the Yankee said, "for bringing the last of your furs to me instead of taking them to that thief William Sublette, you're going to get yourself a one-day bargain in trade goods—the likes of which you'll never see again!"

Throughout the rest of that morning they arm-wrestled on the value of the last of Bass's pelts, then on the price of each and every item Scratch had pulled from the crates and barrels of trade goods. And when it was over, they both could smile and have themselves a drink, toasting their mutual fortunes.

"I'll be trapping up in Crow country," Bass explained, eyeing the number of crates and bales in Wyeth's camp. "My wife's people. If'n the furs are good up there, I'll stick close to home for spring too. You gonna haul this hull outfit around, supplying 'em from your winter camp?"

Wyeth stared at the last of his whiskey shimmering in the bottom of his cup a moment, then declared, "I suppose I have no choice—seeing how I've been left with all these trade goods, abandoned by a faithless group of bastards who are refusing to honor their contract with me."

"Goddamned shame a man's word ain't wuth near what it used to be," Bass commiserated.

"So what does such a man with all these trade goods do, Mr. Bass?"

For a minute he reflected on the possibilities. "I been out to the Columbia where you said you was going to meet that ship of your'n."

"You've been to Vancouver yourself?"

"Yep—so I don't figger a savvy nigger would wanna build hisself a post anywhere near the white-headed Doctor."

"McLoughlin," Wyeth said thoughtfully. "Yes. It wouldn't make a lot of sense, would it?"

"Mayhaps a man with all this plunder to trade"—and Bass swung his free arm in a semicircle to indicate the profusion of goods—"should stake out his own ground."

"His own ground?"

"Find hisself a spot where he won't have no one near to bump up again' him in business."

Wyeth's eyes shone wide and bright. "Yes, yes!"

"Someplace where he would plop hisself down and be there with his post and his goods for the trappers what wander by," Bass explained, seeing that fire of excitement flicker boldly in the Yankee's eyes. "Someplace where that post of his would bring in the friendlies."

"The friendlies?" Wyeth drained his cup, setting it aside.

"Tribes what cotton up to the white man."

"Yes! Like the ones here," Wyeth cheered. "Flathead, Nez Perce."

"Snake too."

"Why, the Shoshone roam that Snake River country."

"Good place as any for a man to be when he's got him a passel of trade goods."

Slapping both palms down on the tops of his thighs, the Yankee vaulted to his feet suddenly. "A good place where I'll raise my fort—squarely in the middle! Right between the Hudson's Bay at Vancouver on the Columbia . . . and the post Sublette and Campbell are raising at the mouth of La Ramee's Fork! God bless you, Titus Bass! God bless you!"

"W-what the hell you bless me for?" and he found his cup being filled by the exuberant Yankee.

"All is not lost! Don't you see?" Wyeth swept up his own cup again, pouring some amber fluid into it from a clay jug. "From the other outfits come here to rendezvous, I've somehow managed to add another thirty men to my brigade . . . and now I know where to base my operations! By building my own fort squarely in the western country!"

As for Wyeth, the Yankee did have little choice but to swallow the bone he had been thrown at this turn of life's trail.

There truly was no recourse against those who had conspired against him, just as he himself admitted in correspondence written to his financial backers in the East over the last few days, "For there is no Law here."

Fair play and honesty had apparently counted for nothing under the hot summer sun that second of July as the Wyeth brigade set out for the Snake country, escorting Jason Lee's party of five Protestant missionaries bound for the land of the Nez Perce with what remained of their horned cattle.

A hungover Bass had finished loading up the last of the goods he had traded from Wyeth that morning as the Boston merchant eagerly prepared to pull out for the west, accompanied by a pair of naturalists he had escorted from St. Louis: Thomas Nuttall, a botanist, and John Kirk Townsend, a Philadelphia ornithologist.

Grittily shaking hands with the two partners who had done nothing to stop Sublette's underhanded scheming, Wyeth grimly prophesied to Fitzpatrick and Bridger, "You will find that you have only bound yourselves over to receive your supplies at such price as may be inflicted on you, and that all that you will ever make in this country will go to pay for your goods. You will be kept as you have been—a mere slave to catch beaver for others."

Upon marching away from that rendezvous in the valley of Ham's Fork, the Yankee tipped his hat and smiled at Sublette and Campbell, those who had done everything in their power to destroy the success of his business enterprises, vicious competitors who out of some species of curiosity had come to see him off.

To them and the remnants of the Rocky Mountain Fur Company partners, Wyeth vowed, "Gentlemen, I will roll a stone into your garden that you will never be able to get out."

His was a threat that would echo even louder across the years to come.

The unmerciful August sun stung Bass's eyes with the burn of mud-dauber wasps as he stepped from the cool shelter of the cottonwoods along Ham's Fork to watch the approach of those eighteen Frenchmen and half-breeds moseying unhurriedly behind Thomas McKay and Jarrell Thornbrugh. The seething orb had just emerged from the ridges to the east, but already the motionless air felt stifling.

"Not a good day for the trail!" Titus called out as the ragged column approached.

"We better get out while we still have some fat on our bones!" Thornbrugh roared, and brought his tall horse to a halt. He swiped a hand down his sweaty face. "Not one of us used to this bloody heat, Scratch."

"Figure we can stay and sweat in the shade," McKay declared, "or we can start back to our country—"

"Where it's cooler," Thornbrugh interrupted, "and green too!"

For a moment Bass regarded the austere beauty of the burnt-sienna bluffs that rimmed the valley, shoved up like massive, mighty shoulders against the pale summer-blue of the morning sky. "Green there all the time, ain't it?"

"Winter or summer," McKay agreed.

"You can keep it," he told them. "I'll stay on here where there's real seasons. Much as I hate the summers—I'd rather have me my seasons."

"The snows don't get deep in Oregon country," Thornbrugh chided as he started to rock out of the saddle. "And the snows don't stay near as long as they do in your mountains."

"You ain't got me to worry about moving in with you, Jarrell!"

"If not, will we see you next rendezvous?"

He watched the Englishman step up before him. " 'Less I've gone under—that's for sartin."

"You have all you'll need for another year, my friend?"

"Believe I do."

"Powder and lead—"

"Yep."

"Blankets and beads?"

"Yes, Jarrell," he answered with a smile. "Even got some girlews and geegaws off Wyeth in my trading."

"That Yank's sure to trouble the Company," McKay snarled. "I just know it, Jarrell."

Thornbrugh turned back to Bass. "You'll watch what you got left for hair?"

"I got me others to watch over now," Scratch replied.

"They're beauties, let me tell you," the tall man exclaimed with admiration. "Good thing the wee one takes after her mother—gorgeous as she is."

"Wouldn't do to have a sweet babe like that take after her mud-ugly ol' man, would it?"

And then they stood there, motionless a long moment longer, staring at one another, growing in the unease of knowing the time had come once again.

"I said my fare-thees to you twice't a'fore, Jarrell," Bass stabbed the silence between them as the men sweated and the horses stamped in a semicircle around the two of them.

"What's that you're trying to say?"

"That this may be a fare-thee too, but it's also a promise to cross your tracks again."

Titus held out his hand between them, but Thornbrugh shoved it aside roughly and seized the American in both of his massive arms, pulling the smaller, thinner man into a ferocious embrace. At that very moment Scratch was grateful Jarrell nearly squeezed the breath out of his body. For that moment Thornbrugh choked off the sob that threatened to overwhelm Titus.

When the big Englishman pulled back, their arms outstretched between them, Bass blinked several times, squinting as if troubled with the intense light. But it was the fire of those sudden tears that stung his eyes now.

Thornbrugh inched back another step. "I'll hold you to that promise, Titus Bass—true lord of this great wilderness! If God doesn't take me, and the good Doctor so chooses, I'll be back here to your rendezvous next year."

"I'll be here, friend. Lay your set to that." And he studied the way the huge man moved as Thornbrugh turned and stepped back to his horse, taking his reins from McKay, then rose to the saddle.

"Give my respects to the Doctor."

"I will do that," Thornbrugh agreed as he urged his horse away slowly.

"He's a good man . . . for an Englishman!"

Jarrell bawled with a crack of sudden laughter that split the hot air. "You aren't a bad sort either—not for a wretched American!"

Then he called out, "Watch your backtrail, Jarrell!"

Thornbrugh turned and smiled hugely with those massive teeth of his like whitewashed pickets surrounding a settlement house. He waved one last time, then twisted back around in the saddle and was swallowed up by the rest of those bringing up the rear of that column.

When Bass finally felt the fiery touch of the sun against the side of his face, he reluctantly wheeled about and started for the shade, finding Waits-by-the-Water standing in the shadows, the sleeping infant at her shoulder.

"It pleases my heart so much that you have such friends as these," she said as he came into the shade.

Laying an arm over her shoulder, he turned to watch the small brigade slowly move away, disappearing into the shimmering heat rising in waves from the sunburnt landscape.

"First Maker has blessed me with a few good people through all my days," he responded in Crow. "The sort of friends that show me, no matter all the mistakes I made in my life, just how the Grandfather still smiles on me."

"A man's life is not all horses and battle honors," she said. "In the end, a man's life must count for more than that, husband."

"Yes," he agreed, turning with her now, heading back to their bowers as the valley fell quiet once more. "Good friends, and this wonderful woman who has blessed me with a beautiful child."

"A child who has no name."

"But not for long," he said, squeezing her against him.

Breathless, she turned within the yoke of his arm. "Have you chosen a name for our daughter?"

"Tonight when the sun settles to the edge of the earth, we will celebrate for her."

FOUR

It seemed as if the rest of the world held its breath.

With the sinking of the sun and the arrival of twilight, that faint afternoon stirring of the air grew still. From the burning cottonwood limbs a dizzying array of sparks popped free, each dancing firefly swirling upward without torment in its dazzling ascent.

The baby talked and talked, more than she ever had, playing with her hands, reaching out for the distant sparks as if to snatch them from the darkening sky. Ever since arriving there at rendezvous a handful of days ago, she had suddenly taken to chattering, more every day it seemed. A happy, cheering babble.

This evening as the baby talked to the sparks and those leaping blue-yellow flames, Titus sat with his daughter on his lap, cradled against him, his back resting against a downed stump as Waits-by-the-Water completed the last of her chores at the edge of the fire, stuffing utensils, root, and leaf spices away in her rawhide bags, then looked over at her husband and sighed.

"This has not been an easy day," she admitted.

"Why?"

"It is hard to wait," the woman confessed. "Knowing she would finally have a name."

"She's always had a name," Bass explained.

Waits stared at him a moment more before asking, "What do you mean, our daughter has always had a name?"

"One Above has had a name for her all along, perhaps even while she was growing in your belly—preparing for her arrival in the world."

Rising sideways, the woman got to her feet and moved around to his side of the fire. There she settled at his knee, facing Bass, her legs tucked to the side in that woman way of hers.

"If she had a name from the beginning," Waits asked, "why didn't we know it?"

"First Maker was waiting for us to find out what her name is," he declared.

"We had to find out her name?" and she smiled at him, the lines of confusion disappearing from her forehead.

"All we had to do was find out what the Creator had already named her."

"Was this easy for you to learn what her name was?"

"No, not easy at all," he admitted. "I was wrong three times."

"Three? How . . . how did you know you were wrong?"

He shrugged, presenting the baby one of his gnarled fingers. She grabbed it readily. "Only from the feeling I had inside."

"You felt this three times?"

With a nod Bass said, "At first I thought of *daa'xxa'pe.*"

"Little Red Calf?" and she chuckled behind her fingers.

"Remember how red she looked for a long time after she was born," he explained. "Just like the little buffalo calves when they are born."

"Yes," she said with a smile. "It would be a good name for a girl."

And he agreed with that. "I know—but I eventually figured out that she was not named Little Red Calf."

"What was the second name you thought she had?"

Clearing his throat, Bass declared, "Spring Calf Woman— *daa'xxap'shii'le*—because she was a little yellow calf dropped in the spring."

"Yellow? How is this little one yellow when you just said she was a red calf for a long time?"

"Her skin was red for so long. But look at her hair," he told her. "Is it as black as a raven's wing like yours?"

"No," and Waits shook her head. "But it isn't the color of her father's hair either."

"I agree—but it is easy to see that her hair is lighter than a Crow's, and may even have some light streaks in it as she grows up and her hair grows longer."

"So . . . yellow?"

"Yes—because my sister and one of my brothers had blond hair. Yellow as riverbank clay."

"I think I am glad we did not find out her name was Spring Calf Woman," Waits replied thoughtfully. "That is far too much to say for a little one. I remember how hard it was for me, how long it took to learn to say all of my name when I was so small."

"Most parents give little thought to what trouble they may cause their child when they name them," he explained.

"And I suppose you would say that most parents do not try hard enough to find out what their child is already named?"

"Yes!" he responded with glee, pedaling his hands up and down for the baby who had a fierce grip on his two index fingers.

Waits laid a hand on Bass's knee, took the girl's foot in her other hand, and caressed the tiny toes. "What was the third name you wanted to give our daughter before you found out it did not belong to her?"

"Cricket."

"The happy insect?"

"Yes," and Titus laughed easily, thinking about it again. "For the last few weeks coming here, I have listened to her as she began to make sounds."

"Sounds?"

"Just sounds. But most times they were happy sounds. I was re-minded of a tiny cricket hiding somewhere under our blankets, or in my beaver hides, chirping so cheery and happy."

She echoed the name as if trying it out—"Cricket."

"But at dawn this morning after you fed her and she did not go right back to sleep," he explained quickly, "I had the feeling that cricket was not her name. Something told me."

"Grandfather Above told you."

"Yes," he replied. "And as she sat in her cradleboard watching you, and looking at me too—talking to us like we understood everything she was trying so hard to say—the Creator finally agreed that I had found our daughter's name."

"After three others, you are sure this is the one?"

"Yes, *ua,*" he answered, using the Crow word for *wife.* "I discovered the name she has had all along."

"So, *ak'saa'wa'chee,*" she addressed him as a father, "are you going to tell me just what this little person of ours is named?"

"I think you should bring me my pipe and tobacco," he suggested.

She clambered to her feet and knelt among the rawhide parfleches and satchels. "See?" Waits proudly held up the small clay pipe. "I know where you keep this safe."

"There's some new tobacco I traded for, laying there in that new blanket we now have for the baby."

Waits pulled back the folds of the thick wool blanket, fingering it a moment. "She will stay warm this winter."

"Gonna be colder in Crow country than you were down in Taos while I was gone."

Pulling apart the crumpled sheet of waxed paper, Waits selected one of the twisted carrots of tobacco, then refolded the rest and stuffed it back beneath the layers of that new blanket. "No, husband. I was colder there in Ta-house than I will be this winter among my own people because I did not have you with me."

He sensed a stab of remorse, recalling the wrenching conflict he had suffered after deciding to leave his pregnant wife behind while he attempted a midwinter pilgrimage to hunt down some old friends in St. Louis. "No more should you fear, for we will spend the rest of our winters together, *ua.*"

As she returned and laid both the pipe and tobacco beside his knee, Waits rocked forward and planted a gentle kiss on his bare cheekbone. "I promise you the same, *chil'ee*. Until death takes me, I will spend all the rest of my days with you."

Then she scooped up the infant and lifted her from his lap. "Let me hold this little girl while you fill your pipe. Then I can finally discover what the First Maker has named our daughter."

From the narrow tail of that twist of dried tobacco he had traded from Nathaniel Wyeth, Bass crumpled a little of the dark leaf between a thumb and finger, dropping each pinch into the bowl of his clay pipe. Although fragile, these pipes had long been a staple of barter between the white man and the red—going back some two hundred years. While they might break if a man did not carefully pack his pipe among his possibles, they were extremely cheap. Bass, like most of those trappers who hunted this mountain wilderness, owned several of the creamy-white clay pipes. From its months of use, the inside of the bowl of this one had taken on a rich earthen tone, while the oils and dirt from Scratch's hands had given the outside of the pipe a softer, hand-rubbed, sepia-toned patina.

Accustomed to watching how her husband practiced his habits, Waits-by-the-Water was prepared when he nodded his approval of having packed the bowl just so. From the edge of the coals she pulled a short twig she had propped there, suspending its tiny flame over the bowl as he sucked the fire into the tobacco. As he did, Bass looked sidelong, finding his daughter staring at the pipe, perhaps more so the bobbing flame she reached for with both of her tiny, pudgy hands.

"She wants to smoke with you," Waits said, amusement in her voice.

"Tell her she's not old enough," Bass said when he took the stem from his lips, ready for their ceremony. "But you can smoke with me tonight."

"M-me?" she replied. "I've never . . . unless one is a member of a woman's lodge, w-we don't . . . never smoke—"

"You are a member of my lodge," he declared. "Better still, I have become a member of your lodge, woman. When I married you, we became our own clan."

"B-but . . . I never before—"

"Tonight you will," Bass interrupted. "This is for our daughter."

"Smoking is a sacred thing," she explained with a slight wag of her head, as much doubt written on her face as in the sound of her voice. "Men smoke together to deliberate on an important matter. Or to offer prayers."

He chuckled as he leaned to the side, noticing how his daughter's eyes remained fixed on that pipe in his hand before he looked closely into his wife's eyes. "That is exactly what you and I are about to do. This is a sacred thing—this naming of a child, is it not?"

"V-very sacred, yes."

"And we have deliberated on this matter of a name for some time?"

"You have deliberated," she admitted, "and I have prodded you for an answer to your deliberations—"

"See, I am right," he interrupted with a chuckle. "And now the two of us who belong to the Titus Bass coyote clan are about to offer a prayer for welcoming a third member to our clan."

"Yes, a prayer."

In one hand he held the pipe up to the sky as black as the gut of a badger. "First Maker, we offer our prayer as thanksgiving for showing us our daughter's name."

Then he placed the stem between his teeth, drew in a short breath, and let it out a little at a time, to each of the cardinal directions. That done, Bass handed the warm clay stem to his wife. For a moment Waits studied the pipe—until the baby reached out for her mother's hand that held that interesting object.

"Smoke to pray for our daughter," he said. "You see by her hand touching you and the pipe that she understands the importance of you smoking for her."

Slowly the woman pulled her hand away from the baby's tiny fingers, placing the stem against her lips.

"Don't draw in much," he advised. "Just a little. I don't think the spirits will mind if you smoke only a little. Surely what is important is not how much you take in, but that you did pray with the smoke."

Waits wrinkled her nose at the bitter taste as soon as she drew some smoke into her mouth. This she quickly expelled in one direction. Then followed suit with three more short puffs to finish her circuit of the directions as the child in her lap began to fuss.

"She wants that pipe," Bass said as his wife handed it back to him. "Or she wants your attention."

"When will I learn what her name has been all this time?" she asked, licking her lips and tasting the strong tobacco.

"Patience, my wife." Then he raised the pipe to the sky again. "Grandfather Above—we offer this prayer to ask that you guide our steps in protecting this child as she grows."

Once more he smoked, exhaling four light puffs to the four directions, then watched as Waits again completed the offering of her prayer as the baby began to fuss, kicking her legs and balling her fists as she flailed her tiny arms.

Quickly Waits handed the pipe back to Titus. "Now she wants only my attention."

With a smile Scratch said, "Take her clothes off."

"That isn't what is going to make her happy."

"As we offer our daughter to the Grandfather," he explained, "she should be as naked as the day she came to be with us."

Without a word of protest, Waits-by-the-Water released the knots in the soft strips of antelope hide that secured the sections of cloth around the child's body. First that strip under the babe's arms, then the one around its belly. And finally those that held absorbent grass stalks around the infant's legs. With a dry scrap of wool, Waits quickly wiped her daughter's bare bottom, then handed the squirming bundle over to Bass.

Completely dark beyond that small corona of firelight, hemmed in by a great encompassing wilderness where no sound was heard save for the yonder call of the mournful song-dogs, the quieting buzz of insects among the rustling leaves, and that muted babble of the nearby creek—Bass laid her tiny head in the palm of his left hand, stretching her little, lithe body along that forearm so that a leg fell on either side of his elbow. With the fingertips of his right hand, he gently caressed her forehead, cheeks, and under her chin, slowly soothing the fussy child, quieting her. Down each arm he lightly rubbed, fingertips pressing softly as he progressed.

When he looked up at Waits, he found admiration in his wife's beautiful black-cherry eyes. Then he gazed down at his daughter once more and continued massaging her plump little body while he whispered to her the nonsense that makes no difference to an infant who knows only that she is the center of her own universe at that moment. Down each hip and on down each leg, Titus didn't finish until he had gently rubbed every small toe.

He raised her head, and kissed the tiny brow, watching the babe's wide, wondering eyes roll upward as he lowered his hairy face toward her.

Then Bass clutched the infant in his two strong hands and slowly raised her above his head until his arms were outstretched. She began to squirm again, her legs kicking, arms pumping, fists flailing in discontent, a little brown-skinned ball of anger at the end of his arms, held here against the black sky in the fire's light, her flesh lit red as Mexican copper.

"We honor this gift you have given the two of us, First Maker!" he said now.

"This little one who you knew would make a place for herself in our hearts."

Slowly, the baby slowed her leg's gyrations, quieted her fussing.

"You gave this little one her name at the very beginning—even from the start of time . . . and you have waited for us to discover her name for ourselves."

The child cooed, reaching for those sparks that spiraled upward from the flames leaping inches from Bass's knees. Then he realized his daughter was no longer trying to catch the daring, dancing sparks. Instead she reached for those twinkling bits of light just beyond her reach, those stars flung against the blackened backdrop.

"Help us protect her, to raise her right, strong, and straight. Help us to teach her to know you," he said, feeling the first tear spill from his brimming eyes.

The infant was talking again, not chattering at her father, but babbling at those flecks of light in the sky above her. Just beyond her reach.

"We know she is our child for only a short time, Grandfather. We know you have been so kind to part with her while she comes to us for a short time. Help us both to see that she walks the right trail. And help us to make her happy."

At the end of his arms the babe stretched out her arms again and again, flexing her tiny, pudgy fingers, trying to scoop up the glittering specks of brilliant light as her happy, constant chatter grew all the bolder.

"So you have told me her name," Bass said, both eyes streaming now as he gazed upon his daughter. "We ask your blessings on this child who will be called . . . Magpie."

Quickly he looked over at his wife. Tears suddenly spilled from her eyes too as she brought the fingertips of both hands to her lips, smiling and sobbing at the same time. Waits nodded to him, then looked at their daughter there above them both in the copper firelight.

Past the happy sob clogging her throat, Waits-by-the-Water pushed the word, "M-magpie."

"Magpie," Bass repeated as he lowered the babe into his wife's arms, "this little talking one called Magpie has come to be with us for a while."

As they followed Ham's Fork down to its mouth to depart the valley, Bass had kept his pony close to Waits's horse. The rendezvous site was crowded with coyotes, a few lanky-legged wolves, and flocks of big-winged, wrinkled-necked buzzards flapping and cawing out of the sky all around them.

Zeke strained at the length of rope tied round his neck, yanking on the strong hand that restrained him as Titus led them east. "Easy, boy. Easy."

From far and wide, what had called in those predators was the stench.

Those streamside camps once filled with over six hundred white men along with some three-times-that-many Indians was making for quite a feast of carrion. Several snarling wolves or angry, flapping, snapping vultures clustered around every butchered carcass or gut-pile left behind. So bold had these predators become with their feasting that the sound of the horses' approach did not drive off the four-legged and birds, much less the sight of those horses and humans as Scratch took his family past the refuse of each of Rocky Mountain Fur's progressive camps, Wyeth's camp, and finally what had been American Fur's camp where Ham's Fork poured into Black's Fork.

It was good, he thought, so good to leave that place where so many had crowded together with all their noise. That place of grass trampled beneath so many moccasins and hooves, what grass hadn't been cropped and chewed by the thousands of horses. But given a winter to lie fallow beneath the snows of this high, arid country, those meadows along the creek would cloak themselves in a thick coat of green come spring's torrents.

How much he had been looking forward to their return to Absaroka.

All the memories flooded together as they crossed the Green and made for the southern end of the Wind River Mountains where they climbed up the west side of the southern pass and crossed over to the Sweetwater before striking due north for the Popo Agie, following it as they rose into the eastern slopes of the mountains.

For several weeks they leisurely clung to the high country, working their way north by west through the rugged Wind River Range until they reached the country where the passes either carried them west to Davy Jackson's Hole, or north into the forbidding fastness of the hulking Absaroka Range. Instead they turned southeast around the end of those mighty hills and made for the Owl Mountains.

For another month he had them mosey north along the foothills of the Absaroka Range, stopping to camp for a night or two along every stream where they found the beaver active, at the edge of every flooded meadow where the flat-tails had erected their dams and lodges, felling their trees and raising their young.

Before leaving camp for his traplines each morning, Bass freshly primed a pair of smoothbore fusils and their two extra rifles, along with a brace of pistols, leaving them propped here and there against their shelter, or astride beaver packs—somewhere easily within her reach. Besides those usual chores of tending to the baby's needs, bringing in firewood, making repairs to moccasins and clothing, or preparing meals for her ravenous husband, Waits-by-the-Water again proved herself an invaluable camp keeper by expertly fleshing every beaver hide he dragged in, cleaning it of fat and excess connective tissue after Scratch pulled the heavy green hide off the carcass at streamside. Last fall in the Bayou Salade he had taught her how to lash the green hide inside a large willow hoop, threading a long rawhide whang round and round as she stretched the beaver skin to dry.

At most camps they snuffed their fire by twilight and warily slept out the night in a darkness that made those autumn nights feel all the colder. As sociable as the horses were, as gregarious as was young Samantha— Bass figured it was nonetheless far better that he picket each animal in a separate place from dusk's deepening till dawn's first light. If some thieving redskins happened to stumble across them, far better was it to lose one or two than to have the whole bunch driven off together. Better to count those horses' ribs than to count their tracks.

As soon as Magpie was sleeping soundly on the far side of her mother, lying close at hand for those times when the child awoke hungry during the night, and Waits-by-the-Water was nestled beneath their blankets, Titus always slipped quietly into the frosty darkness. One by one he made the rounds, checking on the horses, then the mule, before bringing the buffalo pony with the spotted rump right into camp. Dropping a loop of rawhide rope around its head, Scratch played out the rest of the rope as he settled back among the blankets and robes with his wife and child. After tucking the end of the rope securely beneath his belt, the trapper could finally close his eyes, assured that he would be jolted awake with the pony's slightest tug on the rawhide rope as it grazed through the night.

A man who wanted to keep what he had left of his hair, who wanted to protect his family, didn't much worry about sleeping out his nights in peace. He could sleep the night through come next summer's rendezvous, or come this winter with the Crow. No man long in tooth, be he white or red, ever let a little thing like some lost sleep nettle him.

Better to awaken after a few hours of sleep in fits and starts than not awaken at all.

If it wasn't Magpie fussing with an empty belly, or Samantha snorting to announce she had just winded some nocturnal animal like a raccoon, skunk, or porcupine, that awakened him, most times the trapper would come to, suddenly aware of some seminal change in the nightsounds drifting around their camp—even if it were nothing more than the rustle of an owl's wings as it prowled on the hunt through the branches overhead or a change in the wind's pitch as it soughed on down the valley below them.

Season after season, the senses of those who hadn't gone under became honed more finely, polished to clarity, become virtually instinctual.

Too many times in these last nine years he had simply reacted, not given the luxury of a moment to plan, to consider and reflect on what course to take. Here he was alive after so many had tried to kill him simply because Bass had absorbed the virtual wildness of this wilderness. The way of those beasts around him, that survival of the quickest, the most wary, those most cunning.

He had survived in this wilderness where lesser men were swallowed up simply because he had become wild enough to reach across that gulf between man and beast.

They had autumn beaver, a damned good start on what prime pelts he'd trap come spring. Maybe even do this winter what he hadn't done in recent years—slip off for days at a time and search out those high country meadows and damned streams where the beaver were laying out their winter safely burrowed in their lodges. A man could bust open the tops of those lodges, then shoot or spear the big flat-tails he caught inside. But those efforts always left a trapper with furs something less than prime—punctured by a gaping hole or two. Something that would pare down the price of his plews come rendezvous next summer.

And with what he had seen of the high cost of necessaries coupled with the slide in the dollar that a man's beaver could bring, Titus Bass didn't figure he could chance anything else robbing him of what prime he had left among his plews.

South of the Yellowstone River where the Crow would winter, down toward the Stinking Water around that region the trappers called Colter's Hell, he was sure he could run onto some creeks and streams fed by warming springs, even those wider rivers where the banks bore plenty of beaver sign plain as paint and the water remained open throughout the cold months. A week of hard work here, and a week there, returning to the Crow camp to turn his hides over to his woman, nestle himself down in the robes with her naked, full-breasted warmth for a few days before he would set out again in search of another stretch of winter trapping.

Sure sounded like it had the makings of some fine winter doings. He'd revisit his old friends among the Crow, stay off and on with Waits-by-the-Water and his in-laws . . . but when he got that old itch to be on the tramp again, why—he could pack up a mess of dried meat and pemmican before heading south with Samantha in search of brown gold.

"Husband," she called out, the word catching in her throat.

She had seen the smoke a heartbeat before he spotted it. Down the slope to their left, rising among the last few leaves still clinging to those cottonwood branches—faint spirals of wood smoke. Bass imagined he could already smell its fragrance like a wispy perfume on the cold autumn wind gusting along the ground, kicking up icy streamers across the top of the most recent dusting of snow.

"They are camped right where we believed we would find them," he said with a smile. "Let's ride on down there and show your family this little girl of ours."

FIVE

Arapooesh was dead.

It slapped him with the same brutality he had experienced in losing Ebenezer Zane, Mad Jack Hatcher, even the canny old preacher Asa McAfferty.

Rotten Belly simply wasn't the sort who rode off half-cocked, spoiling for a fight, taking stupid chances. No, he had always been a warrior's warrior, a prudent fighter who persisted in considering the odds and planning every detail of the battles he led against the enemy.

But the Crow had many enemies, and they were strong. Rotten Belly's mountain band of the Crow required a vigilant defense. For a man like Arapooesh that meant more than sending his young warriors into battle—it meant leading them himself.

Rotten Belly had been killed in battle against the Blackfoot.

Waits-by-the-Water's parents welcomed them into their lodge that first night of celebration and homecoming. Grandmother and grandfather could not take their eyes and hands off little Magpie, playing and talking with the child until she grew hungry and ready for bed. Across the fire, Bass did his best to join in with their talk from time to time—but for the most part he sat silent, staring at the flames, listening to the crackle of wood and the wolfish wind howling without the buffalo-hide walls. He wondered on Rotten Belly's spirit. Where it was on its journey. Would he have already reached the end of that long star road to spend out the rest of eternity with the likes of Zane, Hatcher, and McAfferty, even with all of those Arapooesh himself had killed in battle?

That first night he awoke, fitful and damp. Slipping from beneath the blankets, Bass sat up in the dull red glow of the coals in the fire pit where he laid some small pieces of wood and watched the low flames till dawn when Magpie stirred, awakening her mother.

"I must go away for a few days."

"We only arrived," she said, lifting the baby to her breast.

On the far side of the lodge her parents stirred. The old couple sat up, but remained silent in the dim light, curious. Waits stared at her husband's gray face, his sleepless, red eyes, trying so hard to read something there that would allow her to understand.

With his empty hands gesturing futilely before him, Bass said, "I must do something."

"Give yourself a few days to rest," she pleaded. "You have worked so hard, been on the move ever since we left the place where all the white men gather."

Wagging his head in despair, Titus tried to explain. "I am torn. I do not want to leave you and Magpie—but something tells me I must be alone with this terrible news we were given last night."

"Is this your heart crying out in hurt for He-Who-Has-Died?" she asked, referring to the departed without speaking his name.

Staring into the fire pit, he admitted, "Yes. I must go away to mourn for him—"

"Stay and mourn for him here," she begged, patting the blankets beside her. "Ever since last summer my people . . . his people have mourned for him in his own camp. It is good to shed the tears among others."

He crabbed closer to her, leaning against her shoulder. "My grief comes easy."

His wife's parents stirred. Her father, Whistler, left their blankets to scoot next to the fire. His black hair had only recently begun to show the iron of his considerable winters. He said, "Mourning does not belong only to women."

Crane, her mother, added, "Tears should never frighten a strong man."

With her free arm Waits-by-the-Water pulled Bass's brow against her cheek. "My father speaks good words. Your tears tell me you are a strong man, strong enough to show how much you miss He-Who-Has-Died."

"I raised my daughter to show her heart," Whistler said. "But she must realize that we all grieve in our own way. If you believe you must ride into the hills to mourn, then that is where your spirit calls you to go."

Waits tried to speak for a moment, but ultimately admitted she was not going to convince her husband that he should stay. "I will miss you. Hurry back to us."

She turned away quickly, a gesture that tugged plaintively at his heart. Scratch knew she hoped to hide her face, those sad eyes, from him. He watched her back as she settled upon their blankets and gathered the baby to her breast.

He laid a hand on her shoulder and said, "I have lost so many in my life, friends. I don't want to lose you, lose even your love."

She laid her hand upon his, finally turning to gaze up at him, her eyes brimming, half-filled with tears. "When you left our camp two winters ago," Waits-by-the-Water said, her voice no more than a choking whisper, "when you went away angry at me—I realized I never wanted to know that pain again."

"I don't want to hurt—"

"And when you went east to follow the trail of those who had cheated you . . . I vowed I would never let you leave me again. I promised myself that I would always go with you."

"Before you realize, I'll be back," he promised, watching the tears spill down her cheeks, drops she licked as they hung pendant from her upper lip.

"I know," she whispered, and squeezed his hand. "You must go to mourn the loss of another friend."

As his wife finished nursing Magpie, Titus Bass hurriedly lashed a blanket inside a single robe. He made certain he took a little tobacco and his own clay pipe, stuffing them deep into his possibles bag with his flint and steel. Seeing that his horn was filled with powder and his shooting pouch weighed down with lead balls, Scratch stepped outside into the early light as Zeke leaped to all fours there beside the door.

"C'mon, boy," he whispered to the dog as he knelt, scratching its ears, gazing into the animal's attentive eyes. "Let's go fetch up Samantha."

With the mule, man and dog hurried back from the tiny corral where he had confined their stock. After cinching the riding saddle around her, he lashed his bedding behind the cantle, then ducked back inside the lodge.

"I want you to take my pipe," Whistler pleaded as he stepped up to the white man. "I smoked it when I grieved for my brother's death. Now I want you to take it into the hills with you so you can offer your grief with it."

Eventually he took the pipe from Whistler's hand suspended between them. "By giving me your pipe, you do me a great honor."

"By mourning my brother, your friend, in your own way, you do his family a great honor."

As the two men gripped one another's forearms, Crane said, "Remember to drink water, or eat the snow. If you cut yourself in grief, you must drink water."

"I'll remember."

Quietly Crane explained, "It is winter. You will need lots of water if your flesh weeps in sorrow too."

For a moment Bass looked at the two of them, then asked Whistler, "Where did you leave his body?"

"South of here. Near the Grey Bull River. He-Who-Has-Died is lying in his lodge until his body returns to the earth and winds."

"Perhaps I will go look for this place where you left his lodge," Bass replied, then heard the surprised squeak of air escape his wife's throat.

Turning to step up to Waits-by-the-Water, Titus vowed, "I will return when I have grieved for He-Who-Is-No-Longer-Here."

As Bass knelt to gather his wife in his arms, Magpie reached out to seize that single narrow braid he always wore at the right ear. Bass kissed his daughter, gently tugging her hand free of that bound hair. Then kissed his wife's lips, long and lingering.

"I will think of you both, often," he said, then turned on his heel and ducked into the sunshine as Zeke whirled twice round his legs, clearly eager for the trail.

Miles away to the south along the gurgling creekbank, Scratch turned into the hills rising sharply in the west. The higher he climbed, the deeper the snow became—changing from no more than a windblown skiff to an icy crust deep enough to brush his calves by the time Samantha had tired and he'd dropped to the ground at the edge of some rocks jutting from the barren side of a hill that overlooked part of the valley below. Here where only some clumps of sage dotted the white, pristine slope, nothing obstructed his view. With a brilliant autumn sun overhead, Bass pulled the camp ax from the back of his belt and trudged to some nearby brush where he hacked off a number of branches he dragged behind him when he returned to the boulders.

Thatching those limbs across one another on the snow, he constructed a crude platform that for the most part would keep him out of the snow, dampness, and cold through the hours and days to come. Retrieving his blanket and robe, Titus loosened Samantha's cinch, then tied her off in some brush down the slope a ways where she could graze on some grass blown free of snow. He was winded by the time he and the dog made the slippery climb back to his perch where he spread out the robe across the small platform, fur side up.

Next he used his bare hands to scrape the snow away from a small circle directly in front of his platform. Zeke inched forward, sniffing with intense curiosity at that patch of earth Bass was clearing.

"G'won," he told the dog. "Lay over there so you'll stay outta my way."

Zeke turned and circled the man twice, eventually settling on the snow near the rocks where he could watch his master.

In the crude circle he had cleared, Bass piled small twigs and slivers of bark he broke off the limbs beneath him. With enough small wood near at hand, Scratch unfurled the blanket and clutched it around his shoulders before he settled down upon the platform. By bunching the robe around him, Bass was ready to load Whistler's pipe with his trade tobacco.

Once the tall redstone bowl was filled, Scratch laid a sliver of charred cloth on the top of his thigh, striking the fire-steel against the flint, sending a tiny shower of sparks onto the blackened char. Quickly laying the cloth with its glowing ember over the top of the bowl, Titus sucked steadily on the stem, drawing the fire into the tobacco and smoke across his tongue, sinking deep into his lungs.

Then he pulled the glowing char from the top of the bowl, laying it on a small piece of pithy wood. Blowing on the ember, he quickly ignited the dry pith. With it smoking readily, Bass stuffed the wood beneath the center of the fire pit he had cleared in the snow and laid several of the smallest twigs over the smoky embers. Leaning to the side to blow across the pith, the dead twigs suddenly burst into flame. He added more, larger twigs, then leaned back and sucked on the pipe.

With the smoke held momentarily in his lungs, Bass gazed out across the valley. On his left sat the sere bluffs and red-hued rimrock marking the valley of the Yellowstone. Off to his right rose the great bulk of the Absaroka Range. And before him in the middistance sat the Pryor Mountains. This had been Rotten Belly's country—a land held by the might of an able chief at the head of a powerful people.

As the sun continued to crawl toward midsky, Titus smoked the last of the tobacco in that pipe bowl, with each long puff recalling some memory of He-Who-Had-Died. Both good times and tragic. Remembering how Arapooesh had told visitors that this land of Absaroka was in the right place: not too cold and not too warm, not so far east onto the plains that the Crow could not gather in the cool shadows of the mountains. Remembering how the chief had stepped into the middle of his people's grief and fury, offering two white men the challenge of bringing back the hair of a third white trapper, the hair of a murderer.

Arapooesh, who winters ago had accepted Bass as a brother. This man Rotten Belly who had adopted Josiah Paddock as one of his own relations.

When the pipe went out, Titus turned the bowl over and tapped it against the heel of his hand, knocking the ash and blackened dollop into the tiny fire before him. With a twig he scraped some of the growing mound of ash to the edge of the snow he had cleared from the bare ground. Setting the pipe aside on the robe, Bass dragged the coyote-fur hat, then untied the faded blue of the silk bandanna, from his head, laying both by Whistler's pipe.

Now that his naked skull was exposed to the winter sky, he carefully scooped up a little of the warm ash into both hands. Slowly he dumped the ashes on top of his head, using both hands to smear their warmth through his hair, rubbing it across that pale patch of bone.

Reaching around to his back, Bass pulled free the long, much-used skinning knife from its sheath. Seizing that narrow braid he wore at his right ear, he dragged the blade of his knife across the middle of the braid, hacking it free. After flinging it into the flames at his knee, Scratch grabbed a handful of his long graying hair, sawing it loose, then tossing it into the fire where the strands sizzled and smoked, choking the cold breeze with its terrible stench. Clump by clump, he continued to work around the base of his head, crudely chopping off his curly hair until what remained hung just above his shoulders in ragged, uneven tatters, most of it choked with ash.

For a long time that early afternoon he continued to sit there, adding pieces of limb and branch to his little fire, sensing the breeze blow cold across the flesh of his neck where he had sawed off long sections of his hair, exposing his skin to the teeth in every gust of wind. Eventually he loaded Whistler's pipe a second time and smoked, remembering other friends he had lost across the years.

Good men who had welcomed him into their lives and their hearts without conditions. Men who had become a part of Bass's life, friends now become the chinking in so many of his memories. Old friends who had loved their life and their freedom as much as Scratch loved his.

Puff by puff he drew the strong, stinging tobacco into his lungs, then slowly exhaled as the breeze whipped the smoke away while he offered up his remembrances like a prayer. One by one he asked each of those who were gone to look down upon him now and in the months and years to come.

Strange, he thought, but when he was a youngster back on the Ohio after running away from home, he had always believed life was bound to get easier the older he became. Then he managed to collide with the wrong women—females who discovered his weakness, his need, and what unerring devotion he offered them—women who took and took until they left him behind. Certain that wisdom had come after every broken heart, Bass instead found a newer, deeper hurt with each new love. Instead of life growing easier, he discovered that life offered him no simple answers, no respite from the painful learning as he was knocked about.

How innocent he had been in earlier years, to believe that as he put mistakes behind him, he would find life all the easier. But for every woman who had scarred him, for every misstep he had made in life, there nonetheless had been a good friend who stood at his shoulder.

Those faces were monuments to the seasons of his life. Men who had remained steadfastly loyal through shining times and walks with death.

And now he had lost another.

Quickly Titus tugged at the bottom of his long buckskin shirt, dragging it over his head and from each arm. Yanking back the sleeves of his faded woolen underwear as the cold wind startled his bare flesh, Scratch gently dragged the knife's blade across the back of his forearm. Then a second narrow slash close beside that first just beginning to bead and ooze with blood. Then a third, a fourth, and more he cut, slicing a series of slashes on down that forearm before he repeated the process on the other arm.

"He was the greatest of all Crow chiefs," Bass whispered with a sigh, feeling the cold wind bite along the oozy wounds as he turned to glance at the dog. "Now he's gone."

Bass set the knife aside to stare at the tops of the far hills across the valley.

You are a man who understands that there is no use in lingering in this life when one's time has gone, he remembered Arapooesh declaring when Bass and Josiah were about to set out on McAfferty's trail after Asa had murdered the chief's wife. *Why should a man linger, like the wildflower in spring holding on to hope of passing the heat of summer and the cold of the coming winter? Only the earth and sky are everlasting.*

"So many," he whispered now. "So many it makes a man feel he ain't got friends left."

It is men that must die, Arapooesh's voice reverberated in Bass's head. *Our old age is a curse.*

Sensing the burn of tears, Titus said, "Times like this, I feel older'n I really am. And I feel any more years is a goddamned curse . . . living without them what's gone is a hard thing. Too hard."

Again, Rotten Belly's words whispered in his head, *And death in battle is a blessing for those who have seen our many winters.*

In the death of a great chief, Crow tradition dictated that the band mourn across four days. The entire camp would grieve any man killed by an enemy—but especially a beloved chief like Rotten Belly, felled as he was in battle with their most hated enemies.

That first day of public grieving, the chief's lodge had been painted with wide horizontal red stripes. Inside where no fire would ever burn again, the body was cleaned, dressed in his finest war regalia, then laid on a low four-pole platform. In his hands was placed a fan of eagle feathers, and his chest was bared to the spirits. There the body rested while his people expressed their utter sorrow at his death, their unrequited anger at the Blackfoot who had killed their leader.

Across those nights and days, Rotten Belly's warrior society conducted elaborate ceremonies in his honor. The Otter Clan saw to it that the dead man's treasured war totems lay beside his body, and assured that his face and bare chest were painted red. For hours they beat drums throughout the camp. Wailing, mourners pierced the skin at their knees, others pierced their arms to draw blood. Some jabbed sharp rocks against their foreheads, making themselves bleed. For four days a somber pall fell over the entire camp.

Then on the morning of the fifth day, the Crow had torn down their own lodges, abandoning the site on the Grey Bull River and leaving the chief's lodge to decay with the elements through the coming seasons. While the dead man's relations would continue to grieve in their own way, the rest of the band went on with its life and a new leader stepped to the fore.

From time to time as the sun sank from midsky and disappeared in the west this cold day of his own private mourning, Bass left his perch to scour both sides of the bluff for deadfall poking from the crust of snow, wood he could drag back to his fire pit. After each short trip he found he needed to rest longer and longer, sucking on more and more of the icy snow as he heaved for breath. Once he was ready, Scratch clambered to his feet and trudged off again. Exhausted, he returned from what he knew would be his last trip as twilight darkened the sky and threw the land into irretrievable shadow with night's approach.

"C'mere, boy," he called, patting the edge of the crude lattice platform beside him.

Zeke eagerly lunged up through the snow, then went to his belly at his master's knee, laying his jaw on Bass's thigh where he knew he would receive a good scratching.

"I'm glad you come along, ol' fella. You'd been a mess for her back there in camp if'n I'd left you behind. Got yourself in the way but good, staying underfoot. Better the woman didn't have you whining and moaning after I left."

He watched the first stars come out before he grew too tired to watch any longer. Bass banked more wood against the fire, then rearranged the robe and blanket on the platform that kept him out of the snow.

"Lay here, Zeke," he instructed, patting the robe.

The dog came up, turned about, and nested right next to him. Then Scratch pulled the other half of the robe and that heavy wool blanket over them both. Laying his cheek down on his elbow, Bass closed his eyes, listening to the distant sounds of that cold winter night—an utter silence so huge and vast that he felt himself swallowed whole by the open sky above them.

He tried to imagine what she was doing right then, if Waits-by-the-Water had Magpie on her knee as she helped her mother prepare supper. Or if the baby was sleeping. Perhaps even talking more than ever. He wondered if his wife was thinking of him right at that moment. Surely she was, for that had to be the reason his thoughts had turned instantly to her.

And he thought on how warm it was lying next to her skin in the winter, even cold as deep as this. It saddened him to think of all those winter nights Arapooesh had endured after his wife was murdered. Knowing how hard it would be for him to endure two long winters without Waits-by-the-Water.

Perhaps Rotten Belly had sought out his own death. Some men did just that: seeking an honorable death on its own terms. Like Asa McAfferty.

Bass wondered if he would have the courage to seek out his own death when the time came.

Then he thought on his woman, and their child—knowing because of them he now shared the promise of life.

The dog lay warm against him, breathing slowly.

As the Seven Sisters rose in the northeast, low along the horizon that first night of early winter, Bass dreamed of sunlit high-country ponds and the slap of beaver tails on still water, the spring breeze rustling those new leaves budding on the quakies, and the merry trickle of Magpie's laughter.

Dreamed with the pleasure of his wife's lips on his.

And that joy of crossing into a span of country where he knew he was the first man ever to set foot . . . as if it were the day after God had created it all, made that world just for him.

There was little choice but for Scratch to put out the call—asking warriors to join him in making a raid deep into Blackfoot country.

In those first days following Bass's return to the village, Whistler not only readily offered to go along on the journey, but volunteered to spread the call.

"I will be your pipe bearer," declared the man not all that much older than Titus.

"That means you are the one who will take responsibility for asking others to join you?"

"Yes," Whistler explained. "I will carry the pipe throughout the village and ask all who wish to join us in this blood journey to bring tobacco to our lodge."

"And you'll smoke the tobacco of those you decide will go with us?"

"*We* will smoke their tobacco, offering our prayers for a successful venture."

Bass felt humbled at this honor. "Whistler makes me proud, agreeing to act as pipe bearer on this war trail led by a white man."

"You are a son-in-law who gives me honor," the warrior protested. "The loss of my older brother and my own selfish mourning blinded me to what must be done for my brother's memory. Now you have returned to us after many seasons. And you have mourned as my people grieve: cutting your hair and drawing your own blood. You offer to ride into the land of the enemy to take revenge in the name of the One-Who-Is-No-Longer-Here."

"He-Who-Has-Died was a good friend," Bass explained. "For such a friend who treated me like his brother, I am without honor if I do not go in search of Blackfoot scalps in his name."

After four nights in the hills beside his little fire, with only Samantha and Zeke for company as the sun rose, climbed, and fell each day, as the stars wheeled overhead each night, it was such a sweet homecoming to lie next to Waits-by-the-Water. To tell her how he had yearned for her closeness as he endured those days of isolation, eating snow and the dried meat he had packed along, moving from that rocky point on the brow of the hill only to gather more wood he lashed on the mule's back twice each day: first with the sun's rising so he would have enough for his little fire until dusk, and later as the sun began its tumble into the west so he had what he needed to keep his fire going through the long winter night.

Darkness spent dreaming of his wife and Magpie, slumber troubled with frightening memories and terrifying visions that awoke him in the cold and the blackness to lay more wood on the struggling flames. Clutching the old dog against him beneath the buffalo robe, Scratch sorted through the dizzying glimpses of blood and loneliness, those confusing and blurred images of violence, despair, and loss.

Each time the haunts visited him, he somehow managed to drift off again—reminding himself that he would never be frightened for himself, fearing only for those he loved.

Strikes-in-Camp was the first to volunteer. This tall, haughty warrior had reacted with violent jealousy when Arapooesh chose Scratch and Josiah to go in search of McAfferty. Whistler's firstborn, Waits-by-the-Water's brother, and now one of Bass's relations, Strikes-in-Camp nonetheless remained cool and distant to the white man.

"I came to say I will go with you to take Blackfoot scalps," the young warrior announced the afternoon of that first day Whistler spread the call across that camp of some three thousand souls. But he spoke only to his father, rarely allowing his eyes to touch the trapper.

Whistler glanced at Bass, then asked his son, "Are there any others in your society who will join us?"

"Some," the warrior answered. "And they will come to join for themselves. I am not here to speak for them. Only for myself. You must understand that I do this not for my brother-in-law," he explained, clearly refusing to mention the white man by his Crow name. "I go to take revenge on the enemy because they killed my uncle."

When Strikes-in-Camp had gone, Whistler settled at the fire again and continued drinking the strong coffee he and Bass shared every afternoon, an anticipated and much-enjoyed treat the trapper brought from the rendezvous where the white men gathered.

After some reflection the aging warrior declared, "My son has been shamed, perhaps."

"Shamed?"

"Yes, perhaps. Because you were the first to announce you were going to take Blackfoot scalps in the name of He-Who-Has-Died."

For some time Bass did not answer. How best to walk the straight road with his words without offending Strikes-in-Camp's father. Eventually he said, "Your son could have raised the call as soon as the four days of mourning were over, as soon as this village moved on and left the chief's lodge behind. He could have convinced many of his warrior society to join him, and he would have been well regarded."

Whistler could only nod in agreement. "But I think he was too busy with other things more important than family and honor."

"We were young once, Whistler," Bass sympathized. "The two of us, we both grew older, we both came to know there is nothing more important than family . . . and honor."

Across the next five days more than ninety others came to Whistler's lodge on the outskirts of the Crow village to ask that they too could ride along, men old and young. Some were men of such considerable winters that they had long since given up the war trail, content to let younger men do battle in the name of their people. Most of these Whistler turned away with his thanks, acknowledging that they had already given many years serving in defense of the Crow nation. And there were many of the very young, really no more than boys—most tall and lithe, of ropy, hardened muscle, but every one of them smooth-faced.

"Some mother's son," Whistler would say when he had turned them away and promised that he might lead them on the next war trail. "I am a father, and I know what fear I had in my own heart when Strikes was just as young, believing he was ready to take scalps for the first time. I remember how Crane wept, begging me to keep him from going. How she pleaded with me to go in secret and demand the pipe bearer turn our son away, to prevent him from going along."

"Each man must have his first fight," Scratch said as he savored that coffee. "My first blooding was against the Choctaw."

"Ch-choctaw? I have not heard of these people."

"They live east of a great muddy river, so far away that your people have no name to call that river," Bass explained. "I was nearing my seventeenth winter."

"That is a good age for a young man to go on his first pony raid."

Titus nodded with a smile, saying, "I wasn't a pony holder, even though I was with older, wiser men. None of us were out to steal horses. I was alone, hunting supper when the Choctaw found me—chased me—and wounded one of the others."

"Did you kill any of your enemy?"

"Later," he said, remembering how the canoes slipped up alongside the flatboat in the dark, warriors sneaking onboard to initiate their fierce and sudden attack. "I lost a good friend in that fight."

"And you killed your first man that night?"

"Yes, I know I killed. There was no doubt."

"Blood you spilled, to atone for the blood of your friend the enemy spilled," Whistler observed grimly.

Scratch gazed into the older man's eyes. "Yes. Sometimes the only thing that will do . . . is blood for blood."

"Now we ride this trail together," Whistler said quietly. "Together and alone, we go to do what old warriors know must be done."

SIX

From the moment they forded the half-frozen *Iichii'-likaashaashe*, every last one of them realized he was leaving Absaroka behind. With every mile, every step, every breath taken north of the Yellowstone, they were inching closer to enemy country.

North by northwest the war party marched from the moment it grew light enough to ride till it became too dark to safely cross the broken landscape. If there was a place where rocky outcrops or the shelter of trees would hide the flames from distant eyes, then the older men allowed the warriors to disperse and start half a dozen fires where eight to ten men gathered to warm their dried meat, their hands, their stiffened joints from sitting too long on horseback. Fire or not, through the endless winter nights they talked in low tones as Whistler and the white man moved from fire to fire, group to group, reminding the young that they were on an honor ride, calling upon the veterans to be watchful of the young men when it came time to fight.

Every morning three or four proven warriors were chosen to mount up before the others. In the dim light of dawn-coming, these wolves would make a wide-ranging circle of their camp to learn if they had been discovered, searching for any trail of enemy spies. When they had reported back that all was safe, the scouts for that day would lead out ahead of the others as the sun brightened the winter sky. Riding ahead on both sides of the march, their task was to choose the safest path of travel through dangerous country, scouring for sign of the enemy, some telltale smoke on the horizon.

Day after day they trudged farther and farther north, encountering nothing more than last autumn's fire pits lying cold in old camps. Ahead they watched the clouds boil around the snowy peaks of two mountain ranges, then struck the south bank of the Musselshell.

As they stopped to water their horses at a spot along the river's edge where the water slowed, remaining unfrozen, Whistler sent the scouts across to the north. He said, "We follow the *Bishoochaashe* toward its headwaters and cross to the far side of those mountains. From there we should see the *Aashisee*."

"What your people call The Big River?" Scratch asked.

"I have heard it flows north for a long way," Whistler explained as they started across the Musselshell with the rest, "then it turns east, through the land of the Assiniboine and the Arikara before it curves south at the land of the Hidatsa and finally enters the country of the Lakota."

"From what you describe, that must be what my people call the Missouri."

"Miss-you-ree," the older man slowly tried the word out on his tongue.

"Good," Bass said. "The Missouri. I lived beside that river for many winters. More winters than I should have before I broke free."

Whistler smiled. "This *Aashisee* is a good river this far north . . . before it goes far to the south where it enters the land of the white man. But on the other side of this Miss-you-ree, we must hold tight to our hair."

With a grin Bass said, "Many Blackfoot wanting our scalps, eh?"

Whistler glanced at the top of the white man's head. "But this is nothing new for you, son-in-law."

"No," Bass replied as their horses slogged onto the north bank of the Musselshell and shook themselves like big dogs. "More times than I can count, these Blackfoot have tried to take what I have left for hair."

Around the fires that last night before they reached the Missouri, the older warriors, those contemporaries of Rotten Belly and Whistler, spoke of Arapooesh. Not only did they speak in reverent tones for one who had died, but they recalled the departed chief's sharp, cutting sense of humor, the youthful jokester he had been in years long gone. And they talked of his many war deeds.

Not content merely to defend Crow land from encroachment, Arapooesh was constantly organizing war parties to venture into enemy territory on pony or scalp raids. East toward the land of the Lakota, southeast to steal from the Arapaho and Cheyenne. Southwest to sneak into Bannock country. And there was always the northern land of the Blackfoot.

"He-Who-Is-No-Longer-With-Us made himself very popular among our people many long years ago by bringing back so many enemy horses," Whistler explained to the curious young men come along on their first war trail.

Another old warrior, Turns Plenty, spoke. "Very rarely did he lose a scalp to the enemy."

"Every young man wanted to ride with him," Whistler observed.

"If a man steals the easiest horses," Strikes-in-Camp said, "then he never has to worry about fighting the enemy."

Biting his tongue for some moments, Whistler glared at his impudent son, then said, "Your uncle often showed he was as good a war leader as he was good at stealing horses."

Yellowtail agreed. "He-Who-Is-Dead always chose the best men, put them on the best ponies, made them carry the best weapons . . . so his war parties would be ready to fight for their lives if necessary."

Whistler continued. "Those times we rode into enemy land, my older brother always chose at least two ways to get out of that country so we could make our escape with the ponies we stole and our hair. He figured out places where we could all meet after we had split up to throw the enemy off our trail."

"But if escape did not work," Real Bird declared, "He-Who-Has-Died was ready to turn around and fight. That's when his leadership proved itself—for he had made the effort to choose only the finest warriors with the best weapons."

"Like us," Strikes-in-Camp boasted.

Whistler gazed at his son. "Sometimes it is better for a warrior to let others do his bragging for him."

"Perhaps it was that way in your day," the young warrior argued, teetering on the edge of disrespect. "But today, with the coming of the white men and the Blackfoot pushing hard against us—I think our people need warriors who aren't afraid to speak for themselves."

Whistler opened his mouth to speak, but Bass put his hand on the old warrior's forearm and got his words out first. "A man who speaks too much for himself might find that there isn't anyone else willing to speak for him."

Glaring at the white man as if his hatred for Bass was smoldering anew, Strikes-in-Camp announced to the group, "Perhaps we shall do better in the land of the enemy than He-Who-Is-Not-Here ever did. Perhaps our deeds will far outshine his."

Scratch watched a few of the young heads nod, young faces smile.

Then Whistler stepped over to stand beside his son. "Maybe you are right, Strikes-in-Camp. Who knows? We who are old horses, like *Pote Ani* and me, have tired bones, so it's not so easy making war anymore. Perhaps you are right that war is a job best left for the young men."

"My father sees the wisdom in my words, does he?"

Whistler put a hand on his son's shoulder. "Perhaps. I will trust that you will be there to save my life if an enemy warrior is about to take my scalp."

Swelling his chest like a prairie cock, Strikes-in-Camp said, "I will watch over both of you who are too old to make war—my father and the white man who has married my sister."

Moving on around the circle, Whistler stopped behind Bass and Pretty On Top to say, "He-Who-Is-No-Longer-Here was never the sort to boast pridefully. Though he had many war honors, he rarely spoke of them before others."

Bass added, "He made no big show of all that he had done, never prancing up and down like some young colts out to prove how strong they are."

"As I said, white man—I will even save your life since you are married to my sister."

"No wonder you don't understand what your father is trying to teach you," Scratch uttered with regret. "Your uncle was so much more a man than you will ever be."

"But he was the one who taught me many things!" the young man snapped.

Whistler shook his head and said, "So why didn't you learn to be more like my brother?"

"Because I am going to be a man in my own right," Strikes-in-Camp spouted.

Bass watched Whistler turn and move into the darkness, heading for the nearby fire where another group sat out the long winter night. Looking back at Strikes-in-Camp, he said, "You have shamed your father with your selfish disrespect."

"My family has shamed itself, white man," he snarled. "My sister shames herself by fornicating with you. My mother and father shame themselves because they accept the white man who shamed their daughter into their lodge."

"Your sister and I are married."

"By the white man way?"

"No, not in the white man's church," Bass reluctantly admitted the truth. "We have promised our hearts to one another—"

"You white men are like rabbits in heat," the warrior sneered. "You will say anything to our women to get your manhood under their dresses—"

Scratch found himself bolting to his feet before he realized it, but two sets of hands appeared out of the darkness to stay him. Struggling to free himself, he turned first to the right, finding Turns Plenty holding his arm. On the other side stood Whistler.

"He is not angry at you," Whistler explained. "He is more angry at himself."

"The white man is a coward," Strikes-in-Camp said. "That day in our village, two winters ago, he could have fought us like an honorable man. Instead, he let us tie him up, him and his friend."

"You will also remember how my brother came to free the two white men," Whistler protested as he let go of Bass's arm. He stepped over to stand before his son. "Already the white man and I have talked," he told the young man. "There will be a ceremony for your sister when we return from this war trail to avenge the killing of He-Who-Is-Not-Here."

"Ceremony?"

"She will marry the white man in the way of our people," Whistler declared.

Bass swallowed hard, choking on the surprise of it.

"No matter," the young warrior growled. "Too late to make my sister anything better than a whore who lays with white men—"

Scratch was lunging across the snow when he was jerked backward by Turns Plenty's hold on his right arm. But as he shrugged that arm in a second attempt to free himself, he watched Whistler's arm dart into the fire's dim light, slashing out. His hand struck Strikes-in-Camp's cheek with a pop as loud as an old cottonwood booming in the cold of a February night.

"Don't ever do that again, old man," the son snarled, laying his hand against his bruised cheek.

"Or what?" Whistler asked. "Perhaps it is you who should heed a warning. Maybe you should look over your shoulder more often when you are in enemy country. A man who so openly shames his family is surely the sort of man who has no friends to protect his back."

That early morning when they crossed the frozen Missouri in the darkness, Bass discovered the tight knot in his belly along with the unshakable remembrance of that old shaman who had walked among the half-a-hundred warriors at dawn on that morning they had started north on this war trail so long ago.

Then, as now, it was snowing fitfully: not with huge, ash-curl flakes, but with those tiny, icy spears of cold pain as the wind whipped the glassy slivers sidelong across the ground. Slowly the old man moved between the rows of ponies and warriors quietly mumbling his songs as he shook an old rattle made of a buffalo bull's scrotum. In his other hand he held a bull's penis, stretched to its full length by inserting a narrow wand of willow. Both were his potent symbols of the bull's power—the largest creature known to these people. The provocative maleness of those two objects, their utter masculinity plainly exhibiting that strength shown by the bull in his battles to assure his right to the cows, would now transfer their spiritual power to those men who were plunging into Blackfoot country.

So many more had wanted to come along, some who had all but begged Whistler to be included in the war party. Those he hadn't selected for this dangerous journey had to stand back with the others in a wide cordon pressing in on either side of the five-times-ten who were the objects of a raucous send-off: cheering men, keening women, those boisterous children and yapping dogs darting in and out between the legs of the restive ponies.

Arapooesh's successor, Yellow Belly, had parted the joyous, singsong crowd to stand before Whistler and the white trapper, holding aloft Rotten Belly's sacred battle shield. No longer did it hang on the man-high tripod of peeled poles that stood outside the chief's lodge. Instead, it had been passed down by the dying Arapooesh as a symbol of his office, as a token of the transfer of his power.

For a few minutes the noise had grown deafening as Yellow Belly held the shield aloft, hand drums beating and wing-bone whistles blown with shrill delight. Then as the chief lowered the shield, a hush fell over the crowd.

"Before you ride against our enemies," Yellow Belly said, "each of you must touch the shield, touch the power of He-Who-Has-Died."

First Whistler, then Bass, gently laid their hands on that round hoop covered by stiffened rawhide. Nearly the entire circle was covered with a pale-red earth paint; at the center stood a human figure with oversized ears and a single eagle feather, representing the moon who had come to the great chief in a vision and described the construction of this powerful shield and its medicine.

"Is it true," Bass now asked Whistler as they pushed up the trail scuffed in the new snow by their forward scouts, come to that deadly land north of the Missouri, "true what your people say about the shield of He-Who-Is-Not-Here?"

"Its power to tell us the outcome of an event yet to happen?"

"Yes—I was told about the raid your brother wanted to lead against the Cheyenne in the south."

Whistler stared into the cold mist ahead, then explained, "In the middle of camp he stacked a pile of buffalo chips, almost as high as his head. On the top he placed his shield and told us that he would let it roll to the bottom. If it landed with its painting against the ground, he would not lead the war party."

"But years ago He-Who-Has-Died told me that his shield rolled down that stack of buffalo chips and landed with the paintings facing the sky."

"Yes, and my brother led us to a great victory over the Cheyenne far to the south." Then the warrior sighed and adjusted the heavy buffalo robe he had wrapped around the lower half of his body while they rode on horseback. "That shield was powerful enough to foretell its owner's death."

"How did he know he was going to die?"

"That summer morning we left to steal Blackfoot ponies, my brother again stacked up some buffalo chips, this time in the privacy of his lodge, and called his headmen to meet with him. When he laid his shield on top of the pile, he told us that if the shield rose into the air without his touching it, then his medicine had told him he was going to die in battle."

Turning slightly in the saddle, Bass stared at Whistler a moment before he asked, "Is that what happened to your brother, to my friend?"

"We all saw the shield rise there before He-Who-Is-No-Longer-With-Us. No one touched it as it floated as high as the chief's head. And no one spoke until I told my brother he should not lead the horse steal-ers."

"Why didn't he listen to you?"

"The One-Who-Died said that his death was already foretold," Whistler declared. "He could not call off the raid. He would not allow his people to believe he was anything but brave enough to face his own death."

Despite knowing the shield had predicted his death, Arapooesh nonetheless pushed ahead with the raid. And as much as other warriors tried to protect him once they were confronted by superior numbers of the enemy, Rotten Belly did not hang back and let others do his fighting for him.

Scratch gazed at Whistler, sensing that this same trait of honor must also course through this younger brother's veins—

Suddenly two of the advance scouts bolted out of the trees a half mile ahead, sprinting back toward the head of the march. They raced their ponies around in a tight circle, then slowed to a walk to explain their excitement.

"We have discovered a trail!"

Whistler asked, "An enemy trail?"

"It must be," explained the second scout. "Many riders."

"Is it a fresh trail?" asked Yellowtail as he rode up and brought his animal under control.

The first scout nodded. "Very little snow in the tracks."

"Are they dragging travois behind them?" Scratch asked.

"There are a few," the second scout declared.

Bass looked at Whistler. "It might be a small band of the enemy."

"Women and children—they are our enemies too," Strikes-in-Camp said.

Turning suddenly on the young warrior, Titus asked, "So now you kill women and children too? Does this make you a mighty warrior?"

"Those children will grow up to be fighting men and the mothers of warriors. Those women will bear the seeds, giving birth to more of our enemy—"

"Quiet!" Whistler demanded, clenching a fist in his son's face. The group gathered round them fell silent. "We won't kill the women, nor children. Mark my words: a warrior kills only the warriors."

"Those women—"

This time Whistler drew his hand back, prepared to slap his son across the cheek, but he suddenly stopped his hand inches away. "I should take your weapons and your ponies from you—make you walk back to Absaroka."

It was so quiet Bass could hear some of the horses snort in the cold air, the vapor rising from their nostrils like gauzy wreaths as the sky continued to snow.

"But I won't do that, Strikes-in-Camp," Whistler continued. "Not because you are my son . . . but because you need to learn how a Crow makes war on his enemy that is more numerous, an enemy that is stronger."

Strikes-in-Camp glared at that hand Whistler lowered. Yet he did not utter a word to his father.

"I am the leader of this war party—not my son," Whistler announced. "We are here to revenge the death of my brother. Not to stain the honor of our people by killing women and children. No—we will capture those women and children, take them back to our country when we turn around for home. The young ones will grow to become Crow. And the bellies of those women will give birth to many Crow warriors!"

The half-a-hundred immediately yipped and trilled in triumph with a great ululation of their tongues.

Then Whistler turned back to those two scouts, asking, "How far away do you judge the enemy to be?"

"Before the sun is in its last quarter of the sky and the winter moon has climbed out of the east," the second young warrior explained, "we could reach them."

"Return to the others," Whistler commanded. "And tell them to follow the trail carefully until they have found where the enemy will camp tonight. We will continue on your trail into the time of darkness. Only when our enemies have stopped for the night are you to return to us."

.   .   .

Whistler's scouts found the Blackfoot on that broad plain just north of the Sun River.

As the dimming orb continued its descent toward the horizon, the Crow war party crossed the frozen river, then cut sharply west toward the uneven rim of bare hills that bordered the narrow valley, following the young men who had raced along the backtrail to bring up the rest. As predicted, by late afternoon Bass and the others neared the crest of those hills with their weary ponies, hearing the faint, distant boom of the enemy's guns.

"It is a good thing my brother realized how important it would be to have good trade with the white man," Whistler huffed as they neared the brow of the hill on foot, having left their horses below with the others.

"Powder and lead," Bass agreed. "To fight your enemies."

"And guns!" the warrior cried in a sharp whisper as he went to his belly. "He-Who-Is-Not-Here decided long ago that we needed to be friends with the white man because we needed the white man's guns."

Dropping to his belly in the snow, Scratch inched to the brow of the barren hill and peered over. As the reports of the large-bored muzzle loaders echoed from the surrounding slopes, the scene below opened itself before them.

"That is not a village on the move," Whistler declared quietly, his breathsmoke a thin stream of gray against the deep-hued blue of the winter sky that outlined the handful that had crabbed to the hilltop to join the white man.

"No, these are hunters," said Pretty On Top. "Men. Warriors. And they are delivered into our hands!"

"But there are some women," Bass warned.

On the far side of him Strikes-in-Camp scoffed, "Is this the warning of a woman who is afraid of the fight to come?"

"Take care that your father does not mourn your death in battle before the sun falls from this sky," Scratch growled.

Strikes-in-Camp chuckled, saying, "I will be an old, old man before I will ever heed the woman words of the white man!"

"You will hold your tongue!" Whistler snapped. "And you will obey me as the leader of this war party, if you will not obey me as your father."

"Perhaps the white man is afraid we will learn he is too afraid to fight the enemy—"

Whistler interrupted his son. "No more of your angry, foolish talk about my friend, *Pote Ani!* Time and again he has proved himself a friend to our people, a friend to He-Who-Has-Died, and a friend to our family. I will not have you insult him."

For a long moment Strikes-in-Camp was silent, unmoving; then he rolled onto his hip and slid away from the rest, hurrying downhill to rejoin those who waited with the horses.

"Forgive my son and his words," Whistler begged as he peered at the Blackfoot below him.

"You are a good man, Whistler," Titus told him. "I would not be near so patient as you."

The older warrior chewed his bottom lip in contemplation, then confessed, "I feel it is my fault Strikes-in-Camp has become the man he is."

"He is a man," Bass reminded. "He cannot blame who or what he is on you. And neither should you. Your son's sins will not fall upon his father's lodge—"

"More are coming!" Pretty On Top announced, pointing across the snowy bowl.

Instantly they turned, the distant figures magnetizing their attention. On the far hillside a short string of horses and some twenty people started down at an angle, the figures stark across the brilliant snow shimmering with a golden hue as the sun continued its fall.

Wheeling to gaze at the west, Bass ripped off both blanket mittens, laid the edge of one hand along the horizon, then set the other on top of it. The sun was racing toward its rest.

They didn't have long.

"If we are to fight these people," Scratch said, yanking on the mittens in the severe cold as a gust of wind slashed over the bare brow of that hill, "we must do it soon."

"Yes. For if any escape our slaughter," Whistler agreed, "we might not find them in the dark."

Real Bird asked, "How will you attack?"

The warrior considered that for some time, then pointed. "They have come from the north, looking for these buffalo. Their village must lie in that direction because we have not come upon it. So half of us will ride around to those hills and cut off their escape."

"I will lead those men," Pretty On Top volunteered.

"No. The white man will lead," Whistler deferred. "But I want you to ride at the right hand of *Pote Ani.*"

The young warrior smiled, his eyes flashing at the white man. "This is good. After all these winters . . . we go into battle together."

"And you will lead the rest?" Titus asked Whistler.

"Yes. We will wait until you have reached the far side of those hills across the valley."

Bass nodded. "We must hurry to be in position."

"Then I will bring the rest with me, riding through that saddle, and sweep down on the enemy."

With a smile Scratch said, "Driving them right into our trap."

"I see the fear in their eyes already!" Pretty On Top exulted.

"I can smell how they have soiled themselves in fear!" Whistler echoed.

"No more dried meat for us," Windy Boy cheered youthfully. "Not only has the First Maker delivered this enemy into our hands to revenge the death of He-Who-Is-No-Longer, but tonight we can end our diet of cold meat."

"Pretty On Top," Bass said, tapping the young warrior on the shoulder, "it's time to set our trap."

Back among the others and the horses, Whistler and Turns Plenty divided the warriors, being sure there were proven veterans and newcomers to war in both groups.

"We will do our best to be in position before you ride down on the Blackfoot," Bass assured Whistler as his warriors were mounting up behind him. "We don't have much light left in the day."

"Defend yourself, *Pote Ani,*" Whistler pleaded before he turned away to his group. "Both of us must return to our wives."

Titus reached out and grabbed the warrior's arm. "Know that in my heart, I am married to your daughter."

"I don't claim to know all what lies in a white man's heart . . . but I believe that you truly love my daughter—"

"All you have to do is tell me what you want of me, how I am to marry her—I'll do it."

Whistler smiled. "I know. But for now, we have some Blackfoot to kill. We'll talk again of this marriage upon our victorious homecoming."

Backtracking to the south for about two miles, Bass was able to lead his band north again behind the range of low hills until he struck that trampled trail the enemy had taken through the snow to climb over the heights and drop into the valley where the Blackfoot had encountered the buffalo herd. From time to time the boom of distant guns echoed from beyond the heights. Minutes later as the sun was easing down upon the crowns of the western hills, they heard a massive volley of shots.

"That isn't a buffalo shoot!" Bass roared, kicking his thick winter moccasins into the ribs of the pony with the spotted rump.

"Time to take scalps!" Bear Ground bellowed, leaping away with Pretty On Top.

Like water bursting through a beaver dam, some two dozen of them had their weary ponies lunging up that last slope, reaching the top to look below. On the western side of the valley Whistler and Turns Plenty were leading the others in a mad gallop that was just reaching the valley floor where the Blackfoot hunters had been engaged in shooting the snowbound buffalo while others, mostly women, were at work on the outskirts of the herd, skinning and butchering in tiny, trampled circles of crimson snow.

Enemy horsemen were mounting up, charging toward the onrushing Crow to throw a buffer between them and the women as those figures on foot hurtled themselves around and lunged away with their horses dragging half-laden travois of meat and heavy green hides. Calf-deep snow clawed at their legs, slowing their retreat as the Blackfoot horsemen closed ranks behind the women, then rushed the charging Crow in a full front.

As Scratch and his warriors swept over the brow of the hill, he watched the Blackfoot line collide against Whistler's Crow with a great crash—men yelling and grunting, horses crying out, guns blaring and handheld weapons clattering.

Then the Blackfoot were behind the Crow lines, several of them yelling to the rest, ordering their comrades to halt and circle around on the rear of the Crow.

Just then the women fleeing from Whistler's men spotted Bass's Crow horsemen fanning out across the northern hillside, realizing they were being attacked from two directions. With a howl they dragged to a halt, screaming, turning round and round in fear and confusion.

Down, down the slope Bass's line flowed as it raced toward the women who wailed and cursed the Crow warriors as those horsemen peeled past them in a blur, tearing on down to the valley floor where the buffalo were suddenly turning blindly, lumbering toward the southwest, making for the narrow saddle that allowed them their only escape from the snowy bowl.

Behind them the women shook their knives in their bloody hands, shouting their oaths at the Crow backs.

"Perhaps you'll find a wife today!" Scratch hollered at Pretty On Top. "These Blackfoot love to copulate with brave Crow men!"

The young warrior laughed.

On the far side of him Windy Boy said, "I saw a pretty one! Maybe I will take her back to my lodge and we can make many Crow babies!"

Having raced halfway across the trampled snow on the valley floor, Titus realized several of the Crow and Blackfoot riders had been unhorsed in the brutal collision of their lines. In the midst of the butchered buffalo carcasses and the milling, riderless horses, the warriors were crawling out of the snow, whirling about in search of an enemy. Voices rang from the slopes, overwhelmed by the roar of smoothbore English fusils and American-made trade muskets. Once the weapons were empty, most of the combatants did not stop to reload. Instead, they pitched their empty firearms aside and pulled out a bow, a long-handled war club, a tomahawk, or a knife before they rushed on one of the enemy.

Even in the swirling maze of confusion, it was easy for Scratch to pick Crow from Blackfoot, even with both sides bundled in heavy blankets or capotes. The enemy was dressed for winter hunting, while the Crow were painted for war.

In shock, the Blackfoot warriors were realizing they were caught between the pincers of a trap rapidly sealing off their chance for escape.

Those still on horseback were forming up, yelling boldly to one another, kicking into a gallop as they started across the snowy ground toward Bass's mounted warriors.

If they collided with the Crow line and lunged on past it, they would rejoin the women and the chase would be on. The battle would then be a running fight instead of a decisive victory.

"Halt!" Scratch cried, his throat immediately sore in the superdry air. "Halt!"

He was waving as a handful of the warriors took up his cry, the Crow waving at the rest to return up the slope, to re-form in a ragged line somewhere between the fleeing women behind them and those oncoming horsemen sweeping across the valley floor.

"Hold the line—do not charge!" the white man ordered.

Bear Ground shook his head in confusion. "You want us to stand here while they ride down on us?"

"Yes!" he demanded. "If they get past any of you, if they break by our line, then they have escaped."

"*Pote Ani* is right!" Pretty On Top yelled. "None of us wants to chase after the enemy! We must stand and fight them here!"

SEVEN

He saw the fear in their eyes as the Blackfoot raced toward his line.

But on their faces was written a stoic anger.

Time and again Bass had seen that loathing the Blackfoot held for the white man. No, their hatred for Americans.

The tribe put up with the British to the north, endured the Hudson's Bay traders and fur brigades because those white men brought all sorts of useful goods, most especially the guns, powder, and lead. But the Americans traded with every enemy of the Blackfoot. With the arrival of the Americans, the Crow, Shoshone, and Flathead found a supplier of those firearms necessary to even the balance after decades of mountain warfare while a mighty, well-armed confederation of Blood, Piegan, and Gros Ventre sought to crush its poorer neighbors.

In the fading of that afternoon's light, the Blackfoot were discovering that their firearms gave them no advantage if they could not reload them on the run. Caught unaware in the surprise attack, these hunters found they had no choice but to use weapons that would bring them face-to-face with the Crow.

Those Blackfoot closest to Bass suddenly realized there was a white man among their enemy. Just before the lines clashed, some of the warriors yelled to the others, pointing at the lone trapper—singling him out for certain attention.

"They don't like you!" Pretty On Top shouted beside Bass as his pony pranced, barely under control.

Titus growled, "Never worried about what dead men think of me!"

A half dozen were converging on the trapper as he poked the trigger finger of his right hand out through a slot cut in the palm of his blanket mitten.

As Scratch struggled to calm his own frightened horse, an arrow slapped his leg, painfully pinning the meat of his calf against the animal. The horse sidestepped away from its pain, trying to rear back. Each time it jolted back onto all four hooves, a shock wave of nausea bolted through his stomach. Then the wounded leg popped free and he was able to swing it up, clutching the long shaft in his left hand. Snapping it off, he quickly bent down to try pushing the damned thing on out the inside of his calf when a second arrow raked along his rib cage.

Staring at the shaft fluttering there in his thick elk-hide coat, he wondered if he'd been punctured. Seizing the arrow in his left mitten, he steeled himself, ready to snap it off against his belly, when he discovered that it had pierced only his coat and buckskin shirt.

From behind him unearthly shrieks rolled toward him like a land-slide.

Twisting partway in the saddle, he raised the full-stock rifle, pulled back on the rear set trigger, and clumsily waved the Derringer's muzzle at the closest Blackfoot screaming down on him. Yanking back on that front hair trigger, Scratch watched the heavy .54-caliber ball slam the warrior back onto the rear haunches of his pony for a heartbeat before the man tumbled backward off the animal into the trampled snow.

Now as the others closed on him, in that long flintlock rifle Titus found himself holding no more than a long and very heavy club. Leaning to the right, he dropped out of the saddle and landed with most of his weight on the uninjured leg. But when he slapped the pony on the rump and sent it away, then started to step backward as he clawed at his side for the powder horn, the wounded calf gave way as soon as his weight was momentarily shifted onto it.

Pitching into the snow, Scratch realized he had no time to reload the long-range weapon. He dropped the rifle to the ground beside him, rolled onto his knees, and futilely tore at the flaps of his coat with both mittens, scrambling clumsily to seize the weapons tucked in that wide leather belt secured around the outside of his coat. Stuffing each of the mittens under an armpit, he tore them from his hands just before dragging the two big pistols from his belt, raking back the hammer on the right one.

At that moment the Blackfoot collided with the two ends of the Crow line, smashing into those two horns of the crescent.

Scratch took aim at a target closing on him, a round-faced warrior wearing a blanket cap and swinging a stone war club with a long elk-horn handle. That first pistol ball struck the warrior under the armpit, spinning him so violently he struggled vainly to clutch at the pony's mane as the animal clattered past and the man bounced loose. Ten yards behind Bass the warrior spun to the ground, tumbling across the snow.

More shrieking yanked Scratch about to find another warrior with his bow strung, its arrow drawn back against its string to form a sharp, two-sided vee. Swapping the pistols, Bass ripped the hammer back and pulled the trigger—an instant after the string snapped forward.

Flinging himself backward, Bass fell into the snow as the arrow slammed into the icy crust between his knees.

For a heartbeat he stared at the quiver of the shaft and its fletching, then jerked up to find the bowman on top of him, slashing out with the bow. Twisting to the side out of its way, Titus watched the warrior coming off the pony, flying spreadeagled through the air, that bow at the end of one outstretched arm.

He slammed into the white man, driving the air from their lungs as Scratch rolled them over, throwing his arm behind him to find his knife. Instead, his fingers struck the frosty head of the belt ax.

The muscular Blackfoot grabbed the white man's throat with one hand, his fingers closing around the windpipe as the warrior began to flail at the white man's head with the bow in blinding flashes.

Dragging the ax into his hand, Titus swung wildly, eventually slamming the side of the blade against the warrior's head. In bringing his arm back for another blow, he twisted the tomahawk in his hand. This time the blade sank deep, splattering hot blood and brain matter into Bass's face.

He had to unlock the dead man's legs from his before he could struggle to his knees and wrench up the first of the pistols. With some of the Blackfoot retreating back down the hill into the flat where more of their number were fighting furiously against the trap that had closed around them, some of those who were dismounted were taking cover behind the huge buffalo carcasses rising like dark, hairy boulders against the bloody snow.

With that first pistol reloaded and stuffed into his belt, Bass lunged across the Indian's body to scoop up the second pistol. After blowing snow from the pan, he reloaded it, snapped the frizzen down over the pan again, and jammed it into his belt. Back up the hill a few yards lay the rifle, its barrel buried in the snow right up to the lock's hammer.

"White man!"

He looked up to find Strikes-in-Camp gleefully reining his pony to a halt nearby.

The young warrior asked, "Where is your horse, white man?"

"I fight better on foot," Bass growled.

"Forget your firearms," Strikes snarled. "Come with me and fight the enemy close today! Come fight like a real man!"

With a wild laugh the warrior spun his horse around savagely, kicking it in the ribs as he shot back down the slope toward the hottest of the fighting.

By then Pretty On Top and the others had driven the Blackfoot back, throwing them against the warriors Whistler and Turns Plenty led. They had the Blackfoot surrounded. On the hillside above him the women were screaming, keening, crying out to their men.

Surrounded by the enemy, goaded by their women, the Blackfoot could only be made bold by their desperate straits—or stupid, willing to grasp at any chance before they died.

One of them was about to do just that.

Near the center of that buffalo killing field the Blackfoot warrior stood, waving his smoothbore fusil at the end of his arm, his mouth a wide *O* as he hollered at the rest who were beginning to withdraw from the shelter of their buffalo carcasses and stream toward their leader. It reminded Scratch of a black cloud of sparrows as they dipped this way, then that, low in the sky overhead. Suddenly the leader took off, his warriors strung out on either side of him, racing for the hills.

In an instant Bass could see that they really weren't making for the distant slope. Instead, they were sprinting for the weakest part of the Crow line where Strikes-in-Camp and a handful of others were all that stood between the Blackfoot and escape. On the far side of the valley, Scratch could tell that Whistler saw things taking shape at the same moment. The old warrior was yelling and waving even as he started his pony loping to head off the enemy.

Bass was already on his way down the hillside, whistling in the cold air, licking his lips to whistle again for the pony which raised its head and started his way.

Instead of waiting for the others, instead of slowly backing up the slope to delay the clash, Strikes-in-Camp taunted his fellow warriors into joining him in a headlong dash toward the Blackfoot spearhead coming their way. Near the bottom ground the enemy swept around the half-dozen Crow, swallowing them whole the way a mountain lion swallowed a deer mouse in one bite.

The Crow warriors disappeared beneath a roiling mass of arms and weapons, dragged one by one from their horses.

Whistler and the others were closing in on the slaughter as some of the Blackfoot broke from the six unhorsed Crow and lunged up the slope to make their escape. The older warrior waved at the enemy seeking to flee—sending more than ten of his fighters to seal off any chance of escape. Then Whistler continued into the fray to save his son and the others.

Dragging himself atop the pony as the injured calf cried out in pain,

Scratch slapped the rifle's buttstock against its rear flank to put it into a gallop as they raced across the bottom, weaving through the bloody buffalo carcasses.

As more Crow reached the scene, the Blackfoot spread out to meet the charge the way a pebble dropped into a still pond would radiate widening rings around it. Bodies struggled on the ground at the center of the melee, Blackfoot finishing off the six Crow.

Into that contest Whistler plunged on horseback, swinging a long war club first on one side of his horse, then on the other, as he desperately cut himself a swath through the enemy to reach his son.

Bass was starting to rein up when he saw that Blackfoot leader who had rallied his warriors leap to the side, coming into the open. The short fusil he had been waving was now shoved against his shoulder. And aimed at Whistler.

Smoke puffed from the muzzle.

Even as the low boom rang out, Bass watched the impact jerk Whistler up straight, his war club tumbling from his hand as he fought to stay atop the horse. With both hands he clawed for the single horsehair rein he had dropped. In desperation both hands knotted themselves into the pony's mane as it pranced round and round in a tight circle, more Blackfoot closing in on the war-party leader.

Scratch drove his pony over two, then a third warrior, spinning them aside, crushing one beneath the runner's hooves as he lunged to reach the injured Whistler. Reaching the scene as a pair of the enemy on foot were clawing at the wounded horseman, attempting to yank Whistler off the back of his frightened horse, Scratch pulled the loaded pistol free, aimed, and fired at a narrow back. The enemy warrior nearly crumpled in half backward as he spilled into the snow beneath the pony's hooves.

Reining aside, Scratch swung the empty pistol, smashing its barrel against a second warrior's head with the loud crack of a heavy maul striking tight-grained Kentucky hickory. The warrior stumbled backward, wheeling round to gaze up at the white horseman as he collapsed across a jumble of legs and arms as others wrestled in the snow.

"Go!" Bass ordered Whistler. "Get to the hillside—"

"I . . . I can't hold on," he said weakly, beginning to sink off the side of his pony.

"Get to the hillside!" Scratch repeated. "Don't let go until you are at the top of that hill!"

Then the white man slapped the back of the pony with the pistol's long barrel, making it leap away. He watched Whistler clutching both his arms around the horse's neck as it bounded through the milling warriors. Shiny blood streamed down the Crow's leg, slicking a huge, dark patch that ran down the pony's side as it raced up the gradual slope, away from the fighting.

A few yards away the Crow were just striking the Blackfoot who had swallowed up Strikes-in-Camp and his companions. The six were nowhere to be seen. Titus figured they were likely dead already as he jabbed heels into his pony's ribs and loped toward the bitter hand-to-hand fighting as the Blackfoot suddenly turned from mauling the few to preparing to meet the many.

Racing in at an angle, Bass reached the enemy just as the Crow clattered into the Blackfoot formation. Slowly, slowly the enemy backed, swinging, slashing, shrieking with all the fury they had left as their women continued to yell and scream from the nearby hill.

On the ground nearby, two of the enemy still struggled over one of the Crow, both of them working at pinning down the arms and legs as they swung their weapons for the kill. Dragging their victim over onto his side, one of the Blackfoot struck the back of the Crow's neck with a glancing blow. Scratch watched all the fight pour out of the valiant warrior. The second Blackfoot raised his heavy tomahawk at the end of his arm, its iron blade glinting dully in the falling sun as Scratch pulled out his second pistol, dragged at the big gooseneck hammer, and seized the trigger.

He felt it buck in his hand as it spat fire and a billow of gray smoke.

Clawing at his back, the Blackfoot twisted about wide-eyed to stare at Bass a moment before he pitched into the snow, dead beside the Crow he was ready to kill.

Yet the first was already seizing hold of the Crow's tall, greased, provocative forelock, yanking the warrior's head back as he dragged a huge dagger from its scabbard, prepared to cleave the Crow's throat like a bled pig his grandfather would prepare for the smoke shed.

Scratch threw the empty pistol at the Blackfoot. Its barrel slashed across the warrior's cheekbone, making him jerk aside for an instant, gazing up at the white man descending on him.

That instant was all Bass needed.

He rode the pony right over the Blackfoot, shoving himself sideways out of the saddle as the warrior fell backward the moment the horse stomped over him. Seizing the hand that held the dagger in both of his, Scratch slammed it against the snowy, frozen ground again and again until the knife tumbled out. Then with a bare fist he smashed the warrior in the face, watching the man's cold skin split and ooze blood across the nose, over an eye. Again and again he smashed that young warrior's face until the Blackfoot no longer struggled.

Scooping the dagger from the snow, Titus raked it across the warrior's throat, opening a gush that flooded the ground beneath his knees, the snow turning a dirty brown beneath both the dead Blackfoot and that Crow he had been ready to butcher.

Dragging his wounded leg beneath him, Bass grabbed the dead

man's shirt and pulled him off the Crow before he seized the Crow's shoulders and turned him around.

Strikes-in-Camp.

The dark eyes fluttered open, crimson ooze seeping from a big gash over one eye, snow crusted against that bruised, puffy side of his face. His shirt was bloody where a long gash had been opened up in his side, and his breath came short and labored as those eyes struggled to focus on the face of the man who had just saved him.

Bass realized his mistake the instant Strikes-in-Camp recognized him.

The young warrior's eyes narrowed into slits and his bruised face drew up into a sneer.

There would never be any gratitude from that man for the one who had saved his life.

"Why were *you* the one who saved me?" Strikes-in-Camp growled as he shoved away the hands of those warriors who were steadying him on his feet.

Bass turned away, shaking his head in disgust. "Your father needs help."

"Why did it have to be *you*, white man?" the words slammed him in the back.

The white man stopped, turned to confront Whistler's son. "You are a Crow warrior," Scratch explained as it grew still around them. "Your uncle was my friend. Your father, he is my friend."

"Perhaps it would have been better for me to die than to be saved by you!"

Grimly Titus said, "One day you might just get your wish, Strikes-in-Camp."

"Pote Ani!"

He spotted Pretty On Top and Windy Boy riding his way through the litter of carcasses and bodies, both Crow and Blackfoot. "Both of you, up the hill—help Whistler!"

The young warriors turned, spying the older man. Immediately they kicked their ponies into a lope across the side of the knoll. Leaping to the ground, the two of them helped steady the wounded man who held fast to his horse with only his arms, his legs no longer able to respond. As Scratch started up the hill, Whistler put out one arm to grip Pretty On Top's shoulders and leaned off the horse, sliding to the ground with a deep pain graying his face.

"Rest, friend," Bass said softly as he knelt beside his father-in-law. Quickly he turned to Windy Boy. "Go—bring us one of the Blackfoot travois and a pony to hitch it to. And bring two of those green buffalo hides. We must make Whistler as comfortable as we can for his ride home."

The young warrior leaped onto his pony and wheeled away as Pretty On Top stepped up behind the white man's shoulder. Across the valley the women were screaming wildly, turning to flee like a scattered nest of sow bugs as the victorious Crow warriors galloped toward them, sweeping up on both sides to capture the enemy squaws.

But here on the slope with Whistler, it grew still while the sun eased out of the sky and the air seemed so very cold of a sudden.

The warrior reached up and gripped Scratch's forearm. "I don't know if I can make that long journey home."

"You will."

"My s-son?"

"He is alive, and he will live," Bass responded, placing his hands on Whistler's bleeding hip. "Just as you will live."

"Did . . . did my son fight well? Or did he fight foolishly?"

Titus looked up at Pretty On Top.

The young warrior bent down to declare, "Strikes-in-Camp fought well against the enemy, Whistler."

The old warrior closed his eyes, then clenched them tight as a spasm of pain volted through him. When it had passed, he sighed and opened his eyes. "I am glad. It would not be a good thing for us both to be killed in the same battle."

Bass could see that the lead ball had crashed through the side of Whistler's hip but had not exited. It lay somewhere inside his gut. And the top of that left leg had been shattered by the bullet's path. Of all the men he had known who survived injuries to live full lives without part of an arm, without part of a leg . . . Titus had never known of a man who had lost all of a leg, right up to the hip.

The warrior whispered, "You will tell Crane?"

"You can tell her yourself—"

"Tell Crane that I loved her."

"We'll be back to the village soon—"

"Promise me you will tell her," Whistler interrupted, squeezing on Bass's forearm with a bloody hand.

Titus felt the bitterness start to fill his chest, the utter senselessness of it. And again he realized that a man knew when he was about to die. No matter what he might say, there was no convincing Whistler that he would make it home.

"Promise me you'll tell my daughter what happened here," he pleaded. "And in the summers to come, you'll tell your daughter about me."

Scratch started to choke. "I . . . I'll tell her what a fine man she had for a grand . . . grandfather."

"It's so cold," he said.

And Scratch remembered how Josiah had uttered the very same

words. "We'll have you warm soon. Just hold on to me and we'll get you some robes, and start a fire—"

"Where is my son?"

"He'll be here soon—"

"I want to see my son before I die."

"We'll get him," Bass promised. "Now, you just do your best not to fall asleep yet."

"But I am tired," Whistler confessed. "So very tired."

"A man should be tired. It was a long journey you led us on," Scratch said, turning quickly to see more than a dozen others coming up the side of the slope toward them. He could feel the sting of those first tears. "And a mighty battle you took us into."

"Wait . . . I find it hard to see you, *Pote Ani*—"

"I'm right here, Whistler."

The warrior sighed again, the death rattle in his chest. "I hear your voice, but I do not see you so well anymore. But there, just ahead of me—wait. I see the green hills."

Turning slightly, Scratch looked to see where Whistler was pointing with his shaking hand. Nothing but the deepening indigo sky behind the cold, barren, snowy hills.

"Yes," Titus said in a harsh whisper, his throat clogged suddenly. "I—I can see the hills too, Whistler."

"Do you see him?"

Bass turned and looked off again in that direction. "See who?"

"There," the warrior whispered. "It's my brother."

"You see Ara—" Suddenly he caught himself in saying the dead man's name, realizing the grim significance of that vision. "You can see He-Who-Is-No-Longer-With-Us?"

Whistler lowered the hand he had been using to point into the distance. "And he has seen me too. He is waving to me. My brother . . . he is walking this way. He is coming for me."

Whistler had died during that long, cold, cold night.

By the time Strikes-in-Camp came up the slope to where his father lay, Whistler was unable to speak, but he must have recognized the sound of his son's voice. They touched hands, gripping one another while the warriors parted and allowed Windy Boy and Pretty On Top to bring the travois close.

On the far side of that range of hills where they had first spotted the enemy, the Crow war party chose a place for their camp where they built their fires, roasted some of the meat the Blackfoot had dropped in the valley, and put a guard around the eleven captured squaws. Five were tied together, and six were tied in a second group. Except for the quiet sobbing, the low-pitched keening of those women, it was a quiet, subdued camp.

Little was said the next morning as Turns Plenty ordered that the rest of the enemy horses be rounded up, that more of the travois be brought in with the green hides on them, along with more of the hump ribs and fleece from those buffalo the Blackfoot hunters had killed.

They would be going home with the squaws as their prisoners, with the enemy's ponies and more than thirty fresh hides . . . but also dragging with them the bodies of eleven Crow dead.

The war party found their village south of the Yellowstone, hard under the Pryor Mountains. For more than an hour the war party stopped to prepare themselves to enter the camp, putting on fresh paint, stringing out the forty-six Blackfoot scalps on lances and medicine staffs. While the others were eager to push ahead, Bass chose to hang back among those who were dragging the eleven bodies behind their ponies. From one of the older warriors he borrowed some red paint, smearing it on his face.

Pretty On Top, then the ten other riders tending the wounded, stepped up and dipped their fingers into the white man's palm, taking some of the red ocher and bear-grease mixture to daub across their foreheads, down their noses, over their copper cheekbones, and finally on their proud chins.

While Turns Plenty led the others into the village, Bass and the eleven brought up the rear of the procession with their war dead. As the column neared the outskirts of camp, women and children poured out to yell and cheer, trilling their tongues in celebration to see so many enemy horses and those robes. Then the first of the women realized she was not finding her loved one among those riders. She had not spotted a familiar face.

Then another, and another, and more.

Those eerie, bone-grating wails began as the squaws took to sobbing, the children to crying for lost fathers or uncles or brothers.

Solemnly the eleven entered the camp where more than three thousand Crow had formed along the route. Now the crowds parted as the travois rumbled slowly through their midst. On both sides of the procession women flung themselves on the ground, wrenching at their hair, wailing to the skies, crying so piteously it made the hair stand at the back of Bass's neck where the cold wind tousled the ragged ends of the curly hair he had chopped off in mourning.

As the last man in the march, Scratch desperately searched the throng for Waits-by-the-Water, fearing more than anything that she would not see him and immediately suspect that he was among the eleven dead. Looking for her face in the crowd, any young woman wrapped in a blanket and holding an infant . . . eager to spot the lodge of Whistler and Crane.

Of a sudden he spotted her. Relief washed over him as he raised his arm to signal. She saw him, then stepped closer to her mother. At Crane's other shoulder stood Strikes-in-Camp, supporting his mother as the travois bearing the dead started past. Crane clamped a hand against her mouth, as if attempting to stifle her cry, to swallow down her grief.

Strikes-in-Camp bent to say something to his mother just before Crane started toward one of the travois, her feet leaden, almost refusing to move.

Suddenly she crumbled there on the muddy snow, all the strength flushed out of her. Waits and Strikes-in-Camp knelt beside their mother as Bass leaped to the ground, sprinted the last few yards to the woman's side.

The trapper turned to Waits as he started to scoop his arms beneath the small woman. "I can carry her to the lodge if you will lead—"

But Strikes-in-Camp shoved his arms aside. "I will carry my mother to her lodge."

Standing and moving back a step, Scratch watched the young warrior lift his distraught mother from the snow into his arms. How tiny Crane looked, how frail and helpless, cradled there in her grown son's arms.

For an instant Strikes-in-Camp's eyes flashed at Bass as he started away with his mother, saying, "You are not of our blood. Go from here. You will never be our blood. You are not part of this family. So you must turn and go from here."

EIGHT

At times through the rest of that winter and early spring, Crane's mourning was almost more than Waits's husband could bear.

Torn between her own grief and the love she felt for this white man she did not always understand, over time Waits-by-the-Water learned to relinquish her husband to the lonely hills for days at a time once more. All she knew was how important it was that she was there for him each time he rode back to rejoin the village.

In those four days following the war party's return, Crane stayed with Strikes-in-Camp in his family's lodge. The widow could not bear to enter, much less eat or sleep in, the lodge she had shared with Whistler. But it should only be a matter of time, Waits realized, before her mother would return to her home. After all, it was her lodge. Not Whistler's.

She only hoped that her mother would be content to stay with Bright Wings and the children until spring pulled the white man back into the far recesses of the mountains. Until then Waits and Magpie would have a home, a place where the young mother welcomed her man for a night or two each time he rejoined the village. But all too quickly he grew restless, packed up, and rode off again, leaving behind a stack of hides for her to scrape. Those beaver pelts filled her days while he was gone into the hills, along with making repairs to clothing and sewing up extra pairs of moccasins, or fashioning tiny dresses and leggings for little Magpie.

By the time the war party had returned, Magpie was crawling, able to scoot about the lodge so well that Waits and Bass had to firmly scold their daughter to keep her from the fire pit. And by late winter she was already standing. Then one early spring afternoon as Bass rode back into camp to find Waits and Magpie enjoying the warm sunshine outside the lodge, their daughter stood shakily with Waits's help, taking those first few awkward and wobbly steps toward her father as he dropped from his pony and Zeke loped round and round them.

Together all three laughed and hugged there on the damp ground as thunder rumbled across the sky as it did every afternoon at this time of year while the seasons turned. It was a good homecoming that night when rain struck the taut lodge skins like drumsticks beating on a hollow tree. All evening Magpie chattered and lumbered around the fire, falling often, but always climbing back up with a giggle, so happy was she with herself.

That night Waits again released the animal in her, hungry for his touch, impatient to have him deep and warm inside her. When he had spent himself and they both lay there exhausted by the glow of the fire, Waits-by-the-Water clung to him like a tick burrowed deep in the curly fur of the buffalo. So afraid to let go, but knowing that come a morning all too soon he would be leaving.

She could not bear to think of how hard it would be to go on if he should die. As much as she tried, Waits was less than successful in squeezing out those thoughts of life after her man's death, the way Crane now existed without her husband. Would she too go through each day as if made cold to her marrow, feeling small, having no desire to eat, little need to sleep, hardly speaking to anyone, staring off at the hills and beginning to cry for no more reason than a sudden, painful remembrance?

Each time Bass left them to ride off for some distant stream, Waits-by-the-Water found it harder and harder to wait. To know exactly where her man was going on a hunt or to steal ponies or perhaps to raise some scalps—that was one thing. But not to know where her man was headed when he went in search of the beaver? That was something so altogether different.

What if her husband was killed by an enemy and his body was left where he had died? What if his pony fell and crushed him and he had to lie there in agony until he drew his last breath? Or what if he was attacked by one of the mountain predators that might scatter his bones?

She would not know where he was, how he had died, where to find his body before the wolves, a mountain lion, or a great silver-haired bear would tear his body apart. This separation was far more excruciating than when she had waited for Bass and her father to return from Blackfoot country. Each time he left to disappear in his hunt for the beaver, she had no idea of her husband's fate until he chose to return to the village with more pelts.

Would she be a widow? Would Magpie be raised without her father?

Late that spring she decided it was far better that the two of them no longer stay behind when he left for the lonely places.

"We are going with you when you leave," she bravely told him this cold, damp night as clouds scudded across that patch of starry sky they could see when they gazed up at the place where Crane's lodgepoles were joined in a great inverted cone.

"It would take so much time to gather—"

"Everything we own is packed," she explained. "Only our blankets, and these robes. We've done it before: with our ponies, we can carry it all."

"Yes," and he grinned at her. "We have done it before. I was planning to do some work trimming the ponies' hooves—"

"Then . . . we can go with you?"

His face turned gray with sudden concern. "What of Magpie?"

She rolled onto an elbow, raised herself up, then gazed down at him as her breasts gently brushed the skin of his chest. "Your daughter already rides in the saddle with me."

"How long has she been doing this?" he asked with a grin.

"Long enough."

Bass smiled at her. "So behind my back you women have made ready to take to the long trail?"

She bobbed her head enthusiastically, afraid to tell him just how much she was wanting to leave the Crow village, needing to flee the daily reminder of her mourning mother . . . afraid to let him know just how much she needed to be with him, no longer able to let him go.

"Promise me, husband—promise that you will never leave me, never leave us behind with the Crow when you go to trap the beaver."

For a long time he peered into her eyes. "That is what you want? You don't want me to leave you behind with your people?"

She shut her eyes a moment. "I don't belong here anymore." Then opened them, gazing into him. "You are my people now."

"So you want to go where I go from now on?"

"Yes," she admitted in a small voice, looking away. Then looked back at him again suddenly, saying strongly, "Promise me—that you will never leave me a widow like my father did."

He stroked her high cheekbones with his rough hands, then eventually said, "I promise you, woman. If it is what you want, you and Magpie will be at my side wherever I go."

"The rest of it—the most important—tell me the rest of your promise to me," she instructed breathlessly.

"And I promise . . . never to make you a widow."

Laying her head against his chest, Waits-by-the-Water listened to his breathing, listened to his heart beating for a long time—slowly realizing that she had just made him give a vow no man could keep.

"Strangers are coming!"

At that first announcement Bass shot to his feet, dropping the crude iron files he had been using to trim the animal's hooves, and leaped atop his pony's back. They raced into the village toward the sound of the excitement.

A large crowd was gathering on the outskirts of camp, some of the people pointing to a dozen riders slowly making their way up the valley toward the Crow village, leading a handful of packhorses.

Waits-by-the-Water spotted him, waved her husband over. "Are they white men?"

Shaking his head, Bass studied the horsemen and said, "They don't ride like white men. No stirrups on their saddles."

"But they are coming from the north," she replied. "Perhaps they are enemies who are lost and don't realize they are about to ride into danger."

"No, I think these riders have come to do some trading with your people."

Within minutes more than fifty Crow warriors had mounted and were loping toward the strangers. When these camp guards were within rifle range, the distant horsemen raised their weapons in the air and fired, puffs of smoke jetting from each muzzle a heartbeat before the booms echoed from the far hills.

"They come in friendship," Bass declared, laying his arm around her shoulder in relief.

No better sign of friendship in this wilderness than for a man to empty his weapon upon approaching a camp.

The small band of strangers halted as the Crow guards swirled around them. They exchanged handshakes and slaps on the back before the entire group continued for the village. In short order it was plain to see these riders were not only Indian, but Crow.

*"Peelatchiwilax'paake!"** a voice exclaimed in recognition as the horsemen approached.

But Bass studied the packhorses more than he did the riders. "Appears they've got some trading on their minds."

Upon entering the village the visitors dismounted as the Crow

---

* *River Crow*

guards turned aside with their ponies. Stopping near the center of the camp circle, the spokesman for the newcomers gestured for quiet before he started to speak.

"Friends! Fellow *Apsaluuke!*" he cried in the Crow tongue. "We bring you good wishes from the River band of Long Hair!"

That voice.

Bass stepped closer so he could peer at the speaker, pricked by something recognizable about the man. Whispering to his wife, he asked, "You know him? Ever see him before?"

Waits wagged her head and shifted a squirmy Magpie in her arms.

"Where is Yellow Belly, your chief?" the visitor asked.

"I am here," the band's leader exclaimed as he shouldered his way through the crowd. "Who is asking for me?"

"Medicine Calf," the spokesman declared.

Scratch remembered hearing that warrior's name. . . .

Yellow Belly stepped closer to the visitor. "You are the one who was taken as a child and returned to Absaroka as a beaver trapper?"

"So you have heard my story?" Medicine Calf bellowed beneath the huge cap he wore, made from the entire skin of a mountain lion that spilled clear down his back. "Then you know I am one of you, know that your people are my people too!"

"We have heard the stories of your life with the River band," Yellow Belly replied. "And how famous you are with the women! Why have you come? Did you bed the wrong woman and now you are forced to leave that village?"

"No!" and Medicine Calf laughed uproariously. Something about that laugh pricked another familiar chord in Bass. "I have come with presents for the chiefs, goods to trade."

"To trade?" Real Bird asked as he stepped up beside Yellow Belly.

"I come here with these presents and goods from the trading post the white man calls *Cass* at the mouth of the *Iisaxp'uatahcheeaashisee.*"*

Strikes-in-Camp shoved his way forward to ask, "Why did the white man send you?"

"I work for him," Medicine Calf answered truthfully.

Turning to his wife, Bass said, "Now that's something a mite peculiar. A Crow warrior working for the white trader—"

The visitor continued. "The trader pays me money to see that the Crow bring their furs to his post."

Titus touched his wife's arm and whispered, "Wait for me here." Then he parted the crowd and started for the visitor, saying loudly in English, "Who does this goddamned trader work for?"

Medicine Calf wheeled in surprise at the question, his eyes narrow-

* *Bighorn River*

ing to a squint in his dark-skinned face. In English he said, "I figgered it had to be a white man asking jest such a god-blamed question! Ain't no Absaroke gonna know our tongue near that good. Trader hired me, he works for American Fur—"

Suddenly the English-speaking Crow stopped talking, holding his breath as Bass drew near.

"By the stars—it's . . . yeah, you're the one called Scratch, ain'cha?"

Now it was Titus's turn to be dumbstruck. He stopped, peered the stranger up and down twice, trying his best to recognize something about this warrior called Medicine Calf. "Where the hell do you know me from?"

"Shit, Scratch!" the newcomer bellowed as he started for Bass, some of his bewildered Crow companions stepping back. "I knowed you from your first ronnyvoo."

Now Titus was confused as hell. "Never met me no Crow early as that."

"But you knowed me!" the spokesman exclaimed, stopping right in front of the trapper. "You was riding with three fellas—not a one of 'em liked Negras."

That hit Scratch like a lightning jolt. This Medicine Calf claimed to know him back of a time when he was riding with Silas Cooper's bunch.

Cocking his head to the side warily, Titus asked, "How the blazes you know that?"

Holding out his hand, Medicine Calf said, "Hell, it's me, Scratch! I'm Jim Beckwith! D-d-don't you 'member me?"

"Beckwith?"

The mulatto lunged a step closer and snagged Bass's right hand in his, then pumped mightily. "One and the same, you ol' dog!"

"Jehoshaphat—I ain't see'd you in . . . by damned—I did hear tell at ronnyvoo you was took prisoner by some Crow what thought you was their long-lost son!"

The mulatto slapped his chest. "That's me!"

Bass pulled Beckwith against him firmly, pounding the mulatto on the back several times before he stood back and took it all in again. "If'n you don't look like some Crow dandy, all gussied up!"

"Ain't I purty, Scratch?"

"So what's this consarn 'bout you working for some trader?"

"Name's Tullock," Beckwith explained. "Trapped way back of the early days, but now he's gone to work for American Fur. Has his post down on the Yellowstone near the mouth of the Bighorn."

"You come here for him, did you?"

Beckwith nodded. "Don't do much trapping no more. Say, with you being so handy with this here band, you think you could get all the headmen and chiefs together round noon so I can tell 'em about the good prices Tullock's gonna give 'em on their furs?"

"You come to stir up some business for them American Fur men?"

With a shrug Beckwith confessed, "Hell, coon—I'm an American Fur man my own self."

"Easier'n wading in cold streams, ain't it?"

"Got me a passel of Crow wives too," and he grinned. "They been keeping this child's pole stropped on winter nights! Why—I even go out to steal ponies and take scalps with the rest of 'em."

"Sounds to me Jim Beckwith's took right to the blanket!"

The mulatto smiled broadly, then asked, "Ain't you, Scratch?"

"Naw."

The skin between Beckwith's eyebrows furrowed. "But ain't that why you're living here 'mong these'r Crow? Ain't you got a mess of Crow wives fighting to climb on your wiping stick ever' night?"

"Just one, Jim," he said. "And I ain't gone to the blanket a'tall. Why, we're fixing to light out for the high country 'nother day or so."

"Damn—finding you here, I just naturally had you figgered for making life easy after all them years you been scratchin' round for beaver."

"Plain to see how you're took to the Crow yourself."

"So a'fore you make for the hills, won't you help me get these chiefs sat down for some palaver 'bout their furs and Fort Cass?"

"I s'pose I could," Titus agreed, seeing no harm.

"There's sure to be something in it for you, old friend," and Beckwith took a step back, motioning to the packhorses being held by the Crow men who had accompanied him from the trading post.

Turning to Yellow Belly and those leaders gathered behind him, Bass grandly slapped a hand on Beckwith's shoulder. "The Medicine Calf speaks good white man talk to me, but he wants to speak from the heart as a Crow. He comes here asking for a council with the chiefs—to talk about bringing your furs to the white man's post."

Later that evening when Titus returned from the afternoon conference where Beckwith passed out good things to eat, beads and tobacco, cloth and powder, Waits-by-the-Water asked him, "How long till the white men gather to trade their beaver?"

"Not for more than three moons," he said, settling back in the blankets and patting the robe beside him.

As she slipped her dress over her head, Scratch felt his eagerness stir, sure to overwhelm him. Hungrily, he pulled her face down so he could kiss her mouth.

"Good," she sighed, nestling her head against his chest, curling up beside him to scratch the small patch of graying hair in the middle of his chest. "Then we have lots of time to lay our traps in all those streams flowing down from the foothills as we ride south for that great camp of the white men."

Stroking her fragrant hair for a few minutes as he stared into the distance, Titus finally answered, "Before we do, I think we ought go to the mouth of the Bighorn."

"Why should we go east, husband? Did the Medicine Calf tell you there were more beaver there than in the mountains south of us this spring?"

"No," Titus answered, brushing his fingers along the curve of her breast until he felt the nipple. His touch quickly made it rigid. "Some time back I heard talk of a new post on the Bighorn. I didn't figure it for the truth, not this far south of the Missouri."

"Yes—some of our men learned of the new post a long time ago."

Bass could tell she was beginning to experience that tingle of excitement starting to spiderweb its way across her flesh as he continued to caress the engorged breast, to tantalize that hardened nipple. "Have any of your men gone there?"

"Yes, a few. But the River Crow where Medicine Calf lives, they travel to this post to trade many times."

"If the trader has powder and guns to fight off the Blackfeet, then I'm sure the Crow will do a lot of trapping, will take all their furs there for even more powder and guns."

Her fingers tiptoed down his belly until she found his flesh and began to stroke it gently with her fingers. Bass wondered if she wanted him to grow as desperate for her as she must be for him.

Waits said, "So like the River Crow you will take your furs to this trader on the Bighorn?"

"I figure we'll wait to trade until rendezvous," he confessed as he felt his hardened flesh warm dramatically with her touch, "but I am still very curious to see for myself just how strong and powerful this fur company has become here in these mountains where once only the free men reigned."

"Why should this bother you, husband? You are not a man who goes where the company says, like this Medicine Calf."

"You know I never will be."

"Then you are a truly free man. And you should not let this trading post concern you."

"No," he answered with a sudden gust of exuberant laughter, no longer able to endure the delicious anticipation. He rolled her over on her back and positioned himself between her legs. "I could never truly be a free man again—not when you hold my heart captive!"

"If you're a man what can keep them Crow busy with their hides," the trader explained, "the job's yours, Mr. Bass."

Scratch wagged his head. "Didn't come for no job, but thankee all the same, Mr. Tullock. It's been too many years since I last worked for anyone but my own self." He peered around at the crates and canvas-wrapped bundles piled across the earthen floor. " 'Sides, with you packing up your goods, I'd say you're fixing to leave this country."

Great disappointment crossed Samuel Tullock's long, overly thin face. "Could use you at the mouth of the Tongue."

"That where ol' Astor got you headed?"

"Astor don't own American Fur Company no more," Tullock groused.

That surprised Bass. "If'n he don't own it, who does?"

"Goddamned Frenchmen down to St. Louie. Same ones what've give up on this post," the trader grumbled as he snatched up his pipe and turned in search of his tobacco pouch. He found it, turned with a disapproving grunt. "They figger to pull back east a'ways, figger it'll be better pickin's there. I sure as hell don't read it that way—what with that damned Beckwith gone to the blanket the way he done."

Watching the man light his pipe with a twig he held in the small stone fireplace, Bass asked, "I figgered Jim to be just what you needed: a man what them Crow adopted for one of their own, someone in the company's pay too."

Tullock sputtered a derisive burst of laughter, spewing smoke from both nose and mouth. "Shit! Maybeso it worked at first when McKenzie heard Beckwith lived with them Crow and could get them Injuns to bring all their furs in to trade at the company posts. But things didn't stay friendly for long."

"Friendly?"

"Hell, the longer that Negra was living with the Crow, the more Crow he got! So busy playing warrior and Injun chief, he up and forgot he was working for the company what was paying him good money!" Tullock snorted. "Trouble was, 'stead of making them redskins work hard as a white man, Beckwith got lazy as them bastards when it comes to trapping plews!"

"For the life of me," Bass replied, "still can't figger out how your bosses callate they can get as many plews from these red niggers as they can harvest from a brigade of white men."

"Oh, McKenzie and them St. Lou Frenchmen only making sure they cover all bets. 'Sides having the Crow and other tribes out trapping the country, the company booshways always gonna send out its own outfits."

"Sure as sun you can't be no greenhorn," Titus observed. "Beckwith said you laid a few traps in water your own self."

"Come north in twenty-six on the river—was hired on to work for McKenzie's Upper Missouri Outfit. Pushed into the mountains with my brigade the following year," the trader declared.

"I was at that ronnyvoo in twenty-six."

"Didn't see my first ronnyvoo till the next summer," Tullock admitted. "That fall we was trapping up in the Snake River and Portneuf country. Just bumped into some Hudson's Bay fellers under Ogden when winter blowed in early on and we got trapped. Started eating our dogs and horses. Damn, if that bastard Ogden didn't do ever'thing he could to get our boys to come over to him with their pelts! Charged us double on his goods and only give us a poor price for our beaver. We tried twice to make it out on foot but was turned back. Son of a bitch Ogden wouldn't even sell us no snowshoes. We'd had some snowshoes, we'd walked outta there!"

"What come of your outfit?"

"Weather finally opened up come late January, so we finally backtracked on down to Bear River after being holed up more'n two months—eating dog and horse. After a time we run across Campbell's outfit headed north to trade with the Flathead for the spring. From him we got enough to get by till our summer train come out from St. Lou."

Bass gazed a moment at Waits-by-the-Water as she sat in the corner nursing Magpie. Then he asked, "This Fort Union that your booshway McKenzie built up at the mouth of the Yallerstone really all I heard folks say it is?"

"It's one fancy place, that's for certain," Tullock agreed, beaming. "But McKenzie ain't there no longer. After all the liquor problems up there, his Frenchy bosses needed to get someone's head on a platter, and it turned out to be McKenzie's."

"What's the trouble with liquor up there?"

"Ain't s'pose to be no liquor in Injun country—which reminds me," the trader said as he turned aside and headed behind some crates where he held up a clay jug momentarily before he plopped it down and began scrounging for some tin cups.

Bass snorted a great gust of laughter. "No liquor in Injun country! Damn if that ain't some fool's bald-face notion!"

"No, it's true," Tullock protested, finding the cups with a noisy clatter, turning back to Bass. "Now, you understand what I'm offering you here ain't liquor."

"That ain't likker?"

Clearing his throat, the trader explained, "Let's just say this here don't come from the company. Only be something between two friends."

Taking his cup and holding it out as Tullock began to pour, Scratch said, "Ain't no liquor in Injun country! Damn—then what the hell Ashley and Billy Sublette been bringing to ronnyvoo all these years?"

Tullock started laughing so hard he sloshed the whiskey and had to stop pouring till he composed himself. "That's the biggest crock of shit the Injun department's ever done out here! Astor was sore afraid of his competition that he got the Injun department to make that law what says no liquor can be transported to or made in Injun country!"

"But you and me both know traders been bringing whiskey to ronnyvoo for years now!"

"Damn right, Mr. Bass. But Sublette gets away with it because Astor's law got a crack in it."

He took the cup from his lips to ask, "What crack?"

"Law says a trader can bring whiskey into Injun country for his voyageurs—his boat crew."

Nearly spitting the whiskey he was savoring on his tongue, Bass shrieked in disbelief, "Sublette ain't got no boat crew! Ain't a Frenchy parley-voo come overland with him!"

"Him and Campbell been smuggling whiskey to the upper river for years now, coming overland—bringing their liquor to both their posts to trade with the Injuns."

"Why didn't McKenzie just do the same?"

Tullock topped off his cup and sat atop a crate with a sigh. "Hard to smuggle whiskey upriver on them supply steamers, Mr. Bass. Government agents all flutter over the river while they ain't keeping much watch for overland outfits."

"So how'd McKenzie get his head on the plate?"

"I s'pose he figgered since he couldn't sneak no whiskey up to Fort Union, leastways he'd make his own right there," the trader explained. "Brought up the still on the supply steamer, and he grew his own grain at Union. His plan was working fine till word drifted back downriver. I allays figgered it was Sublette or Campbell stabbed McKenzie in the back that way."

"From all I learnt 'bout Sublette at ronnyvoo last summer, I'd say he's one real oily nigger, the sort what'd cut you off at the knees just to get his hands on a few more beaver plews."

"Astor's cut him a deal with Sublette and Campbell," Tullock admitted. "Now the company has a year with no competition on the upper Missouri, while Sublette's free to work the mountain trade alone."

"Jehoshaphat! That oughtta suit them two beaver thieves!" Bass exclaimed. "What's to become of the trade now that Sublette drove Astor and McKenzie out of the business and got all the ronnyvoo trade to themselves, while the Frenchies gonna run their business right from their posts way up here on the rivers? Damn if the whole lot of you don't got a free man hamstrung two ways of Sunday!"

"Like I said, maybeso you should think about coming to work for me," Tullock said, grinning wryly.

Scratch held up his tin cup. "Like hell I will, Tullock. Your whiskey may be good, but Titus Bass ain't never been a man to get cozy with honey-fugglers like Sublette or your parley-voo bosses."

"Face it: fellas like you gonna be doing business with Sublette, or you're dealing with American Fur—one or the other," the trader warned.

"Maybe a nigger like me needs to take his pelts off down to Taos or Santy Fee."

"What?" roared Tullock. "And have them Mex'cans take half your plews for Mex'can taxes? You think you're being savvy riding all the way down there to trade your furs off?"

Shrugging, Titus asked, "What's a man to do when you Americans is driving up the price of trade goods and stomping down what my pelts bring?"

"I s'pose a man like you fights till he realizes he can't fight no more."

Bass stared at his whiskey for some time, watching its pale amber color shimmer in the light of the three flickering oil lamps Tullock had lit. Then he looked at Waits, how she clutched their daughter across her lap as the child lay sleeping, her tummy warm and full.

"Damn you all," Scratch said with quiet dignity as he held up his cup in toast. "I may have to trade with your kind at ronnyvoo, but I don't have to become one of you."

"True, not yet," Tullock admitted. "There's still some ol' throwbacks like you around."

"Allays will be," Bass claimed, taking another sip.

"Maybe, maybe not," the trader argued. "Look what happened to Rocky Mountain Fur."

Reluctantly, Titus had to agree. "Yeah, Sublette killed them too, didn't he? Your booshways come in and scooped up the pieces."

"Fitzpatrick—and Bridger hisself working for the company!" Tullock bellowed. "Can you believe that'd ever come to pass?"

"Why, I figger the company hamstrung Fitz and Gabe so bad, they was bamboozled into leading them company brigades. No matter, for them two niggers is still trapping beaver, by damned!"

"So here's to them niggers what're hanging on to the mountain trade with their fingernails!" and Tullock raised his cup.

Bass clinked his tin against the trader's. "By bloody damn! Here's to the sort what'll never give up the high country. To hell with all your trading posts while there's still flat-tails in the mountains!"

NINE

Waits-by-the-Water watched in rapt fascination as the blood oozed out of the wound in the trapper's back where another white man delicately worked the point of his honed knife.

Surely the one wielding that instrument must be some sort of shaman, if for no other reason than the trapper he was cutting on sat there so calmly, without the slightest movement nor flinch, as the bloody knife scraped deeper and deeper into his upper back. There must be some magic that kept this terrible, painful ordeal from hurting!

From time to time she glanced up at her husband, to gauge his thoughts by the wondrous expression on his face as they stood among those hundreds of awestruck trappers and gaping Indians who stared transfixed, witnessing what truly had to be a powerful magic.

"I've had arrows pushed and pounded right out of me," Bass whispered to her as that bare-backed trapper wrapped his whitened knuckles around a tent pole two others held upright for him. "But I never have seen anything like what's being done to ol' Gabe right now."

Waits repeated with growing proficiency in her English, "G-gabe?"

"Bridger. Jim Bridger."

"Bri-ger," she echoed, then asked him in her tongue, "You know Bri-ger?"

"Known him a long time. Good a man as they come. The sort I'd want at my back in a hard scrape."

"Is this magic? This shaman cuts on Bri-ger and it doesn't hurt?" she inquired, picking Magpie up from the ground to put the girl astraddle her hip.

"Naw," he answered. "Bridger's just taking it bravely. Look there at his teeth—see how he's biting down on a thick chunk of rawhide real hard."

"So the cutter is not a medicine man among the whites?"

With a grin Titus brushed a little of Magpie's brownish hair from the girl's eyes. "Yes, the cutter's a medicine man. A shaman who does his work with knives, sometimes mixing up potions to drink like a Crow medicine man will do."

Still confused, she asked, "No magic?"

He chuckled softly as he took Magpie from her arms and hoisted the girl onto his shoulders where she settled high above the attentive crowd. "No magic. Just Bridger's cast-iron will."

The white shaman wiped a damp cloth across the trapper's back, smearing the glistening blood from the edges of the wound.

"All this, to pull out the Blackfoot arrowhead," she observed wryly, wagging her head.

Bass had come to fetch her late that morning. When he sprinted into their camp, he was flush with excitement as he told her she must grab Magpie and mount up, to follow him back to the big camp because there was about to occur something he wanted her very much to see. By the time they reached the two huge awnings that were stretched overhead in the cottonwood trees near the bank of New Fork as it meandered toward its junction with the Green River, a boisterous crowd of white men were already encircling that shady spot they were keeping open, holding back those curious members of the Ute and Shoshone who were joining the Nez Perce of Tai-quin-watish and Insala's Flathead who had come to witness this magic.

Two tall, muscular trappers trudged in with a thick section of a cottonwood trunk and pitched it onto the grass in the middle of the open ground. Bass had called out to one of the two, saying his name was Meek after the man waved to her husband. By then four men had moved toward the log where the one called Bri-ger settled and removed his faded cloth shirt. As a pair of trappers set a tall shaved pole near Bridger's feet, the fourth man began to probe with a finger at a spot between Bridger's shoulder blade and his backbone.

Then the medicine man waved another out of the crowd, a trapper carrying a small iron kettle filled with water that steamed even as the day's temperature continued to rise. From it the shaman extracted a short-bladed knife, flung off the excess water, then asked something of Bridger who sat hunched over below him.

When the trapper shoved that piece of rawhide between his teeth, then gripped both hands around the tent pole, the medicine man laid the point of his knife against a particular spot on Bridger's back and made his first cut—a gesture that caused every one of the hundreds of onlookers to fall silent at that very instant, the entire circle of them craning their necks forward.

From time to time the medicine man and the trapper shared a few words; then the knife continued its work.

And now the medicine man inched around in front of Bridger, kneeling so he could peer closely into the trapper's eyes, and began to speak as his bloody hands appeared to make signs.

"What is he signing?" she asked her husband in that expectant hush of the crowd.

"He isn't signing," Titus explained. "Just telling Bridger that the arrow point he's digging for is stuck deep, buried in the bone."

She swallowed hard, vividly picturing that—having seen enough of the iron arrowheads that had wedged and embedded themselves into the thick bones of the buffalo her people hunted through the seasons.

"He says the tip of the arrow is bent, stuck in Bridger's back," Scratch continued. "And Bridger just said he figures that's why they couldn't get the arrowhead out three years ago."

"Three years," she repeated, transfixed on the medicine man's hands as he crooked a finger, describing something to the trapper.

"The medicine man is telling Bridger it's gonna be even harder to get the arrowhead out than he first thought."

"Why?" She gazed up to pat her daughter's hand before she stared back at the doctor who was getting to his feet and returning to his work at the trapper's back.

"Can't think of the Crow words for it—but there's some new bone what's growed around the arrowhead," he explained, stabbing a single finger on one hand between two other tight fingers to show her.

Waits nodded in understanding. "Three years the bone has grown around the arrow, yes."

With Bridger chomping his teeth on the chunk of rawhide as never before, the medicine man pressed on with his cutting, delicately working the tip of his knife down and around the wound that was freely flowing now. Then, by slicing sideways and prying slightly, after agonizing minutes of torture the medicine man pulled from the wound a dark, glistening object he immediately held up at the end of his arm.

Her husband and the others instantly hooted and hollered, screeched and whistled, as Bridger shuddered, huffing deeply after he spit out the thick slab of rawhide. He grumbled at the medicine man who stepped to the trapper's knee and handed the bloody object to the bleeding man.

"Goddamn, if that ain't some!" Bridger commented quietly, as if much of his strength had just been tested.

"Damn right!" the one named Meek roared as he lunged over to slap the medicine man on the back, then held up the shaman's bloody arm while the trappers went wild again with their whooping and shrill Indian calls.

"That was 'bout as slick as warm buff tallow!" her husband bellowed at those old friends of his who stood nearby, these trappers he had traveled the high places with in years gone by before he had chosen to journey the mountains and plains with her.

Now he turned to her quickly, chuckling, his eyes filled with wonder, his face lit with exuberance as he said, "A friend just told me that medicine man is named Whitman. He's one who reads the book of God."

"A holy man, yes," she said, finding it made perfect sense for a true holy man to possess such remarkable healing powers. Among her people the spiritual men healed the physical body.

Bass whispered to her, "The knife cutter just told Bridger he is amazed the arrowhead didn't cause more trouble in the last three winters . . . but Bridger claimed his back only hurt when the winter cold was deep and long."

"Just as your wounds hurt you a little more with every winter?"

"As long as I have your fire to warm me, woman—I'll never mind the coming winters," he told her, gathering Waits beneath his arm.

As she gazed up to smile at Magpie, four of her husband's old friends pierced the crowd that was breaking up and stopped around them. She recognized a few of those words they spoke back and forth as the white men looked upon Magpie with smiles of admiration, touching the girl's dusty feet or rubbing her bare arm as they cooed at her and jabbered with her husband.

Bass slipped the child from his shoulders and saddled her on his hip. Cupping her chin in his hand, he asked Magpie in Crow, "You want to come with me to visit my friends?"

Then it sounded as if he asked the same thing in the white man's tongue.

"I don't think she understands me," Bass sighed.

"One day soon she will understand what we say," Waits explained, taking the child into her arms. She watched her husband turn away and dig among his things in search of something. "And when she gets older, I hope she will know just how special she is to learn two languages while she is still a child."

From a rawhide pouch Titus pulled a greasy deck of cards tied with a narrow whang cut from his legging fringe, and said, "With these, sweet woman—I just might win something extra from my old friends in a game of chance."

"Chance? Like the game of hand my people play?"

"Just like it," and he bent to kiss her. "Wish me your luck so I can bring back a present for you and one for little Magpie too."

"Just bring yourself back, husband," she said with laughter lighting her eyes. "And I will give you a present beneath the blankets tonight."

He kissed her again. "Do you realize how special you are? To let your husband go off to gamble with his friends?"

"A man needs to be with his friends," she replied. "You are with us the rest of the seasons—I think it is good we come here each summer so you visit your old friends. A man like you—to live alone in the mountains and on the banks of the far rivers away from the village—such a man needs a few good friends."

For a moment her husband sighed, his eyes looking over the four white men who stood around them. Then Titus gazed at her with a sad smile and said in Crow, "As I grow older, I greet fewer friends here every summer. So it is right that with the passing of the seasons, what friends I have left grow more special to me, grow more dear in my heart."

"If'n that hoss don't take the circle!" Elbridge Gray roared as he and the others joined Titus in recounting the missionary doctor's operation on Jim Bridger four days before.

Half bent over with laughter, his copper beard dusted with cornmeal, Rufus Graham demanded, "Say it again, Scratch—what Gabe told that sawbones preacher."

"When Whitman asked Bridger why that arrowhead didn't give him more fits in the last three years"—Scratch could barely sputter between side-aching guffaws—"Bridger tol't him—meat don't s-spoil in the m-mountains!"

All five of them pounded their feet on the ground or drummed their thighs, clutching their bellies as they laughed.

"Caleb would've loved seeing that!" Isaac Simms said with a great chuckle, then realized the sad import of what he had uttered.

"Damn them red buggers anyways!" Bass swore as they all went serious with the flicker of a jay's wing. "Cutting down a good man like Caleb Wood—right in his prime."

For a few moments the five grew thoughtful, staring at the ground, or out at the sky, perhaps up at the leaves dancing in the warm breeze that wound its way through the American Fur Company camp.

Finally Solomon Fish said, "Jack would've bust his gut to stand there and hear that story too."

"Shit," Titus bawled with a huge smile. "Mad Jack was the sort stepped right up there and offered to cut that goddamned arrow right outta Gabe's back for him his own self!"

The others looked up to find Bass grinning, and in an instant all of them were chuckling again. It was a good feeling, being there among old friends who had stood at his back when together they had faced down Comanche and Blackfoot. Now these friends sprawled around the fire, drinking their potent whiskey, smoking harsh trade tobacco, and stuffing themselves with the beans, cornmeal, and pumpkins Lucien Fontenelle's mules had packed all the way from the settlements.

"That's purely some, fellers," Scratch declared, fighting the sob in his throat as the group fell silent once more. "Chirk up, boys! It shines to laugh when you're thinking 'bout an old friend. What would Mad Jack and Caleb think of us if we was to get all mopey and down in the tooth whenever we was to 'member on them?"

"Bass is right," Elbridge reminded them as he turned those slabs of aromatic pumpkin frying in his skillet with a fragrance that reminded them all of a home long ago left behind. " 'Specially Jack."

Scratch bobbed his head. "Hatcher was the life-lovin' fool now. And Caleb loved playing the sourpuss for Hatcher too."

"Ain't that the saint's truth?" Isaac agreed, wiping more of the dark yellow-brown streaks of tobacco juice into his pale, whitish beard. "When Jack was gone and Caleb took over this bunch, why—that's when Caleb started getting a funny bone hisself."

"Damn them Blackfoot," Bass growled, brooding again on how the four had described Caleb Wood's horrible death at the hands of the Blackfoot early this past winter.

Ever since Scratch had thrown in with Jack Hatcher's bunch back in the summer of twenty-seven, one by one they had been whittled away: first by Rocky Mountain tick fever, then two had decided they would fare better hanging back to Taos with their Mexican wives, and finally their last two leaders had fallen to the enemy—Hatcher in the Pierre's Hole fight* and now Wood had gone under as Bridger's brigade hacked its way back out of Blackfoot country. Where they had once been ten—now there were but four. And as much as they had hoped their lot would improve by throwing in with Bridger's men seasons ago, things hadn't gotten any better at all.

"Damn good thing Jack ain't around to see what's become of the mountains," Solomon grumbled. He swiped at his hatchet of a nose dotted with huge pores forever blackened with fire soot and dirt.

"Trader's got us crumped over a barrel with his high prices," Scratch groaned.

---

* *Carry the Wind*

"And our beaver ain't ever gonna be wuth much anymore," Rufus added with a faint whistle between those four missing teeth.

"Time was, we free men was the princes in this land," Elbridge declared beneath that big bulb of a nose scored with tiny blue veins. "But now we're so poor we're barely hanging on with our toenails."

Simms wagged his head, complaining, "Man cain't hardly make a living catching flat-tails no more."

All too painfully true. This year almost a fourth of Bridger's and Tom Fitzpatrick's trappers had declared their intentions of dropping out of the brigades, choosing to return east with the fur caravan, waiting until they reached St. Louis so they would be paid in cash rather than take out their wages in trade goods for the coming season. Hard to believe that more than eighty men, not to mention Fraeb and Gervais—Bridger's and Fitz's old partners—were giving up on the mountains!

"Let 'em run on back," Scratch had snorted when Elbridge Gray told him the surprising news. "There'll allays be them what don't belong out here. I say hurraw for all of 'em skedaddling with their tails a'tween their legs—goddamned flatlanders anyway!"

At rendezvous this summer there were no more than two hundred company trappers and well less than a hundred free men. For damned sure those Hudson's Bay men who had followed Thomas McKay and John McLeod there again didn't count. Where once more than six hundred red-eyed white hellions had run wild with rendezvous fever, buying whiskey and bedding squaws until they were sore-dicked, hungover, and once again deeply in debt . . . rendezvous this summer paled when compared to those robust carnivals of recent years. Not near the fun, nor near the trade goods and liquor. And even if there had been plenty of supplies and grain alcohol, there simply wasn't all that many men who could afford the rampant, glazed-eyed sprees of bygone years.

Plain as summer sun this August of 1835, no longer was there anywhere near the beaver there had been.

Why, if it hadn't been for that Presbyterian missionary Dr. Marcus Whitman cutting that iron arrowhead more than three inches long out of a three-year-old growth of bone and cartilage in Jim Bridger's back, so far there had been little to make this rendezvous remarkable in more than a decade of summer fairs.

No sooner had he finished running spidery threads of elk sinew through holes he'd jabbed in Bridger's skin to close the wound than another American Fur trapper stepped up to Whitman and yanked his own grimy shirt off to point at the lump of cartilage hardened around an arrowhead right under his skin—a wound almost as old as Bridger's. And for the next three days this quiet man of God from the East had entertained one gamy patient after another—both white trapper and redskin alike—performing his minor operations and dispensing calomel to those who had

grown bilious, even bleeding others. The Reverend Doctor Whitman had
made a lifelong friend in Jim Bridger, and convinced the others that while
all the rest of the religious Bible-thumpers who came west for the Nez
Perce country were the sort to glower down their noses at the little fun
these men allowed themselves every summer at rendezvous, there was at
least one missionary who took the chalk.

It wasn't long before news began to circulate from the American Fur
camp that Lucien Fontenelle's supply train might well not have made it to
rendezvous if it hadn't been for the good Dr. Whitman. Back along the
Missouri, even before turning west along the Platte River Road, cholera
had begun to burn its way through the caravan. And though he had little
strength remaining in his own reserves, Whitman began to nurse the sick
and dying, able to save all but two by the time every last man in Fontenelle's train had been laid low by that terrible scourge.

They had lost a month there on the bluffs overlooking the muddy
river: at least two weeks to let the epidemic run its course through the
hired hands, and another two weeks until the men recuperated enough to
continue their journey for the mountains.

To those unlettered laborers who had muscled Fontenelle's wagons
and mules west, to those illiterate but savvy princes of the wilderness,
Whitman became no less than an unvarnished hero. As he began the next
three days of recovering from the crude, open-air surgery, no less a mountain veteran than Jim Bridger himself had declared that the doctor would
clearly do to ride the river with.

That praise was enough for any man jack of them there at the mouth
of the New Fork.

Then, as if having that arrowhead cut out of his back four days ago
wasn't enough, Bridger handed the camps another reason for celebration.

"C'mon!" the burly trapper bellowed as he lunged back among the
blanket bowers and canvas-covered shelters where Bass sat among old
friends and company men.

"Grab yore guns!" roared the flush-faced man scurrying up on Joe
Meek's heels.

"Injun trouble?" Isaac Simms shrieked as he scrambled to his feet.

"Shit," Meek huffed, coming to a halt. "Just bring your guns to shoot
off when the marryin' is done!"

"M-marryin'?" Rufus asked.

Robert "Doc" Newell leaned an arm on Meek's shoulder, huffing as
more than fifty company trappers hurried close to hear the news.
"Booshway's give us a half hour to gather a crowd, boys. Then he's gonna
let a ol' hide-thumper marry him off to a gal he's took a shine to."

"Booshway?" Bass repeated. "You mean that ol' whitehead Fitzpatrick? If that don't beat all—Broken Hand's getting hisself hitched!"

"Goddammit—Doc here didn't say nothing 'bout Fitz tying the knot with a squaw!" Meek snorted.

Scratch shook his head. "But he said booshway—"

"Bridger, gol-dangit!" Newell bawled. "Bridger's taking him a bride!"

Gabe must have been feeling more than pert. What with having that arrowhead cut out of his back, he must have been feeling downright cocky.

After more than a dozen years in the mountains, after bedding squaws every summer at rendezvous and occasionally of a winter encampment, Jim Bridger likely decided he was ready to settle down with a squaw. And not just the first one that caught his eye, Scratch discovered. This beauty was the cherished daughter of Flathead chief Insala.

Bass hurried back to camp where he fetched Waits-by-the-Water and Magpie, all three of them quickly donning their finest clothes. As his wife finished brushing her own black tresses, Titus dabbed a little purplish vermilion dye along the part of their child's hair after he had dragged a porcupine-tail brush through her locks already reaching her shoulders. Then he tied Zeke to a tree with a long length of rope and gave the dog a new antelope bone to content himself with before the three of them mounted up and loped off for the Flathead village erected on the far side of the American Fur Company encampment.

Beyond Insala's people stood more camp circles crowding this lush bottom ground: Nez Perce, Ute, Shoshone, and even a few lodges of Arapaho who were dared come trade with the trappers rather than to fight the white men. More than a thousand Indians all told, and most of them were streaming into the Flathead village with close to two hundred of the company trappers who were singing a variety of discordant songs, pounding on brass pots and iron kettles, one man even blowing reedily through an out-of-tune clarinet while several men dragged air through concertinas and others sawed catgut bows across the strings of their violins as the many processions threaded their way toward the center of the camp like throbbing spokes on a wagon wheel.

It was there the Flathead were not to be outdone as the old rattle shakers and thick-wristed drummers were already taking up their chants and high-pitched songs while the crowds shoved together, shoulder to shoulder, neck-craning to get themselves a good gander at the bridegroom riding into camp with an escort of the most dandified trappers Bass had ever seen. Wearing war paint of their own, feathers tied in their long hair as well as in the tails and manes of their horses, with strips of blue and red wool tied around their arms and legs or bands of brass wire encircling their wrists and upper arms, those half dozen who accompanied Bridger were a sight to behold.

Then all went hushed as Bridger and his men halted before the central lodge, dismounting. Handing their horses to those in the crowd, the booshway and his best men strode up to the handful of old counselors who stood at the lodge entrance. Dressed in the spanking-new knee-length morning coat and canvas pantaloons Lucien Fontenelle had purchased in St. Louis specifically for him, Gabe respectfully removed his hat to bare his hair greased back and freshly combed for this momentous occasion. Swallowing audibly, he spoke as clearly as he could those halting Flathead words, stuttering nervously.

A wrinkled oldster turned and called out to the lodge, whereupon a middle-aged warrior emerged to stand before Bridger.

"That's Insala," Bass declared in a whisper as Waits stood on tiptoe to have herself a better look through the expectant crowd.

In but a moment Bridger turned and waved his arm—signal for more of his men to push their way out of the crowd with more than a dozen ponies, two of them laden with blankets he pulled off and laid before the Flathead chief. Upon the blankets the best men then spread a glittering array of knives and tomahawks, kettles and beads, cloth and ribbon, finger rings and hawksbells. Packets of vermilion and indigo ink joined the rest as Bridger stepped back, gestured across his gifts, then crossed his arms and waited ceremonially for the chief's answer.

Dramatically, Insala stepped forward and knelt at the first blanket, fingering this, inspecting that, closely peering at most everything before he moved on to the second blanket . . . slowly, thoughtfully studying it all while the crowd murmured quietly, the hundreds upon hundreds of witnesses waiting in the bright summer sun as the chief decided if the gifts were enough compensation for this sale of his daughter.

Eventually the old warrior stood and moved over to stop inches from Bridger, gazing into the white man's eye as Gabe dropped his arms to his side and gulped, clearly showing his anxiety, his face bright with sweat.

Suddenly Insala raised his arms and brought his hands down on Bridger's shoulders four times as the Flathead people set up a huge roar, laughing and cheering, women keening while the drums began thumping again. While Bridger grew wide-eyed, the chief quickly turned and pointed to his lodge door, calling out in his tongue.

As one of the old counselors pulled aside the flap, a head emerged, just as the crowd fell silent once more. In that noiseless pause the chief's beautiful daughter came to stand beside her father, a red-striped white trade blanket folded over her left arm. Taking it from the bride's arm, Insala nudged Bridger a step closer to the shy young woman. Then the chief unfurled the blanket so he could wrap it around his daughter and her new husband.

Taking hold of Bridger's wrist, Insala stuffed two corners of the blanket into the trapper's hand so the white man held the blanket around himself and his new bride—then the chief suddenly raised both of his arms into the air and shouted.

His Flathead people answered in kind and took to singing once more as they surged in and began circling the newlyweds, shoving against one another, against members of the other tribes, against the outnumbered white men, everyone slowly dancing in a great sunward swirl as Bridger self-consciously put his forehead against his bride's brow and gazed into her eyes.

"By damn," Scratch exclaimed to his friends nearby as they all craned their necks for a good look through the throbbing, dancing, celebrating masses, "if'n it don't look to be that Gabe's a'blushing!"

"It's his wedding day, goddammit!" Rufus Graham snarled.

Elbridge Gray bellowed, "I figger he's thinking 'bout his wedding night!"

"She sure be a purty-enough gal to make a feller get all het up," Isaac added.

After a matter of minutes Bridger and his escorts started to knife their way slowly through the celebrants who spread out in a wide cordon along either side of the path the bride and groom were now taking to begin their journey back to the American camp. Drumming and singing continued, laughs and snorts and wild music floated on the afternoon air all along those two miles of valley bottom ground where the tall grass, bluestem, and wild flax waved in the summer breeze.

By the time the parade had reached the trapper camp, most of the Indians were turning about, making their way slowly back to their villages where fires would be kindled and supper put on the boil. Meanwhile the trappers were streaming around a large open meadow where a few were feeding wood to huge bonfires and beginning to stake out slabs of meat to roast, some rolling up small kegs of whiskey and stumps for that time when the musicians would settle around the leaping fires while the sun continued its fall toward the western hills.

Of a sudden Bass became aware of a change in the tone of the celebration when a knot of trappers nearby began shouting, cheering, jeering, hollering in that way of angry, worked-up men.

"You stay with Magpie, here," he told his wife, lifting the child from his shoulder, passing the girl to Waits-by-the-Water. "I'll be back soon."

Motioning the four old friends to follow him, Titus loped with many others toward the growing commotion. Back and forth the crowd surged, stretching itself this way and that so it always left just the right amount of open ground for the brutal, bare-knuckled sport raging at its center. On the ground lay three white men, by their vivid dress plainly some of Fontenelle's and Drips's French voyageurs. Of the trio, two sprawled across one another, clearly unconscious, while the third struggled clumsily, attempting to drag himself from the ground as he wagged his head. In their midst a fourth voyageur gamely tried to duck as he flailed away with wild, ineffective haymakers at the lone man the four of them had been fighting off.

A tall tree trunk of a man—a frightening, slab-shouldered giant bigger than Silas Cooper had been, a giant every bit as imposing as was Emile Sharpe, the half-breed Red River *Metis* who had come west to the Green River in search of Josiah Paddock.

Laughing sinisterly, the giant quickly stepped aside as the lone voyageur lumbered past, grabbing the shorter man's hair and using it to hurl his victim around in a tight circle as the Frenchman shrieked in torment, clawing at the big man's wrist. But as the monster of a brute guffawed and spouted in broken English, it was immediately clear he too was a Frenchman.

"Enfant d'garce!"

Slowly the giant raised his left arm, hoisting the voyageur by the hair until the shorter man dangled, his toes barely brushing the ground. Mule-eyed, the voyageur clung to the giant's left wrist, completely helpless as the monster roared his foreign French oath, spat a wad of phlegm into the small man's face, then flung his maul-sized fist squarely between the struggling voyageur's eyes.

Then let his victim go.

Stunned senseless, the short man crumpled to his knees, watery-legged and totally oblivious as the giant shadowed him once again, looped a big hand around his throat, then flung him up at the end of his arm again where the voyageur swung freely. This time the giant smashed his fist into the middle of the small man's face with a sickening crackle of cartilage and bone, blood spurting from the crushed tissues.

Again the monster cocked back his arm, ready for another blow—

"Shunar!"

A hush descended upon the spectators like a blanket.

The voyageur hung limp as a length of buffalo gut at the end of the huge tormentor's arm, as if no more than a clump of oiled canvas swaying in the hot afternoon breeze. Slowly, the Frenchman turned from the victim he had imprisoned at the end of his left arm to stare narrow-eyed at the one who had cried out his name.

Amid the sudden silence, Isaac Simms leaned in and whispered to Bass, "That's Drips—company booshway!"

Still this giant named Chouinard did not release his fourth victim.

"Let 'im go, Shunar!" Drips demanded as he stepped within six feet of the giant, his hand resting on the butt of his belt pistol.

It was as if the entire crowd of hundreds, white and red alike, waited to draw a breath—watching this small, spare man dare to stop within easy reach of the monster.

Slowly considering the command, Chouinard gazed at his prisoner for a long moment, then flung the voyageur to the ground with an audible snap of bone.

"Goddamn you!" Andrew Drips shrieked as he went to one knee beside the crumpled victim.

Immediately the giant took a step to loom over Drips. The company leader jerked his head up to glare at the giant and yanked that pistol from his belt—holding it out at the end of his arm, the hammer coming back to full cock with one swift motion.

"I'll kill you," Drips said with studied coolness. "You big pigheaded Frenchman, don't you doubt that I will shoot you between your god-damned eyes where you stand."

"Maybe I grab your gun first," Chouinard growled in reply, "keel you before you can pop your leetle gun."

The pistol held steadily on its target as Drips slowly rose to his feet, never taking his eyes off the giant, nor the muzzle of that pistol from that spot between the giant's slitted eyes.

"I'll let you have this chance, you parley-voo bastard," Jim Bridger said as he stepped from the edge of the crowd with his pistol drawn, flanked by the huge, bear-chested Meek and the smaller tow-headed Carson. "You so much as move torst Drips—I'll drop you."

"Lookee here," Meek said on the far side of Bridger, wagging the end of his short-barreled smoothbore. "This here's what I call a camp clearer, you son of a bitch. Loaded with a good handful of drop shot. I touch this'r trigger and it'll cut you in half."

"That's right," Carson added, his blue eyes flashing with menace. "Then the whole crowd gonna see you piss on yourself while you breathe your last."

Drips slowly lowered his pistol, eventually stuffing it into his belt again as he said, "I figure Shunar here can see the deck's stacked again' him, don't you, Frenchman?"

The giant smiled wickedly as his dark eyes glowered at Bridger, Meek, and Carson. "Amereecans. Like buffalo dung—you Amereecans are everywhere."

"I oughtta shoot a gut-load of drop shot in you just for that!" Meek snapped.

"There'll be no more blood here today!" Bridger ordered.

"Jim's right!" Drips said as he knelt again beside that fourth victim. "Damn you anyway, Shunar. You better pray these men of mine recover enough to ride out of here for the fall hunt."

"I have some fun—"

Shooting to his feet, Drips stood all but toe to toe with the giant, staring up at the huge man who stood more than a head taller, interrupting the Frenchman with a fist he shook beneath Chouinard's chin. "And I'll kill you if it happens again! I might kill you yet—goddamn you! Costing me four men. Even you aren't worth four goddamned men!"

Drips lowered his fist, spun on his heel, and furiously spat, "You go costing me my men—I'll put you down my own self!"

"If you want some help, Drips," Meek growled, "I'll be glad to kill him for free."

Chouinard immediately raised his two fists like mauls and took a step toward Meek, but Carson and Bridger lunged forward a step at the same moment Drips whirled on the giant.

"I'll give you a five count for you to get out of my sight, Shunar," the booshway ordered.

"Ahh, but I come here to dance and drink some with—"

"There'll be no dancing for you here today," Bridger warned. "This here's my wedding, and you ain't welcome round here no more. Go back to your camp and make your own fun there."

A childlike look crossed the monster's face, something hurt, wounded. "Shunar no dance? No sing and drink?"

"You heard the booshway!" the bandy-legged Carson snarled, glaring up crane-necked at the giant who stood more than a foot taller than he. "Get outta here, Frenchie!"

For a moment more his breath heaved in his ironmonger's barrel of a chest; then Chouinard hurled himself around and flung his way through the crowd, knocking men aside if they weren't quick enough to leap out of his way.

"Damned good thing he's gone," Bridger sighed, relief in his voice.

Dragging a hand through his shoulder-length light-brown hair, the thirty-year-old Carson glanced at Meek and the others who stood close at hand, then glared at Chouinard's back as the giant disappeared through the crowd. "That there's a killing just waitin' to happen."

TEN

"Where is that black-hearted sonuvabitch!" Carson roared.

Bass jerked around there in the shade of that awning strung over the trading blankets where he was consumed that morning with selecting between bolts of the fine woolen tradecloth or some of the coarser ginghams and calicos. Red-faced and slit-eyed, the diminutive Carson suddenly appeared, on the verge of exploding, as Meek, Newell, and others leaped to their feet, surrounding Kit.

"Who you looking for?" Tom Fitzpatrick demanded as he stepped around a plank counter toward Carson.

Shaking with anger, Kit growled, "The Frenchman! Shunar!"

"We got rid of him yestiddy, Kit," Meek declared soothingly.

"Run him off," Carson concurred. "But—he went and made trouble for hisself in the 'Rapaho camp."

" 'Rapahos?" Newell repeated. "Where you been sparking that purty squaw?"

A dark cloud immediately shadowed the short man's countenance. "When Shunar left here, the bastard went down by the crik, close by the 'Rapaho camp. He laid a'wait there for dark to come, watching for Grass Singing."

"She the squaw you had your eye on?" Meek asked.

"He figgered to catch her in the brush," Carson declared, then went on to explain the rest of the story.

After breakfast that morning he had decided it was about time for him to take himself a wife, just like booshway Bridger had done the day before. After all, Kit reasoned, he had been in the mountains four years already, and a man could do with a good helpmate. So he had taken account of all that he possessed and what credit he could wrangle out of the company clerks, then packed it all aboard two ponies he led over to the Arapaho village.

"She had to know I'd be coming," Carson told them. "I could see it in her eyes ever since them 'Raps come into ronnyvoo. The gal knowed I had my eye on her too. Already I been over to smoke twice't with her pa."

"But you don't speak no 'Rapaho!" Meek hollered.

"Don't have to," Carson shut him off. "Plain as sign to the ol' man I was there for his daughter. After coming two times, he sure as hell figgered I'd be back with my presents, be back to buy her for my wife."

But when Kit had shown up at the lodge with his gifts earlier that morning, the girl's father spurned Carson's offering, angrily signing enough of the story to explain why he and his daughter wanted nothing more to do with white men. The old warrior made it plain enough as he held two fingers projecting from his lips to signify the forked tongue of the pale-skinned trappers, then ordered Carson to leave just before he began to sing a war song to his bow and quiver of arrows.

Fitzpatrick asked, "What got the two of 'em so damned fractious over white men?"

"Shunar." Carson spat it as if he had just spoken the most vile word in his vocabulary.

Meek asked, "What's that horse's ass got to do—"

"I tol't you!" Carson barked. "We run him off from here, so that snake-bellied coward went right down to the crik and waited for Grass Singing to show up for water."

For a breathless minute, more than a hundred men stood there in absolute silence beneath the morning sun, watching Kit quake in anger— knowing all too well the outcome of that story.

"So the Frenchie . . ." Fitzpatrick began. "He—"

"He tried," Carson interrupted. "Her pa signed that Shunar tore her skirt off, scratched her all over when he throwed her down in the bushes and got hisself ready to poke her. That li'l gal ain't never had a man afore!"

"How you know for sure?" Meek inquired.

Suddenly glaring at his tall friend, Kit snapped, "Grass Singing wears a virgin's horsehair knot," gesturing around his waist then between his legs to symbolize the knotting of an Arapaho chastity belt. "She showed me herself, Joe. When the big bastard went to grab for his knife so's he could cut her belt off—"

"She made her play," Bass finished Carson's sentence.

Kit looked over at Titus. "That's right, Scratch. Her pa signed that she somehow wriggled away from him like a tadpole, what with Shunar just having him one hand to hold her down."

"So for sure he didn't . . ." Fitzpatrick began.

"No," Carson answered, staring at the ground in the midst of that swelling crowd. "But my gut tells me he'll try again till one of 'em is dead."

"One of 'em?" Bridger asked. "Who you mean?"

"Either she's gonna kill him," Kit replied, "or Shunar's gonna kill her."

From the catch in the young trapper's voice, Titus thought he understood how Carson must feel: terribly wronged by someone so easy to loathe, so easy to hate.

Looking then into the distance over Carson's shoulder, he saw the figures coming. Sure that it had to be—that tall one in the middle, a dozen or more clustered around on either side of him like saplings around the tall oak.

Scratch gazed directly at Carson. "So you figger to make sure Shunar don't get that chance to kill the gal?"

"She and her pa," Kit explained, "they don't want nothing to do with me, not with no white man now—so this ain't about getting myself a squaw no more." His eyes went cold. "Now it's about putting a bad animal out of its misery, fellas. It's 'bout killing someone needs killing in a bad way."

Pointing with one arm, Scratch pulled a long-barreled smoothbore pistol from his belt with the other hand and announced, "There comes your chance, Kit."

Carson jerked around with the rest of the crowd to see Shunar striding up with his hangers-on.

Bridger said, "That'un's bad as Blackfoot. Big mouth, but he shoots center too. Best watch 'im like a snake."

Kit whirled back to look at Bass, gazing down at the big pistol. He took it in both hands, snapped back the hammer to half cock, flipped the frizzen forward, and peered down at the priming powder in the pan. "Thankee, Scratch," he whispered with deep appreciation as he stuffed the loaded weapon into his belt.

As Carson turned to watch the giant's approach, Bass was struck with how big that huge pistol looked hanging from the belt of the five-foot-four-inch trapper. The young American stood some eight inches shorter than Scratch, and Chouinard easily towered a foot or more over Titus. Suddenly Titus was reminded of an ancient, dramatic image from his long-ago childhood, a visage come as clear as rinsed crystal from those days he'd sat with his brothers and sister at their mother's knee while she read by the fireplace from that huge family Bible draped over her legs like the curved wings of a great bird come to rest in her lap.

How vivid that image had been to him as a child: visualizing those colorful hills and armies of thousands blackening the valley, tents arrayed for as far as the eye could see as the enemies of Israel sent forth their hero—a giant called Goliath. To meet him there between the lines went a young shepherd boy, the smallest among that army of Israel. Instead of arming himself for battle with a shield, and bow or lance . . . David carried only three smooth stones and his leather sling—

"Amereecans!"

The crowd turned as the distant figure hurled the word like a profane slur. Slowly the Americans stepped to each side like the parting of a flock of wrens when a hawk descends through them. Carson, Meek, and Bass stood at their apex watching the monster lumber across those last fifty yards.

If this duel started close-up, Scratch knew Kit didn't stand a snowflake's chance in a boiling spring. He turned to the short man. "You don't have to do this—"

"Yes, I do, Scratch," Carson cut him off, not taking his eyes from the giant. "I ain't running."

From afar Chouinard pounded his chest twice and bellowed, "I want Amereecans to beat! Crunch my teeth on Amereecan bones, speet them out!"

Around the giant that motley array of cowered voyageurs and pork-eating Americans laughed as they came on in their hero's gigantic shadow. From the glistening of the brown molasses pasting the Frenchman's black beard, it was plain to see he'd been punishing the whiskey that morning. But as liquored up as he might be, the brazen Chouinard carried no rifle, had no pistol in sight.

"He ain't armed," Carson said.

Meek shook his head. "You can't count on that."

Ripping the big smoothbore from his belt so suddenly, it caused Chouinard to freeze nervously, Kit returned the weapon to Bass before he took a single step forward, empty-handed. "Here's one American what's ready to have you try chewing on me, Shunar! Look around you: Bridger's brigade is full of men what'd thrash you good, but you've got 'em buffaloed. Ain't got me fooled! By God, I may be the smallest one in this camp, but I'm gonna make you choke!"

Throwing his head back so far his tonsils showed, the St. Louis Frenchman howled with an evil laughter lusty enough that it had to make his throat raw. With a few more long strides he stopped again less than ten feet from Carson.

"You make me to laugh good, leetle Amereecan bird," Chouinard growled. "Thees is good to laugh with your leetle bird chirping."

"Don't figger I said nothing wuth you laughin' for," Carson snapped.

The giant lost his sickly grin. "These Frenchmen here, no fun to flog no more. Now I come to crunch me Amereecans."

Carson demanded, "What you want with an American?"

Inside his black beard Chouinard wore that same mad grin he had on his face yesterday afternoon as he mauled the four voyageurs. Pointing at the nearby brush, he snarled, "I go to trees, there. I get switch. I bring it back and switch all you Amereecans!"

"I'm standing right here. You don't see me running, you yellow-backed bastard," Carson rasped, his voice growing quieter each time he spoke. "Go fetch your switch and try to switch me."

"Y-you?" Chouinard sputtered, turning left and right as his followers started to laugh with him. "B-but you are so small! Make me laugh to switch Amereecan so small!"

"I ain't gonna take that talk from no goddamned Frenchman!" Carson bellowed, his voice grown loud once more. "There's more'n two hunnert Americans in this camp, and any man of 'em can take your switch from you and shove it right down your goddamned throat."

"Ho, ho!" Chouinard roared, covering his mouth as he laughed.

"Take your words back or I'll shove 'em down your throat too!"

That only made the Frenchman laugh all the louder. "Sounds like leetle fly buzzing 'round Chouinard! Leetle fly says he stick my switch down my throat!"

"That's right, I'm the smallest there is," Carson declared, "but even I can brass-tack a coward like you."

Glaring steely-eyed again, the Frenchman snorted his curse, *"Enfant d'garce!* I grind your bones first—let all these other peegs watch—then I see it more Amereecan peegs fight Chouinard! *Moi!* I beeg bull of thees lick."

"When you gonna stop talking and go fetch your gun, Shunar?" Carson demanded.

"Gun?" the giant echoed, slowly pulling his big butcher knife from its scabbard at his side. *"Sacre bleu!* I like to cut when I keel."

"You say 'nother goddamned word about crunching bones or stomping an American," Kit warned, "I'll blow a hole in your head, then take that goddamned knife of yours and rip your guts out with it right here and now! Leave them guts for the birds to peck over while you're sucking your last breath!"

"I step on you like leetle bug," the Frenchman boasted, stomping one moccasin into the trampled grass, grinding his heel into the dirt.

Carson rocked forward on the balls of his feet and hunched his shoulders menacingly. "All you can do is talk? Draw your goddamned knife, pork eater! For days now you been getting likkered up and bullying this hull camp—but now you've rubbed up again' a real fighting rooster 'stead of some corn cracker's barnyard pullet!"

For a moment Chouinard's hand flexed and relaxed, flexed and relaxed around his knife handle.

Bass roared, "Gut 'im, Kit. Cut his heart out."

His nostrils flaring, Carson growled at the towering Frenchman, "You're big bull of this wallow?"

"I beeg bull of—"

"Shit!" Carson cut him off. "You ain't much of a man, Shunar. Cain't even take no horsehair belt off no li'l gal! You ain't no bull no more! G'won and pull your knife so I can leave your guts out to dry for the jays!"

Chouinard drew his shoulders back, taking in a long breath as his chertlike eyes slowly ran across the crowd behind Carson. Only when he had done that did he peer down the short American's frame before crawling back up to glare at Carson's face. That look of undisguised contempt was suddenly replaced by a grin.

"No fight now, Keet," he said almost apologetically. "I like your sponk. Maybe we be friends, *ami? Friends, n'c'est pa?"*

To Bass's surprise the Frenchman turned on his heel without uttering another word and brutally shoved some of his followers aside as he stomped away.

Struck dumb at the suddenness of the giant's retreat, Scratch listened as a smattering of laughter began among the Americans. In a heartbeat more than a hundred men were guffawing as loudly as they could, hooting and catcalling after the Frenchman and his embarrassed followers who scrambled to catch up to Chouinard in his retreat.

"Why, if that hoss don't take the circle, Kit!" Scratch marveled as they watched the giant's back grow smaller. "The bastard was just about to wade into you till you spoke your piece 'bout that 'Rapaho gal."

Meek asked, "Figger that's what made him run off with his tail 'twixt his legs?"

"No matter—he's gone now," Bridger announced. "Let's have us a drink for that bastard showing us the white feather!"

"Dunno, but something tells me this ain't over, Gabe," Bass warned, sensing that gnawing in his belly about the suddenness of the giant's back-stepping once the squaw was mentioned. He turned to Kit, saying, "Best you watch your back."

But Bridger and Meek jointly yoked their arms over the shorter man's shoulders and cheerily dragged Carson off toward the whiskey canopy.

"There's other gals you can poke," Joe declared.

Newell caught up with them. "Allays other squars, Kit!"

Wagging his head, a bewildered Titus Bass sauntered back to the awnings where the trade goods lay, sensing that nothing had been settled between the two. Chouinard's attack on Grass Singing had served to irritate a wound that had been opened and kept oozing for some five long weeks while the Bridger and Drips brigades sat on their thumbs, impatiently waiting for the long-overdue supply caravan to reach the mouth of New Fork.

The camps already sat atop a powder keg of emotion.

During those long days of waiting, rumors had begun to circulate that Sublette and Campbell had indeed given up the mountain trade in an agreement with Astor's successors in St. Louis. Another story confirmed that the partners were even selling the fort they had built on the North Platte last summer to the new firm of Fitzpatrick and Fontenelle—quitting the fur trade completely to become landed gentry and mercantilists back in St. Louis.

First it was General William H. Ashley who had pulled out after he made his fortune, and now Sublette and Campbell appeared poised to do the same. Could it be, rumor had it, that the two of them were following Astor's lead: getting out while the getting was good because there was no more money to be made in the mountain beaver trade?

A man had only to look around that sprawling rendezvous camp as they waited through those last days of June, on through the entire month of July and the first week of August, to see that the bales of beaver were small, and few. More and more of the grumblers in the company camps announced their plans to cash in their chips once the caravan arrived. And once Fitzpatrick showed up more than a month late on August 12 with those pack animals swaybacked beneath trade goods, one of Fontenelle's St. Louis clerks busied himself telling all who would listen a depressing tale that served to thicken the aura of gloom already hanging over that rendezvous of 1835.

"Back home it's all the talk—a story come upriver from N'orleans 'bout a French duke what was over visiting the Chinee last year," the wag related to his rapt audiences. "Seems that Frenchie lost his beaver-plug hat over there, and them Chinee didn't have nary a beaver-plug hat to sell him."

The clerk went on to describe how the French diplomat had a tall hat specially made for him from the silk of those productive worms, a hat he proudly wore upon his return to Paris where it became all the envy, and the fashion conscious clamored to have one just like it. In droves the best dressed of Europe had begun to abandon their beaver felts and were ordering hats of Chinese silk.

By now, the clerk explained to slack-jawed trappers, this frightening trend was gripping the States. Silk was all the rage.

Any half drunk who cared to give it a thought couldn't help but reckon what was at that moment being scrawled on the wall: if beaver was no longer in demand, then it stood to reason that beaver men were soon to become an endangered species.

In light of all that disgruntling talk of silk, the groaning about the poor price for plews, and the moaning about the high cost of possibles, it didn't take all that much mulling over before Scratch decided he wasn't about to trade off all his pelts to the company then and there. What with the low dollar beaver was bringing, coupled with the exorbitant prices demanded for what trade goods were being offered, he figured instead to hang on to half of his plews he might well end up trading off at that new Fort William raised down on La Ramee's Fork. By any reckoning that post lay closer than Tullock's new fort going up at the mouth of the Tongue, and much closer than either Taos to the south or Fort Union in the north.

There sure as hell had to be somewhere a man could squeeze a better dollar out of his pelts.

What with having a family now, why, a man needed to give due consideration to such matters—not as he had done in past summers when he would take what value was given, trade for his possibles and some whiskey at the prices demanded, then disappear for another year.

But the more he cogitated on it now in the shade of those awnings, the angrier it made him, realizing that the fur company, the traders, all of those who acted as middlemen to supply this to, or do that service for, the trappers were lining their palms and stuffing their pockets with fruits harvested through the risks taken by others. Those with the oiliest tongues turned out to be the richest at others' expense.

And while he had galloped west many years ago hoping to leave that obscene inequity behind, with every summer Bass was coming to realize that the monied minority and their lackeys would always find some way to reach out from the settlements and exploit those who called this wilderness home.

Beaver had to come back, he told himself as he made his final decisions with more hope than horse sense. Beaver just had to come back.

"Run this up and tell me what I owe you," he instructed the clerk after turning back what he hoped would be more than half of the necessaries and shiny presents he had picked out for his women.

"With all this fur of yours, you've got much more credit than these few purchases."

"I ain't trading all my furs," he interrupted the man. "Gonna keep some for—"

"The Frenchman's coming!"

Bass turned at that warning cry stabbing the hot summer air from beyond the tree line.

"Shunar's coming!"

More of them took up the call as Titus swung around, his eyes digging, scratching, searching for Carson as he lamented, "Goddamn— there's gonna be a fight now!"

Once more Bass scanned the trees, finding the giant just emerging a few hundred yards off on horseback. Even at this distance he could make out the shape of the firearm Chouinard had braced atop his right thigh as his horse loped toward the trading canopies.

At the sound of footsteps and loud voices Scratch turned, finding Carson hurrying past, out of the shade and shadow, to stop in the intense light as clouds continued to scud toward the sun. Behind the Frenchman came a growing crowd of the curious. The shelters poked back in the brush and trees now began to spew many more white men as well as Indians who had been visiting the trapper camps.

"Leetle Amereecan!"

Even at this distance they could all hear the bite of Chouinard's voice in the dry, hot air.

A wisp of graying cloud brushed the face of the sun, sucking some of the intensity out of the afternoon light.

"Get my horse, Doc," Carson ordered without turning.

While Newell hurried away, Bass stopped behind the short man, offering his weapon once more. "You want my pistol?"

Carson turned slightly, patted the butt of the big pistol he had stuffed into his belt this day. "Got mine, Scratch."

Fifty yards away now, Chouinard shook the rifle overhead. "I keel you Amereecan! The squaw—she is mine!"

Turning suddenly, Carson snagged a handful of Bridger's shirt. "Gabe, if'n this don't turn out . . . promise me you'll take my ponies, my plunder, over to that 'Rapaho camp."

"What the hell for—"

"Promise me," Kit begged. "Give it all to the ol' man and try to tell him I done what I could to kill this bastard."

"He ain't gonna kill you."

"Gimme your word, Jim," Carson pleaded. "Tell him all white men ain't lyin', thievin', snake-tongued bastards."

"Awright," Bridger agreed reluctantly.

"Keep what you want from my possibles," Kit instructed. "It's your'n, friend."

With a snort from its nostrils, the horse was led up, and Newell quickly passed the reins over its ears as Carson leaped to the saddle. He yanked on the reins, and the animal lunged back against some of the growing crowd.

"Watch his eyes!" Bass shouted above the tumult.

"Scratch is right!" Bridger echoed. "The bastard's tricky, so watch his eyes."

Thin-lipped with determination, Carson nodded. "Them eyes'll tell me when he's gonna shoot."

"Send 'im to hell, Kit!" Meek bellowed as Carson spun the nervous horse around and shot through the crowd.

Bass growled, "Make meat out of the nigger!"

The gathering throng had grown noisy as their numbers swelled. But the moment Carson burst into the meadow atop his horse, an even louder call burst from more than half-a-thousand throats.

"He got a chance, Scratch?" Bridger asked in a whisper.

"If'n he gets in there close, I'll lay he's got a chance."

Kit began circling off to the right slowly, raising himself in the stirrups so he could instantly spring that way or this.

"Shunar! Am I the American you're looking for?"

Wagging his big shaggy head of black hair, the Frenchman, for some reason, recanted. "No."

"You're a goddamned liar!" Carson snorted with some mean laughter. "And a yellow-livered coward!"

Chouinard hurled his curse as his horse pranced closer, lowering his rifle to make certain of his shot. "Peeg! I will crunch your bones in my teeth!"

"Ain't much of a man, are you, Shunar?" Carson taunted as he bobbed back and forth in the stirrups, intently watching where the giant swung the muzzle of his smoothbore fusil. "Cain't even untie the knot on a young gal's chastity rope!"

"Beeg lie!" the giant spat, flecks of spittle collecting at the corners of his thick lips.

Kit sang out, "So you're the big bull of this wallow, eh?"

"I chew your bones—"

"Not when a li'l Injun gal get herself away from you!"

Jerking back on his horse's reins, Chouinard stopped only a few yards from Carson. With steely conviction he said, "I gonna like to keel you, leetle bird."

Kit inched his frightened horse to the left, transfixed on the muzzle of the rifle that followed his every move. He held the pistol close, ready.

Already the crowd was shouting, calling out to one antagonist or the other, hooting and whistling and goading until Bass could barely hear what Chouinard and Carson were shouting at one another while they worked themselves up to that deadly moment.

"You're nothing more'n a puffed-up bag of wind, Shunar! Some young gal can spook you!"

"I keel you, Keet! Cut your heart out—"

"Gonna stuff that rifle up your ass, Shunar!"

"—cut your heart out and show it to the squaw!"

Bringing his horse up beside the American's with a leap, Shunar rested the rifle's barrel across his left elbow, propping it there for his shot.

"I crunch your bones today!"

Now both animals were touching, their riders making the horses shove against one another, snorting and pawing up clods of dirt and prairie grass as the two men spun them in a tightening circle, slowly wheeling round and round.

"Gonna put you in hell today, Shunar!"

Turning constantly, this way and that, each dueler twisted in his saddle to keep an eye on his enemy.

"Leetle Amereecan bird chirping till I keel him!"

Suddenly Chouinard jerked his rifle back from his left arm, inverting it to slam the butt of his fusil against the neck of Carson's horse.

Yanking a foot free of a stirrup, Carson lashed out with a moccasin at the Frenchman's buttstock, failing to connect. "Buzzards gonna pick your bones clean a'fore sunset!" When Kit kicked a second time, the blow landed solidly against the flank of Chouinard's horse.

The giant's animal sidestepped in a leap as the Frenchman struggled to regain control of the frightened horse. He twisted in the saddle to face Carson, dropping the fusil's barrel back into the crook of his left arm again as it spat a tongue of yellow fire.

But the American had fired an instant before as that fusil was descending. Carson was already swinging to the side as his pistol erupted.

With the fusil tumbling from his hand, Chouinard shrieked in pain, clutching his bloody right arm. For a moment he gazed down at the path the bullet had taken: entering the wrist, traveling through the forearm, then exiting the elbow as it smashed bone. As his eyes glazed in agony, the Frenchman turned round to find Carson now some twenty yards away, stuffing his empty pistol into his belt.

"It's over, Shunar!" Andrew Drips shouted, loping toward them on foot.

"No! I keel him!" the Frenchman cried like a wounded, terrified animal.

"Leave it be!" Drips commanded as he came to a halt beside the giant's horse.

Instead of turning away, Chouinard cocked his leg back and kicked out at the company commander, sending Drips sprawling across the grass. Then the giant slowly sawed on the reins with his left hand before reaching for the scabbard at his back with that one good hand left him. The other arm hung useless, dripping gouts of blood onto the trampled, dusty grass.

"Reload, Kit!" someone hollered from the crowd.

But Carson hadn't carried his pouch or powder horn into the fight.

"Shunar gets Kit close enough to use that knife," Bridger grumbled, "he'll make meat of Carson."

Slashing his big heels into his horse's ribs, Chouinard leaped toward the small American until his animal collided with Carson's, wildly slashing the huge knife through the air. Kit was just regaining his balance from that blow when the Frenchman lunged out with that left arm, swinging low enough with the big butcher knife that Carson had to lean backward in the saddle.

Back and forth Chouinard slashed at the American, forcing Kit to dodge side to side so fast he could not regain his balance—eventually spilling from the saddle. Pitching headlong into the grass, Carson struggled to yank his foot from the stirrup as Chouinard savagely kicked at the American's prancing horse, hurrying to get around to the other side where Carson hung from the saddle.

Terrified, Kit's horse sidestepped again and again, for some miraculous reason keeping itself between Carson and the Frenchman's horse in those frightening seconds as Kit battled to free his foot twisted in the stirrup.

He pulled his moccasin free just as the Frenchman sawed his reins in the opposite direction, deciding to spin around the rear of Carson's horse. Kit stood, his right hand scraping at the back of his belt, fingers finding his scabbard empty. Somewhere on the ground nearby lay his knife.

But as clouds loomed across the sun, so too the Frenchman loomed over Kit. With a powerful grunt Chouinard brought his left arm down at the American who dived between the horse's legs, rolled on a shoulder, then sprang up in a sprint.

Bass was already on his way, tearing away from the crowd the moment he realized Carson didn't have a weapon left. "Kit!"

Right behind Carson the giant was goading his horse into a gallop, its hooves thundering like hailstones the size of cotton bolls on a hide tepee. Scratch could see Kit wouldn't have time to reach him before Chouinard would ride Carson down from behind with that knife.

Meek yelled, "Behind you!"

The moment Kit turned his head to find Chouinard all but on him, Carson stumbled, sprawling in the grass as the Frenchman shot past. The giant reined up, his horse gone stiff-legged as the Frenchman yanked back on the reins. Kit grasshoppered out of the dirt, sprinting toward Bass once more.

When Kit was no more than ten yards away, Scratch hollered, "Now!" in warning, and heaved the heavy smoothbore pistol into an arc.

Both of Carson's arms came up as he plucked the weapon from the sky, drew the hammer on back from half cock, and wheeled about in a crouch at the very moment Chouinard raced up, leaning off the side of his horse, attempting to impale the short American on that long knife.

But Kit dropped to one knee, gripping the huge pistol with both hands at the end of his outstretched arms, pulling the trigger point-blank in the Frenchman's face—the force of that blow driving the giant off the far side of his horse as the huge lead ball entered just below the left eye socket before it flattened to splatter out the back of his immense head an instant later.

Kneeling there with the smoking pistol still in his hands, Carson remained motionless as the big man drooped farther and farther in the saddle, then suddenly collapsed into the grass.

From one side rushed Bridger and from another came Drips, both of the company booshways reaching the Frenchman as some in the hushed, murmuring crowd pressed forward, step by curious step.

Drips wagged his head as Bridger stood and announced, "Bastard was dead a'fore he hit the ground."

The crowd erupted.

Meek was at Carson's side, pulling Kit onto his feet. "Shot him in the saddle, Kit! By jump—you been shot too!"

Staggering a moment, Carson regained his balance and touched the side of his neck. "Just a graze, Joe."

Newell, Bass, and a gaggle of others were crowding in on Carson now as Drips was ordering some company men to drag the body away. In a moment Bridger shouldered his way through the clamoring crowd, each one of them loudly reliving the frightening seconds of that duel, all at the same time.

"Damn—if this don't call for a drink!" Bridger hollered above the noise.

"Maybeso later tonight, Gabe," Carson announced as he turned to Bass, his hands shaking. Passing the pistol back to its owner, he said, "Thanks, Scratch. I'm beholden to you. Saved my life."

"Maybeso, Kit—you'll have yourself a chance to save my ha'r one day."

Joe Meek draped a mighty arm over Carson's small shoulder. "C'mon with Gabe—we ought'n have us some whiskey wet our gullets now that bastard's dead, Kit!"

Carson finished shaking hands with Scratch, then turned to Meek. "We'll all have us that drink together after supper, Joe. Right now I got something I better tend to."

"Tend to?" Newell echoed, scratching the side of his head. "What you gonna do that's better'n wetting down our dry with Bridger's whiskey?"

Carson winked at them, saying, "Right now, boys—I'm on my way to buy me a wife!"

ELEVEN

Nine days after his partner Thomas Fitzpatrick had reached the rendezvous at the mouth of New Fork River on the Green, Jim Bridger started north with his brigade.

With his sixty men went not only his new wife's family and Insala's band of Flathead, but the Nez Perce who had once again visited the white man's rendezvous in their unremitting hope that a man of God would come to live among them, to show them how to earn their eternal reward. After two disappointing journeys to the trappers' rendezvous, these Nez Perce were finally returning to their native ground with just such a man and his medicine book.

Reverend Samuel Parker.

This dour, humorless fifty-six-year-old evangelist had just volunteered to press on into the wilderness while his younger associate, Dr. Marcus Whitman, returned east to enlist more recruits for their mission work among the heathen savages of the Northwest. While Whitman might not approve of all the earthy and raw habits of the mountain trappers, the doctor nonetheless chose not to preach to or condemn them—unlike the bookish and haughty Parker.

Extending an uncharacteristic and polite patience to the

good reverend, a large number of the unrefined trappers listened attentively as Parker discoursed on their need to immediately abandon those worldly ways he found so deplorable, including how the white men squandered away their hard-won wages in an orgy of whiskey and debauchery, having nothing left to show for their labors than the baubles they purchased for their pagan wives and half-breed children.

Shocked less at the violence he had witnessed in that bloody duel between Carson and Chouinard, the reverend fierily preached his brimstone on the evils he had seen at rendezvous—in particular scolding the trappers on the practice of some who held up a common deck of playing cards before the visiting Indians as the white man's holiest book. Able to purchase several of these inexpensive packs of cards from the company's trader during rendezvous, many trappers convinced gullible Indians that unless their wives and daughters were not lent for carnal pleasures, then the white man's powerful God would hurl down all manner of fiery and eternal torment suffered among the flames of hell. Time and again, without refusal, the women were turned over.

Those sins of the flesh, magnified by the sin of bearing false witness!

But just as Parker was working himself into a ranting lather, a horseman rushed up to announce that buffalo had been spotted up the valley. Without a by-your-please, the reverend's grease-stained congregation leaped to their feet, grabbing rifles and horses, racing off to run those buffalo. Their sudden exit left the disgruntled Parker reassured that he was taking the right course in going to preach and convert the Nez Perce rather than attempting the salvation of those profane trappers who showed absolutely no hope of God's redemption.

To better make his case for continued donations and funding from the American Board of Missions, Dr. Whitman was overjoyed to discover a Nez Perce boy who spoke a smattering of English. After securing permission from the youngster's father for the trip east, the doctor christened the lad Richard. During that ceremony a second Nez Perce father promptly presented his son to accompany Whitman east where he could be taught the white man's religion. The doctor baptized this second companion John.

Six days after Bridger's departure for Davy Jackson's Hole with his Flathead family and the rest of the tribe, Fitzpatrick started for Fort Laramie with the company's fifty men, some two hundred mules bearing the year's take in beaver along with some buffalo robes, and more than eighty former employees who were abandoning the mountains. Accompanying them on their journey was the party of scouts and hunters employed by Scottish nobleman Sir William Drummond Stewart. That long snake of men and animals strung out through the valley and beginning to wind up the hills made for an impressive leave-taking that late August morning.

Gone now was the jubilation that had rocked this fertile bottom ground like a prairie thunderstorm. Some began to realize just how late it was in the season. As far back as any man could remember, the trader's caravan always reached rendezvous anywhere from late June to early July. But this summer's delay translated into five lost weeks—weeks the brigades and bands of free trappers weren't able to use in tramping to their fall hunting grounds. Now they would have to labor long and hard to make up for that lost time.

With Elbridge Gray and the other three already gone with Bridger nearly a week, and with Fitzpatrick just starting east to turn the caravan over to partner Fontenelle who was recuperating at the company's Fort William, Andrew Drips led his eighty-man brigade south by west for the fall hunt among the Uintah and Wasatch ranges. No man among those white Americans, French voyageurs, and half-breeds would leave any record of their travels that winter.

No more trace than what any of those bands of free trappers would leave behind on the banks of the New Fork: the cold, black smudge of a string of long-abandoned fire pits and faint moccasin-clad footprints quickly erased by the ever-present autumn wind or buried beneath untold inches of icy snow. No tales of their passing were left for generations yet to come.

They might as well have been ghosts chasing down the moon.

As Zeke roamed along either side of their path, Scratch hurried Waits-by-the-Water and little Magpie east across that trampled and familiar path. Striking a little south of east, they crossed the Big Sandy, then climbed that barren saddle of the Southern Pass where they struck the first narrow channel of the Sweetwater which took them east, down to the North Platte. Day after day for two weeks they descended, following Fitzpatrick's trail, encountering the great sprawl of his campsites until they finally caught up with the caravan one day before the entire cavalcade came within sight of La Ramee's Fork.

Near the river's mouth stood the tall cottonwood stockade that the year before had been christened Fort William in honor of one of its original owners. But in leaving the mountains for more sedate business ventures, William Sublette and Robert Campbell relinquished this massive post to the victors who would stay to the bitter end.

While Fitzpatrick's caravan plodded on down the gentle slope toward the impressive timbered walls, Titus pulled the pack animals to the side of the march and halted. Waits reined up beside him.

"That's some," he gasped in English.

Removing the hand she had clamped over her mouth in awe, she repeated, "Some."

"Only see'd two other forts," he continued in his native tongue. "One on the Missouri called Osage, and that post of Tullock's they call Cass. Both of 'em small."

She nodded, wide-eyed with wonder. "Cass." And made a sign using her two hands, "Small."

He chuckled and said, "Nothing like this. This here's a hull differ'nt place, woman. A hull differ'nt place."

Scattered across the plain within a half mile of the stockade walls stood the lodges of those bands invited there to trade—three camp circles, along with their separate herds, where riders moved to and from the fort, women and children streaming back and forth along the shady riverbanks for water, bathing, or to swim naked in the glistening waters. It struck Bass as a damned fine idea that hot afternoon.

"Who are these people?" Waits asked in Crow.

"They look familiar?"

"Those are not Crow lodges," she said guardedly.

"I didn't figure they would be," he replied, a little cold water suddenly dashed on his ardor. "This ain't Crow country."

"Ak'ba'le'aa'shuu'pash'ko," she said. "Your northern people call them Sioux."

"What northern people?"

It took her a moment to consider how to explain that. "They do not talk like the men from your country," Waits said. "Their skins are fair, like yours and your friends', but their tongues speak a different language—"

"Parley-voos!" he roared, remembering a dim tale told here and there. "That's right. Them parley-voos call 'em Sioux."

But the sound of the word did little to bring him comfort. Not that he had ever had a run-in with the tribe, but he had heard a few stories from those who had bumped up against these powerful warrior bands pushing farther and farther west across the plains until they now had virtually reached the foot of the Rocky Mountains, claiming that prime hunting ground by right of might.

They would just do their best to stay clear of any what might stir up some trouble.

Pointing at a piece of open ground to the southwest of the fort, Waits-by-the-Water asked, "What do your people call those boxes with the round white tops and large rosettes on the side?"

With the one good eye Scratch squinted a little into the distance obscured by the summer haze, then chuckled. "We call them wagons. The rosettes turn and roll—hoops called wheels. They carry the wagons."

"Do men push them?"

"No," he said, and scanned those six wagons, finding that not one of them was hooked to a team. Instead, all sat abandoned, motionless on that open bottom ground, their tongues either pointed heavenward, or lying hidden among the tall grass. "Horses pull them. Most times, four horses or more. The people ride, just the way we ride a horse, or your people pull someone on a travois."

She nodded as if beginning to understand. "I see: they are the white man's house that he takes with him the same way my people move our lodges from camp to camp?"

With a grin he agreed. "Jehoshaphat, but you've got it right."

"God dit," she repeated with a wink.

As they ambled toward those fifteen-foot-high palisades, Titus could not remember the last time he had seen that red-and-white-striped flag. A banner every bit this big had flown from the top of the Fort Vancouver flagpole, but he figured he hadn't seen America's flag since reaching St. Louis to track down Silas and Billy more than a year back. With every tug of the wind, the huge flag snapped taut for a moment, allowing him to count another row of stars until he tallied up twenty-four. With each star representing a state, Bass reflected what new states had joined the union since he had abandoned the settlements back in twenty-five.

Craning his neck as they came alongside the walls, he peered up at the huge bastion that hung over the top of the northwest corner. He found another like it constructed at the southeast corner. And midway down the southern wall stood the massive gate where he reined to a halt and gazed up to take in the massive blockhouse perched atop the wall more than fifteen feet above them.

"Ho!" he called to a face he saw watching from the west window cut in the blockhouse.

"Ho, yourself," the shaggy graying man called down.

Pointing at the gaping southern window, Scratch asked, "That your cannon?"

"It's a cannon—but it ain't mine," the man replied. "Only here to visit. C'mon up an' get yourse'f a good look-see for far an' wide."

"Holler down and have 'em open up the gate for us," he asked.

Hanging partway out the window, the man shook his head. "They ain't gonna open up these'r gates, on 'count of all them Sioux out there."

Bass turned in the saddle to peer once again at all the lodges. "Afraid them Injuns'll rush the fort?"

"I s'pose they are," the man answered. "Most of 'em belong to a chief name o' Bull Bear. Campbell invited 'em down from their country north of here to do some trading."

"And now these fellers here won't trade with 'em?"

"They been trading with them bucks last couple of days," the man declared. "But the company don't let very many come in at one time. No more'n a dozen I s'pect."

"So how's a man to get in?"

"She with you?" the stranger asked.

"My wife and our daughter."

"Likely you come on round to the back side where you come in the corral gate."

"Someone there to open up?"

"There will be in a shake or two," he responded as he pulled his head back in the window and disappeared.

"We ride to another gate," Bass explained in Crow.

On the river side they found a pole corral constructed along the entirety of that northern wall. Pulling back one half of a suspension gate wide enough to admit a wagon, Scratch was able to lead their animals into the corral where no more than a dozen horses grazed on dwindling piles of cut grass.

The narrow door behind them creaked open, and the older man poked his head out, looked this way and that, then spoke. "Tie off your critters there, then you come on in with me."

Once they passed through the narrow door, the three of them entered a cool and shady part of the fort. The stranger started them for a low-railed balcony. Beyond it Titus caught a glimpse of the huge open courtyard.

"Name's Bass," he introduced himself, sticking out an empty hand.

"I'm Creede. Langston Creede."

"How long you been working here?"

"Oh, I don't work here," Creede explained as they stepped onto the porch leading to the balcony. "I been trapping for the company. American Fur Company, that be."

"Ain't much else in the mountains these days," Titus replied as they stopped at the low rail and peered into the bright September sunshine. "You come in with Fitzpatrick from ronnyvoo?"

The man nodded. "With him till four days ago when some of us got half-froze to get here on our own," he said. "That pack train of theirs was dawdlin' a leetle too slow for our likin'."

"So you're with them what're leaving the mountains for good?"

"Naw," and Creede leaned back to settle on the top rail of the balcony. "Ever' three years me and a ol' friend meet back to St. Lou and have ourselves a winter spree. Get some women, sleep on a real tick, and have some more women. Man gets a hunger for a white woman . . ." Then he caught himself, his eyes softening apologetically. "Sorry. Didn't mean nothing again' your woman here."

"No trouble took by it, Langston. So have yourselves a good spree, then come back out to the mountains, eh?"

"I do, but Levi had him his job upriver—"

"Levi? You said your friend's name is *Levi?*"

"That's right. Levi Gamble," Creede declared.

"G-gamble?"

"Ever you run onto him?"

"I'll be damned," Bass exclaimed in wonder with a grin growing big as his beard. "I knowed a man named Levi Gamble of a time. But that were so long ago, it couldn't be the same man."

"The nigger I know is older'n dirt," Creede exclaimed with a chuckle. "But a damn good man. We been workin' for American Fur a long time, Bass. Upper Missouri Outfit. The Western Department—no matter what them booshways called it, they always had plenty of work for us over the years."

"Levi Gamble," Titus sighed, staring at his toes and calculating the years, trying to sort through a jumble of feelings and recollections that name stirred in him. "Had to been the summer I run off from home."

"How long ago was that?"

"A mess of winters," he replied, his eyes moistening with remembrance. "Eighteen ten."*

"That's going on twenty-five years now, mister. I ain't been out on the upriver near that long, but Levi damn well has."

Bass grew excited. "Y-you think it's the same feller?"

With a wag of his head Creede confessed, "Chances be, chances be. If'n the Levi Gamble you knowed first come up the Missouri to work for that Spanyard, Man-well Lisa."

"That's him, by damned!" Titus roared with a booming clap of his rough hands. "Levi was coming through Boone County back to the summer of eighteen ten, and I just 'bout beat him in a shooting match."

Langston's eyes narrowed suspiciously. "You say you just 'bout beat him in a shooting match?"

"Come this close," and Bass held up a thumb and fingertip all but touching.

Creede shook his head. "Had to be a differ'nt Levi Gamble . . . or you must be one center of a shot," he replied with a tinge of admiration in his disbelief. "In all these years I ain't never knowed another man to shoot better'n Levi Gamble."

Eagerly he asked, "So you're meeting Levi back in St. Louie for your spree?"

"Come the end of winter we'll be heading upriver again, on the first steamboat bound away for Fort Union," Langston explained. "I ain't gonna be trapping no more." The man flexed his back with a sigh, "Find me 'nother way to make a living up on the high Missouri."

"Levi still traps?"

"Not now, not for a long damned time," Langston said. "You was saying how he beat you in that shoot?"

"Yeah—by the skin of his teeth!"

* *Dance on the Wind*

"Wasn't long afore the booshway at Fort Pierre found out just how good Levi was and hired him for to be fort hunter. Since then Gamble's sashayed on up the Missouri and been working for booshway McKenzie. But McKenzie ain't gonna be around no more now, so I don't know if Levi can figger on having him that sweet job no more. I s'pose I won't know how McKenzie's settled his dust till I meet up with Levi back to St. Lou."

"When's that?"

"We allays lay plans that come the first of November the year we're spreeing, when the snow's flying and it's time to hunker close to a fire, we're gonna ronnyvoo up at the Rocky Mountain House."

"As likely a place for a hurraw or blood spillin' as you'll find in St. Louie!" Scratch bawled in merriment.

"That's the God's truth!"

"Listen now, hear? You gonna tell Levi you run onto a feller he knowed from long, long ago—"

"Eighteen ten. Summer."

"That's right. The summer I come this close to whupping him in the turkey shoot. It was down to just him and me. That summer he was off to St. Louie for to join Lisa's brigade bound for the high Missouri."

Creede held out his hand. "Chances are I'll see you round the next few days while Fontenelle's getting everything throwed in his wagons for the trip back, but if I don't bump into you, it was good meeting you, Bass."

"You get a chance, come look me up next day or so. I figger we'll find us a likely place to camp down by the river. But no matter what, you tell Levi I'll give it my damnedest to look him up to Fort Union next year or two."

"We'll keep our eyes out for you on the skyline!" Creede said as he turned and clattered down the steps into the sunny courtyard.

"I understood some of what you said to the other man," Waits explained when Creede was leaving. "What is this *Levi?*"

"Levi Gamble. A nice man I knew many years ago back in the land of the whites, even before you were born."

"He is an old man now," she said as she adjusted Magpie on her hip.

With a grin Bass replied, "I'm getting to be an old man now too, woman!"

Together with Waits and Magpie, Titus explored the fort interior that afternoon, stepping down from the railed balcony into the dusty quadrangle. At the center of the courtyard he stopped momentarily to stare up at the tall pole that so reminded him of those sky-scratching masts bristling with monstrous sheaths of canvas at the port of New Orleans.

Staring up at that flag being nudged by the wind suddenly gave him pause, realizing that until this moment he hadn't thought of this western wilderness as belonging to the United States, a place and people who lay more than a thousand miles away, back there in his past.

For the first time in more than ten years, Bass sensed the first pang of regret—not for having left his country behind to flee to this untamed frontier . . . but regret in reluctantly coming to understand that the civilized, gentrified, pacified country he had abandoned was inexorably creeping west on his heels, slowly swallowing all of what was still, at least for the present, a vast and feral unknown, for this moment known only to his breed.

When he tore his eyes from the twenty-four stars of that flag and gazed around the quadrangle, he found that in many ways this massive wood stockade reminded him of the huge adobe fort built by the Bent brothers on the north bank of the Arkansas River. Here too buildings ringed the inside of the walls, some for trading, others for sleeping quarters or storage of furs, with space for a powder magazine, blacksmith's shop, and a cooperage.

From the base of that immense flagpole he led his wife across the trampled ground for the main entrance. To the left of the massive covered gate hung a wide set of stairs leading up to the roof over those rooms built against the interior of that front wall of the fort. Atop the roof the stairs continued upward at a right angle, leading the two of them to the central blockhouse poised across the main gate, perched high on a pair of massive cottonwood posts.

Stepping through the blockhouse door into the cool, shadowy interior, Scratch found several other white visitors, all clad in greasy buckskins or shabby woolens, leisurely peering from the windows cut in three sides of the blockhouse.

"You fellas in from the mountains?" Titus asked as he stopped in the center of the shady room with Waits at his elbow.

One of them quickly looked the woman over, then replied, "Heading back to St. Lou with the fur train."

Moving to one of the windows with his wife, Bass declared, "My, but I never see'd anything like this out here, even back there in St. Louie neither. Can't remember stepping higher'n the first floor of anything since I was a tad and we all had our sleeping ticks up in the rafters of our cabin."

"That were in Missouri, ol' man?" a fresh-faced settlement type asked, the hint of a sneer on his mouth.

Titus eyed him and smiled disarmingly, saying, "That was back to Caintuck. Likely afore you was even born."

With a haughty huff the ruddy-faced youngster agreed, "Don't doubt it, ol't as you appear to be."

"I'll 'llow as you got so much green behin't your ears that you don't know how to talk respectful to your elders," Titus explained as the blockhouse grew quiet around them. "Maybeso you just bumped up again' someone ol't enough he could cut you two ways of Sunday a'fore your guts'd ever spill out on this floor."

Flicking his eyes side to side, the youngster realized his companions had inched back from him. He chewed on a lower lip for a moment more, then apologized. "I didn't mean nothin' by it, mister."

"I figger you didn't know no better, son," Bass said. "One thing a pup learns as he grows is when to bark, and when to shut his jaws. There's a time for barking, and by damn, there's a time for keeping his yap closed and his ears open."

An older man dressed in greasy wool britches and a tobacco-stained calico shirt had been watching it all. He now stepped up from the far window to the youngster's shoulder. "Those are good words anyone can live by, Joseph."

Joseph nodded once at him and said, "I didn't want you thinking I'm backing down a'fore this feller, Pa. Don't go—"

"I ain't thinking that at all, son."

Bass cleared his throat. "Your boy?"

"Yep," the older man said as he clapped a hand on Joseph's back. "His first trip to the mountains this summer. Likely filled his head with wild ideas."

With a smile Scratch agreed. "Gonna be hard taking your boy back there to them settlements and St. Louie where a young man can't stretch his arms when he wants."

"Still, the trip done him good," the man replied, gently starting Joseph away toward the blockhouse door. "He's found out there's a big world out here where I been coming last few years. Trouble, though, Joseph still gotta learn his place in that world."

"Don't ride him 'cause of the way he riled me," Bass pleaded, feeling a bit guilty now as Joseph shambled out the door and clattered down the noisy wooden steps. "Ever' man's gotta find his own way, make his own mistakes in the world."

"If he don't make the sort of mistake that takes his life."

For a moment Bass glanced at Magpie, then thought of Josiah. "It's allays good when a man takes a step back 'cause he figgered out he's tempted Lady Fate long enough on his own."

"My name's Clement," the pecan-skinned man introduced himself as he approached.

A low, menacing growl rumbled at the back of Zeke's throat, stopping the stranger in his tracks.

"Hush, boy!" Scratch snapped, motioning the stranger on.

"Antoine Clement," the man said, pronouncing it with that richly expressive roll the tongue gave to *Clah-mah.*

"French name," Bass declared as he stood beside the fire he and Waits-by-the-Water were starting. "Titus Bass be mine."

"My father was a Frenchman," the half-breed explained. "I'm chief scout taking a Europe nobleman across the west. We are camped nearby, so he sent me to ask you for supper with him tonight."

"Supper, you say?" Bass replied, glancing at his wife. In Crow he explained, "We've been invited to eat with another camp."

She nodded enthusiastically.

"Seems my wife thinks it's a right fine idee, Mr. Clement. When you want us to show up?"

"Soon as you're able," and the scout turned to point to the nearby bend in the river where the grassy meadow was rimmed with wild currant bushes laden with thick clusters of resplendent red fruit. "Can't miss us. My boss has a few unusual tents pitched in a half circle around our fire."

Bass rose, dusting his palms on the front of his greasy leggings. "We'll be along shortly."

In no more than a matter of minutes did Waits-by-the-Water have herself and Magpie ready to go visiting. After looping a short length of hemp rope around Zeke's neck, the four of them set off into the last of the day's heat as the sun sank upon those dark timbered heights resting along the western horizon, known to the mountain men as the Black Hills.*

"Stewart is my name, Mr. Bass," said a slight and shorter man as he stepped away from the big fire to greet them. "William Drummond Stewart."

"Call me Titus, baptized Christian back in Caintuck," he explained. "Or call me Scratch—you might say I was baptized that name when I first come to these here mountains."

"Scratch, is it?" Stewart repeated with a wry smile. "I believe I've heard your name come up among some of your American compatriots. Perhaps Bridger himself mentioned you."

"Me and Gabe go back some," Titus declared. "Run onto him clear back to twenty-six."

With a look of warm approval filling his kind eyes, Stewart cast his gaze upon the woman and that young child she clutched against her side. "And this is your wife? What tribe is she—wait. Let me see if I can guess by her clothing." He considered a moment, studying Waits-by-the-Water up and down, then finally wagging his head. "I'm not sure, but suppose she might be Shoshone?"

---

* *Today's Laramie Range, not the mountains in present-day South Dakota, which after the era of the mountain man would come to be known as the Black Hills during the great Indian wars.*

"Naw, she's Crow."

"Crow!" Stewart clapped his hands together exuberantly. "I haven't had much acquaintance with the Crow in my travels, even the journey I made through a corner of their country. But come, come! All of you." He pointed to some ladder-back wooden chairs arranged around the fire. "Let's sit and talk away the evening."

Stepping behind one of the chairs, Stewart gripped its back and looked at Waits with a broad smile.

"He wants you to sit on it," Bass explained in Crow, unable to come up with a word for *chair*.

"Sit?"

"Among the white men, this is how they sit. They have many chairs."

She regarded the piece of furniture suspiciously, then glanced at Stewart, and down at the chair again. "Why sit on this—when they can sit on the ground, can sit on a blanket or robe?"

"Don't make much sense, just like a lot the white man does. But"— and he shrugged—"white folks partial to this way of sitting. Go on, sit— and we'll be good guests for this visitor from a land far, far away."

After she had settled, Bass and Stewart took their seats as a half-breed servant stepped up with a silver tray on which rested four large pewter goblets.

The nobleman took his from the tray as the half-breed stepped between Bass and the Crow woman. "Try this, Scratch. It's a very nice wine I brought with me. If you shouldn't like it, we can find you something else to drink."

As it turned out, Waits enjoyed the taste of her first glass so quickly that Bass had to warn her the white man's powerful drink might either make her sick or cause her to act like the trappers she had seen become silly fools after guzzling at rendezvous.

"You've covered some ground, William," Bass declared later as the half-breed attendant poured steaming coffee in china mugs after an elegant supper of elk tenderloin garnished with canned oysters and slabs of a tart cheese on the side. He had never seen Waits-by-the-Water eat near as much as she did once Magpie was nursed and laid to sleep on a blanket spread beside her chair.

"You said you've been out to Vancouver. So you must have met Doctor McLoughlin?"

"That ol' white-headed eagle? Sure did. A good man—even for a Britisher."

"Lord, he's not a Britisher!" Stewart corrected. "He was born in Canada. Which might explain why he might well share no more love for the crown than do I."

"You're Scots, are you?"

"Not a drop of John Bull in me," Stewart said proudly.

Scratch sipped at his coffee, then said, "My grandpap allays told us we was Scot too—leastways, back some in the family."

At that Stewart hoisted his tin cup and merrily proposed, "Welcome to the tartan, my friend!"

"You said you been far yonder to the west, and clear up to Fort Union at the mouth of the Yallerstone," Scratch declared. "How far south you been? See'd Bents' Fort?"

"Indeed I did. Spring of thirty-four. We came north after a winter sojourn in Sante Fe—"

"Jehoshaphat! We was close by ourselves—down to Taos that winter!" Titus exclaimed. "That's where our li'l Magpie was born. I first come through Bents' Fort that spring of thirty-four too, on my way back from St. Lou."

"We visited Taos a few days on our way north for rendezvous on Ham's Fork," Stewart declared. "Quite an undertaking the Bent brothers have assumed with their fortress, not unlike the construction of this post. Back in Scotland, I'll have you know, my brother is building himself a new castle. Murthly he's calling it."

"What brung you all the way out here?" Scratch inquired after draining his mug. "All the yondering you've done, from the Missouri to the Columbia and on down to the greaser diggings—that's a passel of tramping."

For a moment Stewart ruminated on the question while he gazed into the fire, the thump of distant drums softly floating across the open meadow from the villages that lay beyond.

"I'm not the firstborn of my family, you see, Scratch. Among the wealthy, landed class that means I must make my own way in the world, unlike my brother John. Were it not for my gracious and loving aunts, I would still be making a career for myself in the British army. I was a captain—and I suppose it was my service in the wars of our empire that first stabbed me with this incurable appetite for travel and adventure."

"Adventure—damned sure to get your fill of that out here!" Titus replied.

"So in turn I'll ask you the same question: what brings you here?" Stewart inquired, his eyes intently studying the American. "Come for the beaver?"

Wagging his head, Scratch answered, "Some time back I realized it ain't the beaver. There's some what come for the plews, but that ain't what makes a man stay."

Stewart sighed, gazing now into the flames. "You Americans have something here in this country of yours that doesn't exist anywhere else in the world." He peered up at Bass. "Something that doesn't even exist back east, back there in the rest of America."

Bass shook his head emphatically now. "But I don't callate how this here's the United States, William. It ain't like nothing else back there. Another land, this."

The Scotsman abruptly raised his cup. "Huzzah! Huzzah! Here's my toast that this country out here will never become anything like that country back east!"

With a stab of some sudden, undefinable pain sending its icy finger through the middle of his chest, Scratch gazed at the black night sky and replied, "Aye, I damn well pray this never will be anything like that land they ruin't back east."

TWELVE

Perhaps it was all for the best that his brother-in-law hated him for his white skin, loathed him because he was not Crow.

Bass looked over the party slowly passing by the fort on their way to one of those small clusters of buffalo-hide lodges that dotted the south bank of the North Platte. In the lead rode a white trapper resplendent in his leggings and war shirt, the unfurled wings of a black-and-white magpie adorning his bear-hide cap. Behind him on her own prized pony rode his first wife. To her right sat a child so young the boy's legs barely reached over the wide back of his small pony. And behind them came a woman who had to be another wife followed by her own three children on their horses. Perhaps a widowed sister of the trapper's first wife. At least ten or more riders brought up the rear of that slow procession. Old ones and young, male and female both, some goading travois horses with their peeled switches, poles kicking up hot streamers of dust that hung in the still morning air.

When a man took an Indian woman for his wife, he married her whole damned family. That meant promising to provide for his new kin. Clearly, that poor trapper had wanted a wife and had ended up with the responsibility of close to twenty of her relatives.

Scratch turned to Waits-by-the-Water with a grin. "I just decided it's a good thing your brother hates me."

"But Strikes-in-Camp gives my mother a home," she said. "If he is killed, there will be no one but me to care for her now with my father and uncle gone."

"When that time comes, you and I will see that she is warm, that she has food for her belly," he vowed.

"My mother will not be a burden on you?"

He bent and kissed her cheek, then said, "I have no others, so your family is my family. We will take care of our own."

"But you do have family, husband," she reminded him. "The daughter who stays among the white men, to the east."

"Yes," he fondly remembered Amanda. "I have a grown daughter. A woman by now, she probably has given me a grandchild or two."

"But this child," Waits said, handing Magpie to her father, "she is your daughter too."

"How about that!" he said to the little one with a grin as they continued toward the fort gate. "A man old enough to have grandchildren of his own has been blessed by the First Maker with you, my beautiful child. Let's take your mother inside to find something so pretty she can't live without it."

Fort William's trading room was a long, narrow affair, with a plank counter running down the entire length of it. The company employees reached the area behind that counter through a door that passed into a storeroom. Directly behind the three clerks rose a solid wall of shelves and cubbyholes stuffed with goods and spanning the entire length of the room, a display that extended all the way from the ceiling overhead to the bottom shelf, which served as a second narrow counter about as high as a man's waist. From there down, the wide openings were stuffed with bales of folded blankets, small kegs of powder, along with bolts of coarse and fine cloth.

For a moment the two of them stopped there in the cool shade of that September afternoon while the clerks attended to other visitors. Bass watched his wife's face as her eyes slowly climbed up the extent of the shelves, in utter awe of the grand display. She had seen a few of the white man's trade goods laid out in display at the last three annual rendezvous they had attended, but most of the items were always kept back in crates and bundles and bales, covered with sheets of canvas to protect them from dust or a fickle summer thunderstorm. Here everything could be taken in at once—all of it on display, right out in the open. Each item lay little more than an arm's length away, just beyond a person's fingertips. Taunting, luring, entirely seductive.

Where to begin, he wondered.

"Lemme see your finger rings and bracelets," Bass replied when a clerk moved over to ask what he could do for the trapper.

With a noisy clunk the young employee dropped a large, three-foot-square, wooden tray atop the counter. Narrow dividers partitioned the huge tray into sections where lay a glittering array of brass and copper rings, bracelets and necklaces, silver gorgets and dangly earrings, ivory brooches and other large decorative pins fashioned in the shape of sea serpents, winged dragons, snakes, and peacocks displaying their finest plumage.

Slightly breathless, Waits turned to ask her husband, "M-may I touch them?"

"Touch them all you want."

"You trading pelts?" inquired the clerk as the woman picked up some earrings to examine.

"They're back to our camp," Scratch explained. "When she figgers what geegaws she's took a shine to, I'll have you put 'em back for me so I can go fetch my plews."

One by one Waits chose those items that most caught her fancy. Eventually she took a step back from the counter and the tray, raising her eyes to her husband with a smile. "These are the prettiest."

"You want these?"

"For me, and for Magpie—yes."

Turning to the clerk, Scratch asked, "How much?"

Computing the cost, the man announced his total.

"Forty dollar?" Bass shrieked. "So what's plew by pound?"

"Dollar a pound for prime."

He gulped. "And you dress it down from there?"

"It ain't prime, it don't bring a dollar," the clerk explained.

"Damn," he sighed. "Prices ain't no better here'n they are to ronnyvoo."

A second clerk stepped up to ask, "You figgered to cut yourself a better deal here?"

"I did," Bass admitted. "Ain't never see'd prices so high, never see'd beaver drop so low."

"Dollar worth the same here as it is on the upper Missouri," the second man declared. "The company sets what we charge for goods at ever' post. And they say what we give for furs."

"Beaver's on a slide," the first clerk said, starting to scoop up the brass, copper, and silver jewelry into one hand.

Scratch snagged the man's wrist in his hand. "Hol't on. Don' put those away just yet. Forty dollar, you said."

"Yep."

"And a dollar a pound for beaver."

The first man repeated, "Be it prime."

"Damn if that don't cut deep," Scratch grumbled, staring down at the jewelry spread across a square of black calico dotted with tiny yellow, red, and blue flowers.

"You got any buffler robes?" asked the second clerk.

"Trade for them too, eh?" Scratch commented.

"They're bringing better money than most anything right now," the man explained. "Just figgered you might have some robes, what with the woman here."

"We got robes for damn sure," he told them. "But them robes keep us warm through the winter. Can't sell 'em off."

As he started to amble away down the counter toward a man just come through the door, the second clerk advised, "You decide to sell those Injun robes, we'll give you good dollar on 'em."

Pursing his lips with resentment, Bass nudged the jewelry toward the first clerk. There was no way he could bear to see her face, that disappointment in her eyes if they walked away without that foofaraw.

"Keep all them shinies for me," he ordered. "I'll be back with 'nough plews to pay you your forty dollar a'fore you can finish your coffee."

Returning Waits and Magpie to their camp beside the Laramie River, Bass untied the rawhide ropes looped around one of the last two packs of furs. Whacking the dust from them the way his mam used to smack the dirt from their cabin rugs, he quickly sorted the pelts, selecting twenty of his best. They should easily bring more than the forty dollars it would take to trade for those geegaws.

Returning to the fort alone, he flung the small bundle atop the end of the counter and waited for the clerk to finish with another customer. Eventually, the man pulled out fifteen of the pelts, laying them beneath one arm of a scale. Quickly adding weights to the other arm, the man found that he had to remove one of the pelts.

With a sigh he turned back to Titus. "I can get 'er down to forty-two dollars."

"For the differ'nce gimme one of your best-looking glasses and the rest in your newest 'baccy. None of that ol' stuff."

"That ain't gonna get you much in tobacco, mister."

"Just treat me fair and we'll call it even," he said, taking up the ends of the rawhide rope he knotted around the plews left on the counter. "Fella don't stand a chance no more," he groused. "Appears your company is the only outfit trading in the mountains and at them posts in the upcountry. No good when you run all the other traders out."

"Our company ain't the only ones in the mountain trade," protested the second clerk who had sauntered over to rest his elbows on the counter.

"I know," Scratch said miserably. "I been to that fort the Bents got— but it's a piece of riding, way down on the Arkansas."

"It ain't the only one," the first clerk explained as he spread the small square of black calico on the counter.

"I don't figger on riding all the way north to your Fort Union neither."

"So I s'pose you ain't heard," the second man confided. "News come in the other day. We just heard some folks is raising a small post down on the South Platte a ways."

"South Platte," Titus echoed. "And it ain't your company's post?"

"Don't belong to us," the first man said. "We hear it belongs to one of Billy Sublette's brothers."

"Him and his partner, Louie Vaskiss, was here with Campbell last spring," the second one explained. "I figger the two of 'em are throwing in together, what with big brother Sublette and Campbell calling it quits for the mountains."

Titus tied up the four corners of the calico scrap and stuffed it into his possibles pouch. With a pat on the flap he told the clerks, "Thankee, fellas. For the geegaws, and for laying out the trail sign on that new post."

"You gonna head that way?"

Nodding, he replied, "Figgered to do some trapping south of here anyway."

"Good luck to you," the second man cheered.

"Thankee—but after all these winters I know luck ain't got much to do with me saving what I got left for ha'r," Scratch declared. "Hard work, never giving up, and good friends . . . they been what keeps this nigger's stick afloat through the years."

"Of all the mistakes I have made in my life," Sir William Drummond Stewart explained as darkness fell and the stars came out around them, "only two do I truly regret. All the rest I have atoned for, corrected."

This last evening prior to Fitzpatrick's departure for St. Louis, the Scottish nobleman had invited Bass to join him and a few guests for a final dinner before setting off for the east come morning. As soon as the sun fell, the air took on a new quality, growing crisp and chill, enough that he welcomed the fire's warmth and the coffee that steamed in his cups.

While the conversation among Stewart's guests had remained cheery and buoyant for some time, as the night wore on the nobleman grew more pensive.

"A child don't get to be our age 'thout making his share of mistakes," Bass reflected, sensing how the host was down in his mind. "Measure of a man is what he learns from the times he's stumbled and snagged his foot."

"Why do you say that, Titus?"

Shrugging, Scratch replied, "Don't seem like you're here. What's eating your craw?"

"I'm sorry," Stewart said, then turned to Marcus Whitman, saying, "I apologize, Doctor—and to the rest of you too. Perhaps I am brooding at the realization that with the morrow I will be abandoning these mountains, this western country where I have spent these past three summers, as well as that one winter at the mouth of the Columbia. I've hunted for and shot every big-game animal in this wilderness, including grizzly and elk, antelope and bighorn, mountain goat and more than my share of buffalo. More times than I can count I've stood shoulder to shoulder with you mountaineers, taking part in at least a dozen skirmishes with the redskin natives."

"Can't you ever plan to return west?" Whitman prodded.

"I will certainly do my best to return, once I've seen to some nagging family and financial affairs back east," the nobleman answered, grown all the more melancholy as they watched.

"Mayhaps you should shet yourself of what nags at you," Bass suggested. "Put it behind you here and now, no matter if you don't make it to another ronnyvoo."

Sighing thoughtfully, Stewart eventually nodded. "I came to my first rendezvous with George Holmes—a traveling companion. Since setting off across the plains, we had tented together. Poor George. In rendezvous camp I had arranged a liaison . . . arranged for a squaw to come to our bower for the night, so I prevailed upon George to sleep elsewhere."

Stewart related how Holmes had taken this request for privacy in good humor, carrying his blanket with him to a grassy spot near their bower, and lain down to sleep beneath the light of a nearly full moon. Sometime in the deep of early-morning darkness, the barking of dogs, shouts of men, and hammer of running feet awoke the nobleman. With a curious crowd he hurried to the commotion, finding a rabid gray wolf glaring at its victim without showing the slightest fear of the men rushing up. A few feet away sat George Holmes—his face torn and bleeding.

Turning to Whitman, Stewart explained, "There was nothing our Dr. Harrison could do for poor George but bathe his wounds and bind them up. In the next few days I couldn't shake the sickness I felt in my soul that I had been the cause of this tragedy."

Although Holmes's wounds healed quickly, his normal, lighthearted mood began to worsen. Over the next few weeks, the nobleman explained to his audience, George began to grow more morose and despairing, expressing his certainty that he was bound to die of hydrophobia.

"It wasn't until weeks later that poor George suffered his most terrifying fit," Stewart declared. "He tore off his clothing, ripped out his hair, scratched at his skin as he ran shrieking into the timber. We immediately went in search of . . . but we never found a trace of him."

"Not uncommon," Whitman replied. "There is nothing anyone can do once the hydrophobia attacks the brain."

His eyes begging for sympathy, Stewart said, "Never has a day gone by when I haven't reproached myself for that sad, sad night."

"Like the doctor said, I don't figger you can blame yourself for what the wolf done," Bass declared. And thinking that he should change the subject, he asked, "You said you made two mistakes. What of the second?"

For some time Stewart stared at the flames, then spoke with guarded resignation. "I have shot men in the heat of great battles, where I have run them through with my sword—looking them in the eye as I killed by my own hand. But never before have I indirectly done harm to another, much less caused their death. Not only did I bring about the ruin of George Holmes, but with heedless words uttered in the heat of my anger, I as much as pulled the trigger on the gun that killed another."

From the corner of his eye, Scratch watched Antoine Clement suddenly turn away and step into the darkness beyond the fire's light as if he were no longer able to endure his employer's self-inflicted pain.

"Don't mean a damn—you didn't shoot the man yourself," Tom Fitzpatrick consoled gruffly.

Stewart waved off that comfort and said, "I might as well put the gun to Marshall's head."

"Marshall?" Whitman repeated.

"It was the English name I gave to the servant who had been with me since thirty-three when we first crossed the plains for these mountains. He was of the Iowa tribe," Stewart explained. "From time to time I caught him stealing some trifle from me."

"The man is responsible for his own death," Clement argued, suddenly stepping into the firelight as if to set the record straight. "For some time you knew he was a thief. No one made him steal your horse."

Rising to turn his rump to the flames, the nobleman began his story. "My party was working our way north after a winter in Sante Fe, several days north of Bents' Fort when Marshall—for some unknown reason— decided that he wanted to steal my prized thoroughbred, Otholo."

On their way north along the Front Range, Marshall stole off one night on the Scotsman's prized horse, also purloining Stewart's favorite English rifle. When the nobleman discovered the loss the next morning, the short fuse of his anger flared. Exploding in a fury, he roared that he would offer a five-hundred-dollar bounty to the man who brought him the thief's scalp.

"Unfortunate that Markhead was in the sound of my voice," Stewart declared sadly.

Although there was no braver man than this Delaware Indian come west to trap beaver, many would question if he possessed even a modest strain of common sense. As a guide for the Scottish nobleman, Markhead evidently took it as his personal quest to hunt down the young horse thief. Besides, five hundred dollars was nothing short of a fortune to him.

Without saying a word to anyone, the Delaware slipped away from camp on his own.

Two days later Markhead returned, leading Stewart's thoroughbred and brandishing Marshall's scalp at the end of the recaptured English sporting rifle.

"My thoughtless words, spoken in a fury, killed that Indian boy," Stewart groaned.

Disgusted and sickened, the Scotsman tossed the scalp into the brush, but eventually paid Markhead that handsome reward so rashly offered.

"I don't figger you can lay claim to knowing what's in the addled brain of another man," Bass declared, thinking back on an old friend of his own, Asa McAfferty. "Can't none of us know what another'll do."

"Two deaths by my hand, as surely as if I held the payment of their eternal debt in the balance." Stewart stood and stretched, holding his palms over the flames. "To die in battle, under the honor of arms, is one thing. But here in this wilderness, I've learned there is no certainty of an honorable death. What a bitter lesson this has been for me, gentlemen: learning how quick and capricious, and truly senseless, death can be."

Whitman stood beside Stewart, asking, "Is death anything but capricious?"

The British soldier gazed at the missionary physician and said, "Men ride into battle, finding they can smell the nearness of that horror. In war, death is not capricious. It is an absolute, a veritable truth. But here in your American wilderness . . . I have seen truth stood on its head."

Snowflakes big as cottonwood shavings landed on his back and shoulders, slowly seeping into his deer-hide shirt as he hunched over the last of the trap sets.

The flakes fell slow and heavy, almost audible when he held his breath, when he stilled his frozen hands and clenched his chattering teeth. Soaked all the way to the scrotum, Bass listened as the storm tore itself off the high peaks above him, careening down the slopes toward the foothills below him. Listened to these first newborn cries of another winter storm a'birthing.

Two more days and he would have enough beaver collected that he could ride back to her. They would spend a few nights together; then he would pack Samantha and take off again to try another one of those streams that tumbled down from the timbered slopes along the Front Range here below the barren hood of Long's Peak—named by that intrepid explorer who ventured across the Central Rockies in the wake of Lewis and Clark's expedition through the northern mountains.

For the past several months he had forged this pattern: six or seven days alone among the spruce and pine and barren quaky, then returning for two or three nights in her arms, days spent bouncing Magpie on his knee, teaching the girl and her mother a little more English by the fires at night.

Each time he rode off, Bass left behind a stack of hides for Waits-by-the-Water to scrape while he was gone. Gone long enough for a man to grow lonely for the sound of the woman's voice, long enough for him to become ravenous for her flesh. Each time he returned, she seemed surprised with the fury of his coupling, yet responded to his hunger with an insatiable appetite of her own.

Here, deep in his forty-second winter, it seemed that he took longer to convince his joints to move each morning as he awoke in that cold loneliness before dawn. And it took all the longer for his bones to forgive him their immersion in the freezing water, longer to warm themselves when he returned from his trapline. But he nonetheless continued to find the beaver, though forced to ride farther into the hills, deeper still into rugged country. Those days of endless meadows clogged with beaver dams and lodges were gone. Gone too were the huge rodents who yielded pelts so big the mountain men called them *blankets*.

Gone were the days of easy beaver.

Now it was enough that a man catch something in a trap every two or three days. Not near enough beaver sign that Bass could expect to bring one to bait every day, but he still figured these long winter sojourns into the hills were worthwhile. Every winter pelt was one plew more that he wouldn't have had if he had dallied until spring began to thaw the high country.

Maybeso the trapping would have been all the better up north in Absaroka this past autumn, but then they would have been obligated to lie in for the winter with the Yellow Belly's Crow. Which would rub him right up against Strikes-in-Camp. And Crane too. Scratch didn't figure he was ready to see that much grief on one woman's face, not ready to find out how it would tear his own wife apart again. Better all around that they had turned south from Fort William, making for the South Platte where they ran onto Fort Vasquez, the new post founded just that autumn by partners Andrew Sublette and Louis Vasquez.

Louis was one of twelve children born to a father who had migrated to Canada from Spain, where he married a Frenchwoman before migrating again, south this time, to St. Louis on the Mississippi where his children grew up around that heart of the fur trade.

Andrew was the younger brother of the legendary William and Milton. After making his first trip west with his eldest brother to the Wind River rendezvous of 1830, the last for the firm of Smith, Jackson & Sublette, Andrew next accompanied Bill on that ill-fated 1831 trip to Taos that saw the tragic death of Jedediah Smith on the end of a Comanche buffalo lance. By 1832 and the famous rendezvous fight with the Gros Ventres in Pierre's Hole, Andrew was becoming a mountain man in his own right.

The following year found him pushing upriver with his brother's partner, Robert Campbell, to challenge the might of the American Fur Company on the upper Missouri by establishing some rival posts adjacent to the company's established forts. Their eye-to-eye challenge to Astor's empire quickly bore fruit, and the two competitors agreed to divide the fur company between them. Andrew was chosen to carry the articles of agreement, along with all the property the partners were turning over to the company, up the Yellowstone to Fort Cass in the summer of 1834.

From the Bighorn he had pushed south for Independence Rock on the Sweetwater, then on to the North Platte to reach the new post being constructed by his brother and Campbell by the last week of September. Later that fall, when Andrew first met the older Louis Vasquez at Fort William, Sublette and Campbell were already considering their withdrawal from the mountains. Back and forth they discussed their belief that the fur trade had reached its zenith, with profits sure to continue their slide.

Eager to step out of his brother's shadow that autumn, Andrew marched south with Vasquez, striking the South Platte, where they constructed a temporary post they christened Fort Convenience, trading for buffalo robes from the Arapaho and some Cheyenne hunting in the area.

Then in late December of thirty-four, excited by the heavy packs of furs and their prospects, the partners set out overland for St. Louis after briefly considering whether or not they should attempt to float the furs downriver in mackinaw boats. Surely they had proved to themselves that there was a vast potential for raising a post squarely between Fort William to the north and Bents' Fort south on the Arkansas. The future seemed theirs for the taking.

By April of thirty-five Andrew had returned to Fort William with Robert Campbell to assist with the transfer of the post to Fitzpatrick, Bridger, Drips, and Fontenelle. Early in the summer Louis was back in St. Louis where they both presented themselves to William Clark, petitioning for a license to trade among the tribes. Returning to the South Platte by late summer, the new partners started on their stockade with the help of a few men hired in St. Louis, struggling to raise enough shelter before the first winter storm rumbled down the slopes of Long's Peak to batter them.

Reaching that high ground east of the river, Scratch and Waits-by-the-Water found workers furiously felling trees and dragging those cottonwood timbers back to an open patch of ground where they were raising stockade walls.

"Soon as the frost is gone from the ground next spring," explained the stout Vasquez, "we can start making 'dobe bricks. Like the Bents done on their fort."

Titus told them how he had been to that post on the Arkansas, had seen plenty of adobe construction for himself down in San Fernando de Taos.

"You bring your furs here," the thinner Andrew Sublette promised, "beaver or buffalo—we'll give you top dollar."

"You don't go so far away, not down to Bents'," Vasquez said. "Get furs in these hills, trade them here too."

"We'll be back," Scratch promised. "Maybeso camp for the winter."

After resting nearby for two days watching the construction, Bass led his wife and animals across the sandy bottom of the South Platte and pushed into the foothills where Long's Peak brooded over them for the next ten weeks as he worked this stream, then another. Gradually pushed down from the high country a little farther day by day, Scratch and Waits-by-the-Water worked feverishly, rising well before first light to wolf down some food before he trudged away into the dark and she began her hide scraping before Magpie awakened. Each night found them working on the hides, cleaning the weapons, making repairs in clothing and adjustments to the square-jawed American traps or those manufactured of Juniata steel.

By the middle of December when the cold had grown serious, they traipsed down from the foothills, returning to the banks of the South Platte to find that the laborers had thrown up enough of a shelter to protect the traders and their goods from winter's furies.

Reaching the edge of the prairie at the foot of the mountains where the river meandered north, they chose a spot to camp out the rest of the winter near the new stockade. In a small copse of old cottonwood they chopped down the saplings they needed and cleared out a clutter of underbrush before erecting their shelters. The smallest protected the beaver pelts he caught and she grained and stretched. A partially enclosed bower gave her a place to work throughout the day as she cooked and tended to Magpie's needs close by their fire. And on the opposite side of the fire pit sat their sleeping shelter, where they could lash down all the flaps the better to withstand the passing of each icy gale winter hurled at them.

In less than a week he rode off again, this time on his lonesome. Bass turned once, looking behind to find the child standing hand in hand with her mother. Waits bent to say something, and when she straightened, both of them waved. He knew the woman was crying, probably angry with herself that she could not stop the tears that might frighten Magpie.

Back again after eleven days of trapping, he moseyed up to the post one afternoon, hungry for some male conversation.

"I don't think much of your big brother," Bass told Andrew Sublette. "He done all he could to ruin the fur trade for other men. And now he's run off back east when the running's good."

The handsome twenty-seven-year-old failed to protest. Instead, he reluctantly nodded. "I don't agree with all what Billy's done, but I can't figure him for a bad sort."

Dryly, Louis Vasquez asked, "All's fair in love and business, eh?"

Andrew glared at his partner a moment. "No matter what any man says, Billy made a go of everything he done. So maybe if we're gonna make it out here our own selves, you better savvy we'll need some of Bill's determination to see we don't come out second-best."

Scratch wagged his head. "How your brother cheated that Yankee fella named Wyeth, same time Billy was throwing your other brother Milton square into the middle of it—"

"Milt was already in the middle of it!" Andrew fumed.

"Don't put that underhanded back stabbing on Milt," Bass growled. "I heard the story of how Billy slipped around seeing to it that Rocky Mountain Fur Company refused them supplies they told Wyeth to bring out to ronnyvoo. Then your brother Billy made Milt out to be part of all his bamboozling!"

"Billy had no other choice," Andrew answered defensively, yet without much conviction. "Don't you see? Those five partners still owed him a debt from previous years. So when Billy learned they arranged to have the Yankee bring out their supplies, he figured they was breaking their contract with him when they was already bound to him—"

Vasquez interrupted. "Even though Billy Sublette was determined to keep every last one of them a prisoner in his grip?"

"If Billy was a better businessman than them partners were, so be it," Andrew admitted grudgingly.

"That strikes center, it does," Bass added. "I'll agree that Gabe and Fitz and the rest of 'em, they was better trappers, better *men* than they was businessmen."

"Don't you remember, Andrew—how the two of us decided we wasn't gonna be the sort of trader your brother was?" the Spaniard asked in that tiny trading room where more than a dozen men sat smoking their pipes and drinking coffee to wile away a winter afternoon.

"Billy don't run me, Louis," Andrew vowed. "We don't need him no more."

" 'Sides, I heard him and Campbell ain't ever coming back to the mountains," Bass said.

"That's right," Vasquez declared, looking at Scratch evenly. "Seems them two're buying up land back in St. Louis. Gonna be country gentlemen. So maybe Andrew's right after all: we ain't gonna worry 'bout Billy Sublette making trouble for anyone out here no more."

THIRTEEN

Each time Scratch returned to Waits-by-the-Water throughout the rest of that winter, bringing in more beaver pelts from the streams and creeks ribboning the nearby slopes, he couldn't help but notice how the ricks of buffalo robes multiplied in the fort's storage house when he rode over to the post for the sound of male voices, some man's talk, or just to hear a bit more English than he could wring out of his wife.

And with the mountain man's every visit to the stockade, young Sublette gently prodded Scratch. "Ain't you getting a little old to be traipsing off all alone into them snowy hills anymore?"

Bass's eyes would twinkle, and he'd wink at the older Vasquez when he replied, "I ain't so old I can't take care of myself, you pup."

"Man smart as you," Sublette chided, "I would've thought you'd figured out some easier way to make a living."

On that Louis Vasquez would agree. "Trapping's gotta be some of the meanest work any man can do, Scratch."

"Hard work never kill't no man I know of," he grumbled over the lip of his tin cup.

Every visit Sublette would say, "Don't you figure it's time

you quit scratching out a living with your hands, and start making your living with your wits?"

"I told you, I ain't fit out to be no trader," Bass told them, a little stronger this third time, as they sat out a storm.

At the stockade walls a wolfish wind howled as dawn approached. The sudden subfreezing gale had come on so fiercely that Scratch abandoned their camp and hurried his wife and daughter through the moaning trees that loomed out of the darkness to reach the walls of the fort. In the last few hours Waits-by-the-Water and Magpie had slept snugly in a far corner of the trading room behind two bales of buffalo robes while he had dozed fitfully, his back propped against a pack of beaver in another corner.

Once Vasquez had awakened, he shoved open the plank door to start some coffee brewing over the fire Scratch kept going in the mud and river-stone fireplace. Two of the fort employees had abandoned their blankets to sit before the flames, kneading their cold hands and inhaling the luring fragrance of brewing coffee.

It wasn't long before Sublette himself had appeared at the ill-fitting door where a sudden gust billowed a rooster tail of snow around him as he struggled to shut off the wind, forced to throw his shoulder against the rough planks. Even as he sat and accepted his tin cup from Vasquez, Sublette had begun to prod the old mountain man.

"When you going to admit you're just the man Louis and me need to trade with the bands hereabouts?"

"There's traders, and there's trappers," Titus snapped. "And one ain't fit to be the other."

Then he sat silent while Vasquez moved from man to man with the huge coffeepot, filling each steaming tin before moving on.

"Pretty plain our friend doesn't want us to beg him anymore, Andrew," the Spaniard stated with a wry look of amusement on his face. "The matter's dead. Isn't a concern to Scratch that the bottom is getting torn out from under the beaver trade. He doesn't have to worry with none of it."

"Damn right," Scratch grumbled. "I'll stay on trapping what I can, trading for what I need. I ain't been a hired man in almost eleven years. So I ain't about to sign on now."

"You got a family," Andrew lobbied. "How you figure to provide for them when beaver goes to hell?"

"Just the way any man would!" he shrieked, then realized how loud his voice had grown and sneaked a quick look at the far corner where wife and daughter slept. Whispering, he continued, "We ain't gonna starve, long as I can hunt."

Sublette asked, "How do you propose to pay for lead and powder? For your coffee and tobacco, sugar and salt—not to mention those nice things your wife deserves?"

Bass snorted with a grin. "Damn, if you ain't got a lot of your oily-talkin' brother Billy in you, young Sublette," and he hoisted his coffee cup in salute. "Comes to it, a man with a strong back and his wits about him can allays find himself work."

Vasquez said, "We got work for you right here."

"Dammit, boys—ain't neither of you give thought I got me a Crow wife? How you ever 'spect me to take a Crow woman into them 'Rapaho and Shian camps?"

Sublette shrugged, muttering, "I . . . I—"

"You doing your damndest to make me think you got horse apples for brains, ain'cha?"

"It ain't so foolish as you're making it out to be," Sublette argued as he glanced over at his partner, finding Vasquez grinning in his dark face. "You been riding off from her to trap all winter long. Come back to your wife and her camp when it pleases you. Tell me what's so different with going off to find some villages and trade for their buffalo robes?"

"Long as there's beaver in the hills, there's lots of differ'nce," he answered firmly. "I'm a man gonna choose how he makes his living, how he works out the rest of his days."

Vasquez came over and squatted down next to Titus. "Ever you consider trading with the Crow up north? You're married to one, gotta know plenty of them bucks too. It might work out well for you and us."

But he wagged his head. "Things ain't so good 'tween me and them Sparrowhawks right now. Ain't none of you been paying no notice I spent the winter here, 'stead of up there in Absaroka? Don't that tell you nothing?"

"Just figured we might help you and you help us," Vasquez explained. "I traded among 'em myself couple winters ago. Lost two of my men to the Blackfoot, but damn if that spring of thirty-four I didn't haul better'n thirty packs of buffalo up to Campbell's post at the mouth of the Yellowstone."

"Crow trade ain't wuth the trouble," Bass declared. "Not long after the company bought out Campbell and your big brother Billy, they found things so tough up there on the Yallerstone in Crow country that they pulled back from the Bighorn—moved their post to the Tongue."

Andrew whistled low. "Don't say?"

" 'Sides, the company booshways already got 'em someone living with the Crow. He sees they trade their furs off only to him and the company."

"That Negra Beckwith," Sublette grumbled, then grinned. "But I'll bet you'd do fine working for us up there."

Titus dug a fingernail at his itchy scalp. "Trader at Fort Cass, fella named Tullock, he asked me 'bout taking Beckwith's job last spring."

Vasquez leaned close. "Company isn't happy with him?"

"Tullock says Beckwith spends too much time making war on the Crow's enemies," Bass explained. " 'Stead of making them Crow warriors trap beaver for the company. Tullock ain't figgered it out: up there near the Blackfoot country, there ain't but one choice for them Crow. They can trap flat-tails, or they can protect their families."

"But down here," Sublette replied with gusto, "Injuns don't have the Blackfoot to fret over! You agree to be our trader, you can see that the bands in these parts bring us their furs instead of taking them down to the Arkansas, or up to Fort William on the North Platte. You make 'em see how good they'll have it trapping beaver for us, making buffalo robes for Vasquez and Sublette."

"Naw," Scratch answered with a dull echo as he brought his tin cup to his mouth. Waits-by-the-Water settled beside him. She kissed his cheek and rested her head against his upper arm.

"Magpie asleep?" he asked her in English.

She nodded and spoke in his tongue. "Yes. She hungry soon."

"Storm's 'bout played itself out," Bass said, gazing at that one window in the room where a sheet of thin, translucent rawhide had been tacked over a square hole sawed in the cottonwood logs to serve as a crude windowpane. "Figgered to pack up and move out this morning anyways."

"But now the snow will be so deep," she protested in Crow, gripping his arm fiercely, as if she would physically keep him there.

"The two of us, we've been through worse," he answered in her tongue. "So don't you worry. There's beaver yet—believe me. And I mean to trap my share of it."

He set his empty cup down, looking at Sublette and Vasquez. To them he said in English, "I mean to trap my share of what beaver's left, no matter that traders like you don't give me much for my plews no more."

With winter retreating up the slopes more each day, Bass was able to push farther into the recesses of that eastern front of the central Rockies. As the days lengthened and warmed with the arrival of spring, he stayed out longer, visiting their camp on the South Platte for shorter stays.

While the sun warmed the earth late those mornings he spent near the stockade walls, Bass loved to grab his daughter and her soft doe-skin ball Waits-by-the-Water had sewn together, slowly trudging hand in hand over to a patch of open ground where they tossed and kicked and even batted the ball across the ground with limbs he snapped off of some deadfall. Although she couldn't move all that fast, stumbling and pitching into the new grass more than her share, Magpie nonetheless scrambled back to her feet laughing, chirping, eager to continue their exhausting play. Without fail, their game always ended with Titus chasing after his daughter, arms waving over his head, fingers crooked clawlike as he bellowed the battle roar of a grizzly, eliciting ear-shattering squeals and giggles from the little one as she peered over her shoulder at the terrible man-beast pursuing her.

At the edge of the meadow stood Waits-by-the-Water, always watching, smiling, laughing with them each time either father or daughter spilled, rolling in the cool, wet grass. Day by day Magpie got better at smacking the ball away from him, better at staying on her feet, better able to dodge and sidestep her father until he would collapse on the ground, huffing from exhaustion while she leaped upon his chest to pull at his long hair or his beard.

"Popo play! Popo play!" she would cry in English, unable yet to call him *papa,* as she tugged at his graying curls as if to drag him to his feet so he could continue their game.

"Popo tired, Magpie," he would mimic her pet name for him. "Popo sleep now."

Then Titus would shut his eyes to feign sleep until she bent over his face, gently nudging back an eyelid to inspect his condition. Each time she did, Scratch would immediately roar and leap up, snatching her into his arms, hoisting her overhead, spinning, spinning until he made himself so dizzy he had to collapse again, both of them laughing as Waits-by-the-Water leaped on them both.

These warming days of early spring were good. Though their times together were brief because the beaver were sleek with winter coats, he did his best to make the most of every visit before he rode off again. One day soon, he promised, they would start north for rendezvous in the valley of the Green, not so much to trade furs off for their necessaries as much as he hankered to see familiar faces again—to learn what old friends had gone under, who had abandoned the mountains, and who remained steadfast as this way of life slowly burned itself out like the final ember in a fire that had flared far too hot.

Far back in the hills again, he had encountered sure sign of Indians for something on the order of a week, moving his camp a little each day. At first he saw the smoke of distant fires. Then spotted some far-off riders. And even crossed a fresh trail that came down from the saddle above him two days back. Four of them, perhaps five. At least there were five horses. No telling how many riders. Might only be hunters, their packhorses laden with elk as the game grazed farther and farther up the slopes with each week's warming.

But for the past two days of making cold camps—chewing on dried meat, going without coffee, and sleeping without a fire—Bass hadn't run across any new sign of the horsemen.

"Likely 'Rapaho," he grumbled to himself now as he pulled the trap sack loose from Samantha's packsaddle, the way he had grumbled countless times in the last week. "Taking furs in to trade with Sublette and Vaskiss. Get 'em more powder and shot."

More than once Bass had returned from his trapping forays to find Arapaho lodges pitched outside the walls of Fort Vasquez, come there to trade for what they needed, perhaps wheedling for what they coveted, willing to steal what wasn't nailed down when the white men turned their backs.

Losing some of his hair made his gut burn with an unquenchable hatred for the tribe. Finally Scratch had taken his revenge upon the very man who had scalped him nine years ago.

How cleansing it had been to exact that brutal retribution.*

And even though the red bastards had put an arrow in his shoulder more than two winters back, somehow Titus always managed to hurt the Arapaho more than they had hurt him.

Over the years he had come to learn there were tribes and bands he could deal with, and tribes who meant trouble straight up. Even among the Crow, he had discovered there were good and there were those whose hearts lay in a dark and shadowy place. He figured it had to be just that way with the Arapaho. A man had to be on the watch for Bannock too, a bunch who always did their damndest to run off with what they could. Then there were the Ute, a peaceable enough people. And those Shoshone who had healed him, perhaps saved his life, though Slays in the Night had inexplicably turned on him later: stolen Bass's horses, tried to kill his old white friend.

Maybeso there really was good and bad in each bunch, he had begun to believe this long, wet winter. Just as there were good men who were his friends among the company brigades, there would always be men like Silas Cooper or that parley-voo Chouinard. Skin color didn't make no difference, he allowed.

Except when it came to the Blackfoot.

They were the foulest creatures God ever put on the earth. Why, those red sons of bitches had butchered more good men Scratch knew of. If ever there was a tribe that deserved the iron fist of God's own wrath rubbing them out in one fell swoop, he believed it was the Blackfoot. Evil incarnate.

Late in the day after lying back in the shadows wrapped in a robe, Titus led Samantha out of hiding, heading downhill for the swampy bottom ground where he set more than a dozen traps that morning. The beaver had been busy there in the shade of the leafless quaky, stirring from their winter lodges to fell the saplings they fed their young. That half of the meadow the sun could not yet reach this time of the year was still slicked with inch-thick ice. The rest of the clearing warmed enough to become a bog by day, but refroze each night.

Now he needed to gather all his traps before returning to camp;

---

* *Crack in the Sky*

tomorrow he'd be on his way even higher. What with the way the tiny freshets were feeding every little stream, how so many of them wove together to form gushing creeks that spilled on down the slopes, Titus figured the high country had to be melting. And if the snow was softening, then there surely had to be a way of punching his way back into that country where the beaver slumbered, yet undisturbed.

When he pulled up that first trap, Bass found it empty. Into one of the two trap sacks it went, clattering softly as the iron jaws and chain settled against Samantha's side where the deer-hide sack hung suspended from the elk-horn pack-saddle. The second clutched a fat, sleek beaver captured in its jaws. Glancing at the sun, he figured he had enough time to skin the animal out there and then. That done, the trap went into the other sack with the green hide he had rolled tightly. On and on he went, collecting at least two beaver for every three traps he pulled from the water—

Samantha's ears came up as she froze.

Bass held his breath. Stilled his hands over the carcass he was skinning in the cold, damp grass beginning to slick with ice here as the sun's light continued to fade from the sky. For the longest time he listened, his eyes searching the brush, the trees, always coming back to look at the mule—watching her eyes, her nostrils, until she finally snorted and dipped her head to tear contentedly at the grass.

He breathed again, relieved, and went back to trimming the hide from the two back legs, then sawed off the huge tail. But instead of pitching this tail out with the gut-pile, Titus decided to save it, perhaps cook it tomorrow after they had climbed high enough, far enough that no skulking redbelly would follow.

Gathering tail, hide, and trap, he stood and heard his knees crackle in protest. The years of cold, wading and working in frozen streams, were exacting their toll on his joints. Tortured more every season with aching, icy stabs of pain, he worried how long his body would be able to endure, how long before he could no longer provide for those who counted upon him.

He glanced over at the big Derringer rifle leaning against the brush, then decided against gathering it up, pushing instead for the pack mule, his arms already burdened. At Samantha's side he dropped the trap with a clatter, then spread the green, sticky hide across her wide rump, hair side down. On the gummy flesh he laid the beaver tail and quickly rolled it within the hide.

Pulling back the top of the trap sack, Titus dropped the green plew inside—crying out with pain as the iron tip of the arrow slashed a furrow along his right shoulder, pinning his right hand against the wide wooden packsaddle support.

Gritting his teeth with that exquisite trail of fire scorching its way up his arm, Scratch jerked around, hearing the war cry burst from the brush at the edge of the clearing. Just one voice. A lone figure among those leafless trees, nocking a second arrow against the bowstring.

Twisting back to look at his right hand, bloodied and impaled on the arrow shaft that quivered with every pulse of his bright red blood, quivered with every shudder of uncontrollable pain that sent its tremor through the arm. Gently he flexed the fingers a little, finding that every one of them still moved. Just a little, what with the pain it caused—but they moved.

He seized the shaft with his left hand, slid the fist down until it smeared the blood oozing from the wound, and pulled. The arrow did not budge.

When the second arrow struck the mule's flank, they yelped in pain together as Samantha jerked, kicking a hind leg, slashing his shin with her hoof as she tried to escape the cause of her torment. With each buck she made and tremor that shot through her muscles, he grunted anew with his own pain.

Behind him the warrior suddenly screamed again, shouting this time a rhythmic, off-key war song as he jabbed another arrow against the bowstring and brought the weapon up.

Slapping the mule, driving his knee up against her belly, Scratch got Samantha turned a quarter circle before she threw her weight back against him, angrily twisting her head around to stare at him with wide, cruel eyes—as if she couldn't understand why he wasn't doing more to ease her pain.

The third shaft struck the far side of the packsaddle with such force that it quivered as she lunged in a sidestep against him, knocking his feet out from under him, suspending her master from that shaft buried in the wooden packsaddle frame.

Grunting in torment, he scrambled to regain his footing. His wet moccasins slipping on the damp grass, Bass choked down the hot ball his stomach hurled against his tonsils. A wave of icy pain had begun to numb his brain. Scratch's eyes glazed over with stinging tears as he finally planted his feet and stood, instinctively reaching for the belt pistol with his left hand—yanking the weapon free as the mule twisted, shoving him backward so hard he lost his balance again.

Pushing himself upright, Titus blinked his eyes clear, finding the warrior dropping his quiver off his shoulder to the ground.

At that moment Bass went dry-mouthed, suddenly hearing the approach of another pony, another voice—this second still disembodied somewhere in the trees behind the first attacker.

Narrowing his gaze on that bowman who was straightening after removing the quiver so he could drag a brass-headed tomahawk from the back of his belt, for the first time Titus realized how the cards were stacked against him.

One-handed.

With only one shot.

And now a second warrior had appeared back in that dapple of light and shadow among the skinny lodgepole and bone-bare quaky.

The bowman was already in motion, his arm cocked overhead as he sprinted toward the white man and the mule, screaming with guttural bravado over a sure kill.

No more than fifteen yards between them.

Scratch firmly squeezed his sweaty left hand around the pistol butt.

Ten yards . . .

But he had to relax that grip to clumsily thumb back the hammer mounted on the right side of the weapon.

Five yards—

With the frizzen flush against the pan, and the hammer back to full cock, he didn't allow himself the time to hold and aim as he plopped his pistol arm down atop the mule's rump.

The warrior dodged to his right, starting to career around the rear of the mule.

Whirling to his left with the target, Scratch pulled the trigger.

Samantha shuddered, jerked sideways at the gunshot, prompting another wave of nausea through him as the icy pain flushed clear up to his shoulder the moment she settled back to all four.

On the far side of the mule the bowman skidded to a stop, backed one step, then a second, when he collapsed backward, a dark stain spreading on the left side of his chest. There he thrashed and gurgled a moment before the second attacker emerged from the tree line.

Free of the tangle of lodgepole and aspen, the horseman brutally kicked his pony. This second attacker did not wear a war shirt—only a buffalo-fur vest that flapped open with the rhythm of the gallop as he brought the forestock of his muzzle loader down to rest on the crook of his bare left arm—racing toward the open ground where the white man and that mule began to dance in a tight circle.

Yelling at Samantha didn't help settle the mule, but it was nonetheless as loud as that Arapaho war cry.

Flinging the empty pistol aside, the trapper wrapped his left hand around the shaft and gave it another mighty heave. Unable to budge the arrow.

He had no weapon but his knife now. His rifle was propped against the distant brush, his camp ax lay a few yards closer among a small pile of float-sticks. Both weapons might as well have been on the other side of those peaks for all the good they could do him now.

If he couldn't free the arrow from the packsaddle, he had to free his hand.

Clenching his teeth, Scratch threw a shoulder into the mule's ribs to turn her, putting Samantha between him and the oncoming horseman for the moment—then snapped the shaft off just above his bleeding hand.

He tasted sour, stinging bile as he dragged his right hand up the short section of arrow, over the frayed splinters, and it was free.

Dragging in a huge breath to push back the warm, liquid unconsciousness he realized was about to overwhelm him, Titus looked at the rifle. Saw it was too far. And realized the camp ax lay too far away too.

Now that the mule had danced them around part of a tight circle, Bass found himself staring down at the dead warrior.

Leaping aside, dodging right, then left, as the horseman approached, Titus gave the warrior nothing more than a moving target as he raced by.

Once the horseman shot past and was wrenching back on his single rein, Scratch lunged for the dead bowman. Skidding onto his knees, he peeled back those fingers locked around that tomahawk handle, one by one, until he ripped the weapon free of the death grip.

Wheeling in a crouch, he found the horseman had turned, kicking his pony savagely, coming back for another try with his short-barreled rifle. Bass dodged, the warrior swerved, swinging the weapon's muzzle toward the white man as he started his pass—

Scratch was already leaping, that left arm swinging, planting the brass-headed tomahawk under the two bare brown arms crooked to hold the rifle on its target.

Sensing the broad blade crunch through bone, Bass drove the weapon into the naked chest with all that left arm and both shoulders could muster—toppling the horseman as he ripped downward with the tomahawk.

Even as the rider landed on his back, he had both hands locked around Bass's wrist as he struggled to pull the tomahawk from his rib cage. Spewing bloody, gurgling oaths, the warrior struggled with an unheralded fury in his final moments.

With his strong left arm imprisoned by the enemy, Bass reached at the back of his belt with the injured right hand for his thin-bladed skinning knife, pulled it from the sheath decorated with brass tacks.

In that instant the trapper's knife hung frozen above him, the warrior relaxed his grip on the white man's left wrist—staring transfixed at the weapon poised above him.

Driving the blade deep into that notch at the base of the Indian's throat, Scratch yanked and pulled with all his might, savagely tearing back and forth, slashing the windpipe that wheezed with a last rush of air, severing thumb-thick arteries that gushed free those last tremulous pumps of a heart not yet stilled.

Hot blood splattered him with such force that he was blinded as he tumbled back from the horseman's body.

Landing on his side, Bass heaved for wind. Resting on his right elbow, he dragged his left forearm across his eyes, clearing them of crimson spray.

A few feet away the warrior lay motionless on his back—totally still but for the quivering flex of the fingers on both hands that once had gripped the white man's wrist, still but for the tremble of his lips as they fought to speak unuttered words in that deadly silence suspended between killer and killed.

He began to catch his breath, the thunder slowly diminishing in his ears. Staring at the dying man, Scratch grew aware of the breeze quietly nuzzling the branches of the surrounding trees. Aware that the warrior's pony had come to a stop near Samantha and contentedly tore at the short new grass emerging at the border of the old snow still crusted in a dirty, ragged line at the edge of the tree shadows.

Eventually he realized that in staring at the horseman's bloody chest, he was noticing something odd, something out of place. There above the abdomen smeared with the splatter of glistening crimson, some of the copper flesh was not near as dark as the rest.

Rocking onto his knees, Titus crabbed over to the warrior and studied that skin. Scarred—perhaps by hanging himself from a sun-dance pole. Then he suddenly realized those scars covered more flesh than sun-dance punctures high on the pectoral muscles.

There was even something of a pattern to them.

With his bloody right hand Scratch swiped at some of the spatter of thick, congealing blood. It took another swipe with his left hand to remove enough of the blood to see what lay beneath it.

That lighter skin did form a pattern across the warrior's cinnamon-colored chest.

Shoving aside both flaps of the warrior's buffalo-fur vest, he quickly rubbed away more of the blood.

"Goddamn," he whispered, stunned.

Scratch raised his face to the sky deepening suddenly with the sun's last whimper, its crown just disappearing over the distant peaks.

When he opened his eyes again, Bass laid both of his palms flat against the two scars.

"This were a brave man, Grandfather," he said in no more than a whisper. "He lived them many winters you gave him after I handed the bastard back his life. Tol't him to go back to his people, so he could tell 'em the story of all I done to the nigger what took my ha'r."

Removing his hands from the scars, Titus gazed down once more at *T* and the *B* he had scraped in this warrior's chest many summers ago when he had finally taken his revenge on the scalper.

"I hope you saw fit to let him have children, Grandfather," he whispered. "Brave man what had to drag hisself back to his village. Maybeso he crawled till someone come out looking for him. A brave man ought'n have children."

Such a warrior had some mighty powerful medicine.

Bass sensed the chill drag its finger down his spine like a drip of ice water. He turned suddenly to look over his shoulder as if he had been warned.

Likely more of them. Where there were two, there would be more. And if they didn't start looking for these two dead men tonight, they surely would be coming at first light. From the sign he had run across the last few days, these two might even belong to that hunting party working this side of the mountain.

With a shudder he stood, already feeling regret that he would have to endure another night wrapped in his buffalo robe and blanket rather than enjoying the comfort of a small fire. He needed to get back up to the rocks where he had camped, throw everything together, and get as far from there as he could before sunup.

The Arapaho's pony was skittish as he approached, but with its long loop of rein played out on the ground, Scratch was able to bring the animal close and tie it off to Samantha for companionship. Slowly inching alongside the nervous horse, he stopped. Brushing his hand across the half robe the warrior had draped across the horse's back, the trapper suddenly realized what he had yet to do.

"Easy, boy," he whispered as he gently dragged the long section of buffalo hide from the animal's back, turned, and gazed at the line of trees gone to shadow.

There in the dusk he knew he didn't stand a chance finding any of those lodgepole or aspen with limbs big enough. And he sure didn't have time to waste cutting branches and lashing together some lattice to construct a tree scaffold. Besides, he told himself, the others would be coming along tomorrow, and odds were they would undo all that Bass would attempt to do now.

Still, he realized he must do what he could do.

A brave man deserved a proper burial, especially if he was buried by the man who had killed him.

What one warrior did for another.

As an inky twilight deepened, in the distance he spotted a tangle of boulders that had torn themselves away from the mountainside above him aeons ago. The top of those rocks would have to do. As good a place to offer up the body to the elements as any man could ever want, as good as any brave warrior could ask.

As he struggled to lift the body, to hoist it over his shoulder, then onto the back of the pony, Titus found his right hand growing numb, the hot pain diminishing the more he demanded of the hand. After making his first ascent to decide upon the best route to reach the top of the boulders, Bass laid the buffalo hide on the gently arched crown of the highest rock, then returned for the body.

Looping the end of his rawhide rope under the dead man's arms, he dragged the body to the bottom of the boulders, then began to climb. As he reached a narrow shelf, he would turn and haul back on the rope, bringing the body up behind him. Once it lay at his feet, Scratch climbed a little higher. Then hoisted the warrior too. Higher and higher still, until he finally heaved the body onto the edge of that tallest boulder.

Turning his back on the faint light of that band of sky in the west, he stared to the east and smiled with satisfaction. It was good: here the sun would not be blocked as it rose come morning.

Flipping the buffalo robe fur side up, he stretched it out to its full length, then dragged the body atop the hide so the warrior's feet would point to the east, greeting the morning sun.

For a few minutes he remained there, catching his breath while the air grew cold, that last bit of early-spring warmth sucked out of the earth with the onrush of night. Finally Titus started to slide back down, knowing what he had to do.

He would gather up the enemies' weapons, strip the first man of any tradable clothing, then search for the second Arapaho pony before he led the two animals and Samantha back to the rocky outcrop where he had pitched his temporary camp. There he would tie everything onto the mule and ponies, then ride downslope through the night.

Maybe the time had come for him to get moving anyway.

Wasn't going to be healthy for him to lollygag around this part of the country for some seasons to come.

FOURTEEN

"White wim-men?" she parroted back the two English words she heard so many of the trappers around her shouting at that moment.

"Yep," Bass told his wife. "They say some white womens gonna be here soon."

Waits-by-the-Water noticed how his green eyes narrowed with concern as he stared toward the mesa bordering the eastern edge of the river valley.

In Crow she asked, "You Americans really do have white women?"

He looked at her quizzically. "Course we do. Mothers and sisters. Only ones what don't grow up to be wives are the ones what become whores."

"Whores—I never heard that word from your tongue before."

"A woman what lays with a man for the money he pays her," and he turned his eyes away, staring at the growing bustle of activity as the electrifying news spread.

"Women who open their legs for men?" she asked in her language, still somewhat bewildered. "Indian women who take the beads and ribbon to open their legs for you white men?"

"Maybeso," he admitted as he turned back to gaze down at her face. "I laid with my share of white whores back east in my day. But as long as I been out here in these mountains, as many Injun gals what I laid with, never have I thought Injun women was whores the same as white women—"

"Why not?" she interrupted, scratching the top of the dog's head. "If I opened my legs for you men so I could get a new knife or some hawks-bells, wouldn't I be a whore like your white women?"

After some thought he eventually wagged his head. "Somehow, it don't seem the same to me. Them whores all the time stay where the men come to lay with 'em. It's what they do to make their living—like I trap beaver to make mine."

"In that land where you came from, are there more whores, or more wives?"

He grinned a little, saying, "I s'pose there's many more wives."

She sighed, grinning herself as she snuggled against him. "A long time ago when I was a young girl and the first white men were coming to visit my people, many of us came to believe that among your people there must not be very many women."

"Not many, eh?"

With a nod Waits explained. "We decided you must not have many women where you come from because you white men had such an appetite for *our* women."

Squeezing her shoulder, he replied, "There are more'n enough white women back there. I sure as hell knew enough of the worst for me to decide I like Injun gals best."

Gazing up at his greenish eyes, Waits felt consoled enough to say, "I am glad to hear you tell me this. When I heard the riders shouting that white women were coming, I grew afraid."

"Afraid? Of what?"

"Afraid that you white men were growing tired of Indian women so your traders were bringing white women here to lay with you men in trade for your beaver."

He snorted with laughter, throwing his head back a moment, then clutched her securely in both arms as the first of the riders started peeling away from the trappers' camps, in a mad dash for the mesa that lay on the eastern rim of this valley of the Green River where the trappers and Indians always found an abundance of wood, water, and grass for their animals. Here at the mouth of Horse Creek, the Green flowed roughly west to east. South along the banks of the creek stood the lodges of two of those four visiting tribes, while west along every twist and bend in the river itself the company trappers had crowded their camps.

"I'll lay a year's wages that the women coming to ronnyvoo ain't whores, woman," he reassured her.

If not the sort to lay with men who gave them presents, she decided, then the newcomers had to be wives.

At the first noisy announcement from those riders galloping into rendezvous, Waits-by-the-Water had been very scared, believing that with the arrival of these white creatures, the trappers would have their pick, forsaking the Indian women, abandoning their Indian wives.

In her people's oral history, it was told the white man first sent horses among the Crow, then sent firearms to the Absaroka, followed by bright, shiny, wonderful trade goods. It wasn't long before the white man himself came among them. Each of these arrivals caused volcanic changes for her tribe. So it was natural now that she should convince herself the white man was bringing as many of his women as he had brought horses, or guns, or tin cups and hanks of beads.

Understandable that if the white man didn't bring the women there to lie with the trappers at their summer gatherings, then the women would have to be wives. She had imagined a trader caravan chock-full of pale-skinned women, enough to provide one partner for every trapper. And some of those white women would likely have hair on their faces, just as the majority of white men she had seen in her life grew hair on their faces.

Among the Crow, neither gender grew facial hair. In coming to view beards and mustaches as a characteristic of the white race, it seemed very natural to assume that many of the white man's women would grow the same beards and mustaches on their faces.

Still, her greatest concern about that long trader caravan bringing an untold crowd of white women the way it brought a dazzling and innumerable array of trade goods lay in her fear that the white men would abandon their Indian wives, forsake their Indian children, and return to their own kind. Waits-by-the-Water did not want to think of life without Ti-tuzz.

"The women are here to marry white men?"

He answered, "Naw, I figure they come with their husbands."

"Among your people, can one man steal the wife of another?"

"Yes," he answered, then suddenly looked down at her with some alarm. His eyes quickly softened as he must have read the hurt that had to show on her face. "But don't you worry 'bout me and them white women. I had near all I could stand of their kind back east." He embraced her fiercely. "No white woman ever gonna take me away from you."

She gripped him tight, pressing her cheek against his chest, feeling safe there, safe enough to tell him of an old fear.

"When you left me behind with Rosa two winters ago, I was so afraid I would never see you again," she confided as more shouts reverberated in the distance. "I feared you would be killed and I would be left to live among strangers in a land I did not know. But even more frightening, I was afraid you would stay in that country from where you came—you would find a white woman and forget about your Crow woman."

She felt him rub his chin on the top of her head.

"You are the one I love," he said to her in his halting Crow. "Maybe it's only my poor luck, but every white woman I've knowed has been faithless to me, one way or another. For more winters than I can count, I've looked for one woman who would remain loyal to me, a woman who could show me that I was the most important person in her heart."

"You are all my life," she told him.

"You won't be scared of no white women?"

Gazing up at him, Waits replied, "No. You have given me your promise."

"How 'bout me taking you and Magpie to have yourselves a long look at them women?"

A slow smile crossed her face, and Waits nodded. "Yes, let's go now and see these women creatures with their pale skin and their hairy faces."

By the time they were saddled up, with Magpie riding behind her father, loping up to that flat mesa across the Green, more than half-a-hundred mounted trappers were racing for the head of the caravan in the middistance. Hundreds of mules and horses, along with many small two-wheeled objects her husband explained were called carts. As the trappers kicked their horses into a furious charge on the front of the pack train, Waits spotted a new sort of two-wheeled cart that appeared to be a small box sitting on its wheels, the front of the box laid open so two people could control the pair of horses attached to it.

All those trapper guns erupted with smoke, and a heartbeat later she heard the distant weapons boom from the caravan in a ragged order. Then her husband was laughing, harder than he had laughed for some time.

"Damn if them pilgrims don't figger those boys are Injuns on the attack!" he roared, his eyes moist with tears. "Lookit 'em! Stopping that pack train and circling them carts right there to make a fight of it!"

A handful of figures at the head of the march stopped, turned, and were yelling at the pack train.

"I'll wager the pilot for that outfit is telling 'em just what a bunch of softheaded idjits they are—being skairt of them white fellers come riding out, whooping and hawing!"

That broad front of bare-chested trappers was continuing to race for the caravan, unslowed, shouting and shrieking just like warriors as half of their number swept down one side of the incoming train, the other half tearing like demons down the opposite side. Both ends of their charge circled the other and continued their gallop back up the line of march until they reached the head of the procession where they slowed to match the pilot's pace.

When the ceremony began. The white man sure put a lot of importance in this matter of shaking hands and pounding one another on the back, she thought.

"C'mon, woman," Bass said with excitement. "Let's go show Magpie how a white gal looks."

His pony was already bolting away, with Magpie clinging to her father's back the way a small, chubby tick would grip the hide of an old bull as Waits nudged her horse into a gallop.

In nearing the head of the march, she expected him to slow down to the crawl the caravan was taking, but instead her husband kept galloping right on past the leaders. At times he waved that hat he had torn from his head, but he did not ease the pace.

In front of them some strange creatures bolted, starting to peel off to the right and scatter, lumbering with an ungainly gait as two young Indian boys started after the animals, yelling and whipping the air with long sticks. Then they were close enough that she recognized the scattering, bawling animals, those strange creatures the white man brought out to rendezvous every summer to pull his wagons or to give him warm milk. Strange that a race of people so prepared to fight and defend themselves like the whites would have so docile and tranquil an animal while her people grew up among the wild buffalo.

Her husband was slowing as he neared that strange small box set on its four small wheels, his horse jogging sideways to a halt with Magpie laughing merrily at the exhilarating ride. Bass waved to her with his hat. As she came racing up to yank back on the reins, she thought the white man who rode a horse beside the box wagon looked familiar. The rider pushed his hat back from his face. She smiled, recognizing the holy man who had cut the arrowhead from Bridger's back last summer.

The holy man was smiling, waving her over, at the same time saying something to those in the shadow of the box wagon.

As Waits slowed her pony to a walk beside her husband's horse, she felt her eyes grow big, and her chin drop. On one side of the box wagon sat a thin, sour-faced, bony creature who peered out at her with suspicion and alarm from beneath the brim of a black hat that nearly wrapped itself around the woman's face. Dark circles hung like ugly pendants below her glaring, accusing eyes. Waits wondered if this person had ever smiled in her life, much less laughed.

Was this a white woman? No wonder the white man had such an incurable hunger for Indian women!

But the creature seated next to the hard-eyed one caused Waits to gasp. The holy man and her husband were talking at once, shaking hands while Bass dipped his head and introduced their daughter . . . but Waits could not take her eyes off the radiance of the fair-skinned beauty who sat alongside the mousy-haired, mean-eyed, dried-up pucker of a creature.

To her surprise this second white woman pulled her hat from her head, revealing hair the color of which Waits had seen on some white men—but never in such tight curls and ringlets. She reached up and touched one of her own black braids wrapped with strands of blue and red ribbon, bewildered to discover she almost coveted hair like this white woman's—

"Waits-by-the-Water . . ."

Upon hearing her name, she turned to her husband.

"You remember Dr. Whitman?" he asked.

"Yes," she answered in English, and dropped her eyes, adding in Crow, "he is the holy man."

Bass translated her comment to Whitman in English, then continued in Crow for her. "This woman closest to us is the holy man's wife. Both of them are wives of holy men."

"Not whores?"

"No," and Titus shook his head with a wry grin that put Waits at ease with her questioning. "This is Whitman's wife. Her name is Narcissa. Nar-Sis-Sa."

"Nar-Sis-Sa."

The moment the Crow woman repeated it, Narcissa Whitman smiled at her and wiped her brow with a large red bandanna, cheerfully saying, "Hello. What is your name?"

Slowly Waits repeated what her husband had taught her of the white man sounds to her name, "Waits-by-the-Water."

Twisting halfway around on the back of his horse, Bass had managed to loop an arm about his daughter, and she was crawling over his hip to sit in front of him on the pony's bare back.

"This here's my daughter, Magpie," he announced. "Tell these good folks you're pleased to meet 'em, Magpie."

"Pleased mee'cha."

At the child's tinkling reply both Marcus and Narcissa laughed, but neither the sour-faced woman nor her dull-eyed husband showed anything more than indifference bordering on contempt. Ahead of them the column was already resuming its march.

"This year we push on for the Nez Perce country," Whitman explained to Titus as they all set off once more, continuing their descent to the river bottom. "Has Reverend Parker come in to meet us?"

With a shrug Scratch replied, "I ain't see'd him. But I can't say for sure, Doctor. Likely wouldn't know him less'n someone said that's who he was."

"I pray he has returned," the physician added. "He vowed he would—so to lead us back to where we are to establish our mission."

"We will make our way through the wilderness without him if we must," said the woman with the happy eyes.

Waits-by-the-Water found she liked the light-haired one more and more as they pressed on to the rendezvous. But the other woman's glare made her feel self-conscious, as if that dour woman did her best to hold herself above all others by the way she peered down her nose with such haughty disdain.

When they reached the campground chosen for the supply train, the two women were helped down from their wagon while trappers scurried to provide a place to sit in the shade where the women were brought water to drink. Nearby others began to erect a large conical tent. It struck Waits as more and more white men came to gawk at the new arrivals, how those trappers fell over one another to keep the white women from having to lift a hand to help themselves.

Perhaps it was best that these two white women were hurrying on through this mountain west, she decided, best they were bound for the land of the Nez Perce far, far away. Waits-by-the-Water believed it had to be a good omen that the women did not belong to trappers, better instead that they belonged to those who were only passing through. It was plain enough that neither of the white women belonged out there—even Narsis-sa, despite her open friendliness. Both of them looked . . . soft. Not hardy enough to withstand much trial or hardship. And that was pretty much all life held in store in this brutal land.

The white men who had come to this Indian country to catch the beaver had either toughened themselves enough to survive, or they had died. Her husband explained how some of his kind had turned around and fled back to the land of the whites. Waits doubted these soft women raised inside their immobile lodges could endure a nomadic life lived outdoors through all seasons.

For now these two clearly seemed relieved to have reached this raucous white man's gathering. Neither of them appeared to have any children, and it was pretty apparent that neither Narcissa nor the glowering one would have to raise a hand to do much of anything in caring for themselves. In fact, their hands weren't soiled at all. Not the way dirt and soot permanently etched every knuckle and scored every wrinkle on Waits's hands. No doubt these women didn't know the first thing about graining a hide, chopping wood, or removing the organs of an antelope without pricking the bladder or rupturing a bowel. These white women had men who leaped right in to do everything for them. With all those trappers fluttering around like hummingbirds at a vine of sweet blossoms, it was no wonder these women didn't know the first thing about taking care of themselves.

They didn't have to.

The more Waits-by-the-Water watched the comings and goings in that camp, the more she decided it was a very, very good thing these women weren't staying. Almost laughable, she thought, how these hardy, coarse men became such different creatures around their white women. Waits contented herself that the women were only passing through.

And she hoped the white men would bring no more of these soft creatures to this land.

For the first time since Bass could recollect, there were nearly as many free men come to rendezvous as there were company trappers. And a damned sight fewer of both camped this year near the mouth of Horse Creek.

Slightly more than a hundred Americans had come in with the Bridger and Drips brigades, along with no more than fifty Frenchmen between them. With the supply caravan, Tom Fitzpatrick brought in another seventy hands to wrangle more than four hundred horses and pack mules, but the lion's share of those men would be turning right around for the States once the beaver was all bought up.

At Fort Laramie, Fitzpatrick had abandoned the long train of wagons, packing everything they couldn't fit into nineteen two-wheeled carts onto the backs of their mules for that last leg of the journey over the Southern Pass and on to Green River. Milton Sublette, courageously recovering from the recent amputation of his leg, bounced all the way into rendezvous in one of those carts. Before he slid to the ground, Milt strapped on the cork leg purchased for him in Philadelphia by Hugh Campbell, Robert's brother.

It brought some hot moisture to Bass's eyes to watch that man, an unvarnished hero four years before at the Battle of Pierre's Hole, now wobble and waver on that one good leg as old friends rushed up to hug and shake his hand as if it were a pump handle on a long-ago dried-up well. Especially the tall, slab-shouldered Joe Meek and his Shoshone wife.

Titus remembered the story fondly told of this woman and the two inseparable friends. Seasons ago *Umentucken,* the Mountain Lamb, had married Milton Sublette, known as the "Thunderbolt of the Rockies." Back in thirty-two she and their young child had been with Milt's brigade that summer morning in Pierre's Hole when they chanced to bump into a large band of Blackfoot.

Eventually Sublette's leg refused to heal from an arrow wound his friends claimed was poisoned. Reluctantly deciding to return east to have the infection cared for, not knowing if he would ever return to the mountains, Milt gave his wife over to his best friend, Joe Meek. For the last few years Joe had cared for this beautiful woman, raising Milt's child as he did his own.

Shyly now, the Lamb stepped out from behind her new husband and inched up to embrace Sublette.

Not one man there mentioned the tears they saw well in Milt's eyes, or the way he bravely snorted and swiped at his nose as the crowd pounded on his back and gawked at his new cork leg.

"By damn!" Scratch roared. "You ever think you'd have one'a your legs make it to hell afore you!"

"Shit! Don't matter I got only one good leg," Sublette chortled, "I can still outrun the devil hisself!"

"That's right, Scratch!" Bridger agreed. "With you and Meek galloping to keep ahead of the devil, Milt don't have to worry none about running the fastest . . . he only gotta be fast 'nough to stay ahead of *you!*"

"You figger I'm so slow, the devil gonna get his claws in me, eh?"

"Damn right he will, Bass!" Milton bawled with laughter.

"One of these days, mayhaps," Scratch confessed with a grin. "But not till I'm so old and stove-up I can't outrun him no more . . . and all you niggers are already there to greet me!"

By the following day Fitzpatrick's hands had fixed up the largest of a handful of squat log structures first erected a short distance from the Green by Captain Bonneville's fur brigade back in the spring of 1832. Rather than hacking any windows in the crude eighteen-by-eighteen-foot square, the builders settled for what light streamed between the unchinked timbers or through the only entrance: a six-foot-wide, two-foot-high rectangle laid on its side some four feet off the ground. It was through this lone opening that furs were passed in and trade goods handed out, the better to protect against pilfering. For a roof Fitzpatrick's Frenchmen had stretched some oiled sheeting across the timbers they laid overhead in an attempt to protect the valuable goods from those fickle summer storms known to visit this high valley.

All told, more than thirteen hundred Indians were in the valley to greet the incoming train. The Shoshone and Bannock had camped along Horse Creek, while up the Green near Bonneville's Fort both the Flathead and Nez Perce had raised their lodges.

Moseying over to have himself a good look at the trade goods Fitzpatrick had packed out from St. Louis, Titus watched the man in fancy buckskins dismount from his showy white mule and walk up to shake hands with Bridger and Drips. Together the three of them ambled toward the awning where Milt Sublette sat in the shade.

"Who's that in them foofaraw booshway clothes with all the red wool and blue beads?" Scratch asked of a familiar face who had turned from Bridger's side and was walking his way.

"Name's Joshua Pilcher," the tall man said when he stopped beside Bass. "I hear he was on the upper Missouri with Lisa afore Ashley ever come west. When the Spaniard died, Pilcher took over Lisa's company, and they did well till Immel and Jones got butchered by the Blackfoot in twenty-three. Drips and Fontenelle, even one of them Bent brothers, they all worked for Pilcher one time or other. Some time back I heard talk he offered the English up north he'd trap this side of the mountains for the Hudson's Bay."

Glaring at Pilcher, Bass grumbled, "On American territory? That'd make him a traitor to his own country and his own kind!"

"The English turned him down, but a couple years back they made him agent on the upper Missouri for all these Injuns," the big man declared.

"That what brung him here?" Scratch demanded. "Something to do with the Injuns out here?"

"Naw. Says he's come here to buy out Bridger and the rest."

"B-buy 'em out?" Scratch sputtered in surprise. "With whose plews?"

The tall man shrugged. "Sounds like it's St. Louie French money."

"Damn if that don't take the circle." Turning to stare up into the younger man's eyes, Titus said, "I see'd your face at many a ronnyvoo, round some fires, over at the trade tents. But I don't recollect I ever caught your name."

"Shadrach Sweete," the man replied. "And you're Titus Bass."

"How you know me?"

Sweete chuckled. "Hell, anyone runs with Jim Bridger's brigade knows who Titus Bass is."

"But I ain't never trapped with Gabe."

"Don't matter," Sweete replied. "I recollect how we run across you a time or two through the years. Ain't that many of us been out here long as me or you have. 'Sides, Gabe thinks the world of you. Why, ever' time he tells that story of you losing your ha'r, or how you run onto that red nigger years later . . . whoooeee! Them tales keep the greenhorns from sucking in a breath!"

They laughed together; then Scratch asked, "You figger Fitz got his whiskey kegs open yet?"

"I seen him crack 'em my own self," Sweete said.

"You think my word be good as plews with Fitz?"

"Damn if it wouldn't be better'n most."

Bass slapped the tall man on the back. "Then, what say you, Shadrach—let's you and me go have us a drink of that saddle varnish these traders claim is whiskey!"

Sweete struck him as a gentle man shoved down inside a grizzly bear's body. A little taller than Joe Meek, and so wide of shoulder too that Scratch wondered if he could lay a hickory ax handle across that broad beam with no hickory left to hang off at either end.

"Just like you, I come to the mountains myself in twenty-five," Bass replied as one of the clerks poured out the whiskey into a pair of brand-new tin cups.

"But I bet you wasn't no fourteen-year-ol't pup like I was in twenty-five!"

Astonished by that admission, Titus asked, "How the hell you hire on with Gen'l Ashley when you was fourteen?"

"Just lookit me, you cross-eyed idjit!" Sweete bellowed with a disarming smile, standing back to spread his arms. "Even as a pup—I was big for my age!"

"You're still a goddamned pup!" Titus growled at the man who stood a good half foot taller than he did and nudged something just shy of three hundred pounds.

After a long moment of quiet Sweete sighed. "Where's the beaver gone, Scratch?"

He looked at the big man, then took another sip of his whiskey. "There's beaver still, Shad. Up high. Back in a ways where no man's yet gone. There's beaver."

"They say the easy beaver's been caught," Sweete agreed. "Ah, shit—we're on the downside of our trade, what with folks back east wanting silk hats."

"Beaver's bound to rise, Shad," he said with more hope than he felt. "Bound to rise."

"If it don't—what the hell'm I gonna do?" the big man asked. "I come to trap beaver when I was fourteen. What the hell'm I s'posed to do when I can't make a living no more trapping beaver?"

"Let them others get all lathered up, run on back to what you run away from," Bass said. "They just leave more beaver for niggers like you and me!"

At the sharp ring of the voice they both turned and squinted into the sunlight washing over everything beyond that shady copse of trees. A lone rider galloped up, shouting.

"The Nepercy! They're fixing to come over with a parade!" the man huffed as the distant sound of drums first reached them. "Gonna show off front of them white women!"

"I'll bet that'll be some!" Bass exclaimed, bolting to his feet and swilling down the last of his whiskey before handing the empty tin to Sweete. "Be off to fetch my wife and girl so they can see."

Zeke was straining at the end of his rope the moment Titus and his horse hoved into sight, yipping and prancing side to side, his big tail whipping mightily at the return of his master.

"You're gonna have to see this!" Scratch called as he kicked his right leg over and landed on both feet.

He knelt as Magpie lumbered up toward him, clenching a well-moistened strip of dried meat she had been sucking on in one hand. He swept her into his arms and turned to his wife. "C'mon. Get your pony."

"Where are we going in such a hurry?"

"Bet Magpie's never see'd the Nepercy strut like prairie cocks. Likely you ain't either."

He positioned the girl in front of the saddle before he stuffed a left foot into the stirrup and swung his leg over, settling her onto his lap as he came down into the saddle. "Here," he said to his daughter, wrapping her tiny hands around the thick latigo leather. "You hol't on to the reins with me."

Waits came up beside them, leading her pony. When she had leaped onto its bare back, she asked, "Why are the Pierced Noses making a procession?"

"They want to show off for the white women."

He watched how that suddenly soured the expression on her face.

"For the white women," she repeated. "Now the Pierced Noses are gone strange in the head for the white women."

Titus leaned over and gripped her forearm sympathetically. "Don't think nothing of it. Just wanted you and Magpie to see the show."

For a moment Waits gazed at her daughter's cheerful face, then said, "Yes. Let's go see the show these Pierced Noses put on for the white women."

As it turned out, all four tribes eagerly joined in the grand procession as it worked its way toward the site where the missionary women were camped. By the time Scratch and Waits dismounted and tied off their ponies, the front ranks of the march were approaching. Having started their ride at the west end of the valley, the Snake and Bannock passed through the Flathead camp, then the Nez Perce village, sweeping up more and more participants until some four hundred yelling, chanting, shrieking warriors boiled up and down the sides of the parade column.

Stripped as if for the hunt, they wore no more than their breechclout and moccasins, many painted with vivid colors, tying birds and feathers in their hair, wearing the skullcaps of wolves, badgers, even buffalo upon their heads. Shaking lances strewn with the scalp locks taken from vanquished enemies, the horsemen strutted as proudly as any war hero might. Old men rode stately at the center of the march, singing their battle songs as they beat on hand drums or shook buffalo-bladder rattles filled with stream-bottom pebbles. Younger men who had taken no scalps brandished their bows or war clubs or fusils, to which they had tied long strips of red and blue cloth to flutter in the summer breeze.

Within a nearby copse of trees, Captain William Drummond Stewart and Bridger assured Marcus Whitman and Henry Spalding that this noisy, bellicose charge was every bit as harmless as the charge made on them by the trappers racing out to meet the caravan. Both wives appeared at the flaps of their tall conical tent sewn of bed ticking and large enough to comfortably sleep all seven of the missionaries. But the moment pale and sickly Eliza Spalding spied the approach of the screaming warriors, she emitted a pained yelp, slapped a hand over her mouth, and turned on her heel—disappearing back into the sanctuary of her tent.

"Curse these godless savages for their nakedness!" the prim and proper one shrieked in horror as she ducked from sight.

But Narcissa Whitman of the twinkling blue eyes and ready smile clapped her hands together with glee before hurrying on her husband's arm to the edge of the meadow to watch the approach of that cavalcade assembled in honor of the missionaries.

Closer and closer the warriors came, growing noisier, shrieking louder as they drew near until the front ranks spotted the holy man's fair-haired wife. Like the reflex of a muscle, they put their ponies to the gallop, shouting anew as they raced toward that bed-ticking tent, shaking weapons and feathers, scalps and coup-sticks, tearing out and around, leaping again and again over clumps of gray and green sage, spurts of yellowish dust flaring from every flying hoof. When no more than ten yards away, the first chiefs in the parade suddenly swept to the side without slowing in the slightest, careening their snorting, wide-eyed ponies in a maddening loop that took them entirely around the tall conical tent held fast to the prairie with wooden stakes.

Now more than four hundred warriors raced in a crude oval round and round the campsite as Narcissa laughed and clapped and spun with the excitement and color of it all, made immensely happy at this exhibition in her honor. At first a few warriors, then more, reined up in a spray of dust and dismounted, walking their ponies over to examine the Dearborn carriage the missionaries had succeeded in bringing all the way from the States. Outside and in they inspected it, some even crawling in the grass beneath the carriage to get themselves a complete study of it. Others rubbed the top, dragged their fingers across the soft leather-covered horsehair-stuffed seats, or repeatedly picked up and dropped, picked up and dropped the double-tree that harnessed the carriage to a single horse.

"Waits-by-the-Water!"

They both turned to find Narcissa and her husband approaching with quite a crowd in tow. The doctor's wife called out the Crow woman's name again just as they came to a halt before the trapper.

"Please tell your wife it is so good to see her again," Narcissa exclaimed. "I was hoping to before we depart for Oregon country."

Bass translated and Waits nodded self-consciously.

"Mr. Bass," Marcus Whitman began, "my wife and I would like to invite you and your family to have dinner with us tomorrow evening. If that isn't convenient, we'll make it the night after."

"No, 'morrow evening will set just fine by us, Doctor."

"Good," and Whitman smiled genuinely. "Tomorrow it is."

Narcissa took a step forward, reaching up to touch Magpie's bare foot as she sat on her father's shoulders. Then she took up Waits-by-the-

Water's hand and squeezed it, smiling with her whole face. Together she and her husband turned and moved once more into the crowd that inched its way back to that conical tent of blue-striped bed ticking.

"Tomorrow," Waits repeated after they had started back for their ponies.

"Won't it be fun for you and Magpie too?"

"Yes," she answered in English, then turned to face him fully after he lifted Magpie from his shoulders and set her atop his saddle.

Waits-by-the-Water took his empty hand and caressed the fingers gently, looking into his eyes as she said, "It will be a good night to celebrate our happy news."

"What happy news?"

She laid his hand on her belly, pressing it there as she had done once before. "Ti-tuzz . . . you are going to be a father again."

FIFTEEN

A father again?

Why . . . he had a grown daughter back in St. Lou, a woman herself, old enough to give him grandchildren.

This momentous news, all tangled up in his blissful igno-rance of how a woman came to be with child, purely con-founded Titus. While most of his fiber rejoiced at his wife's happiness, there was nonetheless a narrow but hardy spider's thread of baffled wonderment and befuddled concern for the health of a child born of so old a father.

Not that such a thing was so rare in his family; why, at the time his grandpap was born, his great-grandpap was fifty-two! Though Titus never knew the man, he had indeed known his grandpap, hale and hearty, every bit as lean as whipcord and tough as sun-dried rawhide till that fated evening he had told his wife he figured it was time for him to accept God's rest and took to his bed. There he had closed his eyes as if to sleep, slipping away to his mortal rest before morn.

His grandpap's was truly the first dying Titus had ever witnessed, but far from the last his eyes were to behold. Times were Scratch had fervently prayed God would grant him a pass-ing every bit as much at peace as his grandpap's had been. Each time, however, he would realize that simply wasn't the way of a man's seasons out here in this big yonder.

Would folks be awestruck that this man the color and toughness of a lean strop of saddle leather could still father a babe? Would a great number of them stare all mule-eyed and wag their heads in judgment while some would snigger behind their hands when they learned he was going to be a father again?

In the end he supposed these things did not matter—none of those fears or doubts, and surely none of what others thought of him. He was reminded that the way of such things wasn't his to decide, but the doing of something far greater. Not his, but God's. When a man and woman coupled, then Bass figured God eventually saw fit to give them a young'un. As surely as Jim Bridger's wife was now heavy with child.

He glanced over at Cora again as the shadows deepened, finding her still reluctant to join her husband and the others at the missionaries' fire. Instead, the young Flathead princess stood in the shadows behind Bridger, not saying a word, nor joining in the lighthearted talk and bantering laughter. Titus figured she, like Waits-by-the-Water, had grown dismayed by the way the white men acted so differently around the white women.

Maybe later he should pull Gabe off to the side and remind him to assure Cora that he still loved her.

All in all, he had explained to his own wife, it was natural the way the trappers grew so adolescent or fiddle-footed around the white women. Natural because Narcissa Whitman and Eliza Spalding reminded these men of loved ones left far behind in the States. Perhaps a lost love who had broken a young man's heart; maybe a beloved older sister or auntie. Or perhaps an adored mother who had always smiled and caressed and wiped away a little boy's tears.

Natural for a white man to act somewhat childish around those white women, he had explained to his wife, since those white women reminded a man of those he had once loved a lifetime long ago.

After a supper of mountain mutton and elk tenderloin, sliced with their belt knives and eaten using forks made from peeled, forked twigs, Sir William Drummond Stewart opened some of his treasures and brought out more of the exquisite and exotic foods he had packed to the mountains from last winter's sojourn in New Orleans. Besides the savory selections of game, the Scotsman had provided his guests with a sampling of sardines and cured ham packed in newfangled airtight tins. For dessert he had prepared platters heaped with a variety of dried fruits, green mango pickles brought from Caribbean islands, and a butter-colored marmalade made from Seville oranges shipped all the way from Spain.

"Why do you suppose there is such unhappiness on Cora's face?" Titus asked his wife in Crow as Stewart's servant made the rounds with a coffeepot.

For a long moment she gazed at the pregnant Flathead woman. "Among my people a woman lives a step behind her husband."

"That does not tell me why Cora looks sad and angry at the same time."

With a sigh Waits explained. "Don't you see? Her husband is talking too much to the white woman, laughing with her. Maybe Cora thinks her husband would be happier with a white woman for a wife."

"Because the women are from the same people we are?"

For a moment Waits pursed her lips, considering. "Maybe because this husband doesn't talk so much to his wife, doesn't laugh so much with her as he does with the white woman. Perhaps Cora thinks there is something only you whites understand, something we wives will never share with our white husbands."

"So this fear can hurt a woman's heart?"

"Yes," she answered, gazing fully at him as he took the sleeping child from her arms and cradled Magpie in his. "If Cora married one of her own people, they would talk more, maybe even laugh more together too."

"Like we laugh?"

She smiled. "Yes, like us. But not all white men are like you, Ti-tuzz."

He still found that it tickled him each time she stuck her own English pronunciation of his name at the tail end of all her Crow.

As he sat there watching the guests, glancing too at the dejected Cora, Scratch figured he couldn't blame the booshways and trappers from fluttering around the woman. Not only was Narcissa Whitman a treat for the eyes, but she did her best to put them at ease around her, from the highest of company partners to the lowliest of skin trappers. It continued to amuse him how, after more than two days, these hardened mountaineers who annually bought or traded for squaws with carnal abandon were suddenly acting like bashful little boys, or performing like strutting, over-confident adolescents suffering their first schoolhouse crush around Narcissa Whitman.

"So did Black Harris tell you all about my peetreefied forest on your way west, ma'm?" Bridger asked the missionary.

Titus grinned and sipped at his coffee, amused to know what was coming.

"No, not rightly, Mr. Bridger," Narcissa replied. "Each night around the fire Mr. Harris did tell us many a story on our way across the plains. But he claimed he dared not tell any of your stories because no one could do it better than you."

Bridger glanced up at Harris, pilot for that year's supply train, and winked. "Why, thankee, Black."

"G'won and tell the lady 'bout your forest, Gabe," Harris instructed. "I told her: good as I was at spinning a yarn, Jim Bridger still be the champeen spinner."

Grinning, Bridger took a sip of his coffee, then set down his cup as his eyes danced over the five greenhorns from the States. Then he began his tale by explaining how he and his brigade came to find themselves in a new stretch of country up near Blackfoot territory. Gabe told how he was out hunting when he came across some game birds singing sweetly in the trees.

"Pulling down my sights on one, I fixed to shoot it in the head, so I wouldn't ruin the meat," he declared. "And I did just that, shot the damn bird's head right off—excuse my language, ma'm."

"Yes, of course. Please—go ahead," Narcissa pleaded, anticipation bright on her face.

"Durn if I didn't see the head go flying off in a hunnert pieces," Bridger continued. "And when the body went toppling off its branch, why—just like the head, it broke in more'n a thousand pieces when it hit the ground."

"B-broke into pieces?" Dr. Whitman echoed with a disbelieving sputter.

"Well, now—I walked right over there and couldn't find my bird," Bridger declared. "But laying there at my feet was pieces of that bird, pieces laying all over the place. Like it was a broken rock. I picked some up and studied 'em real hard. Weren't like no bird I'd ever laid eyes on. Hard as rock."

"Gone to stone?" Narcissa asked with a gasp.

"I 'spect so," Bridger answered. "Looked up at the tree where that li'l bird was sitting, singing its pretty songs. When I tapped on that tree with my knuckles—found it hard as rock too."

"The tree was made of stone too?" Henry Spalding inquired with a bemused haughtiness.

"Not just the tree and that bird," Bridger carried on with a wag of his head. "Right about then I heard more birds and their pretty calls. Ain't shy to tell you I stood there with my jaw hung down so far I was 'fraid I'd step on it. For the longest time I waited right where I was, staring up at them peetreefied trees where even more of them peetreefied birds was singing more of their peetreefied songs!"

It felt so good to laugh with all the others who roared, stamping their feet, slapping one another on the back, dabbing at the tears in their eyes from laughing so hard. Even Cora had to grin a little behind her hand when the others hooted and whooped at her husband's whopper.

Scratch said, "Say, Gabe—why don't you tell these folks 'bout that looking-glass mountain you run onto one day you was out hunting elk."

"Did you tell 'em that story, Black?" Bridger asked.

Harris shook his head. "I had 'nough of my own tales to tell 'em 'bout walking to St. Lou with Billy Sublette and that poor ol' dog we had to eat to stay alive! So you go right ahead and tell 'em 'bout your looking-glass mountain your own self."

Jim explained that one autumn day years before, he was out on his trapline when he noticed a fine-looking bull elk with an impressive array of antlers grazing not all that far upstream. Carefully, quietly he made his stalk, stopping every few steps to peer out from behind the brush to assure himself the elk hadn't winded him or heard his approach. Even as Jim slipped well within rifle range and stepped from the edge of his cover, he was surprised the bull still did not bolt and run off, preferring instead to graze contentedly.

"With that big critter turned sideways to me, close as I was, I couldn't fail to plug him in the lights," Bridger confided. "My pan made fire, so when I brought my rifle down, I 'spected to see that bull drop, maybeso run off on the chance I'd missed. But there he was, big as all life itself—still chewing on his grass like I hadn't hit him."

"What did you do, Mr. Bridger?" Narcissa asked.

"I was downright disgusted with myself for missing that shot offhand the way I done, so I reloaded and stalked up a might closer to that bull. When he still didn't pay me no mind, I aimed to drop him for certain, and pulled the trigger."

Dr. Whitman asked, "And?"

With a shrug Bridger said, "Damn bull kept right on chewing his grass like I wasn't nowhere around throwing lead at him. I was a mite angry now, not knowing if my sights been knocked wrong, so I reloaded and walked right up to where I knowed that lead ball couldn't miss."

"Did you kill the elk?" Spalding asked.

Wagging his head dolefully, Jim admitted, "Nope. Missed him three times! I was so mad, I was choking on fire. Decided if I couldn't shoot that bull with my rifle, then I'd go bang him over the head with my rifle. I started off on a run, holding my gun over my head like this."

He waited an extra moment as the group fell to a hush, assuring himself that he had every person's rapt attention before he continued.

"I was running like nothing you ever seen when I smacked square into something that throwed me back a good twenty feet."

"What was it?" Whitman asked. "Did you run into a tree?"

He looked over at the missionary with a dead-serious look on his face. "Weren't no tree I run into, doc."

"A bear?" Spalding prodded.

"Weren't no bear neither," Bridger explained. "Didn't know what it was, cause there weren't a thing 'tween me and that bull. Open as all get-out 'tween me and him! So I picked myself up off the ground, grabbed my rifle up too, dusted myself off, and started running to knock him in the head again—when, bam! I'm throwed off my feet again."

Bridger went on to tell how angry he was when he yanked up his rifle and started racing for the elk a third time, only to find himself hurled off his feet once more.

"Now, I'll admit this here fella ain't the smartest child ever come to the mountains, so I figgered it was time to go a leetle slower at this," Jim told them gravely, the way a man confided a deep secret. "I started walking slow toward that elk . . . when of a sudden I come smack into a wall."

"A wall?" Whitman repeated.

"Weren't a wall, 'sactly. But it were a solid mountain, clear all the way through. Took me near all the rest of that day, but I got over that mountain, where I saw that elk chewing his grass on the far side. Why, that bull had to be more'n twenty mile away from me when I'd tried to shoot him!"

Spalding snorted dourly. "Twenty miles? How could you even see the animal?"

"Don't you see, Rev'rend?" Bridger said respectfully, grinning a bit as he pulled on the pilgrim's leg. "That there mountain was so big, clear as glass, that it were just like a giant looking glass that made the bull seem big and close—just the way folks use a looking glass to see things far, far away!"

"Your looking-glass mountain!" Narcissa squealed with glee, clapping her hands. "Marvelous, marvelous!"

"How true, Mrs. Whitman," agreed the tall man in the showy buckskins as he stepped to the edge of the fire pit. Holding out his tin cup, Joshua Pilcher said, "Bridger is a consummate storyteller. And one of the finest booshways these mountains have ever seen. I'm sure Jim will join me in proposing a toast now that he and his partners have wrapped up our business and we no longer have to keep our talks under wraps."

"Why all the secrecy, Joshua?" Stewart asked.

"My benefactors demanded it of me," Pilcher explained. "At least until we came to terms, shook hands, and the matter was sealed."

Stewart turned to Bridger, asking, "What matter, Jim?"

"We sold our company to Joshua's bosses," Bridger confessed. "Today."

"Pratte, Chouteau and Company," Pilcher said. "But they'll continue to be known as the American Fur Company out here in the mountains."

"Because they'll be the only American fur company out here in the mountains," Tom Fitzpatrick added.

"So here's to a united front," Pilcher proposed, lifting his tin cup. "One American company, to face down the threat of that giant Hudson's Bay Company."

"Hear! Hear!" slurred Lucien Fontenelle, clearly inebriated already.

Andrew Drips reluctantly nodded and held his cup high as Fitzpatrick stood.

Bridger finally got to his feet. The smile that he had worn while he'd been regaling them with his whoppers was fading quickly. In its place this veteran of the mountains wore a grave expression of defeat.

Bass instantly felt a sharp stab of sorrow for the younger man who had made an honorable name for himself after a youthful indiscretion had marred a reputation yet unborn. At seventeen Bridger had come upriver with Ashley and Henry. Green as a willow, he had volunteered to stay behind with the badly mauled Hugh Glass, then agreed to abandon the old frontiersman—running off with rifle, pistol, knife, and shooting pouch. But unlike most, who would have made excuses for the wrong they had done, year by year Bridger put in a yeoman's work protecting those under his care.

But no matter the times that Bridger had attempted to better his lot by joining in one partnership after another, Lady Fate steadfastly refused to smile on him. Once again the fickle dame had turned her face from him. It damn well didn't seem fair, not fair at all.

"Here's to success, to our American company," Pilcher repeated, then swilled down the potent libation from his cup.

"No," Bass demanded as he stood and held his cup up to Bridger. The others froze. "I won't drink to no bunch of tie-necked booshways back east, or the fancy two-faced struttin' prairie cocks they send out here to do their thievin' for 'em."

Pilcher's face went ashen, his eyes dark in that sullen face. "Are you r-referring to me, sir?"

For but a moment Bass glared at Pilcher; then he quietly said, "You damn well know I am."

The partisan's ashen face flushed red with anger in the firelight. His lips moved, but it was a moment before the words came out. "Are—are you a company man?"

With a snort of laughter Bass said, "Hell, I'm a free man, Pilcher! Ain't no turncoat like you!"

"How dare you—"

Already Bass was turned to Bridger and Fitzpatrick, interrupting the angry cackle from the company lackey by saying, "It ain't gonna be no goddamned rich niggers like them parley-voos back in St. Louie, and it won't be bastards with a high opinion of themselves like Pilcher here what's gonna beat John Bull at the beaver business. Mark the words of this one man. What's gonna drive Hudson's Bay outta the mountains, and keep 'em out, ain't fellas like Joshua Pilcher and all his snuff-snortin', sheet-sleeping kind."

"Hear! Hear!" bellowed Shad Sweete with a bull's roar.

Warmed to his toast, Scratch continued. "It's gonna be men the likes of Jim Bridger what keeps the beaver trade alive in these here mountains. Brave and honorable men like Jim Bridger what pertect this here land for America!"

Two days later, John Bull rode into rendezvous again.

As they had done for the last two years, half-breed Thomas McKay and factor John L. McLeod led a small brigade of guides and trappers to visit the annual American trading fair during their three-year-long expedition through the Snake River country. When Scratch rode over to look up an old friend, he was confronted with a pair of surprises.

The first was finding Kit Carson and his young Arapaho wife riding in with McKay's outfit.

"We wintered over at Fort Hall," Carson said. "So come spring, seemed a good idee for me and Godey, 'long with four others, to throw in with the Hudson's Bay brigade."

That news was nothing short of astonishing to Titus Bass. From time to time faithless belly-draggers like Joshua Pilcher offered to work for the British, but no one the likes of Christopher Carson who had stood up for the flag back when that Frenchie Shunar was boasting he would switch any American who chanced to cross his path.

It struck him hard. "S-so you trapped for John Bull, Kit?"

Carson shrugged. "We worked all the way down the Mary's River this spring. Didn't get but a few beaver and we near starved. Come close to eating ever' last horse we had, so McKay headed for Fort Walla Walla to get some stock. Meantime, we managed to make it in to Fort Hall. McKay come there with plenty of new mounts so we could ride on in here to ronnyvoo."

"Damn if that don't take the circle," Bass brooded. "You going over to the Englishers."

"Not that way at all," Thomas McKay said as he stepped up. "Carson doesn't want to go back with us."

With a nod and a grin Kit explained, "I'm gonna look for Bridger. See if Gabe'll have me back. I've had enough of starving in that English country."

Just then the Yankee trader, Nathaniel Wyeth, approached. He too had just arrived with the Hudson's Bay brigade that mid-July day. Bass anxiously looked over the brigade dismounting to start dropping packs from their mules. For this second summer in a row he didn't see the familiar face of his old friend.

"I'm asking after Jarrell Thornbrugh," Titus announced as Wyeth came to a stop near McKay and McLeod.

Then he saw how the men dropped their eyes, their smiles disappearing as they self-consciously turned away.

Scratch swallowed and tried his best to make his words sound cheerful. "That big son of a bitch ain't come to ronnyvoo again, and here I was—fixing to get him good and drunk like before!"

"I'm afraid Jarrell's dying a slow and terrible death," disclosed the half-breed McKay, John McLoughlin's stepson.

"I looked for him here last summer," Bass explained, his voice starting to quiver. His eyes were already pleading when he asked, "He at Vancouver where the white-headed doctor can care for him?"

McLeod said, "Far as I heard, Thornbrugh's still at one of our trading houses south of the Columbia where he was taken ill. We all fear it was the arrow that found him in a fight with some renegade Umpqua."

"Took an arrow?" Bass said.

"A year ago spring," McLeod continued. "Heard he didn't feel so poorly until it came time to set out from the Siskyou country to meet us inland for our last journey to rendezvous."

"He never reached us in time to come along," McKay declared. "But we really didn't know he was in such a bad way until after we returned last fall."

"None of you see'd him for two summers?"

Both McKay and McLeod shook their heads. The half-breed said, "Doctor McLoughlin fears it can only be a matter of time."

In his mind he was plotting the grueling distance and the exhausting months of travel that journey would consume if he chose to stab his way across the Snake River wilderness, down to the Columbia, pushing west to Vancouver where he might learn just where Jarrell was dying, somewhere far to the south of that British fort. The man might be dead by the time he reached his side. If he wasn't already.

And what of Waits-by-the-Water and Magpie? Now that his wife carried another child, he couldn't fathom taking her along on such an exhausting quest. So if he were to go alone, what was he to do with his family? Take them all the way north to Crow country before he hurried west.

As much as he felt compelled to ride to Jarrell's side, Titus was pulled in the opposite direction at the same time, realizing he now had stronger loyalties to consider. Unlike that solitary winter's journey to Fort Vancouver in hopes of putting McAfferty's ghost to rest, now Bass was no longer alone in life. He had family—a wife, his daughter, and another child on the way. Weighty responsibilities to the ones he loved.

"If'n I'd wanna write Jarrell some thoughts, could one of you see my letter'd get to him?"

McLeod nodded. "We'll see it's carried back with our annual express."

"Are you learned?" Wyeth quietly asked the American trapper. "Can you write your friend that letter?"

Scratch pursed his lips, reluctant to admit that shortcoming. Eventually he shook his head. "Use to write a bit. I can read a mite, but it ain't much. I figger to find someone what can help me—"

"I'll write your letter for you," the Yankee interrupted enthusiastically.

"I'd be in your debt, Nathaniel. Much 'bliged." He felt an instant and overwhelming gratitude for this man who had been so wronged by William Sublette.

"When you're ready, all you have to do is tell me what you want to say to the man, and I'll transcribe it, word for word," Wyeth stated. "When would you like to start?"

He wagged his head, unsure, then asked, "How long you gonna be here afore you turn back for Fort Hall?"

Wyeth smiled with a hint of wistful regret. "The fort is no longer mine. I've sold it to the British. That's how I came to ride in with McLeod and McKay. I plan to head east from here—make Boston by autumn. Which means I'll be around until the fur train starts back for St. Louis."

"So John Bull drove you out too," Titus said sadly.

"Perhaps. But if I am put out of business, then the blame must be squarely laid at the feet of the two men who have already fled the mountains for gentler climes and far easier money."

"Sublette and Campbell?" McLeod asked.

"Yes," Wyeth answered bitterly. "But I feel some small measure of pride knowing that those cowardly thieves fled the mountain trade long before business reversals now force me to leave this country. Years ago when they defrauded me, I vowed I would roll a stone into their garden . . ."

When Wyeth paused, Bass said, "And there ain't never been a stone bigger'n the Hudson's Bay Company."

The Yankee smiled, gratitude written in his eyes now. "It will be an intriguing and most exciting contest to watch, won't it, Bass? These two long-surviving fur giants, one American and the other British—locked in this final, mortal combat for mountain peltries. A fight to the death."

Scratch shuddered. "I'm a'feared it'll be a fight to the death of us all."

Time was when men like General Ashley could reap immense harvests of beaver without establishing permanent posts. But the easy beaver was taken, and Ashley retired.

Now those men who came west hoping to grow rich so they could retire back east had to climb higher, penetrate farther into the fastness of the mountains, or dare to slip around the edges of that forbidden Blackfoot country. Smith, Jackson & Sublette had failed: the first dead on a Comanche lance, the second off to have a try at Spanish California, and the last escaped back to St. Louis, having pillaged the fur business of every last dollar he could squeeze, finagle, or steal from it.

Their successors, the Rocky Mountain Fur Company, had gone under as well—two of its partners eventually giving up on the mountains. And now Bridger, Fitzpatrick, and Drips had shown the white feather, becoming nothing more than hired trappers for the rich moguls in St. Louis.

Where once there had been a handful of big companies along with those small outfits working on a moccasin string, now there remained only one.

The tragic scenario was playing itself out just as he and Bridger had figured it would. With fewer beaver reaching rendezvous every year, and the market for those pelts diminishing with each rendezvous season, what with the price of supplies and trade goods continuing to escalate at the same time, only the biggest company of them all had pockets deep enough to stay in this fight for the Rocky Mountains.

First the traders brought milk cows, then two-wheeled carts, and freight wagons, and even a Dearborn carriage! And now, not only were the preachers come to the mountains to deliver their hellfire and sulfurous brimstone sermons . . . but they'd brought white women along too!

What would these mountains come to?

Looking back now, Scratch could see how in the last few winters the trade had undergone such dramatic changes that he and Gabe hardly recognized it anymore. Now there were posts and forts sprouting up at the mouth of this river or that, stockades where the company's traders successfully lobbied the surrounding tribes to harvest beaver so they no longer had to rely solely on the labors of white trappers—indentured employee or free man, neither one.

Maybeso these rendezvous were on their way to playing out as the fur was playing out itself.

"Boys, I'm 'minded of that time I first come to the mountains—how I made a turrible mistake," Bridger said the next afternoon at his fire, looking up at Bass and Shad Sweete with such sad eyes. "I 'member looking down at that ol' wolf, Hugh Glass, his breathin' like a death call in his chest, chewed up so bad there weren't a ghost of a chance of him survivin', just a'layin' there beside his own shallow grave in the sand—sure to die."

Jim drew in a long sigh and poked among the ashes at the edge of the fire pit. "Maybeso this here business is just like ol' Glass. It's fixin' to die, run outta time there beside its grave, just hanging on somehow, one breath at a time."

"But Glass didn't die that way, Gabe," Shadrach argued.

"That's right," Bass agreed. "He went down years later, fighting on the Yallerstone."

"Mayhaps you're right, boys," Bridger admitted. "But even ol' Glass went under . . . eventual'."

"You figger the end's coming, Jim?" Sweete asked.

Bridger nodded his head. "Take a good look around us, boys. See what Sublette and Campbell and them St. Louie parley-voos are doing to choke the life out of us. Don't figger it's a question of *if* the trade's gonna die. Only be a question of *when.*"

That had set Scratch to brooding, down in his mind and dwelling on matters he hadn't given much thought to over the last few years. He just couldn't bring himself to accept that his way of life was changing and would never be the same again, that the way he had lived might actually be dying, never to resurrect itself again.

"You one-eyed idjit nigger," he scolded himself sharply late of an afternoon. "You been half-blind to it!"

All a man really had to do was look around at those gathered for rendezvous to read the sign. If he didn't count in the Frenchmen who trapped for the company, and didn't tally up those settlement fellas who came and went with Fitzpatrick's supply caravan—there was a damn sight fewer white men come to rendezvous this summer of thirty-six than ever before. And even more revealing, for the first time he could remember, there were almost as many free men gathered in the valley of the Green as there were company trappers.

More than anything, that hammered home just how many were giving up and fleeing the mountains. Would this mean the company posts controlled the rivers, and the company brigades controlled their chosen territories in the high country? Would these changes now force the last of the free men to trap where they wouldn't run the risk of bumping into the booshways and their hireling skin trappers?

How long now had he refused to see what was right before his eyes? This fur business was being slowly strangled. If it wasn't the big, powerful companies that would kill it, then surely the death was coming as the beaver were wiped out. Already there was talk of areas stripped clean, nary a flat-tail to be found.

If that didn't sound like a wheezing death rattle in those last gasps of the fur trade . . . Bass wasn't sure what did.

Wasn't a day went by when he didn't walk past some conversation, or overhear someone at the trading post talking about the latest dire news straight from the tongues of those St. Louis clerks.

"They say for the last two years, the first time ever," a wag pontificated before some two dozen company trappers, "buffalo robes are selling better than beaver."

For top dollar, merchants and middlemen were buying up every last robe brought in from the prairies, no question about it. This, while beaver was moving poorly, no longer regarded with as much favor as the robes.

"Them fur buyers back there been seeing how slow this beaver is to sell lately," agreed another clerk. "What with Campbell's brother living in Philadelphia, I'll bet he's the one who's been feeding Billy Sublette all the news of them eastern markets."

"Don't know how long this company can afford to keep buying your beaver, boys," a third settlement type pronounced. "Silk is all the go of the day back in the States, and with robes in high demand, beaver don't stand a chance to last much longer."

How long had he been refusing to admit that the market wasn't just flat, but on a downhill slide?

How long did he have before the fur trade breathed its last?

And if he didn't trap no more, just how was a man to go about providing for his family?

SIXTEEN

Six days after they reached rendezvous, McLeod and McKay turned their brigade around and departed for the northwest. This time the Hudson's Bay men would be guiding five missionaries and their two young Indian boys on to the land of the Nez Perce.

Scratch and Waits-by-the-Water, like hundreds of whites and Indians, watched the short procession of pack mules, horses, sixteen milk cows, and that oddly misplaced Dearborn carriage wind its way out of the valley of the Green River, followed by the Nez Perce village dragging their travois, a hugh pony herd bringing up the rear. It made for a noisy, heartfelt farewell from the trappers who turned out for one last look upon those church women, a departure that left behind such an awful silence when the dust clouds eventually disappeared beyond the northern hills.

So quiet, Bass could hear the quiet gurgle of Horse Creek along its bed, or Zeke's fitful panting in the oppressive heat, or the buzz of the deerflies that tormented and bit, leaving behind hot, painful welts. So unlike those last few frantic days after Wyeth had introduced McLeod and McKay to the American party.

"This must surely be God's answer to our prayers!" Marcus Whitman exclaimed. "Praise the Almighty for His blessings!"

Henry Spalding concurred. "We've been praying that He would provide us a way to reach the Walla Walla country."

"That's where Sir Stewart suggests we settle our mission," Whitman explained. "Up the Walla Walla some twenty-five miles north of your post, at a place he says the Nez Perce call *Waiilatpu.*"

"A good spot: plenty of ground for your crops and graze for your cattle," John McLeod replied enthusiastically. "It's agreed—you can join our brigade when we leave on the eighteenth. From here we'll march for the Walla Walla by way of Fort Hall."

"Thank God, thank God!" Narcissa cried, and clapped for joy.

"There is one thing I must require, however," McLeod declared more sedately, quickly glancing over the few Americans who happened to be visiting the missionary camp at that moment.

"If it's about money," Whitman began, "I'm afraid we don't have much of any to—"

"This isn't about your money," McLeod interrupted. "Only that I must have your guarantee on something before I commit to lead you into Oregon, into Hudson's Bay Company territory."

Spalding's brow knit. "A guarantee?"

"We cannot have you encouraging any of these American hunters and trappers to come to the Columbia River to settle," McLeod drew a fine point on it. "We do our best to have nothing at all to do with the American fur men, nothing in any fashion."

"B-but you've come here to their rendezvous," Whitman observed.

"The better to see to the nature of the American business on this side of the mountains," McLeod declared.

Whitman shook his head. "Why shouldn't we have the right to encourage any man who might want to make a home for himself among our mission—"

"Reverend," McLeod said, "we know from past experience that any of these American hunters who would come to the Columbia country only cause trouble and difficulties among our Indians. They always have before."

"But I have been thinking that we might need some help in building ourselves the church and meeting hall, putting up our simple homes too," Whitman stated.

McLeod was waving his hand, ready to speak. "Should you need any manual labor, be it workers for your fields or men to assist in putting up your buildings, the Hudson's Bay Company would rather furnish you with what you need than to have you encourage and invite any of the Americans to migrate into the Columbia country."

It was clear, from the set of McLeod's jaw and the determined cast in his eyes, that should the missionaries desire the assistance of his brigade in delivering them to the land of the Nez Perce, those missionaries would have to toe the company line.

Whitman cleared his throat to announce, "Then I have committed something of an error I will have to correct."

"What error, Doctor?" asked half-breed McKay.

"I've asked some men to accompany us to Oregon country," Whitman explained, "enlisting them as employees to help us raise shelter before winter arrives. Now . . . I'll have to tell them I won't need their services."

"We believe that's for the best," McLeod responded. "For all concerned. Our enterprise, and yours."

So the Whitmans marched out of the Rockies, across the interior basin, and on to Oregon, passing into the lore and legend of a fading era.

How quietly did two great upheavals glide by that summer, all but unnoticed on the turbulent river of history.

Having crushed all remaining American competition in that year of our Lord 1836, Astor's St. Louis successors in this western trade would themselves end up closing the door on a glorious era. The end of an age had come.

Yet at this same July rendezvous another door had been cracked open, one never to be shut again: white women, wheels, and cows had crossed the Southern Pass.

From here on out, the West would never be the same.

Within days of the missionaries' departure, Thomas Fitzpatrick and Milton Sublette packed up their furs and started for the post on La Ramee's Fork, now no longer called Fort William but renamed Fort Lucien when Fontenelle and his partners purchased it from Sublette and Campbell back in thirty-five. While the one-legged Sublette would remain as *mayordomo* at the post, Fitz would pilot the pack train to St. Louis. With this fur caravan went Nathaniel Wyeth, who carried a pouch of letters written to loved ones back east, most transcribed for those who could neither read nor write. The intrepid Yankee promised to have them in St. Louis by October, as he was heading south to Taos by way of Bents' Fort. Bound too for St. Louis and the States were Stewart, the Scottish nobleman, and his guide, Antoine Clement.

The most significant transaction there on the banks of the Green River was not the trading of furs for sugar and coffee, powder and lead, but that sale of Fontenelle, Fitzpatrick & Company to Joshua Pilcher, agent for Pratte, Chouteau & Company. With no more than a whimper the grand and raucous rivalry that had raged between competing outfits was now a thing of the past.

A new American Fur Company had won the pot. But while those wealthy St. Louis Frenchmen might have defeated their less-well-heeled

American competitors, Pratte, Chouteau & Company still did not have the fur country to themselves. With Hudson's Bay continuing to skulk around the edges, this business of beaver pelts was bound to be not only a competition between two companies, but a sharpening of the rivalry between two countries.

While Andrew Drips once again led a small brigade south by west past the Snake River country for the Wasatch and Uintah ranges, Lucien Fontenelle departed with Kit Carson and some thirty men for a fall hunt on the Musselshell, intending to winter on the lower Powder, a favorite with trappers because of its protection from the winter winds and the numbers of buffalo that grazed there throughout the cold months.

"Due north, where we'll stab our way into the gut of Blackfoot country again." Thus Sweete explained where Bridger's brigade was heading as he held out his hand, preparing to move out at first light that late July morning.

"Got us plenty of time to trap a'fore we winter somewheres over on the Yellowstone," Jim Bridger added as Bass shook their hands in farewell.

Scratch embraced his old friend. "You boys gonna watch your ha'r up there in the land of Bug's Boys, ain't you, Gabe? Maybe we'll run on you come winter. Spring at the latest."

"You'll be up north too?" Sweete asked.

With a nod Bass said, "Fixing to winter on the Yallerstone with my wife's people. Crow, they are. We lost her pap to the Blackfoot two year ago. Time we got back up there to see to her mam."

Bridger glanced at Cora who sat atop her pony nearby. "Reckon I know how your stick floats when it comes to your wife's family. Many don't just marry a woman."

"He ends up hitching hisself to all her kin," Titus concluded. "It's a good thing too, Jim—what with that doctor's wife gone to Oregon now. Shiny-eyed gal like that being around just naturally made my woman jealous. Yours too."

"What? My Cora?"

"Yep. Reason I know is, my wife had a good talk with me—worried all sorts of white gals was coming west and I wouldn't want her no more," he explained, watching Bridger turn to stare at Cora.

"I had me no idee I done anything to make her worry."

"She's carrying your child now, Gabe."

Jim nodded and said, "So I made her worry I was gonna leave her high and dry with a young'un?"

"Take it from a feller what has one pup and 'nother on the way— carrying a child makes a woman act like she was bit by the full moon for no reason at all. Best for you just to figger she's gonna bawl at nothing, scream at you for nothing too."

Grinning, Jim commented, "I know my way round the mountains, know a Blackfoot mokerson from a Crow, know when to fight the niggers and when to run . . . and damn if I ain't a fool to think I knowed women too!"

"At times, Gabe—there be no sign writ on a woman's heart, so it's for us to find out for our own selves."

"Thankee, Scratch," Bridger added, shaking Bass's hand again before he turned, swung into the saddle, and waved his arm as he hollered for his brigade to mount up.

"Time for the trail," Sweete said as he crawled atop the strong, jug-headed Indian pony, the man's legs so long they all but brushed the tops of the meadow grass as he reined away for the column starting out of the valley.

Titus waved, crying out, "See you boys on the Yallerstone!"

Some of the finest moments in his life were spent sitting on a hillside such as this, listening to autumn pass with such a hush that most folks simply weren't aware of its journey across the face of time until winter had them in its grip.

Now that summer was done, every few days Titus dawdled among the shimmering quakies, leaning back against a tree trunk there in the midst of their spun-gold magnificence to gaze out upon the valley below where he ran his trapline. Since leaving rendezvous, he had keenly anticipated this season of the year, this season of his life.

The quiet murmur of the land as it prepared for a winter's rest. The frantic coupling of the wild creatures big and small before the coming of cold and hunger. That soul-stirring squeal of the bull elk on the hillside above him. Those heart-wrenching honks of the long-necks as they flapped overhead, making for the south once again to complete a grand circuit of the ages.

As he sat there today, gazing down at how the wind stirred tiny riffles across the surface of the stream, Scratch remembered the ancient Flathead medicine man who had died early that July morning his village was preparing to depart the white man's rendezvous. Only the day before the old man's death had Bass gone to the Flathead camp with Bridger, Sweete, and Meek, who had come along with Cora to visit some of her kinfolk to have a divination, a portent of their autumn hunt.

The ancient one unexpectedly called the trappers to his shady bower where he lay suspended on his travois of soft blankets and robes beneath a buffalo-hide awning. His daughter, old herself, remained at his side.

"My father wants to talk to you," the widow had explained, looking up at Bridger, then the others, with tired eyes.

"Who is your father?" Sweete asked in sign.

And Bridger inquired with his hands, "Why does he want to talk to me?"

"Come," she gestured. "He will tell you everything."

The old man reached out a frail, bony hand, looking more like a bird's claw, the moment he heard his daughter return, heard the trappers shuffle up and position themselves self-consciously around the travois.

"Touch his hand," she signed, rubbing the back of hers with her fingers. "So he knows you are here."

Bridger knelt and rubbed the back of the ancient one's veiny hand. Then Scratch touched it, amazed at how the dark cords stood out like tiny ropes against the sheen of the malleable brown skin.

"Does he hear?" Bass said, then remembered to make the sign.

The woman nodded and laid a hand on her father's cheek, spoke to him softly in Flathead.

When he began speaking, it was only a few words at a time, almost as if he was having to fight for breath between each phrase. And when he sighed, resting, the old woman translated with her hands.

"He says to you: it is good that you come to listen—you leaders of the white men who are strangers to this land," she signed.

"Many long winters ago when I was a boy, I remember the seasons as good. Then the first white men arrived.

"Your kind came to our country as no wild creature ever came to our villages before. And we did not understand.

"The white man did not stay at the edges of our camps like other creatures, but he came straight into our village. He ate the beaver and all the animals in our mountains with his iron teeth.

"Because the white man has such a great appetite for everything in our country, now my grandchildren and great-grandchildren are hungry."

While the old woman signed these last words, her ancient father wiped his watery eyes and clutched a tiny tortoiseshell rattle against his chest as if he had finished. Sweete, Bridger, Bass, and Meek began to rise—but the daughter motioned them to remain.

"Do not think my father is done. So tired is he with his years, he only needs a little rest now."

For a long time the soft, wrinkled eyelids remained closed in that gray-skinned, skeletal face. Then, just when Scratch was growing restless, the medicine man finally spoke again, in even more of a whisper this time, his voice grown all the weaker. Eventually the daughter turned her attention from him to the white men and made sign.

"If the mountain lion or the great silver bear ever came to our villages the way the white men have . . . the lion or bear goes down under our arrows and lances.

"But the eye spirits in my dreams tell me we do not have enough arrows and lances for the many white creatures who have come boldly into our country, you who do not stay on the edges of our camps. My dreams tell me we can never kill all of those wild white creatures who have come to change things forever.

"We do not understand," she translated into sign. "Once we were masters in our land. Now we are hungry, and afraid. Above us in our skies, the sun has set on our faces. Night has forever fallen across our land . . . never again will we ride the moon down."

As if she knew he must be thirsty from all the talk, weary from all the effort, the old woman gave her father some water from a horn ladle, then settled at his elbow where she made sign.

"He is done. All done, what he wants to say to you. Farewell."

The next morning the ancient seer was dead. Chances were good that his last words were spoken to some white men he believed were chiefs among their people. While Meek, Newell, and Sweete had joked with Bridger on their way back to camp about Gabe's being a chief among the trappers, Bass wondered instead why the old man hadn't sent for the rich or the noble, the holy or the powerful, among the white booshways and traders, sportsmen, and missionaries camped along the Green River.

Perhaps the old man had no desire to talk to the loftier sort who had never truly penetrated to the heart of the mountains. Maybe he wanted more so to speak to those who had trapped and crossed his land, those who had invaded and thereby changed life as his people had known it.

Funny—until this moment Scratch hadn't remembered the old rattle shaker. But now, here among the glittering but dying yellow leaves, watching the rhythms of death slowly overcome the seasons of life, he suddenly imagined that the old man and his people were very much like the beaver. Unlike those tiny worms said to spin their threads of silk for hats, the beaver had to be sacrificed for others to reap their harvest. A man took the hide and discarded the rest.

The rattle shaker must have figured the trappers had come to his country to take what they wanted in the way of furs and women, discarding everything else when they moved on. Perhaps his people were like the beaver.

So the old man's dream began to disturb him in that season of dying before the onset of winter—a terrifying vision of perpetual night that held no hope of a moonset, no prayer that any of them could ride the moon down and bring about the coming of day.

This autumn, more than any before, Scratch sensed the cold stab him to the marrow.

"What the hell's a man call this godforsaken place of yours, trader?" Bass roared as he ushered his wife through the narrow doorway cut into the clay-chinked cottonwood logs and threw his shoulder back against the crude door planks to batten it against the wind.

Samuel Tullock looked up from the floor where he was sorting through some buffalo robes a handful of Crow warriors had brought in. All six of them stood to peer at the new arrivals.

"That you, Bass?"

Tearing the bulky coyote hat from his head, Scratch slapped the fur against the tail of his elk-hide coat, knocking loose a cloud of snowflakes. Despite the best efforts of the stone fireplace at the corner of the small trading room erected there on the north bank of the Yellowstone opposite the mouth of the Tongue River, their every breath was a greasy vapor in the winter air.

Tullock stepped around the warriors and that scatter of robes as Waits-by-the-Water set Magpie on the floor of pounded earth. As soon as she pulled back the deep hood of her blanket capote, three of the warriors instantly recognized her. She settled onto a small wooden crate, tearing at the knot in the sash around her waist. Bass held out his hand to the trader.

Tullock shook with him, affectionately laying his frozen club of a left hand on Titus's forearm. "I ain't seen a white face in weeks."

"Down to ronnyvoo, one of them brigades made plans to spend the winter over on the Powder," Titus explained as he tore open his heavy coat and dragged it from his arms. "Figgered they'd been through here a'fore now on their way to winter camp."

Tullock shook his head and took a step back. With a sigh the former trapper said, "Good to see a white man every now and then. Likely them company boys come through eventual', if'n they're in this country. Coffee?"

"Some for both of us, thankee." Scratch watched the trader turn and step around the pile of robes, moving behind the group of warriors who had stepped over to chatter with Waits. He caught every third word or so, fast as they were talking—happy and animated. It made his heart glad to see such a smile on her face, hear that cheer in her voice. Back among her own kind.

"Trading been good?" he asked as Tullock handed a cup down to Waits, passed a second to Titus.

"Spring was a mite slow," he admitted. "But it's been picking up here of late now that the cold has come for certain."

"So you ain't been hurt none closing down your old place and moving over here?"

"Near as I can tell, these fellas say their people gonna bring in their furs no matter what."

The steam of his coffee warmed his face as Scratch held it beneath his chin. "These Absorkees ain't got nowhere else to go, Sam'l. They ain't about to ride north through Blackfoot country to trade at the Marias post, so if you wasn't here—they'd be banging on the gates of Fort Union for powder and coffee."

"It ain't powder and coffee these bucks come for," Tullock growled. "They don't believe I ain't got no whiskey."

Titus snorted with laughter and glanced over at Magpie standing at her mother's knee, gazing up at the warriors. He sensed that the girl must realize how those men looked more like her than did her father.

"Whiskey, is it? Ain't that just what we taught 'em? We done our best to make these poor niggers want what's the wust for 'em."

"You was down on the Green?"

"Yup, a hot, dry one too, that was."

"What's news from ronnyvoo?" Tullock asked. "Last boat of the year, word down from Union said St. Louis has gone and bought up ever'thing."

After sipping at the scalding coffee, Titus declared, "Your outfit owns the hull mountains now. It be a'tween you and Hudson's Bay."

The trader patted, then settled back against a stack of folded buffalo robes. "Beaver's 'bout done."

"I ain't give up, Sam'l. Gonna ride this horse till it drops dead a'tween my legs."

"What brings you here to the Tongue?" Tullock asked. "You been trapping nearby?"

"Been up the Rosebud, hung round the big bend for a few weeks till I trapped it out and weren't wuth the trouble putting my steel in water. We moseyed north for the Yallerstone. Aiming to make it downriver to Fort Union. Look up an old friend."

"Who that be?"

"Levi Gamble. You hear of him?"

"Never thought you'd know Levi," the trader responded, stepping over to the ill-fitting door to brush away some of the snow sifting in around the jamb. "A fair man, good of heart too. Gamble's been out here longer'n most."

Nodding, Bass replied, "Met him back in Caintuck when he was on his way to St. Lou. Gonna meet up with Lisa and ride up the river for to be a beaver hunter."

"That man's got him some rings, all right," Tullock declared with his back turned.

"Didn't ever figger to run onto him," Scratch admitted. "It's been over twenty-five year now."

The trader turned from the door as the wind keened all the more loudly, rattling the crude planks, whining as it shinnied through the chinking, moaning as it sulled around the sharp corners on this low-roofed log hut. "Figure it's better for you and your family to stay here the night."

"Thankee, Sam'l," Scratch replied. "Gonna be dark soon."

"You speak better Crow'n me—why don't you tell them others they can bed down right here with us if they choose."

After translating for the warriors, Scratch removed his buffalo-hide vest from his shoulders. Settling near the fireplace, he held out his arms to Magpie. A smile instantly blossomed on her face, her black-cherry eyes glowing as she trundled across the uneven floor, tripping once and catching herself before she reached her father's arms, giggling as he smothered her face and neck in kisses.

Two of the Crow followed Waits over to the fire and squatted cross-legged on the ground as the woman leaned against Bass's shoulder.

"You will have another child soon," one of the Crow said, nodding toward Waits's belly. "Perhaps it will be a boy."

Smiling, Titus patted the rounding belly. "Yes. A boy, perhaps."

"A good thing, this—your wife birthing a boy," the second man commented. "He will become a Crow warrior."

Scratch took his eyes from the young man and stared at the flames. "Better that the boy become a beaver trapper like his father."

"Just who in hell's asking for Levi Gamble?"

Gazing up at the man yelling down at him, Scratch craned his neck there beside the wall of that massive wooden stockade rising some twenty feet beside the hulking stone bastion erected at the southwestern corner of the fort. A second and third man now joined the first to stare over the top of those pickets near the bastion's stone wall. All three studied the visitors in that cold swirl of a ground blizzard.

For much of the day he and Waits-by-the-Water had struggled through the storm, making no more than a half-dozen miles, fighting to reach the walls as the afternoon light waned.

"An old friend," he shouted at the trio above.

"You speak good English, friend," a voice called down, the words all but hurtled away before they reached Bass at the foot of the giant timbers. "Better'n any Injun I know can speak English."

"Well, now—I figger you for a white nigger too," Titus growled. "My wife an' young'un near froze out here, so what say you crawl on down here and let us in a'fore we can't move no more."

"Said you was a friend of Levi Gamble's?"

"From a long time ago," he replied. Bass was relieved when he saw the speaker's head disappear. The other two faces peered at him for a few seconds more before they were gone as well.

The snow stung his eyes as it flung itself against the wall, ricocheted off with a glancing blow and a howl of fury, then hurled sharp, icy shards at him from several directions at once.

He heard Magpie whimper again inside his coat where he clutched her against his warmth. Patting her back with one hand, Scratch pulled the buffalo robe more tightly around her. The moment the storm had descended upon them that morning, he had stopped, turned the girl around so that she faced him, her little legs straddling him in the saddle. Untying the flaps of his elk-hide coat so he could admit her, he had Magpie loop her arms around him, burying her face and head into the furry warmth of the buffalo-hide vest. When he had retied the coat around her, Bass dragged a buffalo robe across the neck of the pony, positioning it over Magpie's back, wrapping it securely around their legs as the wind began to shriek through the cottonwoods that lined the northern bank of the Yellowstone.

Able to see no farther than their ponies' noses, they had taken the better part of the afternoon to locate a place where they could ford to the north side of the Missouri, upriver from the post. Now they stood waiting on the tall, barren bluff overlooking the muddy river, at the mercy of the cruel wind, their animals caked with a brutal mix of ice from the Missouri and frozen snow.

"Over here!" a voice called gruffly as the wind died momentarily. "Hurry, goddammit!"

Through the swirling, wispy gauze of the dancing ground blizzard, Bass spotted a dark rectangle appear in the solid bank of wall timbers. He blinked and the rectangle disappeared. But as that gust of wind died, the dark rectangle reappeared, beside it now a figure swathed in a furry coat, his head like a huge, disproportionate grizzly's resting atop his shoulders.

"C'mon!" Scratch snapped at Waits, reaching for her reins.

Their head-bent, tail-tucked ponies and Samantha required some extra nudging, heels and yanking both, to encourage the animals to move.

Near the fur-wrapped figure at the gate Scratch dropped to the ground with the girl in his arms. "You got a place in there for these here animals?"

"How many you got?" the voice grumbled beneath the hood of fur.

"Six. Less'n I take 'em somewhere back down the bank outta the wind, they ain't gonna make it."

"Bring 'em in," the man relented. "We'll make room for the night. Soon as the storm lets up—"

"I'll pay for their k-keep," Bass stuttered, shifting the little girl in his arms when she whimpered with the cold.

"That your young'un you got in there, mister?"

"My daughter."

Beneath the frost-glazed brow of his bear-fur cap the man peered up at the Crow woman now. "You better get them both in here outta this wind."

Scratch watched the man reach out and seize the reins to Waits-by-the-Water's pony, removing them from Bass's thick glove. The stranger turned and led the woman's horse into that narrow rectangle, pushing aside the huge gate only wide enough to admit the animal and its rider who sat hunched over in the howling fury of the storm.

Hoisting the small child into his arms, Titus struggled to clutch the buffalo robe around them both as he started forward, tripping on the robe and dropping it.

"Magpie?"

"Yes, popo?" she said in English, her voice faint, muffled against his chest.

"I'll get you warm soon," he told her as he turned to discover the mule and the other ponies slowly drifting away before the wind, angling from the wall toward the tall fur press, its top completely obscured in the foggy swirl of snow.

"Get in here, mister!" the stranger bellowed as he reappeared at the gate, waving violently.

As a gust of wind died, Bass cried out, "Samantha!"

He tried to whistle, but his swollen, bleeding lips would not cooperate. Instead he called her name a second time, then started for the dark slash in the wall where the man stood holding open the gate.

Magpie shivered against him. "Popo?"

"Said I'll get you warm soon."

"Cold. Cold," she whimpered, shaking against him.

Of a sudden that word reminded him how Josiah had whispered in his ear in the bloody aftermath of chasing after an old friend, moments after killing Asa McAfferty.

"M-my wife?" he stammered as he inched through the gate the stranger held open.

"She's safe. I put her in the trade room round the corner," the man said, bracing his arm against the wall to his left, propping open the heavy gate. "Take your young'un round there too."

His weary arms barely able to hold on to Magpie, his legs stubborn and leaden, Scratch shuffled through the door with Zeke at his heels. As the sudden warmth brushed his bare cheeks, Titus noticed how the shriek of the wind disappeared behind him. This place smelled of coffee and beeswax, gunpowder and new wood slats on the crates of every trade good imaginable.

"Leave the child with its mother," the stranger ordered.

Waits sat side-legged on the floor, wiping the melting snow from her damp face as she pulled back her hood. When he stumbled toward his wife, she looked up, held out her arms. Waits pulled aside the flaps of his coat and vest, reaching inside to grab the child, murmuring at Magpie in Crow.

He eased the girl into her mother's lap with a whimper, then turned slowly.

"C'mon, mister," the stranger said. "Let's get them animals put up or they're lost."

It took long minutes of struggle to account for the five horses and Samantha, cajoling them toward the walls, through the gate, then into the crude pen to the right of the gate where they joined some other stock. Together Bass and the stranger tore at the knots lashing their meager possessions and packs of beaver to their backs until everything had been dropped.

"Now," the man gasped, brushing some of the frost from his gray beard and mustache, "s'pose you tell me who the hell this friend is what's looking after Levi Gamble."

"My name's Bass. Titus Bass," he gasped, winded, weary, and more than half frozen.

"Bass. Say you know Gamble?"

"Knowed him a long, long time ago."

"How long?"

"Back to eighteen and ten it were—"

"Jesus and Mother Mary!" the stranger exclaimed. "How the hell you 'spect a ol' man to remember that far back? So how you know him?"

"We shot at a mark together, once," Bass explained, dragging a coat sleeve across the lower half of his face. It wasn't near so cold there, out of the wind the way they were. "No more'n sixteen was I, but still I nearly whupped Levi that summer—"

"The Longhunters Fair?" the stranger suddenly blurted.

Bass licked his lips, surprised at the interruption. "Y-yup. Levi come through Boone County. We shot at the Longhunters Fair they hold every summer—"

"You that skinny whiffet of a green-broke young'un nearly outshot me that summer day?"

Scratch blinked again, closely studying the stranger's face in the dim, fading light of that stormy afternoon. Those tired eyes, their deeply etched crows'-feet and liver-colored bags of fatigue, along with that massive, un-kempt gray beard and tangle of iron-colored hair beneath the crown of black-bear fur.

"Levi?" he croaked. "Levi Gamble?"

"Goddamn, it's been so long and you changed so much," Gamble apologized. "I'd never knowed it was you even if you'd come up and punched me in the nose!"

Bass opened his arms and flung them around this man who was a stranger no more. "Damn if it ain't good to see a old friend!"

Gamble flung his arms around Bass, squeezed, then pounded Scratch on the back with both thick mittens. "I'll declare, Titus Bass! What the hell took you so goddamned long to look me up?"

SEVENTEEN

"You want me to believe this man nearly shot the pants off you, Levi Gamble?" demanded Kenneth McKenzie, the undisputed king of the high Missouri.

"That was more'n twenty-six summers ago, factor," Levi apologized after he had introduced Bass to his employer the next evening following Scratch's arrival at the Fort Union gates. "We was both better shots back then—wasn't we, Titus?"

Bass grinned and winked at Gamble. "More'n half my life ago, Levi. I'm sure we both was better at a lot of things than we are now!"

"Like with the women, eh?" asked Jacques Rem, a half-breed hunter in his early fifties, better known around the fort as Jack.

"We menfolk just like dumb-witted animals," Bass declared. "We learn slow when it comes to women: gotta make a lotta mistakes a'fore we find ourselves a good one."

"What ever come of that purty gal you had snuggling up with you that summer at the Longhunters Fair?" Levi inquired. "I recollect how she purt' near had you tied into a husband knot herself."

Titus wagged his head. "We never . . . I run off on the

Ohio a'fore I got roped into that, Levi. Been the wust to happen: marry that gal and turn into a farmer like my pap. Live and die right there never knowing what lay over the far hills."

"Here's to what lays over the far hills!" Gamble roared, and hoisted his pewter cup filled with a hot blend of illicit trade whiskey and strong coffee they had been drinking at this gathering of fort workers.

"And here's to them gals what keep their men back east!" Titus bellowed.

"Levi's got him a young family," Rem stated. "He didn't get married until he was an old man. So now he has young wife, young chirrun."

" 'Bout like you, Titus—with a young'un on the way," Gamble said.

"Oh, don't let him fool you none," Jacques continued with an evil wink. "Levi Gamble gone through more'n one woman ever since he come north on the river many year ago!"

"Don't listen to this soft-brained half-breed, Titus," Levi warned with a grin. "He's got him a big family awready—growed kids and gran'chirrun too. So now Jack's a man with a tired pecker he can't get hard no more—and that means he don't care nothing 'bout women no more."

"Hrrumph!" Jack snorted as he stood and grabbed his crotch. "Maybe better I go crawl under the blankets with your wife, eh, monsieur? Show you which of us can still be a man with the women!"

"You ain't no older'n me, Jack," Levi said. " 'Cept that you used your pecker so much it got whittled down to nothing a long time ago!"

Rem slapped Gamble on the back as he stood, starting for the door. Turning, the half-breed looked at Titus and said, "Maybe you should shoot another match against this bag of hot wind, eh? He is so old now, he can't shoot straight with his rifle."

"But, Jack—you are so old you can't shoot straight with your pecker!" Levi bawled.

"Don't stay up too late tonight, my friend," Rem warned. "We must be off at dawn to find some buffalo."

"You crazy ol' Frenchman," Levi said. "You know I'd never let you down. We'll ride at dawn."

Jacques Rem slid back the iron bolt in its hasp and dragged open the door, then slipped into the night. A cold gust of air knifed into the room as the half-breed slammed the door shut again.

All through the previous night of the blizzard Titus had stayed close to Waits-by-the-Water and Magpie, unfurling their robes and blankets to sleep on the floor in what Levi called the Indian room. Early the following morning after Gamble showed up with the bail of a coffeepot gripped in one hand and three tin cups suspended from the fingers of the other, he and Levi set about hauling in Bass's packs from the corner of the fort's courtyard where they had dropped them during the storm.

Next they led the mule and ponies out of the fort's cramped stables, struggling across the drifts of wind-crusted snow in that first dim light of day, leading the animals to the post's main corral which stood more than a hundred fifty yards east of Fort Union, constructed from timbers brought there from nearby Fort William, the post abandoned by the Sublette & Campbell more than two years before. McKenzie's laborers had dismantled the opposition post, then rebuilt its stockade, a blockhouse, and three small cabins, in addition to an extensive corral where most of the post's stock was kept when they weren't let out to graze on the extensive plateau surrounding the site.

On reaching the corral with his stock, Bass felt the back of his neck burn with warning. Turning to glance over his shoulder, he spotted eyes watching from the dark windows as he and Levi dragged back the gate and led the animals through.

"Friendly folks?" he asked Gamble.

"Them?" Levi asked, stopping to look at the windows.

Scratch said, "Gives me the willies, looking at us like they are."

Levi took a few steps until he was inside the gate, turned and glanced at a couple windows before he said, "Don't pay 'em no mind. Just ol' man Deschamps and his kin. His two boys and a nephew. Their 'Sinniboine women and all their chirrun."

"My animals safe here?"

"This here's McKenzie's country, Titus. Deschamps figgers to stick around, wants to keep his ha'r, he knows better'n try stealing from Mc-Kenzie—"

"I asked about my horses."

"That's why I come over here with you, let 'em see me," Gamble explained. "Anything happen to your stock, the Deschamps know I'll be busting down that door to take care of it on my own. And if I come over to square it, they know McKenzie will send over all the help I need."

"So this bunch don't cause you no trouble?"

"I didn't say that," Levi added grimly, glancing once more at a pair of faces that disappeared from a nearby window when Levi caught them watching him. "But your animals gonna be safe here. Safe as any of Kenneth McKenzie's horses."

Later that morning Levi came to fetch Bass and his family from the Indian room, explaining they were invited to bed in with Gamble's family. Just to the east of the flagpole and a twelve-pounder cannon in the middle of the compound stood five buffalo-hide lodges, their smoke flaps blackened by countless fires, snow piled more than three feet high in sculpted drifts around their bases. Nearby, to the north of the flagpole, stood the one-story factor's house where McKenzie lived, along with his favored clerk, Charles Larpenteur, and Larpenteur's family.

At daybreak that morning after the storm blew through, McKenzie had most of his sixty-some employees out with shovels, clearing icy snow off the pitched roof of his bourgeois house. Next they moved to clear the snow from the roofs of the storage rooms, apartments, trading stores, stables, and the barracks, all of which huddled under a long roof along the east wall. Finally they moved on to scrape the roof of the apartment range where the clerks and interpreters, the carpenter, tinsmith, and tailor, as well as seasonal laborers, all lived, another long building that extended most of the length of the west stockade.

By evening all the snow had been swept from the bastions and that massive blockhouse overlooking the main gate, supported on gigantic cottonwood uprights. Just before twilight most of the deep, drifted snow that had swirled into the courtyard had been removed in carts and wheelbarrows, muscled from one of the two gates, where it was dumped onto the prairie.

He was ravenous at the end of that long day of constant cold and shoveling, lending his hands to help his hosts. As the sun eased beyond the horizon and the temperature plummeted even farther, stars began to twinkle in a cloudless black sky. As their Indian wives prepared to put the children to bed, scrubbing the youngsters with the last of the hot water in a brass kettle steaming beside the fire, Gamble suggested to Bass that they mosey across the courtyard to the laborers' quarters where they could smoke their pipes and drink a little whiskey, all the while catching up on those many twisted miles the two of them had walked since that fine summer day beside the Ohio River at the Boone County Longhunters Fair.

"I never told you something that night after you won the money what would take you to St. Louis . . ." And Titus's voice dropped off as the chill left the room following Jacques Rem's departure.

"Told me what?"

"Just how sad it made me you wasn't a Boone County man," Bass admitted, then sipped at more of his coffee and whiskey.

"Why'd that disappoint you?" Levi asked.

"Right after I'd found a fella what seemed to be just like me . . . I learned you was only passing through," Scratch tried explaining why he had been drawn to the tall frontiersman and the lure of the unknown frontier in much the same way he had been drawn to the lure of Amy Whistler's flesh. "You wasn't like the others, them farmers, not even them Ohio boatmen I come to know that autumn."

"Neither was you, Titus Bass. I hailed from Pennsylvania, looking for somewhere different, just like you was looking. You met me when I was off to a far country filled with more beaver and Injuns and hellfire adventure to last any man's lifetime."

"Damn, but didn't that light a fire under my mokersons!" Bass confided. "Just knowing that I'd run onto someone else what had the same deadly fear I did, fear that I'd take root in one place and die right there 'thout seeing all I wanted to see."

Gamble stared wistfully into his coffee cup. "Family and friends told me I ought'n stay on that side of the river and leave this here country for the Injuns. But I hankered to see just how much country was left over here, a'fore it got changed like that country we left back there got changed."

"I'll bet this was some in them early days, Levi."

With a grin he said, "A sight few men ever see'd—and no man will ever see again."

"It's changing awready . . . ain't it, Levi?" Bass asked sadly. "I see'd it some my own self, and I ain't been out here near the time you have."

"Others is coming, Titus. They always come. One or two families at first. Then a handful after them. And the word keeps on spreading. They come like bees to the honeycomb. Next thing there's towns where there was only campsites. River ports and steamboat landings along this high river. Wagon roads where once there was only game trails or Injun footpaths going from one place off yonder t'other."

"I 'member an old farmer telling us the land is bound to change . . . when man comes to it."

They sat quiet for some time, each man lost in his recollections, in this portent of the future.

"You think it's 'cause of us, Titus?" Gamble finally asked. "Is our kind to blame?"

"Blame for what?"

"For coming here first. We're the ones to open it up and point the way. Maybe we're gonna be to blame for ruining it all."

"How we to blame, Levi?" he asked defensively. "All our kind ever wanted was to go someplace where men ain't changed the land yet. To go where that country is so old and untouched that it's brand-new at the same time."

Wagging his head, Gamble said, "Maybe you'll see it one day, Titus. See how there's always been two kinds of men. Them few that comes to a place first—to discover that new land. And then there's the others who come by the hundreds and hundreds, and even more'n that—they come pouring in like ants once a place has been found, come to settle down. And the few what come first like us, that's when we gotta move on."

For a long moment Bass didn't say anything. He sat there stunned, letting the cold pain of that realization settle in. "You're saying them what come first are to blame for opening the door for them others what come after to ruin it all?"

Nodding, Gamble said, "The others always come where we left our tracks for them to follow."

"That don't rightly make much sense—"

"Dammit if a man don't get on in winters like me and he looks back to see what a god-blamed fool he's been bringing on the ruin of everything he's ever wanted in life."

"You ain't ruin't it, Levi. None of us has. This country ain't like that soft country back there. This here's a hard, hard land what don't easily forgive. Folks won't ever leave them dark forests and that black earth where they can grow their corn and taters and 'baccy. This here country's left for the rest of us what ain't found a home in such a soft land."

"Maybe you're right," Gamble relented, his tired eyes showing how much he wanted to believe. "Maybe their kind will try, but find out there's too many Injuns, or the winters're too cold, or the snows're too deep . . . and they'll skedaddle back to that soft life back yonder in the East."

"These mountains already kill't their share of pilgrims what figgered they had the ha'r we got, Levi."

Gamble grinned. "Only 'cause our kind is so crazy, we don't know no better, Titus Bass!"

"You give me a chance to live to be a old man back east, or to die a young man out here—you damn well know there ain't but one choice for me."

His grin disappeared, and Gamble pursed his lips in resignation for a moment, then said, "Can't help but think we're the last of a breed, friend. A breed come to set a foot down beside streams where no white man ever walked. But that day's gone too. Like the sap that riz up in us when we young."

"A differ'nt time, this is now," Titus added.

"No more do booshways send out brigades to trap beaver. Now the booshways plop down their fur posts beside the big rivers and trade robes with the Injuns. One day this'll all be dead, and they won't even need me to hunt buffler to feed 'em."

It scared Bass the way Gamble sounded. "You're talking like you're touched by a fever, Levi," he protested. "Like a man gone soft in the head."

"Ain't much use for the like of you and me no more, Titus Bass."

"Damn if there ain't! Your booshways can go right ahead and build their posts where they want. Don't make me no never mind. Beaver's bound to rise, I say. The fur trade damn well ain't dead while men like Jim Bridger is leading brigades off to the high lonesome. Long as there's traders to buy beaver, there'll be trappers like me to catch them flat-tails."

"And when there ain't no more beaver?"

"Ain't gonna happen," Bass snapped.

"When there ain't no one to buy what's left?"

He stared hard at Gamble a moment. "What's took over you, Levi?"

"You're right, Scratch," he apologized, the tone of his voice softened. "Been out here on this river most of my life," he explained. "Them years when Lisa retreated downriver, I worked in Fox or Osage or Pawnee country. I've seen more'n my share of winters in this wild county . . . so maybe what I see coming hurts me more'n it hurts men like you—"

The door flung open with a noisy racket and a gust of cold wind as two men leaped inside.

"They killed Papa!"

Leaping to his feet, Gamble rushed up to the young man who had spoken. Seizing the front of his blanket capote, Levi demanded, "Jack? Someone killed Jack?"

"*Oui!*" the young man growled.

Around Titus the rest of the interpreters and clerks had bolted out of their beds, forming a tight crescent surrounding the two young men who stood shaking with fury in the open doorway.

Levi demanded, "Who, Paul? Tell me who!"

"Who else you think?" Paul Rem replied with a snarl. "The Deschamps!"

"You gonna help us, Levi?" the second son asked. "There's too many of them—we need your help. They threaten all of us now—say they kill any friend of Jacques Rem!"

"We need men and guns too," Paul demanded. "Give us the powder to blow all them devils to hell!"

"Hold on," Gamble attempted to calm them. "Tell me how you know it was them what killed Jack."

The second son, Henri, laughed in a harsh gust, then said, "Ol' woman Deschamps's boys wanted to kill Papa for long time after Papa kill ol' man Deschamps! Now she done it. We find him outside the wall—his face beat so bad, cut up so much, we not sure it was him at first."

Shaking his head in disbelief, Gamble silenced the angry murmurs in that room gone cold with more than the wind. Eventually he stared round at the fort employees. "This here night been a long time coming, fellas. We got some business to see to."

"You gonna help us kill them all?" Henri asked, grabbing Levi's arm.

"The squaws and their young'uns—let them go," Gamble ordered. "The rest, they don't deserve to live to see another sunrise." Turning to the interpreter named Bissonette, he said, "Louis, go to the arsenal. Get a rifle and pistol for every man who wants to be a part of this fight. Horns of powder and plenty of ball too. The rest of you what need weapons, go with Bissonette—*now!*"

They flooded past on either side of Gamble and Bass, streaming out the door behind Henri and Paul Rem. Outside on the frozen courtyard stood Jacques's wife and daughter, comforted by several Indian women and half-breed laborers.

Titus felt rooted to the spot, stunned. "Their father . . . he was just here. Drinking with us, telling stories, laughing with us."

Gamble's eyes glowered as he ground a fist into an open palm. "Come with me, Titus: I'm going to tell McKenzie that Jack's dead. So he knows we're going to burn out that nest of rattlers once and for all. Then we'll go to my lodge and fetch our weapons. Time has come to kill all the rest of Deschamps evil seed."

On the way to the bourgeois's house, Levi started to tell Bass how the Deschamps clan had shown up on the upper Missouri about the time Kenneth McKenzie had been building his fort. Since then they had been in the thick of every foul deed: murder, robbery from the post stores, robbing and killing friendly Indians camped nearby, as well as continually committing adultery with one another's wives. Eventually some bad blood arose between the clan and the Rem family, going back a few seasons when one of Jack's sons was killed during a drunken spree with some of the Deschamps band.

"The old man is the root of their evil. He's named Francois, Senior, and it's said he's the one killed the British governor up at the Red River colony in Canada when Northwest Company was fighting Hudson's Bay. The Deschamps all escaped down here after that bloody deed. There ain't no rakehellions like that clan."

Kenneth McKenzie, Levi explained, was able to soothe the pain of the murder and put the simmering feud to rest for some time until one of the Deschamps boys stole the Indian wife from Baptiste Gardepie, a friend of Jack Rem. Old man Deschamps and his son Francois went to the cuckolded Frenchman, offering a horse in exchange for the squaw, saying she was no more than a slut anyway and not really worth a good horse.

Seeing red, the aggrieved Gardepie refused the horse as settlement. But as Francois and his father turned to leave, he swept up an old rusted rifle barrel and clubbed both of his enemies. As the elder Deschamps lay dying, the infuriated Gardepie yanked out his dirk and finished his revenge—disemboweling the patriarch.

"Gutted him like a hog for a smoke shed," Levi described with relish.

Titus asked, "So Gardepie killed the son too?"

"No. And that was a mistake," Gamble answered, going on to explain how *engagés* from the fort rushed from the gate, saving Francois from a similar fate.

Once more Kenneth McKenzie leaped into the middle of the feud, demanding a truce between the warring families, each wary and fearful of the balance of power between them. For the better part of a year, an uneasy tension had existed around Fort Union.

"But last fall two fellas what married Jack's daughters rode off to the Milk River to do some hunting for robes and pelts," Levi declared.

Titus asked, "The Deschamps kill 'em?"

"Nawww—Blackfoot got 'em."

With those two out of the way, the Deschamps clan began to feel stronger, growing more insolent by the month, increasingly resentful of McKenzie and arrogant in the face of all attempts to keep the feud at rest.

"Just the other day one of them bastards was over here at the post, bragging big as could be," Levi said. "Told us his mother called all her boys together and said they wasn't really men less'n they took revenge on the man who goaded Gardepie into killing their pa."

"Jack Rem."

"Right," Gamble growled. "And now them bastards done it."

By the time Levi awakened McKenzie and Larpenteur, bringing them to the door of the factor's house, the Rems had appeared to demand use of the cannon that stood beside the flagstaff.

"Very well. Just go finish it," the bourgeois told them. "Leave off the women and children . . . but you have my permission to take the twelve-pounder with you and finish this, once and for all."

With a jubilant shriek of blood-lust, the Rem brothers whirled about with their comrades, leaping over the porch rail onto the frozen courtyard, rushing for the cannon they began to push toward the front gate while Bass and Gamble hurried to Levi's lodge for their weapons.

The group had dragged the fieldpiece some seventy-five yards, halfway to the old Fort William stockade, when Titus and Levi caught up with them. As the *engagés* struggled to muscle the heavy cannon around a tall, icy snowdrift, a volley of shots split the clear, cold night, wounding one man.

"Get that loaded!" Henri ordered.

After stuffing a small pouch of powder down the breech, Paul Rem jammed a spike down the touchhole, piercing the pouch, before he threaded a short piece of fuse through the touchhole and into the pouch. Down the throat of the cannon another man rammed a ball.

"Back! Get back!" Henri Rem bellowed, waving one arm in warning as he ripped a sputtering torch from the hands of a friend.

"Wait!" Levi ordered. "Don't touch that fuse till we get the helpless ones out!"

Paul Rem fumed a moment, glowering at the old man. "They deserve to die with the rest! Like that ol' woman too!"

Gamble seized Rem's arm, flinging him around to stare into his eyes. "I wanna see 'em all dead just as bad as you, Paul. But this ain't right to kill them women what ain't part of this feud."

After a moment Rem reluctantly yanked his arm from Gamble's hold and turned toward the stockade walls where his enemies hid. Shrieking at the fort, he warned, "You bastards ain't got much time to get them women and children outta there!"

" 'Less we blow you all up together!" Henri Rem bellowed.

From the distant walls came the muffled shouts of protest and cries of terror. Above them all rang the angry, profane curses of the Deschamps boys, and the shrill taunts of their matriarch.

Beneath the silvery light of a half-moon Bass and the rest watched the first dark silhouette appear. In a moment more spidery figures emerged from the rectangle.

"They opened the gate!" one of the *engagés* announced.

One by one the distant figures slipped away from the wall, tearing pell-mell across the bluish snow, clumsily vaulting drifts and spilling over the far side, stumbling headlong for the cluster of lodges where a small band of Assiniboine had come to camp for the winter.

Paul Rem pointed into the moonglow with his rifle. "Go, Henri! The women and children can go free! But see no men get away!"

With a whoop Henri Rem bolted off, three others right on his tail. A rifle shot split the freezing air, its muzzle flash hot and white from a loophole in the stockade fence. All the French and German laborers hurled themselves to the ground, taking cover by the cannon carriage or diving behind snowdrifts as the Deschampses opened fire.

In a heartbeat Paul Rem leaped to his feet. "Shoot! Shoot! Kill them all! Shoot!"

In the distance the women and children were screaming as Henri and his followers caught up with them. As quickly as they had sought to scatter, they were herded back together, shrieking, imploring, crying piteously. From the stockade the Deschamps men were yelling at the women. Another shot rang out, a muzzle flash from one of the dark windows near the corral.

A voice bellowed a French curse at Henri as those around Paul Rem and the rest fired a few rounds at the dark squares along the stockade timbers, sure they were gun ports or windows.

"They just say to my brother he should hang on to his pecker," Paul snarled. "Goddamn Deschamps tell Henri they cut it off while his heart still beats."

"Not if we can pen 'em down till they're all dead," Gamble bellowed.

"Are all your women and children out now?" Henri hollered as he led his men back toward the cannon to rejoin his brother.

"You are cowards!" a female voice shrieked at them.

"Mama Deschamps?" Paul yelled.

"I will spit on your grave this night!"

"This is your chance to run, Mama Deschamps!" Henri explained. "Get out now before we kill all your family!"

"*Non!*" she screamed. "I stay to help them kill all of you!"

Gamble yelled now, "You don't leave, eh?"

"My boys die, I die too, Gamble," she yelled in reply from the darkness of the far stockade. "I watch my boys kill you!"

Paul shouted, "I am happy Gardepie kill your husband!"

"Oui!" the woman shrieked. "Me happy too! Now I can sleep—my sons have killed your father!"

"Shoot them!" Henri roared in fury. "Shoot the old she-bitch too!"

At that moment it grew so unearthly quiet that Levi got to his feet. "Listen!"

It seemed they all held their breath. Bass put his ears to the breeze, hearing the faint sound of scraping, the piercing of the earth's hard crust with a metal shovel. "That's digging, Levi. They know you're bound to use the cannon!"

Gamble wheeled, crying, "You gonna shoot that gun, Paul—do it now!"

With a streak of light the older brother dipped the spitting torch to the fuse which stuttered as it threw off sparks for a moment before the cannon belched, spewing a muddy yellow tongue of flame into the freezing darkness, enough that they were all blinded momentarily. Titus was just beginning to see again when the hissing ball tore through the stockade wall with a clatter. Inside the main cabin men hollered and the aging matriarch swore profanely.

"May your mother couple with dogs in hell for all eternity!" she bawled at the Rem brothers.

"Reload the son of a bitch—now!" Gamble ordered.

As three of the laborers went to swabbing and reloading, the sounds of digging resumed.

"We blow down that wall," Henri vowed, "we'll go right on in and finish 'em all."

While they were preparing that second charge, a scattering of shots came from the Deschampses. Bass knelt, selecting a black square where he had seen a muzzle flash. He held on it, released half his breath, held until he had about given up hope—then the moment that far opening lit up with another bright flash, Scratch squeezed the trigger. The ball struck bone and flesh with a loud, unmistakable smack accompanied by a shrill cry.

The twelve-pounder roared a second time. Then shots from the stockade. With more guns firing back at the Deschampses.

"Levi—they got any other way out?" Titus asked.

"Maybe we ought'n be sure they don't try sneaking out the back of the corral where we can't see 'em."

Running in a crouch around the far side of those drifts the wind had sculpted near the river bluff, both Bass and Gamble managed to slip right up to the southeast corner of the corral without being spotted. Inside, the animals were already frightened, milling anxiously with the nearby gunfire, all the shouting and screams. In the distance the cannon roared a third time. Followed by shrieks and moans from the stockade, more curses from the Rem forces.

Back and forth the battle swung for the next three hours as Bass and Gamble waited out the fight—keeping their eyes trained on the back side of the stockade. Henri Rem lobbed shell after hissing shell into the tattered compound, ripping ragged holes through that western wall of the cabins. Though the cannon was causing a lot of damage, the Deschampses nonetheless managed to fire back from time to time in the midst of their interrupted digging.

"I don't figger 'em for being smart enough to wanna escape," Levi growled in a whisper, shivering with the intense cold and inactivity while the two of them lay prostrate in the snow.

Bass glanced to the east, finding the sky graying. "Hope this is over soon. My belly's hollering for fodder awready."

That next hour dragged by as the sky lightened and it seemed the stars were gradually snuffed out by the approach of dawn. Every few minutes the fieldpiece roared. Men yelled in the battered cabins; women screamed from the Assiniboine camp pitched far on the other side of the stockade. Back and forth the Rems hurled taunts at the Deschampses, and the Deschampses flung their curses at the Rems.

"Look!" Levi yelled, suddenly rising to a crouch, then darting away in a lope. "It's the old woman!"

Bass bolted to his feet, following the moment he spotted the matriarch appear, emerging from the dark rectangle into the ashen light of dawn. Overhead at the end of her arms she held an object.

"Is that a pipe?" Titus asked as they trotted along the south side of the corral.

"That ol' she-bitch!" Gamble snapped. "After all the thieving and murders, she wants to smoke the pipe with the Rems!"

As she walked away from the wall, Madame Deschamps continued shouting at her enemies. But instead of hurling down curses upon the Rems now, she was begging them for mercy, vowing she could keep the obligations of the pipe if only they would smoke with her—

A single rifle shot rang out, a bright jet of orange flame spewing from the muzzle of Henri Rem's gun.

A cheer erupted the instant those with Henri and Paul could see that the old woman had stopped in her tracks. Slowly her arms came down as she started to stumble forward, a dark patch spreading over her chest. Just as she had the pipe at chin level, Madame Deschamps spilled forward, her open, speechless mouth closing around the end of the pipe. As she collapsed facedown onto the snow, dead where the bullet caught her, the bloody end of that pipe pierced the back of her throat and tore out the side of her neck.

The instant she spilled onto the bloody snow in that gray light, a cheer rose anew from the Rems and the *engagés*. Men jubilantly jumped up and down around the cannon as Paul Rem stepped forward a few feet.

He stopped, shook his arm at the dead woman lying halfway between him and the stockade. "There's the end to that mother of devils!"

New shouts and taunts erupted from the stockade, then a sudden volley that drove the Rems behind their snowdrifts.

"Some still alive!" shouted one of the laborers named Emile Vivie as Gamble scurried up with Bass on his heels.

"Only way is to burn 'em out," Henri Rem warned.

"I'll take the torch and some powder," Paul Rem volunteered.

"Go to the northwest corner, brother," Henri suggested as he handed Paul three pouches of the black-powder cannon charges and the sputtering torch.

"I go with him too," Vivie shouted as he followed Paul away from the cannon.

A few futile shots followed them across the snow, but in a matter of moments the two had reached the side of the stockade where Paul handed the torch to Vivie while he ripped open the powder charges and spilled the grains at the base of the wooden pickets. As the sky brightened to presage the dawn, Titus watched the two Frenchmen leap back a few yards when Paul hurled the torch at the bottom of the wall. With a huge gush of flame and smoke the old, dried timbers of the stockade were on fire.

Inside the cabin men shouted in fury, cried out in terror, groaned in their death throes.

With the sun's coming the wind stirred along the Missouri River valley, goading the flames over those next few electrifying minutes as the noise from the cabin rose to a crescendo, then fell off to silence.

Most of that bombarded stockade had been consumed by flame by the time Gamble led the Rem faction toward the smoking walls. Behind them as the sun emerged over the prairie, more than half-a-hundred faces watched from atop the east wall of Fort Union, another sixty-some peering from behind the safety of their lodges in the Assiniboine camp.

Suddenly Scratch heard the sound of running footsteps and a man's grunts as he fled the burning building, escaping his enemies.

"He's going for the bastion!" Henri Rem announced.

"I'll kill him myself!" Emile Vivie boasted.

The young *engagé* was the first to reach the east bastion of the old Fort William stockade where he called out, "Which one of you do I get to kill this morning, eh?"

"That you, Vivie?" screamed the voice from within.

"Ah, it is you, Francois!" Vivie shouted back at the man cowering inside the bastion. "Baptiste Gardepie should have killed you the day he killed your father!"

"Hah!" he bellowed with mad laughter. "I got to see the eyes of Jacques Rem when I ran my knife through his guts. I killed him for my father!"

"Y-you killed Jacques?"

"*Oui!* His blood is still on my hands, Vivie!"

"Arrrghgh!" Emile growled, whirling about to search for a narrow opening between the pickets through which he could shove his rifle.

But inside, the murderous Francois Deschamps had already discovered just such a tiny gap. The muzzle of his gun was waiting when Vivie stepped up to the wall. As Francois pulled the trigger on his rifle, the force of the ball picked Vivie off the snow, into the air, to land more than six feet away.

As the snow beneath Vivie turned to a brownish slush, his legs thrashed and wisps of steam spiraled from the hot blood rushing from his terrible wound. Then he lay still.

"Merciful God," Henri prayed there at the wall near the bastion, and made the sign of the cross.

"God demands vengeance this day!" Paul Rem shouted as he whirled, waving at the *engagés.* "Bring the cannon!"

A handful of fort employees finally managed to muscle the fieldpiece across the crusty snow into position, aiming it at the bastion where Francois kept up some pitiful gunfire until his gun fell quiet.

"The bastard's out of ball or powder," Bass announced.

"No matter—he must die with the rest!" Henri growled.

At that moment Paul Rem touched the short fuse which sparked, sputtering its way down the touchhole an instant before the cannon leaped back, belching with a smoky roar. The ball tore through the side of the bastion with a clatter of old timbers and river rock, then a horrifying shriek from Francois Deschamps.

Then a hush fell.

The others stood around the Rem brothers for a few moments as the cannon's roar faded in the dawn. Then Henri started for the bastion. Paul was right behind him.

In little time they were dragging the mangled body from the wreckage of the bastion, smearing the trampled snow with the dead man's blood seeping from a dozen wounds. Around the corner of the stockade they pulled the body until they were within feet of the leaping flares busily consuming the cabins. As Henri grabbed the dead man's arms, Paul seized Francois's ankles—both of them heaving the body into the crackling flames.

"Now bring that old she-bitch over here!" Henri Rem demanded, his voice shrill with retribution and blood-lust.

Madame Deschamps was the last of her family the victors consigned to the flames that shockingly cold, clear dawn coming out of the east red as a butchered buffalo.

"That makes nine of 'em," Levi announced in a harsh whisper as he stood beside Bass, watching the others dance and twirl, hearing them sing and shout their utter joy. "Let the devil do as he pleases with 'em now!"

Sensing that corona of warmth washing over him from the rising flames, Scratch turned to gaze at the eastern walls of Fort Union, thankful he did not find his wife's face among those watching this funeral pyre.

But despite those waves of heat, Bass shuddered with the subzero chill, staring at the charred bodies as they were consumed.

"Revenge," he told Levi, "be the cup a man best drinks cold."

EIGHTEEN

It brought some rest to a place inside her heart to return to her people. Two summers had passed while Waits-by-the-Water had been away, and a winter spent in that southern land of the Arapaho.

Days ago she and her husband had turned south from the white man's fort at the mouth of the Yellowstone. It had not been a happy time for her there. So many half-breeds and Assiniboine, she never felt welcome. Better that a Crow woman stay safe inside the walls of that fort until Ti-tuzz could take them back across the Missouri and ride for Absaroka.

As they began their journey south, the weather turned mild for many days, but winter had resumed its fury by the time they found the village sprawled among the cottonwoods towering on a neck of land along the southern bank of the Yellowstone.

"It was near this place where we first talked," she said as they halted to gaze at the welcome sight of those brown lodges.

Drawing in a long breath of the cold air scented with wood smoke and the fresh dung of hundreds of ponies, he looked about at the surrounding river bluffs—then gazed at her and smiled. "Yes. I remember. Now I want us to be even happier this winter than we were when we realized we needed each other."

Over their seasons together Waits had grown even more patient with how slow he sometimes was to put his thoughts together in her tongue. She knew Magpie would have it easier than either of her parents, growing up with both languages spoken to her as they were.

Looking up, she found him staring at her still, his eyes twinkling. Then she realized he was watching her hand. She had been rubbing her huge belly unconsciously, thinking of this child to come.

"It will be born this winter, yes?" he asked.

With a nod she answered, "I think sometime in the next moon, perhaps."

Urging his pony over beside hers, Bass tore off a blanket mitten and stuffed his bare hand beneath her buffalo robe, laying it upon that swollen belly beneath her capote. "You are so big—how many little calves do you have in there?"

She giggled. "I think there is only one, but it will be a big child."

"A boy?" and his eyes sparkled.

"Perhaps," she said. "If it is a boy, you will not forget your daughter?"

Bass twisted round to gaze back at the girl who sat behind him, clinging to his elk-hide coat. Patting the child's leg beneath that half robe he had wrapped securely around her, he said, "This little one? I could never forget what she means to me! Tell me, daughter: by spring when the snows melt, will you be ready to learn to ride on your own?"

"Ride a pony by myself?" she asked in Crow.

"Yes," he answered her in English, the way many of their conversations took place: mixing the two tongues together while they conversed, as if it were as natural as could be. "I think you will be old enough to learn, Magpie."

"How old was my mother?" she asked in Crow.

Bass turned to look at Waits. "When did you have your first lesson on a pony by yourself?"

"My father . . ." Then Waits suddenly felt the sharp ball of sadness spring to life again in the middle of her chest. Of an instant her eyes were welling up. Waits barely got the words out of her mouth. "He taught me when I was almost f-five summers."

"Should we come here to be with your people, to see your family?"

She nodded and wiped the tears from her cheek, trying bravely to smile. "It hurt when I remembered my father." And she looked at Magpie sitting behind her father. "Remembered how he held me on his lap, how he smelled when he hugged me . . . I never want Magpie to forget anything about her father."

"What?" he protested in English with a grin. "I'm not going any-where! I don't plan to die for a long, long time!"

But she knew a man never did.

It always came suddenly, unexpectedly—as it had with her father's death in Blackfoot country. And Ti-tuzz could have died last spring when those Arapaho attacked him. Waits had learned about that when she'd discovered the two scalps and the weapons hidden among some green pelts he'd brought back to their camp one cold spring day. And he could easily have been killed when the Frenchmen and half-breeds had fought outside the big fort at the mouth of the Yellowstone.

How many times would she say good-bye to him before she could finally accept that he might not return one day?

Waits looked into his face as he laid his hand on her arm.

He said, "It is good to come back to your people."

"I am happy to see my mother."

"My heart is glad to bring you back here," he said, looping his arm around Magpie to pull the small girl over his hip and into his lap where she quickly gripped on to the round pommel with her tiny blanket mittens.

"Let me have the reins, popo?"

"Here," and he laid them inside those tiny mittens. Then he turned to Waits, saying, "My family is very far away. It has been a long, long time since I saw them—when I was a very young man and ran away from them. I do not think my father and mother are still alive. Maybe my brothers, or sister, still live. But that family did not want me to belong to them very much, so I left them long ago. Now you have become my family."

"Me too, popo?" the girl asked in his tongue, pushing back against him.

"Yes, Magpie. You, and even your little brother too."

"My little brother? Where is little brother?" she asked as she peered on one side of the horse, then the other.

"Perhaps your little brother who is hiding in your mother's belly will come out soon so you can play," he told Magpie.

"When, Mother?"

Waits-by-the-Water looked at him with mock disapproval and scolded, "See what you have started, husband? Now she thinks I am carry-ing her playmate inside me!"

"It will be good to give Magpie a little brother," he told her as they put their animals in motion once more. "To have a family that loves one another is a good thing. I cannot remember having much of that. My mother worked hard, cooked for us and sewed our clothes. And my father worked very hard too, brought us food, kept us warm and dry—but I do not remember being touched by them, do not remember being held." He squeezed Magpie there at the end of his words as his voice cracked.

"It is important that a child is held and touched, especially by its father," Waits declared.

His eyes brimmed with moisture. "I know you must miss He-Who-Is-Gone very much. I can never take his place in your heart, nor will I try, but—I never want you to forget that I will protect you, provide for you, watch over you till the end of my days, woman. That is my promise."

She felt stunned, sensing how his words made her heart pound faster in surprise as she turned to look at him. "Ti-tuzz, those are words I never knew a man would say to a woman."

"Are you silly, wife? Surely when a man falls in love with a woman, he tells her . . . no, he tells her family and all her people that he promises to care for her until he can no longer watch over her."

Wagging her head, Waits said, "No, there is no promise like that made between a man and woman who marry among my people."

"What do they promise each other?" he asked.

For a moment she thought, then finally shrugged. "I have never known anyone to make a vow to another when they want to live with that person. A man may buy a bride, or a man can kidnap another man's wife and make her his own, but most times among my people, a man and woman just decide they will start living together."

"Is that what we did?" he asked. "When you came with Josiah to look for me after I left your village with a very sad heart?"

"Yes. When Josiah came to find you, I knew what I wanted. And I believed you wanted me. You never had to say any words to make me want to search for you after you ran away from my village. When I saw how glad you were that I had come to find you—I knew I had found my husband."

"Waits-by-the-Water?"

"Yes?"

"Would it be better for a man who wants a wife to give presents to that woman's family?"

She looked at him in the cold wind, studied the frost that formed an icy ring that clung to the graying hair around his mouth. Softly she said, "Some bring gifts to the woman's father."

He stared ahead, not looking at her for some moments, then asked, "What if that woman's father is no longer alive?"

She swallowed hard. "I am not sure, but I believe the man would give presents to the eldest in the family—asking to marry the woman."

Waits's breath came hard in her chest, her heart was beating so fast as she studied his face.

Finally Bass looked at her again. "I have decided something, *bu'a*. It is time that your people hear me make my vow to you. I think your family should hear me promise myself to you."

She could barely whisper, "Husband."

"You are my family, Waits-by-the-Water." His eyes softened, brimming again. "I will go to your brother. I will take him gifts. And I will ask his permission to be your husband . . . to take you as my wife."

Titus couldn't remember the last time he felt his knees rattle this bad. He was sure the others would know, that they would laugh behind their hands at this white man shaking with fear to get married.

Bass glanced to his left. At his elbow stood Pretty On Top. To his right stood Windy Boy. He was relieved when the young warriors offered to stand with him outside the lodge where Waits-by-the-Water was among her mother and friends, preparing for this ceremony.

Surrounding the three of them were more than fifteen hundred Crow, talking and laughing, come here to witness what Waits had described to everyone as a *promising*. Women waited patiently, having donned their very best, men stood stoic and expectant in their ceremonial dress, while the children darted between legs, chasing after dogs, throwing clumps of icy snow at one another, giggling, diving, sliding at the feet of their elders.

In less than a month he would reach his forty-third birthday. Which meant that Christmas was almost upon them. Titus fondly remembered his first Christmas with her down in Taos—the warmth of all those flickering candles, the fragrant smells drifting from Rosa Kinkead's kitchen, such soft music from the Mexican's cathedral and their nativity procession through the small village . . . then came the new year and his tearing himself away from her to travel far and long in hopes of putting old ghosts to rest.

But these people did not celebrate such annual events, nor did they have any similar religious festivals to mark the progress of each year beyond the tobacco ceremony of their women. Instead, these Crow celebrated war, perhaps the birth or naming of a child, maybe even the success of a war party or pony raid, nothing but that tobacco planting ceremony to track the march of the seasons the way the white man did.

From beyond the far edge of the crowd came a growing murmur. He turned to watch the witnesses part for a group of men resplendent in their very finest war clothing.

"Sore Lips," whispered Pretty On Top. "Strikes-in-Camp's war clan."

As more than twenty of them emerged onto the open ground that surrounded Scratch, he glanced at their faces, finding each man painted, feathers and stuffed birds tied in his hair, an animal head lashed onto his own with a rawhide whang tied under the chin. All but one of them carried a tall staff—some crooked, some straight—but each bearing feathers tied at right angles to the poles, wrapped in otter fur, arrayed with enemy scalps.

Only Strikes-in-Camp—who stood at their center—remained empty-handed. He crossed his arms, looked at the white man, and waited.

"Now," Pretty On Top whispered.

Scratch looked over at the young warrior. "The presents?"

Pretty On Top nodded.

Wanting to ask that handsome young warrior to wish him luck, Titus suddenly realized the Crow had no concept of luck, much less the crazy notion of one person passing on that luck to another. Instead, he turned to his right and stepped up to Turns Plenty who held the halters of two ponies. The old man handed the white man those halters, then stepped over to join Pretty On Top.

With his heart beginning to pound, Bass started for the far side of the open ground at the center of that huge crowd suddenly growing breathlessly quiet, so quiet Scratch could hear the whine of his winter moccasins on the old, icy snow, hear the slow plodding of each one of the eight hooves with that pair of ponies behind him. Somehow he made it across the arena at the center of the village and stopped a few feet from Strikes-in-Camp.

"These horses are for you," he said as confidently as he could muster it, having practiced and rehearsed the words over and over the past two weeks, to get them just right for this day.

Pointing to the scalp hanging from the halter beneath the jaw of each pony, Bass continued. "And these scalps—they belonged to the Arapaho warriors who rode these ponies against me last spring. The horses and the scalps of two brave warriors I now give to the mighty warrior I ask to become my brother-in-law."

Strikes-in-Camp took a few steps forward, moving around one of the ponies, then came back between the pair, lifting a leg here, touching a flank there, staring into the eyes of these gifts. When he turned and walked back to where he stood in the midst of his Sore Lip warrior society, Strikes-in-Camp recrossed his arms.

Anxious, Bass flicked a glance at Pretty On Top. The young warrior made a quick gesture with his hand.

Scratch turned back to Turns Plenty, then stepped up to Waits-by-the-Water's brother and held out the halters to those two ponies.

For a long moment the man stared at Bass, then looked over the white man's shoulder at Pretty On Top, Windy Boy, and Turns Plenty behind the trapper. Finally Strikes-in-Camp took the halters, held them a heartbeat, and passed them to one of the painted warriors who stood beside him. The man started away with the two Arapaho ponies.

By the time Strikes-in-Camp recrossed his arms and stared again at him, Bass realized he could barely hear—his heart pounded so loudly in his ears while he started to turn slowly around on those shaky legs of his, reminding himself he must not stumble, must not fall there in front of her people.

Less than three steps brought him back to Windy Boy, who held out his left hand. In it he clutched the halters to another two ponies. Quietly clucking for the pair to follow, Bass slowly started back to Strikes-in-Camp, stopping again a few feet from the warrior and his Sore Lip comrades.

"I bring more gifts to Strikes-in-Camp," he said in a studied cadence with the Crow words. "Two more horses."

"Two more horses," Strikes-in-Camp repeated, not budging, moving only his eyes as he looked from the white man to stare at one of the ponies.

Turning, Bass pulled the oxblood blanket from its back and held it before Strikes-in-Camp as a soft murmur came from the crowd. "This will keep your wife warm on those nights when you take the warpath against our enemies."

Strikes-in-Camp brushed the blanket with his fingers, lifted a corner, inspecting it as if to ascertain that it truly was new.

"Two moons ago I traded for it," Titus explained, scrambling for these words not in his planned script. "From the Crow trader—Tullock—at the mouth of the Tongue River."

Eventually Strikes-in-Camp took the red blanket from Bass's arm and passed it back to one of his warrior society. "Yes, it will keep my wife warm when I am not with her."

Bass thought he saw a little softening in the man's eyes. His heart leaped. For days now since he and Waits-by-the-Water had discussed this ceremony with her mother, Titus had steadily grown more apprehensive. From the beginning Strikes-in-Camp had frostily objected. He had even refused to talk to his mother about the white man's wanting to ask for his sister in marriage.

Three more times Waits had prevailed upon her mother to ask Strikes-in-Camp, hoping to wear him down. But each time he had grown a little more insolent. Then, yesterday, both of them had gone together to speak to him.

Waits had returned alone to pull back the flap to their shelter and clumsily squatted on the bedrobes. "Strikes-in-Camp says he will take your gifts."

Titus hadn't been sure he'd heard the words correctly at first. So he asked, hesitantly, "Your brother said he would give you away to be my wife?"

Then she was smiling not just with her mouth, but with her whole face, flinging her body against his as the tears gushed down her cheeks. He wasn't sure which of them cried more at that moment, but yesterday had lifted much of the gray pall that had settled about him since their arrival in Absaroka.

"But I don't understand—he refused three times before," Bass said, wagging his head, happy and confused all at once. "What made him—"

"I reminded him that you and I were already married in the way of our people, that we didn't need any ceremony," she told him, gripping one of his hands in both of hers while Magpie snuggled up next to them both. "Then I reminded him that you had no responsibility to ask anyone for me when I had no father."

"What did he say?"

"He scolded me again that I should not have given myself to a white man."

Bass gazed down at her belly, touched it, and said, "It's a little late for that now."

She grinned radiantly. "Then I told him you wanted to do your *promising* before my family, before all my people—whether or not he gave me to you."

"You told him I was going to promise myself to you before all your people no matter if he was there or not?"

"Yes, I said those words to him."

"That's when he agreed?"

But she wagged her head. "No."

"What made him decide?"

"Not until I told my brother that you were honoring him before all our people. You, the man he hated almost as much as any Blackfoot or Lakota warrior. You, the man he had no good words for. You were honoring him by coming before our whole village to offer him presents, to show our people that my brother was a man worthy of his respect. I told him that you would be showing our people that he was a man of true stature now, not just a young warrior trying to make a name for himself."

"And?"

"I told him how important that would be in front of our village—to see you, a white warrior with many scars and many, many coups, honoring him by asking for me in marriage."

"That's what changed his mind?"

Nodding, Waits-by-the-Water said, "I think he finally realized that it would be an honor to have you in his family, a man who would offer him presents despite all the bad that he has spoken of you, all the bad he has wished on you."

And now, before this hushed crowd, Bass stepped back to the second horse, carefully raising the rolled-up blanket of a brilliant medium blue he had tied across its back. He carefully unknotted two rawhide straps that secured the blanket to a single braided-horsehair surcingle lashed around the horse's middle.

Stopping before Strikes-in-Camp, the white man said, "And this blanket is for your mother. I hope that it will keep Crane warm when you are away to fight the enemies who killed her husband, the enemies who killed your father."

The warrior touched the blue blanket, laying his palm on it where it rested across Bass's forearms. "It is a good color. My mother will like this blanket."

As Strikes-in-Camp pulled the blanket roll from the white man's arms, a rifle emerged from the tube of blue wool. The stunned warrior froze with the blanket draped over his forearm, staring at the rifle.

"What is this you hide in the giveaway blanket?" Strikes-in-Camp asked. "Another present for my mother?"

Bass smiled, swallowed, his mind scratching to recall those words he had practiced. "This rifle is for the brother of the woman I want to take for my wife. A rifle for the man who is the head of her family now. May it kill many of our enemies, Strikes-in-Camp. This rifle . . ." And he stopped, dragging a long-barreled pistol from the wide, worn belt he had buckled around his elkhide coat. "And this short gun too."

"It . . . it too?" the warrior asked in surprise.

Nodding, Titus continued. "Both are gifts for a brother-in-law I honor today as a brave and fearless warrior who stands between his people and their enemies."

Like Strikes-in-Camp, the crowd was stunned into silence.

Quickly passing the blanket back to a comrade, the young warrior first took the pistol, giving it a cursory inspection before he stuffed it into the wide, colorful finger-woven wool sash knotted around his blanket capote.

Then with both hands Strikes-in-Camp took the smoothbore fusil from Bass's arms with something resembling reverence. Those more-than-twenty other members of the Sore Lip Society crowded in on both sides, murmuring in admiration, touching the musket's freshly oiled barrel, its gleaming stock, the graceful curve of the gooosenecked hammer that clutched a newly knapped sliver of amber flint.

Scratch grew anxious, standing there before the warrior, waiting for some words to be spoken, something to be done. Had he gotten all the words right? Oh, how he had practiced and practiced them—

Suddenly Strikes-in-Camp leveled his eyes at the white man. "These gifts . . . they are truly fit for the daughter of a chief."

"He-Who-Is-No-Longer-Here was not a chief," Bass struggled with the words, tongue-tied and nervous as a field mouse cornered by the barn cat, "but she is the sister of a man who will be a chief someday."

The warrior's dark eyes actually smiled at the white man. "You came here to honor me, *Pote Ani*. But in many ways you have honored my whole family. And you have brought honor to our people. The Absaroka are known not only by the strength of our enemies—the Blackfoot, the Blood, Gros Ventre, and Lakota . . . but we are known by the strength of our friends: the white men who stand with us to fight our enemies."

Laying the new rifle in the crook of his left elbow, Strikes-in-Camp reached out and seized Bass's forearm with his right hand, clutching it fiercely.

"Now I go to bring my mother to this place. Together we will bring my sister to you. So that there can be what you call the *promising*. So that she becomes your wife before all our people."

Before Bass could respond, Strikes-in-Camp had turned and was moving back through the crowd that parted for him.

It truly felt as if it took forever, more than an hour—although he realized it was but a matter of minutes before he heard the admiring rustle washing his way through the crowd. Yard by yard he watched the hundreds move aside, every one of them falling silent but for their hushed whispers. Finally those members of the Sore Lips stepped aside. Through their ranks emerged Strikes-in-Camp. Behind him stood Crane. Beside her, Waits-by-the-Water.

Titus gasped at her beauty.

Both wore their very best. His wife wore a blue wool dress he did not recognize, something big enough to fit over her swollen belly. Front and back across its heavy yoke were sewn the milk teeth of the elk. Red strips of ribbon were tied across its skirt, each tassel blowing gently with the winter breeze. And Waits had smeared the deep-purple vermilion not only in the part of her gleaming hair, but in a wide band that ran from her hairline down her forehead, continued down the bridge of her nose, and ended at the bottom of her chin. Two more purple lines started at the bottom of her eyes, dropped across the high cheekbones, then ended at the jawbones.

Scratch found her radiance so stunning that he had to remind himself to breathe.

Strikes-in-Camp moved aside; then Crane brought her daughter forward. Now Strikes-in-Camp's wife, Bright Wings, stepped up behind him, the brilliant oxblood blanket around her shoulders. From her arm she took the new blue blanket, handing it to her husband. Strikes-in-Camp passed it on to the white man. Together they unfurled it, and the two of them laid it across Crane's shoulders as the old woman gazed up into the white man's face and smiled, her eyes misting.

Scratch could not remember the last time he had seen her smile. It had been so long ago, before Whistler had led the revenge raid on the Blackfoot. Then he realized that until today Crane had had no reason to smile.

With her new blue blanket wrapped about her shoulders, Crane reached out, took hold of her daughter's hand, and raised it waist level, presenting the hand to the white man.

Without any urging Bass seized Waits's hand—not sure of a sudden if he would remember all that he wanted to tell her, all that he had rehearsed saying before her family and her people.

"Among the white man, when two people want to share their lives together, they stand before their families, stand before their friends, stand before a holy man in the sight of the First Maker . . . and they give promises to the one they love.

"These promises are not a simple thing the two can easily ignore or leave behind, because their promising is a bond that the friends and family hear them make."

He felt his eyes starting to sting with tears.

"I do not have any family to join me today. You and our children are my only family. But I have friends among your people—friends I trust to stand at my back when we fight our enemies. From this day on I hope to have many more friends among the Crow.

"Before your family, here before your people—I make this promise: that I will protect you, provide for you, shelter you from storm and cold and hunger until I am no more. This promise I will keep all of my days, even unto my final day. Our children will not know want, nor will they know fear. Instead, they will know the love of their family until they are grown and leave us to walk a road of their own making."

He reached up with a roughened fingertip and gently wiped that first, lone tear spilling from one of her eyes. Bass wasn't sure how to read the look in them—so filled with love were they at one moment, filled with surprise at his words the next.

"I promise myself to you all the rest of my days," he concluded. "I will be your husband. Will you be my wife, the mother of my children?"

Then he noticed how she was clenching her bottom lip between her teeth.

When she finally spoke, Waits-by-the-Water whispered, "I will be your wife, Ti-tuzz. Mother of your children. For all of our days—"

And he felt her grip him with tremendous force as she quivered slightly.

Concerned, he said, "Waits-by-the-Water?"

"I must go with my mother now—"

"Your mother?"

Reaching up to touch his face with her fingertips, Waits's eyes softened, and she said, "The rush of warm water has come, *bu'a.*" She looked down at her feet.

When he gazed at her moccasins below the edge of that blue wool dress, he saw the puddle softening the snow between her feet, how the moisture had soaked the bottom of her leggings and moccasins, how the pool of it steamed in the cold air.

"I promise you I will stand at your side for all the rest of your days," she gasped, her face pinching as another cramp swept over her. Crane moved up to take her elbow, to steady her as Waits said, "But . . . your child will not wait any longer."

"This one is so big!" the elderly Horse Woman announced as her bony fingers pushed, prodded, squeezed the belly.

Waits groaned from the ripping torment within, the stabbing of the fingers without.

"Sit up now, woman," Horse Woman commanded.

Together Crane and the old midwife each pulled on an arm to bring Waits to a sitting position.

The old one asked, "Do you want to push?"

"Y-y-yes!" she gasped as the next fiery rush of pain crossed her belly. Crane pulled one arm, then the other, from the blue wool dress they had borrowed from a large family friend. It hung around her neck as she shuddered with the passing of that long tongue of fire coursing through the center of her.

She knew it would be soon. Her body shuddering with the easing of the contraction, Waits remembered when Magpie was born in that land far, far to the south. "Wh-where is Magpie?"

Crane explained, "She is with my sister's family. I told her she will have a baby brother or sister to play with before the sun sets on another day."

Growling with the flush of another fiery tensing, Waits blinked away some of the tears in her eyes and watched the old wrinkled woman crawl up close before her with a long stake in her hand, a hand-sized stone in the other. Horse Woman drove it into the bare ground inches from Waits's knees, in front of the robe she had been sitting upon.

"Hold on to this," the midwife demanded, taking both of the young woman's wrists in her bony hands and yanking them away from the bare, swollen belly, pulling them toward the stake.

"Hold on—then you can push," Crane added.

They pulled the blue dress up and off her head, then quickly draped an old, much-used blanket over her shoulders, stuffing part of it between her shaking legs, beneath her where spots of blood began to appear. Horse Woman and Crane both bent so low, their cheeks rubbed the floor of the lodge, peering between the young mother's thighs.

"He comes!" Crane cried out in joy. "He comes now!"

Suddenly Waits was blowing like a horse after a long run as the pain rumbled through her like a swollen knot that grew bigger, ever bigger. Then she felt as if she were being torn in half and could not think of how she could save herself—

"Its head is here," Horse Woman announced gruffly.

Waits was so faint, gasping with such shallow breaths, wondering how she could hold on to the stick any longer—

"You are almost done," Crane cooed beside her daughter, her arm around her shoulders, whispering in her ear. "Remember Magpie. Remember that this will be over soon."

"One more push," Horse Woman demanded. She was hunched over between Waits-by-the-Water's knees, crouching there with her hands supporting the newborn's head. "One more—and this child will be here to see you."

Starting to groan with the recognition of that next tensing, Waits felt the pain rise like a crack of far-off thunder within her, shoving its way into her throat like summer lightning before it pushed downward with a sudden clap. She was sure this huge child was ripping her apart as the fire became more than she could bear.

Shuddering, trembling, suddenly collapsing onto her bottom, Waits found she had no more strength left. This child would have to do the rest on its own—

The baby cried.

Blinking again, Waits swiped at her eyes swimming in tears, peering at the old midwife crouched between her knees. The gray head pulled back, the nearly toothless mouth grinned, the baggy eyes smiling anew. She held up the tiny squalling newborn, legs and arms pumping, its head thrashing side to side. Down its belly her eyes dropped quickly, finding that purplish white life cord attached to its belly.

Pushing the life cord aside, Horse Woman held the child up for the young mother's close examination. "See, woman?"

Crane was sobbing, her face swimming into view through Waits's tears. "You have a boy!"

Breathless, Waits whispered in a weary gush, "Ti-tuzz . . . has a boy."

NINETEEN

"I think you should've hightailed it outta here while you had your chance, Scratch," Jim Bridger huffed as he scurried up in a crouch.

Bass watched his old friend settle in beside him at the breastworks. "And leave you boys to have all this fun?"

At Titus's other elbow Shadrach Sweete said, "Maybeso we ought lay back on Titus, Gabe. I been jabbin' him 'bout it since he come running in here."

"I don't rightly think you're an idjit," Bridger declared with a grim smile. "Just figgered you for more sense when it comes to fighting Blackfoot."

"I fit my share of the bastards, that's for certain," Titus said. "Ain't had a year in these mountains what Bug's Boys hasn't troubled me and mine."

"I tol't Titus he could still slip off when it gets dark tonight," Sweete explained.

"Shadrach," Bass said with a grin and a doleful wag of his head, "you goddamn well know them red niggers got us surrounded, so there ain't no slipping off come dark for any coon."

"The man's right, Shad," Bridger agreed. "There ain't

gonna be no leaving for any of us now. If there's gonna be a fight with all these here bastards—I for one am sure as hell glad to have Titus Bass and his guns here with us."

Scratch nodded at Gabe with appreciation. That simple gesture was all the thanks he needed to express for those words from an old friend. Sweete himself patted Bass on the shoulder, then turned to the side, staring over the brush and log breastworks the brigade had hastily thrown up the day before.

The very day Titus had ridden into the brigade camp, making a midwinter's social call on old friends.

For hundreds of miles around, the land lay locked in winter, frozen and silent. From time to time over the last couple of months Scratch had ventured out to try trapping one river or another, believing that he would find some beaver out of their lodges. But with the hard freeze that held on week after week, even the Yellowstone had turned to ice.

Restless as a deerfly in high summer, Titus finally decided he would mosey upriver to visit Bridger's camp. Before the hard freeze had descended upon this country, Scratch had bumped into some of Gabe's men scouting for sign of beaver a few miles up Pryor Creek from the Crow village. They had informed him where the brigade had made its camp on the north side of the Yellowstone, just west of the mouth of Rock Creek— no more than a long day's ride from the mouth of the Pryor.

A week later he had hugged Magpie, kissed Waits-by-the-Water, and given the little boy-child a squeeze before he was off. Sometimes a man just needed to move.

At first Scratch had smelled the wood smoke, then spotted the gray tatters of it clinging among the tops of the leafless cottonwoods upriver. From the sideslope of a hill he had spotted the brigade's camp no more than two miles ahead. It was late of the afternoon, which meant he was saddle weary, hungry, and half-froze for coffee, not to mention how keenly he anticipated the palaver and storytelling they'd do around the fire that night.

He had nudged Samantha into a brisk walk, reining her down the gentle slope toward the bottomland where he lost sight of the camp as he emerged from the brush along the south bank of the Yellowstone and dismounted. He had dropped the reins and stepped onto the ice by himself. A good ten yards out he stopped, then jumped and stomped, assured the stuff was thick enough for them both.

Skirting some spongy patches, Bass had gotten the mule to the north bank, the wood smoke grown all the stronger in his nostrils, when his ears caught a sound that shouldn't have been on that cold wind. Not that trappers didn't yelp and whoop and holler themselves when they took a notion to . . . but those voices sure didn't sound like white men at all.

He had swung into the saddle cinched on Samantha's back, pitching his leg over the thick bedroll of two robes and a blanket, and was just settling his left foot in the wide cottonwood stirrup when a screech jerked him completely around—his heart suddenly in his throat as more than two dozen warriors on snorting ponies broke from the brush thirty yards ahead of him. Smack-dab between him and the brigade camp.

It was die right there, or go under making a stab at pulling his hash out of the fire.

Without thinking, Titus had banged his heels against the young mule's flanks. Samantha bolted away, eyes big as beaver dollars, ears standing straight and peaked as granite spires in the nearby Beartooth Mountains.

Damn, if he hadn't surprised the bastards by charging right at them. They had milled a moment, ponies whirling as they reined up, then split in as many directions as there were horsemen. Bass had Samantha into the brush again, whipping the mule back and forth through the cottonwoods before the warriors could regroup and turn around to pursue him. But there had been more ahead of him before he'd made it to the end of the gauntlet—wondering every step of the way what the hell he would have done if he had decided against charging on into that camp, or if he hadn't had those old friends to run to.

"Hol'cher fire!" some man had bellowed as Bass burst from the willows and buckbrush, lying low along Samantha's neck, clinging like a fat tick to the mule that carried him on a collision course for the piles of deadfall, logs, and leafless brush Bridger's men were stacking up on all sides of their compound at that very moment.

"It's a g-goddamned white man!"

"Bridger!" Scratch had screamed as he neared the breastworks. "Sweete! Ho, Meek!"

"Damn betcha it's a white man!"

Of a sudden a half-dozen of them had shoved their way into the buckbrush wall they had been throwing up, suddenly heaving against the thorny barrier to force open up a narrow path just wide enough for a man to slip through sideways . . . then forcing it a bit wider . . . and finally just wide enough that he knew Samantha would make it.

It seemed as though a many-armed creature had reached up to drag him out of the saddle, so many hands were raised as he brought the mule skidding to a halt inside the brush corral . . . a sea of faces, all of them fuzzy and out of focus, blurred by the wreaths of frost that clung about every head.

"I'll be the devil's whore if it ain't Titus Bass!" growled Joe Meek.

Standing just that much taller beside Meek was Shad Sweete. "Come to pay us a social call, have you?"

Bass had gotten his land legs back there on the frozen, compacted snow, working his knees a moment to assure himself they would hold his weight after the long, cold ride. "Nawww, you soft-brained niggers! I come to tell you boys you're plumb surrounded by Blackfoot!"

Wrinkling his brow with the gravest look of worry Titus could remember ever seeing, Sweete had replied, "Blackfoot? Blackfoot? Where the Blackfoot?"

"We don't see no dram-med Blackfoot!" Bridger roared with laughter as he had come stomping up, holding out his bare hand.

"You niggers are lower'n a bull snake's belly, thinking you're so goddamned funny!" Titus had grumbled as he'd knocked Bridger's hand aside and they embraced quickly. "Man comes riding in here to help you boys, Blackfoot stuck on his tail like stink on a polecat . . . and all you can do is rawhide him like you're doing to me?"

"Don't take no offense," Sweete pleaded with a grin as big as sunrise. "Me and Joe didn't mean nothing by it. Glory, if we ain't all pleased to see your butt-ugly mug, Titus!"

"And his guns," Joe added, slapping the thin man on the back. "If'n there's a man what shoots center and kills Blackfoot, it be Titus Bass."

"We can sure stand to have us 'nother gun, Scratch," Bridger observed grimly, much of the good humor gone.

"From what I saw back yonder, you boys need ever' gun you can get," Bass replied.

Sweete shrugged. "Last we figgered a while ago, Gabe and me cipher we're on the downside of odds twenty to one."

With a low whistle, Scratch wagged his head.

"Good thing you didn't catch these'r arrers yourself," George W. Ebbert commented as he stepped up behind Bass.

He turned, finding "Squire" Ebbert stopping at the rear of a prancing Samantha, three arrows quivering from her bloody flanks. Quickly he snagged hold of her halter, holding it tight just below her jaw as he stroked her muzzle, scratched a moment between her eyes and ears, cooing at her. Then he stepped back to her hindquarters, inspecting the three wounds.

"I figger I can quit all three of 'em outta her," Titus proposed. "Ain't a one too deep the shaft'll pull off."

Bridger winked, commenting, "Just didn't give 'em a good 'nough target, Scratch."

"Don't ever plan to, neither." He stood at Samantha's head again, stroking her neck. "You boys got your stock in here with you?"

"All of our critters," Sweete explained.

"I'll drop my bedroll and possibles off yonder by those trees—then I'll cut these here arrows out. Please tell me you'll have some hot coffee for me when I'm done."

Dick Owens poured him a cup as Scratch walked up more than a half hour later. The sun had gone down before Bass had begun his bloody work on the mule's flanks, and it had grown cold as all get-out. He sipped at his coffee, holding it under his face to let the steam warm the frozen rawhide of his cheeks and nose, sensing the painful return of feeling to his fingertips as he clutched the tin cup in both hands.

Finally he asked those close by, "How you fellers get yourselves in such a fine fix as this?"

Around that fire Shad Sweete and some others began to relate the story of how forty of Bridger's brigade had run into a small band of Blackfoot, some twenty of them sniffing around in Crow country, a few weeks back. Those forty trappers had rushed off to ambush the war party, pinning them down on a narrow, timbered island in the middle of the Yellowstone, then nearly wiped them out.

"But something tells me a few of them niggers got away," Scratch declared, "and they rode hard for home to bring the rest of these devil's whelps."

Squire Ebbert nodded. "They left the dead ones behind—four bastards the rest shoved under the ice covering the river. But from all the patches of blood on the snow and the scratches of them travois they made when they hauled off their wounded, easy to tell we cut 'em up purty bad."

"I'll say we cut 'em up real bad," Shad snorted. "Next day when we had us a look where they forted up, we found plenty of brains and blood."

"That war party didn't have a horse left between 'em after we run off their stock," Meek explained by the fire. "So they was dragging them travois outta there on foot."

"Way we tallied it," Sweete reckoned, "there wasn't but a handful got outta there 'thout a scratch."

"Don't look like it matters now," Bass grumped. "If'n only one got away to bring the others, you're still in the soup, boys."

"Look who's in the soup with us!" Ebbert bawled, slapping his knee.

"I'm glad he is," Sweete observed.

After sipping some more of his steamy coffee before it went cold with the rapid drop in temperature, Scratch asked, "So how long you fellas been hunkered down here?"

"Three days now," Meek disclosed. "Ever since we run off them Blackfoot, Gabe's been like a nervous ol' woman: ever' day he'd go up on that bluff yonder with his spyglass. Looked over the country far and wide."

"Only a matter of time afore they come to even the score," Sweete groaned.

Early that next morning on his climb to the bluff, Bridger discovered the plain downriver boiling with Blackfoot, with even more warriors streaming across the ridges. Hurrying back to camp, he started his men building the breastworks of deadfall and buckbrush, laboring long and hard to hack clear a wide no-man's-land completely around their fortress. Inside, the trappers chopped down nearly every cottonwood for the walls.

Then yesterday Bridger had slipped out to learn what he could of the

Blackfoot, discovering that even more of the enemy were arriving, seeing that the warriors had moved their camp no more than two miles from where the white men waited out the brutal, subzero cold.

By that third day the sixty-man brigade had a bulwark that stood almost six feet high, enclosing a square some two hundred fifty feet to a side. If they were going to die there, they sure as hell planned on making it tough on the Blackfoot to rub them out.

"Goddamn 'em and their war songs," Sweete grumbled beside Scratch now. "They been playing them drums ever' day they had us surrounded."

While the intense cold settled into his every joint this evening of his second day within the breastworks, Titus had to admit those never-ending drums were starting to bother him too as the trappers sat in the fading glow of that winter twilight. Listening to the distant singing, shouts, and high-pitched shrieks, Bass chuckled and said, "You're 'bout as grumpy as a bear 'thout your sleep, ain'cha?"

"Cain't none of us sleep much since they showed up," Bridger explained as he came up at a crouch. "Shad's got good reason to be grumpy—he's allays been the one made sure we always had half the boys awake while the rest got some shut-eye."

Night fell on the Yellowstone valley, a second coming of darkness for Bass here among Bridger's sixty. Men came and went around the fires burning at the bottom of pits scooped out of the sandy soil so none of them would be backlit as they moved about their fortress. More than two dozen of the men had already curled up in their robes near one or another of the ten fires, desperately trying for some sleep because they were scheduled to go on watch later that night.

Bass lay there in a cocoon of his own robes and blanket, shuddering until the fur finally warmed with his body's heat. For the longest time he could not get comfortable enough to sleep, listening to the low voices of those keeping a watch at the walls, the snuffling of the cold animals gnawing on scraps of peeled cottonwood bark nearby, the crunch and whine of footsteps made upon the trampled snow. And through it all he thought of Waits-by-the-Water, how she was faring with Magpie and her newborn brother.

He wondered when the First Maker would show him a name for the child, then brooded that he might never make it back to the Crow village to give that name to the boy.

There wasn't a man among those sixty-two of them who didn't know the deck was stacked against them. At his last count Bridger announced there had to be more than a thousand Blackfoot ready to charge the breastworks. Chances were the warriors had worked themselves up with the singing and dancing and drum pounding for better than three days so they'd attack in the morning—the fourth. Plenty of horses and guns, powder and blankets to win as the spoils of battle when they wiped out the white men.

He thought about how grim the mood had become just that afternoon as the sun sank in the west and the trappers saw just how clear that terrible night would be, driving the temperatures far below zero. It grew so cold the water in the trees froze, and they began to pop. From time to time through the night a big cottonwood split as the cold continued to plummet—booming like that throaty twelve-pounder at Fort Union when it had raked through the cabins where the Deschamps clan took cover. Smaller trees popped like the smoothbores these Blackfoot traded off the English north in Canada.

How he wished he were back beside his woman. Smelling her skin, feeling himself grow hard and hot against her flesh. How he missed her. How he would miss her if this were the end.

Scratch knew he had to stay there among friends who were glad to have one more man, one more gun. If these men were going to hunker down to the bitter end, taking as many of the bastards as they could with them when the end came . . . then Bass decided he belonged there.

After all, there was no better place for a man to reach the end of his string than among his fellows. No better time to have his candle snuffed out than in giving his life while protecting his friends—

"Bass!" the voice whispered sharply in his ear.

Instantly coming out of the thick fog of sleep, blinking his eyes, ripping back the buffalo robe, and poking his face into the cold blackness, he found Osborne Russell kneeling over him.

"Bridger sent me for you."

His mouth was as pasty as the scum of bear tallow at the bottom of a week-old kettle. "Yeah," he groaned. "Bridger—"

Suddenly Titus realized something was different.

The whole damned fortress was bathed in an eerie crimson light. The pale-red glow shimmered and pulsed, turning Russell's face, his squat beaver hat, the upturned collar of his buffalo coat . . . everything tinged red as fresh blood.

Titus was scared right down to his marrow. But it wasn't the cold that made him shiver as he kicked off the robes and blanket to stand.

"W-where's he?" His teeth chattered, clacking more from fright than cold. Scratch admitted he hadn't been this scared since Asa McAfferty had first chattered about hoodoos and malevolent spirits slipping through that crack in the sky from the other side of existence.

"C'mon," Russell said as he snugged his hat down over his ears.

There wasn't a man asleep now. Every one of the sixty-one either stood watching the sky, or sat dumbfounded in his robes, having been awakened by the others.

"How long this been going on?" Titus asked with a gulp.

Meek turned at his approach. "Just started."

"Damn, it's almost purty," Scratch whispered quietly. "If'n it didn't scare the piss outta me."

Then he realized he did need to relieve himself and turned away to the breastworks. He urinated on the brush, not once taking his eyes off the dancing, shimmering lights that slowly extended their crimson paint across more and more of the northern sky.

"Ever you see something like this?" Sweete asked as Bass stepped up beside him.

He wagged his head.

"Neither've I," Bridger agreed.

"Damn! Lookee there!" Levin Mitchell exclaimed nearby.

At the very center of the corona the lights no longer merely pulsed. Now to the east of north, bands of crimson lights began to stream skyward from the edge of the earth—brilliant fingers of red, rust, orange, and blood-tinted gold. Every streamer of color wavering, pulsing, expanding, and diminishing, then expanding again as the trappers murmured among themselves.

"Listen," Bass said after a long time of watching the heavens.

"To what?" Meek asked.

"I don't hear a thing," Russell commented.

"That's just it," Titus told them. "I ain't heard them goddamned drums since you come woke me."

"I believe Scratch is right," Bridger declared. "Sons of bitches ain't pounding and dancing no more."

"They see'd this sky too."

"Bound to, Scratch," Shad said. "Lookee there—them red lights are brightest over in their part of the sky, off to the east yonder."

For a long time Titus brooded on the heavenly show, then said, "This here gotta be some big medicine to them Blackfoot, fellas. The way Injuns read sign—this bound to be 'bout the biggest medicine any of them niggers ever laid eyes on."

In all his natural-born days, this eerie display of the northern lights had to be the most frightening exhibition of celestial fire he had ever witnessed. Up to this moment the most dramatic night phenomenon he had seen had been back in the autumn of thirty-three, when the sky rained fire. One shooting star after another, a handful at a time, almost from the moment the sky grew dark enough to spot the starry trails right on till dawn when the coming light made the sky grow so pale the meteor shower was no longer visible.

Remembering how Josiah's little boy had cried with wonder and fear that night . . . Joshua.

Bass wondered on him now. The child would be . . . close to four years old. Walking and talking, likely riding a horse too. How he hoped

Josiah had fared well down there in Taos with Matthew Kinkead and that free man, Esau.

Safer there were they all than he up here in Crow country where the damned Blackfoot had come to raid.

He whispered a curse on that thousand surrounding Bridger's brigade, a breathless curse on their women and children, on their old and on their young who would grow into warriors, an especially hearty curse on their women—for it was they who gave birth to generations of fighting men.

"What did you say?" Sweete asked, stepping over.

He immediately realized he had been muttering in a whisper. "Just asking God to do something for me is all."

"Never knowed you to be a religious man," Shad replied.

"I ain't, not like most."

"You was asking God to do what?" Bridger inquired.

Scratch sighed. "I asked the same God what made that bloody sky up there to wipe out all them red niggers."

"You a praying man, Titus Bass?" Meek asked when he stepped close.

Titus thought a moment, then said, "I s'pose I am when it comes down to it, Joe. Leastways—like I said—I'm praying God rubs all them sonsabitches off the face of the earth."

"I figger ary man can pray for that too," Bridger added quietly.

And quiet was just the way it remained inside those breastworks for the rest of the night. So quiet, a man could swear he could hear the hum of that northern sky as it pulsated and wavered red as blood. From downstream floated the distant songs and chants, the hearty rhythms as some of the Blackfoot pounded sticks on rawhide parfleches serving in place of drums. They too had to be watching the portent of this terrible sky.

Gradually the east began to lighten, and with the coming of dawn the brilliance of the northern lights softened from crimson to a pale rose. Eventually there were no more streaks of red in the sky as the sun made its appearance downriver. And with that newborn light Titus saw how the frightening cold had settled along the Yellowstone itself, seeping among the trees, its foggy mist clinging in dirty-white smears through the bonelike cottonwood and brush.

"Here they come!"

At the warning cry the sixty-two were instantly jerked into motion, crowding toward that wall of the breastworks where the call had been raised. No longer were these fur men quiet. First they muttered to themselves, then talked low to others nearby.

As those first ranks of Blackfoot emerged from the swirling, icy mist downriver, several of the trappers cursed. Two hundred yards. More and ever more filed behind them. It had to be just as Bridger pronounced. A thousand. Mayhaps even more than a thousand. The enemy ranks filled the wide riverbed from bank to bank, trudging toward the white man's fortress on foot through the snow, using the Yellowstone's unobstructed frozen surface to make their approach.

"This be the day, boys!" Bridger bellowed.

"Take some of them niggers with you!"

All around Bass the trappers were screwing up their resolve now—yelling at one another with that sort of encouragement doomed men give to friends and comrades as the end looms near. At the center of the breastworks the trappers' squaws began to keen quietly, the young half-breed children whimpering pitifully.

"Hell is where I'll send as many as I can!" Shad roared.

Popping a half-dozen lead balls into his mouth for the coming fight, Titus vowed, "By God, I'll see my share in hell a'fore noon!"

On the Blackfoot came. At the center of that first column walked a figure in a heavy white wool blanket, wearing a headdress constructed of numberless white ermine skins to which had been attached polished buffalo horns. Attached to the narrow cord of sinew between the horn tips was a single eagle feather that trembled on each wisp of cold breeze.

No more were any of the Blackfoot hidden by the fog. Now the whole of them paraded in full view of the white men waiting behind the bulwark of their brush fort. What an impressive sight they made: their faces clearly painted, feathers and scalps streaming from lances, bows, and shields, war clubs and rifles at the ready.

"You ever faced anything like this?" Meek asked.

"Shit." And Bass shook his head. "I ain't ever see'd this many Blackfoot in one place a'fore."

Then, just beyond a hundred yards, the one in the white blanket waved an arm, shouting something to those around him, and that first rank of warriors turned aside. Slogging onto the snowy bank, they pushed on through the brush until they reached the open prairie as the wind kicked up old snow around their ankles and calves.

"You figger 'em to work around us, Gabe?" Ebbert hollered.

"I can't figger 'em for nothing," Bridger answered. "No telling what they're about."

It did indeed mystify the trappers to watch the succeeding ranks of the warriors follow the first. Instead of some going this way while others went that in what Scratch had assumed would be their attempt to surround the breastworks, the Blackfoot all followed the one in the white blanket. Eventually the entire war party had abandoned the frozen river for the open prairie more than a hundred yards from where the trappers stood waiting the attack.

By then the first warriors to reach that open ground were starting to sit. As the hundreds arrived in waves, they too settled into the snow around their leaders, forming a huge council circle in that open-air amphitheater.

"Don't that take the chalk!" Scratch cried.

"What you callate they're up to, Gabe?" Sweete asked.

"Can't say as I know," Bridger replied.

"Yellow-backed sonsabitches!" Bass flung his voice over the breastworks at the enemy.

Suddenly emboldened, other trappers began to taunt the Blackfoot. "You're women!"

"Cowards!"

"Can't fight us like real men!"

Titus screamed with the others, "You ain't got no manhood!"

"Come on and fight!" Sweete bellowed.

Louder and louder the white men became in their insults. But still the Blackfoot remained in their huge war council just beyond rifle range.

"You want we should fire some bullets at 'em?" Squire Ebbert inquired.

"Just a waste for now," Bridger declined.

Scratch agreed, "You'll need your lead soon enough, boys."

"Damn," Sweete growled, "I'll bet there ain't one of them niggers knows any American talk."

"Too bad they can't unnerstand what we're calling 'em," Meek added.

With a grin Bass passed his rifle off to Osborne Russell. "Hold this for me."

"What you fixing to do?" Russell asked.

Turning to Meek and Sweete, Scratch gave instructions, "You two 'bout the biggest niggers there is out in these here mountains. Both of you pull aside some of that brush wall over there."

"What the hell for?" Meek demanded.

"Them Blackfoots don't speak no American, so they don't unnerstand us, right?"

"Right," Sweete replied, still mystified.

"So I'm gonna talk to 'em in sign so they damn well know what I think of 'em."

"Shit," Bridger grumbled, "they too far off! None of them red niggers gonna see you talking in hand sign!"

Smiling hugely now, Scratch shook his head and said, "Them bastards bound to see my sign, Gabe!"

"C'mon, Joe!" Sweete cried, bolting away. "Help me pull this here brush back!"

The moment the two of them had muscled the logs and branches apart, Scratch lunged through. Right behind him Meek and Sweete popped through the narrow opening as every last one of the trappers surged to that wall to have themselves a good vantage point to watch Bass's "sign making."

Instead of stopping just outside the breastworks, Scratch kept right on going, halting only after he was more than ten yards beyond the wall— alone and in the open, where he began to attract the attention of those warriors on the outer flank of the council.

Emerging from the breastworks empty-handed, the lone white man unbuckled his belt and flung it to the ground beside him, then yanked off his elk-hide coat. Spinning about in the swirling ground-snow to face the fortress again, Bass dropped the coat and dragged up the long tail of his war shirt, tugging aside the blue wool breechclout to expose his rump. With one cold bare hand he slapped the faded wool longhandles.

From afar came the first shouts of fury. He was certain they understood his sign.

"Come kiss my ass, you yellow dogs!" he screamed as he bent over, staring between his legs at the Blackfoot. "Come kiss my ass!"

Behind Titus, both Meek and Sweete were doubled over, roaring with laughter. At the walls of the brush fort, every one of those sixty-some trappers were screaming at the Blackfoot now, many gasping for breath as they guffawed and yelled, guffawed and bellowed some more. This was damn well about as much fun as a man could have before he went under.

When his rump and bare hands grew numb from the terrible cold, Bass finally stood, wheeled about, and raised the front tail of his war shirt, grabbing his crotch.

"This here's a man!" he shrieked at the enemy. "You ain't got a pecker like me 'cause you're all women!"

"Women afraid to fight!" Sweete cried behind him.

Eventually Titus picked his coat out of the snow, buckling the belt around it, then turned again, bent over, and gave his rump one last slap before he slowly trudged back to the breastworks—accompanied by the hoots and hollers and uproarious cheers of those sixty-one other men.

At the walls Meek and Sweete slapped him on the shoulders, teary-eyed, they were laughing so hard.

"Up with him!" Shad ordered.

With that the two of them firmly seized the smaller man and hoisted Titus high into the air. Confused for a moment, Bass thrashed as Meek and Sweete stepped directly under him, settling the skinny man atop their shoulders where he caught his balance.

The cheering grew even louder as two dozen more emerged from that narrow gap in the breastworks, pushing back on it to carve an entrance wide enough for those who carried Bass aloft. Many of the trappers were already growing hoarse from shouting and laughing so lustily in the dry cold air, surging around Meek and Sweete, some bending over and slapping their own rumps to copy how Bass had taunted the enemy.

Back inside the breastworks, Sweete and Meek started around in a wide circle, still carrying Titus on their shoulders, when Bridger suddenly hollered above the clamor.

"Someone's fat is in the fire, boys!"

The noise ended abruptly and Scratch leaped to the snow, hurrying to the wall with the others.

The warriors were parting slightly, allowing that warrior in the white blanket to step through their numbers. Halfway between the Blackfoot and the breastworks he came to a halt and began to wave his arms.

First one, then another, of the white men translated the chief's gestures.

"Says they ain't gonna fight!"

"Can't fight us today."

More signs were made.

"Gonna go back to his village now!"

Shaking his head in wonder, Scratch reflected, "You s'pose them Blackfoot figgered that red sky over their camp was bad medicine for 'em?"

Sweete snorted with a gust of raw mirth and said, "It sure weren't your skinny ass what scared 'em off!"

As the white men watched in fascination, the chief turned aside and started across the bottom ground for the slopes bordering the valley, starting west for the Three Forks of the Missouri. At the same time less than half of the warriors began to move away in the opposite direction, marching downriver to the east.

"That bunch ain't going back home," Meek commented sourly.

"This gotta be a trick," Ebbert said.

"We'll wait 'em out and see," Bridger declared.

A few minutes later, as the last of the Blackfoot were disappearing around a bend in the Yellowstone, Sweete came up and threw his arm around Bass's shoulder. "You scared 'em off with that bony ass of your'n, Scratch."

Thin-lipped and melancholy, Bass wagged his head. He pointed downriver. "Not that bunch, Shad. They ain't running off for home. Them niggers is making for Crow country."

TWENTY

Not trusting the Blackfoot any farther than he could throw one, Jim Bridger had his brigade maintain their vigilant watch across the next three days, wary that the enemy would lay a trap for the unsuspecting whites. Then, on the fourth day, Bridger called for a small detachment of volunteers to venture from their breastworks and reconnoiter the surrounding countryside for sign of the war party.

Joe Meek, Kit Carson, and the others returned at twilight to report they hadn't seen a warrior. But what they had found sure made them grateful those northern lights had spooked the Blackfoot.

"Joe's the one with some proper learning, so he ciphered it out," Carson explained. "When we come across all them war lodges that bunch had downriver, we could make out how each one was big enough to hold least ten men. Meek went to counting straightaway . . . and he tallied up enough of them timber lodges to make for twelve hunnert warriors!"

But for that deserted encampment of conical brush, branch, and log shelters, there wasn't another sign of the Blackfoot. Six days after the enemy had abandoned the country, Bridger's brigade crossed the Yellowstone at the mouth of

Clark's Fork and started east. Bass marched with them those first few days until they reached Pryor Creek where he hailed his farewells. The sixty-one would push east for the Bighorn with plans to hunt buffalo while Scratch turned Samantha downstream to look for the Crow camp, anxious to rejoin his family.

That spring, after caching their winter goods, Scratch took Waits-by-the-Water, Magpie, and the infant boy north for the Musselshell country where the beaver grew sleek, their pelts much darker than anywhere to the south. At the site where he had been mauled by a sow grizzly seven years before, Bass sat beside the river with his family and the old dog, burned some sage and sweetgrass in a small fire at their feet, then smoked his pipe while the boy nursed in his mother's arms. Here in this place, with the sleepy child's tummy filled, Titus decided the time had come for him to name his son.

"For a long, long time," he told Magpie, who sat in his lap, "I thought I should name your little brother *isappe.*"

"Woodtick?" his wife asked, looking up as she removed her glistening nipple from the sleeping child's mouth.

Bass grinned as he looked up at his wife, nodding. "Isn't he always sucking at you? Just the way a fat little tick sucks blood till he's so full he falls right off to wait for another deer to walk past."

Magpie looked closely at her baby brother as he slept, then watched as Waits slipped her breast back inside her dress. With a giggle she looked back at her sleeping brother. "Woodtick. That is a good name, popo."

"But I will not give him that name," Scratch corrected, resetting her on one of his knees as Zeke laid his chin on Bass's other leg. "Next, I thought he should be named for a bird—just like his sister."

"Yes!" Magpie cried exuberantly. "What bird?"

"*Ischi'kiia,*" he replied. "Snowbird."

Waits smiled. "You thought of this because he is our winter baby?"

"Yes," Scratch declared. "For a long time I thought it would be good to name our children for birds—because they are about as free as any animal I know."

But Waits asked, "You don't want to call him Snowbird?"

"No." Titus wagged his head. "Later I finally figured out our son should have a name that wouldn't cause other children to make fun of him when he grows a little bigger and starts to play with other youngsters in the Crow village. For a boy, better that it be a strong name."

"What did you decide for him?" his wife asked.

"*Bish'kish'pee,*" he replied.

Waits gazed down at their son. "Little Flea?"

"Look at him," he explained. "See how he clings to you, just like a flea clings to a dog."

"That is what every child does to its mother," Waits explained.

Then Scratch continued. "When Flea gets old enough to understand, I want to give him a white name."

Magpie looked up into her father's face and asked, "Why do that?"

"I want to give my children the sort of name a white child would have."

The girl scrambled to her feet there before him, taking some of his beard in each of her tiny hands and holding her face close to his. "Are you going to give me a white name too?"

"I thought I would, one day when you grow bigger, Magpie," he confirmed. "But I won't if you are still happy with your Crow name."

She thought about that for a while, then said, "No. I like Magpie. It feels like it should be my name. Maybe when I am older, you can give me a white name. But while I am a little girl, I am Magpie."

He grinned. "That's just how I feel about it too." And gave her a squeeze. "Go sit with your mother."

When he took the boy in his arms and Magpie settled in her mother's lap, Titus said a prayer for them all, asking for a special blessing on the child he was giving the name Flea. When he was done with that simple ceremony, Bass was content to hold the sleeping child across his arms as the air warmed that late afternoon, birds chirping in the budding branches overhead.

After sitting in the exquisite silence for a long time, her daughter dozing in her lap, Waits asked, "Do you think Magpie will marry a white man?"

"In many ways, I hope she doesn't," he eventually admitted.

"But my life with you has been very good," Waits declared. "If I had married a Crow man, I would not travel as far as I have, nor would I see anywhere near as much as I do with you."

"Doesn't it make your life harder to stay on the move with your white husband?"

She grinned and shook her head. "No—life would be much, much harder with a Crow husband. A white man takes care of his wife much better, and he treats his woman much better too."

"Then you hope Magpie finds a white man to marry?"

Nodding, Waits said, "Not just any white man. If she can find a man as good as her father, then I want her to marry him."

Aroused from her brief nap, the little girl stretched, then toddled over to her father and clasped her arms around one of his. "Maybe you marry me when I grow up, popo?"

He laughed a little and hugged her close. "I can't marry you because I am your father. But I can make sure that the man who does marry you will treat you just as good as I treat your mother."

"Then I won't marry anyone. I will always live with you and my mother," Magpie vowed.

Bass grinned at Waits. "Maybe you should tell our daughter that there will come a day when she will be very anxious to leave us so she can go live with a young man."

"There is no sense in explaining that to her anytime soon, *bu'a,*" she replied with a grin. "Soon enough your daughter will find out about men all on her own."

Marching south from the Musselshell after a successful spring hunt, they recrossed the Yellowstone early that summer, hurrying through the lengthening days, putting every mile they could behind them, riding from dawn's first light until dusk forced them to stop for the night. Striking the Bighorn, they continued on down the Wind River to swing around the far end of the mountains where they crossed the Southern Pass. On its western slope they struck New Fork, following it to its mouth, then turned north on the Green to reach Horse Creek, site of that summer's rendezvous.

From the high benchland he could see that the Nez Perce were already there, their village raised in a horseshoe bend of the twisting creek beyond the scattered camps of company and free men.

"Where are the many?" Waits asked.

"Didn't figger us for coming in early," he told her in English, his eyes narrowing with concern. "Trader ain't come in yet neither."

"I am tired of the long journey," she told him. "We'll stay awhile. Wait for the trader."

"Yes," he said, relieved to know she wasn't impatient after the long journey. "I promised you a new copper kettle. We'll wait for the trade goods."

Beyond the first few camps of free men, he ran across the sprawling settlement of lean-tos and blanket bowers where the company men sat out these midsummer days, watching the east for signs of the caravan. Just beyond Bridger's brigade Bass found a small copse of trees that would do while they joined the wait. After a day occupied with setting up their shelters and dragging in some wood from down the valley, he spent a morning untying the rawhide whangs from his packs of fur, dusting and combing each pelt for vermin, then carefully repacking them until it came time for the St. Louis men to attach a value to his year's labor.

By afternoon it was time to ride over to look up those friends who had shared a cold winter siege with him along the Yellowstone. Zeke settled in the shade with him as Kit Carson, Joe Meek, Shad Sweete, and others came up to have themselves some palaver and a little of what whiskey remained in the American Fur Company kegs.

"Jehoshaphat!" Bass growled as his cup was filled, looking round at those company trappers who hadn't been with Bridger's men last winter on the Yellowstone. "If the sight of them Blackfoot skedaddling wasn't call for ol' Gabe to pour out a extra ration of Pratte and Chouteau's whiskey!"

Holding the small keg beneath one arm and doing the pouring now, Sweete added, "Damn me, boys—but this child won't ever again have me cause to get likkered up on one poor cup!"

The two of them were holding court there beside the Green River that hot July day, eighteen and thirty-seven, telling and retelling the tale of that just-about battle with those Blackfoot some twelve hundred strong. One bunch after another of Andrew Drips's brigade showed up to hear the story of when one white man's bony rump turned back the biggest war party ever heard tell of in the mountains.

"More Injuns than ever these eyes see'd in one place," Bridger testified.

One of Drips's trappers regarded Bass warily, demanding, "You really the one showed his arse and made them Blackfeets run away?"

Before Titus could reply, Shad slammed a hand down on Scratch's shoulder, sloshing some whiskey as he answered for Bass. "Just the sight of this coon's arse turned them niggers' hearts to water!"

Nearly every one of those doubters who came to hear the story looked Bass up and down, plainly struggling to believe the tale because Scratch wasn't near so tall, nor anywhere as big, as Meek or Sweete. And besides—Titus was a damned sight older than every other trapper most knew out there in the mountains. The skeptical listeners clearly had trouble believing the story . . . until Carson or Meek, Sweete or Bridger, told them about those northern lights and that terrifying crimson sky.

A legend was a'borning—but all the more a tale about that frightening celestial display than a tale about one man pulling aside his breechclout to insult the enemy.

"Gabe!"

The whole bunch turned with that cry of alarm from Meek. Joe stood just beyond the circle of their shelters at the edge of the prairie, pulling a looking glass from his eye. More than a hundred men fell silent in a blink. That tone of warning and danger in the big man's voice damn well didn't belong at rendezvous. Here they came to relax among companions and friendlies. But those who remembered the deadly battle in Pierre's Hole knew how quickly a summer's tranquil stillness could be shattered.

"It's them Bannocks again!" another man cried.

"Bannawks?" Grabbing Sweete by the arm, Bass demanded, "What's going on?"

On Shad's face was a look of murderous determination. "Trouble. You bring your gun?"

"Right over there. But I didn't figger I'd ever—"

Bridger interrupted everything with his bellow. "Where them Nez Perce?"

"Over here!" George Ebbert answered.

"Keep 'em outta sight, Squire," Bridger ordered. Turning round to the rest, he commanded, "Lick your flints and prime your pans, boys. This can't be no social call."

Not with the way those three dozen Bannock warriors were coming on at the gallop.

Unlike the rest of the suspicious trappers, Scratch kept expecting the horsemen to raise their rifles into the air, firing them in that universal sign of friendship upon approaching a camp.

"This ain't gonna be good, Shad," Bass said as he eased up beside the taller man. He quickly licked the pad of his thumb, ran it along the underside of the flint in the gun's hammer to swab it clean of burned powder smudge. "S'pose you tell me what lit a fire under their asses."

"Few days a'fore the Nepercy village ever come in for ronnyvoo, six of 'em come on ahead of the rest to find out for sure where the white men was camped. Them Bannocks already had their village on up Horse Crik, and some of their men run onto the Nepercy," Shad began. "So those Bannocks up and took the Nepercy horses and most everything else they had too."

"Even though both tribes was coming in to ronnyvoo?"

"Damn right," Shad replied sourly. "Put afoot, them six run on in here, asking us to protect 'em till their village got here. Fact be, while we was making our own way here, we heard this same bunch of Bannock bastards been doing some thieving: raised some traps and plunder from some Frenchies working Bear River last month . . . so Gabe was more'n happy to help out them Nepercy."

"How so?"

Sweete answered, "Them six Nepercy waited till dark a couple nights ago, then slipped off to the Bannock camp to see what they could do 'bout getting their ponies back. We didn't see 'em till next morning when the six of 'em come in with their horses."

"They'd stole 'em back from the Bannawks?"

Sweete nodded. "Damn right. I s'pose them Bannocks didn't figger no one'd dare try, so most of the warriors was off hunting when the Nepercy stole their ponies back. Them Nepercy bucks rode right in here, told us to be ready for a fight with the Bannocks, and give the finest horse to Bridger hisself."

"That was a stroke of medicine," Bass said as the Bannock warriors neared the tree line. By now he could see the horsemen were painted. Not a good sign at all.

Seizing the halter of the Nez Perce gift horse, Bridger hollered, "Grab tight on your horses, boys! I'll wager these buggers aim to run 'em off!"

With war screeches, snorting horses, and the slamming of hooves as they brought their ponies to a dusty halt, the horsemen careened into the trappers' camp with bluster enough for twice their number. Two of their group waved their weapons, yelling at the rest, sending the warriors this way and that through the camp. Each one of the three dozen naked warriors bellowed threateningly, shaking his old fusil or bow or war club at the white men.

Damn if those Bannock didn't try their best to frighten the horses, bullying the white men by swinging their own mounts at the trappers who remained on foot among the shelters. One of the leaders, a barrel-chested youngster, halted his pony near Bridger, hollering down at the brigade leader.

"Get over here, Mansfield!" Bridger ordered. "I need someone what knows this red nigger's tongue!"

Cotton Mansfield trotted over to begin making sense of the youth's shrieking bravado. "Says he don't want no trouble with you—with no white man. But he come for the ponies, them horses took from his camp."

"You tell him I don't know nothing about horses took from his camp," Bridger snarled. "Tell him his manners is bad and he better get his ass outta here till he can act better."

Shouting among themselves, the Bannock slowly regathered around their leader at the edge of the trapper camp.

Mansfield whispered to Bridger from the corner of his mouth, "They didn't figger to have to fight white men, Gabe."

"That big young'un told you that?"

Nodding, Mansfield said, "They only come for to kill them Nez Perce and get their horses back—"

"Tell 'em to get!" Bridger growled, the short fuse on his anger all but gone.

"Watch out, Gabe!"

Bridger whirled at the warning from one of his men, finding the second leader of the bunch loping up atop his pony. He was shouting at the rest of the horsemen.

"Jim!" Mansfield whispered sharply. "He knows that horse of yours come from the Nez Perce!"

"To hell with him!" Meek yelled as *Umentucken,* his Shoshone wife, cautiously stepped from their shelter and stood beside her imposing husband to watch the confrontation.

Bass could see the dark cloud suddenly cross the second, older Bannock leader's face. His dark, chertlike eyes narrowed on Bridger as he came to a halt beside the gift horse and began to mutter something to the others.

Scratch turned to Carson, saying, "That nigger looks to be bad from mouth to headwaters, Kit."

Mansfield translated, "This'un says you got his horse—"

"Tell him it ain't his," Bridger snapped. "Belonged to the Nez Perce and they give it to me. A present what's mine now."

They watched the way Mansfield's translation struck the Bannock leader. Furious, he drew himself up atop his pony and shouted to the rest.

"He's just told 'em they come for horses or blood!" Mansfield warned.

"Get ready, boys!" Sweete ordered as everyone braced in a crouch, weapons ready.

Slapping his quirt along his pony's flanks, the older Bannock leader forced his horse between Bridger and the Nez Perce pony. As Bridger's hand was wrenched from the lariat around its neck, the war chief seized the bridle.

All around the two of them trapper rifles came up, and the last of the hammers were snapped back to full cock. Before any of the horsemen could react, one of the guns rang out—no man would later admit to firing the first shot—a deafening boom beneath that canopy of leafy cottonwood. Atop his horse the Bannock chief stiffened, arched backward, and spilled to the ground, a red smear on the center of his chest.

The wolf was out, and no way to put him back in his den.

With throaty screams the Bannock fired their smoothbores, aimed their bows, and fired their arrows. Some hurled their war clubs at the trappers who were diving this way or that as the air filled with gun smoke and shrieks, arrows and curses.

But in less time than it would take for a man to fill and light his pipe, the horsemen had turned and retreated, leaving six of their dead behind in the white man's camp. Many of the trappers dashed from the trees, stopped, and leveled their long guns on the backs of the fleeing warriors. Another half dozen fell before the Bannock were out of rifle range.

"Ah-h-h, Joe!"

Meek and the others spun at Squire Ebbert's pained call. The trapper was slowly lowering Joe's wife, the Mountain Lamb, to the ground. The front of her beaded shawl was dark with blood around the shaft of an arrow Ebbert held, his hand already slicked with crimson.

Collapsing beside her in an instant, Meek cradled his wife across his legs as he gently laid her upon the ground. Plainly, she had taken an arrow intended for him.

"Oh, God!" Joe whimpered as he peered down into her glazed, fluttering eyes. "Don't die! Please don't die."

Shocked, Titus stood there with the others in a ring surrounding the man and woman as the sting of acrid black-powder smoke hung in the summer air, remembering the story of this Mountain Lamb and the two inseparable friends. Now the woman Joe loved, the mother of his own children, lay gasping in his arms, gurgling for air as a thin trickle of blood oozed from the corner of her mouth. She reached up with one hand to touch Joe's face. Her fingers lightly brushed his thick beard before the arm fell limp.

"No-o-o-o!" Meek cried piteously, crumpling over her.

The sound of that moan, the sight of this big, powerful man brought to his knees with the death of his wife—it tore right through to the marrow of him. Of a sudden Bass realized how he would suffer should he lose Waits-by-the-Water. After all they had been through together . . .

Here was this friend of his, a man with whom he had shared the very real prospect of death. Someone who had stood at his back, and he at Meek's.

"Shad," Bass whispered harshly as he swallowed down the grief, allowing the anger through. "I reckon we got us some niggers to rub out."

Sweete was the first to turn away from the circle, but with him came many others: Doc Newell, Squire Ebbert, Kit Carson, Isaac Rose, Cotton Mansfield, Dick Owens, and at least fifty more. There was no need of talk among them, much less any deliberation. Silently the half-a-hundred slipped off to catch up their horses and joined Bass at the edge of the prairie.

In the distance a smudge of dust clung to the horizon, the only sign of the fleeing Bannock.

Looking around at those grim-faced, determined men as they climbed atop their horses, Shad Sweete said, "We're all friends of Joe's. He'd do the same for any of you."

Then Bass told them, "Want you to remember them young'uns what ain't got a mother now! 'Sides Blackfoot—there ain't no wuss thieves in the mountains!"

Suddenly a handful of them howled like wolves, raising their rifles. The rest joined in, yipping and shrieking, half-a-hundred horses prancing and sidestepping nervously.

"Let's go raise some Bannock hair for Joe!" Titus bellowed, savagely kicking heels into the pony's ribs.

Away they all shot, dirt flying in clods, streams of it spraying up in cockscombs, streaming down in golden-lit clouds as they spread across the prairie at the gallop, that lone gray-white dog struggling to keep up with the lean, long-legged horses driven in furious pursuit of the Bannock.

Men after blood, revenge boiling in their veins.

By the time the fifty had crossed that four miles of river-bottom land, the three dozen Bannock had reached their village and issued their warning. Young boys were already driving in the small herd of ponies. Old people were gathering up the children. Women were frantically yanking lacing pins from lodges, tearing stakes from the ground, dragging lodge skins and poles from the anchor tripods. At the moment the first one of them spotted the oncoming trappers beneath the dusty cloud in the mid-distance, she raised a pitiful shriek.

In a flurry the women entirely abandoned their lodges and belongings, wheeling through the line of warriors, racing for the nearby bank of Horse Creek. Into the knee-deep water they churned on foot, turning upstream toward a narrow sandbar of an island where a few warriors beckoned, urging them on. Once onto the sandbar, the women took out their knives or tin cups, starting to dig in the soil while others tore at the skimpy willow and buckbrush, piling up all they could to construct some sort of shelter that, though it would not stop a bullet, would nonetheless hide them from view.

As Titus came off the pony in a run with the others, he slapped the horse on the rump, turning it away as the first of the arrows hissed overhead. He turned at the shrill whimper, expecting to find a friend he knew had been hit.

Instead he discovered Zeke, an arrow shaft trembling from a front shoulder. The old dog stumbled sideways, seized by pain and fear. As Bass whistled and headed for him in a sprint, Zeke tried biting at the shaft until he lost his balance and collapsed onto his side.

Lunging onto the dog, Bass flung his rifle aside and seized the shaft, tugging on it gently at first. Good—didn't feel as if it had buried itself in bone. Quickly he spread his legs out and laid most of his weight atop the struggling animal while he folded Zeke's muzzle into the crook of his left elbow, then ripped the arrow from the fleshy muscle.

Bright red blood slicked the grayish fur, oozing for a moment till Bass pushed a bit of the tobacco quid he had been chewing into the hole. Quickly he looked at the arrow he had tossed to the ground. The stone point was still attached—not enough time for the sinew to grow damp enough that the shaft would pull free.

As gunfire began all around him, trappers swearing and Bannock yelling, crying, wailing, and shrieking, Scratch rubbed the old dog's ears.

"Ain't your day to die, Zeke," he whispered into the closest ear. "This ain't your fight neither. G'won—you get back with them horses."

Slowly Titus came onto his hands and knees, rocked back to let the dog lick at the oozy wound. Zeke peered up at him, then struggled to stand, throwing his head a few times before he managed to stand.

"G'won, get!"

Scratch flung an arm toward the horses peacefully grazing more than a hundred yards off. Reluctantly the dog started away, hobbling on three legs, favoring the one wounded foreleg. Zeke stopped once, some distance away, peered back at his master, then kept on.

Scratch dragged a hand under his nose, smearing the dribble, and cleared the clog in his throat—thanking the First Maker that the dog hadn't been taken from him. Magpie and Flea needed a dog to play with and watch over them. Good thing that old mongrel was tough as he was. Scarred and stove-up though they were, the two of them made a handsome pair.

The hot afternoon breeze struck him full in the face as he raced the few yards toward the riverbank where he finally joined the rest. The smell of those Bannock was strong on the wind, a day rank with the stench of blood and dying.

Hour by hour the siege went on. Lead sang into the brush on that island. Every now and then arrows whined out of the willows on the sandbar, arcing down from the summer blue. Sometimes they struck a man in the leg, or a foot, perhaps pinned an arm to the ground until someone else freed him and wrapped the ragged wound.

"Goin' back—get us some water," George Ebbert said with cracked, dry lips as he crawled past the clump of red willow where Bass and Sweete held down their post.

"Take 'nother man with you, Squire," Shad ordered. "Bring back what water you can. And load up with some ball and powder too."

Bass nodded, his tongue starting to swell with thirst just the way it had on that death march he had made with McAfferty down on the Gila. "We're gonna be here for a spell."

The warriors were too far away from the white men to make sure kills with their arrows. And every time one of them showed enough of his brown body to make a target, a trapper's rifle roared. Someone grunted on that island of misery. A woman cried out, wailing—until more warriors shrieked their war songs anew, drowning out her grief with their unremitting fury. On and on it went as the day aged and twilight came on.

Ebbert returned with water in some Mexican gourds and a few tin canteens. Meek and three more men had chosen to join him on the ride back from camp, their packs filled with lead balls of different calibers and horns of powder to resupply those who were laying siege to that bloody island. The sun continued to sink behind the western hills, and the first stars appeared. Finally it was dark, with nothing more than a thin rind of a new moon rising overhead.

"They'll slip off now, won't they?" someone asked in that still summer darkness.

"Not if we fire at that goddamned island from time to time," Meek suggested, his voice uncannily flat and even.

"Joe's right," Sweete agreed. "Teach 'em not to budge. Keep their heads down."

On into the night the half-a-hundred white men lay along the west bank of Horse Creek, taking their turns firing at the island where the

Bannock had forted up, continuing to dig their foxholes. And all through that night the women wailed quietly, men sang war songs softly, and children whimpered. Bass felt sad for the children—they didn't know no better.

But them big folks, men and women both—they were bad two ways of Sunday, and they deserved to die—stealing horses from the Nez Perce, a people what had been good to the white man since the first explorers with the Corps of Discovery crossed these mountains. And now they'd gone and killed a white man's wife . . . an innocent woman who meant them Bannock no harm.

For that, this whole damned shitteree of brownskins was due a lesson.

Every minute or so one of the trappers fired his rifle at the island, keeping the enemy on the move, terrifying them as the short summer night dragged on. There would be no escape from their burrows on that sandbar.

Those first streaks of dawn fingered out of the east, and with them came a few arrows arcing out of the willows.

Then late that morning Bass grew concerned and slid over to Carson, telling him he would return after he rode back to camp. "My woman's gonna be fretting. Likely she's heard the shooting and gone looking for me."

"Take your time," Kit said. "We both got wives, so I know how they can worry a man."

Waits-by-the-Water loped barefoot onto the sunny prairie toward Bass the moment she spotted him in the distance. She was crying by the time he lunged the horse to a halt and vaulted out of the saddle. Clumsily she hurried into his arms, Flea on her hip, Magpie wrapping her arms around her father's leg.

Tears streamed down the woman's cheeks as she mumbled words he didn't understand; then suddenly she went silent, pulling back from him, hands brushing across his bloody shirt.

"It's Zeke," he confessed immediately, turning to point at the prairie. The dog was in the distance, gamely coming along the best he could on those three good legs.

"The dog, he is wounded?"

After explaining how Zeke was hit with the arrow, Waits cried all over again as the dog came up. Magpie leaped on him, locking her arms around his thick neck, smothering him with her tiny kisses.

Waits pressed her cheek against Bass's neck. "We worried about you—"

"I come to tell you I'm fine," he said. "But it isn't over."

While he wolfed down some of the meat she had cooked last night while waiting for him, washing it down with cool creek water, Scratch told her of the siege—its cause, the death of Meek's Mountain Lamb. Then declared that he would be going back. And he made sure she knew why.

"I'd 'spect any friend to do the same for me if'n it were you to die," he said quietly. "Any man what's got him a woman. Any man what's ever lost him his woman. I'm going back to do my best by Joe Meek."

After tying Zeke to a tree with a length of rawhide lariat, Bass filled up three more horns of powder and snatched up another two pouches of balls from his possibles. First he bent to kiss wide-eyed Flea on the fore-head, then knelt to sweep Magpie into his arms, holding her aloft as he kissed both her cheeks.

Setting her back on the prairie, Scratch handed his rifle to the little girl who stood only half as tall as the tall weapon. He turned to embrace his wife. Pulling back from her, he said, "Close your eyes."

When she did, Bass kissed each eyelid gently.

She opened them and he said, "That's until those eyes see me coming back to you."

He turned, took up the rifle, and leaped into the saddle again. Bass heard Zeke howling as he galloped away, the hot moisture streaming down his cheeks. And he thought he heard Waits crying far behind him where he had left her.

A sound that made the guard hairs stand at the back of his neck.

TWENTY-ONE

They ended up pinning the Bannock down on that island for another two days and nights. Through those hours of darkness when they could not see their enemies, the trappers smoked their pipes and talked about their chances of wiping out that band of lying thieves.

"Why they ain't getting hungry?" George Ebbert growled with dismay. "We had 'em trapped in there for better'n three days!"

"They're killing their ponies," Bass explained matter-of-factly.

Shad Sweete agreed. "They got enough horses in there to last 'em a long, long time."

"Water ain't no problem neither," Joe Meek observed resentfully. "Bastards can hole up in there just as long as we can hold out up here."

"I always knowed the Bannawks was about the stealingest red niggers," Scratch observed, "but I never knowed 'em to be near so stupid that they'd sashay right on into a white man's camp just as bold as you could be and try to steal some horses!"

"Only way to write a treaty with their kind is in blood," Jim Bridger grumbled.

"That's right," Osborne Russell declared, patting his half-stock per-
cussion rifle. "Best way to write a treaty with them Bannock is with this
here rifle. It's the only pen what will write a treaty the bastards will
keep."

Sometime after the moon had set that third night and men were
snoring around him, Bass sat in the brush remembering a summer night
long ago when he had remained behind with Josiah and a few others who
were maintaining their vigil around those Blackfoot they had surrounded
in Pierre's Hole. But unlike that band of thieves and murderers, these
Bannock hadn't all slipped away the first night.

"Scratch!" came the sharp whisper from that chunk of shadow crawling his way out of the gloom.

"Who's that?"

Sweete's big grin took form in the starshine. "Something I wanted to
tell you ever since this little fight got rolling—but Joe's always been close
by."

"He sleeping?"

Sweete nodded and settled in beside Titus with a sigh as one of the
trappers fired a shot at the island. "Think it's the first time he's shut his
eyes in the last three nights."

"That man's taking this real hard," Scratch commented in a whisper.
"Can't blame him none."

"That's why I figgered I wouldn't tell you the story 'bout Joe and his
Mountain Lamb till he wasn't around," Shad declared.

"She was the woman these Bannock killed?"

"Yep. And late last winter he killed a Crow nigger on count of her
too."

"Crow?"

"Thought you might'n heard tell of it—what with you being up there,
married to a Crow gal and all."

Titus shrugged. "Didn't hear a peep of it. There's two bands of them
Crow. Since I didn't hear tell of the trouble, I figger it was Long Hair's
bunch."

"Yep—one of Long Hair's band. Happened up the Bighorn a ways.
Some time after you turned off from us, we run onto their village. They
had that trader from Fort Van Buren with 'em—"

"Tullock?"

"That's him. He'd come out from the Tongue and hooked up with
'em late that winter. Was doing some trading," Sweete explained. "But
that big war party what come along with Tullock to visit us weren't good
Crow."

"Trouble?"

"Sonsabitches brung the devil right into our camp. While Tullock
had his blankets out and most of them young bucks was trading with

him or with Bridger, one of 'em takes a shine to Mountain Lamb of a sudden."

"That's bad," Scratch clucked softly. "Don't ever wanna get wrong-ways with Joe Meek."

"That crazy buck walked over to Mountain Lamb's shelter, strutting his best to get her attention," Sweete declared. "When she wouldn't look up from the moccasins she was sewing up for Joe, that Crow bastard took to walking back and forth in front of her—sure he'd get her to look at just how purty he was."

"So Joe got jealous when she looked at that Crow buck?"

"No," and Sweete wagged his head. "Mountain Lamb never did give that son of a bitch a look-see. Fact was, Joe was sitting right inside their shelter, watching it all—and getting a real tickle from it too, what with the way that bastard kept trying harder and harder to get Mountain Lamb's eye."

"So what caused the trouble?"

"When the gal kept on refusing to look up at that buck, it burned his powder so bad that he walked back on over to her and slapped her 'cross the face with his rawhide quirt."

"Damn!" Bass moaned. "Sure as rain, that red nigger picked the wrong woman to play Injun with."

"Yep—Joe pulled up his fifty-eight and shot the bastard where he stood right over Mountain Lamb holding that quirt in his hand," Shad said. "I don't figger he ever knowed what hit him at that range."

"But I reckon all hell broke loose then."

With a wag of his head Sweete said, "The wolf was let out to howl—right there in our camp. By the time Bridger and Tullock got the shooting stopped, we had one man dead, and there was two more Crow rubbed out. The trader finally got them red niggers out of our camp when Gabe passed out a bunch of presents to pay for them dead Injuns."

"When it was a goddamned Crow buck what started it?"

"That were their country, Scratch," Shad replied. "We was on the Bighorn, right in the heart of Crow country."

"Ain't never a call for bad manners," Scratch said softly. "No matter they be a cocky Crow or not."

"Time was a white feller could count on folks in that tribe," Sweete said, regret heavy in his voice. "Past winter or two, I ain't so sure no more."

"Time was we all counted on the beaver staying seal fat and sleek," Titus whispered with some of that same regret. "We counted on the price of plews staying high. But the years has changed things, Shad. The years gone and changed us too."

For the most part they sat in silence the rest of that night, taking turns curling up to catch some sleep while the other kept watch. All along that riverbank some slept while the rest stared at the island, a few even firing an occasional shot at the brushy sandbar just to let the Bannock know the white man hadn't cashed in his chips and pulled out.

Bass shivered slightly in the gray light of dawn-coming and rubbed both of his gritty eyes. How he wished for some coffee, some whiskey, something that would cut the awful taste in his mouth. He hacked up some of the night-gather clogging his throat and turned toward the island to spit into the willow. That's when he spotted the movement.

"Shad!" he said sharply. "Shad!"

Others had seen it too as Sweete came awake, rolling onto his hands and knees, blinking his bleary eyes.

"Lookee there," Bass instructed.

Up and down the riverbank in the dim light other trappers were peering closely at the sandbar, trying their best to make out what the shift in shadows and the rustle of willow meant. A mourning cry grew louder and louder. That wailing was like a gritty mouthful of cold sand lying in his belly—something he knew he was bound to bring up sooner or later.

A rustle came from the brush near his end of the island, and an old woman parted the bushes to step into the open as dawn's light swelled around them that summer morning. The front of her dress smeared with blood, the ancient one clutched a long pipe in both frail hands. Raising it to the riverbank above her where the white men huddled in the brush holding siege on her people, the old woman called out in a reedy voice.

"What she saying?" a man yelled.

"That's Snake," Scratch answered. "I catch some of it."

"But she ain't a Snake," Ebbert grunted.

"I s'pose she figgers some of us'll know some Snake," Bass said.

"All of you!" Meek hollered. "Keep quiet so us what knows Snake can figger out what that ol' woman's saying!"

"You heard him!" Bridger ordered. "Hush!"

Moments later Joe explained, "She's telling us we've killed all their warriors. But the bullets keep killing."

"We ain't killed all their men!" Rube Herring snorted. "Some of 'em must've run off!"

Waiting a moment while she repeated the next part to be certain what she said, Meek continued. "Now she's asking if we wanna kill the women too."

"Maybe we oughtta kill 'em all," Robert Newell suggested.

But his best friend, Joe Meek, grabbed Newell's arm and snarled, "Don't you see? That'd make us no better'n them nigger dogs to kill a woman the way they done!"

"Hold on, Joe!" Bass ordered. "Listen: the ol' woman's saying if we wanna smoke with women to make peace, she has a pipe and some tobaccy too."

Meek stood, disappointment graying his face. "If'n there ain't a man left in there—I s'pose I done all I come to do, boys. Time for this child to mosey on back to camp."

Up and down that west bank close to a hundred trappers slowly emerged from the brush, starting for their horses they had tied here and there within the deserted Bannock camp they had plundered during the days of siege.

Scratch walked over and grabbed hold of Meek's elbow. "I figger it's time to think 'bout putting your woman to rest, Joe. You need any help— count on me."

Not uttering another word, Meek laid a hand on Scratch's shoulder for a moment, then turned away, climbed atop his horse, and rode off alone.

"Every man finds his own way to heal a broke heart," Scratch declared several days later when he overheard a few men at the trader's tent talking about the way Meek had chosen to mourn the loss of *Umentucken,* his Mountain Lamb. "Ain't for me to say he shouldn't climb right back in the saddle again. Ain't for none of us to say he ain't grieving in his own way."

Just that morning, only one day after Tom Fitzpatrick brought in the caravan that had embarked for rendezvous from Westport, Joe had loaded up a horse with finery and ridden right over to the Nez Perce camp where he had taken a shine to a pretty young woman. Not long after her father had approved of the marriage, Meek was back in the company camp with his new wife, celebrating his good fortune that he wouldn't remain lonely for long at all.

After weeks of horse racing, gambling at cards or a game of hand, not to mention endless hours of yarning while they waited beneath the shady trees for the long-overdue trader, it damn near brought tears to Bass's eyes to see how small Fitzpatrick's pack train was as it descended off the bluffs and made its way down to the junction of Horse Creek and the Green. No more than twenty small two-wheeled carts pulled by mules, tended by some forty-five men trudging along on both sides of the procession.

"Poor doin's," Titus muttered as Fitzpatrick escorted Sir William Drummond Stewart west for another rendezvous. "Poor damned digger doin's."

Maybe the trade would hold for another year or so. If only long enough that the fur business could get itself straightened out back east and folks found out that those new silk hats couldn't hold a candle to prime beaver felt. Beaver was bound to rise. All the old hivernants were saying it. Sure as hell, beaver was bound to rise.

Just like the goddamned prices the company was charging for what little they sent west with Fitzpatrick.

"Two dollar a pint for sugar!" Scratch roared at the red-faced clerk. "How much your coffee?"

"Same—two dollars."

"Damn," he grumbled in disgust.

Blankets were going for twenty dollars while a common cotton shirt cost a man five. Tobacco was damned pricey at two dollars a pound, but the toll on whiskey hadn't gone up over the last few summers: holding at four dollars the pint. He figured those parley-voo traders were pretty savvy about that: hold down the cost of liquor and most men simply wouldn't mind all that much if the price of everything else climbed sky-high.

What kept Scratch from throwing up his hands at those mountain-high prices and refusing to trade for anything at all was the fact that the company offered five dollars a pound for prime pelts, four dollars for poorer plews. That meant his Musselshell beaver brought him top dollar at the trading tent that afternoon when he brought his family along to look over the beads and rings, ribbon and hawksbells.

While Waits-by-the-Water picked through the merchandise to find herself a new brass kettle, Scratch stood at the other end of the long counter with Magpie as the girl chose several hanks of new ribbon to wrap up her brown braids, along with a new handkerchief of black silk to tie around her head the way her father tied a faded blue bandanna around his.

Then she spotted the tray of shiny, multicolored beads.

"Popo! Look!"

With the way she gushed and stuck out her hands to touch the beads in each compartment, Bass knew he was already in trouble.

"Purty, ain't they?" he asked.

She gazed up at him a moment, imitating the word, "Pur-r-r-ty."

"That's right. I s'pose you want some too."

"Yes," and she nodded emphatically. But when she dug her fingers in and pulled out a handful of the deep cobalt-blue beads, along with some of the oxblood variety with their narrow white centers, Magpie surprised him by saying in Crow, "For you, popo—these so pretty on your ears."

"On my ears?" he repeated, confused a moment.

Reaching up to tug on the tail of his shirt, Magpie pulled him down far enough that she tapped the small hoops of brass wire he wore through both earlobes. "Beads hang there."

He straightened, smiling. "Damn fine idee, little'un. Put some pur-ties on my hangy-downs."

Turning back to the tray, Scratch scooped up a big handful of the Russian blues and the white-hearts, laying them atop several yards of calico he was buying for Waits-by-the-Water. Next he picked out several dozen brass tacks for decoration and some tiny brass nails to make repairs to saddles, packs, and other equipment. Then he took Magpie over to stand before the tray containing the tiny hawksbells and large coils of brass wire.

Picking up one of the bells, he shook it in front of her. "Want some?"

Grinning hugely, Magpie snatched the bell from him, holding it forth to shake it herself. "Two?"

"I said you could have some. How many?"

For a long moment she stared down at her tiny hands, then handed him the bell and held both hands before her, all the chubby fingers extended.

"Ten?"

"Ten," she repeated that English word with certainty.

"If that don't beat all," Shad Sweete chirped as he came up and stopped at Bass's elbow. "This li'l gal is already learning what a woman does best."

"And what's that, Shadrach?"

The tall man spit a stream of brown juice into the dirt behind them and dragged a dirty sleeve across the dribble on his lower lip. "Them womens learn early to hold a man right in their hands, don't they, Scratch?"

"Ain't no better reason for me to spend my money," he replied with a wink. "Don't matter if it be a little woman like Magpie here, or her mama."

Rubbing his hand across the top of Magpie's head as she grinned up at him, Sweete said, "Maybe one day I'll take me a squaw, have me young'uns too."

"Man like you don't deserve to be alone, Shad."

With a shrug the big trapper explained, "I run off to the brush with a few gals ever' ronnyvoo. Sometimes I take a shine to a squaw when we hunker down for winter camp too. But I ain't ever found one I wanna pack along with me."

"One of these days," Bass declared, "you'll be ready to pack a squaw with you, raise some pups too."

"Maybe so." Sweete brushed his hand down Magpie's cheek, then looked into Scratch's eyes. "Where you figger to mosey come time to light out for the fall hunt?"

"Been thinking I'd wander on down to the South Platte again."

"Gonna see if you can run onto more trouble with them 'Rapaho, eh?"

"That weren't no big ruckus, Shad," he protested. " 'Sides, I always do my best to stay outta their way."

For a moment Sweete's eyes flicked to the back of Bass's head. "I s'pose any man what's lost his hair to them red niggers is gonna be extra careful he don't lose the rest of his hair to 'em."

"Come on over to our camp for supper?" Scratch offered. "That is, less'n you got plans to drag some gal back into the bushes with you this evening."

"No plans particular' now," he answered. "Was gonna be a trial on one of the fellas."

"Trial?"

"Yep—one of Drips's men got hisself drunk last night and kill't a Frenchman. But there ain't gonna be no trial now."

"Drips figgered to let the nigger go free?"

Wagging his head, Sweete explained, "The murderer run off. I s'pose he figgered he stood a better chance out there on his lonesome than he did standing for a murder charge with the rest of us as his jury."

"Some men might figger him for a coward," Bass reflected. "But I figger he's run off to find his own way to die."

"Maybeso that's what he's done. Sure saved us the trouble of stretching some rope off a tall tree."

"Whyn't you come look up our camp later," Bass suggested. "We'll have some meat on the spit 'long about sundown."

"I'll bring a little whiskey along," Sweete offered with a grin.

"Ain't no better way for friends to wash down some fat cow."

Sweete scooped Magpie off the ground, hugged her, then whirled once around with the child before he set her back on her feet. He winked at Bass. "This here's the purtiest gal I got my eye on, Scratch."

"Hell with you, Shadrach," he growled. "Ain't no way I'm gonna marry off my daughter to someone the likes of you."

"Here I thought you liked me," he whined with mock wounding. "Thought I was your friend!"

"You are, you mangy, flea-bit, wuthless bag of polecat droppings," Bass roared with a grin. "But that don't mean I'd ever want you for a son-in-law!"

"So you're gonna raise up your daughter to have a proper husband, are you?"

Bass pulled Magpie against his leg as she jingled a pair of tiny bells, oblivious to the English conversation above her. "Only thing I'm sure of is I want her to grow up safe and happy, just as happy as her mama's made me."

Shad knelt before the girl and gently pinched her cheek. "Your camp up Horse Crik a ways?"

"No more'n a mile from here."

Standing, Sweete brushed off the knee of his legging and said, "See you come sundown."

"You're not one of Monsieur Fontenelle's company men, are you?" asked the young man as he stood, shoving the long pad of paper beneath his arm. He poked a narrow wand of artist's charcoal behind his ear and held out his hand.

"Name's Bass," Scratch announced, craning his neck around and bending to take a closer look at the pad where the man had been sketching when he finally realized Titus had crept up behind him, mesmerized at how that hand clutching a simple stick of charcoal was creating such magic. "And no, I ain't one of Fontenelle's outfit."

"I'm Alfred Miller."

He gestured to the sketchpad. "Lemme take a close look there, Alfred."

"This?" and Miller took the pad from beneath his arm and held it before him.

It was nothing short of purely amazing. For a moment Titus stared at the thousands of tiny charcoal scratches on that long sheet of paper, at how they all came together in patterns that gave such reality to the sketch. Then his eyes lifted from the page to that scene occurring right over Miller's shoulder. Back to the paper once more, then again to the scene out on the prairie where Indian and white riders were conducting horse races.

"I ain't never seen anything like this," Scratch whispered with abject admiration. "That there . . . with only your hand and that piece of charcoal . . . it's just like what I'm seeing right out there."

"Thank you, Mr. Bass," Miller replied as he turned back to gaze at the scene he had been sketching. "I'll take that as a real compliment."

Scratch inched up to the young man's elbow again. He tapped the paper lightly with a lone finger, saying, "Them lodges there, you drawed 'em just like they are over there. And those fellas down there running footraces too. All them Injuns over there—all of it damn near like it is right here a'fore my own eyes."

"So you've never seen a painting before?"

"Not that I can rightly say," he admitted as Miller resumed his scratching at the paper with his charcoal. "And what I have seen, it only be sticks and such to stand for folks."

His head still bent in concentration at his work, Miller asked, "If you don't work for the fur company, then you must be what they call a free man?"

"That's right," he answered. "How you come to be out here to the Rocky Mountains, making your pictures on paper? You come out with the trader's caravan to see ronnyvoo, then gonna turn around for the settlements?"

Miller shook his head. "I've been engaged by a Scottish nobleman who wants me to—"

"Stewart?"

The artist looked up at Bass in amazement. "You know of Sir William Drummond Stewart?"

"He knows me too," he boasted. "We et together a time or two."

With a smile Miller nodded, then went back to his sketch. "Perhaps I should draw you sometime."

"Me? Naw. Naw—what you do is far too fancy for you to go and draw me," he replied, then touched the edges of some sketchpad pages that had been stuffed in behind the one Miller was drawing on at that moment. "What's these? Other'ns you already done?"

"Yes," the artist replied, dragging out some of the crude sketches.

The first showed a mounted trapper, behind him a squaw on her pony.

"Who's that?" Bass asked. "Looks like someone I know."

"I think his name's Walker. I sketched him yesterday."

"Joe Walker, good man," he commented.

As the next sheet came up, Titus stared at a drawing of two young Indian women playing in the shade of a tree, neither wearing anything more than a skirt, both bare-breasted as one of the two swung from a tree limb by her arms, carefree as could be.

"This the first you ever see'd any Injun gals?" Bass inquired.

Miller smiled, his cheeks flushing with embarrassment a little as he answered, "First time ever beyond the Mississippi. Come up from New Orleans with Sir William."

Miller shuffled another sketch to the top, this one a scene where a seated trapper held out his hand to a young Indian woman who appeared shy, even coy, as she peered back at him from behind her eyelashes.

"What's this'un about?"

Clearing his throat, the artist explained, "This trapper's taking a bride. Buying her from her father. That's the father standing beside his daughter as the white man offers presents for her hand in marriage."

"You seen this happen too?"

With a nod of his head Miller said, "I've seen all of these." He shuffled through the stack of thick paper and brought out another page. "In fact, Mr. Bass—I've seen all manner of things out here in the West I never saw anywhere back east."

"You must've see'd lots of griz," Titus commented, looking at the scene of trappers flushing a huge silver-tip from some brush. "I lost some of my own hide to a griz, fingers too."

"Miller!"

Together they turned at the call, finding the half-breed Antoine Clement jogging up on horseback.

"Miller! Sir William sent me to find you."

"Something wrong?" the artist asked, his face grave.

"Nothing wrong," Clement said. "But he wants you to come back to camp so you can draw something for him."

Turning to stuff the large pad of paper into a narrow leather valise, Miller asked, "What is it this time?"

"He's getting ready to make a present to Bridger."

"Stewart's gonna give Gabe a present?" Titus asked.

The handsome half-breed nodded, leaning on the flat pommel of his Santa Fe saddle. "Sir William had something shipped all the way from Scotland just for Bridger."

Swinging into the saddle, Miller gazed down at Bass. "You feel like coming to see for yourself what this gift is?"

"Go most anywhere, long as I can watch you draw some more," Bass pleaded.

With a broad smile young Miller said, "Grab your horse, Mr. Bass. Let's go see what Stewart had shipped all the way from his native land to present to Jim Bridger."

In a matter of minutes they had reached the company camp where a crowd was gathering.

"Let Miller through!" Stewart yelled as soon as he spotted his artist returning. "Let the man through, dammit!"

The young artist dismounted and handed his reins up to Clement. Stepping aside, the trappers allowed Miller to pass through the ring they had formed around an open patch of ground where company operators Fontenelle and Drips stood, joined by partisans Fitzpatrick and Bridger. The Scottish nobleman called forth two of his servants, bearing a large round-topped leather trunk.

"Jim—Jim Bridger!" Stewart called, waving the trapper to his side. "Join me here, would you?"

From his perch atop his horse at the outskirts of the crowd jostling and shouldering to get themselves the best view, Scratch watched an embarrassed, self-conscious Bridger step up to Stewart's elbow.

"Jim, the first time I returned to your eastern cities after meeting you, I posted a message to my home in Scotland," the nobleman explained. "I dispatched my request that they send me what I'm now going to present to you."

"This come all . . . all the way from Scotland?"

"Aye," Stewart replied, his burr crisp above the murmuring throng. He turned, stepped to the trunk, and threw back the domed lid.

More than a hundred heads craned forward as the nobleman drew forth the odd-looking apparel. Stewart turned to hold the metal plate to Bridger's shoulders.

"Wh-what's this?"

"Cuirass," he answered.

"Kwee-rass," Bridger repeated, his face flushing with embarrassment again. "What's it for?"

"It's part of an ancient suit of armor, Jim. Here, help me. I'll show you how to put it on."

Red-faced, Bridger began to mutter as Stewart removed the trapper's broad-brimmed hat and handed it to one of the servants. Instructing Jim to raise his arms in the air, the nobleman lowered the armored breastplate and back protector over Bridger's head and down his arms until it settled on Jim's shoulders.

Bridger shifted it slightly. "Damn, if that ain't heavy."

"Meant to turn a pike or protect you from a claymore."

"What're them?"

"A pike is very similar to an Indian's lance," Stewart explained as he turned to bend over the trunk once more, accompanied by the sound of clinking metal. "And a claymore—why, it's a very long, double-edged broadsword my Scottish tribesmen have used in battle for untold centuries."

At that moment the nobleman straightened and wheeled back to stand before Bridger. Between his two outstretched hands he held a shiny helmet that glittered in the summer sun. From its top sprouted a broad decorative plume crafted from the tail of a horse and dyed a brilliant crimson.

"Here, Jim—I'll help you with this."

"That? It goes on my head?"

Stewart had it started down on Bridger's head before he answered. "Noble knights of old needed such protection when they rode into battles of honor."

Once the helmet had settled on Bridger's shoulders, Stewart raised the slotted mask. Inside, the trapper's eyes were wide with wonder.

"I'll bet this'll turn any damned Injun arrow," Jim remarked, slapping his palm against the breastplate.

Shadrach Sweete cried out from the crowd, "You dang well could've used all that truck back when you took that Blackfoot arrer in yer shoulder, Gabe!"

Stewart had already turned to Miller, saying, "Alfred—are you getting all of this?"

"Some of it, sir," Miller admitted. "I think a better composition would be to have Mr. Bridger mounted on horseback."

"Splendid!" Stewart cried with an enthusiastic clap of his hands. He instructed his servant, "Go quickly to the wagon and fetch up the pike. Mr. Bridger must wear the whole outfit now!"

"P-pike?" Jim echoed. "The spear we was just talking about?"

The nobleman dragged his hat from his head and bowed at the waist before the brigade leader. "Indeed, my dear friend. Once we've finished dressing you in the entire suit of armor, I want you to carry that pike I brought for you to carry on horseback."

From inside the helmet Bridger's words had a dull ring of doubt. "You . . . want me to get on a horse with all this on?"

"By Jove I do!" the Scotsman cheered. "This suit of armor was worn by generations of ancient warriors in my family—a gift from me to a present-day warrior. I have fought against Napoleon's finest soldiers in battles on the Continent of Europe, yet never have I found any braver breed than you and men like you, Jim Bridger. My hat's off to your kind, noble sir!"

Suddenly Joe Meek leaped to the center of the open circle, pounding Bridger on the back, waving for the crowd to join him in their congratulations. "Sing out with me, boys—sing out for these Shining Mountains and our noble few!"

The throng answered the call, "Huzzah!"

And Joe cried again, "Huzzah for the Rockies!"

"*Huzzah!*" the voices echoed all the stronger.

Then a third time Meek exhorted them. "For the mountain man!"

When came the deafening roar that rocked this valley of the Green River: "HUZZAH!"

TWENTY-TWO

Times were in the past year he had reckoned on just what Bridger did with that heavy suit of armor the Scotsman gave him. Wondered what would have happened when all that foofa-raw got too heavy to pack around in Blackfoot country, just where Gabe would have abandoned the damned thing. Bass didn't think Jim would have cached it. A whole damned suit of old armor wasn't the sort of plunder a man figured on coming back for any day soon.

Back when that rendezvous of 1837 broke up, company partisans Andrew Drips and Lucien Fontenelle elected to swap places. That summer while Drips accompanied the fur caravan back to St. Louis, the volatile Fontenelle commanded a brigade in the field. With Bridger as his pilot, they set out for the Blackfoot country of the upper Missouri with one hundred ten trappers and camp keepers. Osborne Russell and Doc Newell joined a smaller outfit that headed northeast for the valleys of the Powder and the Tongue—some of their favorite country.

Every summer when the pack train arrived, those men who had fled from a life back east nonetheless clamored around the caravan pilot, eager to learn if they were to receive any mail from family or friends so far away in the States. If the booshway didn't have any mail for a fella, then he could usually get his hands on one of the public papers of the day, packed in thick bundles and transported halfway across the continent to men who could barely read but were nonetheless ravenous for any news of home. At rendezvous a man who could read was damn near reading all the time: ciphering letters written to those who could not understand the strange marks on the paper, or relating stories from those newspapers that recorded long-ago events in faraway places.

But the heady days of these raucous midsummer fairs were breathing their last.

In those last few days before Bridger steered his brigade north, Scratch purchased a dozen of the small iron fishhooks the traders offered, then went onto the prairie with Shad Sweete in search of grasshoppers. The two of them ended up having almost as much fun catching the hoppers as they had using those insects for bait on the hooks they dipped in the Green River and Horse Creek. On lazy afternoons they fished and sipped some Monongahela rum, a rare treat in the mountains, sweetened with a heaping spoon of brown sugar stirred into each cup.

"I can't recollect ever fishing since I was a young'un," Scratch admitted.

"Where was that?"

"Caintuck, right on the Ohio."

Sweete said, "I figger it's just like riding a horse. You fall off, but you don't ever forget how to crawl back on."

At times the two of them gathered a small crowd of curious Indians and trappers who collected on the shady banks to watch their amusing efforts. More often than not the small native trout and grayling weren't shy about taking the wriggling bait that floated on the surface of the water. It never failed to surprise Titus when a sharp tug pulled on that twine he had knotted at the end of a peeled willow branch.

Eating the tiny fish was a different matter altogether. What with all the little bones, he soon decided it was far more work than was worth the effort. Antelope or elk or buffalo it would be from here on out. Just as long as the fish didn't ever get greedy and start eating beaver, Scratch figured he would leave those fish in peace.

By late fall, after trapping his way through the Wind River Mountains and up the Bighorn, he had his family back on the Yellowstone and in the heart of Crow country. The weather had grown cold early that autumn, then moderated as the days sailed past. Instead of turning west, where he believed he might run onto Yellow Belly's village, he started east for the Rosebud and the Tongue. Since winter appeared slow in arriving, Titus decided he could steal a final few weeks of trapping out of the season, working their way toward Fort Van Buren before they had to turn west, searching for the Crow in their winter camp.

Even though the water in the kettles lay covered by a thin ice slick every morning, the sun always rose, warming the earth blanketed by autumn-dried grasses, lacy collars of old, dirty snow strangling every bush or tree trunk. Along the Tongue the beaver were starting to put on a heavier coat, that protective felt nestled below the long guard hairs growing all the thicker. As the days passed, Scratch read the sign plain for any man who took a notion to pay heed.

A hard winter was due.

So when the faraway horizon threatened many days later, Scratch quickly hurried back to camp where he loaded their plews and possessions on Samantha and their horses, then lit out for Tullock's post. They might well have as much as a day. From the looks of that gray-blue skyline rearing its ugly head out of the north, they should have enough time for the journey before the storm clobbered them. Down, down the Tongue they hurried, their noses pointed for the Yellowstone, riding straight into the teeth of the coming fury as the wind began to quarter around, carrying with it that distinct metallic tang of a high plains blizzard.

Reluctantly he agreed to stop that night short of their goal. Lighting a fire, Bass figured to give his family and the animals a few hours' rest before sunup. But Scratch had them moving again before night had been completely sucked out of the dawn sky.

By the middle of that second morning the storm's first sullen tantrum was taunting them. Snowflakes sharp as iron arrowheads slashed this way and that at their bare cheeks as they rode hunched over, head-tucked into the softly keening wind.

"How far, popo?" Magpie asked, her tiny voice muffled against his chest where he had the girl wrapped beneath the buffalo robe covering them both as the horses plodded forward one slow step at a time, icy heads bent against the mighty gale.

Each time he blinked, his eyes cried out in pain—the wind-driven shards slashing across them. By now his eyelashes were little more than heavy crusts of ice he struggled to keep open. Scratch figured there was no sense in telling Magpie the truth. Better to tell his daughter what she needed to hear then and there.

"I think I see some familiar hills ahead," he lied in Crow. Truth was, he couldn't see much past the end of his pony's nose.

Worried suddenly about Waits-by-the-Water, Bass twisted in the saddle. The gusty wind almost tore the coyote-hide cap from his head.

Back there a matter of yards from his pony's tail root, Titus thought he saw the movement of her shadow, barely making out Samantha's dark outline plodding flank to flank beside his wife's pony. The moment the wind had first come up that morning, he had knotted a rope to both of those saddles, looping the other ends beneath his left leg before he knotted them around the large pommel the size and shape of a Spanish orange at the front of his Santa Fe saddle. He had strung the rest of the pack animals out behind the mule, connecting each one to another animal in front and another in back with more rope. Since starting in that frozen predawn darkness, Bass had brooded that the storm might well cut the strong animals from the weak.

Because one or more of the ponies might break free and turn about with the force of the wind, he had packed what they needed to survive on Samantha. The rest he could go in search of after the storm's fury had played itself out. But the mule carried what might well save their lives even if all else were taken from them.

"My mother, she is near?" Magpie asked.

He figured she became frightened when he turned to look behind him.

"She's with us, daughter," he reassured her, his teeth chattering like bone dominoes in that horn cup Hames Kingsbury loved to rattle while floating down the river.

He wondered if Kingsbury was an old man now. If not—where he was buried. Perhaps even put to rest in the Mississippi the way they had consigned Ebenezer Zane's body to the river back in 1810. Or maybe on that thieves' road known as the Natchez Trace. Would any of the others still be alive . . .

Dragging the ice-crusted wool blanket mitten across his eyes, then under his red, swollen nose, his raw, chapped, ice-battered skin shrieked in torment. Suddenly Titus held his breath, put his nose back into the wind, and breathed deep.

Wood smoke.

By damn, it was wood smoke.

That meant a fire. And where he would find a fire, there must be humankind. Somewhere he could get out of the storm and warm up his nearly frozen wife and children. A lodge, even a windbreak . . .

"You smell that?"

After a moment his daughter asked, "Smell only you in here against your heart."

"Magpie," his voice cracked, "I smell wood smoke."

"A f-fire, popo?"

"Yes—a fire." He spoke it like a promise. "You'll be warm soon."

His mind racing, Scratch sorted through the possibilities the way he would sort through his pelts: thinking of the worst that could happen, pushing that aside to cling to the best. At the very least he knew that with this wind blowing into his face, that fire had to be due north of them. A blind man could stumble across it now. Even if it were nothing but some hunter who found himself caught out in the storm and quickly erected a crude windbreak, such a shelter would be more than the four of them had right then anyway.

Too—he considered—a praying man might beg God that they would find a fire glowing inside a Crow lodge where they could huddle out of the wind while the storm exhausted itself just beyond their sanctuary of poles and buffalo hides. But then he admitted that Titus Bass never had been the sort to get down on his prayer bones and taffy up to the Lord the way his mam had tried to teach her young'uns to do.

But at times like these when a man simply could do no more on his own to protect those he loved, when it was simply beyond his own power . . . then he supposed it wouldn't hurt to see if the All-Maker was listening. Just as long as the four of them made it to shelter and lived out the storm, as long as this storm didn't take his wife, or his daughter, or that little baby boy, Bass promised he would do anything in return. All God had to do was show him what was expected.

A man what didn't spend much of his time listening to anything the Almighty had to say wasn't the sort of man who could easily read the All-Maker's sign. Not like Asa McAfferty—now, that was a fella who could cipher the Lord's word plain as sun. But someone like Titus Bass might well be hard-pressed to figure out when God was talking to him, or even what tongue the Everywhere Spirit chose to speak in.

Nonetheless, if God saw his family through, Bass vowed he would do his best to be attentive to what God might ask in return, where- or whenever.

As strong as the fragrant tang of wood smoke grew in his sore, drippy nostrils, Scratch believed they had to be getting close. Step by step, stronger and stronger.

At times it became difficult to keep the bank of the Tongue close by on their right, what with the way the trees and willow forced them to ride several yards from the riverbank, sweeping slowly this way and that as they needled their way through the underbrush. The pack ponies began to protest now, pulling back on Samantha—making her bray in distress or anger at the way they were attempting to turn about and flee in the face of the brutal wind. For a moment he stopped, just long enough to loop the mule's rope twice around his left wrist, clutching Magpie against him with his right arm, the pony's reins held short and tight in that right hand as he struggled to get the horse started again into the teeth of the storm.

Out of the swirling gray gloom leaped the flickering glow of the fire, a corona of yellow glittering in the midst of the wavering, white-diamond air as snowflakes darted about in wispy, wind-driven trails. As they approached, Titus could tell that the fire had been huge not so long ago, nearly a bonfire fed by huge trunks and limbs of downfall someone had dragged to this small riverbank clearing. But now the man-high inferno had whipped itself so furiously that the firewood was nearly exhausted and on the verge of dying.

No one here to attend it. Like a beacon lit, then abandoned.

For barely a moment as he halted the exhausted pony again, Titus spotted two meat-drying racks erected back against the cottonwoods . . . then the blackened crowns of those small rocks arranged in a crude fire-ring where a lodge might once have stood. Injuns.

Should he stop here—get the three of them down by that fire—then push on by himself into the teeth of the storm?

There on the far side of the fire, that wall of ten-foot willow offered the only windbreak he could see in the fury of wind and snow. Right where those who had abandoned this place had raised their lodge. Perhaps Waits could huddle with the children beneath the three robes he could drape over them, waiting there for his return as the snow continued to build.

When he kicked the pony in the flanks, the animal failed to move. It shuddered the next time he kicked it with the heels of his ice-crusted buffalo-fur moccasins. A third hammer to its ribs finally got the animal lunging away a hoof at a time, slowly stepping around the perimeter of that dying fire, flames wildly licking up the huge logs, sparks spewing from the rotted wood like muzzle blasts, quickly swallowed by the wind, extinguished by the cold like galaxies of dying fireflies—given life in one breath, gone with the next.

On the far side of the fire, upwind, he tugged back on the reins and twisted stiffly in the saddle, his left arm wooden as he raised Samantha's rope, clumsily trying to find the pony's lead rope he had looped beneath his belt.

As the wind battered the side of his face, Scratch searched and dug at the side of his elk-hide coat. His cold mind slowly grasped the horror: the pony's rope was gone! It had somehow disappeared, dragged from his belt without his realizing it—

"W-waits!" he cried hoarsely in English. Even as the word escaped his lips, it was swept away by the gale, swallowed by the keening wind.

"Popo?"

Swallowing hard, he whispered to his daughter, "I'm calling your mother."

"Is mother there?"

"Y-yes," he lied again, feeling his eyes pool.

"And little brother?"

"Yes, Magpie."

God, I told you I would do anything you asked. Spare them. And if you must take any of us, then see they live and you can take me.

Her voice drenched in anguish, the girl whimpered, "I want my mother."

"Hush, now, Magpie," he scolded her sharply, angry and bitter at himself as much as he was angry and bitter with the All-Maker. "There's a fire here where I can get you warm."

"And my mother too."

"Yes, daughter—"

"Ti-tuzz!"

Her raspy voice slipped through a lull in the wind a frozen heartbeat before her shadowy, ghostly form loomed out of the blizzard.

"Woman!"

"Ti-tuzz!"

Bending his head down, Bass reassured his daughter, "Your m-mother is here."

She was sobbing against his breast. "Now you can get all of us warm."

"Yes," he gasped as he turned the pony around, watching the black form inch closer. "Now I promise to warm all of you."

He dropped the mule's lead rope and held out his left arm, so crusted it felt as if he had been lifting a thick stump of cottonwood. She brought her pony to a halt at his left side, leaning against him beneath that arm, sobbing.

"I thought I'd lost you in the storm," he said, rubbing that flap of the buffalo robe where her head was buried in the crusted fur. Then he heard the faint whimper of the baby.

"The boy, he is cold. I know he is scared too," she pleaded as she drew back the fur and tried to gaze up at his face in the storm.

"There is a fire where you and the children can stay while I go in search of shelter. You will be safe here till I can come back for—"

"We will be safe with you."

"The animals are tired," he begged her. "Better that I go on alone. I don't want to lose any of you to the cold and wind."

She interrupted, "*Bu'a*, out there minutes ago, I knew we would not die. My heart knew to believe in you. We will go with you."

Instantly his heart rose to his throat. "No. You must do as I say. Trust me and stay here. I will be back—"

That's when he dimly realized he was still smelling the wood smoke.

Bass immediately twisted in the saddle, away from his wife, turning his face into the wind once more—sniffing the terrible, metallic teeth of the fury heavy with moisture. Water. Nothing but a dry winter storm that had just crossed a wide river on these high, desertlike plains could smell quite like that.

Yet how was it that the beckoning fragrance of that wood smoke remained strong in his nostrils now that he stood upwind of this abandoned fire?

There had to be another fire to the north. Close to the Yellowstone that relinquished its wind-whipped froth to the storm.

"Come!" he cried. "Stay beside me. And talk to Flea! Keep talking to him so I can hear your voice and know your pony is staying near mine."

Harder than ever now, he struggled to get the animals moving, horses that acted as if they were no longer ready to bolt from the teeth of the storm, but had decided they were giving up the fight and would die there. Yelling, lashing out with his icy moccasin, he goaded Waits's pony and his own into lunging, uncertain steps as the white veil grew thicker around them, the wind no longer keening like a bitter, disembodied widow.

Now it howled in anger, sang out in a shrill fury.

At times over the next half hour, which seemed to be an eternity, the wood smoke grew stronger for a few moments, then disappeared altogether—only to return on the back of the wind just when Bass became convinced he had wandered off the path, or had passed the fire by. All through those next anxious minutes his mind tugged at it the way the current of the powerful Platte had tugged at his two horses, eventually claiming one—moving blind into the whiteout.

Suddenly he realized they had stepped off the shallow riverbank, their horses lunging into the Yellowstone. Icy water surged against their legs, washing against their bellies and ribs, swirling around his own left leg, spray and drops freezing instantly as the animals snorted in fear, whinnied in fear—plunging headlong for the north bank without a shred of hesitation. Only blind terror.

Waits cried out, a shrill yelp she stifled as her pony sidestepped there in the middle of the river where it found a deep pocket and swam back out, continuing to battle the current from the west and that blizzard born out of the north.

Stronger and stronger still the odor grew, then disappeared as the blizzard twisted this way and that—

Just as his horse's front legs floundered and he sensed it was going down, Bass heaved back on Magpie with that left arm as she started to slip away from him, onto the animal's withers. But with the next step the horse rocked back and shuddered, its front legs clawing—seizing ground, lunging onto the north bank with the last of its strength!

Out of the ghostly curtain emerged the dark shadow of the low, hulking block of neatly stacked timbers. He was almost upon the wall when it appeared right before them.

A few more steps and he stopped. Reached out and touched the chinked timbers with his crusted mitten.

"Halloo!" he croaked, barely audible as his cracked lips split even more painfully.

There against the wall, for the moment, they were out of the worst of the wind. He cried again, louder now, "Hal-halloo!"

It had to be Tullock's post.

Bass reached over and tugged on the other pony's rope now, getting their horses started again there in the lee of the log wall.

Fort Van Buren. Mouth of the Tongue. North bank of the Yellow-stone.

"Halloo! Tullock!"

They reached the end of the wall, where the dark shadow of the timbers disappeared in the blizzard as the wind screeched itself around the low log structure.

"Tullock!" and the wind carried his cry away again—

"Who? Who goes there?"

Titus swallowed, ready to cry as he glanced over at his wife, squeezed his daughter tighter.

"B-bass!" he whimpered into the might of the storm. "Titus Bass!"

"Titus Bass?" the disembodied voice came to him around the corner of those timbers.

The ghost figure suddenly took shape. "I ain't see'd your hide for longer'n I can count!"

"Tullock?"

"No!" and the tall, rail-thin figure stepped right around the corner of the post, stopping at Scratch's knee to peer up at the frozen man from the hood of his capote. "It's Levi, Scratch! Levi Gamble!"

The two tiny rooms that made up Fort Van Buren were gloomy with the blizzard's blotting out the sun. Little light but for the four smoky oil lamps, a pair of flickering candle lanterns, along with that stone fireplace where two Indian women and a half-dozen children sat basking in the warmth.

Gamble shooed them back, clucking in Assiniboine, clearing a path through them as he ushered Waits-by-the-Water from the creaky door and had her settle right in the middle of the hearth where she dragged the crusted buffalo robe from her shoulders as the ice adhering to it began to sweat and dribble to the hardpacked floor. She bent her head, kissing the boy's face, wiping her tears from his cheeks.

"I'll see to this'un, Titus Bass," Samuel Tullock offered with a kindly growl, kneeling and putting his arms out to accept the young girl as she emerged stiff and frightened from the buffalo robe and elk-hide coat Scratch had clutched around them both.

"I . . . I thankee," Bass whispered, his throat clogged with appreciation—to Gamble, to Tullock. To God. "I truly do."

Then he turned back to the door with Levi.

Outside the two of them stumbled after the animals already drifting before the wind that hurtled the men around like wood chips on a mountain stream. Lunging after the mule's lead rope, Scratch managed to yank Samantha back toward the cabin.

The other ponies reluctantly turned when she did, following her as they would a bell-mare, while Gamble hollered and slapped and cajoled

them from the rear as they busted through the snowdrifts already accumu-
lating waist high at the corner of the fort. It was there the wind whipped
and eddied. There along the south wall they tied the ropes off to iron
swivel rings pounded waist high into the unpeeled logs.

For a long moment Bass stood there, shading his eyes from the wind
and frozen snow with a mittened hand, staring at the ice caked on their
legs, around their bellies. Howling snow and crossing that damned river—

"Ain't nothing more you can do now!" Levi yelled above the deafening wail of the wind as it careened around the corner of the wall with a
constant white slash.

For a moment Bass stood there, looking at all of them, the way the
ice crusted their eyes, forelocks, and manes, how wind-scoured ridges of it
lay gathered against the packs and even across the broad flanks all the way
down to the tail roots.

Then he said, "If they're meant to make it—they'll be here when the
storm's passed."

"C'mon," Gamble urged. "Get on inside with your family."

Some of the drifts were already tall enough that the deep snow billowed out the long tails of his coat, his legs busting through until he stood
crotch-deep in the shocking cold, snow seeping down inside his breechclout and leggings. They had to kick with their toes, dig with their heels, at
the thick, icy crust forming at the foot of the doorway. Eventually the two
of them together were able to pry the door back toward them far enough
to allow them to slip through sideways, then drag it closed against the
square-hewn jamb.

Both Gamble and Bass sank to the floor, gasping, pummeled by the
wind, worn down with the subzero cold, suddenly back inside where a man
could hear his own heartbeat again, could hear the crackle of burning
wood in that fireplace. Where a man felt relief at finding himself still alive.

Scratch's face started to hurt as his breathing began to slow. He
dragged off the coyote cap and that long strip of blanket he had tied
around his head and over his ears, working at the frozen, crusted knot
under his chin. Across the room at the fire, Waits-by-the-Water nursed
little Flea in the flickering glow of that fireplace as she talked in low tones
with the women. A young half-breed girl sat with Magpie, a pair of dolls
between them.

Titus gazed into his wife's face—her eyes saying that her faith in him
had not been misplaced. As he worried the big antler buttons from their
holes and pulled the flaps of his coat aside, his daughter looked over,
stood, and started his way.

"Popo," she said as clear as she ever had, coming into his arms.

As Magpie laid her cheek against her father's chest, Titus sighed.
"That's a second time you've took my family in from a winter storm, Levi.
How's a man s'pose to repay you for kindness like that?"

"I'll figger something out," he gasped with a weary smile.

"We damn near thought you was the wind," the trader said as he came over to the two of them with a long-necked clay bottle in hand. "Till Levi claimed it weren't the wind calling my name out there."

Bass gazed at Gamble. "I'd found the fort a'ready, by damn, Levi—no sense you coming out in that storm to fetch me."

"Like your ass weren't half-froze to the saddle as it was, Titus Bass," Gamble said, reaching up to take the bottle from Tullock as the trader squatted between them, shoulder to shoulder. He sniffed, smiled, and tilted his head back as he drank long and slow with eyes closed. Levi licked his lips when he passed the bottle on past the trader to Bass.

"You'll like it," Tullock declared.

"That there's good company rum, Sam'l," Gamble observed. "Not the sort I'm used to drinking up at Union."

"It ain't for the trade," Tullock explained. "This here what's made for the factors."

"That's some fine rum, mighty fine," Scratch said as he wiped the back of his hand across his lips and mustache. "Don't much care where it come from, Sam'l—long as it warms up that cold man inside me."

"If *that* stuff don't warm you up, then the nigger inside you is awready dead!" Tullock swore.

After he took a second slow swallow, Bass handed the bottle to Tullock, licked the droplets on the ends of his mustache, and asked, "What brings you down here this season, Levi?"

Gamble tore his eyes away and glanced at Tullock. The trader nodded, placed the clay bottle on the floor between Levi and Titus, then stood and moved off toward some crates in the corner as if he were going to busy himself elsewhere.

When Gamble finally looked back at Bass, Scratch already had a cold rock of something resting at the bottom of his belly.

"I been down here going on two weeks already, Titus."

Scratch was afraid it had nothing to do with good news when he asked, "Little late in the season for you to be bringing trade goods upriver from Fort Union, ain't it?"

Tullock still had his back turned when he said, "I ain't gonna get no trade goods this year."

For a long moment he studied Gamble's face. "S'pose you tell me what you're doing down here, Levi. You didn't go and kill nobody, did you? Didn't go and get yourself in trouble with your booshways?"

Gamble stared at his knees, then answered. "It don't have nothing to do with any of that."

Suddenly Tullock wheeled and blurted, "They got smallpox on the river! Smallpox." And as suddenly he turned on his heel and disappeared into the darkness of a small adjoining room.

Stunned silent, Titus watched the white-faced trader go, then looked at Gamble. "Sm-smallpox?"

Levi nodded. "Come upriver on the summer boat, *St. Peter's.*"

Bass quickly glanced at Waits, at the boy suckling at his mother's breast. Staring in turn at those other women and children as the fear climbed out of the pit of him. "Y-you ain't . . . ain't got no smallpox in you—"

"No," Levi interrupted, laying a hand on Bass's forearm a moment. "But I did have me a terrible fight with it."

"Fight?"

With a struggle Gamble rose, moved off a couple of steps, and brought back an oil lamp where a smoky wick burned in rendered bear grease. Bringing the flickering light near his face, Levi knelt in front of Scratch. "You see what it done to me?"

Gamble's face, the shape of that nose and those eyes, they remained unchanged. But the cheeks and the forehead were deeply scarred, pitted with the ravages of the scourge.

"I ain't never knowed no one had the pox," Bass admitted quietly, awed by his fear.

"Pray God you never do, Titus," he said, putting the lamp aside and settling back against the wall, sweeping up the clay bottle to throw down another drink.

Scratch stared through the dim, flickering light provided by the lamps and that fireplace, gazing at the Indian women, at the children. "Your wife, your young'uns—they get it just like you?"

"Neither of them my wife," Gamble admitted sullenly. "They be Tullock's woman and her relations. They was awready here ahead of me when I come in. Don't you worry: they ain't got no smallpox. Be down with it awready, but they ain't—"

"So wh-where's your family, Levi—"

"Gone. All gone."

"The pox?"

Gamble nodded and finally looked at Bass, handing Titus the clay bottle. "Here, drink up with me, 'cause it don't help no man to drink alone."

Wondering what he could say, suddenly made to think of other men like Asa McAfferty and Joe Meek, men who had had their women killed, had their hearts ripped right out of their chests . . . Scratch took the bottle from him. "No man's ever gonna have to drink alone when his heart's been broke."

Levi stared at the floor. "Titus, there's a hole inside me what I don't think I can fill with all the rum in the world."

"How . . . how'd the pox come up here?"

"They said one of the men on the boat. He come down with it, and they didn't turn back because they had just so much time to bring trade goods upriver, had furs to take down to St. Louis. Brung the pox to Fort Clark. The boat brung it on up to Fort Union."

"Your woman . . . how many others?"

"More'n anyone can count," Levi whispered like a death knell. "Before fall come, it destroyed the Mandan down at Fort Clark, the Arikaree too. Ain't any of 'em left we heard of."

"The Ree too?" Bass thought on the people of that rattle shaker Asa McAfferty had killed many a winter ago.

"When the boat reached Fort Union, they quickly unloaded the goods bound upriver for Fort McKenzie, then loaded 'em on the keel and pushed on up the Missouri."

Bass shuddered. "You telling me they took the pox into Blackfoot country?"

Gamble nodded. "Word coming downriver says Culbertson tried to warn them Blackfeets away from Fort McKenzie—but the niggers was suspicious the company was stealing powder and lead from 'em. Powder and lead they needed to make war."

"War on the Crow and Flathead. War on the white men," Bass said quietly. He looked into the thin man's sallow, gray face—recognized the torment there. "Hard to believe. Your wife . . . and all your young'uns."

Gamble only nodded silently.

"How's a man . . . make sense of that, Levi? Watching your family get took by the pox? Get took by something you can't fight?"

"The day after the boat come, a few of us went out to tell the villages in the area not to come in, warning 'em something terrible would happen to 'em if they did. But a few days after we told 'em not to come in to trade, some young bucks rode on in to steal some horses. Halsey—the new booshway up there—he put up a reward for those horses. One of the men who was 'bout to come down sick went out to catch them horse thieves."

Titus watched Tullock trudge back into the light, another clay bottle clutched in one hand as the trader grumbled, " 'Stead of the pox staying there at the fort, that ignorant bastard give it to the horse thieves—and them young bucks took it back to their village."

Bass wagged his head. "But that wasn't how your woman, your children, got took."

"First one to come down with it was Halsey hisself," Levi declared, courage in his voice. "One of the other booshways claimed he knowed how they could 'noculate everyone else from Halsey's sores. So we done that, all of us—hunters, interpreters, coopers—all of us . . . and our families too. A simple thing: make a small cut in our skin and rub a little of Halsey's pus in that bloody cut. They told us it was gonna keep us all alive."

What did you say to a man who had watched his wife and children come down with the raging fever, the boils that erupted into pustules, unable to save even himself from the disease—forced to watch as all those he loved were ripped from him, while he somehow survived.

Titus asked, "How . . . how come you . . . you—"

"Lived?" Levi finished the question. Then shook his head. "Ain't none of us can answer that. Maybeso the white man got a stronger constitution, Titus. Most of the whites come down with it lived. And near ever' one of the Injuns what got the pox . . . they're gone."

Settling to the floor nearby, a grim-lipped Tullock set that second clay bottle between the three of them.

"So now the company's give the pox to the Blackfoot," Scratch repeated the ominous news as if to make some sense of its unreality. Then suddenly it struck him at the pit of his belly where that cold stone still lay. "What about the Crow?"

"So far as we know," the trader said as he leaned back against a bundle of robes, "the pox ain't come no farther up the Yellowstone."

"F-far as you know?"

Both of them nodded. "None of the Crow been in to trade with me since late summer—'bout the time I heard first rumors of it up at Fort Union. I was on my way north to find out why the boat didn't come down with my year's goods."

"No Crow?" Scratch echoed, hopeful. "Maybeso they heard and they're staying away."

"Can't count on that, Titus. Someone's gotta tell 'em," Levi advised. "That's what me and Sam'l been trying to sort through last few days. Where to find 'em—how to tell 'em to stay away."

"And someone's gotta tell 'em to stay away from the Blackfoot," Scratch declared solemnly. "Can't go make war on them what's got the pox."

He watched both Tullock and Gamble nod as they glanced at one another.

Levi turned back to gaze at Bass. "We figger you're the one, Titus."

"The one for what?"

Gamble sighed. "Go tell the Crow the white man's brought sure death to the mountains."

TWENTY-THREE

Those ghastly, unspeakable images Levi had burned into his mind continued to haunt Bass, day and night.

Scratch even believed he could somehow smell the stench of those dying people, wriggling maggots starting to nibble away at their decaying bodies even before they had taken their last breath.

Once those who had been inoculated with Jacob Halsey's illness began to sicken with the maddening fever and die, the fort workers were ordered to remove their families at the first sign of the disease. The half-burned Fort William barely standing a hundred-some yards east of the Fort Union stockade became their sick haven. This post where the Deschamps clan once reigned soon became a den of death.

Most days, Levi had explained, the winds in that country came from the west, occasionally out of the north. But on those rare days when the wind did not blow at all—or worse yet, the upslope breeze drifted out of the east—the stench of putrefying flesh of those too ill to do anything but lie in their own human excrement mingled with the unbearable reek of decaying bodies.

This matter of odor, even stench, was something of such

immediate vividness to one who lived among these mountains. Outdoors, here beneath this restless sky, in a land where the air *always* moved, for a man to describe to another the overwhelming power of that decay made it so vivid that Titus believed he truly could smell death's most gruesome, repulsive retribution in his own nostrils.

From the ramparts of Fort Union the company employees watched many of their loved ones and friends, watched those friendly Assiniboine stricken with the unbearable fevers, all go stumbling down the barren slope to the boat landing at the Missouri where they plunged themselves into the cold waters, their dulled minds seeking somehow to snuff out the unquenchable fire. Most who plunged into the river simply never returned to the bank. Their constitutions weakened, sapped by the pox's destructive power, then shocked by the brutal cold of the powerful and capricious spring-fed currents, one after another they vainly flailed at the river as they were swept away to a watery end.

And that moaning Levi described—the uncanny wails drifting night and day from the blackened walls of Fort William, from those hide lodges where death's angel touched the Assiniboine one after another—and from the dusty banks of the river where the few went to mourn the many who had crawled to the Missouri to die.

Through the hours of that winter blizzard, Gamble described the pitiful whimpering of the dying children, the groans of the women no longer able to care for their little ones. How the horror of it floated on that dry summer wind both day and night without ceasing.

"Like a haunting," Levi quietly explained.

An undeniable wraith that would not depart, could not be driven away. Unceasing until its ravenous appetite had consumed all and there were none left to cry out for mercy.

"What become of 'em?" Titus had asked as winter's fury howled outside those log walls of Fort Van Buren. "Y-your family."

"After more'n a day of quiet—not a sound from anyone or any-thing—I went to the stockade. Looked in through the window at all that was left of them what went there to die," Gamble whispered. "There was nothing moving but for the scratch of the mice at the food we'd brung to leave at the walls for the sick'uns."

"They . . . your wife and chirrun . . . was all took?"

"Aye, Titus. Some of us, we soaked our kerchiefs in coal oil and tied 'em around our noses, done our best to remember to breathe through our mouths. But still that stink . . . that stink."

"You done what you had to do to bury your own family," Scratch said barely above a whisper.

But Gamble shook his head. "No. Rolled my little'uns onto them poxy blankets. Found ever' one of 'em being et up with maggots awready. Their skin oozy and bleeding from the sores, the maggots swarming and wriggling in every hole on their flesh. Nothing else to do but drag 'em all out to the prairie where the village stood, and we built us a big fire. Throwed downed trees and logs, lodgepoles and hides too on that fire till the flames climbed clear to the sky and the smoke reached even higher."

Then for a long moment it seemed the very breath had gone out of Levi's body, and he could not speak as he was reliving the ghastly horror of it.

Titus swallowed. "A fire?"

Staring at a spot between his moccasins on the earthen floor, the aging frontiersman explained, "We throwed the dead on the fire. Prayed we'd burn the pox till there was nothing for the pox to live on no more." Levi shuddered. "The way it ate on humankind—just the way we humans eat the flesh of the poor dumb creatures we kill."

Scratch found himself unable to escape Gamble's gruesome, heart-felt descriptions, haunted every mile he took his family west from the mouth of the Tongue. Those grisly images continued to prey upon his mind like frightening specters from that world beyond his own. Terrifying images all too real: the stench of filth and rotting corpses, the horror of those hideous and oozing pustules writhing with maggots, and finally the purifying heat of that raging bonfire as the sanctifying flames consumed loved ones.

Each day Titus found he repeatedly turned in the saddle to assure himself Waits-by-the-Water was still behind him, to confirm that she held little Flea in her arms or that his cradleboard swung from the tall pommel of her prairie-chicken saddle. Every night when they made camp and Waits busied herself at the fire, Titus clutched those children more firmly against him; later he wrapped himself more securely around his wife as they slept in their robes.

To lose them the way Levi lost his woman, their children . . . was a prospect far more terrifying than the possibility of losing his own life. Better was it that he die himself than to face a future lonely, stark, and bleak without the three of them.

It was to be a winter when the way of the mountains was turned on its head.

Fort Van Buren had been no more than a day behind them when Scratch hustled their ponies into a copse of cottonwood and brush on the south bank of the Yellowstone. No more than a quarter mile ahead he spotted some horsemen picking their way along the bottom ground at the foot of the rimrocks along the north side of the river. After leaving the others in hiding, Bass ventured out on foot to have himself a look before he made himself known. If the bunch was Crow, he could ask them where he would find Yellow Belly's village.

But turned out they were Blackfoot.

Studying them closely with his small, leather-covered brass looking glass, Titus noted those greased forelocks standing stiffly, provocatively erect as a challenge to any would-be enemy, daring an opponent to attempt removing the scalp. Behind more than two dozen riders came at least that many riderless horses, the whole cavvyyard moving east at an easy pace. Close as he could tell, none of them were wearing paint. Moseying the way they were, nary a one of them displaying his special medicine, Scratch doubted they could be a war party. A bunch of bucks out for scalps and plunder didn't drag along some pack animals. He figured that after they had wrapped up their raiding and were hightailing it on out of Crow country, then they planned to pack their stolen goods atop those extra horses.

But this bunch was loping east—toward the farthest reaches of Absaroka. If he didn't know better, he might figure they were riding for the Tongue.

Letting them pass well out of sight before he emerged from hiding to hurry back for his family, Bass brooded how odd it was if the Blackfoot might actually be making for Tullock's post. They had their own fort well up on the Missouri. Then again, these might well be some Blackfoot what belonged to a band who hadn't gone in to trade with Culbertson at Fort McKenzie last summer when the pox's prairie fire was igniting. This bunch might be from a village that later brushed up against some of those who got themselves infected from Culbertson's men and the company's goods.

If these horsemen had witnessed how the white man's scourge devastated their brothers, it was possible they had sworn off packing their furs to Fort McKenzie some six miles upriver from the mouth of the Marias where old Fort Piegan stood abandoned and decaying, deciding instead to haul their robes and plews south and east to trade for powder and lead, guns and blankets at the Crows' trading post.

Damn, if the pox hadn't pulled the pegs right out from under the whole teetering balance of things here in the north country.

Power might well be in the process of shifting already. As the scourge ate its way through the Blackfoot, it would kill off a sizable number of their warrior bands—Blood, Piegan, Gros Ventre. Never again would they be as mighty as they had been from that day Meriwether Lewis's party of explorers chanced to bump into them on the expedition's homeward trek to St. Louis. With every year since that unfortunate tragedy in 1806, the tribe had grown more than intractable.

The Blackfoot had gone after Americans with a vengeance.

With fewer and fewer warriors, as well as fewer women to seed future generations of fighting men, this once-most-powerful confederation in the Northern Rockies could do nothing but watch their mighty strength slip through their fingers like overdry river-bottom sand. Without their overwhelming numbers, the Blackfoot would be hard-pressed to maintain the pressure on those American brigades daring to nibble hungrily around the edges of that once-forbidden beaver country where a man most certainly was gambling with his life.

All the more white men would come to shove back the Blackfoot frontier, season after season, assault after assault.

Those superstitious Blackfoot still alive after the pox had run its course would naturally believe that Fort McKenzie was the seat of the disease and their devastation. So they would seek out other traders, to the north among the English, and to the south among the hated Americans. Especially if that post lay in a region abandoned by the Crow who had been terrified enough to stay as far away as possible from Fort Van Buren.

If the Crow had heard of the disease and were avoiding Tullock at all costs, then they wouldn't be trading to the benefit of the greedy company, nor trading for the powder and ball they themselves needed to hold back any Blackfoot encroachment upon Absaroka. Their superstition or their ignorance would keep them away from the mouth of the Tongue.

Could he blame the Crow for their fear? Not with the pox raging upriver and across the prairies as the Blackfoot carried it right into the heart of the Rockies.

Titus didn't know how the devastation was transmitted. Never had understood such matters. Did the Blackfoot have to touch the Crow to pass along the infection? Or . . . could it be something as simple as the wind? Was this terror no more than a matter of the air in the Blackfoot country drifting over the hills and down the river valleys to reach Absaroka? Like a windwhipped grassfire, this scourge might well race from village to village on the air they would breathe, seeping stealthily from lodge to lodge. The infected would believe if they ran fast enough, if they fled far enough, they would stay ahead of what death loomed on the backtrail.

Then one night as Scratch banked their fire and slipped beneath the robes beside Waits, the cold of it suddenly struck him: if the Crow were as afraid of Tullock as they were of the company traders at Fort Union, how in heaven were the Crow going to react to him . . . one of the race who had brought this terrible epidemic to the mountains?

How could they believe that he wasn't carrying the disease? Would they even trust in Waits-by-the-Water?

Or because they so desperately feared the pox brought by the Americans, would the Crow warriors do everything in their power to prevent him from reaching their village?

Instead of risking that gamble, would the Crow decide they must kill him?

Scratch had begun to wonder if they ever would find Yellow Belly's people.

For the better part of a month they had been scouring the river valley, west all the way to the Big Bend of the Yellowstone then back to Clark's Fork, with no sign of either village. Not a clue on the River Crow; no Mountain band either. For the past two weeks he had begun to despair of finding them at all, much less finding the village in time to warn them of the danger from the north.

But Bass swallowed it all down, refusing to let her know of his doubts. On and on they plodded from first light to last, halting only when it grew so dark he dared not stumble on through the broken, icy country. At the mouth of every tiny creek they passed, he brooded on what he should be doing instead of this fool's errand Tullock and Gamble had talked him into accepting.

This was clearly a time when a man should be stalking the flat-tails. Plain enough the animals would have grown a thick coat, as brutal as this winter had become. Why didn't he just admit he had failed and go off to do what he had done for the last few winters—spend a handful of days away from the lodge to trap on his lonesome, then return with the pelts for her to scrape and stretch, play with the youngsters, couple with her each night until he felt that itch to leave again?

But every time he tried talking logically, rationally, to himself about it, reciting the litany of reasons why he should put this futile search aside and get on with the white man's business of trapping beaver . . . Titus felt that sharp pang of remorse in his belly—the way something distasteful soured his meat bag. He knew he would never be able to look his wife in the eye if he gave up.

Should they not find the village until spring, so be it. More important than his beaver was this matter of his duty to Waits-by-the-Water's people.

For three more days they moved up Clark's Fork, traveling some seventy miles south of the Yellowstone. Odd that they hadn't run across any sign of hunters, much less sign of the village itself. That many people camped for the winter somewhere near the valley of the Yellowstone had to leave some evidence of their passing. So many hundreds upon hundreds of bellies to feed, thousands upon thousands of ponies needing pasture. So far, not a sign along the Yellowstone, nothing from the Tongue to the Great Bend and back again to Clark's Fork.

They had come to the very foot of the mountains. Instead of pushing on to the south into the narrowing valley, Scratch turned east. Climbing with the rising ground on the sunrise side of the fork, they dropped into a high rolling country. To the west lay the Stinking Water and what the trappers called Colter's Hell, a route that would lead a man into the region the Crow revered as the Land of Spirit Smokes. To the east lay the valley of the Bighorn. Ahead to the south lay the Greybull basin.

"Have your people ever come this far south to winter?" he asked her that night after they had camped among some hot pools of sulfurous water.

"Twice, when I was much younger," Waits said as she stood from pulling off the last moccasin.

She grabbed the bottom of her hide dress and raised it over her head. When she had shimmied out of her blanket leggings, Waits tested the water's temperature, sticking her toe into the pool where he sat submerged to his armpits. Around them a gauzy steam wisped into cold midwinter air.

He glanced at their children sleeping a few yards back from the edge of the pool. "Come here."

As she glided through the smoky water, he reached out and pulled her to him. "Why would your village ever come so far south?"

"If the winter was terribly cold," she explained as she settled across the tops of his thighs. "They will always go where there is meat, where the winds won't blow so long and hard. Where spring might return a little sooner."

He bent, kissed the tops of her breasts as they shimmered at the surface of the water. His flesh stirred.

"How far south would they go?"

"I can remember wintering one time in the shadow of the mountains."

He pointed off to the south. "Those mountains still far away?"

"Yes," she answered, but her voice had lowered an octave with that huskiness born of hunger as she took his hardening flesh into her hand, kneading it.

"Then we should go until the River of the Winds turns west at the foot of the mountains?"

"At least that far."

He sighed with the delicious pleasure she was bringing him as she rubbed his flesh against herself, as she began to squirm a little in anticipation of him. "I am sure this is the season we spent together in Taos, the happy celebration before I left."

"Ta-house," Waits repeated the word in English. Then in Crow she said, "I remember the sweet foods Rosa made for us, the smells from her warm cooking, the flavors she put in her coffee so strong, sweet, and milky."

"You are milky too," he said as he gently raised one of her breasts, then sucked at the nipple while she groaned, suckled gently until he tasted the warm, sweet, sticky milk.

She reminded him, "Th-that is your son's milk."

"But this is his father's breast."

"So whose is this?" she asked, squeezing his manhood firmly as she rose a little, positioned his hardened flesh, then settled down on him with an agonizingly delicious slowness.

He rocked his hips upward, squirming to seat himself within her. "I think it is yours now."

"Then we agree," she said devilishly as she began to rock more insistently upon him. "It does belong to me."

The following morning they pushed on south, marching upriver for the mountains that loomed ever larger to the southeast, a chain stretching across the entire horizon, their pinnacles and slopes blotted by an unbroken mantle of snow extending from hoary crests all the way down to the valley floor. At the mouth of the Popo Agie they turned north by northwest, following the Wind River along its foothills. After a snowfall two days later they crossed a large trail. Hunters. If it wasn't the Crow, he figured it might well be the Snake.

They followed the tracks north for another day, then made camp after sundown, once it had grown too dark to follow those tracks left by more than a dozen horses. That night when he stepped away from the fire to look after the animals, Scratch stood among the ponies, rubbing Samantha's withers. After a few minutes he became aware of the faint fragrance of wood smoke drifting in on the wind.

Turning this way, then that, Titus realized he wasn't smelling his own fire. Instead, it had to be smoke wafting over the hilltop just beyond their campsite. His heart leaped.

Crunching across the surface of the frozen ground, he loped through the trees toward the crest where the black of the night sky collided with the pale blue of the icy, moonlit snow. By the time he reached the top, Scratch was out of breath, huffing as much from sheer anticipation as he was with the exertion. At first it did not strike him what he was seeing, those tiny specks of light appearing as so many points of starshine reflected off the endless smear of snow in the far valley.

Slowly he realized they had to be campfires. More than a hundred of them. A few glittered brightly, but most had a translucent, opaque quality to them.

"Lodges," he whispered as excitement gushed up within him.

Then turned on his heel and hurried downhill through the animals for their campfire.

"Woman!" Scratch cried lustily as he came bounding up. "Woman— I see a village below!"

"Ssshhh," she warned, pointing to where the children lay sleeping, then asked, "Are there many lodges?"

He gulped for air, swallowed, and said, "It must be Yellow Belly's camp. There are hundreds of lights—many, many fires and lodges."

"I think I will have trouble sleeping tonight," she said, leaping to her feet and throwing her arms around him.

"It makes my heart glad to see how happy this makes you," he declared, squeezing her tightly. "Tomorrow you will see your mother, you will see Strikes-in-Camp and his family too."

Burying her face against the crook of his neck, Waits-by-the-Water confided softly, "I have been so afraid that they were no more, husband. I feared they had been swept away like the others who have been touched by the white man's death."

"But they haven't disappeared," he consoled her.

"Until now, a big hole in my heart feared that very thing," she admitted. "I did not want to trust we could find them. As the days became many, I grew more afraid we would find empty lodges, skeletons of bone wrapped in tattered clothing, every one of my people eaten by this terrible sickness."

"We found them alive. They are safe," he reassured her, his own tangible relief lifting a great weight from his shoulders. "Tomorrow we will rejoin your mother, your brother, and his family. And tomorrow night we can laugh at your fears as we gather around their fire, all of us, and throw these fears of yours into the flames."

"Tomorrow," she echoed the word in a whisper. "I was so afraid tomorrow would never come."

That dawn came cold and gray, a hulking bank of clouds the color of a ripe bruise hovering halfway down the mountain slopes. By the time Flea had nursed and Magpie finished chewing some cold meat from last night's supper with her father, Bass had the animals packed for what should be a short ride.

He had been anticipating this morning ever since the day they put Fort Van Buren behind them. Afraid he would only deepen what he could see was his wife's own growing anxiety, Scratch kept his fears to himself. Day by day he had become a bit more morose—swallowing deep the slightest image his mind conjured of their searching endlessly, eventually to stumble across a camp of Crow lodges, entering the circle to discover that it was now home only to magpies and robber jays, coyotes and wolves, as the flocks and packs of predators worked over the bodies of three thousand dead.

In his own way Scratch had been praying every day that when they finally found Yellow Belly's camp, they would not find a village of ghosts. Afraid that after saving them from the blizzard, God would not now succor his newest prayer.

With the way the wind was quickly quartering around to blow out of the northwest, the smell of wood smoke grew strong once again. Far behind them now stood that ridge crest where he had peered into this valley as the unnumbered fires twinkled in the clear, subfreezing night air. Ahead, in that bottom ground where a creek flowed out of the tall, cloud-covered mountains to pour itself into Wind River, stood the camp. Hundreds upon hundreds of smoky spires rose from the lodges, each column quickly absorbed by the belly of those low-hanging clouds momentarily hued with a reddish-orange tint as the sun foretold its emergence from the east.

"Camp guards," she announced, pointing to their right.

He turned in the saddle, finding the eight horsemen bursting from the timber, loping their way.

More hooves clattered to their left as another half dozen broke into the open. These, like the first, carried shields at their left elbows, war clubs or bows in their right hands, while a few held aloft long lances festooned with scalps and brightly colored cloth streamers made all the more brilliant in these moments of the sun's brief journey between earth and cloud bank.

At first he did not recognize any of the young men coming their way, afraid this was not a Crow village. But as the riders approached, he recognized the hairstyles, the special markings on a shield here or there. And then he heard a camp guard yelling at them in his wife's tongue.

These were Crow!

But instead of welcoming, the voices shouted in warning, two of them now—both voices strident and . . . afraid.

"What are they telling us?" he asked of her, beginning to pull back on the pony's reins uneasily.

"We must stop," she said in dismay, her eyes as wide as Mexican conchos when she looked to him for explanation.

Of a sudden Titus was afraid he knew the answer.

Fourteen warriors fanned out in a broad front as they came to a halt fifty yards from them.

"Popo?"

"Ssshhh," he rasped at Magpie.

He felt the girl pull herself against his back more tightly as she tilted her face up so she could whisper to him.

"Why is my mother so afraid?"

Scratch looked at Waits-by-the-Water and had to admit she did look frightened.

"I think she is excited about—"

"Do not come any closer!" interrupted the warrior beneath the swelling wreath of frosty breath that encircled his head.

"But we are friends," Bass hollered in reply, watching one of the guards rein about and kick his pony into a lope, heading back to the village.

"I know you, Waits-by-the-Water," the first warrior admitted. "When my younger sister was a little girl, you and she played together with your tiny lodges and horses and dolls. But you cannot—"

"Three Iron?" she suddenly asked. "Is that you?"

"Yes—"

"Then you know us!" Waits interrupted. "Why don't you invite us into the camp? I have waited a long time to see my mother again, to show her how much her grandson has grown."

"I can't invite you into the village," he shouted.

"But—you are my people!" she cried.

"Your husband is not," Three Iron explained.

Far behind the camp guards Bass saw two riders emerge from the village, coming their way at a gallop. He turned to look quickly at the dismay on her face, realizing he must try to talk some sense into these warriors.

"You say you know me," Titus began, hearing Magpie start to whimper quietly against his back. "Your people have always welcomed me—even when I came on foot chasing horse thieves."

"I am Red Leggings," shouted one of the guards near the end of the crescent. "I was with Pretty On Top the day we rode off with your animals many winters ago."

"Then you must explain why you will not allow me to bring my wife and children into your camp to see their relations."

Halting, one of the arriving horsemen announced, "It would be dangerous."

"Strikes-in-Camp?" she wailed. "Is that you, my brother?"

"Yes, sister. I am here."

She nudged her pony forward, saying, "How I longed to see you and my mother—"

At that instant Scratch lunged over and grabbed the pony's halter, pulling to a stop.

"Stay there, sister!" Strikes-in-Camp demanded. "You can come no closer."

"Brother!" she shrieked, covering her face with a hand.

Magpie began to wail behind him.

"Why won't you accept your sister into the camp of her people?" Titus asked in a strong voice, words hanging brittle as ice while the clouds lowered over them. The sun was disappearing, rising into the blue-black, as if all the warmth of that crimson light was being snuffed out. Tiny lances of ice darted about their faces, stinging the cold flesh.

Strikes-in-Camp explained. "She might be sick."

"S-sick?" Waits sobbed. "Only my heart is sick to be treated so badly by my people—"

Afraid he already knew, the trapper asked, "How do you think your sister is sick?"

"She is with a white man," yelled another man.

"How will that make her sick, Strikes-in-Camp?"

"In that hottest part of the summer, we heard the stories of the white man sickness killing other tribes," his brother-in-law explained, his pony pawing a hoof at the frozen, snowy ground.

Pausing as he thought, Bass suddenly said, "But you can see I am not sick—"

"We have heard the white man does not grow sick and die with this terrible affliction," another warrior interrupted. "Only the Indians. Mandans, Arikara, Assiniboine, even Blackfoot too. Now that you have come, white man—this evil has followed us here."

"You ran away from your fear of it, didn't you?" Titus asked.

"The old men believed it the wisest," the young warrior declared. "The oldest among them remembered the tribal stories of another time long, long ago when our people lived close to the great muddy river—a time when this same evil sickness of the seeping wounds and fever swept through the villages along the river."

"The Crow have known about this sickness before?"

"Yes," the young warrior said. "Our old men say only a few died because our people quickly scattered onto the prairie, running faster than the invisible terror that had come to kill us all."

Bass nodded. "So your chiefs decided you should run again."

"And stay as far away as we can from the white man who once more brings this evil to kill Indians who are his enemies," Strikes-in-Camp said. "Even Indians who are his friends."

"Look at me. I am not sick."

"You are a white man. You carry the sickness in you," he said, waving his arm in frustration. "While it doesn't consume you, it will kill us."

Stretching out his arm to indicate his wife, Bass said, "Look at your sister! She is alive! We have been to Tullock's post and she did not die. Our children are still alive. There is no disease in them!"

Clearly frustrated now, Strikes-in-Camp roared, "You must stay away!"

"B-brother!" she keened, her voice rising even as the black belly of the clouds tore open with the first falling of an icy snow.

"If I take my wife into your camp to see her mother, what will happen to me?"

The warrior said, "I will have to kill you."

Bass swallowed hard. "And if my wife comes to see her mother without me?"

Drawing himself up, Strikes-in-Camp said, "I will have to kill her."

"We are not your enemies," Bass snarled, feeling angry at his help-lessness.

"The white man brought this sickness to the mountains. You must stay away from us."

Scratch reached over and took his wife's forearm in his mitten, gripping it reassuringly. "Tell your mother . . . say we send her our love and want to see her face one day soon."

"Perhaps one day," Strikes-in-Camp said sadly.

Waits began to cry, covering her face with a blanket mitten as she wheeled her pony around and started on their backtrail.

"Strikes-in-Camp," Titus called. "You must be careful."

"Of other white men like you?"

"No," he replied. "I bring a warning that the Crow must be careful of the Blackfoot."

"Not the white man?"

"No," Bass said. "The Blackfoot carry this terrible sickness now."

TWENTY-FOUR

A wolf called that gray morning as the icy snow fell softer, then beat no more against the side of the brush-and-canvas shelter where he lay with her and the children.

Winter was old, almost done. Yet it hung on and on, refusing to give itself to spring.

For weeks now Waits-by-the-Water had hardly spoken a word. She still sang to Flea to put him to sleep at night, and she held Magpie in her arms too. She even made love to him with the same ferocity she always had . . . but she did not talk much at all.

Never, never about Yellow Belly's camp. Not one word about her people.

Better to let that wound be, he decided, hoping it would heal on its own.

That wolf howled again, perhaps a different one. It was a plaintive call, anguished and lonely.

If it had been raining—instead of snowing—Titus might be more concerned, even afraid. A wolf that came out to howl in the rain was the spirit of a warrior killed before his time. So if it were raining instead of that weepy snow, it might well make him venture from these warm robes and blankets, push into the cold timber in search of that restless, disembodied spirit.

Up there in Blackfoot country was damn well going to be plenty of wolves to howl in the rain come spring. Maybe the cold of winter had killed all the pox. Nothing like that was going to live through the long, deep cold of this northern land. If the Blackfoot weren't all dead from the disease, then at least the pox was finished now. And what was left of the tribe was nothing more than a pale shadow of what they had been.

Ghosts.

Mandan, Arikara, Assiniboine, and Blackfoot. And now the Crow.

Yellow Belly's people might as well have been ghosts too. Day after day, week upon week, he and Waits-by-the-Water never could get very close to the village before camp guards rode up shouting, threatening, until she explained that she only wanted one of the warriors to bring her mother to the edge of camp. Just to see Crane's face in the distance, to know she was still alive. To show her mother they were still alive and well. So Crane could see they were not being eaten by a terrible sickness.

The children waved to Crane across that distance, and their grandmother waved back—then suddenly turned, slump-shouldered, and hurried back into the village with her daughter-in-law's arm around her shoulder. That retreat always made Waits-by-the-Water even sadder.

Something on the order of a week later Bass had finally convinced her they had no business keeping a vigil around the fringes of that camp of frightened people.

Ghosts, he thought. His wife's family might as well be ghosts.

That last time Crane brought the rest of them with her, all of Strikes-in-Camp's family. Bright Wings and the children waved before they turned to go. Then, before she retreated into the village, Crane pointed to an outcropping of rocks several hundred yards from the village. She gestured expansively, struggling to make herself understood.

Then Waits began to cry and held up little Flea to wave to his grandmother. Titus helped Magpie stand tall upon his shoulders as she signaled to that small, distant person. In the end the girl even blew kisses to her grandmother the way Titus taught her to do. Waits turned away with Flea, and they returned to their camp where his wife sobbed until close to sundown.

When they remembered the point of rocks. Hurrying there, Waits discovered a newly smoked antelope skin wrapped inside a piece of oiled rawhide. Within it rested several small gifts Crane had bundled together: a tiny deer-hair-stuffed doll for Magpie and a stuffed horse for Flea, two small whistles carved from cedar, while beneath them all lay a badger-claw necklace.

Her breath caught in her throat when she saw the necklace, pulled it slowly from the antelope skin.

"This belonged to my fa—" But she quickly remembered. "He-Who-Is-No-Longer-With-Us," Waits explained, holding the claws and beads reverently across the palms of both hands.

"It is a very great thing for your mother to want you to have this," Bass said. "Did he carve these whistles?"

"I think he must have," she replied quietly, rubbing their red wood with a fingertip. "That was his name. I remember how our people knew of him because he could blow on a whistle he made with his own hands—blowing a sound just like the bull elk calling from the mountainside in the autumn."

"Waits-by-the-Water," he sighed, "your mother wanted you to have something of him to show our children."

"Yes," she sobbed, "a totem to show Magpie and Flea when we tell them about their grandfather."

She put it on, and he realized she meant never to take it off. Right from the moment she dropped the necklace over her head, Scratch knew that somehow it made her feel closer not just to her father who no longer lived, but to her mother. Closer to her people.

But he never uttered a word about his deepest fear, more a regret. Titus never mentioned how afraid he was that in leaving those gifts for her daughter and grandchildren, Crane was saying that she realized she might never see those loved ones again. Then time and again he argued with himself, thinking the old woman hadn't really been trying to say good-bye, believing they would never meet again.

So each day he wondered how long the Crow would keep them apart, and he worried if Yellow Belly's band ever would allow Waits-by-the-Water back among her people, back in the arms of her family. For weeks now as winter softened its fury, they had remained no more than a day's journey from the village. When it migrated to a new campsite—requiring more wood and water, more grass for their herds—Bass packed up his family and followed, never drawing close enough to cause the camp guards alarm, never working streams so close that the Crow village might spoil his trapping haunts.

Camping no more than a day's ride from her people . . . just in case they might have a change of heart.

Every few days as he tended to his trapline, Scratch went to some high ground to scour the country for sign of the camp, the lodge smoke, any horsemen out for game until the Crow had run all the game out of the area. Sometimes the hunters, or those scouts who constantly patrolled the hills and ridges for sign of their enemies, would run across the lone white man at work in the icy streams, or on his way back to his camp with his beaver pelts. Never did those hunters come anywhere close enough that he could make sign, much less call out to them. Instead, they always stopped upon recognizing the trapper, turned about, and rode off.

Over and over he reminded himself that he couldn't blame them. As cruel as it must feel to his woman, Scratch told himself he didn't have the right to blame her people for their fear of him—and what poison they believed he represented.

After all they had somehow heard about the horrors of the pox, both those tribal legends of long ago and the fresh tales of summer's terror on the upper Missouri, the Crow had reason to be cautious. Worse still, this new calamity fed the superstitious fear of those among the Crow who proclaimed there was now every excuse to drive the white men out of Absaroka. More and more of the Crow were ready to believe the leaders who spoke against the trappers and traders.

Where he once was welcomed, now he was feared, shunned, even hated. Perhaps Waits-by-the-Water did not truly know what hate was because she had never before experienced the hatred of others. Bass doubted she herself had ever hated anyone before. But he knew full well the power of hate. He understood how hate goaded a man into acts of revenge against those he despised, or acts of retribution against those who despised him.

Titus hoped she remained innocent, hoped she never knew either side of hate.

Sadness rode with them that winter—which meant that its hand-maiden, called bitterness, could not be far behind.

That morning she didn't say much in either tongue as the wolf awoke him before dawn. Titus pulled on his clothing, then quietly told her he would not return before sundown. He kissed her, feeling something in Waits-by-the-Water's embrace of her longing to explain how bewildered she was. Instead of speaking, however, she only held him tight, kissed his mouth, then released him to the darkness.

As the black became gray, Bass dismounted, tied the horse and mule to the brush, then trudged toward the creekbank. The only sounds in the forest were his footsteps on the sodden snow, the slur of his elk-hide coat brushing against the leafless branches as he neared his first set. Of a sudden he grew concerned.

Standing at the snowy edge of the stream, he couldn't make out the trap pole he had driven into the bottom of the creek several feet from the bank. Kneeling as he shoved his right sleeve to the elbow, Scratch stuffed his bare forearm into the ice-slicked water. Back and forth he carefully fished, his fingers searching—unable to feel the square bow of the iron trap, the wide springs, the pan or trigger or long chain.

"Goddamned beaver got away with it," he grumbled as he got to his feet, flinging water off his arm before it turned to ice.

Later, when the light grew, he'd come back and wade on into this wide part of the stream, to try locating where in this flooded meadow the animal had dragged his trap. Somewhere out there in the faint smear of dawn one of the creatures had freed the trap from the pole, then drowned, sinking to the bottom with the weight locked around its paw. It was only a matter of his wading far enough, long enough, in the icy water to find both trap and beaver.

For the time being there was enough work pulling up the other fourteen traps, taking yesterday's catch back to camp for his wife to begin her work fleshing, graining, and stretching. That started, he could return and look for his trap. As costly as such hard goods were in the mountains, a man simply couldn't stand to lose one of his traps. Sweeping up his rifle and the rawhide trap sack, Scratch backed out of the thick willow and turned upstream.

A moment later he was standing on the bank, staring out at the glistening surface of the water, bewildered that he was getting so old he had forgotten where he had made the second set. Turning on his heel, he peered across the ground, discovering the stake he had driven into the bank to mark the location of his trap sites. Now he whirled, angry and confused, staring at that point where the frozen ground met the surface of the water, gazing into the stream with a squint to search for the tall pole that always marked the extent of the trap chain that prevented the beaver from reaching the safety of his winter lodge. Out there in the deep water, the creatures would drown—

But at this second set there was no pole, no trap. And no beaver.

Angrier still at his growing frustration, Titus flung himself out of the brush and sprinted upstream for the third set. He stood at the stake in the bank and peered at the widening pond pocked with the prickly domes of mud-and-branch beaver lodges. No trap pole there either.

Furious, he shoved his right arm into the water where he found only the narrow shelf he had carved for the trap. Empty.

Flinging water from the sleeve, he stood and whirled around, his breath coming hard. Heart pounding faster.

And in the light of day-coming Scratch spotted the tracks.

Hurtling forward, he pitched to his knees among them, studying the hoofprints, the moccasin tracks, blowing a little crusty, ice-laden snow out of the prints. Yesterday.

He had come across some tracks two days back, a heavy man riding a pony with a cracked hoof. Altogether there were more than ten horses and riders making that trail he had discovered a good distance north of the Crow village. Hunters were all over that part of the country. Likely the Crow were keeping an eye on him too.

But now he found evidence that same pony, if not the same rider, had visited his traps just yesterday, even though Bass's camp and this stream were both east of the Crow village.

Balling a fistful of snow in his mitten, Titus stood and flung the snowball angrily at the ground. The bastards for sure spied on him. Circling his camp. And now they'd even gone to honey-fuggling with his trap sites, taken to stealing his traps. Three of them would take some plews for a man to replace, especially when that man was already down three traps.

Feeling his anger rising to fever pitch, Scratch feared the Crow had taken them all. Every last one of his traps, from every one of his sets, along with the beaver snared in them.

Pretty damned plain. No longer were they merely content to hold him at arm's length. Not satisfied to keep an eye on him and prevent him from infecting them. Now the warriors were beginning their campaign to drive him off, muscle him as far away as they could, right on out of Ab-saroka. Away from her people.

Standing there over those tracks around the fourth set, his blanket mittens gripping the stock of the big flintlock, Bass sensed he held his deepest fury for Strikes-in-Camp. This was no way for the son of a bitch to treat his sister.

The first rays of the sun suddenly pierced the timber, sending shafts of saffron light across the snow, illuminating every hoofprint, every mocca-sin track. Eight, ten, maybe as many as a dozen—horses and riders. God-damned bastards. They'd skulked around behind his back, waited for him to put in all the time to prepare and make his set, watched him turn his back and leave for camp, then swooped on down and robbed him.

Cowards! Traveling in packs like predators, sneaking up behind him—afraid to take him on even though they would have him on the downside of some bad odds. That was all part of their plan, he figured. They didn't want to confront him in the open, so they committed their foul deeds in secret. Probably even Yellow Belly or the warrior-society chiefs left orders that the white man was not to be hurt, even killed, because he had once been a friend of the Crow. And, after all, he did have a Crow wife. Better to steal what they could from him, make it so tough to work his traplines that he'd pack up and ride off for other country.

Would he surprise them!

Just as soon as he rode back to camp to tell Waits-by-the-Water he wouldn't be returning that night—not until late the following day because he had a long way to ride—he planned to tear right into that village and demand his property.

And if they didn't allow him into the camp, if they didn't return what was his . . . why, goddamn them niggers—there'd be some dead Crow!

How many thieving red niggers was an iron trap worth?

One for one? Or maybe as high as two of them smart-assed, cocky bucks for every trap they stole from him?

Angry as he was getting with every mile, Bass figured any of them got in his way, they'd find out this was one white man more dangerous than any of the white man's smallpox.

"Keep the guns near you," he reminded his wife as he tied the last knot on Samantha's packsaddle.

She gazed up at his face. "Where are you going?"

"I'll be back before the sun sets tomorrow."

"Why is your face like a stone, husband?"

He tried to smile, but it didn't work, so he turned away so she would not see his eyes.

"Is your heart an angry stone too?" she asked. "Are you riding somewhere because of your anger?"

"Yes," he said, knowing he could not tell her a lie. The best he could do was to keep from telling her all of the truth. "I'll be back by sundown tomorrow."

She had pressed herself against him, clutching desperately. He sensed her fear, and in that moment Bass felt deeply guilty for the leaving. Since her own people had shunned her, Waits-by-the-Water had no one else but him. Now he was riding off without explaining, leaving her feeling as alone and lonely as she had ever felt.

He whispered, his lips against the top of her head, "Have Magpie help you with the boy."

But the little girl at his side heard and wrapped herself around his leg. "Come soon to us?"

"Yes," he said, bending to kiss her forehead.

Then he pressed his mouth against Waits-by-the-Water's, turned, and vaulted into the saddle. Kicking his pony out of camp, Bass knew he could not turn and look back.

He wanted this to be over. Not just to have his traps returned, but to have his wife and children back with Waits-by-the-Water's family and people. Disillusioned that everything could not be as it was before, Scratch started cross-country for the Crow village, knowing that he could be there before sundown if he stopped to rest the animals no more than twice on this journey through the snow.

Shame of it was, he didn't know who he should be angry at, who he could get his hands on, to bloody them with his bony knuckles, to wrap his fingers around their necks and squeeze the breath right out of them. Who to blame? The sick man who had boarded the *St. Peter's* down in the settlements when the company's summer boat carried the dreaded scourge upriver? Or the booshways at the posts along the high Missouri who ended up putting their future trading dollars ahead of the lives of those tribes they traded with?

Could he blame white men like Gamble and Tullock for being a part of a giant sprawl of cogs, men who were essentially as powerless as he once the prairie fire was ignited? Could he blame the Blackfoot for their suspiciousness, their anger that they were being lied to by the white man when they were ordered to stay away from Fort McKenzie?

But shouldn't he hold his deepest bitterness for the Crow who turned against their own because she had married a white man?

The Blackfoot and the booshways were already his enemies, already the target of much of his wrath. But what of Tullock and Gamble? If the Crow didn't return to Fort Van Buren, then the trader was ruined, the company would close the post down, and Samuel was out of a job.

And hadn't Levi lost enough already? Bass didn't figure he could hold any bitterness for the old friend who had already paid the highest price a man must pay for another's mistake.

But the Crow had no goddamned reason to steal his traps, to make it tough on him to provide for his family. Despite their fear of the pox, they had no call to keep the woman and their children from the village. Never could there be any justification strong enough that would allow the Crow to—

He yanked back on the pony's reins, his breath caught in his chest, ears straining. Samantha blew, wisps of frosty steam jetting from her muzzle. As the sound disappeared, he heard more gunfire. Shouts. Screams and cries.

Scratch turned left, listening. Then right and listened some more.

Muffled by the distance, shielded by the slopes before him—those noises originated from the far side of the knoll that stood between him and the sounds of battle.

"Hep! Hep-hepa!" he bawled at the animal beneath him, and at the mule he yanked into motion.

With a bray Samantha shot into a rolling gait as they burst from the timber at the bottom of the hill, galloping up the slope on a slant, clods of icy snow kicked up by every hoof, streamers of it slapping against his blanket-wrapped leggings. Both animals lunging, their breath chugging as he ripped the long fringed gun case from the muzzle of the rifle, twisting about to stuff the cover beneath his ass.

Reaching the top of the knoll, he peered down, his own breath ragged as he tore back on the reins and stopped the animals.

Here the sounds were more distinct. Beyond, where the creek knotted itself into a horseshoe bend then loosened itself again and disappeared from sight around another hillock, Bass saw blurs of movement. Legs and arms, horse tails and manes, shields and war clubs, lances and bows. Another gun boomed. Indian smoothbore.

Yips and growls of men in a fighting lather. Grunts and wails of the wounded or dying, men left underfoot, abandoned in the war-lust.

Common sense stated that one side of that bloody fracas had to be the Crow. And whoever their enemy was, those Crow warriors appeared to be getting their arses whipped but good.

Stabbing his moccasins into the pony's ribs, Bass bolted off the crest of the hill, thundering down the slope toward the sparse creek-bottom timber where more of the combatants emerged, fleeing in his direction before they turned and set themselves to meet their attackers.

From their hair, the markings on their clothing, he figured the bunch readying for the onslaught had to be Crow. No more than a handful of them now, if there ever were any more when the scrap had begun. Likely a hunting party, he thought. Maybe even the bunch who had stolen his traps before moseying on back to their village.

Twice their number burst from the shadows at the edge of the timber, shrieking as they fired arrows, flung war clubs and tomahawks at the four Crow still standing, the last to put up a defense. One of the warriors who had his back to Scratch screamed with such fury that it made the tiny hairs stand at the back of Bass's neck. The warrior was standing there as arrows rained down around him, rallying the others.

Titus reached the bottom ground, yanking the flintlock's hammer back to full cock.

From the snow at his feet the Crow warrior pulled an enemy arrow, clutched it overhead, and screamed his challenge to those about to overrun him.

With a click Bass set the back trigger.

Then the Crow rammed the arrow point through the long decorative flap at the bottom of his leggings—pinning himself to that spot. This warrior-wanting-to-die was proclaiming he would go no farther. Here he would die, never to retreat unless one of his friends released him from this death vow by pulling up the arrow for him.

The enemy were all over the four Crow in the next heartbeat. No way to tell them apart as Scratch yanked brutally back on the reins, lifting his leg to release Samantha's lead rope as she burst on past and clattered away, looping to the right in retreat. As his pony quartered to the right as if to follow Samantha down the backtrail, Scratch squeezed the animal with his knees, shoved down on the stirrups—instantly stopping the horse.

By the time he got the rifle to his shoulder and peered down the low top flat of that octagonal barrel, the brave Crow warrior had scrambled to his feet in the midst of his attackers, leaving two of his enemies on the ground. Still there were three, lunging across the bloody snow where they had just smashed in the heads of two of the Crow.

Those odds clearly spelled doom for these last two warriors bravely fighting off what Bass took to be Piegan, all smeared up with paint and gussied with feathers and totems for this bold foray into Absaroka. Likely they'd lain in wait for a small hunting party to come along, then sprung their trap. As much as he hated these two Crow warriors for stealing his traps, Bass figured he hated the Blackfoot even more.

When one of the Piegan pinned the Crow's arms back, a second warrior closed in with a glittering brass tomahawk raised at the end of his arm.

Sweeping the gun's muzzle over the pony's head as it pranced sideways at the edge of the timber, then came to an abrupt halt when he angrily squeezed his knees into its ribs, Bass brushed his fingertip across the front trigger. With a roar and a burst of orange flame, the rifle erupted. Twenty yards away in the open, the warrior with that glittering tomahawk blade vaulted backward into the snow, writhing, clawing at his chest with both hands.

Every warrior jerked around at once—both of the surprised Crow, and those four Blackfoot who were about to complete their slaughter.

In that moment of surprise, one of the Crow swept upward with his knife, catching one of the Blackfoot low in the abdomen, plunging the blade in just above the pubic bone, ripping upward as the startled attacker flailed at his enemy for a heartbeat, then frantically fought to prevent his riven intestines from spilling from the gaping, steamy wound as he collapsed to his knees. Foot by slippery foot of purplish gut oozed over his hands into the reddened snow as the Crow spun on another Blackfoot descending upon him with a stone club.

The other Crow, his arms still imprisoned by an attacker, continued to struggle by kicking both his legs at the last of the Blackfoot who slammed the butt of his English fusil along the Crow's head—bringing the stunned man to his knees for a moment before the warrior fell onto his face in the snow.

As Bass vaulted off the pony onto the frozen ground, the Blackfoot pitched his rifle aside to pull a short bow from the quiver draped over his right shoulder. As that warrior reached back a second time to snag a handful of arrows from the quiver, the Blackfoot who had locked the Crow's arms behind him leaped onto the collapsed Crow's back. As he gripped the warrior's hair with his left hand, the Blackfoot savagely yanked the Crow's head back and jerked the knife from the Crow's own belt.

The muscular neck exposed, the Crow's eyes widened—staring not at the enemy about to slash his throat . . . instead the Crow gazed at the onrushing white man.

Swapping the rifle to his left hand, Titus yanked the first of the big pistols from his belt, sweeping back the hammer to full cock with his left forearm an instant before he flung his right hand forward, already in a dead run for the Blackfoot who was flexing his arm downward, looping the blade around the Crow's neck, inches and an instant from delivering the death blow.

The round lead ball caught the Blackfoot low, just above the bottom rib with an audible crack of bone as it smashed through the Indian's torso, flinging him off the man he was preparing to kill.

Transfixed, Scratch slid to a halt, staring at the face of the Crow sprawled on the ground, the man whose life he had just saved—

"Ooxpe!" cried the other Crow.

That shrill warning ordering him to *shoot* snapped something taut within Bass, yanking him about to find the Blackfoot, dropping to a knee, his bowstring snapping forward.

Without thinking, the trapper hurtled sideways—the arrow springing from its rawhide string. As Bass fell sideways, his empty rifle tumbling across the icy snow, the painted shaft hissed through the thick elk-hide coat. Landing hard enough to knock the breath from him, Scratch dragged his shoulders out of the snow, rocking onto a hip as he spotted the second Crow scrambling up behind the Blackfoot who had another arrow already nocked in his string. Titus pulled the second pistol into his empty left hand, crudely dragging the huge dragon's head hammer backward with his right wrist.

As he looked up, his left arm shooting forward to aim at the bow-man, Scratch found the bowstring snapping, flinging its arrow his way. Holding his breath that instant it took to aim, he fired.

The knapped-stone point parted the gray muzzle blast the way a bolt of lightning might tear through a coal-cotton storm cloud. Titus was moving too late. The arrow slammed through his right forearm, the point stabbing him high in the belly.

Collapsing onto his back, Titus yanked back on his arm, freeing the stone tip from his clothing, relieved to find that it had only caused a wound barely deep enough to bleed, penetrating only the skin, not near deep enough to pierce the thick bands of muscle over his gut.

Suddenly he dragged his legs under him, rolled onto his hip, and reached at the back of his belt for a tomahawk to defend himself from—

The bowman was on the ground, struggling beneath the Crow warrior until the Blackfoot's legs thrashed no more.

The victorious Crow stood over the bowman with a jerk, screaming in triumph as he held aloft the dripping trophy just ripped from the head of his enemy.

Scratch gazed down at his right forearm. From his fingertips all the way to the shoulder, the arm quivered as if with shocking cold. Instead he found this a searingly hot pain, so much so that he swallowed to control his stomach from revolting as he stared down at the arrow piercing the upper part of that forearm. Of a sudden the nausea vanished as he looked up at the second Crow warrior.

"Ti-tuzz!" the young man called as he lumbered off his hands and knees, rising onto his feet to step back from the white man.

"Str . . . Strikes-in-Camp," he said, his mouth gone dry and pasty. There was fear in his brother-in-law's eyes.

"Stay away!"

Bass started to get to his feet. "I don't want to kill you."

"Stay back, I tell you!"

Then he stopped where he was, on his knees, heaving breathlessly. "All right—I won't come any closer. Just . . . just as long as you give me back what your warriors stole from me."

TWENTY-FIVE

"Come no closer!" Strikes-in-Camp bellowed at the other Crow. "Stiff Arm, you must come no closer!"

The muscular warrior shuddered to a halt, bewildered by the command.

"See to the white man," the taller Crow ordered. "He is wounded."

For a moment Bass stared at his brother-in-law, wondering why he demanded the other warrior to stay back too. That didn't make a damned bit of sense if Strikes-in-Camp's bunch had been out stealing his traps. They had him two to one . . . but he suddenly remembered that this was his wife's brother. All Scratch wanted was to have his traps returned. If these bucks just gave them back, he'd figure it was settled.

Then Scratch looked down at the shaft piercing the meat of his right arm and settled back into the snow with a grunt. As Stiff Arm came to a stop to stand over him with that dripping scalp in one hand, Bass grumbled, "Hold the end of the arrow. No—your hand must be near my arm."

With the warrior bracing one end of the shaft, Titus seized the other end of the bloody arrow, gripping it where the cherrywood shaft protruded from the arm. He took a breath, held it in his lungs, and snapped downward with a loud crack.

"Pull!" he cried as the breath gushed from his mouth with a hot pain.

The younger man yanked the fletched end of the arrow through the white man's arm.

It took a moment, but the wound's fiery river subsided to the point where Titus dared to flex his wrist gently, slowly bend his fingers. Lucky that the shaft hadn't cut anything but meat, he thought, relieved that everything still worked.

"We must see to Strikes-in-Camp," he suggested as Stiff Arm helped him to his feet.

But Strikes-in-Camp held out his arm, gesturing for them to halt where they were as he himself took another step backward.

Both of them stopped, bewildered. Titus asked, "Just give me my—"

"This one," Strikes-in-Camp interrupted as he pointed to the dead man lying at his feet, "you will see he has the disfiguring sickness. The other one too," and he kicked the second Blackfoot's body.

While Stiff Arm released Bass's wrist and inched backward in trepidation, Scratch tried to make sense of this shocking news.

"You don't know if they're sick—"

"Both of them touched me," the warrior argued. "This one who held me from behind, he rubbed his face against mine as we struggled—"

Bass swallowed, getting to his feet as he gripped that right forearm. "Let me see him."

Now the tall Crow fell silent for a long moment, then said, "You white men, is it true you cannot get the disfiguring sickness?"

He had only doubt. "I have heard some white men become sick—but they do not die."

"Like the Indian always dies?"

"It will not kill me," Titus explained, taking a step toward the warrior. "Let me see the Blackfoot."

Strikes-in-Camp took three steps to the side, away from the two bodies. Bass walked over, propping the wounded arm across his chest, then knelt beside the first body. The enemy's sallow face was just beginning to erupt with angry red pustules. Not so bad, he thought. Perhaps the Crow had little to fear.

He knelt over the second dead warrior who lay on his belly. Turning him over with a toe, Bass jerked back the instant he got a look at the man's face.

"He was already a dead man," Strikes-in-Camp said woefully.

"Yes," Bass replied, gazing down into that face of death—a ghastly, oozing death mask worn by a man with a day, perhaps little more, left to live.

"Stiff Arm, you must return to the village," the tall warrior instructed. "Tell them what happened here. Bring men with you to see to our dead."

"Y-you will stay here with the bodies until we return?" Stiff Arm asked.

He shook his head sadly. "No. I cannot be here when the others return. You tell them I have gone somewhere to think about the death that is coming to me."

"Where?"

Strikes-in-Camp peered at Bass. "Perhaps I should go to see my sister and her children once more before I die."

"That . . . that might kill them," Bass warned. "Just as it would kill your own wife and children to be close to them."

"Yes," he admitted quietly. "I cannot be with any of my family while I die."

"They would grow sick too—"

"Then I will have to die alone," the warrior said.

"No," Bass argued. "No man should die alone. We can go to my camp. We can make a shelter for you near ours, where you can be close enough to see your sister, but not so close you will make her sick. And I will care for you when you no longer can care for yourself."

"That will be the hardest of all for me," Strikes-in-Camp admitted. "A man unable to take care of himself."

"I will tell your wife where to find you," announced Stiff Arm.

"But no others," Strikes-in-Camp ordered. "No one else must come . . . so there can be no chance of our people all dying."

"Where is your camp?" Stiff Arm asked the trapper.

Bass turned, pointing at the hills to the northwest. "Half a day's ride from this place."

"Then it is a long day's ride from our village," Stiff Arm said. "I will bring them so they can look at you one last time."

Strikes-in-Camp drew himself up and took a long, rattling sigh. "Bring them quickly, Stiff Arm. I want them to see me with my own face . . . not this face of a horrible death. Just look upon this one, the face of our enemy. That is no way for my family to remember me."

She could hear her daughter whimpering. Magpie sobbed in their Crow tongue, softly muttering a few words at a time.

But it was difficult for Waits-by-the-Water to hear what the girl was saying somewhere behind her on another pony. The attackers had knotted a wide band of thick blanket material around her head, blinding her eyes, covering her ears with the heavy dark-blue wool.

"Water, Mother," Magpie said. "Tell them to give us water."

Then she heard a loud slap, immediately followed by her daughter's shrill wail.

"Magpie—be quiet," she chastised the child. "Be strong and do not do anything to make them hurt you."

Just as she had to remind herself. Be strong.

Waits licked at her puffy, cracked lip, tasting the blood again. It reminded her that she had put up a fight before they subdued her. From the corner of her eye she had seen the stick swinging at her; then it all went black. When she awoke, there were at least four of them, more—all around her. One was on his knees between her legs, pulling his breech-clout aside, pulling out his manhood.

She had screamed at what they were about to do. Someone slapped her hard with a flat hand. That's when she tasted the first blood. In the background Magpie was shrieking. She could see her daughter being held back by one of the warriors who had a handful of the girl's hair. Magpie would be forced to watch what was about to happen to her mother.

Suddenly, as the warrior rocked himself forward between her thighs, another attacker raced up on a horse—shouting, barking angrily at the rest. The warrior between her legs snapped back at the man on the pony—both of them speaking in a tongue she did not understand. Then those who had gathered around her to shame Waits-by-the-Water started to inch back, cowed by the anger of the one on the pony.

That's the moment she bolted to her feet and lunged for Magpie, hoping the two of them could make it to the thick timber, where it might be hard for the enemy to follow them—

But the one on the horse wheeled his pony, stabbed his heels into its ribs, and caught up to her just before she reached the warrior yanking her daughter about by the hair. She heard the sound more than felt the impact.

Waits stumbled, tripped, and went to her knees near Magpie's feet. Blinking to clear the brilliant shooting stars, Waits turned slightly when she heard the pony snort. That's when she saw the rider swinging the bow again. It cracked against her cheek and across the temple.

She did not awaken until now, finding her wrists bound together and lashed to the pommel of the saddle she could feel with her fingertips. Around her ankles they had wrapped more bands of rawhide, tying her feet together beneath the pony's belly. Why were they stealing her and her daughter? Who wanted the two of them alive—

Then she remembered, and her heart sank.

"Magpie," she said, her puffy lip and swollen tongue making it difficult, "where is Flea?"

"Safe," the girl whispered.

"One of these attackers stole him too?"

The girl was a long time in answering. "N-no."

Magpie must have known how that news would stab her mother.

Waits reminded herself to keep her voice quiet. In little more than a whisper, she asked, "Not with us?"

"No."

Her greatest fear was realized—to lose another loved one. Especially her husband or a child. The tears began to gush, her nose running as she fought down the thoughts of doing something that would make these attackers kill her, just kill her now that they had murdered her son.

"They killed . . . killed your brother?"

"No—"

"W-where then?" Her heart wanted to believe. "Is he alive?"

"Yes."

Her heart leaped. "Magpie—you must tell me now—"

"Safe."

"Later, you will tell me where your brother is."

Ti-tuzz wouldn't know where to find them, could not know what had happened to them. And her husband surely wouldn't realize what had become of Flea. The boy wasn't with their attackers, yet he was safe. . . .

How she prayed that her daughter wasn't lying to her only to make her feel better. Oh, how she prayed that Flea was still alive.

"Waits-by-the-Water!" Scratch called out as he led Samantha and Strikes-in-Camp off the hillside toward his camp.

He wanted to give them warning that they were approaching, so that she could gather the children, keeping a safe distance from her brother. Bass realized how the suddenness of seeing Strikes-in-Camp, after the man had prevented them from entering the Crow camp for so long, would likely cause Waits to rush headlong to embrace her brother.

But that could not be.

"Waits-by-the-Water!" he cried again.

Simply could not be, since he dared not think of her becoming sick . . . dying horribly, in pain, doubled over with a fever, the flesh on her face pocked with scabrous pustules. Eyes sunken, lifeless even before a merciful death took her—

Through that last copse of trees he saw the camp.

Everything scattered. What wasn't broken appeared to be torn, ripped, destroyed.

Their shelters toppled, canvas slashed. A sour ball collected in the pit of him.

"Where is she?" the warrior asked in a low voice as he came to a halt beside the trapper, his eyes looking over the ruin.

"Something happened . . . I don't know—" Then he suddenly kicked out of the saddle and landed on the snow.

He was on his knees, studying the prints—ponies and moccasins.

"Here. Look," he said to the warrior, motioning him down from his pony. "Tell me these are not Blackfoot."

Joining the white man on the snow, Strikes-in-Camp studied the tracks, peered off to the northwest. Then looked at Scratch's face. "Blackfoot."

"Not just the warriors who attacked you?" It was starting to sink in. "More?"

The warrior stood. "Perhaps all belong to a large war party who came to Absaroka to make war on us."

"And the warriors who attacked your hunting party when you . . ." Bass paused, his eyes narrowing, wanting to select his words carefully. "When your hunting party was on its way back to the village?"

"Only part of the raiders."

"How many?" Bass demanded of the warrior.

"No more than ten here. Maybe less."

He watched the Crow stand, follow the tracks to the far side of the camp where he stopped, gazing off through the trees. Bass joined him.

"Ten horses left here with riders on them, going in that direction. They took the rest of your ponies with them."

Bass whirled, peered through the lodgepole at his makeshift rope corral. "Damn," he sighed. "The rest of my ponies."

"Only ten ponies have riders."

After a moment of studying the hoofprints, Scratch stood. "I count only ten too. No matter: I will chop them off like limbs from the trunk of a tree—one branch at a time . . . to kill one each time they stop or make camp. When I have chopped off a few limbs, then I will attack the rest."

"I am going with you."

"But you are going to . . ."

"I am not sick yet," Strikes-in-Camp protested.

"No," the white man argued, wagging his head. "I can't chance taking you along with me. When you do grow sick—too sick to ride—then you will be like a heavy stone that I must drag along as I chase the enemy."

He watched how his words slapped the proud warrior. In his heart Bass struggled with the thorny dilemma.

"Strikes-in-Camp, you would force me to choose between staying to help you while you are dying a terrible death," Scratch explained, "or leaving you behind to die all alone, when I ride off to find your sister and our children."

"Your children, yes," Strikes-in-Camp repeated bravely. "I am not sick now, Ti-tuzz. If we delay—then I just grow sicker each day I can be following the enemy."

"Stay here and wait for Stiff Arm," Scratch said, turning to place a hand on the warrior's shoulder. "When he brings your family here, you can have him return to your village and bring a war party along behind me—"

"That would be the hope of a fool's hen," the warrior scoffed, shrugging the white man's hand from his shoulder. "You want me to believe that they would have a chance of catching up to you when it won't be until tomorrow evening before they reach here? Then Stiff Arm would need another day to return to the village, a third day to get back here again . . . they will be at least three days behind you—"

"I don't have time to argue with you. I must leave now," Bass interrupted sternly, wheeling around. He was bitter, angry—wanting only to find his family and draw the blood of those who took the loved ones from him. For now, all he could do was wound with his words. "I cannot wait on those who kept my wife from rejoining her people. Nor can I take a sick man who will be dying along with me."

"Do you have any more guns?"

Titus stopped, slowly turned back to gaze at the warrior. "I left some for your sister to protect herself, our children. But the enemy probably—"

"Find them, white man."

"Yes," he said. It made a lot of sense. "I will need every gun I can carry when I catch up to those Blackfoot."

"*We* will need every gun."

"I'm not taking you!" Bass roared, remembering how twice he had told Josiah Paddock he wasn't coming along on a journey into danger.

"No. This is not yours to decide," the warrior said evenly. "I am a man. And a man chooses how he wishes to live. How he will die. She is my sister. Her children are my relations. Your family is my family, white man. Your people have killed the tribes along the Missouri with this sickness. Then your people sent their sickness into the Blackfoot nation . . . and now your people have killed me too—"

"I never meant for any of that to happen . . ." His voice cracked with deep sorrow. He felt the salty burn at his eyes.

Strikes-in-Camp took a deep breath and looked squarely at the trapper. "I do not blame you for any of this. You are my brother, so you must try to understand: this is how I choose to die. We are going together to find our relations."

"T-together?"

"This is not a quest of one man alone against the many."

"No, you are right—this is not for me to do alone." Titus reluctantly accepted the warrior's offer, ripping his mitten off his right hand, holding out that painful, wounded arm between them.

"I will ride at your side, fight at your side," Strikes-in-Camp declared courageously as he laid his forearm against the white man's, gripping Bass's wrist. "And when I can no longer sit atop my horse . . . then . . . you will have to go on alone."

．　　．　　．

The bastards hadn't left much behind.

Blackfoot damn well poked through it all, deciding what they were going to load onto the packhorses, discarding the rest after they had ripped, crushed, or broken what remained in their destructive rage. Good thing the war party hadn't wanted any of Bass's medicines: small skin pouches of his medicinal plants they had tossed about the camp. But they had pitched his bundle of wiping sticks in the fire where the hickory wands had become nothing more than charred cinders, the way they had cut up what little they had left behind.

He couldn't find his pelts. Nor the packsaddles he used on the extra ponies. The Blackfoot must have strapped the saddles onto the horses, lashing the beaver to the frames. They might be figuring to trade them off at Culbertson's Fort Piegan.

Most everything of value had been ripped from him. Losing beaver again, the way he had when Silas, Bud, and Billy ran off with all that he had worked so hard to earn. But once more he realized it wasn't so much those autumn plews . . . after all, he could replace them in another season, still have something to show for the year by rendezvous set for the Popo Agie.

It was his woman, the most important person in the world to him. And those children. There would never be another two who could compare to Magpie and Flea.

Bass realized he could put his possibles back together. He could make do with what traps he had left. And he could catch enough beaver to trade for what he needed across the next few seasons as he got himself back on his feet . . . but he never would be the same again if he didn't get those three back.

And to do that, he could not delay in putting to the trail. Bass could not wait for more Crow warriors to join him. He and Strikes-in-Camp would have to leave at once and make their play against the war party alone.

Already on Samantha's back was a robe and blanket, what he had taken along when setting out to confront the Crow thieves in their village. From the looks of it, the Blackfoot hadn't taken anything with them to keep Waits-by-the-Water, Magpie, and Flea warm during their ride, to wrap themselves in at sundown when they halted for the night to eat, to sleep, to celebrate their captives, to . . .

Damn, Titus reminded himself as he looked about the debris left of his camp. He would have to hold those thoughts at bay, or he'd drive himself mad thinking of what those warriors would do to his wife—make himself so crazed that he couldn't plan and plot, and do it all carefully enough so the Blackfoot wouldn't have time to kill their captives when he caught up to them.

He figured it had to be as if he'd stare straight down the barrel of his rifle, concentrating while he placed the front blade in the bottom notch of his buckhorn rear sight, blotting out everything else—he had to force himself to think about what to do, and when to do it, how to pull this off despite the odds . . . rather than how the Blackfoot would abuse a woman prisoner.

"We should go before it gets any later," Strikes-in-Camp reminded him.

Bass realized he had been staring at the litter of their camp, the scattering of torn robes, canvas, and blankets. "Yes," he answered quietly. "Those bushes—see if there is anything they left behind, anything we can use."

The Crow turned without a reply, moving quickly to the timber, peering into the brush. Bass knelt at the fire pit, poking at that bundle of hickory ramrod cinders. They would be hardest to replace. He kept spare flints in his pouch. Some extra balls and three spare horns of powder in what he had packed on Samantha. But he didn't have any spare wiping sticks should he break the one carried in the thimbles beneath the barrel of his rifle.

That was one thing a man couldn't do without in these mountains. The bastards had burned them, either knowing full well what they were, or the Blackfoot had pitched the bundle into the fire just to destroy what they didn't care to pack along—

He turned at the strange sound, finding Strikes-in-Camp, staring into the warrior's eyes . . . as if Titus believed the Crow had just made that muted, out-of-place noise. More of a whimper. Perhaps the warrior had been suddenly struck by the prospect of his own horrible death—

There it was again. But the whimper did not come from Strikes-in-Camp.

With his heart rising in his throat, Bass scrambled to his feet and sprinted to the rubble of blankets and robes scattered back among the brush across the camp from where he and the Crow had been talking. When Titus heard the next faint, muffled sob, he went to his knees, as if his own legs had been knocked out from under him. To left and right he tossed the scraps of wool blanket, the ruin of the buffalo robes, flinging them over his shoulders until he heard that unmistakable sound again. Clearer still.

Yanking the last scrap of robe back, Titus stared down at the tiny body.

Flea lay on his side, curled up, sucking on the knuckles of one hand, blinking at the cold, gray light as his father bent over him.

Bass started to weep as he gently stuffed his hands beneath his son's small shoulders and hips, pulling the boy against his breast. A few feet from the white man's elbow, Strikes-in-Camp knelt, on his face written the sadness that he could not reach out to touch his little nephew.

"Now we know they have only two," Bass croaked his wife's tongue, swallowing hard at the knot in his throat.

The Crow stood when the white man got to his feet. "What will we do with your son now?"

"We'll take him with us."

"No," the warrior said firmly. "I am a father, like you. We cannot take a young child when we leave to trail the Blackfoot."

"Then you must take him back to your village," Bass demanded.

"I am going with you," the Crow argued. "There are Blackfoot to kill, scalps to lift—because I am going to die soon. I have vowed to take many of the enemy with me when I depart for the other side."

"Then the boy must go with us."

"You cannot take him," he protested. "A young child does not belong when you are going on a war trail—"

"Neither of us are going back to the village," Bass interrupted. "We are going after the Blackfoot. Flea will go with me."

"Think of what you are doing. Let me go alone, and you can come along after you have taken him to the village. Bring the rest of the warriors Stiff Arm went to fetch."

"Flea is going with me, and we are going now," Bass turned, cradling the boy, searching the ground, kicking at the scraps of blanket and robe, hoping to find the remains of the cradleboard.

Strikes-in-Camp darted in front of the white man, stopping a dozen feet in front of him, throwing up his arms to get Titus to stop. "The child will catch the sickness. If not from me, your son will catch the sickness from the Blackfoot we are chasing."

Looking down at his son's face, Scratch said, "Maybe he will not die because he has some of my blood in him."

The warrior asked, "Are you willing to risk that?"

For a long moment Bass stared down at the boy's face. "It's the best I can do, Strikes-in-Camp. If I go back to make him safe, then I won't be able to help the other two."

"Are you willing to risk the life of your son to get the others?"

"I think that is what my heart feels," he admitted. "If Flea loses his mother, his sister too . . . then I don't think he would want to go on living either." Bass took a deep breath. "I know *I* will not want to go on if we cannot save the woman, the girl."

"Then you have decided," the warrior declared flatly, a look of determination written across his face. "A father, a husband, has made his choice for his family. As it should be."

"Yes," he said, looking up from the child's face to gaze into the Crow's eyes. "I will bring all my family back . . . or I will die with them."

.   .   .

He tied the last knot in the rawhide strings that bound the scraps of blanket around the boy's body. After swaddling Flea with some small pieces of the buffalo robe, Bass had encased the child in a large scrap of blanket, then wrapped loops of rawhide around and around the makeshift cradle. From those strips of rawhide, he hung two loops. Now he stood with the bundle in his arms and carried the infant over to his horse where he dropped the loops around the large round pommel on his Santa Fe saddle.

Only the child's face remained uncovered. Scratch bent, kissed the boy on the cheek, then tugged the folds of blanket over the tiny copper face to protect it from the cold and the wind.

"My dog," he said to the Crow, turning from the horse—remembering. "You see any sign of him?"

The warrior hunched over some bushes, his arms stuffed into the brush, pulling branches aside. "No blood. No body. The dog is not here . . . but this is."

He watched Strikes-in-Camp pull a trade gun from the vegetation.

"Is this yours?" the Indian asked, holding it out between them.

Bass took the weapon, examined it, and said, "Yes. I left several weapons with her. They were loaded."

"My sister must have thrown it here."

"Why didn't she use them?"

The warrior bent over another clump of brush, fishing with an arm. "I can only think that Waits-by-the-Water believed she could not shoot the firearms without endangering her children. So she threw them away as the warriors rode into your camp—so the Blackfoot wouldn't have the weapons, and protecting the little ones from the enemy."

Strikes-in-Camp straightened again, this time holding one of the big horse pistols.

"There's bound to be more," Bass said, laying the trade gun and pistol on a piece of the torn blanket. "Search—search it all. Maybe the war party didn't steal any of the weapons before they ran away."

Standing at some more bushes, the warrior asked, "Do you think we scared them away before they could search more carefully?"

"No," and Bass wagged his head. "If they had someone watching, they would have seen there were only two of us. I don't think we would have scared off so many. They would have waited for us."

"Why did they go so quickly—before they found all the firearms, before they discovered the little boy?"

Scratch looked at Flea, wagging his head as he said, "Only thing I know is that finding my son and these weapons are a good sign the First Maker is ready to give me this one shot at getting my family back."

TWENTY-SIX

He prayed it would stay cold, so cold it dared not snow.

Much more often here in the Northern Rockies than anywhere else in the central or southern mountains it grew too cold to snow. His prayer was far more than merely wishing against any snow that might fill in and hide the hoofprints left by the Blackfoot war party. Instead, Bass realized the deep temperatures would keep the tracks from melting during the day, then refreezing at night. What that sort of thing did to the top layer of snow could be cruel torture to their horses' legs. Much better that it stayed so cold it didn't snow.

After stuffing the trade gun and that English fusil under the rawhide whangs on Samantha's packs, strapping the extra pistols across the mule's withers, Titus and Strikes-in-Camp began their chase. Crossing the frozen river, the Blackfoot trail headed straight across the lowlands for the better part of that afternoon—a trail that put both the pursued and the pursuers right out in the open under a hard, gray sky.

There was no way for the two of them to hide right out in the open, the direction the trail took. If the Blackfoot had chanced to leave a scout to watch over their backtrail, he would have spotted the two men coming behind. Nowhere to hide.

But if the bastards did leave someone behind to watch for any pursuers, Scratch figured the Blackfoot would just scoff at two lonely riders trailing after them. They wouldn't feel enough of a threat to lay any ambush.

But that didn't mean the two of them could relax. It just didn't pay not being wary when the trail they were following eventually headed off to the northwest, striking for the foothills. By sundown it was plain to see that the Blackfoot were intending to drive up the heights, crossing the high country to reach the Yellowstone on the far side. From there they would push on with their prisoners and plunder until they reached their homeland. They had killed some Crow warriors. And they had stolen some traps from a white man. Worst of all, the thieves had torn Bass's life apart. They had his wife and daughter.

That first night they found some tall willow and cedar growing at the mouth of a coulee they could use for a windbreak. Unsaddling the animals, both men tore sage from the frozen ground, shook off the icy snow, then used the brush to rub down the beasts, doing their best to dry the horses before their sweat froze with the terrible cold as night deepened and the temperatures plummeted. That done, they laid scraps of the torn blankets over their three animals, then settled back in a copse of gnarled, fragrant cedar to wait out the morning.

"Sit here," Titus whispered to Strikes-in-Camp. "Bring your robe to share with us."

"Th-the boy?"

Scratch looked down at Flea. Then said, "Come, we will share our warmth with him."

Together they spread one robe across the ground in the middle of their cedar shelter, then sat with the bundled infant between them before pulling a large blanket and the bigger of the two robes over their heads to make a tiny tent. Even though some of the bitter cold still wicked up through the robe from the frozen snow, the two of them were able to keep themselves and the infant warm enough that they didn't shudder much.

Whether from the cold, or from his hunger, Flea began to fuss later just as Titus felt himself dozing off.

In that growing warmth of their shelter, Bass blindly felt for the knots binding the infant in his blanket cocoon. One by one he untied them, then pulled the bundled child into his lap. From a pouch he had dragged into the shelter with him, Scratch pulled some dried meat he had taken on his ride to the Crow village. The first small piece he broke off and held in his fingers while his other hand felt around to locate Flea's tiny paw in the dark. Once he found it, Scratch shoved the strip of half-dried elk loin between the pudgy fingers and slowly brought the hand to the child's mouth.

That quickly stifled Flea's hungry sobs as the boy began to suck and gnaw on the meat.

For the longest time their breathing, the boy's slurping on the jerked meat, and the mournful keen of the wind outside were the only sounds in that dark little world of their making.

"Should one of us stay awake?" the Crow asked.

"You sleep first," Bass suggested, considering that some of the Blackfoot might have seen them and would creep back to ambush them. "Then you can listen while I sleep."

"I will be quiet, so you can hear."

It wasn't long before he heard the warrior's low, rhythmic snores. Later he realized he could no longer hear the boy gnawing on his supper. Time dragged as he struggled to stay awake in that tiny shelter. Every now and then Flea awoke, fussing—which stirred the Crow. But Titus always had some jerked meat to soothe his son. But one time the child kept whimpering—not satisfied with the strip of elk. In frustration Scratch reached down with his bare right hand, poking it out under a flap of their buffalo robe where he scraped some snow into his palm. Laying it against the boy's chin, he felt Flea licking at the melting snow, his tongue eagerly lapping across Bass's wet flesh. Twice more he brought some snow to the child's mouth, until Flea wanted no more.

To keep himself awake through those long hours Bass concentrated on things, working them over the way he might examine a piece of streambank for beaver sign, searching for the right spot to make his set. Matters that might keep him alert—thinking on people and places and memories in the forty-four years of his life. Struggling to conjure up the faces of the old friends who had come and gone so long ago, the feel of those women, so many women, their shapes and smells, tastes and textures, so dim now because Waits-by-the-Water had come to dull any remembrance he had of others, the white and mulatto and red alike. It had been so many years since he had picked at these memories.

Likely Amy had herself some grandchildren by now, being a little older than he was at the time she had been determined to set her hooks in him. And Abigail might well be dead by now, murdered or dead of a pox—no way could he figure the life of a riverfront whore was a safe pillow for her nights. Then there was Marissa: another one likely to hook herself a husband . . .

And that set him to thinking of Amanda, the daughter left back in St. Louis. One day he'd have to consider packing up his wife and children, pointing their noses east to see the settlements—

But first a man had to get his family back, he scolded himself.

Amanda. Likely married herself in these last . . . four winters now. He might be a grandfather a few times over by now, with young'uns as small as Flea.

Bass clutched the boy to him, feeling the child murmur there in the warmth beneath his father's coat—where Titus could feel the youngster against his heart.

I'll find her for you, son. I'll bring her back.

Twice he had cracked open his side of the buffalo robe, stuffed his fingers along the edge of the blanket, and peered out at the night sky, hoping to find some of the cold inkiness dissipating from the heavens. Finally a third time, hours later, Bass discovered the clouds had drifted on to the east, leaving the sky cold and clear. In the distance he could hear the cottonwoods booming, the smaller lodgepole popping as the temperatures plummeted.

But overhead, a little to the west over the rolling basin, he located the seven sisters whirling toward the horizon. More than half the night already gone.

"Strikes," he whispered, then repeated it louder.

"You want me to listen now while you sleep?"

"Yes."

The warrior began to stir. "I must wet the bushes first."

"If you hold it in—it will help keep you awake," Bass advised.

Strikes-in-Camp snorted. "If I hold it in, you and the boy will be wet before the sun rises."

"Go. Wet the bushes."

He listened as the warrior rustled out his side of the blanket and robe, scooting away to stand on the snow with a crunch, then heard the hiss of the hot urine splatter the frozen bushes nearby. The steaming liquid would likely freeze before it had melted all the way through to the hard ground.

Then the robe and blanket were pulled back, a gust of cold air accompanying the return of the shivering Indian.

"You should not worry: I won't sleep now," the Crow claimed. "How do you expect me to sleep when my manhood has icicles hanging from it?"

Bass chuckled softly. "Wake me before the first touch of light in the eastern sky."

The wind had died by the time Strikes-in-Camp awoke him. The child was fussing, squirmy.

Pulling back the robe from his head and shoulders, Bass scooped a little snow into his bare hand and let the boy lick at it before handing him another piece of the dried meat to suck on. At first the child whimpered, not wanting to take the jerky, but eventually the boy snatched at it, his belly realizing the elk was better than hunger.

"Get me another scrap of the blanket for the child," Scratch asked.

When the Crow returned with the clean swaddling, Titus did the best he could to clean the boy for the first time in the better part of a day and a long winter night. After tossing the dirty scrap of blanket into the nearby brush, he swathed a clean strip over Flea's genitals, rewrapped the blanket around the child's body, securing the rawhide ties.

After pissing on the bushes and resaddling the three animals, they hung Flea's crude cradle from Bass's pommel and set off.

More than an hour later, when the sun rose briefly at the edge of a crimson earth, the whole basin was momentarily tinted with a pinkish hue. Within moments that dramatic dawn exhausted itself as the sun climbed into the low, snow-laden clouds. Once more the broad valley and the surrounding slopes were bathed in a cold pewter light.

He hoped the Blackfoot had made camp earlier than he had the evening before. And he prayed the enemy were slow in moving out this morning. But most of all he asked that the sky hold back that day—just one more day. What wind there was gusted out of the north with the sharp metallic tang of a hard snow on its way. Give them one more day to follow the tracks before the storm blew in and obliterated the war party's trail. If the snow was held in abeyance, Bass vowed he would use this day to narrow the distance, getting close enough to the Blackfoot to come up with some scheme to free their prisoners.

For some time during that ride he brooded on that first fight he had taken Waits-by-the-Water into, slipping in on the Arapaho who had come to avenge the deaths of some fellow warriors. He and Josiah had chosen to risk it all by striking first, not waiting to be hit by the Indians. But to do that required that their own wives had to take part in the killing alongside them. From slipping in to take down the horse guard, to shooting the enemy as they slept around their fire . . .

Bass asked that the woman be every bit as strong in the coming hours as she had been that long-ago autumn in the Bayou Salade.

Near midday, with the sun behind their shoulders no more than a pewter glob behind the immobile clouds, it became even more plain that the Blackfoot were intent on penetrating the high country rather than taking the long way around the foot of the mountains. While it would be a much easier journey for the horsemen, to take that circuitous trail to the east would place the whittled-down war party in the heart of territory claimed by the Mountain Crow. The enemy was taking the quicker, more direct and dangerous, route home.

By late afternoon they were well into the foothills, each gust of wind stirring the fragrance of cedar, the perfumes of the sage that dotted the open slopes crossed by the Blackfoot trail. Hour after hour Scratch squinted up the hillside, studying those mountainsides carpeted with thick timber, the snow-crusted granite escarpments that poked their heads from the last reaches of alpine tundra where trees no longer grew.

Once again he kicked his heels into the pony's ribs, anxious for a bit more speed from the weary animal.

There was little choice but to narrow the gap before they reached that timberline. If the Blackfoot got to those rugged slopes of scree before sundown, they would cross on over. Which meant that he and the Crow could not follow them into the waning hour of twilight. The animals would simply find the footing too tough in the deepening of dusk. And moving across the shifting talus and loose shale would create the sort of noise that would alert the Blackfoot they had company.

Up till now the sight of two lone pursuers would not have caused the war party any concern. But here as the timber thinned, where the cedar and juniper were battered, twisted, and stunted by constant winds, forced to grow closer to the ground, the Blackfoot might well decide to turn around and smack the two strangers the way a man might finally slap at a troublesome deerfly.

So they kept their eyes constantly moving along that portion of the trail cut in the crusty snow, hoofprints threading through the waist-high boulders and knee-high scrub brush—wary of unexpected sounds emerging from the frozen silence as much as they were watchful of any twist in the rocky path ahead where the enemy could lie in wait—

"Zeke!" he cried.

His voice was louder than he would have wanted, but those sodden clouds hovering just overhead absorbed the sound before it carried up the trail as the gray-white ghost of a dog limped from the tangle of wind-gnarled cedar, then collapsed onto his belly, whimpering.

"C'mere, boy!" he called as he vaulted out of the saddle and passed the reins over to the warrior.

Hitching itself onto its hindquarters first, the dog struggled to rise onto its forelegs. He shambled toward his master three steps, whining—then settled to the snow, attempting to crawl as he flailed against the ground with his front legs. As Bass loped ungainly across the slippery snow and talus, the dog's head rolled to the side, tongue lolling from his muzzle.

He went to his knees beside the animal, noticing the long smear of blood marking the dirty snow from the tangle of cedar to where Zeke lay, his chest heaving.

"Awww, boy—" Titus gasped the instant he spotted the broken shaft embedded in the front of the dog's neck, low enough that the arrow point would have penetrated the chest too.

Surrounding the base of the splintered shaft, blood had darkened, drying and freezing in a stiffened mass of clot and ice wider than two of Bass's outspread hands.

Already the dog's eyes were glazing, half-lidded. Strikes-in-Camp trudged up to stop behind Titus, dragging the two animals behind him. Their hooves softly clattered on the loose shale caked with the wind-scoured ice.

"He followed them," the Indian said quietly.

Bass only nodded. He cradled Zeke's head across a knee, rubbing that spot between the scarred ears.

"I don't think the enemy shot him at your camp," the Crow observed. "With an arrow so deep in him, the dog could not live to make that long a journey."

For a moment Titus gazed up at Strikes-in-Camp, his eyes imploring, begging the unknown. Then Bass looked down at the dog again and said, "They shot Zeke here. Today. Not long ago. They found him following them. See the tracks? One of them turned around and returned here to kill him."

Then the trapper gazed down at the animal, finding that Zeke's eyes were glazed no more—but had somehow become clear and bright. Bass happily rubbed the dog's muzzle, believing the worst was over when Zeke licked his roughened hand, lovingly. But an instant later the eyes glazed over once more and the tongue stopped licking. Then Zeke went limp in his lap. For a moment Scratch watched the eyes, waiting with a hand on the dog's chest—hoping that the heart would resume beating.

Finally, Titus admitted, "He's gone."

The warrior tugged on the white man's shoulder, saying, "We must go."

Bass pulled his knees from under the dog and stood. "Not yet. Zeke must be treated right."

Without saying a word, Strikes-in-Camp stepped back as the white man brushed by him.

Some ten yards away among the twisted, wind-stunted cedar, a shelf of gray granite emerged from the slope. Trudging across the loose talus, Bass reached the shelf where he began to lay one layer of the shale after another until he had raised a low altar. The boy was starting to fuss again by the time he turned from the shelf and started back toward the snowy trail.

"We must go now, before it grows late," the Crow reminded.

"Not till I've seen to the dog."

"You do for the dog what you would do for a man?"

He knelt, hoisting Zeke into his arms. Then stood to stop before the warrior. "I'd do the same for any friend. Just like I put the whitehead your people sent me to kill in a tree scaffold. He was an old friend—"

"But there are no trees tall enough here."

"That's why those rocks will have to do," Titus grumbled, that cold hole growing inside him, pushing past the Indian to trudge up the slope with the dog's body across his arms.

He stretched Zeke across the top of that wide bed of loose shale, then gently laid a hand over the dog's eyes. "We come some ways together," he whispered in English as the wind grew stronger on that bare, exposed slope. "Maybeso you was getting old anyways—your time'd come.

But no man had him the right to kill a dog like he kill't you, Zeke. I want you to know I'll rub out ever' last one of the bastards—"

But he couldn't get any more words out. Angrily, he turned away from the stone cairn and clattered down the slope. After scooping some snow into his bare hand, he let the cradled boy lick at it, swiping at his own runny nose with the back of the other mitten.

Titus bent and kissed the boy on the cheek, then stuffed a foot into the stirrup.

He rose to the saddle, saying, "Let's go get your mother back."

The reddish glow from the two fires below them reminded Scratch of the color of polished Mexican gold. A pair of them, their flames wavering in the distance down among the first line of trees the war party would have reached as they'd descended from timberline at dusk. But seen from above, the flickering light illuminated no more than indistinct shadows.

As they lay watching the fires, Bass and Strikes-in-Camp brooded on how to make their attack.

They couldn't slip much closer without the clattering, sliding shale alerting the Blackfoot in the timber below. Either they would have to leave the animals there and cross the next mile or so on foot in the dark, or they would have to circle wide to west or east to make their approach on horseback.

"Better to take the horses with us. Get close as we can," the Indian said. "We may need them if they see us and ride off again."

Gripping the Crow's forearm, Titus suddenly needed to know, "Why are you willing to risk your life against these great odds to take back your sister . . . when you would not allow her to come into your camp?"

"I am sick now," he confessed. "It does not matter that you are sick or she is sick. I am sick now."

"At your village, before—you were afraid of dying from the sickness."

"No more am I afraid. The enemy who brought this to our country should die. I will kill as many as I can before I breathe my last."

Wagging his head, Bass said, "I don't understand your thinking: how you close your heart off to your sister when she brought you no harm. But now you are ready to die to save her and our daughter."

Strikes stared into the white man's eyes in the starlit cold. "It gives me pain to realize I have been a coward. I want to help free my sister while I still have strength. My skin is beginning to grow hot. Hotter all day."

Pulling off a mitten, Bass reached out, fingertips touching the warrior's face, finding the skin was feverish. "You must last until morning. We'll attack them as soon as it is light enough to see. You must hold on to your strength until then."

The warrior nodded. "I will be strong till then."

"And when it comes time for you to die," Titus vowed, "I will stay with you."

"Stay with me?"

"To your last breath," Bass declared. "Then I will tie your body in a robe, take you back to your people—"

"They must not become sick," Strikes protested.

"But you will not give them the sickness after you have died . . . and your people must know of your courage in the face of the death that you know is sure to overcome you."

"Come, then," Strikes declared as he stood. "We will lead our horses down to the timber along that ridge to the east. We can reach their camp in time to kill them all before sunrise."

Bass followed him back to their animals, where they took up the lead ropes and started down the slope, angling off to the right, walking among the tangle of boulders that stood out in bold relief against the pale, icy-blue snow. By the time they reached the timber and had circled on back to the west, Scratch realized several hours had elapsed. Throughout that long night the stars had slowly rotated in a slow crawl across the heavens.

Stopping to listen again, with their noses in the air, the two of them could hear the snuffling of the Blackfoot ponies, an occasional voice carried on a gust of wind, the same wind that brought them the smell of wood smoke.

Strikes leaned close and whispered, "Leave the horses here. Boy too."

It suddenly struck him: what to do with Flea? How could he think of carrying the child with him—taking the chance of the infant's cry alerting the enemy? But to leave the boy alone with the animals . . .

There was little other choice.

What if the Blackfoot killed the child's mother at the moment of attack? What if they ended up killing the father during the fight? Then it was all the better that the enemy discover the child with the pony and the mule. Flea could grow up among the Blackfoot, marry and have children of his own—

If he did not die of the pox first.

There really was no other choice. Scratch knew he would leave the child suspended from his saddle. And should the boy awaken, perhaps the pony's occasional movement would provide enough gentle motion to lull Flea back to sleep.

Moving slowly, Bass took the loops off the pommel, clutching the blanket-wrapped bundle against him for a long moment. When the child stirred, Titus reached into his pouch and pulled out a small strip of dried meat. He stuffed it into the side of the blanket where the child could find it. Then he held the boy in front of him, kissed Flea on the cheek, and hung the crude buffalo-robe cradle from his saddle once more.

"I am ready."

"I pray morning comes before my strength is gone," the Indian said as they started away from the animals, their arms loaded with weapons.

Instantly Bass held a rifle barrel out in front of the warrior, stopping Strikes in his tracks. "You realize what we are about to do. Remember when you said that you wanted to come as far as you could, and when you could no longer sit in the saddle, you wanted me to go on alone?"

"Yes."

"I am not alone. And neither are you. We will kill them all before the sun rises for the day. Their scalps will be on our belts before another day begins."

Strikes said, "It is good that a man is not alone when he embarks on his last battle."

"I will always remember that you chose to be here to die, rather than to die in your blankets." Then Bass started across the snow for the timber.

They didn't stop until they spotted the glow of the two fires against the treetops. Without a word between them, both men stacked their weapons against a small boulder. Bass tapped the Crow on the breast, then pointed off to the left. Tapping his own breast, the trapper pointed off to the right. Strikes nodded and turned away.

Bass was the first to return to the boulder. In the deep cold he sat shivering, wondering about Flea back with the animals . . . worried about the Crow warrior—his ears constantly alert for any sound emanating from the night, when Strikes finally came out of the cloudy gloom.

"Did you find their guard?" Titus asked.

"Yes. One man."

"I found another on the north side. He walks a little to keep himself warm."

With a nod Strikes whispered, "Did you get close enough to look at the enemy?"

"No, not that close. You?"

"Close enough to see there are no longer ten warriors," he explained. "At least, I saw three bodies tied in blankets on the ground. Away from the campfire, where they tied their ponies."

"A small body?" he asked, his skin cold with apprehension.

This time the Indian shook his head. "No child in the blankets. Three large bodies. Men."

"Did . . . did you see your sister at the fire?"

"No."

"But you did not look at the three bodies—"

"No," and this time the warrior reached out to grip the white man's arm. "If the child is alive, then the mother is alive too."

"Why can you be so sure?"

"A woman can give birth to many Blackfoot warriors."

He stared down at the Indian's hand on his forearm, the words sink-ing in, then gazed back into the Crow's eyes. "All right. To go through with this, I must believe that she is alive. That Magpie lives too. I will trust you on this—even though I don't know that I can ever trust you again."

Strikes-in-Camp was startled. "Why do you distrust me?"

"You are a thief."

The warrior leaned his face closer, nose inches from the trapper's. "What did I steal?"

"You and Stiff Arm, with the others who were killed when the Black-foot attacked, you were going back to your village after you had robbed me of my traps."

"Your traps?"

"You wanted to drive me away," Bass argued. "Because it's not a good thing to kill your sister's husband."

Shaking his head, the Indian said, "I did not steal your traps."

"The others, they stole them for you."

"I—did—not—steal—from—you."

"Not to drive me farther and farther away from your village?"

"You will believe me only if your heart wants to believe me," the Crow sighed. "No one I know stole your traps. The only men in that country near your camp who would have taken your traps have now taken your wife and your daughter."

It struck like a slap of cold wind. "The Blackfoot."

"I am not ashamed to steal a white man's horses, or his rifle if he is careless," Strikes boasted, wiping a hand across his feverish face. "But I would never stoop to robbing anything from my sister's husband."

He had to admit, it did make a lot of sense. The Blackfoot. Too quick to accuse those he knew had shunned his wife, Titus could now see that the jagged edges of those pieces had only seemed to fit perfectly—until this moment . . .

"White man," the warrior said, tightening his grip on the arm, "some time ago you told me you would stay with me when it is my time to die of the sickness."

"Yes. I will stay by your side."

"But you said this to me when you believed that I had stolen your beaver traps?"

"You are the brother of my wife. You honored me the day I made the marriage vow to your sister. Why is it so hard for you to believe that I would stay with you until your death, that I would return your body to your wife and children, to your mother?"

"All this time you believed I was a thief?" the warrior asked in a whisper. "How could you believe that I would rob from you—when you had honored me? Before the entire village of my people the day of your wedding—you honored me. How can you ever think I would steal from you?"

"I . . . I—"

"White man, I would protect you with my life," he explained, gripping the trapper's arm. "You must believe that."

"I want to believe you, Strikes-in-Camp."

"You must," he said to Bass, pointing at the sky graying in the east, "because it is time to put your life in my hands."

TWENTY-SEVEN

How small he felt, nothing less than ashamed, as he crept through the darkness, quietly moving through the trees and boulders, inching his way toward the guard who stood watch north of the Blackfoot camp.

Ashamed that he had ever believed Strikes-in-Camp had become a thief to drive him out of Absaroka.

Bass heard the snuffle of a pony. He stopped, scolding himself that he must remember to concentrate, must pay heed to the rise and fall of the breeze. Couldn't allow the Blackfoot ponies to smell him and raise a warning.

For the two of them to get a jump on the seven, he had to push everything else out of his mind now. Concentrate only on those who had stolen his traps, taken his packs of beaver and his plunder. Robbed him of everything—including his wife and daughter. Mostly his wife and daughter.

Before leaving the boulder, the two of them stripped off their coats and divided the weapons. There were six pistols and four long weapons—two rifles, a smoothbore trade gun and a smoothbore English fusil. Ten balls to account for those seven. Trusting what Strikes had encountered—that three of the Blackfoot were already dead and wrapped in blankets for their final journey home—then the two of them must surely be carrying enough firepower into this fight to tip the odds in their favor.

Titus had Strikes-in-Camp stuff two of the pistols into the sash he knotted around his coat, a smoothbore clutched in each hand. In addition to one pair of pistols Bass carried at the back of his belt, he stuffed his knives and a camp ax. Beneath the front of his belt he jabbed another pair of pistols, then took up the two rifles, nodded farewell to the warrior, and slipped into the darkness.

Slowly letting his breath out now, he felt for the breeze, listening for another sound from the enemy's horses. After an agonizing wait Titus decided the animals hadn't winded him. His eyes slowly crawled across the snow to the next tree—measuring the distance, calculating his route. Couldn't stand to get caught out in the open. He had to bring down the horse guard, maybe even drive the ponies right through the enemy's camp to cause confusion, give the two of them a little more of an edge . . . then he knew he couldn't take the chance of one of those horses trampling right over Magpie in the dark.

She should be sleeping by the fire. And the horses wouldn't go anywhere near the fire. Magpie and Waits might be all right if they were near the fire—

But if they weren't, could he chance it? When the ponies came charging through the camp, wouldn't they know enough not to get anywhere close to the fire?

He heard one of them clear his throat. Low voices drifting over from fireside. A voice calling out to the guard from camp. The guard answered. He could follow the sounds of the one moving out from camp. Perhaps they were rotating their guard—

Then he saw them. They stopped there in the dim light of those broken clouds, nothing more than shadows that moved while the trees and rocks did not. He could drop them both from where he stood, but that would put him too far from camp to make certain none of the Blackfoot killed his wife or daughter at the moment the enemy knew they were under attack. Hard as it was, he swallowed down that instinct to start the killing there and then.

Bass knew he had to reach the edge of the firelight before he opened the ball. He had to see if he could spot which of the shadows around the fire were his loved ones before the terror began. He was trusting in the Crow that he too would do everything in his power to know which of the forms were the warriors before the soft lead balls went smashing into bone and muscle, sinew and blood.

He shivered with the aching cold, staring intently, his breath shallow, afraid of making a sound, of making breathsmoke. Now there was one shadow. It turned and stepped back among the horses where the shadow disappeared.

Scratch was moving at the same moment, hoping that the warrior's movement across the snow might dull the sound of his own approaching footsteps. Tree to tree he crept, waiting and listening for a moment . . . then slipping across the snow another few yards, to the next tree or boulder.

Leaving the two rifles propped against some cedar, Bass crept the last few yards, searching for the guard's shadow among the ponies. The animals parted on the pale ground, exposing the warrior. Scratch started forward with long strides, dragging a heavy butcher knife from the back of his belt.

When he was within two arm-lengths of the warrior, the shadow whirled, a club swinging up at his side, clutched in the man's hand. Lunging those last two strides, with shoulders hunched as he shot forward, Titus crouched to spring—meeting the Blackfoot with a noisy impact that knocked the wind from them both.

Shoving his empty hand beneath the man's chin to shut off any call the Blackfoot might make, Scratch drove the knife low into the warrior's groin and ripped upward with the blade, splattering himself with the warm blood and juices.

The Blackfoot grunted and the club clattered twice against the white man's back, then fell onto the snow the moment the warrior backstepped, his arms clutching at his sundered belly as he went to his knees. Scratch was behind him in that next heartbeat, clamping his left hand around the warrior's mouth, dragging the big blade across the crinkling of cartilage in the windpipe with an audible hiss of air—that last breath to escape the enemy's lungs.

Voices grew louder. Someone had heard.

Stuffing the blood-slicked blade back into its leather sheath, Bass shoved a shoulder against a pony to move it aside as he dived through their midst, racing to the tree where he seized the two rifles. After raking back the hammers, he was in motion through the pony herd—stuffing fingers through the trigger guards, setting the back trigger on that most trusted of his weapons.

He heard them coming. Footsteps whined on the frozen snow. Watching the trees and rocks, his breath coming hard and fast as he raced forward, Titus struggled to discern what shadows were—

Hauling the rifle up, he touched the front trigger with his right forefinger, the rifle exploding with a blinding flare. He was almost on the warrior before his eyes adjusted back to the darkness. The one he had blown a hole through was on his knees, shrieking, his voice crackling with pain. Others answered from the camp as Bass approached the wounded man.

The Blackfoot reached out and grabbed Bass's ankle.

More footsteps coming. A gunshot on the far side of the fires.

Scratch turned about, brought his left leg up and drove it downward with brutal force, smashing the Blackfoot's jaw as he dropped the empty rifle beside the body. The hands freed his ankle and Bass dived forward, sprinting toward a sudden volley of gunfire and yells of men.

As he burst from the timber into the first dim glow of the fire's light, he heard the child's scream, his wife's garbled shout. A shadow landed before him, its batlike flicker causing Titus to jerk the second rifle up, that left finger twitching before he had the weapon fully to his hip.

Orange flame spewed from the muzzle—the shadow before him collapsing with a shriek of pain, clutching at a knee. Pitching the empty second rifle to his left, Titus reached at the back of his belt, clawing the ax free with his left hand as he dragged the first pistol from the back of his hip with the right. Sweeping the hammer to full cock, he dashed across those last two yards swinging the ax downward, its blade catching the wounded warrior across the temple and top of the ear, embedding itself in the man's skull with an audible crunch of bone. He yanked with a twist, unable to free the weapon—then heaved the dying warrior aside.

Magpie was screaming as he lunged into the light. She was scrambling after her mother, spilling onto the snow as Waits-by-the-Water was dragged by the hair to the far side of the fire behind one of the warriors.

He locked his elbow, held the muzzle of the pistol on the moving target that clutched a hand in the woman's hair, a graceful English tomahawk held in the other. The Blackfoot turned to the trapper suddenly in the firelight, his mouth o-ing like a black hole as he shrieked a wild cry.

Eyes darting side to side, Bass could not find Strikes-in-Camp. Nothing but noise, some blur beyond the far edge of the light.

Now Scratch had been spotted by another warrior to his left. The tall enemy whirled, sprinting long-legged toward him with a club in motion over his head. Flung forward, it was already on its way when Bass swept the pistol toward the new target, pulled the trigger. Then rolled to the side as the club tumbled into him, the rawhide-wrapped stone glancing off his hip as he struck the ground, that empty pistol bouncing from his hand.

From the front of his belt he pulled a second pistol as the warrior flew toward him, bare hands extended like claws, grimacing and growling like a wild beast. Titus managed to get the hammer pulled back a frantic breath before the Blackfoot descended on him. Yanking on the trigger, the pistol exploded the moment the muzzle jammed against the enemy's chest. As the warrior collapsed his full weight on the trapper, the Indian's back erupted, blood splattering in an orange spray backlit by the leaping flames of their fire.

With his wife's screams ringing in his ears, Bass shoved the body off him, dropping the pistol and pulling the third from the back of his belt as he scrambled to his knees. The weapon held out at the end of his right arm, he swept the muzzle to the right to find the warrior still struggling with the woman who locked both of her hands around the man's wrist as he fought to free the arm that held the shiny tomahawk, a weapon he clearly meant to use on her.

Lunging to his feet, Bass darted to his right to circle the fire as one of the Blackfoot emerged from the darkness beyond the flames. He stood for a moment looking over the scene, long enough to find the white man—then vaulted past the warrior holding the woman and started for the trapper. Bass brought the pistol to bear on that blur—

But Magpie seized the warrior by the leg, almost tripping him at the moment Scratch fired the pistol. Instead of hitting the man squarely, the ball raked across his shoulder, knocking the warrior backward a step as he cried out in pain. He suddenly rocked forward and seized the child by the hair, dragging Magpie backward until he could loop an arm around her.

"Goddamn you," Titus growled, low and feral in his throat as he dropped the empty pistol. He watched the warrior proudly brandish the knife he clutched in his hand. It was already slick, shiny with blood. He knew it had to be the Crow's. Bass was on his own to finish it now.

How many had Strikes-in-Camp killed? Would any more of them leap into the fight?

With the swiftness of river runoff, the little girl whirled on the warrior, sinking her teeth into his wrist. He held her by one hand, and she bit into his other. Screaming, the Blackfoot shook the girl at the end of his arm again and again, as if trying to dislodge a buffalo tick. He began kicking at her with his feet as he stumbled to the side, screaming at her. Suddenly he bent and planted his teeth on her arm. The child yelped in terrible pain, immediately releasing the warrior.

Bass pulled the trigger, aiming at the blur that was the warrior's back. The man flexed backward, almost as if suspended in midair on one foot, then spun around, dragging the girl down with him as he fell, blood smearing his chest, flecked across Magpie's face.

She lay whimpering beside the dying man as he gurgled, bright blood oozing from his lips while the light continued to gray in the east.

"Ti-tuzz!"

He wheeled, finding the warrior pitching the woman backward onto the ground. The Blackfoot hauled her up by her hair and flung her backward a second time, a little closer to the fire.

Pitching the empty pistol at his feet, Scratch pulled the last firearm from his belt and started around the body of the dead warrior where Magpie cowered, crying as she watched her mother dragged to the edge of the largest of the fire pits.

With the heel of his left hand Bass snapped the huge flintlock hammer back, then extended his right arm just as the warrior hurled the woman into the flames.

With a terror-filled shriek Waits-by-the-Water clawed to hang on to the warrior the moment he freed her, scrambling to escape the fire, the back of her hair and blanket coat already aflame.

Bass leaped across those last few yards, landing squarely upon his wife's back, driving her to the ground, the stench of burned hair and flesh stinging his nostrils.

A shadow blotted out the firelight over the two of them as Titus rolled off the woman, the pistol's muzzle wavering for a moment as the Blackfoot's arm descended with that shiny English tomahawk a glittering blur. Bass hurled himself to the side as the blade whined past, slashing a loose fold of his shirt, slicing through some fringe on that arm bringing up the pistol.

He pulled the trigger there below the warrior's arm, the muzzle no more than inches from the Blackfoot's rib cage. As the bullet smashed through the chest, blood spewed from the man's mouth the instant he was driven backward, landing in a heap.

Watching the warrior's legs twitch for a moment, Bass rolled to the side, finding Waits-by-the-Water whimpering, clutching at the back of her head. Her blanket coat still smoldered as he dropped the empty pistol and took her into his arms there on the snowy ground.

Collapsing against him, she began to cry inconsolably as Magpie staggered up to fold herself against them both.

"Take your hands away," he told his wife as he tried pulling her wrists from her head.

"It hurts so—"

"I won't touch," he reassured her. "Only to look."

A patch the size of his palm had been burned from her head, the flesh red and oozy. All around it the hair was singed close to the scalp. It would grow back—but he figured that patch would soon turn to scar tissue.

"My hair?"

"It will grow back," he told her.

Waits gathered Magpie beneath one arm as the child's whimpers quieted.

"You were not alone," his wife whispered wearily.

"Your brother," he told her. "I am afraid—"

Waits-by-the-Water pulled her cheek from his chest, pointed into the darkness. "He was there."

Magpie sat up, stood, and stared her father in the eye. "Where is my brother?"

Wrapping his arm around the girl, Bass said, "He stayed with our horses. Samantha is taking care of him while he sleeps."

"I want to see him," Magpie pleaded.

Scratch said to his wife, "Why did the enemy take the two of you, but they did not steal the boy?"

"He was sleeping when the Blackfoot rushed into our camp. Magpie was sitting near him beneath a small shelter beside the brush when the enemy came toward me—which gave Magpie a moment to cover up the boy and push him into the bushes."

"You did this, Magpie?" he asked the girl. "You saved your little brother?"

"You found him safe?"

Bass felt the mist at his eyes. "Right where you left him, daughter. Where I could find him. Your father thinks you are such a brave girl, Magpie. When we reached that place, Strikes-in-Camp and . . ." He had suddenly remembered. "I must see to your brother. Stay here by the fire."

"I want to see my brother—"

"Stay here with your mother."

Titus scrambled up and turned away quickly. In a few minutes Bass trudged back into the firelight, struggling under the weight of the large warrior slumped across the white man's shoulders. Slowly he knelt by the others, allowing Strikes-in-Camp to settle back on a robe near the fire.

"He is shot," Bass declared as Waits-by-the-Water knelt over her brother.

The man's eyes half-opened, rolled, then fixed on the woman. "I do not have much time."

Slipping an arm beneath his head, Waits raised her brother into her lap. "You came to help."

Bass told her, "He came even though he was already dying of the sickness one of the warriors gave him days ago."

She turned her head slightly, looking off to the darkness. Scratch realized she was gazing in the direction where the three bodies of the dead Blackfoot lay wrapped in their blankets—felled not in battle, but by a ghastly silent killer.

Strikes gripped his sister's arm. "This is far better: to die fighting our oldest enemy rather than to die slowly with the fever, my flesh rotting with decay. It is not a good thing for a man to die helpless against that terrible sickness."

"No," she sobbed, her tears starting to spill. "I am proud that you will die in battle, an honorable man—protecting our people, protecting your family."

"Sister, I am sorry I wronged you when you came to visit our mother," he whispered, his voice weakening. "Forgive me for my fear."

"This sickness makes everyone afraid of shadows," Bass declared. "I don't think we can blame a man who does something out of fear for his family."

"I w-was wrong," he gasped.

"I forgive you, brother," she said, laying her fingertips on his cheek. "You . . . you are so cold."

Strikes-in-Camp smiled bravely. "A good thing, now that I am dying."

"The enemy, they were consumed by such a hot fever before they died," she explained.

"Better that the cold hand of death take me in battle than the fire in this sickness."

They watched him close his eyes wearily. For a few minutes his breath came more and more shallow, each gasp a wet rattle as his chest filled with blood. Then Strikes half opened his eyes again, stared up at his sister. "Tell my wife I loved her. Tell my children . . . say they must remember the touch of their father to the last of their days."

"I—I will tell them," Waits promised.

"Sister, I go now," he whispered, his lips barely moving. Then his eyes rolled slowly to gaze over at the trapper. "Friend Ti-tuzz . . . I go now to ride the war trail with He-Who-Is-No-Longer-Here."

Bass bent over, laying his lips beside the warrior's ear. "Go now, friend. It is time. Soon you will climb into the forests to hunt with your father forever. Very soon you will ride beside him into battle against the enemy. It is time to go, my trusted brother."

About the time Scratch was returning to the fire with Flea and the two animals early that morning, Stiff Arm came riding in with Pretty On Top and more than thirty Crow warriors. They had spent most of the night high among the stunted cedar and pine on the far side of the pass, waiting until there was enough light to cross over the ridge and continue their pursuit.

With a genuine measure of relief mingled with concern, the white man hurried to prevent the warriors from approaching the infected camp.

"Stay back!" he ordered. "Come no closer—the killing sickness is strong here!"

Stiff Arm and Pretty On Top halted the others, then crossed the last thirty yards on foot to reach Scratch on the far side of the Blackfoot camp.

"How did you make it back to the village, to reach us here so quickly?" Titus asked of the two warriors. "I believed you were going to be at least a full day behind us."

Pretty On Top answered, "Stiff Arm did not have to return to the village. These men were among hunting parties already out in the hills. Some of us were already following the tracks of the Blackfoot when we heard the gunfire of your fight with the enemy. So Stiff Arm did not have to lose time going all the way back to our camp because we met him on the trail."

"You must know that my wife's brother is no longer alive," Bass explained.

"D-did he die from the sickness the enemy gave him?" Stiff Arm asked.

"No, He-Who-Is-No-Longer-Here died killing the Blackfoot."

Stiff Arm nodded. "I told the others the story of the Blackfoot ambush, and how your wife's brother killed two of the enemy who had the sickness from the white man."

Bass smiled as he looked at the many warriors. "And these men chose to come with you—even though they were following the sickness?"

"Yes," Stiff Arm answered. "Most decided to come along, to be as brave as your wife's brother had been. But I really thought you would be in your camp, caring for him. It worried me when the enemy's trail passed right through your camp and we did not find you there. For a long time it worried me that the two of you would bring your woman and children along to track down the Blackfoot—so we hurried fast and hard behind you, sleeping only when it grew too dark to see your trail."

Shaking his head, Scratch explained, "We did not bring my family. The Blackfoot captured them in my camp. The enemy took them from me. He-Who-Has-Been-Killed decided to die in battle against the Blackfoot instead of letting the sickness kill him."

"This camp is not clean?" Pretty On Top observed nervously.

"No," and Bass shook his head. "You and your warriors must stay over here, upwind of the sickness and the enemies."

As the warriors dismounted, Stiff Arm and Pretty On Top reminded them that the Blackfoot were infected. There would be no hacking apart the enemy this day. In silence the thirty-two assembled some distance from Waits-by-the-Water while she finished binding Strikes-in-Camp's body within a blanket and a buffalo robe for the journey back to his village. As Magpie sat talking with Flea, Bass stripped weapons from the Blackfoot, claiming all the firearms, knives, and tomahawks for himself. Bows and quivers he carried over to the war party, dropping the weapons on the crusty snow for the Crow to argue over.

Later, Pretty On Top called the trapper to return to the group. "Ti-Tuzz, none of these men want the Blackfoot weapons."

"They are afraid of the sickness?"

"Yes. Keep them for yourself."

Shaking his head, Bass replied, "I don't want the bows. Don't want nothing else—no clothes, no coats or blankets. I will burn them."

Stiff Arm asked, "Will the flames kill the sickness on them?"

"I can only pray it will."

While the restless, frightened warriors huddled upwind of the Blackfoot bodies, Scratch inspected what baggage the enemy war party had along, searching for what had been stolen from him. A half dozen of his

Mexican traps and most of his beaver, along with a good supply of tacks, lead and powder, coffee, ribbon and beads. Not everything, but enough discovered among the dead to confirm they had already divided what they had plundered from his camp at the time they kidnapped Waits and Magpie.

While Stiff Arm's warriors started fires and ate at the edge of the clearing, the white man finished saddling and packing his animals for the return journey across the pass. Over the back of the dead man's prized war pony Bass tied Strikes's body. Hoisting Magpie into Pretty On Top's lap for the first leg of the trip back across the mountain, Scratch took the blanket cocoon from Waits, helped his wife to her feet, then followed her slowly to her pony. There she seized the tall pommel, preparing to climb into the saddle, but instead gasped as if struggling to catch her breath.

"C-carry the child w-with you," she whispered, her voice low and raspy. "I am v-very . . . tired."

He watched her wearily pull herself into the saddle, then her eyes smiled weakly at him. He knew she had to be exhausted from her harrowing ordeal. Bass turned with Flea's blanket and robe cradle across his arm, starting for his pony when Magpie screamed in fear and the warriors cried out in warning.

Whirling just as Waits-by-the-Water pitched from her saddle onto the frozen ground, the white man darted first to Stiff Arm. "Hold my son," he croaked with dread. "His . . . his mother—"

At her side Bass slowly rolled the woman over, pulled her across his lap, cradling her head against his chest. Gazing into his wife's eyes, he yanked off his mitten, then laid his callused fingertips to her brow.

"I have the fire of this terrible death burning in me," she whispered. "Now I will die."

"No . . . no you won't," he sobbed.

"Leave me here—"

"I can't do that."

"Our children, they must not see me die," she pleaded.

For a long moment Scratch peered at Magpie, silently watching the child's terrified eyes. Gently he started to pull his legs from under the woman's shoulders as he said, "I will tell her, then send the others away, back to the village while I stay with you."

"You must go with the children, to care for Magpie and—"

"I will be at your side while you are sick," he whispered against her ear, "just as I promised I would be at your brother's side."

"The others, they will take our children?" she asked weakly.

"Yes, Pretty On Top, the others, they will care for our children until we can come for them."

"Tell Magpie I love her."

Bass stood, quickly moving across the crusty snow to the horsemen. "Stiff Arm, you must go on without us."

His eyes were heavy with concern. "You are staying till your wife dies?"

"She will get better, then we will come," Bass said angrily.

Pretty On Top clearly read the frustration and anger in the white man's face. "We will go back to our village, and wait for you to return."

Gratitude filled Bass's eyes when he gazed up at his young friend. "My children—take them both to Crane. She and Bright Wings will watch over the children until their mother and I rejoin you."

"The children will be safe with us," Pretty On Top vowed.

Taking a step backward, Bass's eyes touched the front ranks of those horsemen, then he went to Magpie's knee.

"Popo?" she whimpered, still frightened.

"Your mother is too weak to ride now," he comforted, stroking the girl's blanket legging. "We will come to be with you soon. Stay with your grandmother and your aunt. Help care for Flea as your mother knows you can. She will rejoin you both very soon."

"How long, popo?"

Swallowing, he did not want to lie to his child again as he had in the blizzard. But in matters of life . . . and death, he would. "We will be coming right behind you. Magpie, do not be afraid now—because you are with those who will protect you, care for you. For your mother's sake . . . remember to take care of your little brother, always."

"Until you come back to us?" she asked plaintively.

"Take care of him always."

She sobbed, "You will come back?"

"Yes," he promised. Then reached up to pull her face down to his. Bass kissed the little girl on the cheek. "You will see me soon."

Stepping aside to Stiff Arm's pony, the trapper pulled back the blanket flaps and kissed his son's forehead. Looking up at the warrior, he whispered, "If I do not return, you will see that my son is raised to become a warrior like the rest of his people—like his uncle, and his grandfather?"

"Your son is Crow," Stiff Arm said. "But he will always know of the good American who was his father."

Slowly taking three steps back, Bass waved to Magpie. "Go now—all of you. While you have so much of the day left for your journey."

Most of the warriors gave some signal to the trapper as they turned their ponies away and started back up to the pass, but not one of the horsemen uttered another word as the animals snorted, their unshod hooves crunching across the icy snow glaring with the day's new light as the wind soughed through the heaving boughs of wind-gnarled cedar and spruce.

He listened to the sound of those hooves disappear as he held his wife, gently rocking her against him while the sun flooded across that timbered slope.

Later, when it grew quiet but for the wind in the trees, Waits-by-the-Water asked, "My children?"

"They will be safe," he promised her. "The others are taking them back to the village."

"He-Who-Is-No-Longer-With-Us?"

He cleared his throat and said, "They will put him on a warrior's scaffold, to honor him before his family and the rest of his people."

"I know this sickness will not kill you," she said softly. "It comes from the white man . . . so the white man won't die."

"Many, many of my people still die—"

"No," she cut off his words. "You must promise me our children will not die because they were born with white blood in their bodies."

Her eyes implored him so, their hollow, teary recesses begging him for reassurance. Bass realized he had already lied to his daughter in matters of life and death. So he would lie to her too.

"Yes. You are right. Our children will be safe."

"The white man just grows sick for a time before he gets better," she whispered some of the words he had told her long ago. "But the white man does not die."

"He gets better," Bass vowed. "Just as you will grow better."

"Take me away from the fire," she begged, clearly growing weaker.

Placing his hand against her neck, Titus felt the fury of her fever in his fingertips. "I will move you away from the fire so you can rest while I make camp."

She closed her eyes. "Bring me some water soon?"

"Yes. I will be back with some water, soon."

Gently pulling himself away from his wife, Bass got to his feet to peer up the rugged slope of scree and loose gray talus toward the pass. Squinting in the glare of the reflected sunlight, he watched the tiny dark column snaking its way toward the open saddle far above him.

Gazing down at his wife who lay at his feet, Scratch turned and started toward the trees for firewood to melt snow into water. He moved away quickly now.

He did not want her to hear him crying.

TWENTY-EIGHT

Bass swatted at the mosquito, then rubbed a fingertip across the tiny red bump raised on the back of his walnut-brown hand. "I don't figger them Blackfeets gonna bother nary Americans no more."

Unfolding his big kerchief of black silk, old friend El-bridge Gray wiped sweat from his forehead and the ridge of his round bulb of a nose more pocked with tiny blue veins every year. "Come spring, we run across more'n one camp of them bastards. Lodges filled with dead'uns getting picked over by the jays, bones getting dragged off by the wolves. Bridger figgers what Blackfoot ain't been kill't off by the pox gonna be cowed but good. Won't dare make trouble for us now."

With a sigh Scratch nodded. "Ain't like it was afore, El-bridge. Bug's Boys ain't the fearsome bunch no more."

"For sartin the Blackfoot country's open to Americans now," Rufus Graham added, hissing his *s*'s between those four missing front teeth, two top and two bottom. Then he glanced self-consciously at the woman who sat nearby cutting moccasin soles from the thick neck hide of a buffalo robe. "After you and your wife rubbed up ag'in' them Blackfoot what had the smallpox . . . how you two ever come out by the skin of your teeth?"

Titus didn't answer for a hot, still moment, watching the woman at work over her hide. She must have felt his gaze, for she turned to glance at him for but an instant before she smiled and resumed her work.

For the longest time now she had refused to let others look at her, hiding her face beneath the hood of her capote, even as spring warmed the land and dispelled all evidence of winter. It wasn't until early in that second summer after healing from the pox that she had relented and no longer kept her face in the shadow—about the time they started south from Absaroka for this rendezvous on the Green.

For more than a year and a half Waits-by-the-Water had lived her life all but hiding out each day. Ashamed of how the disease had ravaged her face, the woman rarely emerged from her sister-in-law's lodge until twilight. If she did venture out to scrape hides or gather wood and water, Waits tied one of Bass's large black silk kerchiefs just below her eyes, covering most of her disfigurement. It wasn't until Crane died late in the spring of 1839 that Waits heeded the praise of others, finally coming to believe that somehow she really was, in a most tangible way, a heroine to her people.

She had survived—not only the brutal capture and abuse of an ancient enemy—but Waits-by-the-Water had endured the slow, cruel torture, and what should have been the sure death demanded by the pox.

"The men of your tribe, they are proud of their sacrifice scars, yes?" Bass asked her, tapping a finger against his own breast to indicate the sundance torture.

Waits had nodded her head in the firelight of the lodge where she and the children stayed with Strikes-in-Camp's family while Titus was gone trapping in the hills for days at a time.

"And the Crow men," he had continued, "they proudly mark their war wounds with vermilion paint—showing everyone just how brave they were, how great their courage to bear up in the face of death?" Titus waited for her to nod again.

"Yes."

"To your people you are just as brave as a warrior. You faced death but did not die. Wife, you do not have to paint a red war circle around a bullet pucker, a knife scar, or a hole made by an arrow shaft. The great battle you waged against the terrible sickness is a battle none of your people ever win. In your victory that battle has marked you with its scars that show you were every bit as brave as a Crow warrior."

Even though she began venturing out in the day without her black silk kerchief, Titus knew how frightened she had to be—afraid of what other Crow would say or ask when they saw her, afraid more of those who wouldn't say a thing about her face but would instead look upon her with disgust or revulsion—worse yet, pity. The deep scars had marked her cheeks, pitted her forehead and nose.

Yet Waits-by-the-Water's battle with the disease had left her scarred far deeper than the surface of her skin. She had healed from the scourge. Eventually she had begun to live again without hiding her face. But this woman would be a long time in healing the inner wounds.

"I never come down with the pox," Bass explained to that dwindling circle of old friends gathered with him at that rendezvous near the mouth of Horse Creek on the Green River. "Only way I figger the woman come through it . . . maybeso God Hisself knowed how much we needed her."

"Your chirrun?" asked Isaac Simms, brushing back some of his gleaming platinum-blond hair that continued to successfully hide the fact that he was graying.

"They was fine," Scratch declared. "Cain't callate how Magpie come out so good—'thout the sickness getting hold of her the way it done to her mam, what with them both being took together by the Blackfoot."

He glanced in wonder at the woman again, noticing once more how the curvatures of her hips and backside had begun to round out her dress as she worked over the hide on her hands and knees. She had been slow to put back on most of the weight she'd lost to those weeks fighting the pox. No longer was she a raw-boned skeleton with her skin sagging over her joints like proper folks' bedsheets draped over a split-rail bedstead. For a long time there he hadn't believed someone so frail and thin, so downright cadaverous, could ever have the strength to fight off the scourge.

"She's a lucky woman," Solomon Fish observed. "Had you to care for her, pull her back from death's door."

Scratch nodded, taking his eyes from the woman to look at Solomon's long beard of blond ringlets. "I'm a lucky man. She'd done the same to save my life."

And that's what had kept him going through those first hours, then those first long, seemingly endless, days and nights as she grew hotter, weaker, sicker. He kept reminding himself that she would never give up on him, that she would be the sort to chide him and scold him and yell at him to fight back even as he grew weaker.

So he had done just as he knew she would do for him. Always reminding her of the children, of all the four of them had to live for. Over and over doing his level best to convince her of the years left them both.

"I kept that fire going day and night," he said quietly in the shade of those cottonwoods as the flies droned about them. "Didn't sleep much them days—couldn't."

He had been scared, too afraid to rest more than a few minutes at a time even when he grew so weary he could no longer keep his eyes open, no longer able to cradle her head in his lap and wash her face with the scalding hot water that sometimes made her whimper and moan, some-times made her wail and thrash against the grip he had on her.

"I don't have me no idea how it helped, but chopping the wood, boiling the snow, washing her over and over every day and every night . . . it kept me busy—so busy I didn't have much time to worry. I had to keep doing what I could do to keep her alive one more day. Then another come after that, and I knowed I had to keep her alive that day."

The sun had warmed the earth that first morning after Stiff Arm's rescue party left as Titus gathered wood close to their camp, brought the horses close, and started scooping snow into her new brass kettle to heat over the flames. That night, like all the nights that followed for them on the side of that mountain, the temperatures sank well below zero. With it too cold for a man ever to sleep for long at all, he repeatedly awoke throughout each long stretch of darkness to prop more wood on the fire, dragging the kettle near the heat again, repeatedly dipping the coarse linen scrap into the scalding water where he boiled slivers of snakeroot, then scrubbed the woman's face and neck as she grumbled, sometimes screamed—but soon grew too weak to push his hands away.

He had convinced himself the ugly, ofttimes oozing, pustules were filled with a loathsome poison as surely as a gangrenous wound would fill with the poison capable of killing. Over and over he cleaned the sores with the snakeroot broth, gently scrubbing each sore open so he could get at the foul ooze, cleanse it from her body in the hope he could prevent the poison from killing her.

They had begun as red spots, then became hard, angry welts lying just beneath the surface of the skin until the first one erupted as he scoured the coarse linen across it. There were many more by the next morning. And by that night it seemed her whole face had been taken over by the noxious pustules.

Yet he persisted, doing what he could to clean each one with the scalding water that soothed the bones in his bare hands aching so with the intense cold. Slowly too, doing his best to remember that he must wash each pustule separately so that he did not rub poison from one into the next. Each time he finished bathing her, he trudged out of the firelight with that kettle of water and dumped it in the same spot, downwind of camp. When he returned, he draped the coarse linen scrap over the end of a tree branch and held it over the coals of their fire, turning it the way he would a thick slab of elk loin so that the heat killed the poison, cauterized every inch of the cloth.

Rituals so intricate and consuming that they kept him this side of that fine line of insanity, rituals practiced with such fidelity that they pre-vented him from going mad with the terror that he was going to lose her.

At times Bass hunted when she slept, never venturing far. Twice each day he made soup in their old cast-iron kettle, boiling snakeroot with the meat of a bighorn goat he'd shot, later a small cinnamon bear—even the goat and bear bones—making a hearty broth he forced her to sip day after day after day as her cheeks began to sag: that ravaged, pitted, bloodied skin of her face . . . her almond-shaped, oriental eyes growing more sunken, red-rimmed, bags like liver-colored fire smudge wrinkled beneath them both.

Every few hours the fever made her delirious. At times Waits even mumbled with a swollen tongue—so bloated it cruelly reminded him of that deadly desert crossing back when he and McAfferty fled the Apache on the Gila. Plain to see the damned fever was boiling all the juices out of her. She had to drink. He never let her refuse, pouring the cool water over her tongue until she coughed and sputtered, or holding a horn ladle of warm broth against her chapped, cracked lips as she struggled to turn away. But he didn't let her—couldn't let her.

Even now he would not tell these old friends how he cried, or how he cried out at her too every time he had to lock her head beneath an arm, doing his best to scold or cajole some liquid past her lips.

Sixteen long days they remained there. He whittled a notch for each one in the handle of a camp ax. Sixteen days and nights, awaking fearfully from his troubled half sleep, afraid she had died. Anxious to see if she still breathed, resting his fingers over her nose and mouth each time he returned from his hunt through the surrounding timber, or among the boulders and tundra, often times with no more than a marmot or two.

With each morning's arrival he watched the sun climb off the far edge of the earth, thankful that she still breathed in her fitful sleep, that she had survived another day, somehow endured another bitterly cold night. As weak as she became, to find her alive there against him, still breathing shallow and raspy wrapped in his arms, it became no small celebration for his heart.

He wasn't sure why he hadn't noticed it before, but there came one night at the fire while he was scrubbing her face with that coarse rag and scalding water, suddenly aware that he could find no new pustules erupting on her face. And what angry red pockmarks there were no longer oozed and bled near as much as they had in recent days each time he repeatedly washed them.

Two days later she awoke him from his own fitful sleep, whispering with her raw throat and swollen tongue that she wanted some water. As he poured sips past her cracked, puffy lips, later fed her spoons of hot soup and washed her wounds, Waits-by-the-Water gazed at him for the first time in more than two weeks. The love in those eyes dared him to hope.

For sixteen days those eyes had remained shut, never looking back at him, not once opening to dispel his doubts, drive away any of his fears. But after all those nights, she finally opened her eyes and looked up at him, soft and thankful. So weary, she did not try speaking any more that day in her exhaustion, even as he clumsily removed her dress and leggings, replaced them with some of his clothing. All she could do was look at him with those eyes.

Not until the next day did she speak again. "Love Ti-tuzz."

And that evening she asked for help walking to the brush so she could relieve herself. She squatted, then pulled herself up against him, and he supported her as they returned to the fire, where she curled up within a new robe and he dragged off the one she had lain in for all those days.

"What will you sleep in tonight?"

"I'll sleep with you again," he explained.

"We'll need the old robe to keep us warm—"

"Going to burn it before we leave," he said in English. "And them clothes of your'n too. The sickness is all over 'em."

Better to leave as much of the disease as they could right there on the mountainside, among the ashes of their fire. Bass realized he could replace things, like his missing traps he figured the Blackfoot had thrown away, like the plunder they had shattered and destroyed. Just leave the pox and its evil there on the mountain. Trouble was, they would never leave it all behind. Waits-by-the-Water was going to carry a telling reminder of the pox with her till the end of her days.

But they still had one another. And they had their children. So Bass remained confident he could rebuild the pieces of their life together. As long as there was beaver in the mountains and as long as the traders hauled their goods out to rendezvous—he'd carve out a life for them . . . just as long as he and his kind could continue to race across the seasons, as long as they could continue to ride the moon down.

Many times since that late winter of thirty-eight it had haunted him just how many there were who had given up and abandoned the Rockies. Daniel Potts, and even Jim Beckwith. It troubled him to think back on how fewer and fewer showed up come rendezvous with the arrival of each summer. Sad to watch how many didn't choose to reoutfit themselves, deciding instead to ride east with the fur caravan, electing to take their wages in hard money once they reached St. Louis. Every summer at least a couple dozen more admitted they were throwing in and giving up.

"Plunder costs too much," some groused.

Others complained, "Beaver's too low."

Still more confessed that a few seasons spent crotch-deep in icy streams, exposed to that unwarmable cold of the mountains for three seasons a year, had aged them well before their years. Titus felt sorry for those who decided to flee back east to what was, back to who they had been. Yet he realized he didn't have any of that to return to himself.

For the last few summers he saw how those who were giving up simply freed their Flathead, Shoshone, or Yuta wives to return to their villages, to their parents, taking the half-breed youngsters with them when the winters of marriage were done and the white trapper no longer needed the benefits of his dusky-skinned bedmate.

But a time or two Titus had heard tell of a man who did take his wife and their children east with him, perhaps to settle somewhere on the frontier that others claimed was inching right to the edge of the rolling prairie itself. There among the pacified Sauk and Fox, among the Osage or those other bands Andy Jackson had driven west, such an old trapper and his family might better mix in with the life of hardworking folks scratching out an existence along that border of the wilderness. Once they were on that backtrail to the settlements, nothing else was ever heard of those men who had returned east in hopes of recapturing some of what life they had left behind, nonetheless unable to let go of a woman and children who were part of another life they had now abandoned.

Again this summer on Horse Creek, some three dozen company men had turned in their furs, preparing to flee the mountains.

Sitting there talking with these scarred, old friends, Scratch realized he could never return to the settlements. There wasn't anything left back there. No family to speak of—no one to make for a sentimental reunion. There had been no real success in the blacksmith trade with Hysham Troost that would lure him back as this beaver trade slowly sank from its lofty heights. And he ruminated that he could never take Waits-by-the-Water onto that rolling land of the buffalo prairie or beyond to those hardwood forests where corncrackers scratched at the ground and raised their fixed communities.

They were no place to raise children—not back there where the trees grew so tall and thick a man couldn't see any distance at all, back east where a man looked up only to see a portion of the sky. No place for a child to grow tall and strong as they would here in these mountains, breathing this clean, dry air. Back east, he remembered, the men on that old frontier of hardwood forests had a far different look in their eye than these hivernants of the high Stonies. Back there, closed in with the thick timber and small patches of sky that too often turned gray and drenched them with rain— such men did not possess the far-seeing squint of those iron-forged few who made a home beyond the western prairies.

Out here a man quickly took on a decidedly distant gaze. He grew accustomed to gazing across great stretches, searching far ridges, studying the skyline for dust or smoke, game or foe, reading those green threads that beckoned him to water as if they were parchment maps, ciphering each swaybacked, snow-covered saddle that allowed him a pass between the mountain peaks—scratching every mile of the journey into the fastness of his memory. This unimaginably huge land required a man to stretch his eyes far beyond what had been required of him in those closed-in, narrow-bounded forests back east.

Come from what he had been, a man either became much more than what he was back east—or he left his bones to bleach on the banks of some uncharted mountain stream. So again this summer those who realized they had teased and taunted Dame Fate long enough chose to rake in what chips they had left and scurry east. Leaving behind a life. Leaving behind loved ones.

"I vowed that if the woman died," Titus quietly explained to the circle of friends that hot summer afternoon, "I wasn't returning to the Crow."

"What of your young'uns?" Elbridge asked.

He grew thoughtful. "Told myself they'd grow up just fine, took in and raised by them what would come to love li'l Flea and my darling Magpie like their own."

"Couldn't bear to face 'em," Isaac said.

"No, wasn't that a'tall," Bass replied with a shake of his head. "If'n I'd buried the woman in a tree, proper that way for the wind to take her . . . I knowed I would ride on down that north side of them mountains, making straight for Blackfoot country."

Rufus nodded. "Take you some goddamned hair."

"One by one," Scratch continued. "I'd kill ever' last one of them bastards I chanced across. Times were at nights while I kept myself awake caring for the woman, I figured how I'd mark the bodies: cutting on 'em, scraping my letters in each one so they'd come to know who I was and what I was about."

Solomon glanced at the youngsters nearby and asked, "You never figgered to see your young'uns again?"

"No," he confessed. "I was gonna ride and kill till ever' one of the Blackfoot was dead . . . or them sonsabitches kill't me."

Gray sighed. "Lookit your young'uns now, Scratch. Ain't it turned out for the best you didn't leave 'em for the Crow to raise? And you ain't dead and skulped up there in Blackfoot country!"

"And the woman pulled through," Graham cheered.

"Were a bunch more days afore she was strong enough to sit a horse, howsoever," Bass continued his tale. "I got us back over the pass just a'fore another storm blowed down on us. We made it to some good timber and sat it out whilst she got a bit more of her strength back. Don't know how many days that was, for I'd stopped a'counting and carving on that ax handle."

Day by day they had backtracked for the Crow village, become anxious when they didn't find it where the lodges had been standing weeks before when the ordeal had begun. As they were pushing out of the abandoned campsite along the snowy ground churned with travois scars, Titus had spotted the scaffold propped across the branches of a distant cottonwood that stood at the base of the rimrock. And from the way the gnarled tree trunk below that robe bundle was marked, they knew it had to be the body of Strikes-in-Camp.

"Them Crow gave him a decent funeral," he declared, "even if they never did bring his body into camp—feared as they was of the pox."

Beneath the spreading branches of the cottonwood they camped that afternoon, and as Bass built a fire and gathered wood for the night, Waits-by-the-Water knelt and began her mourning. She chopped off more of her hair and tossed it into the wind, those shorn locks grotesquely framing that wounded, pitted face. Tears flowed as she wailed, tearing her coat from her arms so she could slash her flesh until her strength was gone and Bass raised her from the frozen ground, carrying his wife back to the warmth of the fire where he fed her, wrapped her, then rocked her to sleep.

"After the second day I told the woman it was time for her mourning to be done," Titus said, looking over to see his young son toddling his way now. "It was time to be finding our young'uns."

Some two and a half years old by then, young Flea lumbered the last few yards as his father spread his arms to welcome him. The boy vaulted into the air, sailing into Bass's arms where he settled into his father's lap, looking round at the hairy faces gathered there in the afternoon shade as the deerflies droned and Horse Creek gurgled along its sandy bed.

"How long it take you to find them Crow?" Solomon inquired.

"Weren't long, not really," he said, rubbing Flea's bushy head affectionately. "They took off right after the four days of mourning for Strikes-in-Camp and them others the Blackfoot killed in the ambush. But we found 'em eventual'."

It had made for quite a scene when Bass and Waits-by-the-Water showed up near the camp one day late that winter of 1838. As soon as he had seen the camp guards loping their way, Scratch halted, waiting. Among the sentries had been Pretty On Top.

The young warrior's eyes filled with a mist as he whooped, his cry sailing to the cold blue sky of Absaroka as he brought his pony skidding to a stop with the seven others right in front of the white man and his wife who clutched the flaps of her hood over her face, not daring to let these people who had known her from childhood see her wounds.

"My heart sings!" Pretty On Top cheered, slapping his breast. "You are returned with your wife! How is this that she did not die?"

"My husband would not let me," Waits announced from the muffle of her hood, surprising even Titus. "He said I could not die."

"Then the medicine of Ti-tuzz is mighty!" cried Three Iron. "In the stories of our great-grandfathers, when the pox visited itself upon us, very few were spared death before the scattering of the bands. So the First Maker has truly smiled on you, Waits-by-the-Water."

She had looked over at her husband and said, "Yes, I know how the First Maker has smiled on me."

The eight guards yipped and whistled with approval, causing their horses to jostle with the sudden loud exuberance.

Bass found her eyes smiling at him from the shadows of her hood and said, "Yes, woman—the First Maker has smiled on us both."

Little Flea had been at their horses' legs before the two of them even dismounted beside Bright Wings's lodge. And Magpie was already reaching her arms to her father as Bass brought his pony to a halt. He had leaned over, caught her by the wrist, and swung her up behind him, marveling at how much it seemed she had grown. As he kissed and hugged her right there on horseback, Waits dropped to the ground to gather little Flea into her arms, smothering him with her kisses. Not knowing what he was doing, the babbling child pushed back the hood—his own eyes suddenly wide with surprise, even fear.

Around the woman others gasped, fell back a step, as Waits-by-the-Water snatched the hood over her head, beginning to sob because the boy continued to stare at her in shock and fright. But in that next moment Crane emerged from the lodge doorway, her stooped body hurrying to her daughter's side where she flung her arms around Waits—crying, wailing, sobbing, keening, blubbering all at once.

Then Bright Wings was there too, the three of them hugging, their arms wrapped around Flea as he rested on his mother's hip. The moment Magpie and Bass hit the ground, the young girl sprinted to her mother's side, ducked between some legs, and ended up in the middle of all those women happily reunited.

Hugging Flea now before the boy toddled off again, Scratch looked at Magpie as she helped her mother cutting moccasin soles. Back then, upon their return to the Crow after chasing down the Blackfoot, Magpie had been no older than Flea was at this moment. But to look at the girl now, tall and long-legged as she was, Titus found it hard to believe so much time had flowed past since that winter of the Blackfoot . . . realizing again that his daughter was more than four years old.

At times that late winter and on into the spring, Pretty On Top and his companions—Red Leggings, Comes Inside the Door, Sees the Star, and Crow Shouting—would ask to join the white man when he packed up and rode away from the village for two weeks or more at a time. By day the bored young warriors might follow Titus to the icy banks of the flooding streams, amused and intrigued by the trapper's rituals. Most mornings one of the Crow would ride out to spend the day circling the surrounding territory, searching for any sign of enemy encroachment while he hunted for fresh meat.

Days later, with a load of beaver for Waits-by-the-Water to flesh and his own heart yearning to hold her, eager to embrace his children, Bass would turn around and return to Yellow Belly's village. For two, some-times three nights he would remain at the woman's side, each day spent hunting elk and deer or mountain sheep for his wife's big family, coupling with her, wrestling with his children and those cousins who now had no father of their own. Once he was assured the group had enough meat to last them many days, Titus packed up again and headed into the high country—sometimes alone, often joined by the young warriors.

With each subsequent journey as those weeks passed, Scratch was able to push higher into the hills, farther upstream, always there when the beaver emerged from their winter lodges to make repairs on their dams.

"We figgered you'd gone under for sartin," Rufus confessed now. "When you didn't come in for ronnyvoo on the Popo Agie last summer."

"Why'd the booshways move ronnyvoo there 'stead of here on the Green where they said they'd meet the brigades?" Titus asked.

Elbridge explained, "Goddamned company booshways changed it on us when they growed tired of allays having Hudson's Bay show up ever' summer over here in this country."

"Englishers got to be a bit of a problem with the free men, so it seemed," Solomon said. "They was offering a good price on fur over at Fort Hallee, and wasn't asking so much for their trade goods neither."

"Wonder why we ain't see'd hide nor ha'r of John Bull yet this sum-mer?" Bass reflected.

Isaac said, "Maybeso they don't know we're here this year for ron-nyvoo."

"Chances are better them English don't give a damn 'bout coming to ronnyvoo no more," Solomon observed, "what with the trade ain't being what it used to be."

"Damned good to see you're still standing on your pins, Titus Bass," Gray said. "We was a'feared you'd gone under."

"Way things was," Bass began, hoisting the restless boy out of his lap, kissing Flea on the cheek, then sending the naked child on his way, "I didn't figger the woman was much ready to be around white folks. So I had me a choice of coming to ronnyvoo all on my lonesome . . . or stick-ing close to her and the young'uns."

"You said them Blackfoot gone and ruin't some of your plunder," Isaac said. "How in blazes'd you fare 'thout them supplies what you'd get at ronnyvoo?"

He gazed at the two children playing in the grass beneath a great clump of willow. "We made out fine," Bass said quietly. "High summer—when the beaver ain't fit for a red piss—I packed up all I had and rode 'em over to the mouth of the Tongue."

"Tullock's fort?" asked Gray.

Titus nodded. "Van Buren. Me and Sam'l dickered and drank, then dickered some more. All in all, he's a good man. That coon spent plenty of time trapping beaver his own self. Knows how it be to freeze your balls to catch poor plew. Tullock done the best by me his company would let him."

Graham inquired, "He get all your fur last year?"

"Most. Even this summer I could trade it to the company here, or I could trade it to the company at Tullock's Crow post. Don't make me no differ'nce," Scratch confided. "Only differ'nce is, this nigger sure missed his companyeros when he don't come in for that ronnyvoo on the Popo Agie."

"Weren't much of a hurraw last summer," Solomon grumbled.

Rufus agreed. "Lookee round you right here, goddammit. Ain't much to ronnyvoo at all no more."

"Drips come out from St. Louie with a small pack train last year," Elbridge explained. "Had him no more'n two dozen carts an' some seventy-five men."

"Getting smaller and smaller ever' year now," Isaac grumped.

Titus stretched out his legs, his knees aching from those countless seasons spent submerged in freezing water. "That Scotsman feller, Stewart—he come out again last summer?"

Gray's head bobbed. "Sartin sure did. Brung him out some others too. Had 'nother furrin-borned fella with him this time. Name of Sutter.* That'un said he was setting his sights on making it all the way to the land of them Spanyards in California."

Rufus Graham snorted with laughter. "It were funny to hear that li'l rip of a runt grumble and cuss with his funny talk! Why, don't you know he went from camp to camp at ronnyvoo, trying to hire him an outfit of fellers to guide him on to California."

"He have him any takers?" Scratch asked.

Rufus nodded. "A few hooked up with Sutter and give up on beaver."

"You 'member how that li'l pecker called 'em all a bunch of robbers!" Solomon hooted. "He howled that all it seemed most fur men really wanted to do in California was rob churches, stealing cattle and horses!"

"More'n a handful signed on with Sutter leastways," Elbridge said. "And Stewart brung out a pair of young fellers, just to make a trip west."

"Either of them two hap to be a artist—maybeso that Miller fella he had with him couple years back?" Titus asked.

"Just peach-faced boys," and Isaac shook his head solemnly. "Their papa sent 'em out to see the West."

Itching the side of his cheek, Scratch asked, "Who's their papa?"

---

* *Swiss immigrant August Johann Sutter*

"William Clark, of St. Louis," Rufus answered. "Same one took that bunch all the way to the far ocean with Lewis back . . . oh, more'n thirty year ago now."

"His two boys come out to see this country for themselves, I reckon," Elbridge observed with a wry smile.

"I'll bet ol' man Clark sent his young'uns out here to see this here country the way it was when he come through here years ago," Bass grumbled sourly. "See this country a'fore it ain't no more."

"Ain't no more?" Rufus squealed.

"Lookit, boys—nigh onto ever' summer we see'd missionaries coming to ronnyvoo, on their way west with their carts and wagons and milk cows," Scratch declared grimly. "We see'd white women and Englishmen, Bible-thumpers and furriners . . . and for ever' one of 'em come out here—there's just a li'l less wild country left for the likes of you and me."

The others fell silent for a few moments, thoughtful. Then Solomon said, "I recollect Scratch is right on that. Even more of them goddamned missionaries come through last summer too."

"More?" Bass groaned.

Gray said, "Had four white women with 'em too."

"Don't s'prise me none," Bass admitted.

"Even had us a li'l fun when one of them preachers married one of the company fellers to his Nez Perce woman."

"Married her?" Bass said. "You mean like stand-up white folks, read-the-Bible married?"

Elbridge nodded enthusiastically. "Them Nepercy stood around stone-faced and quiet as church mice whilst that missionary said the proper words over 'em both."

"Most off, I recollect how last year them clerks from St. Louis didn't have a good word to say 'bout things back east," Isaac explained. "They was grumping over how bad they was having it with furs."

Simms went on to explain how the eastern hands who accompanied the caravan for that summer trip to the mountains and back were eager to describe just how gloomy the financial picture had become in the East. The Panic of Thirty-seven had the States in its grip. Moncy was tight, times were hard, trade goods were never more expensive, and beaver was falling fast.

"That ronnyvoo last summer no better'n this'un," Bass said.

"Most fellers pretty down, that's for sure, what with all them company clerks was telling ever'one," Rufus explained. "Then we heard tell the company was so disgusted, they wasn't gonna bring out no more trade goods. No more ronnyvoo."

"Disgusted?" Titus repeated.

"Rumor was the company bosses tol't Drips they wasn't much happy with the mountain trade no more," Elbridge took up the story. "They figgered maybeso to do it all from the fur posts."

"Fur posts!" Titus squeaked in disbelief. "Won't be no more ronnyvoo?"

Solomon said, "Ever' year now more and more niggers give up trapping and ride off back east. That means there ain't much beaver for them booshways no more."

"What do Drips and Fontenelle fix to do if'n there ain't no more mountain rendezvous?" Bass inquired.

"Fontenelle's dead," Elbridge disclosed. "I heard he died last year. Drips is the only one still running things in the mountains now."

"He put Bridger out in the field with a strong brigade," Rufus explained. "Joe Walker got 'nother outfit working for Drips. Damn if Walker didn't come in to the Popo Agie last summer with a shit-load of Mexican horses. That was 'bout the best news the company got last summer. Needed them horses in a bad way."

This was all so hard to comprehend. Right from Bass's first year in the mountains, there had always been a summer rendezvous: a place to trade in his furs and barter for what he needed in possibles.

Titus wagged his head, unable to fathom it. "No more ronnyvoo?"

"But don't you see?" Gray asked. "Drips ended up calling ever'one together and telling 'em the rumors was all wrong. Promised he'd be out here to Horse Crik this summer."

Then Isaac said, "But the damage been done by the time Drips stomped on them rumors."

"Damage?" Scratch asked.

"We heard tell of . . . maybeso a dozen fellers what listened to all them stories 'bout the company not having no more ronnyvoo," Isaac continued. "Well, a few of them niggers slipped off from the Popo Agie ever' night or so, taking their company traps and their company guns and their company possibles with 'em."

"Ever' last one of 'em running off with a good number of company horses too!" Rufus cried. "Ain't never been so many deserters as there was last summer."

Isaac said, "I s'pose it's cuz no one was much for sure there'd be 'nother ronnyvoo."

"Fact be, Drips says if we meet up next summer, he'll show up here," Elbridge explained. "Just this morning Drips got all the boys together and said Pierre Chouteau the younger back in St. Louis don't know if he'll send out another supply train next year—but if he does, it ought'n ronnyvoo with us right here where we been many times a'fore."

"Damn if this all don't take the circle!" Bass exclaimed in amazement. "Hard to reckon on them fellas stealing traps and possibles and horses from their brigades."

Rufus shrugged in that easy way of his. "Man hears the company ain't gonna be no more, I guess he reckons it's time to take what he figgers is due him."

"We . . . we even talked 'bout deserting our own selves last summer," Solomon confessed.

"But we didn't," Elbridge stated firmly. "We signed on with the company to the end . . . and that's damn well giving a man our solemn word. We ain't none of us gonna steal from no man—not when we got our pride."

"Makes a fella wonder," Isaac ruminated, "what the hell we're gonna do when the company tells us it don't need us to trap its beaver no more."

"Shit," Bass growled as the others fell silent in the drone and buzz of busy insects. "From the looks of things—this here beaver business gone and sunk so low that white men even took to stealing from white men!"

TWENTY-NINE

"You hear tell Bridger's quit the company?"

For a moment there Titus Bass studied Shadrach Sweete's face for any betrayal that the man was pulling his leg. "Gabe?" he asked in disbelief. "Not Bridger!"

The overly tall man bobbed his head as some others stepped up to listen in. "Can't believe it my own self. I just come from Drips's tent yonder. Last night Bridger said he might just do it—but I didn't figger he ever would."

"Quit the company?" asked an older, lanky man striding up in greasy buckskins.

"Told Drips he'd have to get someone else to guide the brigade this year," Sweete explained as he turned to address the man nearly twice his age. "Bridger's heading back to St. Louis with the fur caravan when it pulls out."

If that report didn't just about beat all the other bad news there was at this quiet little shindig beside the mouth of Horse Creek. First off, Bass had reached this rendezvous site on the Green River to find no more than one hundred twenty company trappers and fewer than thirty freemen waiting the arrival of the supply train. And from the looks of what few camps dotted the valley, one thing was certain as sun: no one had packed much in the way of beaver fur to this rendezvous of 1839.

Really didn't matter, as things turned out, because when a rider hailed the camps a few days back, announcing that the trader's caravan was approaching—Bass, like the rest, eagerly scanned that bench to the east, expecting to watch a long mule train or string of carts snake their way into the bottoms, bringing with them more recruits for the autumn brigades, perhaps joined by another large party of missionaries bound for Oregon country with their damned wagons, carriages, and milk cows.

But what caravan pilot Black Harris led into the valley was instead *four* small two-wheeled carts, each pulled by a pair of mules and carrying no more than eight hundred pounds of the company's trade goods. On either side of each noisy, squeaking cart trudged a dust-coated, parched pair of St. Louis hired hands—no more than eight employees to assist in the exchange of furs across those few days it would take to trade furs for staples before Harris would turn his outfit around for the settlements. Besides those eight clerks, another half-dozen mule tenders were along to care for the cantankerous stock.

And there in the sheets of dust stirred up by them all, bringing up the rear of that pitifully small caravan, came two small carts and some missionaries, after all. In addition to those bound for the fertile fields of the heathens, Black Harris was accompanied by a German physician and his small party from St. Louis who had come to the mountains for a summer of recreation and adventure.

"Damn poor doin's," Scratch had grumbled. From what he could see, he didn't figure he had missed a damned thing on the Popo Agie the summer before.

And now Gabe was headed east.

Maybeso if a man did have him some family back in Missouri country, Titus rationalized his old friend's intentions, there might be reason for him to throw it all in and head back now that the business was no more than a ghost of its former glory. But he figured it had to be something mighty powerful to pull a man like Jim Bridger back to the States—quitting the beaver streams, abandoning his Flathead wife and children, forsaking these mountains for the runty hills of the east.

"You figger Gabe ain't never coming back?" the tall bone rack of a stranger asked of Sweete.

Shad could only shrug. "Bridger ain't said what he 'tends to do. But I don't figger him for staying long back there. Most ever'thing he's ever knowed is out here."

"Damn straight," the older man grumped, giving Bass a close, squint-eyed appraisal of a sudden. "If there ain't beaver to skin and red niggers to skulp in the Big Stonies . . . by God there's allays horses to steal from the greasers out to Califorcy!" And with that next breath he poked his face right into Scratch's and asked, "I know you, pilgrim?"

"Maybeso," Titus replied with a chortle, raising his arms into the air, one on either side of his head, fingers spread like antlers. "—If'n you're that crazy nigger what's gonna turn into a bull elk when you're gone under!"

"I thort it was you," the homely man declared with a grin, holding out a bony paw to shake. "The nigger what's called Scratch. Last saw you down to Taos."

Nodding, Bass shook the strong, lean hand and said, "Shad, this here's Bill Williams."

"Ol' Bill Williams?" Sweete asked. "Ever'body knows of Ol' Solitaire. Man, if I ain't heard a passel of tales 'bout you!"

"Ain't none of 'em the truth," Williams snapped. As suddenly he smiled hugely. "Then again, maybeso ever' last one of 'em be the truth too!"

Scratch looked the old veteran in the eye and asked, "How you read the sign, Bill? Fat cow or poor bull? You figger the mountain trade 'bout to go under with Bridger heading east and all these here niggers running off with horses and traps they stole't?"

Williams snorted. "Maybeso fur is done for a while. But beaver's bound to rise, I allays say. If'n a man needs to, he can find hisself something to do till the plews are prime again."

"What else is a child s'posed to do if'n he don't trap?" Sweete demanded testily.

Regarding the tall man warily, Williams said, "You are a big chunk of it, now, ain'cha?" He put a finger to his temple. "Think on it—and maybeso you'll come up with something to do till beaver comes back."

"What you fixing to do, Bill?" Scratch asked.

"Me and few others been kicking round the idee of riding west for Californy—steal some Mex'can horses like I tol't you."

Sweete wagged his head. "Why horses?"

"Out here a nigger can buy 'em for a rich man's ransom . . . or he can ride back east to get horses for hisself. So there might just be some real good money in it for a child who steals some horses in Californy what he can sell to the forts."

"Mayhaps them greasers shoot your head off too," Bass snorted, "you try riding off with their horses."

"Them pepper beans?" Williams asked with sour laughter.

"Any man gets shot at enough," Titus replied, "I figger the odds gotta mean he's gonna get hit with a lead ball one day."

"Ain't a greaser gun made can hit me," Williams boasted.

Turning to Sweete, Bass asked, "If you ain't gonna steal Mex'can horses like Bill here—you gonna stay on with Drips's brigade now that Bridger ain't along?"

With a shrug Shadrach said, "Been thinking I might just head west a mite—work out of Fort Hall. Hear the British promise to treat Americans right on their prices for goods, on what they'll offer for beaver."

"Some ol' partners of mine said they heard the same thing."

"Goddamn them English!" Williams grumbled. "I'd steal ever'thing out from under 'em and burn down their posts a'fore I'd deal with John Bull!"

"Maybeso I figure to have me *somewhere* to sell my beaver when the Americans pull outta the mountains, ol' man," Sweete advised.

"There's other posts," Williams argued. "Don't have to deal with them Englishers."

"Fort Lucien?" Bass inquired. "St. Louis parley-voos own that'un."

Williams shook his head emphatically, saying, "But the company don't own that Vaskiss post on the South Platte. And they don't run them others down in that country neither."

"What others?" Titus asked.

"Some soldier named Lupton left the army to jump in the beaver trade year or two back," Williams said. " 'Side his, there's two more on the Platte: Fort Jackson and Fort Savary—all of 'em trading with the Cheyenne and 'Rapaho."

Titus asked, "Robes?"

"Beaver from white men, robes from redbellies," Williams answered. "And now the Bents are offering top dollar for all the horses we can bring 'em. Californy or Injun—makes 'em no differ'nce."

Sweete said, "All of them places over on the east side of the mountains."

"And that can be a ride for a man what wants to have somewhere handy to trade his furs," Bass observed. "Only reason I ever traded up to Tullock's post at the mouth of the Tongue was I found myself up in that Crow country."

Nodding, the old trapper said, "Ain't whistling in the dark there, Scratch—but ary man what wants to stay in this here country can allays do his business on this side of the mountains."

Sweete growled. "You just said you wasn't giving none of your business to them English over at Fort Hall—"

"I ain't talking 'bout Fort Hall, you idjit!" Bill snapped. "Ain't either of you heard 'bout them two posts on south of here?"

Bass and Sweete glanced at one another before looking back at Williams.

"No doubt you two ignernt coons been spending too much of your time up in Blackfoot and Crow country!" the old man snorted. "Down near the mouth of the Winty is Robidoux's post . . . and just northeast of there a leetle is Fort Davy Crockett."

"Northeast, where?"

"Brown's Hole. East side of the Green. Fort's been there more'n a year . . . maybeso two year now this summer."

"They in the beaver business?" Titus asked. "Got trade goods?"

"Them fellers all been trappers," Williams declared. "So I figger they know how to treat a man fair. Better'n this goddamned company got this hull country by the balls—squeezing down so hard they're choking the life right out of the beaver trade."

Bass looked at Sweete. "I been there."

"Brown's Hole?"

Nodding, Scratch said, "Trapping might be fair in that country. Chances are a man won't bump into too many Injuns. Maybeso we'd make a pair of it if'n you ain't give up on the mountains—"

"I ain't give up on the mountains!" Shad roared.

"Then you cogitate 'bout heading south with me to trap that Uinty country, go sniff out just how fair a man gets treated down to this Fort Davy Crockett."

"I'll think on it some," Shad replied, screwing up his lips thoughtfully.

"You lemme know next day or so," Bass said. "It ain't like we got a whole lot of choices no more, Shad. There ain't many ways for niggers like us to make our living. We don't trap beaver—we can always turn to horse stealing like Ol' Solitaire here . . . or turn back for the settlements."

"I ain't above stealing horses," Shadrach Sweete admitted two days later when he walked over to Bass's camp of a purpose. "But I don't figger I'll ever turn back for the settlements neither."

"What's that leave you, Shad?"

His merry eyes twinkled. "You fixing to keep chasing beaver?"

Titus nodded with a grin, knowing that Sweete had come to his decision. "For many a year now I always hankered to have me a look over the next hill. Time's come to see some new country. Brown's Hole might be the place for us to winter."

"You don't mind me riding along?"

With a smile Scratch declared, "I been 'thout a partner for many a winter now—back to thirty-four. I'd like to hook up for a spell and catch us some beaver to boot."

Sweete stuck out his hand. "When you fixing to pull out?"

"Two days set with you?"

"All right by me."

"Dawn."

"First light it is."

As events turned out, others were setting out that same morning—men who had taken themselves off the company's books. But Doc Newell, Kit Carson, and a few others weren't riding south for the Uintah. They were instead heading northwest for Fort Hall. Carson had his young Arapaho wife along, while Newell was escorting his own family as well as Virginia, Joe Meek's Indian wife, to the British post while Meek set off to the southwest intending to work the Salt River. If the American traders were withdrawing from the mountains, Meek, Newell, and Carson declared, then it made sense for a man to polish his relationship with those English booshways of the Hudson's Bay Company.

"Maybe we'll see you two down to Brown's Hole late of the fall," Carson declared as he swung into the saddle after shaking hands with Bass and Sweete.

"We're gonna see what the English offer us for peltries," Newell explained as he climbed atop his horse. "If'n they give a man a fair swap, we'll trap the Snake country."

"But if the Britishers don't treat us right," Carson stated, "figure to see us at Fort Davy Crockett a'fore it snows hard."

"That's still good beaver country, Scratch," Newell said as he nudged his horse away, giving a farewell wave. "Bunch of us laid in over to Brown's Hole last winter."

In twos and threes small groups of men peeled themselves away from the once-great monolith of the Rocky Mountain fur trade, like ripping back an onion, layer by layer.

Only a year before on the Popo Agie, the Pierre Chouteau Company had employed some one hundred twenty trappers in the field. But by the time this rendezvous on the Green was over, no more than one week after the caravan had arrived, company partisan Andrew Drips discovered he would be leading fewer than eighty men north to the Three Forks country for the fall hunt. And no more than two thousand pelts would be leaving rendezvous for St. Louis.

Never again would skin trappers be able to turn in their furs for credit, then go in debt for whiskey and trifles for the coming year. This summer on the Green no one could be sure there would be another summer, another rendezvous, or if there would be a mountain fur trade. Little surprise, then, that more than two dozen men simply slipped away from rendezvous with what they could lay their hands on. No longer was there such a thing as company credit.

And damn soon there simply would be no way for most of these men to make a living.

Trying to compete with the British had begun to drive Pierre Chouteau, Jr., out of the business. With the high cost of trade goods back east, the Americans had to offer top dollar for beaver—or lose those pelts to the Hudson's Bay Company securely ensconced at Fort Hall. And to continue offering five dollars per pound when those plews weren't bringing enough of a profit in the eastern markets was nothing less than financial suicide. If American trappers could not only wrangle a better price for their fur from the British, but pay less for their possibles in the bargain, then Scratch figured only an idiot would continue to do business with the St. Louis monopoly.

All around him the Rocky Mountain beaver trade had become no more than a pale reflection of those glory days of old.

Following the course of the Green River, Bass and Sweete had slowly marked the miles that took them through that familiar country. Behind the two of them rode Waits-by-the-Water and Magpie on their painted ponies. Little Flea sat in front of his father, tiny hands gripping the reins the way his sister once had done, assured he was master of all that he surveyed each day.

Over the last two weeks a relentless August sun had tortured this high desert country. With every step the hooves scraped the parched earth, sending up clouds of fine yellow dust that hung suspended in the breathless heat. But every night they camped in the shade of cottonwoods lining the riverbank, cooling not only their aching throats but soaking up to their necks in the revitalizing current as twilight overtook the land.

Eventually they neared the mouth of Vermillion Creek,* where the Green made one of its two great bends in passing through Brown's Hole. In the middistance they discovered a small herd of horses grazing beneath the tall old cottonwoods. Just beyond, through the massive trunks of that stately grove, Bass spotted the stockade of upright logs. As they moved closer, a white man pushed open one side of the narrow gate and stopped just outside the walls, watching the party's approach.

"Shady spot you picked for yourselves," Bass commented as he brought his horse to a halt and the stranger dropped the butt of his rifle to the ground.

"This here place is better'n most to winter," the man said as he came up to Bass's horse, holding up his hand. "Name's Sinclair. Prewett Sinclair."

Shad introduced himself, then asked, "You the only feller here?"

"My partners is gone for 'nother few weeks," the man with the dark, angular face explained.

"Partners? How many of you there be?" Scratch inquired.

"Three. Thompson headed east to the Missoura settlements for supplies last spring, just as soon as he could get north around the mountains. Three weeks back, my other partner named Craig headed over to meet Thompson—planning to meet up at Vaskiss's fort."

* In the extreme northwestern corner of present-day Colorado

"Been there more three winters back," Bass declared.

"So it's only me for while," Sinclair advised. "Me, 'long with what Injuns show up."

"Ever had you any trouble with Injuns hereabouts?" Scratch asked, peering round the narrow valley.

"Naw," Sinclair said. "Snakes and Bannacks come by of a time, and even a few poor Diggers show their faces on the side of them hills yonder."

Bass peered momentarily at the high bluffs across the river. "Up to ronnyvoo we heard you boys raised yourselves a fort fixing to do some trading down here."

"That's right," Sinclair replied.

Sweete asked, "You trade beaver for possibles?"

Dragging a bare forearm beneath his nose, Sinclair said, "We'll take robes too, if'n you wanna trade off your buffler hides."

"We sleep in what we got," Bass declared. "You mind us pitching camp over yonder for the night?"

"Not'all," Sinclair replied. "You figger to stick around long?"

Sweete shook his head. "Planning to head on down to the Little Bear, maybeso find some beaver over on the Little Snake."

"Good luck fellers," Sinclair said, wiping some sweat off his brow. "Not the Little Bear. Likely you'll have to work higher up the Little Snake to find beaver anymore."

"Little Bear used to be good beaver country," Bass observed.

"Been trapped out last two year," Sinclair said.

"That's a shame," Bass told them, with an amused grin. "Had some of my hair took on the Little Bear, many a summer ago."

"That where it was?" Sweete asked.

"Yup. Maybeso we'll go see that spot for ourselves."

"Lost hair, did you?" the trader asked, glancing at the graying curls on Bass's shoulder.

"Just enough to sour my milk," Titus answered, the grin becoming a smile. "After supper, we'll mosey on over and jaw a bit."

That evening Titus and Shad did pay a social call on Fort Davy Crockett, if not to share some stories with that new pair of ears, then to take a look at what the three proprietors had to offer in the way of goods and wares in trade for beaver pelts. Damn, if what few possibles sat on those shelves weren't all English, shipped to Fort Vancouver near the mouth of the Columbia River, then packed overland to the Hudson's Bay post at Fort Hall where they were purchased by the American partners to stock the skimpy shelves of this log-and-mud post erected on the east bank of the Green River.

Little wonder Philip Thompson had traipsed off to buy up what he could back in the States.

No more than two years old, the small fort boasted only three sides, each one no more than sixty feet in length, the high riverbank serving as a barrier on the fourth. Instead of separate pickets, the backs of three low buildings served as the stockade itself, interrupted by a narrow gate that faced the open ground stretching to the east. In that fertile bottom ground formed by its junction with Vermillion Creek, an array of native grasses flourished, thick, if not tall, throughout the short growing season, providing adequate grazing for the post's stock. Nearby along the west bank of the creek lay a profusion of tepee rings where visiting Shoshone and Ute raised their lodges when they showed up to trade.

"You fellers keep a sharp eye for Sioux," Sinclair warned the next morning as the small party saddled for the foothills.

"There ain't no goddamned Sioux over this side of the mountains," Sweete chortled. "Now, over in that country on—"

"Don't be so sure," the trader interrupted grimly. "Last bunch of Snakes through here told me they seen sign of Sioux on their way in here to trade."

"Maybeso they was just having some fun with you," Shad argued.

"I'll lay them Snakes figgered to scare you into giving 'em a good trade!" Bass agreed as he waved and started away. "Sioux country's a long, long ways off, Sinclair. Can't for the life of me reckon why they'd roam all the way over here."

Instead of leaving Brown's Hole through the narrow pass carved over the aeons by Vermillion Creek, Bass and Sweete had decided to continue on down the Green River until they struck the Little Bear.* From there they headed east, closely inspecting the smaller feeder streams for sign of beaver activity. Mile after mile, day by day, they marched upstream, following that river to the mouth of the Little Snake. After stabbing up that winding valley for two frustrating days without finding any evidence of beaver, the two of them turned back for the Little Bear, following it east into the foothills and those timbered slopes still crowned with some of last winter's snow.

Funny, Titus thought more than once, how this country down here got two, three times the snow that fell in Absaroka farther north. No two ways about it—that Crow country sure as hell got colder when it did get cold, but damn if winter didn't batter these central mountains with that much more snow. Maybe that was the reason he had been able to continue trapping off and on through the last of that long winter while his wife had finished healing. On through the spring, a summer, and fall, then another long, full winter he and Waits-by-the-Water had remained with her people: migrating only when the Crow moved camp.

---

* *What the fur trappers called present-day Yampa River*

Once during a warm, dry spell late in the summer of thirty-eight, Bass had loaded two small packs of beaver on Samantha's back and moseyed east to the mouth of the Tongue. He had somehow made his wife understand that he was half-froze for white-man talk, half-froze for white joking and white faces, half-froze for someone who could grasp how it was to be a half-wild white man living among his wife's native people.

Looking back now, Titus knew those few days he languished with Tullock had done him a world of good. He had grown lonely across the months, seeing only that one white man in more than a year and a half. Damn well near the same feeling he had back in the spring of thirty-two after all that time in Crow country, fighting off Blackfoot like vicious, blood-drawing deerflies . . . then ran onto Josiah Paddock, recent of the settlements.

Man gets so lonely, he's more than half-froze for a white voice, his own American language, another soul who might just understand when he admits he's grown scared.

"Scared?" Sweete asked at the campfire that late-autumn night after they had been driven to the foothills by a first, heavy snow.

Titus nodded. "Ain't you growed scared of what's to become of all of us, Shadrach?"

The big man stared thoughtfully at the fire. "When there ain't no more ronnyvooz, then I s'pose a nigger can take his plews to a post, like that Davy Crockett, or over to Hallee."

"Don't you see?" he asked the younger man. "When the fur company don't figger it's gonna send any more supply trains, then that means the company don't figger the beaver business is worth the trouble. And when that happens, the price of beaver sinks in the mud for ever'body."

"Trader'll be back," Sweete said hopefully. "Come next summer, they'll come back to ronnyvoo."

"I don't reckon they will, Shad," Bass whispered, gazing at the red embers of their fire as Waits-by-the-Water and the children slept. "The way things was . . . it's all but done now."

"You care to wager on that?" Sweete said, trying to sound as cheerful as he could.

"Sure. I'll buy you a new shirt, a horn of powder, and get you good and drunk to boot," Bass sighed. "If'n there's 'nother ronnyvoo come summer."

Shad was quiet a while before he asked, "How long you figger till the beaver's done?"

"My boy ain't gonna be very old," he declared, peering across the fire at the two small heads of his children poking from their blanket and robe. "Once there was no forts. Then there was a few. Now they're like ticks on a bull's hump. The time's changed, Shad. And it don't appear there's any going back. Good God in His heaven . . . but I pray this land don't change too. Leastways, till I'm gone."

A few days later they struck a buffalo trail as it angled across the rolling, broken country, meandering toward the headwaters of Vermillion Creek, taking them in the direction of Fort Davy Crockett.

"Shadrach," Bass called out a few hours later, motioning the tall man over as their horses carried them west along that buffalo road. With Sweete come up beside him, he whispered, "Don't make no show, but I want you to look down in the buffler tracks. Tell me what you see."

The younger man casually peered off the left side of his horse, then the right. Eventually he looked at Bass. "Injuns."

"How many you figger?"

"More'n two of us can handle."

"We got a bunch of guns—"

"But there's only two of us to fire 'em," Shadrach interrupted.

"Easy now," he soothed. "We don't even know what they be. Maybeso they're just some Snakes—following that buffler herd to make meat."

Sweete sighed in relief. "You're right. I just let that Sinclair get me jumping at shadows. I reckon that's it: only Snakes, trailing them buffler down to the fort."

"We ain't got no reason to think them are Sioux tracks," Bass warned.

Those recent seasons in Crow country had made for a lot of work for little beaver. Times past, he would have had more than twice the plews to show for his efforts, what with all the miles put behind him. Even after replacing those traps the Blackfoot had discarded, Bass still found he was forced to push higher to find the dammed-up meadows and lodges, forced to plunge farther and farther into the recesses of the mountains to find what beaver remained after years of relentless extermination of the creatures. More than once Titus had cursed others, then cursed his luck, and eventually cursed himself for stripping the creeks and streams and rivers of the flat-tails during those golden glory days.

But how was a man ever going to replace those belongings stolen and destroyed by the Blackfoot if he couldn't find enough beaver to trade for the blankets and traps, kettles and beads, finger rings and hawksbells he had possessed before the Blackfoot had raided Absaroka?

Tullock had treated him more than square in their dealings at Fort Van Buren, but there was only so much the trader could do when the price of beaver was on the slide and the cost of goods was rising with every season supplies came north on the Missouri. No matter the pinch they both found themselves in, the company tobacco was good and Tullock's private stock of rum was the best Titus had tasted since he had learned to drink Monangahela on that flatboat ride down the Ohio and Mississippi to New Orleans.

"I heard Beckwith's back in the mountains," Samuel Tullock had declared that summer evening when Bass rode over to Van Buren for some white company.

"Jim Beckwith? You was the one told me he'd give up on the mountains and gone back to St. Louis."

"He did. But the story is he growed tired of it. Beckwith's come back to the mountains."

"He come back to hook up with that band of Mountain Crow?"

Tullock shook his head as he swallowed some rum. "No. Word has it when he come west last summer, he went out the Platte Road. They say he's down at Fort Vasquez with them fellers—trading to the Arapaho and shining on some Cheyenne gals, I reckon."

"Hard to figger, 'cuz ever'thing I ever knowed of him—he was real tight with them Crow."

"Damn tight. Had him a handful of wives, and the Crow made him a war chief, some such," Tullock agreed.

"Why the hell didn't Beckwith come on back north, where he had him a good life?"

"Only thing I been able to figger since I heard he come back is that Beckwith don't wanna have nothing to do with this country up here where the smallpox was."

"Ain't the pox all done, Sam'l?"

Nodding, Tullock replied, "The pox is done, Scratch . . . but now there's talk around the tribes that it was Beckwith brung the pox to the Injuns up here."

"Beckwith?" Bass squeaked in disbelief. "He weren't even in this country back then. You and Levi told me one of the company boats brung the pox up the river a year ago."

Grudgingly Tullock agreed. "I know. Cain't be Beckwith brung the pox."

"But the truth don't matter none to the company, does it?"

The trader shook his head. "No it don't, Scratch. Truth is, the company done everything it can to pin this terrible thing on Beckwith."

"So now your booshways come out smelling sweet," Bass grumbled at the weighty injustice of it all, "seeing how they made damned sure the tribes believe it were Beckwith brought 'em the spotted death."

Jim Beckwith. Purty Jim Beckwith. Had him a sweet, sweet life with the Crow before he gave it up to try things back in St. Louis—

"Scratch!"

Blinking, Bass jerked at the sound of Sweete's cry, torn out of his reverie. Turning slightly, he found the big man pointing with the muzzle of his huge rifle.

Across the winding bed of Vermillion Creek the narrow valley rose sharply. Atop those low bluffs on the far side at least a dozen horsemen were coming to a halt.

Feathers hung from hair and shields and lances. Scalp locks waved beneath ponies' jaws, tormented by the gusts of icy wind. And every last goddamned one of those warriors sat there in the cold with frost streaming from his mouth as they all began to yell in exultation . . . suddenly jabbing heels into their ponies as they raced down the dull, reddish ocher of that hillside—coming on, coming on—close enough that Titus could see they were wearing paint.

Lots of damned paint. Those red niggers were decked out like no Injuns he had ever seen before.

One thing for certain—those sure as hell weren't Snakes riding down off the hills to make a white man feel welcome!

THIRTY

"Into the draw!"

As that command shot from his lips, Bass was already wheeling his pony in a circle so tight, the horse nearly raked its knees on the frozen ground. Yanking sharply with his right hand to force the horse around, Titus tugged the boy back against him so hard he heard little Flea gasp.

"Hang on, son!" he growled.

From behind, Scratch could hear the horsemen reach the narrow stream, charging their ponies right into the water thinly covered by a wind-rippled slake of dirty ice. How he wished they had one or two more hands along to aim the rifles.

At the brushy mouth of the draw he tore back on the reins, almost dragging the pony back onto its rear haunches in the skid. He waved the woman and girl on past him, followed closely by Samantha and the half-dozen packhorses. For the moment the warriors were bunched as they forded the stream, the first horsemen just then emerging from the Vermillion, leaping onto the bank, pony legs and bellies streaming water— those first painted warriors drawing back the strings on their small bows.

Out in the open between those bowmen and the mouth of

the coulee Shadrach Sweete looked ungainly on his snorting, heaving horse as it lumbered toward the wash beneath its rider's bulk. The big man was sitting funny, most of his weight shifted to that right stirrup where he was all but standing as he bobbed across the last few yards. Inch by inch his saddle shifted farther and farther to the right, the cinch scraping against the pony's belly while that right stirrup dropped closer and closer to the ground with every heaving leap of the horse.

Less than ten yards from the mouth of the wash the saddle spun under the animal's belly and the big man spilled into the gray, weathered sage with a grunt. With its saddle rocking under its belly like a clanger in a bell, the pony clattered into the draw to join its four-legged companions.

"C'mon, Shadrach!" Titus screamed as he handed Flea down to Waits-by-the-Water the moment she hit the ground.

Vaulting from the off side of the pony an instant later, Bass ripped the mittens from his hands and dragged the long muzzle of the flintlock from the blanket roll lashed behind his Spanish saddle. Scratch figured the fall had momentarily knocked the wind out of the man . . . but he wasn't prepared to find Sweete still crumpled on the ground. Unmoving.

"Get the guns, woman!" he flung the words over his shoulder in English, his breath a frosty streamer gone on the cold autumn wind. "All of 'em!"

Whirling, he dropped to a crouch and measured what distance the warriors had to cross before they got to Shad, before they could rush the entrance to their coulee. Drawing back on the set trigger, he brought the rifle to his shoulder just as Sweete raised his head, shook it slowly like a sleepy bear blinking awake of a spring morning after a long winter's nap.

Scratch flicked his eyes to the front blade, laying it within the notch at the bottom of the buckhorn rear sight, and poked his finger inside the front of the trigger guard. The closest horseman was starting to lean off his pony, the bowstring taut, his left arm straightened at his groggy target on the ground.

The moment the rifle roared, Sweete jerked awake. "Balls of thunder!"

Hearing the woman clatter up behind him, Titus turned, finding her arms filled with six long weapons. Leaning the empty rifle against the side of the wash, he quickly took the six from her, standing them in a row. With a loaded one in hand, he turned back to find the bowman had toppled into the sage, those closest around him reining their horses aside as they bawled in rage at the white men.

Shad crawled backward a few yards, starting away from the draw to snag his rifle from the sage, then struggled to stand onto one leg, dragging himself up hand over hand on the long-barreled flintlock. Pivoting, he hobbled into motion, lunging step by step toward the mouth of the wash.

"Goddammit!" Scratch bellowed. "Don't you lollygag, Shadrach!"

As the big man approached, Bass suddenly recognized how pasty Sweete's face was—almost the color of that pale limestone of the Ohio River valley.

Four of them were coming, swiftly snapping into focus over the tall man's shoulders. Bobbing side to side, they weaved atop their ponies, galloping straight for the lone white man. Shoving the second rifle against his shoulder, Bass felt inside the guard, finding this weapon did not have a set trigger. An arrow hissed into the sage at the big man's lumbering feet. Another *phtt*ed against the wall of the wash near Bass's head where it quivered inches from his eyes.

Instinctively, Titus wheeled the rifle, pinning the front blade onto that bowman's chest, and pulled the single trigger.

With a shrill cry the horseman toppled to the side off his pony, bounced once in the sage, then sprawled for a moment before he began to crawl slowly back from the mouth of the wash, blood smearing the frozen ground as he bravely retreated.

Bursting into the open, Scratch sprinted toward the big man. When he reached out with his arm, looping it around Shad, his left hand struck the arrow shaft, causing Sweete to emit an inhuman cry.

"Jehoshaphat—you're hit!"

Swallowing down that gush of pain as they hobbled into the wash together, Shad growled between clenched teeth, "You idjit! Figger I'm out there lollygagging on a Sunday stroll all for nothing?"

"Had me no idee you was out catching arrows, Shadrach," Bass apologized, helping him to collapse onto the good hip. "Woman!"

As Sweete groaned behind him, Waits was there in a heartbeat, handing him a third rifle and standing the empty weapon beside the first. He could see she had looped the strap of her shooting pouch over her shoulder. Turning her back on the men now, she yanked the stopper from the powder horn in her teeth and poured the black grains into a large brass measure that hung by a thin cord from her pouch strap.

Clicking back the hammer on the loaded rifle, Bass glanced at his children, finding Magpie huddled against the side of the draw and clutching Flea on her lap, both of them nearly hidden by a blanket Waits had draped over them and some brush.

Kneeling beside the wounded man, Scratch gripped Shad's knee. "What you figger to do with that arrow?"

"This'un?" Sweete said, holding up the long, bloody, headless shaft. "Damn if you ain't pulled it!"

Wagging his head, Shad said, "Nope—broke it."

"Save the goddamned thing, Shadrach. You're gonna wanna bite down on it when I go to digging in your hip with my skinner."

The big man's eyes went half-closed as he said, "Maybeso I can pray

I'll just bleed to death . . . or pray these goddamned Injuns kill me a'fore you get your knife in me—"

"You gonna be wuth a damn with that rifle of your'n?" he shut Sweete right up as he pivoted onto one knee and brought his own weapon up, hearing the approach of the pounding hooves.

"Them stupid niggers hurt me—" he bawled. "You goddamned right I'm gonna hurt 'em back!"

"I don't wanna waste two balls on one of the bastards," Scratch warned. "Which one you want?"

"You take that'un with the purty feathers round his head, and I'll bust the one with that red blanket."

At the last moment another warrior crossed his pony in front of the one wearing that wild spray of turkey feathers like a halo at the back of his head. Bass quickly shifted the front blade, held for that breathless moment, and squeezed the trigger. With its explosion the rifle shoved back into the notch of his shoulder with a completely different feel than he was accustomed to.

Beside him, Sweete's weapon roared.

Instantly Shad was dragging his pouch away from that wounded hip, the fingers of both hands crusted with his own frozen blood. "Hold 'em off while I reload!"

"Waits!" he shrieked in warning, wheeling the instant he heard the children cry, the empty rifle held out before him.

She was dropping to one knee as the muzzle of the weapon she clutched swung upward in a jagged arc. With the buttstock pressed against her hip, she fired over the heads of the children—aiming at the horseman who had just skidded to a halt at the brow of the wash, directly over Magpie's head.

The lead ball struck the Sioux pony just below the eye, slamming the animal's head to the side as it crumpled, the warrior leaping off as his horse flopped into the sage. With a grunt he clambered off his knees, tore an arrow from his left hand, nocking it against the bowstring he drew backward with one smooth motion.

Lunging to the side, Titus threw his shoulder against his wife, pitching Waits-by-the-Water to the ground as he yanked a pistol from his belt. Dragging back the hammer, he pulled the trigger as the bowstring snapped forward. The arrow pierced the flap of his elk-hide coat as the ball caught the warrior just below the breastbone, crumpling him in half as he was driven backward from the brow of the wash.

"You loaded yet, Shadrach?" he cried as he reached down to pick the woman out of the brush and wheel her behind him.

"I am now!"

Shoving the empty pistol into her hand, Bass dragged the second loaded pistol from his belt, never taking his eyes off the top of the draw where the warrior had landed. Up there the only sound was the gentle pawing of the pony that lay dying in the sage, one solitary leg flexing across the flaky, frozen ground.

"Load," he whispered to her as he stepped away, "then take a gun to him!"

The moment she nodded in understanding, he was moving in a crouch, roostering another ten yards into the brushy wash where he pulled himself up the side of the draw.

Behind him Sweete's rifle roared, and he heard Shadrach whoop.

Slowly he hoisted himself against the hard-packed erosion of that coulee until his eyes could peer over the top. Off to his left lay the pony, totally still now. Far beyond it whirled six or seven of the horsemen, gathering among the willow and brush on the north bank of Vermillion Creek.

In that cold silence he heard the gurgle. Poking his head up a little farther, Scratch spotted the warrior less than five yards away. Lying on his back in the sage, the wounded man had drawn his knees up, clutching his belly with both hands, dark, glistening ooze creeping out between the fingers. As Bass hitched himself over the lip of the draw, the dying man slowly flopped his head from side to side, groaning, gurgling, and coughing as more of the shimmering ooze seeped from the side of his mouth, onto his bronze cheek, spilling down his neck into his unfettered hair.

Hooves pounded on the hard ground with a dull, hollow thud.

Clumsily whirling, Scratch clutched the side of the wash with his left hand as he dug in with the toes of his moccasins. And found another horseman bursting into view on the far side of the wash.

Scratch heaved upward, dragging himself onto the top where he lay on his belly, planting his two elbows against the flinty ground, leveling the pistol at the warrior who appeared surprised to find the white man there.

Yanking back on his rein so suddenly that he almost lost his balance, the horseman struggled to hang on to his pony as it reared, then reared again. Bass fired the pistol as the warrior was catapulted into the air. The pony staggered aside, spilling onto its forelegs. Dragging its muzzle out of the sage, the wounded horse struggled back onto its legs, spinning into a retreat.

Titus immediately wished he had used the lead ball on the warrior who clambered to his feet now and staggered away, dragging a leg painfully, clutching a hip with one hand.

"Where are you, Scratch?"

The moment he twisted to crane his head over the edge of the wash, Bass heard another boom from the mouth of the draw. Below the spreading patch of oily gun smoke, Sweete handed the woman the empty weapon and took a loaded rifle from her. Below him he could make out Flea's inconsolable whimper and Magpie's voice attempting to soothe her little brother.

Realizing his mouth was dry, that he was breathing fast and shallow, Scratch quickly surveyed their plight. While the coulee had given them some temporary shelter the moment the war party had charged, that coulee might well be their mass grave if the horsemen were able to take up positions above them. Like shooting fish in a rain barrel.

There were six or seven of them retreating from the open ground where Sweete had spilled another warrior from his pony. Six of them, he counted carefully now—a half dozen reining up at the tree line. Likely the horsemen didn't know they were still within range of the trappers' big guns . . . then again, they might well realize it but figure the white men weren't going to empty one of their guns attempting to shoot at them across this distance. It appeared the milling warriors were arguing, pointing, planning. Far off to the left he watched the unhorsed warrior hobbling toward the creek, the wind shoving a black braid across the middle of his face.

"Goddammit, Scratch!" the big man's voice called out. "You alive?"

Rolling to his left, Bass noisily slid down the side of the coulee. Magpie choked off a sob in her throat as he skidded to a stop before her, crouched, and hugged the children.

"Stay here," he whispered in Crow. "You're safe right here."

"Hush! Father needs you to be quiet, Flea," she reminded the boy as Titus continued to the mouth of the draw.

"Damn you, Bass!" Sweete growled. "Least you could've done was answer me—"

"I was a little tied up with two of 'em, Shadrach," he snapped.

Sweete's eyes instantly flicked to the deep interior of the brushy wash, up to the bare rim of the gully. "What you figger we can do?"

Glancing down at the blood smear across the big man's blanket capote, he gazed into Sweete's eyes. "I don't figger you're much for getting around right now."

Shad reluctantly shook his head.

"Best you stay here," he explained, motioning Waits to come over. " 'Tween the two of you, keep them rifles loaded—always have two of 'em ready."

For a moment Sweete studied the middistance, staring at the horsemen gesturing and yelling among themselves. One of them broke from the group and started toward the north, racing to reach the warrior who hobbled across the sage on foot.

Shad said, "Two guns. That still leaves four of them niggers. They split up and slip around on top of the hill up there—"

"That's four we know of," Bass interrupted, worried to the soles of his feet. With a burst of inspiration it came to him. "I dropped one of their

horses up there, Shadrach. Maybeso I can hunker down behind that carcass where they won't see a thing till they're right on top of me, and I can
throw some lead at 'em while they skedaddle back out of range."

"You're only gonna have one chance at it," Sweete warned. "Once
they know you're up there, them Injuns either stay shy of you or . . .
they'll come ride you into the ground."

"Here I figured you had some faith in me, Shadrach."

His lips pressed into a grim line, Sweete nodded. "I do got faith in
you, Scratch. Don't you ever doubt it."

"Waits-by-the-Water," he said in Crow, turning to the woman, "are
all the weapons loaded?"

She nodded. "Give me your belt guns and I will load them too."

"When you do, keep them for yourself," Bass said. "If things turn
out badly"—and his eyes flicked at the children—"make sure the young
ones do not suffer from these enemies."

Laying a hand on top of his, Waits said, "We have seen one another
through worse than this, husband. None of us are afraid."

Those words reassured him, perhaps because he himself was damned
scared.

"There are five loaded pistols in my saddlebags," he said, squeezing
her cold hand. "Get them. I will take two with me and leave the others
with you."

Then he turned to his partner and said in English, "Soon as she's
loaded these here two pistols, you'll have five. I'm taking two with me, and
three of them rifles."

Nodding once, Sweete said, "Between us, we oughtta cut down the
last of these bastards purty quick."

Bass glanced at the sky, finding the pale, buttermilk-yellow globe
sinking toward the west beyond the hills on the far side of the creek. "I'd
sure like to drive them off a'fore nightfall. Maybe we could slip on in to
the post when it gets good and dark."

"How far you figger it to the fort?"

After calculating a few moments, he sighed. "Don't know. Maybe ten
miles."

"That'd take half the night, less'n we run flat-out."

"You figger it better to lay here waiting till morning—when more of
'em might show come sunup, or try to slip off and make a run for it?"

Shrugging, Sweete answered, "I don't figger we got anything but bad
choices to make right now."

He laid a hand on the big man's shoulder. "Then let's see how many
of them red niggers we can knock down a'fore it gets dark."

For a moment Sweete laid his bloody paw atop Bass's hand. "You
watch your topknot, Scratch."

With a grin he started away for the rifles. "Keep 'em busy as you can out front, and I'll doe-see-doe with the rest."

"Bass?"

Titus stopped in a crouch and turned there on the floor of the wash. Shad blinked once, then asked, "Who you s'pose they are?"

Peering past the mouth of the draw, Bass eventually said, "From what them Snakes was telling that feller named Sinclair—I figger you and me just been interduced to the Sioux, Shadrach."

"Then I reckon we should teach these niggers they better watch their manners around us free men."

"That's right, Shadrach," he replied, taking two of the loaded pistols from his wife's hands, stuffing them into his belt. "No Injun better go stirring up trouble with the likes of us two."

As he stopped by the stack of rifles to select three of the long weapons, Titus thought how good it was that Shadrach Sweete should now regard himself as a free man. After all these years in the mountains, every one of them endured as a company trapper—from those youthful days as an Ashley man, through that golden era reigned over by the various incarnations of the Rocky Mountain Fur Company, and on to these final days as the huge St. Louis monopoly strangled the last breath out of the beaver business—Sweete was at last his own man.

Not that Titus had ever heard the man complain of his lot. Quite the contrary, for Shad, like Joe Meek, enjoyed a reputation as a merry soul, always seeking the bright side of every dire situation.

Titus sensed a genuine feeling of immense satisfaction that by quitting the company at rendezvous more than four months ago, Sweete now regarded himself as a free man at last. Only trouble was, with a partner, there wasn't any well-manned brigade to scare off war parties. More often than not free men died alone and in pairs. Anonymous. No others to know where their bones lay for the magpies and the wolves to scatter.

Angrily he shut his eyes a moment, opening them to look at his daughter and son. Flea waved innocently to his father, then gazed up at his sister. She nodded and the boy waved again. Bass smiled at them, turned, and trudged away, penetrating the brush at the head of the draw.

Standing the rifles against the side of the wash, he clawed his way up to the edge and peered over—locating the dead pony. After sliding back to the bottom, he carried the weapons to the top one at a time and laid them on the lip of the prairie, finally legging his way over with the third rifle.

In bellying through the sage to the pony's side, Titus passed the fallen warrior. The chertlike eyes stared unblinking at the cold, dimming sky overhead, slowly glazing as they lost their luster in these first minutes following death.

Titus dragged the last rifle between the horse's legs as one of Shad's guns boomed. Below, at the mouth of the draw, the big man yelped, *kip-kip-keeyi*-ing like a coyote. Out on the flat three of the warriors set up their own wolf howl, one of them suddenly nudging his pony into a gallop so he could ride back and forth past the white man in a bravery run. Peering out from that shelter of the dead horse's legs, the smell of its frozen blood not disagreeable, Scratch thought the daring warrior made a fine target of himself. He pushed one of the rifles forward, settling it back against his shoulder.

Then he remembered. As tempting a target as that rider might be, if he did fire, Scratch realized the enemy would know he was up there and his surprise would be ruined. So instead he watched the brazen horseman dash back and forth while the other two looked on—

Two? Them and the rider, they made for three. And that meant there was another trio he could not account for as he studied the creek bottom.

Inching his head a little higher, Scratch cautiously peered across more than one hundred eighty degrees of that river valley, searching for the other horsemen in what light was left to that late afternoon. Try as he might, he couldn't locate them among the trees and brush lining the flat. Down below he heard Waits's voice—likely talking low to the children. And he thought he heard Sweete—more than likely talking to himself, if not to those three warriors.

Maybe the light would drain from the sky and night would fall before they had any more trouble. Then they could just slip away into the dark—

The missing trio of horsemen popped up at the brow of the hill right above him, as if they had sprung right out of the sagebrush itself.

Scratch wasn't hidden behind the horse. No, not with them coming from the opposite direction now.

He stayed flat on his belly, his breath stilled, watching them kick their ponies into a gallop as they broke the crest, beginning to shriek and holler. They weren't racing for his side of the gully. Instead, the horsemen were reining for the far side.

Which damn well might mean they hadn't spotted him lying there in the shadow of the dead pony's legs, smelling its dried blood pungently metallic on the cold wind.

As the clatter of their hooves grew louder, he heard Waits scream at the bottom of the coulee, her yell stifled the moment she realized she had caused Magpie and Flea to cry out. How he wanted to yell—try to reassure them . . . even to turn and look at the flat ground to see if the reason Waits had cried was that the other three were charging in to ride right over Shad.

But Scratch assumed that's just what the bottom three were doing: coming from that direction, holding the attention of the two white riflemen, while another trio swept around and over the top of the hill to trap the enemy in their graves at the bottom of the wash.

Not today, goddammit.

When they were sixty yards away, Bass decided he had two shots to make from the three rifles. Take one by surprise, then get another warrior riding away before a third was too far and chancy in the coming gloom.

Forty yards.

But if he felt really lucky, he might just scramble to the top of the hill to take a shot at that third horseman.

Grabbing a smoothbore for this closest shot, he swung the muzzle across the pony's stiffened leg, resting the forestock atop the foreflank. Snapping the big hammer back to full cock, he laid the stock against his cheek, picked the target, and let his breath out halfway. Held . . . then pulled the single trigger.

With a bright gush of light the pan ignited, but the rifle did not fire.

Suddenly screaming with that discovery of the white man in hiding, the warriors reined up, hooves skidding as Bass pitched the smoothbore aside.

He rose to his knees as the warriors attempted to settle their frightened ponies, trying their best to get a fix on the white man and fire their bows at the enemy. To full cock went the rifle's hammer. This might well be his last chance to drop one of them.

Over the gray cloud he watched a horseman spill backward off the rear of his pony, his long blanket coat and the coil of rope the warrior had tucked beneath his belt becoming entangled with the animal's legs.

Turning to lay the rifle aside and take up the last of the weapons, Bass heard the arrow smack into the carcass right where his left shoulder had been a moment before. Grabbing the loaded smoothbore, Scratch felt that shoulder ache . . . remembering the Arapaho arrow that had fully skewered the very same shoulder more than five winters before.

Sweete's gun boomed again from the wash below.

Another arrow slammed into the flinty ground before him, then one tugged at the coyote-fur cap he had pulled down over his ears, knocking it so the fur slipped down, blinding him. Angrily tugging it back with his left hand, Scratch felt the shaft that had pierced the cap.

"Not near good enough!" he roared at them, tearing the cap from his head before he laid the forestock of the fusil along the horse's shoulder and took aim.

He knew he had the man even before the smoke cleared and he saw that second riderless horse clattering away. The moment the last warrior sat there, daring him, throwing an arm into the air and shaking his bow at the white man—shrieking an oath—Bass cursed the misfire of that first smoothbore.

Leaping up as the fusil tumbled to the ground, Scratch drew the old

English horse pistol from his belt. Of the three, it had the longest barrel—the best chance to make this shot at more than twenty-five yards.

With both hands gripping the butt, he yanked back on the dragon's-head hammer, bringing the end of the muzzle down on his target limned in the fading light, intending to hold a little high. In the instant he was slipping his bare finger inside the big half-round trigger guard, Bass heard the hooves behind his right shoulder.

Not moving the pistol or his arms, the white man turned his head, finding a warrior had forsaken his attack on the mouth of the draw to ride up the slope to the aid of those at the top of the hill.

Coming out of the west, horse and horseman were one liquid shadow . . . the bow brought up—

As Bass whirled, his arms still extended and wrists locked together, he dropped to one knee there in the crescent of the dead pony's frozen legs. With a breathless pause in the cold autumn wind, he heard the rawhide bowstring *thwung* a heartbeat before his finger flexed, firing at that widest part of the shadow crowning the pony.

In that instant before the wind rose once again and the air possessed such a stillness, the ball slammed into its target, driving the air from the man's lungs with a grunt, immediately followed by a second grunt as the warrior smacked the ground. His pony dashed on past as the Indian's body disappeared into that gloom inking the ground with an indelible darkness.

"Balls of thunder!" Sweete called out from the gloom. "How many of 'em you got up there, Bass?"

Even as that breath of frozen wind gusted there in the wake of Shad's words, Scratch heard the rustle of dry sage, the grinding of the flaky ground. All of it meaning that the warrior he had unhorsed was moving, maybe crawling—still alive.

"Goddammit—stay down here, woman!"

Bass spun around at Sweete's warning cry. Squinting hard, he could not make out anything but liquid indigo in the wash below him now that the sun had sunk, leaving nothing more than a band of lavender along the rocky breast of the far hills.

He licked his lips, desperately working to finger just the right words in Crow. "Stay with the children," he ordered her.

"Ti-tuzz—"

"The children! Stay with them until this is over!"

A sigh of relief gushed from him, and that next moment Bass heard the faintest trace of sound from the sage. Almost as if he could hear the man breathing hard as he pulled himself along the frozen ground. Those sounds disappeared the moment Scratch turned, began moving in their direction through the growing darkness.

Bass was all but upon the warrior before he made out the horseman sprawled among the low clumps of sage. Bass stopped there near the Indian's moccasins. His eyes slowly swept the valley, straining to find any more attackers. Realizing his blood pounded in his ears, that he still held the empty pistol at the end of both extended arms, Scratch slowly brought the weapon down—staring now at the warrior who had his eyes fixed on the white man.

"Bass?"

"Up here," he said tersely.

Then softly, so much in a whisper that Titus wasn't sure at first, the warrior began to sing. More a discordant chant as the man huffed his medicine song, obviously in great pain.

"Where you, Bass?"

"Keep coming—you'll find me."

With two more steps Scratch stood directly over the warrior. In the enemy's belt were a knife and a tomahawk, neither of which he had pulled to defend himself. As Titus started to kneel over the warrior, the man jerked his fingers to the handle of that knife, but Bass grabbed the wrist before the weapon could clear the scabbard.

"Goddamn, it got dark quick," Sweete grumbled as he slid over the side of the draw, stood painfully, getting his bearings.

"There ain't no more of 'em to worry about down your way?" Scratch asked as he stuffed his pistol away in his belt, then quickly pried the warrior's fingers loose from the knife handle.

He ripped the tomahawk from the belt and stood.

"There's maybe two still down there in the brush," Sweete explained as he came to a stop on the other side of the warrior.

The Indian's eyes flicked in fear as the tall trapper stared down at him. Then the warrior's eyes quickly filled with loathing.

Scratch said, "I figger it's time for us to make a run for that post."

"Why—we can hold off them two niggers 'thout making our balls sweat."

"Think hard on it, Shadrach," he whispered. "What Injuns did we figger these are?"

"Likely them Sioux the Snakes warned was riding through this country."

"And if them Sioux was coming all the way over here where they never been a'fore . . . you figger there'd be only ten or a dozen of 'em come?"

Sweete sighed. "No. They'd send a whole shitteree of 'em."

"So when these don't show up tonight, things gonna get hot around here," Titus explained. "I'm gonna make a run for the fort with the young'uns."

"What about this'un here? You wanna finish him?"

For a moment more Bass thought on it. "Time was, I would have. Might kill me a nigger like this again one day . . . but this'un I'll let go."

"Just free as you please?"

Of a sudden it struck him what to do. "No. If the rest of them Sioux find this nigger alive—find all the rest of 'em dead—I want this son of a bitch to tell all the rest what happened."

"Like that story you tell when you found the bastard what scalped you," Shad declared.

"I'm gonna make sure this'un will never walk right again." Bass knelt over the man. "So he'll never run in his life. Help me turn him over."

"What you fixing to do?" Sweete asked as he roughly rolled the smaller man over, held the Indian down with his weight.

Scooting down to the warrior's feet, Titus pulled up the bottom of his blanket legging, then dragged down the top of the man's winter moccasin, exposing the taut strap of tendon at the back of the ankle. Grabbing the Sioux's foot with his left hand, he braced it and himself as he brought his skinning knife down, raking it brutally across the back of the tendon, severing it completely as the warrior grunted with a muffled cry.

"Man what can't walk," Bass declared, rising, wiping the knife off across his own legging, "that man can't never be a warrior no more."

THIRTY-ONE

Times was hard. Goods come at a king's ransom and peltries was low. But never would there be a shortage of Injuns!

'Cept up north where some said the Blackfoot was no more. Even so . . . it didn't take both of Bass's eyes to see that the Sioux and Shians could turn into devils their own selves and drag hell right out of its shuck.

That long, cold night Flea rode with his mother. Times when a boy gets scared good, seemed what he needed most was the arms of a woman wrapped around him. Magpie held her own, stayed quiet atop her own pony as they hurried to mount up again, putting out on the trail down Vermillion Creek for the trading post. She'd make some man a fine wife one day, he thought as they urged their horses into a gentle lope that night beneath the cold stars. Already she was a female who did her level best to understand what needed doing . . . and did it without a complaint.

That long night he thanked the sky more than once that Magpie had a lot of her mamma in her.

From where Sweete rode at the back of the pack, grunting down his pain, the big man kept an eye peeled so that no one would slip up on them out of the dark. Then, just before dawn, they loped into the narrow, high-rimmed valley of the Green through this only portal along the Vermillion, and spotted that crude stockade standing beside the river less than a mile off. Shad kicked his horse into a full gallop, racing to catch Bass at the head of the pack.

"Trouble?" Scratch asked, his eyes flicking to the big man, then watching the gray horizon bobbing behind Sweete's shoulders.

"I just been listening hard all night," he announced as he pulled back on the reins to ease his big horse down into a lope alongside Bass. "Think we been follered all the way."

"The two of 'em?"

"Yep," Shad replied. "I figger they dogged our trail hoping to find a place to jump us again when we dropped our guard."

"No figgering to it now," Titus explained. "Lookee there."

Twisting in the saddle, Sweete turned to look behind them at that place along the skyline where Bass was pointing. Two shadowy horsemen reined up atop the bluff as the trappers and their party continued into the valley.

"Thunder's balls—they was there all night, Scratch."

Nodding, Titus said, "Only reason they pulled off was they see'd the fort, see'd all the stock out grazing."

"And they don't reckon to pick a fight when the odds is so bad against 'em."

"Trouble is," Scratch growled, "if them bastards didn't know this here fort was here, they know now."

Across the meadow that surrounded the post on three sides, most of the horses and mules busily grazing in that dawn's light lifted their heads at the clatter of hooves, then began to drift away from the path of the oncoming strangers streaming toward them at a lope. Inside the stockade ahead a voice called out, followed by the bleat of a goat.

Bass hadn't heard that sound . . . since Taos that winter of thirty-four. Better than five years ago. There were traders up and down the South Platte, two posts here west of the mountains, so just how was Josiah faring now? Had he made a go of it with those trade goods down in the Mexican settlements?

The narrow gate at the east side of the stockade was shoved open, and a lone figure stepped out guardedly, a rifle in hand as Bass and Sweete slowed their outfit.

"Who goes there?"

"That you, Sinclair?"

"No," the voice cried as Scratch came to a halt. "Name's Thompson."

At that moment a goat butted its way through the gate and dived out between the man's legs.

"Son of a bitch!" Thompson snarled as he bolted into motion. "Get back here, you!" He was after the goat in a sprint, but within a few steps he slid to a stop and grumbled at the animal, "To hell with you. Go get et up by wolves for all I care."

Easing his mount up close to the man, Bass held down his hand. "You was gone last time we was here."

"Me and Billy Craig got back with supplies from St. Louis more'n two weeks ago," Thompson explained.

"Sinclair said you went for them trade goods," Shad declared as he dropped to the ground, "but he didn't say nothing 'bout you bringing no goats."

Thompson shook hands with the big man, then said, "I joined up with Sublette and Vaskiss's supply train when they come out with their goods. Didn't always intend to bring goats—started with some pigs . . . but them bastards couldn't make it walking all the way. So a'fore I pushed out of Independence, I traded my pigs for some goats."

"You got more'n that one?" Scratch asked as he glanced over at the children, seeing their sleepy eyes widen as they followed the antics of that strange new animal scampering around the legs of their horses.

"Made it with eight," Thompson said. "If'n the coyotes don't get that damned runaway. Maybe we ought'n just shoot it and cook it on a spit."

"Ho!" Sinclair called from the gate, emerging as he dragged leather braces over his shoulders, stuffing his cloth shirt into the waistband of his leather britches. "Bass and Sweete, ain't it?"

"That's right," and Scratch came out of the saddle to step up and shake hands.

Prewett asked, "How was your fall hunt?"

Bass turned to eye the rim of the valley. "Hunt was poor, wuss'n I figgered . . . but the ride in here was enough to pucker a man's bunghole."

"Injuns?" Thompson asked.

Pointing with his outstretched arm, Bass declared, "We left some dead bodies back there at sundown."

"You rode in all night?"

"Two of 'em followed us," Scratch said, "so there's likely more."

"What are they?" Thompson asked.

With a shrug Sweete said, "Sinclair here said the Snakes come through here earlier in the fall lay that they're Sioux."

"That true, Prewett?" Thompson asked.

Sinclair nodded once. " 'Cuz of them, the Snakes gone and left the hole early in the fall. I done my best to keep the stock in close, just in case they made a jump on the fort, till you and Billy got back."

Thompson turned back to Sweete. "That woman and those young'uns of yours likely tired from your ride—"

"They ain't mine," Shad said.

So the trader turned to Bass. "Why don't you boys tie off your stock close to the wall and bring them on in for some breakfast? We'll make a place on the floor of a storeroom for them young'uns to sleep after their bellies is full."

"You got any flour?" Shad asked.

"Got some, yes," Thompson replied.

"Cornmeal?"

"Some of that too," Sinclair answered this time.

Smiling broadly, Scratch slapped Sweete on the shoulder. "Keep your flour for this flatland nigger, trader man. Ever since Taos many winters ago, Titus Bass been half-froze for corn cakes!"

By nightfall it was evident a storm lay across the horizon, and by the following morning a half foot of new snow had blanketed everything. Two days later the first trappers working the surrounding area began trudging in—by and large every one of them men who had forsaken ever again working for the fur monopoly threatening to abandon them. Joe Walker showed up with only his Shoshone squaw along, announcing he expected to stay only as long as it took for the weather to clear before he would turn north to search out the village of his wife's people for the winter. Kit Carson and his bunch straggled in from the southwest, having found the trapping difficult over in the Uintah country. And just past nightfall on the third day Joe Meek and Robert Newell showed up at the gate. The wet winter storm caught them on their way back from Fort Hall where they had left their wives.

Now some thirty-five trappers, along with assorted wives and children, had congregated at Fort Davy Crockett with winter's first hard blast.

From dawn till dusk across those next three days while the weather slowly cleared, either Shad or Titus stayed out with their grazing animals, guardedly watching the tall hills that surrounded the post. For the most part, the partners preferred using that part of the bottom ground just north of the fort, which placed the stockade somewhere roughly between their horses and that Vermillion Creek portal.

If the sun put in an appearance, Waits-by-the-Water and the children abandoned the stockade walls to spend the day beneath the canopy Titus stretched between some of the old cottonwoods. Around a small fire the woman tanned and stretched hides, made extra moccasins for her family, or fussed over a special piece of decorative quillwork while Magpie and Flea played, napped, and played some more there within that small grove.

Each night at sundown nearly everyone bustled back inside the mud-and-log walls for supper and some storytelling until the fire burned low, when folks slipped off for their camps outside the stockade. Every morning when Bass and Sweete untied their hobbled animals and led them outside the walls to graze, one of the three traders dragged their seven goats out to graze. One at a time each animal was led out to a small, low corral attached to the south wall, then tied with a short length of rope the cantankerous goats tried to chew until they were turned loose to spend their day in the enclosure with their own kind.

Just before dawn on the sixth day, the Sioux struck.

"Roll out! Roll out!"

With that shrill cry raised by those camped outside the stockade walls, Scratch flung the blankets and robe aside to scoop up his moccasins. When he had pulled on the outer, or winter, pair, he turned back to kiss Waits on the forehead, then quickly touched both of the children on the cheek.

"Stay here with them," he ordered. "No matter what—you stay here."

Shoving both arms into his coat, he snatched up a brace of pistols and two rifles, looping his shooting pouch onto his left shoulder.

In the fort's cluttered courtyard the seven goats bleated and bawled—but nowhere near as loud as Samantha's bray, growing noisy at the outside corner of the wall where she had been tied and hobbled near their horses.

One weapon boomed on the flat, followed quickly by two more. Sweete was behind him as he sprinted for the gate where one after another the trappers streamed through, joining those who had camped outside the walls. As Shad and Scratch peeled to the left, others tore to the right. Samantha and their nervous horses fought against their hobbles, yanking against their halters as the two darted among them.

"Make sure them ropes'll hold," Sweete called out above the many other voices and sporadic gunfire.

A minute later Titus hollered, "Grab your horse and follow me, Shad!"

Bareback, both of them broke from the rest of their animals, loping to join the many who were on foot, racing after the retreating warriors who were driving off what appeared to be more than a hundred horses.

"They get 'em all?" Sweete bellowed as he came to a halt among the half-dressed men.

"Not all," Meek declared as he peered up at Shadrach.

Carson pointed to the north of the post, saying, "No more'n a dozen horses left back yonder."

Some of the angry trappers hurled oaths, flung fists into the air, while others continued to fire at the backs of the retreating warriors.

"My way of thinking," Bass announced, "you niggers got in a bad habit of letting your stock graze free as you please."

"But there ain't never been no bad niggers in the Hole!" Thompson argued.

"How was we to know?" cried Dick Owens, a partner of Carson's.

"Think about it, boys," Scratch said. "What you figger them Sioux come all this way for if'n it weren't to grab your horses?"

"Them really Sioux?" asked one of the group.

"Ain't no goddamned Snakes gonna steal horses from us!" Walker snorted.

"Likely they was more of that same bunch we run onto," Scratch told them. "They been sniffing round here for the better part of a week, ever since we rode in here."

"How many you see?" Sweete inquired of one of the disgusted men returning from upstream.

"Three dozen."

But another man argued, "More'n that. Goddamned well more'n that."

"We'd give 'em a good fight—they come back to take their whupping," Newell grumbled.

"They ain't," Thompson cried as he stomped up to the group. "Appears they run off least a hundred fifty head of prime stock. Mine and yours all, boys."

"You figger to go after them horses?" Meek challenged.

The trader looked over the group, then turned to Meek. "I'll take some of these fellas with me. You can lead 'nother bunch if you take a mind to, Joe. Maybeso we can trap them redbellies between us."

"If'n they don't outrun us, Philip," Newell observed.

"You giving up a'fore you start, Doc?" the trader snarled.

"No, I'll go with Meek's group—"

"Any the rest of you don't figger you got the balls to go tracking them Sioux, you best stay back here with Craig and Sinclair to mind the post," Thompson flung his challenge at them all. "As for me, I'm gonna get them horses back, 'long with some Sioux ha'r hanging from my belt!"

Scratch and Shad volunteered to ride with Joe Meek, the first band after the thieves. Once they pushed through that narrow portal of the Vermillion, it was plain to see how carefully the Sioux had planned their escape. From that point all the way to the distant foothills, the raiders could push the horses flat-out with little to stand in their way. The Sioux had a good start on them, and it would take more than luck and skill to ever catch up with the thieves.

Still, a man had to try.

They rode down the rest of that day and on into the night, knowing full well the Sioux weren't going to stop until they were assured no one was dogging their backtrail. Dawn came, and the trappers' animals were showing need of rest and water. At the next trickle they found at the bottom of a creekbed, the trappers grabbed a little of both before moving on.

"Joe!" Bass hollered late that second afternoon. "Pull up top of that hill so we can palaver!"

Their horses snorted as the rest of the avengers came to a halt around them.

"What you got on your mind, Titus?"

He asked, "Is it as plain to you boys as it is to me that we ain't gonna catch them Injuns?"

Meek and some of the others squinted into the distance at the wide trail they were following. They hadn't seen the horses or the thieves since sundown the day before.

Joe looked over the others, many of whom hung their heads wearily. He eventually said, "I s'pose we ain't."

"And what if we did?" Titus asked. "Count the heads here—then remember how many riders them Sioux had."

"Where is Thompson's bunch, anyways?" Carson growled, turning in the saddle to look down their backtrail.

Shad spoke up. "They ain't ever gonna have a chance of cutting off the Sioux with us if they ain't caught up with us by now."

"Maybeso we ought go on," Meek suggested, but no more than half-heartedly.

"We do that, Joe," Scratch said, wagging his head, "pushing our own horses so damned hard—we're like' to lose the ones we got a'fore we ever do turn back to the post."

"Bass is right," Sweete declared. " 'Member them two carcasses we come across already?"

"Them were my horses the bastards run into the ground!" Carson squealed. "Sure wanna get me their hair for killing my horses!"

Shrugging, Meek said, "I see it the way Scratch's stick floats. We can keep on chasing them horse thieves and kill what horses we got under us to do it . . . or we can take our lumps and mosey on back to the fort 'thout losing any more."

The bunch grumbled, but no one said a thing against turning around. No one really had to because the choices were clear. Continue the chase and fight the overwhelming odds that they would lose what they still had, or head for Fort Davy Crockett. As much as it stung to turn around, Bass figured those horses weren't worth all of those men dying out there.

"Sure sours my milk to give up," Scratch admitted. "But I got my family at the fort. If I go and run the legs out from under this here horse, chances are good I won't get back there to see 'em."

Many of the others had squaws and children waiting in the shadows of the fort walls too. Grudgingly, they agreed.

"Keep your eyes peeled on the way back," Sweete suggested. "Sing out if'n you spot sign of Thompson's bunch."

But they didn't. Not even a dust cloud. And none of them heard anything that night as they made camp astride the trail left behind by the stolen herd. Nor did they see anything of the others throughout the next day. Meek's dozen riders reached the walls of Fort Davy Crockett late the next day, surprised to find that no word had come in from Thompson's group.

Then a week passed. And another. Finally more than a month of waiting and wondering ground by, and most of the trappers figured on the worst. Even Philip Thompson's Ute squaw had completed mourning her dead husband and was in the process of taking up with one of Joe Walker's men when word of Thompson's men reached Fort Davy Crockett.

"Sinclair!" shouted a man, bursting into Prewett Sinclair's trading room late one afternoon early that winter of thirty-nine. "You better come out and talk with these Snakes."

"Visitors? Tell 'em they can send two in here at a time to trade—"

"They don't wanna trade," the man interrupted Sinclair. "This bunch is 'bout as edgy as a pouch full of scalded cats."

Sinclair glanced about the smoke-filled room. "Any of you know Snake?"

"Used to know a little," Bass admitted. "Spent some time healing up in a Snake lodge long time back."

Walker set his cup down on the plank table. "With what I learned from that woman of mine, I figger I can help you on what Scratch don't know."

"You boys give it a try for me?" Sinclair asked. "See what's got this bunch so riled?"

Sinclair, Sweete, and a half-dozen others followed Scratch and Walker out the gate to find more than twenty warriors arrayed in a wide front some twenty yards from the fort wall. Every one of the horsemen had their weapons in view and their shields uncovered. That was a bad sign in any language.

Scratching at his memory to recall what he could of the Shoshone tongue, Bass called out, "Who leads this group?"

"I do," a man called out as he urged his horse forward a few yards and came to a halt. Two others came up and stopped a yard behind him. "I am Rain."

"The trader invites Rain and his warriors to trade," Walker explained. "Two warriors can come in the wood lodge at a time—"

"I am not here to trade with Sinclair."

"You know the trader?" Walker asked.

"Yes, I have come here often," Rain replied. "My people always thought he was a good man."

"No more?"

Rain shook his head. "Sinclair's friend stole horses from us."

Walker and Bass looked at one another, both bewildered. "Who is this friend stole your horses?"

"The one with the pointed chin," Rain answered.

"What's he saying?" Sinclair asked.

Bass shushed Sinclair as Walker continued. "This one with the pointed chin—you're sure he stole horses from you?"

"Yes. He and others came to spend two nights with us," Rain continued the amazing story. "They said they were on their way south to the white man post on the Sage River.* They were leading some horses they boasted they had stolen from the men at the Snake River fort."

"How many horses did they steal from that fort?"

"At least three times the fingers on my one hand. And when they left our village to continue south, they took more than twice as many more horses from us!"

"This is not good," Bass muttered to Walker, shaking his head.

Joe Walker asked the chief, "What do you want the trader Sinclair to do?"

"We want our horses back," Rain declared firmly. "We came to take scalps—but we want the scalps of those who stole horses from us. They are white men with no honor: to steal from other white men, then steal from Indians they say are their friends. We honored them with our hospitality— fed them, let them sleep in our robes. What sort of man would steal from us after we treated him as one of our own?"

Bass thought a moment, then said, "Their scalps are not worth the trouble, Rain. Will you let us go after the thieves?"

Rain talked low to the warriors behind him, then asked, "You white men will go after the others and get our horses back?"

"We can try," Titus said. "If we find them, we will bring the ponies to you."

"And if you don't," Rain vowed, "my band will no longer be a friend to this place and all who camp here. My men will return to steal the horses from this place."

Grimly, Joe Walker asked, "How long will you give us?"

Peering at the half-moon rising in the late-afternoon sky for a long moment, the war chief finally said, "Indian-talkers, you will have till the moon grows fat. Then we will be back to take the horses that graze in this meadow . . . along with the scalps of every man, woman, and child still here when we return."

·   ·   ·

---

* *What the Shoshone called the Uintah River, in the extreme northeastern corner of present-day Utah, where Antoine Robidoux erected his small fur post near the Uintah's junction with the Green*

"Can't understand how I figured Thompson wrong," William Craig moaned at their fire that third night on their cold ride down the Green.

"Folks change," Joe Walker said as he slid the blade of his knife round and round on the whetting stone.

Robert Newell asked, "You figure to use that knife on Thompson?"

"Maybe he should," Titus Bass roared abruptly, surprising them all. "Man just up and turns his coat like Thompson and them others—maybe it's up to folks like us to kill him."

Walker gazed at Bass wordlessly, no need of language between men of like mind.

"You really fixing to kill them white men when we catch up to 'em?" Dick Owens asked.

"Maybeso we'll see what happens when we get down there to take them horses back," Bass said as he poked a twig into the fire.

"They're just Injun horses," William Craig said. "English horses too. It ain't like they stole 'em from any friend of mine—"

"No friend of your'n?" Bass snarled. "Didn't them English help out the three of you your first two seasons?"

"Y-yes—"

"What 'bout them Snakes?" Walker asked this time. "Didn't they come in to trade with you and Thompson and Sinclair, when they could've come riding in and run off with all your stock?"

Craig regarded his Nez Perce wife a moment, then stared at the fire. "I s'pose I do owe the Snakes some decent—"

"Goddamned right," Bass interrupted. "That's what turned it for me. When Thompson and Peg-Leg stole horses from the English up at Fort Hall, I just figgered the English was a big outfit what could take care of itself. But when them white niggers rode into that Snake village and was treated so goddamned good by 'em, only to take off with some of their horses . . . then I knowed wrong was wrong."

"No matter them niggers are white men," Walker vowed. "Them horses is going back to the Snakes. If'n Thompson and the rest put up a fight . . . I'll kill 'em the way I would any man what stole from my friends. That about the way you sack it, Scratch?"

"Stealing from no-good red niggers like Blackfoot is one thing," Bass agreed. "But I never did cotton to stealing from folks who done me a good turn."

"Maybeso anyone here who don't figure this may come to gunplay better turn back in the morning a'fore we push on," Walker said as he slid his knife back into its scabbard. "Ruther not have such a man along when I need to know who's watching my back in a fight."

"Comes down to it," Meek said, "you can count on me and Doc."

"Me and Dick too," Carson said, angling a thumb at Owens.

"You're in with Bass, ain'cha, Shad?" Walker asked.

Sweete smiled. "Me and Scratch see eye to eye on most things. I'd as soon hang a white turncoat's scalp from my belt as a Blackfoot's. 'Sides—Titus Bass hauled my hash outta the fire more'n once. I'll stand at his back in ary fight he calls me to."

The wind was up the next morning when they tried to restart their fires. Shards of icy snow skittered along the ground, gusting this way and that, scattering the ashes and embers. Finally the men saddled up and pushed on without coffee in their bellies.

Mile by mile they rode south-southwest, almost into the teeth of that storm racing off the horizon. But instead of snow, the lowering sky brought only a deepening cold. No man could claim he was warm punching against that brutal wind. Hour by hour they continued down that ages-old trail the Ute had used for centuries, a trail that was leading them toward the mouth of the Uintah River where three winters before Antoine Robidoux had raised his log stockade. It was there the Shoshone said they would find Thompson, Peg-Leg Smith, and the rest lying low with their stolen horses.

But none of them knew for certain what would happen when they finally found Thompson's horse thieves.

That night, and again the following morning, they had to chip holes in the thick ice sealing the Green in order to water their weary horses. The men huddled sleepless around their fires, wrapped in blankets and robes, remembering high times, talking about the glory days that had been and would never be again.

And they talked about justice swift and sure. These men who were of a breed all their own had written their own code of honor across this raw and lawless land.

"Man don't steal from those what treat him as a friend," Bass explained to those grown cold and hungry and tired of the journey.

"I'd ruther gut me a red nigger than chase after white men what took a few horses from some Injuns," Dick Owens grumbled, once more on the verge of turning back.

For a moment Titus looked at Kit Carson, Owens's friend and partner. Then Scratch said, "Ain't none of us likes what's staring us in the eye, Dick. But white man, or red nigger—wrong is wrong . . . and less'n a man stands up for right in a land where there ain't no laws 'cept what's right, then we might just as well turn this here place over to them sheriffs and constables and preachers and high-toned, honey-tongued lawyers right now."

"Scratch is right," Joe Walker agreed. "If'n we don't do what's right, then we might as well hand this land over to them what'll turn everything bad on us. You better decide a'fore morning, Dick. I figger we'll reach Fort Winty* by late morning tomorrow."

"Dick's gonna ride with us," Carson said firmly, turning to his partner. "Ain'cha, Dick?"

Owens reluctantly nodded. "It don't make a lick of sense for me to turn back now. Not alone, it don't."

"I don't want you along if'n your heart ain't in it, Owens," Scratch threatened.

"It ain't, and that's the truth," Owens admitted. "Them are white men. They stole't horses from the English, stole't horses from the Injuns. They didn't steal no horses from me—"

"They might as well took horses from me, Dick," Titus said. "I know Peg-Leg Smith. Got drunk with him a time or two my own self. But when he and the rest went thieving horses from them Snakes, from Injuns what always done their best to treat us good, that's when Peg-Leg crossed the line."

"But they're white men," Owens groused. "Same as you and me."

"Makes it all the worse of 'em," Titus argued. "I got me a choice, Dick. Either I go get them horses back for the Snakes and make it right by them . . . or them Snakes go do it for themselves."

"What you figger them Snakes would do, Scratch?" Meek asked.

"Start killing white men," he declared flatly. "Snakes been our friends for as long as I've knowed 'em, boys. So if you want our friends to start killing white men, then you go right on back: tuck your tail and turn back for home."

"There ain't no easy way at this," Carson advised. "I'm mad as a spit-on hen that them boys stole horses . . . but I'm even madder at 'em for what might happen if we don't get them horses back to the Snakes."

"Amen to that, Kit," Titus grumbled as he eyed the reluctant Dick Owens. "Amen to that."

Late that next morning as he bellied down atop the sage-covered hill alongside Meek and Walker, Bass focused his long brass spyglass on the log-and-mud fort below them at that junction where the Uintah flowed into the Green. In that subfreezing silence, Scratch could hear the snuffle of their own horses tied behind them, just below the skyline.

He passed the glass to Walker. "Seems they might'n be expecting visitors. Look there at the island in the middle of the Green, just down-river."

"I see 'em," Walker said. "That's where they're herding the horses, Joe." He handed the glass on to Meek.

They waited till the muscular trapper finished looking over the scene

---

* Fort Uintah

below; then Titus asked, "We go for the horses? Or . . . we go to raise hell with them horse thieves?"

For a long moment the wind breasted that hilltop before Joe Walker spoke. "I ain't eager to spill a white man's blood, Scratch. Since they got them horses on that island, I'm for slipping down there and stealing 'em back so none of us is forced to kill one of them thieving niggers."

"I'll go for that," Meek responded. "Get them horses back without fighting them fellers."

Walker turned to Bass. "What say you, Scratch?"

A gust of wind howled over the crest of that hill, then whimpered on its way. "I say a thief is a thief, no two ways to it. But . . . if we can get back them horses without a fight doing it your way, Joe—then I'll be satisfied."

"Glad we all agree," Walker declared.

"Just mark my word, boys," Bass snagged their attention again, "if one of them thieving niggers raises his gun at me, he's damn well dead where he stands."

THIRTY-TWO

For some reason a stretch of the Green down below them wasn't frozen near as solid as the rest. Beneath a thin, riffled layer of icy scum Titus could make out the river's sluggish current.

From the willows where he lay, Bass studied the far bank, listening for any sounds coming from the log stockade where three smoky spires rose slowly into the leaden sky. Off to his left lay the narrow grassy island where the thieves had corralled their horses. No more than a half dozen more grazed near the walls of Robidoux's post.

He stared at the telltale color of that ice again. More times than he could count he had crossed frozen rivers, leading his horse and the mule. Times were Titus Bass had crossed the slurried Yellowstone itself bare-assed naked while a winter storm slammed down on that country. He damn well knew cold water as well as any man . . . likely because it scared the hell out of him like nothing else could.

The pale, translucent green of that ice indicated there had to be a spring feeding the river with a trickle of warm water, causing much of the ice around that spring to grow about as soft as a cotton bale left out on the St. Louis levee in a spring down-pour.

Back when Joe Walker led the two dozen down from the hills into the river valley, Sweete was the first to spot the nearby smudge of smoke hanging in an oily pall beyond the bare ridges. That smoke was a good sign either of a band of trappers camping nearby, or a village choosing to spend out the winter close to this trading post erected by men who frequently used Taos as their supply base. As much smoke as there was, Scratch figured it had to be Indians. Carson volunteered to have a look for himself.

By the time Bass, Walker, and Joe Meek had bellied their way down from the hilltop after glassing the fort and horse island, Kit was riding in from that solitary foray to scout the village downriver.

"I say they're Yutas," Carson explained, handing his reins to Dick Owens and promptly kneeling on the hard ground.

Dragging a knife from its scabbard, Carson traced a line to represent the river, scratched a small square for the stockade across the Green, then gathered up a handful of stones he positioned to indicate where the Indians had erected their lodges.

"How many fighting men?" William Craig asked in worry.

"Sixty, maybe seventy," Carson said, dragging the back of a hand beneath his red, runny nose. "Twenty-some lodges."

Walker turned to Craig, asking, "Why you figger we oughtta worry 'bout them Yutas? They never caused me no trouble."

The trader shrugged. "It's clear some Injuns don't want other Injuns trading for powder and guns—"

"You s'picious them Yutas don't like the idea of you trading with the Shonies up at Davy Crockett?" demanded Meek.

"I dunno how that bunch down there will act when we go riding in there to take them horses from Robidoux," Craig admitted.

"Yutas ain't never hurt no man I know of," Bass interrupted brusquely. "Less'n you shaved that bunch on some deal you ain't told us about, trader—them Yutas won't give our outfit no never mind. We only come for the horses them white men stole't, so we ain't got no truck with that village."

"It's plain as sun Thompson's boys picked up more horses from somewhere," Carson explained as he stabbed the point of his knife into the ground along that line representing the river. "There's better'n fifty on that island now."

"Ever' last one of 'em will make a nice present for them Snakes," Bass growled. "Less'n we get horses back for Rain, his warriors gonna do their damnedest against ever' white man in this country—guilty or not."

Walker nodded. "No man here wants war with them Snakes. We got enough enemies awready."

Meek knelt to lean over Carson's shoulder, stabbing a finger at the shorter man's drawing of the island. "A good thing Peg-Leg and the rest don't have no guard on them ponies."

"That'll make it easy for us to get the horses started away," Walker announced. "We won't have to do no shooting at them boys."

"You come up with a plan, Joe?" Newell asked.

Joseph R. Walker looked over the two dozen of them a moment before he explained. "Half of us gonna cross to the island and wrangle them horses across the ice toward the north bank. I want the other half of you to split off in two outfits. One go with Bass on the upriver end of the island and cross over just below the fort. The other'n go with Carson downriver of the island and make your crossing there. Both you boys'll wait to show yourselves till we get onto the island and start the herd across the ice to shore."

"Good," Meek responded. "That way we'll have them horses penned up a'tween the three outfits so they won't go stampeding off if'n there's shooting."

Walker cleared his throat. The others got to their feet in an uneasy silence. Some coughed softly, others shuffled their moccasins in nervousness.

"Kit—you take your five men on downriver now," Walker instructed, then waited while Carson turned, quickly and silently pointing to Dick Owens and four others. The six pushed from the group toward their horses tethered nearby.

"Take your men off too, Scratch."

Bass peered over them, having already made his choices. Nodding to each man in turn, he picked Sweete, Meek, and Newell, along with two men he didn't know well but who appeared to be weathered veterans of Indian scrapes. Leaving the remaining ten behind with Walker and William Craig, Titus released his horse from the brush and led it on foot toward the broad, shallow ravine that would take them down to the south bank of the Green.

He halted his outfit among the brush growing at the mouth of the ravine where they waited. Anxious to be atop the horse and moving, Scratch found this waiting hardest to endure. He checked the priming in the four pistols he had stuffed into his belt, then flipped back the frizzen to see the rifle's pan was primed.

"There," whispered Sweete.

Titus snapped his eyes to the island, saw Walker's men reaching the grassy sandbar. "Let's ride, boys."

"Walker's plan just may work after all," Meek cheered as they went into the saddle and started their horses onto the ice.

"We get them ponies to the north bank," Sweete declared as they picked their way toward the east end of the island, "we can start 'em off at a run and Thompson's men won't stand a chance of catching us."

But by the time Walker had the first of the horses off the bank, the nervous animals were finding the ice so soft that their hooves were beginning to sink into the spongy surface. Some balked, halting and attempting to turn back as those horses behind them were goaded by Walker's men waving rawhide lariats, or pieces of blanket and buckskin.

When that first frightened horse whinnied, Scratch knew their soup was shot. A handful of the ponies immediately neighed in fear or warning to the rest as they balled up there on the ice that started to sink beneath their combined weight.

In surprise Bass looked down as his own horse suddenly shifted beneath him. They had reached that part of the river where the ice was being undercut by the warmer, spring-fed water. The pony jerked its head, fighting the reins as he jabbed heels back into its flanks. Around him the others struggled with their horses across the next few yards, every soggy step of the way as the riders continued to sink past the hooves, then the pasterns, and slowly up to the knees by the time they reached the middle of the river where the ice was clearly as soft as newly boiled oatmeal on a winter morn.

To their left Walker's men were having a bad time of it, each of them in among the more than sixty horses—whipping, whistling, driving the animals across the river as they continued to sink on the cracking surface, water flooding onto the thick sections of rolling, pitching, floundering ice, splashing the men up to their thighs.

At the distant warning Scratch jerked, twisting to the right. A figure stood just outside the stockade gate, an arm pumping at those inside as he sent up the alarm.

"Wolf's been let out to howl now!" Titus roared.

It was as if the six of them were moving sluggishly, every bit as slow as thick molasses poured over johnnycakes. Sweete and the rest were just turning to look at the fort as both sides of the small gate were flung open and at least fifteen men belched out at once. Instantly angry, they were yelling to one another and bellowing at the horsemen floundering in the middle of the river with those stolen ponies.

"Keep a'coming!" Scratch hollered as they neared the north bank.

Twisting back to his left, he saw Carson's men already on shore. In that next moment Walker's horse was lunging off the ice, clawing its way among the leaders of the herd to clamber onto solid ground. Every animal was dripping, stopping briefly to shudder. But the moment Walker was joined by another four of his men, they had the horses turning.

A shot rang out. A puff of smoke emerged from a muzzle of one of those guns at the stockade as Scratch heard the ball pass his ear.

"Don't shoot, goddammit!" Just outside the palisades a voice was shrieking, perhaps the one of their number shoving down the muzzles of nearby guns. "Them'r white men!"

Closing in on the north bank, no more than a hundred yards from the fort now, Titus could make out the angry clamor.

"Ain't Injuns?"

"Don't shoot—they're white niggers!"

"What the hell they doing with—"

"They stealing our horses!"

Walker had those first horses turned east.

East?

Bass couldn't figure it. Walker and his men had the horses running now—but instead of driving them west along that north bank of the Green, running them away from the fort . . . they were stampeding the wet, frozen, frightened herd straight for the stockade and Thompson's horse thieves.

"Shoot 'em, I say!" a voice cried out at the wall.

"Ain't gonna shoot no white man!"

"I'll shoot any man what steals my goddamned horses!"

The thieves were arguing among themselves, some shoving one another in angry frustration, as Bass's men reached the bank, their own half-frozen, waterlogged horses scratching with their hooves at the icy shore, lumbering onto the flaky ground covered by a thin layer of dead grass.

"C'mon, Scratch!" Walker was yelling off to Bass's left, loping his way as he drove the herd toward Titus's men.

They were no more than eighty yards from the thieves milling in front of the open gates.

"You heard the booshway!" Scratch hollered. "Keep them horses moving!"

Meek, Newell, Sweete, and the rest yipped and bellowed as they kicked their weary, cold horses into motion, stringing out along both sides of the oncoming herd as it overtook them, joining in that gallop toward Robidoux's post.

At the front of the ponies Walker stood in the stirrups, screaming, "Get outta our way, you sonsabitches! Get back! Get back outta our way or you're hoof-jam!"

"What the hell's he doing?" one of the thieves squeaked in a shrill, frightened voice as the horses bore down on them.

In the next instant every figure standing in front of those gates exploded left or right as they realized the herd was making directly for them. Scattering like a flushed covey of quail busted from the underbrush by a coyote, the thieves screamed, cursed, and shrieked in horror as they tumbled out of the way in a roiling mass of elbows and legs, grunts and yelps.

Walker hollered, "Don't stop 'em now, Scratch!"

Before Bass realized it, he was among the lead horses as they shot through the opened gate. Unsure, he reined back quickly as the horses jostled and shoved against each other in this small space where they were suddenly corralled. Here, there, and over there too, men stood pinned against the low-roofed cabins built against the inside of the palisades. Outside the gate men were hollering angrily.

Slowly turning his horse in the milling madness, Bass spotted Carson and Owens reaching the gates, driving the last of the horses into the fort. Walker and three others were already out of the saddle, on their feet, and sprinting along the walls to reach the opening where they heaved against the huge gate timbers, quickly muscling those two sections together and sealing up the fort.

Beyond the walls, just on the far side of those gate timbers, men cursed, some calling out the names of those they had recognized among Walker's outfit.

Of a sudden they were hushed by one voice, a voice that hollered out as the horses snorted around Walker and the rest.

"Billy? That really you, Billy Craig?"

"I'm in here, Phil," the trader answered Thompson.

"What you pulling with our horses, you stupid son of a bitch?"

This time Walker yelled. "I'm the son of a bitch, Thompson."

"Thort that was you, Joe Walker!" a new voice cried.

"It's me, Peg-Leg," Walker announced.

"Best you tell us what's going on with our horses a'fore we bust in there and spill some blood!" Thompson warned.

"Try your damnedest!" Bass hollered. "Them gates is barred shut, boys!"

"What you want with our horses?" Peg-Leg Smith asked.

"Ain't your horses!" Scratch shouted, slowly working his horse through the herd toward the gate.

"We took 'em. Fair is fair!" Thompson argued.

Sweete roared with laughter. "Ain't yours if you can't hold on to 'em!"

"We'll come in and get 'em!"

Walker shouted, "That's one sure way to spill a lot of blood, Thompson. Now, you can think this over and let us ride on outta here . . . or you can pull some idjit trick get a lot of men hurt bad."

"Sure—that shines!" Thompson replied just outside the gate. "You boys go on and ride outta here. Leave the horses and we'll let you go as you please!"

At the gate Titus shouted, "We're taking the horses back to them Snakes you stole 'em from!"

"They ours now!"

"So we're coming in for you niggers!"

"Come right on!" Walker goaded the thieves. "There's a few more of us in here than there is of you boys out there! Make a quick fight of it!"

Just beyond the gate they could hear the thieves arguing among themselves, little more than a murmur of angry voices for a long time until Thompson stomped up to the wall once more and shouted through a crack in the timbers.

"You don't wanna come out to save your hides—that'll be fine by us. We'll get them Yutas camped just down the river to help us bust you outta there."

Walker turned to look at a sheepish Antoine Robidoux. When the trapper pulled a pistol from his belt and brought its hammer back to full cock, the trader shrugged helplessly. Walker held the weapon under the trader's nose. "How the hell you callate them Yutas wanna help you horse-stealers?"

"You ain't so stupid, Joe!" Thompson cried. "Every one of their warriors help us kill you niggers, we'll give 'em a horse. That way we'll get all the horses back and rub you bastards out too!"

Turning back to Robidoux, Walker grabbed a handful of the trader's capote. In a whisper the trapper demanded, "Them Injuns help Thompson like he says they will?"

Robidoux was just opening his mouth to speak when Bass snarled, "I don't know what this here son of a bitch, parley-voo turncoat got to say to that, Joe—but I damn well will wager my own hide that them Yutas won't mix in this here fight."

"That's good 'nough for me, Scratch." Walker let go of Robidoux, shoving the trader back. "Go fetch your Yutas, Thompson! They'll make this here scrap a real interesting fight!"

"You asked for it, you skunks!" the thief cried as if he had been wounded. "We'll burn every last one of you outta there and hang your scalps from our belts when we're done ripping your hearts out!"

After it had been quiet a few minutes, Walker pointed to the trader. "Robidoux—get my men some tobaccy!"

His eyes blinked nervously. "You gonna pay for it?"

"We ain't thieves like Thompson's bunch," Scratch growled. "I figger all you got is that piss-poor Mex tobaccy anyways."

"It come from Taos," Robidoux agreed.

Walker nodded. "If all you got is Mex, we'll leave you one of these here horses when we go. That ought'n pay for some tobaccy and what we'll drink while we're in here."

"What you'll d-drink?" Robidoux flustered, growing more assured. "I don't want nothing from you in trade because Thompson's gonna have your men drove outta here—"

"If he tries that foolishness," Bass vowed, "you'll be the first *I'll* kill."

Turning on Titus with a jerk, Robidoux went white. "Me? Wh-why kill me? I didn't steal no—"

"You took them horse thieves in here!" Walker grumbled. "If Bass don't shoot you, I will."

"Awright," the cowed Frenchman relented as he turned away. "I go get your tobacco now."

"Go with him, Doc," Walker ordered. "See he don't do nothing gonna make me kill him here and now."

"Hey, Robidoux—we'll leave you one of these here scrawny English horses in trade!" Sweete cried as some of the others started to cackle and laugh.

But Walker didn't join in their mirth. "Kit—climb on up there on that wall and see what's going on."

An hour passed. The trader reappeared with Newell to pass out a twist of tobacco to every one of Joe Walker's men. Then a little more time crawled by when Carson suddenly grew animated at the top of the wall.

He shouted down to Walker. "Joe! Joe! Thompson's coming back with some Yutas!"

One of the trappers growled, "Goddamn you, Bass!"

"Shuddup!" Walker whirled on him.

"Sorry, Joe," Titus apologized as the booshway stepped over to him. "Didn't figger them Injuns would come."

Walker wagged his head. "Shit. I didn't figger them Yutas for helping the bastards neither." He turned to yell at Carson. "How many?"

"Twenty. Maybe thirty of 'em I see now."

For a moment Walker fell silent. Finally he sighed. "Scratch, you know any of that tongue?"

"First winter I spent in the mountains," he admitted, "I learned me some . . . from a gal."

Grinning, Walker said, "If'n you picked it up from a woman, then you'll damn well know enough to talk to a buck."

"Walker!"

Thompson's voice came from just outside the gate again.

Joe demanded, "You here to tell me you brung them bucks here to fight us, ain'cha?"

"Last chance! Open up the gates, and we'll let you go a'fore any of you gets kill't!"

"Go to the devil!" Meek hollered.

Peg-Leg Smith yelled, "That's just where we're fixing to send you, Joe!"

Walker grabbed Bass's arm. "Get on up that wall with Kit. Start talking to them Yutas—now!"

"A goddamned mess the way things turned out," Shad grumbled as he followed Bass up the rungs of the narrow ladder to the top of the palisades to join Carson. "White men paying Injuns to rub out other white men."

"These mountains gone to hell, that's for sure," Scratch said as they reached the top and cautiously peered over.

Kit pointed at the last of those warriors just then emerging from the brush downriver. Quickly scanning the horsemen, Bass counted at least forty. That, along with Thompson's thieves, made for some three-to-one odds.

"S'pose it's time to dust off my Yuta," he whispered as he stood slowly. "A mite rusty . . ."

He cleared his throat as the white men started to turn, peering up at him, pointing.

"Ute men," he shouted in the tongue he hadn't used in years. Then repeated the simple address. "Ute men—listen to me. These white men . . . bad."

Bass pointed at Thompson's thieves, who were beginning to murmur as the warriors turned their heads, giving Scratch their attention. He repeated, "Yes—these white men bad. Bad. Steal horses from white men. Steal horses from . . ."

But he couldn't remember the Ute word for *Shoshone.* Instead, he made the wiggling movement with his hand and forearm. Every warrior should understand that universal sign.

"These bad white men steal horses from the . . . and we take the horses back to the . . ." he said, pantomiming the snake wriggle both times.

"White talker!"

Bass turned to find the warrior who dropped to the ground and started toward the fort wall. He asked, "You are chief?"

"I am war chief. Come to help these white men take back their horses from you. These men say *you* are the bad white men. Ask us to help. Promise us horses to kill you bad white men."

"You kill us, you get horses," Scratch said. "But some of you die here. Blood on this ground."

"We rub you out quick, none of my warriors die."

"Perhaps . . ." Bass shouted down sternly, his confidence growing as more of the language came back to him. "But we are here to get the horses ourselves because the other tribe tell us they will come here to get their horses if we don't bring them back."

Titus could tell the man was turning that over in his head, what with the way his brow suddenly furrowed in deep thought.

"Warriors from the other tribe told us they do not want to kill white men, but said they will kill white men because these white men stole from them."

The war chief turned to gaze at Thompson.

"If you help these bad white men," Scratch pressed on, "if you kill us and take some of these horses for yourselves, one day the other tribe will learn that you helped the thieves kill the men who came here to help them."

Now the war chief gazed up at Bass standing at the top of the wall.

"The other tribe will be angry with the Ute—for helping the men who took horses from them, and for taking their horses as a reward for killing us," Titus explained.

"How will they know about us?" the chief demanded haughtily.

"They know about you, because they told us the bad white men had come here."

"They know we are camped here?"

"Yes. So they will come to this place . . . and rub out the Ute who helped the white men steal their horses."

With a whirl of fringe and feathers and unbraided hair, the war chief turned to stomp away, grumbling at a handful of warriors to join him. For long minutes they huddled together, conversed in low, angry tones, until the war chief turned back to Bass.

"We go!"

"You do right," Scratch congratulated.

The moment the war chief and the others leaped atop their ponies, Thompson and the rest set up a pained, furious howl, darting among the forty-some warriors, gesturing at the fort, yelling, patting the Indian horses as if to emphasize that they would earn a booty for their assistance in killing the men holed up inside the walls.

Leaning down from the top of the palisades, Bass announced to Walker, "The Injuns—they're riding off!"

Those men in the compound among the frightened, milling horses set up a wild cheer.

"You sonsabitches!" Thompson roared in anger, hammering the side of his fist against the outside of the gate as Bass, Carson, and Sweete clambered down the narrow ladder to the courtyard.

On the other side of the palisades the horse thieves argued for a long time. It was many minutes before a familiar voice suddenly called out.

"Scratch? Was that you at the top palaverin' with them Yutas, Titus Bass?"

He recognized the voice, but scrambled to put a face with it. Titus asked, "Who's calling?"

"Solitaire, Scratch. You 'member me, don'cha?"

Solitaire, he ruminated on it. "Bill? Ol' Bill Williams?"

"That's me—thought it was you I see'd up there palaverin' with them Yutas," Williams explained. "You done spoil't Thompson's big plan, Scratch."

"To hell with him," Bass snapped. "I'll gut him sure as I'm standing here."

"May get your chance to try, nigger!" Thompson hollered.

Ignoring the turncoat, Bass inquired, "You throwed in with them, Bill?"

Williams's voice came closer to the gate. "I was here when Thompson's outfit rode in with them horses. That's when I tol't 'em the Bent brothers need horses over there on the Arkansas."

Walker asked, "Need horses?"

"Them Bents and Savary sell 'em, or trade 'em off," Williams declared. "So Thompson was fixing to start over to the Arkansas with them horses next day or two . . . 'cept you come breaking things up."

"How's your stick float, Bill?" Titus asked. "You gonna jump in the middle of this?"

For a moment Williams didn't answer. Then he said, "I figger there's 'nough bean-bellies and red niggers for this child to raise hell with. I don't need to kill me no white men."

"You ain't gonna come to Bents' with us?" Peg-Leg squealed.

"Nawww," Williams confessed. "You ain't got no horses now, so I'll have to go off to get me some in Californy."

"I hear them Mex got a passel of horses out there, Bill," Peg-Leg cried. "I'll throw in with you, and we'll steal us some Mex horses we can bring back to the Arkansas."

Outside the walls there arose some disgruntled murmuring, then the noise of footsteps moving away from the walls.

"You still there, Thompson?" Walker yelled.

"I'm here—just figgering a way to kill you, Walker."

"It's over," Walker said. "You ain't got no Injuns to do your killing for you. And from the sounds of it, you're losing some of your own white men too. Why don't you just step off to the side and we'll just ride on out of here with the horses—nobody getting hurt."

"Damn you to hell, Walker!"

Now Bass shouted, "What made you go bad, Thompson? You was partners with Craig and Sinclair—had yourselves a nice post there in Brown's Hole. What went wrong?"

"Beaver's done!" Thompson hollered, his voice cracking with deep regret. "Ain't no future in hunting plews no more. Last year or so, I could see there weren't no future in supplying you trappers neither. Prices too high on goods I brung out, dollar too low on beaver . . . I could see trappers like you fellers wasn't gonna make it, what with the world turn't upside down on us the way it is."

"Maybeso you can make your fortune on horses," Scratch declared.

"Just what I figgered I was doing," the trader snorted. "English horses. Injun horses too."

Walker said, "Go to Californy with Bill Williams and get you some Mexican horses."

"Craig!" Thompson yelled.

"I'm here, Phil."

"S'pose you figgered it out: when I took off to steal some horses, you knowed our partnership was done."

"I thought as much," William Craig responded. "Just me and Sinclair now."

Thompson said, "I wish you boys best of luck."

Craig looked at Walker in wonder. "What you fixing to do about these horses now?"

"I reckon me and the fellas here aim to let you boys ride on by with them horses you can take back to the Snakes," Thompson admitted. "Ain't got no more heart to fight you."

Walker and Meek dragged back the monstrous rough-hewn log some six inches square, withdrawing it from the cast-iron hasps to crack open the gate.

Peering out carefully, Walker said, "You fellas step aside, we'll come on out now and this whole thing be over."

"Awright," Thompson agreed. "You boys come on out and we'll make no trouble. Just see we get our own horses from that bunch you got in there first. We'll need 'em for that long ride to Californy."

"For sure that's a long trail," Scratch said with nothing less than admiration. "You boys will need good horses under you."

By that time the winter sun was sinking and dark was coming on. Walker stepped back and ordered Meek and Sweete to throw open the gate. In shuffled some angry and a few shame-faced horse thieves to reclaim their own horses from the herd. One by one the riding horses and pack animals were broken out until Walker's men were left with thirty-five horses. Thompson reluctantly shook hands with his old partner before Craig mounted up with the others and started wrangling their stock out the gate.

Lean, angular Bill Williams was standing in the long shadows of the fort wall that afternoon as Sweete and Bass brought up the rear of the herd. Titus reined around and came to a halt.

Williams asked, "You gonna hunt flat-tails?"

"Yep. Figure I ought'n till the plews ain't wuth a damn."

"If'n a man can find beaver."

"Yep," Bass said dolefully. "If a man can find beaver."

"Ever you thort of coming to Californy with us?"

"Nawww." And for some reason he felt sorry for Williams, the others too. Then, suddenly, he felt very sorry for himself as well. "When beaver's gone under, then I'll find me something else to do."

"Ain't gonna be long," Williams claimed.

"Not ready to be a horse stealer, Bill. When I can't find no more flat-tails in the mountains, or when the trader says my plews ain't wuth a red piss . . . till then Titus Bass be a trapper. It's who I am, Bill."

"Here's to shining times, then, Titus Bass," Williams said with as much cheer as he could muster, bringing up a long-boned paw.

He shook the offered hand. "Here's to Californy, Bill Williams. Here's to Mexican horses."

The moment he pulled his hand away from Williams, Bass kicked his pony into a lope, riding away feeling unsettled as he stuffed the hand back into a blanket mitten.

It seemed as if he didn't understand this world anymore. While he wasn't watching, wasn't paying attention, the world Titus Bass knew had been changing unseen and unheard. It was as if one of those big prairie winds had picked him up in one place and in one time, then set him right down in a different place and in a different time. . . . Scratch felt un-hitched. Adrift. His belly cold with uncertainty.

No longer sure what the seasons ahead would bring.

THIRTY-THREE

It had taken Joe Walker and the rest more than eight days to get that small herd of horses back to Fort Davy Crockett and the Shoshone. Two of those days were spent rounding up the strays after a freak winter thunderstorm blew in from the southwest—pelting the countryside with a hard, icy rain driven by tempestuous winds and accompanied by flashes of lightning and prolonged peels of thunder that promptly frightened the skittish ponies and set off a wild stampede across miles of muddy ground.

The Shoshone were satisfied.

But Prewett Sinclair was furious that Craig hadn't come back with Thompson's scalp. After some heated debate Sinclair and Craig decided they had best part company. Once their present stock of goods was disposed of, their partnership at Fort Davy Crockett would be dissolved.

Late in February, just before Bass was preparing to set off for the foothills in search of beaver, Sinclair formed a new venture with a trapper grown weary of dangerous work and poor prospects. While Sinclair remained at the post, Robert Hewell loaded more than three hundred pelts onto their packhorses and headed out for Fort Hall to barter for trade goods and supplies.

Down in the spring Shad and Titus had run onto Kit Carson. Because Dick Owens had ended up turning around on them to throw in with Thompson, Williams, Peg-Leg, and those others headed for the California ranchos, Carson had enlisted Jack Robinson as his new partner for the spring hunt. After a night of pitching tales and swapping lies the trappers saddled up to go their separate ways the next morning.

"See you to ronnyvoo on the Seedskeedee!" Bass had cried.

Carson wagged his head. "I can't figger there'll be no more ronnyvoo, Scratch."

"You ain't coming to Horse Creek?" Sweete asked.

"Ain't planning to," Kit confessed. "Don't see no sense in making a long ride to somewhere there ain't gonna be no trader, no trade goods."

Sadly, Titus asked, "So what you gonna do, Kit?"

"We'll see if Robidoux treat us fair down at his Winty post. He better—seeing how we should've burned him out for hiding them horse thieves."

"Fort Robidoux, eh?" Bass brooded. Then sighed as he gripped Carson's hand tightly. "You boys watch your topknots, hear? One day we'll run across your sign again."

"Keep your eye on the backtrail," Carson called out as he and Robinson started away.

The backtrail. That's about all it seemed they had anymore, Bass ruminated more and more throughout that spring and into the first part of summer as he and Sweete started for the Green River. The backtrail. There sure as hell wasn't any future to speak of, what with the way the company had threatened not to show up at all for the coming rendezvous.

When he really got down in his mind, it seemed as if everything he had ever wanted, all that had ever mattered in his life, it all lay behind him. Then he would look at Flea and Magpie . . . or feel Waits-by-the-Water's head rest against his shoulder, and he would grow hopeful anew.

Maybe the beaver were about killed off. Maybe folks weren't wearing beaver any longer and the fur companies didn't give a damn about trappers no more . . . and maybe the only folks who would ever come through these mountains would be settlers destined for the fertile ground of that rainy place called Oregon Territory.

That was all right, he convinced himself as he held her tight through those nights when he couldn't sleep for brooding on the terror it gave him. He had his powder and lead so his family would never go hungry. But what of those pretty things he wanted to provide for her—what if the trader didn't show this summer? Never showed again? Would he have to go to Fort Hall, or Fort Union, or over to the South Platte if he didn't ride over to see Robidoux or Sinclair?

He wasn't sure just how he felt one day to the next as he and Shad continued north. One morning he found himself hopeful, but the next he was sure that life as he had known it was over. His emotions were taking the same sort of ride a broken twig would endure racing down a swift mountain stream swollen with spring run-off.

For all these years he figured he had come to count on things outside himself. Now, Scratch realized . . . he could not put his faith in anything but Titus Bass. In this world turned upside down, that faith in himself might well be all he could count on.

This summer of 1840 the Flathead had come again to the Green near Horse Creek, waiting for the man of God who had been promised to them for many years. In those warm days while they all kept a patient vigil, Bass came to feel sorry for those Flathead, seeing how they sent out riders every day to watch for the approach of the trader's caravan from the States. For years now missionaries had come overland, briefly visiting rendezvous before they continued on to the far northwest to establish themselves, their schools and their churches among the Palouse and Nez Perce . . . always passing the Flathead by. Every summer the missionaries had taken their potent medicine from God elsewhere.

So there was no small celebration in the valley of the Green that thirtieth day of June when the first Flathead rider came racing back to rendezvous screaming with delight.

Those trappers who understood the Flathead tongue quickly translated the happy news emanating from the village. The trader was coming! Carts had been spotted. Many people. And four wagons.

Surely, now, with the white man's lumbering white-topped wagons, there had to be missionaries along. And—dare they hope after all these years—those new missionaries had finally come to bring their power to the Flathead?

Three Protestant ministers and their wives had come west with Andrew Drips and his caravan. But to the soul-flattening disappointment of those joyous Flathead who turned out to greet these arrivals from the States, the six missionaries were bound for the Oregon country. While the Shoshone gave the caravan a raucous greeting, firing guns and racing round and round the column, the Flathead were turning back for their village in despair.

Sympathizing with their unfathomable grief, Scratch watched with curiosity as a lone man peeled off from the caravan on foot, calling out in his heavy accent for the Flathead to stop, to turn around and wait for him. Having walked on foot all the way from St. Louis, the stranger was nothing short of slit-eyed and sunburned beneath his flat-brimmed black hat. With stinging alkali dust coating his long wool frock, Belgian friar Pierre Jean deSmet shook hands with the head men. An amused contentment was written on his face at the joy the Flathead wore on theirs when he announced he had come alone to teach them how to turn their faces to God.

But no one could have been more happy than Titus Bass.

With Flea on his shoulders, Scratch walked out from the trees, Shad Sweete at his elbow. It was as if his hopes, his very prayers, had been answered by the arrival of that caravan. The fur trade wasn't dead. No . . . not yet.

"Truth be, didn't really figger we'd see a supply train this year, Shadrach."

"Me neither. But there it comes, Titus!"

What with the way the company partisans had been grumbling about the poor returns, the dwindling number of trappers to work the mountains, and of course the sinking number and quality of furs harvested, more than half of those men gathered in the valley of the Green River were genuinely surprised that their patience had been rewarded.

For days now the white men had reminded one another that they really wouldn't be disappointed if Drips didn't show. After all, summer was not the time to be chasing beaver anyway. The fur wasn't worth much, so a man might as well follow the Flathead, Nez Perce, and Shoshone on down to Bonneville's old fort on Horse Creek to look up some old friends, share some stories of the glory days, and keep one eye on the horizon.

Maybe Drips would show with a few carts and trade goods and a little whiskey. Maybe the mountain trade wasn't dead yet. Just maybe . . .

Bass turned to his tall friend, tears glistening in their eyes. His voice cracked as he said, "Damn the settlements while there's still beaver in the mountains, Shadrach."

Sweete's moist eyes grew big, his mouth moving with no sound coming forth as he started to point. "L-lookee there, Scratch!" he finally gasped. "It's Jim! By God, it's Jim Bridger!"

"Gabe?" and he squinted into the bright distance. "Damn if it ain't Gabe hisself!"

Patting little Flea on his back, Shad roared, "And ol' Frapp too!"

Sure enough, out in front of the short caravan Andrew Drips was leading into the creek bottom was none other than Jim Bridger and his old partner, German-born Henry Fraeb, whose family had emigrated to America, on to St. Louis when Henry was but a child.

Racing out on horseback to meet the train was Joseph Walker. He tore the hat from his head, waving it wildly as another man on foot suddenly angled away from the wagons and sprinted his way, kicking up dust with his ill-fitting boots. Walker reined up in a spray of yellow dirt, vaulting to his feet where he embraced the stranger who threw down his rifle to wrap his arms around the trapper.

"Who you figger that is with Joe?" Titus asked.

"Maybe its Joe's brother," Shad said with a smile. "You recollect Joe said he'd be on the lookout for his brother, ever since Joe got a letter from him saying he was gonna be coming west to settle in Oregon this summer."

"Settlers?" He nearly choked. "Now there's settlers going to Oregon?"

Shadrach nodded, his smile disappearing. "Maybeso they'll just keep on going, Scratch. And you won't have nothing to fret about. I imagine them folks'll just pass on through and won't ever stop to fill up these here mountains."

"Oregon can have 'em," Bass snarled. "That wet, rainy country is fit for the likes of farmers . . . such as my pap. Fit for the likes of them Bible-spouting preachers too. With their angry eyes, and sad mouths, and their bitter tongues spouting against ever'thing natural a man gonna do. You damn bet their kind better just pass on through. Let Oregon have 'em, I say!"

The next day after their reunion with Bridger, when Drips opened his packs and set up shop, instead of hurrying for the trading canopy, Bass and Sweete turned in a few furs for that first kettle of whiskey, then sat in the shade of a cottonwood calmly watching the bartering begin.

Wiping droplets from his shaggy, unkempt mustache, Titus asked, "You was with Ashley, wasn't you?"

"Just a sprout then."

"I come west in the spring of twenty-five, year Ashley had his first ronnyvoo," Titus explained. "But I didn't see my first ronnyvoo till twenty-six."

"That first'un wasn't nothing more'n the Gen'ral taking in furs and passing out supplies. Not a drop of whiskey. And there sure weren't no such thing as a free man anywhere in sight since we was all Ashley men in twenty-five," Shad reflected.

They fell quiet, listening to the drone of big green-bottle deerflies and the noisy murmur of trappers and clerks, the clatter of beads and tacks, the clink of tin cups inside whiskey kegs.

"Summers, they were good back then," Bass sighed. "For a time there, every new ronnyvoo was better'n all the ones that'd come a'fore it."

"I'll say. Ever' one got bigger. Wilder. More men and mules, more whiskey and women too. If'n a man only got one chance to celebrate all year long in a year of hard, dangerous living . . . then them was the celebratingest times a child could ever hope to have."

And now those days were gone. Bass told himself he had better admit that beaver would never shine again, not the way that beaver had shined back then.

It almost made a growed man wanna cry, it did. Sitting here sipping cheap puke-up liquor, watching a handful of sad, old hivernants try to wrangle themselves a square deal from a bunch of Pierre Chouteau's slick city types out from St. Louis. Men like him and Shad who had seen the sun set on better than five thousand days of glory in these high and terrible mountains . . . men who had withstood freezing winters and blazing-hot summers . . . men who had stared right back into the eye of sudden, certain death and withstood the grittiest test of wills . . . the sort who had always treated every other man fairly and given more than a day's work for what wages the company offered him when it came time for an accounting beneath the trading canopy.

Men who now were all but begging Andrew Drips's weasel-eyed hired hands to realize that for seasons beyond count they had risked their health, their hair, their very lives to trap that beaver the company was buying less than cheap. These last few members of a dying breed, who for a short time in history had stood head and shoulders above any man anywhere in the world, were being told that their labors weren't worth much at all, that the risks they had taken were worth even less than that . . . that their lives had little meaning in a world that was already passing them by.

So rather than openly bawl, Bass sat there and drank. Sip by sip, cup by cup, hoping to numb the goddamned pain of watching those proud men come to the counter to beg for another year's supplies, men willing to turn over their hard-won beaver dirt cheap, willing to pay prices that would choke a big-boned Missouri mule for what possibles might get them through till next summer.

Then Drips came out to stand before less than a hundred trappers gathered there. Bridger and Fraeb stood off to the side, their long faces showing they already knew what the partisan was about to tell the crowd.

"I s'pose it don't come as no surprise to most of you," Drips began before that hushed assembly. "For the past two summers, there's been rumors Pratte and Chouteau weren't going to send out no supply caravan to ronnyvoo."

He waited a moment while some of the crowd muttered in disgust and disillusionment.

"But they was just rumors, men. Rumors. Last summer we come, even when the beaver take wasn't worth the trip. And this spring the company decided to give it one last try."

For a long time Drips looked over the crowd formed in a huge crescent around his trade canopy. It seemed that his eyes touched almost every man there—most he knew, some better than others. Perhaps he was struggling to find the words. Perhaps—Scratch thought—Drips was trying to decide whether or not to use those words Bass was certain the partisan had practiced all the way out to rendezvous.

"Men . . . this here's the last supply train to the mountains."

It was as if they already knew. There was no sudden gasp of surprise or alarm. These men already knew. While Drips himself might have expected anger, a torrent of unrequited rage . . . Bass realized these men likely felt they had been owed more than rumors. They were damn well due the truth. And now they knew for sure. Rather than be hung out on a strand of spider's silk for another year, not knowing. Not knowing.

Now they could get on with what it was they were going to do with the rest of their lives.

"What about the brigade?" a voice cried out in that hot, breathless, midsummer stillness.

"Yeah!" hollered another of those deep voices. "Ain't the company gonna put a outfit in the field this year?"

But Drips stood there, unspeaking.

"Ain't you gonna take us north for the fall hunt?"

Still the company partisan remained mute, staring at the ground.

"Sure they will!" another voice cried, strong with hope. "Bridger's back to pilot!"

"No," Drips finally declared, his face a bland and emotionless mask. "I'm turning back for St. Louis when the trading is done and I can get on my way."

A stunned, quiet pall had overtaken them as every last man of them stood there in numbed silence.

Then Joe Meek took a step forward. "How 'bout you, Gabe?" he asked. "You gonna lead a brigade this fall, ain'cha?"

Bridger hung his head, staring at the toes of his moccasins for some time, eventually pushing himself away from the tree where he had been standing beside the crusty Henry Fraeb. Jim said, " 'Fraid there's no more company brigade, Joe. You'll recollect I quit off the company last year. So I ain't part of it no more. Now I'm . . . I'm just the same as all of you."

"S-same as us?" Robert Newell echoed, his voice rising an octave in grave concern.

"I don't see nowhere else for any of us to go but to the trading posts now, boys," Bridger tried to explain, his voice quiet in that hush of a summer afternoon that stretched out long and warm west of the Continental Divide. "Any man what figgers to go on trapping beaver . . . he's gonna have to trade his plews, gonna have to get his possibles at them forts from here on out till . . . till . . ."

When Bridger's words drifted off into an uneasy stillness, a croaky frog of a voice called out, "Till what, Jim?"

"Till there ain't no more call for beaver."

No more call for beaver?

Jehoshaphat! What had become of the world?

For longer than he could imagine, folks had been wearing beaver hats. Because of those hats, there had always been those who went after the beaver, and those who traded the beaver from them. But now there were nowhere near the beaver a man once found on the streams. Damn, if he and his friends hadn't worked so hard, they'd worked themselves right out of a job.

Scratch was sure Bridger turned away because he felt all those eyes boring into him. Here was a friend who had faced the very worst that winter could throw at a man, faced the very best any painted-up, blood-in-his-eye enemy could hurl his way . . . of a sudden grown self-conscious, maybe even a mite scared, of staring down all those broken-hearted men.

"So can I buy you a drink, Scratch?"

He turned to find Sweete at his shoulder, the big man's eyes brimming above those cheeks of oak-tanned leather.

Titus felt the weariness come of those seasons spent high and alone right down into the bone of him. Quietly he said, "Don't mind if I do, Shadrach."

Men slowly drifted off in more than a dozen directions. Some stepped back to the trading canopy with their plews at the end of each arm, though there really wasn't all that much beaver in camp to speak of. But many more clustered around Andrew Drips now, firing questions at the partisan on how they were to go about getting their pay if they chose not to continue in the mountains, asking how a man might accompany the fur caravan back to the settlements when Drips turned for the States.

Sad questions, Titus thought, questions from confused and bewildered, worried men.

With Shad he returned to their tree, to their kettle and their cups. Returned to their memories of brighter times, shining times. Sip by sip of the potent grain alcohol diluted with some creek water and bolstered by a handful of peppers too made the memories easy to conjure up.

By and large, though they looked weathered and worn and weary, their kind were still young men, most no older than Bridger, who was here in his midthirties. But for a brief time they had been the cocks of the walk. Poor frontier boys from the southern mountains, adventurous souls from far up in New England—some Scotch, Irish, and English too, even a few Delaware and Iroquois thrown in. They had laid down moccasin tracks where few men had ever dared to walk—at least no white man.

In this land as wild as the red men who roamed across it, these few daring souls took on the dress of those who had been there far back in time: some of this reckless breed combed their hair out with porcupine brushes so that it would spill in great manes over the collars of their blanket coats while others twisted their hair in a pair of braids interwoven with colorful ribbons or wrapped in sleek otter skins; across their backs they sported a merry calico or buckskin shirt tanned a fragrant smoky hue; intricate finger-woven sashes or wide leather belts decorated with brass tacks held up leggings of doe skin or blanket wool, even drop-front britches sewn of durable elk hide.

While most coupled with tribal women only at summer rendezvous or in winter camps, some proudly took one or more tribal women as wives. A few hung hoops of wire adorned with beads or stones from their ears, and a handful even painted themselves before every battle, or for every rendezvous debauch. They learned to lavish on their best horse the same attention a warrior would give his own war pony: tying up its tail, braiding ribbons in the mane, or dabbing its muscular flanks with earth pigment. No Indian dandy ever strutted with more swagger than these few hundred had in their heyday.

Moment to moment that afternoon and on into the evening, then through the few following days left them, Scratch and Shadrach, Bridger and Carson, Meek and Newell, talked round the whiskey kettles and the firefly campfires—enthralling one another with stories of tight fixes and derring-do, improbable windies and tall tales, brags and boasts big and small, all those noisy recollections as well as those quiet remembrances of those who no longer gathered with them . . . those gone on ahead to that big belt in the blue. Those who had already made that last solitary crossing of the Great Divide.

Damn, but there were too many of them, Bass thought as he struggled to hold back the tears. And now this would be the last reunion, this final gathering of a very, very small Falstaffian brotherhood.

In the shrinking camps most men made out not to give a damn—drinking hard, laughing loud, fighting and wrassling, doing all they could to hold back the specter of death the way most men are wont to do when they don't know just how they should feel. From the Indian villages came the distant thump of drums, the soft trill of a lover's flute, and a wail of voices singing of birth and war and death. Not the Flathead nor the Nez Perce, not even the Shoshone fully understood, much less believed, that this was to be the last gathering of these summer celebrants. Instead, for the wandering bands it would be life as they had lived it across the centuries: summer afternoons and sweet, cool evenings smoking their pipes, watching children chase and play, scraping hides and sewing beads, telling stories of warpath heroism or creation myths.

Where would they go now? he wondered. Did the tribes go back to the way things had been before the white man came out west with his long caravans of shiny trade goods and powerful weapons?

So bittersweet was that flood of the memories, soulprints of his life made across mountain and plain: juicy hump rib and buffalo tongue around a winter fire, beaver tail and painter meat on the spit, the sharp relish of strong coffee or a handful of high, glacial water so cold it set your back teeth to aching. Games of hand or taking a chance on the well-worn cards of euchre and Old Sledge, foolish wagers on shooting a mark or throwing a 'hawk, running a'foot or racing your horse . . . they were times when a man knew who his friends were and how their stick would float.

But now those sweetest of days were gone like river-bottom sand a'wash come spring runoff, swept away in the rush of the seasons.

So like youth, held here but briefly in one's hand—youth truly experienced by those who believe youth will be theirs forever—the high times in these shining mountains had come and were never to be again. Like impetuous youth, these men did not realize their era had come and gone until the light had begun to fade for all time. And like the young who never fathom the precious gift granted them, these rough-hewn souls had squandered their days, wastrels with those brief seasons allotted them.

Late of a lazy summer morning Robert Newell strode back into camp, eager to share some news with his friends, especially that best of companions.

"Joe!" Doc hallooed as he approached the group lounging upon the ground whiling away these last hours of this last summer reunion.

"You're 'bout to bust at the seams, Doc," Titus said. "Just lookit him, boys. G'won, Doc—spill your beans."

"Them missionary folks what's bound for Oregon country," Newell began in a gush as he knelt in their midst, "well, now—you know they asked Black Harris to guide 'em on west from here."

"Ain't he gonna do it?" Joe asked.

Newell shook his head emphatically. "One of the preachers, named Littlejohn, he fetched me over to their camp and told me Harris was asking far too much to pilot them on to Oregon . . ."

When Newell paused dramatically, excitement flickering in his eyes, Carson said, "Spit it out, man!"

"Them preachers asked me to pilot 'em all the way to the Columbia country, boys!"

Meek bolted to his feet, looking every bit as stunned as he had when Bridger announced his bad news. "You . . . you g-going to take them folks on to Oregon 'stead of trapping beaver with me, Doc? 'Stead of staying in these mountains with us?"

Newell grabbed his best friend by the forearms, gazing intently into Meek's eyes. "Come with me, Joe."

"C-come with you?"

Doc's head bobbed eagerly. "We are done with this life in the mountains, so come with me, Joe."

"Done?"

"We're done wading in beaver dams, done with freezing or starving. Done I say—done with Injun fighting and Injun trading. Look around you, Joe: the fur business is dead in these mountains, and the Rockies is no place for us now."

Meek gasped in surprise, "Doc Newell—fixing to leave the mountains for good?"

"Goddamned right, Joe! We are young yet, and we have all life laid out a'fore us! We can't waste it here when this life is dead!"

"But . . . Oregon?" Meek asked uncertainly.

"We ain't the sort to go back to the States," Newell said, affectionately slipping an arm around the big man's shoulder. "I say come with me, Joe. Let us go on down to the Willamette and take up farms."

"Oregon," Meek repeated the word as if trying out the sound of a mysterious lodestone for the first time. "Oregon, you say?"

"We'll take them preachers and their wives, that Walker family too—all of their wagons on to Fort Hall where we'll gather up our wives and light out for Oregon."

Bass watched the glow cross Meek's face, so contagious was Newell's enthusiasm. It was the look of a man grown so weary and old, suddenly granted new vigor. Where resignation once was scrawled, now Titus could read the hope and joy boldly written on Joe's face.

"There's nothing left for you boys here," Bass charged them as he got to his feet, flinging one arm around Newell and the other around Meek. "Man needs to find him some country what he can call his own. Sounds to me that Oregon is where you two will make your stand."

THIRTY-FOUR

Two days later, when all the beaver had been turned over to Andrew Drips and that sad little rendezvous was quietly dying with a whimper, Reverend Philo B. Littlejohn finally sought out Moses Harris to explain that he had arrived at a most difficult decision.

"My party has decided that to guide us from here to Oregon—your price is simply too high."

"I reckon you don't have no notion just how far a piece that is to pilot you," Black Harris snarled caustically, glaring the missionary up and down. "I figger what I asked is only fair—seeing how I'll miss out on the fall trapping to get you folks through to the Columbia."

"I won't quibble that you asked what you determined was fair for you," the round-faced minister replied.

Realizing that he might be letting a good thing slip from his grasp, Harris suggested, "Maybe we can dicker some more to come up with a dollar more to your liking, but still gonna be fair to me—"

"That won't be necessary now," the preacher declared.

"What you mean: won't be necessary?"

Littlejohn cleared his throat self-consciously, then said,

"We enlisted a pilot for our journey, and for a price much lower than you demanded of us—"

"Lower?" Harris growled. "Who's the bastard cut me outta my goddamned job?"

Red-faced, the preacher exclaimed, "There's no call for your oaths, Mr. Harris!"

Standing there seething, his hands balling into fists before him, the mountain veteran growled menacingly, "Tell me who took my job!"

"His n-name is Newell," the missionary confessed as he inched backward, seeking escape from Harris's fury. "He plans to make a home for his family in Oregon—"

"Not if the son of a bitch is dead!" Harris interrupted as he whirled away in a fury, to start his search of the company camp.

Unsuccessful, he finally headed for the trader's tent. He didn't find Newell there that morning either, but he did find that the clerks were opening up the last of the kegs they had packed west. Harris felt a sudden, inexplicable thirst coming on. Some hard drinking was clearly in order before he continued his search for the man who had stolen his job.

By midafternoon Harris's well-soaked despair had grown ugly. Taking up his rifle, he lumbered away from the trader's canopy intent on finishing his deadly mission. With so few trappers attending this final rendezvous, the search didn't take him long now. He spotted Newell crossing a patch of open ground some seventy yards off near a free man's camp. Harris shoved his rifle against a shoulder, squinted his bleary eyes, and attempted to hold steady on his target.

When the gun roared, the ball went wild.

As a terrified Newell ran for his gun, Harris started to reload while he stumbled after his intended target—angrily cursing and growling his intention to have the younger man's scalp.

"Goddamn you, nigger! Gonna hang your ha'r on my belt before sundown!" the drunk man roared to the skies. "And you're gonna be sleeping with the devil hisself by nightfall!"

Step by step Harris plodded after Newell, clumsily pouring powder down the barrel as he plodded toward the trees where the trapper had disappeared. Digging at the bottom of his pouch, Harris pulled out another ball and set it atop the muzzle. He lunged to a stop as he yanked the ramrod from its thimbles at the bottom of the barrel, preparing to set the ball against the charge when Andrew Drips and a dozen others sprinted up—drawn by the racket as the lazy camps burst into action with the alarm.

"Get me some damned rope!" the trader ordered those behind him.

Someone asked, "You gonna hang 'im?"

"I damn well may do just that!" Drips spat as he dodged side to side each time Harris wildly swung his rifle at those advancing on him. "Get me the goddamned rope!"

Again and again Harris heaved his heavy weapon in a crazy arc at his attackers. The moment the drunk knocked a man down with a grunt, Drips leaped onto him. Five of them jumped in to wrestle Harris to the ground as he spewed curses at them, whipping his head side to side, snapping his teeth at anything that got too close, attempting to clamp down on an ear, a nose, a finger.

"Gimme that rope!" Drips shouted as the others struggled to hold down the figure thrashing on the ground.

"You gonna hang 'im now?" a voice cried.

"No. We'll fix him to that tree," the trader exclaimed as a half dozen of them dragged Harris to his feet.

The bruised and bloodied drunk man spat at Drips and two others, promising to kill them before he went to finish with Newell.

"Son of a bitch stole my job!" the old veteran bellowed like a wounded bull with his balls snagged on cat claw. "No goddamned beaver for a man to trap anymores . . . and now Newell's stole my pilot job!"

A yard at a time they dragged Harris to the closest cottonwood where they shoved him to the ground. Wrapping the rope round and round the trunk, three of them secured him as Harris roared his curses at them, then pitiably cried in despair at the end of the beaver trade—only to suddenly curse some more.

Drips knelt at Harris's side. The drunk man angrily spit at the trader. Wiping the glob of spittle from his cheek, Drips hissed, "I oughtta shoot you right where you are—"

"Go ahead and kill me!" Harris bawled. "Ever'thing's gone anyway!" Then he broke into a sob, "It don't matter to live no more."

The stunned crowd fell to a hush around them.

"Let me tell you why I don't shoot you and get it over with, Harris," Drips explained as he leaned closer. "You been a good man, guiding our supply trains from St. Louis every summer. I figure that's gotta count for something."

"Just lemme kill Newell! Then you can do what you want with me! Nothing counts for nothing no—"

"If you'd killed him, I would have shot you dead myself," Drips interrupted, shaking the man quiet. "Maybe better still, I would have hanged you with that rope holding you to this tree."

"Hang me?" he spat. "I'm wuth more'n a hanging!"

"Look at you." Drips slowly got to his feet. "You sure as hell ain't worth a lead ball now."

"I'll kill you when I get these here ropes off—"

"Let's hope you feel different come morning, Harris."

Once more the drunk trapper whimpered, "M-morning?"

"You'll be good and sober by then," Drips declared, seeing Newell emerge from the trees armed with his pistol and a rifle. "Maybe by then the missionaries will be on their way, and there won't be any cause for more trouble from you."

With their eyes trained on the Columbia country, Newell, Meek, and William Craig started the three missionary couples west at first light, just as Andrew Drips had suggested they do. The rumble of their wagons and the clatter of their leave-taking awoke a hungover, blood-crusted Moses Harris still firmly lashed to his tree.

Red-eyed, the old veteran watched them depart, struggling to keep from showing his utter grief at being left behind. He bit his tongue and didn't utter one word, not one curse, as the wagons rolled from the valley. Joining the missionaries when they set forth on this last momentous leg of the overland journey to Oregon were Joel P. Walker and his wife, along with their four children and his wife's younger sister. They were to be the first family to ply what would soon become a great emigrant road.

With Dick Owens having thrown in with Philip Thompson's bunch who had headed west to steal California horses, Kit Carson found himself alone when the end came. No more would he trap beaver, Kit had decided. Instead, he chose to ride south across the mountains for the Arkansas where he would apply to become a hunter for St. Vrain and the Bent brothers.

But hardest for Bass to take would be Shad Sweete's decision.

"What's come of their gumption?" Titus asked his partner as Carson left their camp after announcing his plans to abandon the fur business. "Won't no one ride into these mountains to trap beaver no more? Looks to be we're the last, Shadrach!"

The moment he turned to peer at Sweete's eyes, Scratch's stomach shriveled as if he'd swallowed a mouthful of pickling salt. He knew, even as he asked, "W-what is it? Why you got that look on your face?"

For a while longer the tall man stood there before his friend, shuffle-footed and dumb, unable or afraid to speak.

Bass said, "Them words are like cockleburrs choking you, so you best spit 'em out now. Ain't nothing you'd say ever hurt me, for you're my friend."

"Beaver's done, Scratch."

"It ain't done," he snapped.

"Then maybeso . . . I'm done with beaver," Sweete explained gently, seeing how he had wounded Bass. "Done splashing round in freezing streams and allays looking over my shoulder for red niggers. I'm done chasing after something I know I ain't ever gonna find."

Titus blinked back the sting at his eyes and asked, "What you been chasing, Shadrach?"

"Maybe I allays figgered I'd make me a little money at this, leastways enough to fix up a post for myself where I could do some trading." Then Sweete shrugged. "But the last few seasons I come to figger the best I'm gonna do is have myself some steady work as a hand for someone else."

"Who . . . who you figger you'll work for?"

He gazed squarely at Bass, seeming a bit more confident. "Been thinking 'bout heading down to the South Platte. Maybeso that post you said Sublette and Vaskiss got."

"There's work down there, Shad," Scratch admitted, choking back the pain already ripping his gut in two at this parting. It never got easy. Damn, but it never got any easier.

"I'll find me something—"

"Bill Williams told us there's other posts down in that country too," Bass said. "Won't be hard for a likely lad such as yourself to find work."

Wearing a look of unashamed gratitude for Titus making it easier on him, Sweete nodded. "I'll hunt for 'em. Maybeso do some trading for Vaskiss. You said yourself that's dead center in the 'Rapaho and Cheyenne country."

"I'd wager my last beaver dollar on you, Shadrach. You'll make a life for yourself on them plains."

"How—how 'bout you, Scratch?" Sweete asked, worry suddenly carving deep furrows on his brow.

"Don't you fret over us none," he said, glancing momentarily at the woman and their children. "Likely stick close by these mountains come fall, maybe winter up down to Sinclair's post in Brown's Hole. I'll lay off that north country till it's for certain them Blackfoot been took by the pox and ain't gonna play the devil no more."

"Things for sure gonna be a mite safer for you in this'r country."

Splitting his shaggy beard with a grin, Titus said, "Won't no Injuns be troubling me anywhere I go, Shad—not as far back in them hills as I plan to hide."

"To get that high, and go back so far, that be a load of work and time on a man."

"Hardscrabble for sure," he admitted. Then, shrugging, Titus pointed at the woman. "But we don't got nothing else to do, nowhere else to be now, but up there where the Injuns ain't likely to roam . . . so it don't matter a lick if I gotta work hard and high to find them flat-tails."

"Bridger told me him and Frapp gonna hook up again, fixing to work the rivers hereabouts. He asked me to join in, but I told him I'd give the traps a rest. Maybeso you'd wanna ride with them?"

Wagging his head slowly, Titus confessed, "I spent me some seasons throwed in with Jack Hatcher's outfit. Since then I got old and set in my ways. Better off on my lonesome."

Slowly Shad Sweete grinned, then flung his long arms around the thin man and squeezed him fiercely. His voice so quiet that it was barely heard over the rustle of the breeze, he whispered into his friend's ear, "Likely you always will be better off, going where it feels right, and being on your own, Titus Bass."

His flesh a war map etched with every wound of arrow, knife, and ball, his sagging face lined and pocked by the deep cold and the high sun, the very marrow of his soul cut, healed, and now scarred . . . Titus Bass clung on. He always would, alone if need be.

Though the seasons he had weathered in this life had mellowed, aged, then died, each one gone the way of the quakies' golden leaves—still his love for this land and this life endured.

Though those summers of rendezvous were now gone forever, though no more than a few beaver had survived the deadly onslaught, though most of the hardy hunters were already scattering east or west . . . still a few would linger, a few would prevail as their world changed around them.

For those few, this then had truly been a love story if ever there was one. Across winters harsh and unforgiving, throughout brief seasons of fading glory, the few had come to love a land, come to love a way of life with such fierce and steadfast devotion that they could not begin to consider ever abandoning their mountain domain.

No more could these few forsake this wild land and this raw life they had come to love with such unspoken fidelity than they could abandon a woman they loved with that same undying passion.

No more could Titus Bass leave these uncharted western rivers than he could leave little Flea. No more could he abandon the valleys teaming with clk and buffalo than he could abandon his sweet Magpie.

And no more could this man forsake the high mountain passes and the hoary peaks than he would ever think of parting from the woman who held his heart in her hands.

There were sunrises and seasons yet unborn.

ABOUT THE AUTHOR

TERRY C. JOHNSTON was born the first day of 1947 on the plains of Kansas, and has lived all his life in the American West. His first novel, *Carry the Wind*, won the Medicine Pipe Bearer's Award from the Western Writers of America, and his subsequent books, among them *Dance on the Wind, Cry of the Hawk,* and *Long Winter Gone*, have appeared on bestseller lists throughout the country. He lives and writes in Big Sky country near Billings, Montana.

Each year Terry and his wife, Vanette, publish their annual "WinterSong" newsletter. Twice every summer they take readers on one-week tours of the rendezvous sites of the early Rocky Mountain Fur Trade, and to the battle sites of the Indian Wars.

Those wanting to write to the author, those requesting the annual "WinterSong" newsletter, or those desiring information on taking part in the author's summer historical tours can write to him at:

> Terry C. Johnston
> P. O. Box 50594
> Billings, MT 59105

Or, you can find his website at:

> http://www.imt.net/~tjohnston/

and can e-mail him at:

> tjohnston@imt.net

DATE DUE

MAR. 05 1999	Sr Center	
MAR. 27 1999	5/7/2000	
APR. 15 1999	OCT. 21 2000	
MAY · 1 1999	NOV. 23 2000	
MAY 21 '99	OCT 06 2003	
MAY 29 1999		
JUL. 07 1999		
AUG. 19 1999		
SEP. 14 1999		
OCT. 07 1999		
OCT. 14 1999		
OCT. 26 1999		
NOV. 09 1999		

GAYLORD   PRINTED IN U.S.A.